Praise for
POLAND

"Mr. Michener is accomplished. . . . As is to be expected . . . there is a depth and richness of detail. . . . An intriguing class-warfare interpretation of the Rural Solidarity movement . . . The sweep of history . . . is faithfully and powerfully captured. And that alone is good reason for anyone intrigued by the Polish situation of today to read it."

—*The New York Times*

"Stunning . . . Michener took extraordinary care with his facts. . . . An unmatched overview of Polish history . . . He can genuinely handle epic sweep. . . . The families themselves come very much alive, and through them, Poland itself. . . . Michener can write scenes of masterful confrontation."

—*USA Today*

"The most successful feature of this . . . panorama is how deftly it weaves the strands from Poland's difficult twentieth century . . . with patterns of more distant years. . . . In his inimitable way, Michener delivers . . . engrossing entertainment. *Poland* is James Michener at his best, prodigiously researched, topically relevant."

—*The Washington Post*

"A titanic documentary novel . . . I, for one, am delighted that Mr. Michener undertook two years of legwork and foraged through hundreds of musty chronicles to give me a total-immersion course in Poland."

—*The Wall Street Journal*

"The way Michener weaves the interaction of the three families with each other and with real historical characters is nothing short of masterful. The result is seven hundred years of Polish history, delivered in an enthralling . . . package."

—*The Dallas Morning News*

"Like a film-maker, Michener uses close-ups and long shots, showing a battle scene as effectively as the hands of a woman grinding wheat, moving from casts of hundreds to the smallest, most significant details. . . . Powerful and disturbing . . . *Poland* is a massive work of fiction, backed by years of research."

—*Los Angeles Times*

"James A. Michener has the passionate intellect, the unquenchable thirst for knowledge, and the quiet intensity normally associated with a college professor. . . . The sweep of history which Michener commands in *Poland* is quite amazing."

—*Los Angeles Herald Examiner*

"If there is a theme to Michener's work, it is Poland has endured. . . . *Poland* is a gallant book, an inspirational saga of a people who not only survived catastrophe, but were capable of building on that very destruction."

—New York *Daily News*

"More than any of Michener's other novels, *Poland* is on top of the news. . . . A panoramic view of Poland's troubled history . . . Michener explores each historic period succinctly and informatively."

—*Business Week*

"A classic Michener production, an expertly synthesized novel weaving fact and fiction into the kind of detail-packed, sympathetic rattling good read one has come to expect from him . . . thorough, enthusiastic, patient, filled with romance and adventure and heroes and villains and lessons in pronunciation, and even a recipe for Polish cherry soup . . . *Poland* shines with interest and pleasure and appreciation of the country and concern for its future."

—*The Detroit News*

BY JAMES A. MICHENER

Tales of the South Pacific
The Fires of Spring
Return to Paradise
The Voice of Asia
The Bridges at Toko-Ri
Sayonara
The Floating World
The Bridge at Andau
Hawaii
Report of the County Chairman
Caravans
The Source
Iberia
Presidential Lottery
The Quality of Life
Kent State: What Happened and Why
The Drifters
A Michener Miscellany: 1950–1970
Centennial
Sports in America
Chesapeake
The Covenant
Space
Poland
Texas
Legacy
Alaska
Journey
Caribbean
The Eagle and the Raven
Pilgrimage
The Novel
James A. Michener's Writer's Handbook
Mexico
Creatures of the Kingdom
Recessional
Miracle in Seville
This Noble Land: My Vision for America
The World Is My Home

WITH A. GROVE DAY
Rascals in Paradise

WITH JOHN KINGS
Six Days in Havana

POLAND

POLAND

A NOVEL

JAMES A.
MICHENER

THE DIAL PRESS

NEW YORK

2015 Dial Press Trade Paperback Edition

Copyright © 1983 by James A. Michener
Cartography copyright © 1983 by Jean Paul Tremblay
Introduction copyright © 2014 by Steve Berry

Published in the United States by The Dial Press, an imprint of Random House, a division of Penguin Random House LLC, New York.

THE DIAL PRESS and the HOUSE colophon are registered trademarks of Penguin Random House LLC.

Originally published in hardcover in the United States by Random House, an imprint and division of Penguin Random House LLC, in 1983.

ISBN 978-0-8129-8670-9
eBook ISBN 978-0-8041-5145-0

Printed in the United States of America on acid-free paper

randomhousebooks.com

8 10 12 14 15 13 11 9

Book design by Carole Lowenstein

INTRODUCTION

Steve Berry

I grew up in the 1960s, a time when the extent of reading material for kids was, to say the least, limited. R. L. Stine, J. K. Rowling, Suzanne Collins, and so many others had yet to come along. In fact, what we now know as the young adult genre had yet to be invented. Back then, at least for me, it was Hardy Boys and Nancy Drew. A limited selection, but what gems those tales were—each loaded with action, adventure, secrets, and conspiracies. Wondrous stories to fuel young imaginations. I devoured them.

Then one day when I was sixteen years old, a friend handed me a dog-eared paperback copy of *Hawaii* by James Michener. Its thousand pages immediately intimidated me, as did the small print. I'd never seen so much information packed into one book. The opening sentence alone contained thirty-six words—monstrous in comparison to the prose of Franklin W. Dixon.

But what a sentence: *Millions upon millions of years ago, when the continents were already formed and the principal features of the earth had been decided, there existed, then as now, one aspect of the world that dwarfed all others.*

I kept reading.

What unfolded was a saga spanning many centuries that described how a tiny group of islands in the Pacific Ocean were formed by nature and then settled by man. The epic involved Polynesians, Chinese, Japanese, Europeans, and Americans. Its massive chapters, hundreds of pages long, featured one expansive episode after another—each intertwined—forming a chronicle that defined both the land and its culture. I read it cover to cover. Then I found more books by this guy Michener and read every one. Eventually, I started collecting them, and now, more than forty years later, I own a first edition of each, save one—*Tales of the South Pacific*. That book is hard to find. Only a few thousand were printed and, if by some miracle one of those 1947 first editions can be found, the price is through the roof. I keep every one of my Michener books prominently displayed, wrapped in plastic. I see them every day. They are a source of pride and comfort. Today, I write modern-day thrillers in which history plays a central role. Without question, the seed for that technique was planted the day I discovered *Hawaii.*

James Michener led an incredible life. Born in 1907, he was orphaned but was soon adopted by a woman named Mabel Michener, who was already raising two other children. Some of his biographers have hypothesized that he was actually Mabel's natural son, the adoption story used to protect both of their reputations. No one knows the truth, and as an adult Michener refused to comment on the subject.

By the time he turned ten, the family had moved to Bucks County, Pennsylvania. They were poor, barely able to put food on the table. His classmates, and even a teacher or two, tormented Michener about the secondhand clothes and toeless sneakers he wore every day. Later in life he recounted that taunting with a sly smile and a twinkle in his eye. He would say that those early years instilled in him an appreciation for life that he never forgot. They taught him about living simply and not attaching too much value to material things. And though he eventually earned hundreds of millions of dollars from writing, he always feared ending up poor.

Before he'd even reached twenty years of age, Michener had traveled across the country in boxcars, by thumbing rides, or simply by walking. He worked in carnival shows and other odd jobs, and he visited all but three states. Of that time, he wrote in his 1991 autobiography, *The World Is My Home,* "Those were years of wonder and enchantment. Some of the best years I would know. I kept meeting American citizens of all levels who took me into their cars, their confidence and often their homes." He would also say that those wandering years spurred inside him an insatiable curiosity about people, cultures, and faraway lands.

In 1925 he entered Swarthmore College, a prestigious Quaker institution, on a four-year scholarship, graduating with highest honors. He attended graduate school in Scotland, then returned home and taught at a school in Bucks County. He eventually ended up in New York City, editing textbooks at Macmillan Publishing.

World War II changed everything. At age forty Michener enlisted in the navy, where he discovered the enchanting South Pacific. He earned the rank of lieutenant commander and was made a naval historian, assigned to investigate cultural problems on the various islands. A near-fatal crash landing in French New Caledonia altered the course of his life. He wrote in his autobiography, "As the stars came out and I could see the low mountains I had escaped, I swore: 'I'm going to live the rest of my life as if I were a great man.' And despite the terrible braggadocio of those words, I understood precisely what I meant."

That brush with death also made him realize what every soldier was experiencing during the war, and that one day, when the danger had passed, people might want to recall those things. So each night he began writing down observations, recording comments, describing people and places. Fifty years later, in 1991, he said:

> Sitting there in the darkness, illuminated only by the flickering lamplight, I visualized the aviation scenes in which I had participated, the landing beaches I'd seen, the remote outposts, the exquisite islands with bending palms, and especially the valiant people I'd known: the French planters, the Australian coast watchers, the Navy nurses, the Tonkinese laborers, the ordinary sailors and soldiers who were doing the work, and the primitive natives to whose jungle fastnesses I had traveled.

All of that became *Tales of the South Pacific.*

The story of how that first manuscript made it to print is typical Michener—an unexpected combination of skill, determination, and luck. Using a pseudonym, he submitted the work to Macmillan, the publisher he'd worked for before enlisting. He omitted his name because he knew the company had a strict policy against publishing anything by an employee. Once the war was over he definitely intended to return to work there, but at the time of the submission he was technically a naval officer and not an employee. So the company bought the book, which was published in 1947. One year later *Tales of the South Pacific* won the Pulitzer Prize for fiction.

Michener changed publishers in 1949, moving to Random House, where he stayed for the rest of his life. More books followed—*The Fires of Spring, Return to Paradise, The Bridges at Toko-Ri,* and *Sayonara.* Also in 1949 he moved to Honolulu and soon began work on his most ambitious project to date. Four years of research and three years of writing were needed to produce *Hawaii.* Its epic scope, length, and breadth proved to be the stamp of Michener's trademark style, one he would master over the next forty years. Legend has it that he finished *Hawaii* on March 18, 1959, the day Congress voted to accept the islands as the fiftieth state.

In 1962 Michener ran for Congress as a liberal Democrat but lost. Then, in 1968, he worked as secretary of the Pennsylvania Constitutional Convention. Outer space was a lifelong interest, and he served on NASA's advisory council, an experience that led to his novel *Space*.

Honors were something Michener shied away from, but in 1977 Gerald Ford bestowed upon him the Presidential Medal of Freedom, the nation's highest civilian award. Eventually, he wrote nearly fifty books, including five on Japanese art. His work has been translated into multiple languages, and there are more than 75 million copies of his books in print. These latest editions, being rereleased with new covers, will only add to that already staggering inventory.

A myth associated with Michener speaks of his cadre of researchers, used to gather the enormous amount of historical detail included in each of his epics. The reality was quite different. Most of the work was accomplished with the help of only three secretaries. He was a disciplined writer, establishing a routine early in his career and maintaining it his entire life. An early riser, he would go straight to work, where he wrote using a manual typewriter. He then had a light breakfast, maybe a meeting or two, and went back to work until around one P.M. Evenings were a time to be by himself. In the final year of his life, at age ninety, he still kept to his daily routine, except he spent three days a week at a renal treatment center, undergoing kidney dialysis.

The treatment proved painful in a multitude of ways, perhaps the most difficult being that it prevented him from straying far from home. The man who'd visited nearly every country could no longer travel. He told an interviewer at the time, "I sit in the TV room and see shows on the big ships I used to travel or areas that I used to wander, and a tear comes to my eye. It's not easy."

And that explains his death—he simply decided there would be no more dialysis. Instead, he welcomed the end.

Michener died on October 16, 1997.

I recall the day vividly. A segment on the evening news reported that he was gone. A sadness came over me, as if I'd lost a close friend—which, in a sense, I had.

In preparation for writing this introduction, I reviewed many articles written just after Michener passed. Most came from folks who'd had some personal contact with him through the years—an experience that had clearly stuck in their memory. All of them recounted what happened as if they had been in the presence of a king or head of state. It seemed a privilege to have spent just a little time with James Michener.

And that legacy lives on.

Though he was known to be fanatically frugal, he gave away more than $100 million. Recipients of his generosity included libraries, museums, and universities. He donated $30 million to the University of Texas for the establishment of a creative writing program. Several million more went to the creation of the James A. Michener Art Museum in Pennsylvania. One wing of that building was named for his third wife, Mari Sabusawa Michener, who died before him, in 1994.

He never really liked talking about himself, and he could frustrate interviewers. "Famous is a word I never use," he would say. "I'm well known. I've written thirty or forty books. I've done a great deal. I let it go at that." He was extremely generous with his autograph, so much so that he once noted, "The most valuable books are those that aren't signed."

Of my own collection, only one bears his signature.

To the frequently asked question, "Which book are you most proud of?" he would just smile and say, "The one I'm working on next."

By no means was he perfect. He could be a difficult man to know. He wasn't the type to start conversations with strangers, and he detested small talk. He had few close friends, and those who counted themselves in that number knew to tread lightly. He could be abrupt, even rude, and quite aloof. After his death we learned that he utilized collaborators on some of the big books, a fact he refused to acknowledge in life. He was married three times and at one point maintained a mistress. He was a multimillionaire, yet he would constantly fret about not having enough money to pay his bills. And though he was an orphan himself and a cofounder of an adoption agency, in the 1950s he gave up his claim to an adopted child when he divorced his second wife.

All of which shows that he was human.

But still, what a remarkable man.

Michener possessed an incomparable ability to simultaneously enthrall, entertain, and inform. Nobody else could write a two-hundred-word sentence with such grace and style. And he chose his subjects with great care: the South Pacific (*Tales of the South Pacific, Return to Paradise*), Judaism (*The Source*), South Africa (*The Covenant*), the West Indies (*Caribbean*), the American West (*Centennial*), the Chesapeake Bay (*Chesapeake*), *Texas, Alaska,* Spain (*Iberia*), *Mexico, Poland,* the Far East.

Like millions of other readers, I loved them all.

I never met James Michener. I would have loved to tell him how he sparked the imagination of a sixteen-year-old boy, which led first to a lifelong love of reading, then to a career as a writer. When, in 1990, I decided to write my first novel, it was Michener who influenced me most. By the end of that decade, though, changes had firmly begun to take hold. Today you won't encounter many two-hundred-word sentences or millennia-long sagas involving hundreds of characters. Instead, in the twenty-first century, story, prose, and purpose are expected to be tight. In the Internet age—with video games, twenty-four-hour news, streaming movies, you name it—there is just little time for thousand-page epics. Toward the end of his life Michener gave an interview in which he doubted he would have ever been published if he'd first started in that environment.

Thank goodness he came along when he did.

Now his stories can live forever.

ACKNOWLEDGMENTS

In 1977 a television company invited me to go to any exotic place in the world to shoot a documentary, and I astonished them by choosing without hesitation: "Poland." When they asked why, I replied: "If you look at its geographical and ideological position, you'll see that it must become a focal point within the next decade."

In succeeding years I visited Poland some eight times, traveling to almost every part of the nation. Private sources provided me with a helicopter for the better part of a week. I used it to fly at a very low altitude over all of Poland. I was encouraged to visit schools, universities, laboratories, art centers, historical sites, and at one point I said that what I needed most was to spend some time with a devout Roman Catholic clergyman who spoke English. By good luck I was taken to see the Bishop of Krakow, Karol Wojtyla, with whom I had a series of productive conversations. Later I spent time with Cardinal Wyszynski and Primate Glemp, and through them was allowed to see the workings of a church within a Communist country.

By accident I spent a beautiful vacation at Lancut Palace and by design an extended tour to some dozen of Poland's magical castles. I also spent an equal amount of time in the heavy industries of Katowice and in the Lenin shipyards at Gdansk. By car I traveled many hundreds of miles to all parts of Poland.

In such work I had the guidance of Edward J. Piszek, an American Pole who, because of his humanitarian interest, had strong ties to Polish affairs, with an entree to almost any facet of Polish life. The car in which I traveled was often driven by his assistant, Stanley Moszuk, a gifted citizen of Poland with a strong knowledge of its art and history.

When the time came in 1979 that I thought of writing a novel about the critical developments in Poland, it was obvious to me that since I did not speak Polish or read it, I would need some kind of bibliographical assistance, and Piszek and Moszuk came up with the idea of asking some dozen top intellects in Poland to draft summaries of recent scholarship in fifteen vital fields. They chose the scholars; I set the topics; and a happy relationship ensued. The scholars received payment for summarizing material they already knew well and I received an unmatched overview of Polish history as local authorities view it today.

They wrote in Polish, which was translated by experts who sometimes knew the field under discussion as well as the writer. From such sources and many others I compiled an impressive body of research data, including some excellent books written in Polish but now available in English.

After I had digested an enormous body of material and felt myself prepared to write the novel which I had had in mind for some years, I returned to Poland in the summer of 1981 and revisited every spot I proposed to write about: Tannenberg, where the great battle took place; Malbork, of the Teutonic Knights; Zamosc, which must be one of the most evocative small cities in Europe; Krzyztopor, a castle of unbelievable dimension; Dukla, of the captivating Mniszechs; Krakow, with its trumpeter; and of course, that section of the Vistula shoreline which would house my story. I mention no Polish place in this novel which I have not visited, and that includes Kiev, which was once Polish.

I followed each mile of Jan Sobieski's military expedition to Vienna, and there traced out his brilliant defense of that city. I went to all borders, followed all the military trails my characters would follow, and lived once more in Lancut Palace, imagining myself a guest of the great Princess Lubomirska, friend of Goethe, Ben Franklin and Thomas Jefferson, all of whom considered her one of the most brilliant women in Europe.

One of my best excursions was with a pair of notable Polish scholars, who spent two weeks with me finding specific and out-of-the-way sites I wished to write about, including remote and towering Niedzica, which used to guard the far Hungarian border.

I had the remarkable experience of being arrested twice within ninety minutes for speeding in Czechoslovakia, once at forty miles an hour, once at forty-five. "Polish license plates will trap you every time," my companion explained. One had to pay the fine in Czechoslovakian currency, of course. But it could be purchased only miles distant from the point of arrest. I left Czechoslovakia just ahead of the police, who wanted to make a third arrest. I left Poland one week before martial law was declared.

The point of these comments is that I was constantly befriended and advised by a sterling group of Polish men and women who discussed with me hour after hour every aspect of Polish history that I proposed touching. Normally, as I have done in my other novels, I would list their names, their impressive occupations, their achievements in research and scholarship, but I cannot ascertain whether in the present climate this would hurt or help them.

I know this: they were loyal Poles; they loved their land; they spoke of it with unbounded affection and never a hint of disaffection. They were patriots of a high order; two of them who had spent time in Auschwitz and Majdanek brought tears to my eyes as we retraced in brutal, infinite detail the day-by-day existence in the latter camp.

This book is dedicated to them, and I hope it conveys some of the passion they expressed in telling me of their Poland.

The completed manuscript was read by Professor Marian Turski in Rome and by Klara Glowczewska in New York, both of whom are entitled to my warmest thanks.

CONTENTS

EXPLANATION

This book is a novel. The three main families—the Counts Lubonski, the petty nobles Bukowski, the peasants Buk—are fictional, as is the village of Bukowo, its two castles, the manor house and its peasants' cottages. Most of the characters on whom the action of the novel depends are also fictional.

Because of the importance of the subject matter and the strangeness of Polish history to the average reader, the identification of certain historical characters, settings and incidents may prove helpful.

Chapter I: Characters, settings and incidents are fictional.

Chapter II: The Tatars Genghis Khan, Batu Khan and Ogodei are historic, as are Henry the Pious, his mother, Queen Hedwig, and his reluctant general Mieszko the Obese. The siege of Krakow and the Battle of Legnica are historic.

Chapter III: The Teutonic Knights Hermann von Salza, Ulrich von Jungingen and Kuno von Lichtenstein are historic, as are Queen Jadwiga from Hungary and King Jagiello and Grand Duke Witold of Lithuania. The Battle of Grunwald is faithfully presented.

Chapter IV: The Swedish king and his ravaging are historic, as are the Polish king Jan Kazimir and his aide Jerzy Lubomirski, and the Transylvanian invader Gyorgy Rakoczy. The sieges of Czestochowa and Zamosc are historic. The Krzyztopor castle existed and was destroyed as depicted and its Ossolinski owners are real, except that the particular members shown here are fictional.

Chapter V: All the principal military leaders on all sides are historic: King Jan Sobieski of Poland, Duke Charles of Lorraine, Prince Waldeck of the Germans, Kara Mustafa of the Turks. Inside Vienna, Rüdiger von Starhemberg and Hieronim Lubomirski are historic. Sultan Muhammad IV is depicted accurately, as is the great battle for Vienna.

Chapter VI: Princess Lubomirska and her palace at Lancut are historic, as are the Czartoryskis at Pulawy, the Zamoyskis at Zamosc and the Mniszechs at Dukla. The Granickis and their castle at Radzyn are fictional, as are the particular Mniszechs at the Niedzica castle, which is very real. The Palais Princesse in Warsaw is fictional.

Chapter VII: Emperor Franz Josef and his mistress Katharina Schratt, who appear briefly, are historic; all else is fictional.

Chapter VIII: The Polish prime minister Ignacy Paderewski and the Russian general Semyon Budenny are historic, as is the crucial Battle of Zamosc, which is not much stressed in most current histories because it involved a Polish-Russian battle in which the Poles won.

Chapter IX: The three centers of Nazi terror in Lublin— Under the Clock, Zamek Lublin and Majdanek—are historic and are depicted as accurately as data permit, except that the specializations of the various fields at Majdanek varied from time to time. Governor General Hans Frank in Krakow and Over-Commander Eric Muhsfeldt at Majdanek are historic, but all other characters, Polish or German, are fictional. When I was far into the writing of this chapter, I learned that the rocket experiments at Peenemünde—which I had dealt with in an earlier novel—had been transferred right next door to the imaginary village I had invented for this book. Polygon was very real, as were the expulsions from Zamosc and the Polish retaliation.

Chapter X: Except for the brief appearances of President Reagan and Pope John Paul II, all characters are fictional, as are the settings and incidents.

THE PEOPLE OF POLAND

During the major part of this narrative the people of Poland were organized in these clearly defined categories.

NOBILITY

Magnates: Owners of vast lands and with many prerogatives, they controlled Poland, with no superior power to discipline them. Ostensibly similar to the great barons of England, they were in fact much more powerful, since they refused to grant consistent allegiance to their king. Because of Poland's geographical position, they often allied themselves, individually, to foreign powers. Thus the powerful Radziwills often represented Russian interests; the Leszczynskis, French. They could be either extremely conservative (Lubomirskis, Mniszechs) or surprisingly liberal (Czartoryskis, Zamoyskis). But they were invariably pigheaded and in the end destroyed their fatherland. The various Counts Lubonski are fictional.

King: Originally an inherited title, it became an elected one, the magnates and gentry doing the voting and preferring to grant the crown to someone outside Poland rather than to one of their own, lest he become too strong. The title was not hereditary, and at the death of any king a riotous election ensued, with foreign powers usually participating with nominees favorable to their interests. This curious system provided one superb king (Stefan Batory of Hungary); one pitiful failure (a weak-willed French prince who resigned after three months); two imbecilic nonentities (from Saxony); three reasonably good kings who brought disaster in their wake (the

Vasa rulers from Sweden); and occasionally some authentic Polish nobleman who ruled at least as well as the outsiders (Leszczynski, Poniatowski). They also elected one Pole of dynamic power who proved to be a most memorable ruler (Jan Sobieski, hero of Vienna).

Princes, counts: Poland conferred no titles, but the papacy, the Holy Roman Empire and surrounding countries did, often at a stiff price, so there were princes, dukes and counts, but such titles conferred no power or standing superior to what the magnate enjoyed. Prince Lubomirski and Count Lubonski had no greater standing than tough old Mniszech of Dukla and were sometimes much poorer in worldly goods.

Minor nobility: Verbally, this category causes trouble. Polish writers use the word *gentry,* which doesn't sound quite right in English. European writers use *petty nobility,* but the adjective has unfortunate connotations. The minor nobility were divided into two groups: those owning land controlling the peasants thereon; and the landless factotums who affiliated themselves with one or another of the magnates. These latter resembled the lesser samurai of Japan, men of good lineage without castles or great estates who survived as hangers-on or as mercenaries. Another useful analogy is with the caballero of Spain, the man with only a horse, a lance and a proud name. The minor nobility provided five functionaries popular in Polish fiction: voivode (powerful governor of a territory); hetman (field marshal of the armies); castellan (governor of a palace and the territory subordinated to it); palatine (palace functionary); starosta (warden or constable). The category includes men almost rich and powerful enough to be magnates, and all intervening levels down to the roving rascal with no castle, no money, no village, no peasants, one horse and pride unbounded. The Bukowski family represents the middle levels and is fictional.

CLERGY

Cardinal, bishop, abbot, monk, friar: Directly linked to Rome, members of this group owned vast estates and whole villages and towns, with all the peasants included. Militantly defensive, they opposed the Orthodox Catholics of Russia, the Protestants of Sweden and Germany, the Jews of their own country and the pagans of the Baltic lands. Toward the famous Uniates of Poland, created by Rome to suborn the Orthodox, they were ambivalent; just as the good Catholics of Spain found it difficult to accept wholeheartedly Jews who converted, Polish Catholics always suspected the turncoat Uniates. In the earliest years of Polish nationalism, the clergy were often the only people in an area who could read and write, and thus they exerted great political pressure, but quickly the magnates and the better nobility educated themselves, often with great sophistication, and then a balance of power developed.

TOWNSMEN

Merchants: Polish writers use the noun *burgher* to designate this category. A growing power throughout this entire narrative, owning their own stores and small factories, they resembled the middle class of all Europe.

Craftsmen: Of considerable skill in Poland, they inhabited the towns, were often owners of their shops, and were governed by their guilds.

JEWS

Financiers: Because the Catholic religion commanded its believers not to charge interest, and because Polish knightly tradition forbade its members to engage in business of any kind (an injunction ignored in the case of wheat and lumber), the handling of money became the accepted responsibility of the Jew. Poland was far more liberal in its acceptance of Jews than most of its neighboring countries, so many found refuge there and prospered, but animosities did sometimes flare.

COUNTRYMEN

Small landholder: Although Polish lands were usually held by either the magnates or the crown, clever farmers managed through adroit behavior, or courage in warfare, or service to magnate or king, to sequester small pieces of land on which they made enough profit to acquire other pieces until they became self-sufficient with their own farms, their own horses, their own rude machinery, and in time, hoards of zlotys which they used for the betterment of their families. Often the money was used as a dowry when an especially attractive daughter was married to a penniless member of the minor nobility.

Peasant: The vast majority of Poles were peasants, like the vast majority of all people in medieval Europe—and down to modern times in eastern European countries like Russia, Poland, Ukraine, Rumania and Hungary. In other countries they were called *serfs, esne, villeins, thralls, vassals, muzhiks.* They were not exactly slaves, but they belonged to the land, rarely owned their own homes, had to work stated days for their master, could not remove to another village without permission, had no education and not even a remote hope of bettering themselves. However, as in western Europe although at a much later time, Polish peasants did gain certain freedoms, release from ancient impositions and a measure of land ownership.

Despite this harsh system in which the magnate owned and controlled everything, a kind of rude democracy thrived in Poland, which was always much more liberal than its neighbors. In England only three percent of the population could be classified as nobility; in France, only two percent; but in Poland a full twelve percent were so qualified, which is justification for the Polish use of the designation *gentry.* And in the towns another ten or twelve percent associated themselves with the nobility, which meant that many citizens had an interest in the government.

The incredible *liberum veto,* by which one man in a Seym (parliament) of hundreds could negate and prorogue the entire work of the Seym by merely crying "I oppose!" was a major cause of Poland's disappearance from the map of Europe, but it was defended as the last refuge upon which a free man (in this case the magnate or his henchman) could rely to defend his freedom. That Poland survived so many fatal reverses was a testimony to its volatile spirit of freedom.

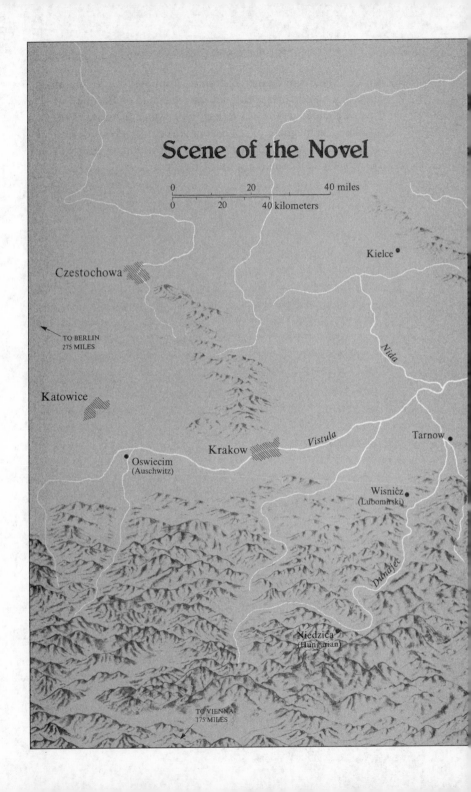

Scene of the Novel

0   20   40 miles

0   20   40 kilometers

Kielce •

Czestochowa

TO BERLIN
275 MILES

Nida

Katowice

Vistula   Tarnow •

Krakow

• Oswiecim
(Auschwitz)

Wisnicz •
(Lubomirski)

Dunajec

Niedzica •
(Hungarian)

TO VIENNA
175 MILES

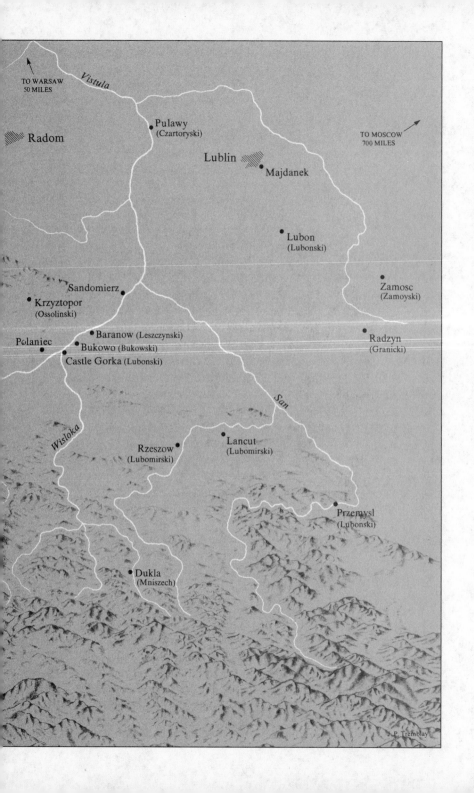

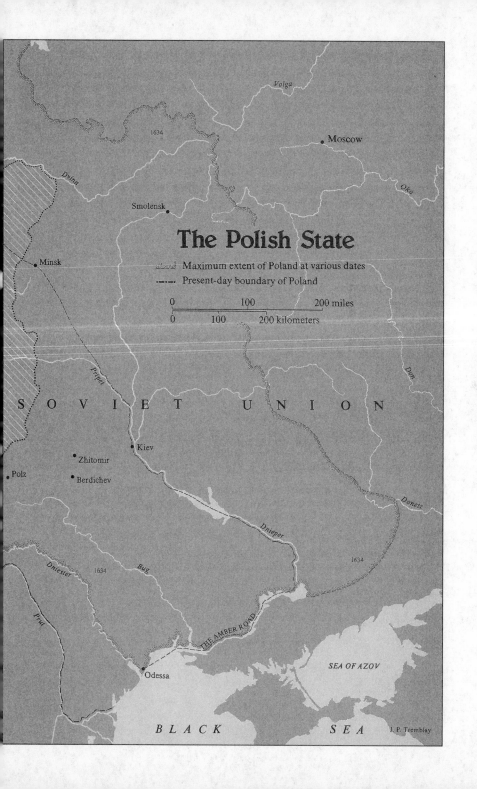

The Polish State

- ▨▨▨ Maximum extent of Poland at various dates
- ▬·▬· Present-day boundary of Poland

```
0              100          200 miles
0        100        200 kilometers
```

Volga

Moscow

1634

Dvina

Smolensk

Minsk

Pripet

Oka

Don

S O V I E T   U N I O N

Kiev

Zhitomir

Polz

Berdichev

Doneiz

Dnieper

Dniester

1634

Bug

1634

Prut

THE AMBER ROAD

Odessa

SEA OF AZOV

B L A C K   S E A

J. P. Tremblay

POLAND

I

BUK VERSUS BUKOWSKI

IN A SMALL POLISH FARM COMMUNITY, DURING THE FALL PLANT-
ing season of 1981, events occurred which electrified the world,
sending reverberations of magnitude to capitals as diverse as Washington, Peking and especially Moscow.

This village of Bukowo, 763 souls, stood at the spot where the
great river Vistula turns to the north in its stately passage from its
birthplace in the Carpathian Mountains at the south to its destiny in
the Baltic Sea at the north. In the little settlement there was a stone
castle erected in A.D. 914 as a guard against marauders from the east,
but this had been destroyed in the early years when those marauders
arrived in stupefying force. Each subsequent owner of the village had
planned at one time or other either to tear down the ruins or rebuild
them, but none had done so because the old castle exercised a spell
on all who saw it, and there was a legend among the villagers that so
long as their ruined tower stood, they would stand. There must have
been some truth to this because there had often been great clamor in
Bukowo, but like its doomed tower, it still stood.

Nearly thirty-six million Poles, of whom eighteen million were of
voting age, were controlled by the Communist party of only three
million members. This minority had made a symbolic concession
right at the start of the present trouble. They agreed to hold the dis-

cussions over farm policy in the very village from which the principal protester came, and this was interpreted by all as a sincere gesture of good will, but as Janko Buk, the leader they were trying to placate, said: "With the steel strikers giving them so much trouble in Gdansk, they can't afford to have us on their backs, too."

The Communists had chosen this village for several additional reasons. It lay in the heart of a large agricultural district and was thus representative. It was also well removed from any big city whose practiced agitators might try to influence or even disrupt proceedings. And perhaps most important, it was near the recently renovated Bukowski palace, with its seventy rooms available for meetings of whatever size might be required.

The three names—Buk for the peasant leader of the troubles, Bukowo for his village, and Bukowski for the family which had once owned the palace—obviously stemmed from the same root, the strong word *buk* signifying *beech tree,* and this was appropriate because from time past remembering, the vast area east of the river had contained a large forest whose principal trees had been oaks, pines, ash, maples and especially beech, those tall, heavy trees with excellent trunks. Through the centuries foresters had selectively cut these trees, sometimes floating the great trunks all the way to the Baltic for shipment to Hamburg and Antwerp, but all the woodsmen had carefully tended a particularly noble stand of beech that defined the eastern edge of the village. Like the castle which they resembled, the beeches of Bukowo possessed a special grace.

The great forest of which they formed such a major part had not borne a name until A.D. 888, when the extremely primitive people who lived between it and the river were frightened by a semi-madman who lived amongst them. He claimed that one evening while returning home with a bundle of faggots collected from under the beech trees, he had been accosted by the devil, who wore about his neck long chains which clinked and clanged, and he convinced them, especially the children, that if they listened closely when the devil was afoot, they could hear the rattling chains.

The dense woods was named the Forest of Szczek in that long-ago year, and everyone agreed that the name was well chosen, for clinking, clanging sounds did often come from this forest, and since in Polish the letter *e*—if printed with an accent, *ę*—carries an *n* sound, the word was pronounced *shtchenk,* which resembles the sound that a chain clinking would make.

The villagers protected the ruins of their good-luck castle and tended the beech trees they loved, but they were proudest of their palace. It had been assembled in rambling style over many centuries by the poor Bukowskis, who had been little better than peasants themselves although acknowledged as petty nobles, and in grand style by the Bukowskis of 1896, who had stumbled upon a fortune.

The palace stood on a slight rise overlooking the castle ruins and the Vistula beyond and was a place of real magnificence, the equal of the lesser French châteaux along the Loire. Shaped like a two-story capital U, the open part with its two protruding wings facing west, its long major base faced east, overlooking the village and the forest beyond. It had been heavily damaged in the closing days of World War II during the German defeat and the Russian victory, but its many rooms had been rebuilt in the 1950s and now functioned as a museum, a rest home for Communist party VIPs and a meeting place for major convocations. A good chauffeur could drive from Warsaw in something under four hours and from Krakow in less than three, so that when government officials selected Bukowo as the site for this important conference they knew what they were doing. Anyone who had visited the Bukowski palace once wanted to do so again.

A major charm of the setting was the village which perched at the edge of the forest. Even before the rude castle had been built or the forest named, a few hovels had collected here, and in the more than a thousand years which had followed, the number had constantly but slowly increased, with the addition of one or two new cottages every fifty years. Improvements came slowly, for the petty nobles who occupied the more permanent buildings that would evolve into the palace cared little about what happened to their peasants. Over a space of eight hundred years no cottage in Bukowo had other than a dirt floor. For nine hundred years none had a chimney, none had windows, and some cottages had passed a hundred years without acquiring a permanent door.

Yet improvements did slowly filter in, a wooden roof to replace a thatch, a slab of precious glass for a rude window, so that in time an attractive collection of harmonious, low, modestly colored cottages grouped themselves artistically about the three sides of a trim central rectangle. As with the palace, the open end faced the Vistula, with the backs of the cottages abutting against the grove of beech trees. Peasants who were born and raised in Bukowo preferred it to any other villages they knew, but this was a limited endorsement because many would have had an opportunity to see only those few that were within a dozen miles. Beyond that perimeter the villagers rarely moved.

That was Bukowo: primeval forest to the east, a splendid grove of beech trees, a snug village, a handsome palace, ancient castle ruins and, dominating everything, the majesty of the Vistula. Here was where the most advanced theories of the contemporary world would do battle.

Sessions would be held in one of the many medium-sized rooms on the upper floor of the palace, and there were six widely recognized clues by which those attending would be able to determine the importance of their meeting. In Communist Poland if guests invited to a formal discussion were of trivial position, only tea was served, in plain cups and from a plain pot. Guests slightly more important saw with gratification that the teacups were placed on a lace doily. Those of medium power sometimes gasped with pleasure when bottles of a delicious black-currant cordial called *sok* (juice) were to be provided, but one did not wield real power until the fourth level was reached: all the preceding plus a bottle of really good brandy.

If the visitors held truly high office, a plate of cookies would be added, delicious things wafer-thin and decorated with sugared designs, but if the official being honored held a cabinet position, or comparable rank in the army or church, or if he was a cinema star or a leading editor, a sixth mark of honor could be reached. In addition to the five customary degrees—tea to cookies—a final one appeared: actual sandwiches, made of the best bread, with thick butter and tangy cheese, or ham, or spiced chicken. Persons attending a meeting where all this was offered did not require medieval trumpets or modern cannon salutes; they knew they came with honors.

For the meeting of the agricultural consultants, sandwiches were prepared and a chocolate cake.

The Communist representatives reached the palace first, and custodians showed them to their rooms; with so many to choose from, it was easy to get one overlooking the castle to the south and the river to the west. Clerks and research assistants received rooms looking toward the beech trees, and some deemed these preferable, for the Forest of Szczek was in its own way as beautiful as the river.

The arrival of the cabinet minister occasioned a good deal of merriment, for his name was Szymon Bukowski, and everyone joked: "It's nice to be in your palace," and he had fun explaining that the

Bukowskis who had owned this showplace were not from *his* Bukowskis, but nevertheless everyone kept calling it his palace.

He was an important member of the Warsaw government, fifty-seven years old, gray hair close-cropped and clipped far up the sides and back, steel-rimmed glasses, heavyset, with slightly hunched shoulders, squarish, placid face, dark-complexioned and with deeply recessed eyes. He wore even in summer a dark, conservative suit made of thick wool and a neatly shaped dark tie. He could have been any Communist official, in any Iron Curtain country; actually, he was Poland's Minister of Agriculture, and it was his job to deal with the rural disturbances which threatened the food supply of his country.

He was a logical choice for the task, a devout Communist who had real appreciation for the difficulties under which farmers labored. He had lived in this village of Bukowo until the age of fifteen, watching his father, who supervised a group of farms, and his hardworking mother, who tilled her own garden patch. In those years he himself had often worked on the farms his father superintended, thus acquiring a sense of what the problems of agriculture were.

After the German occupation ended he had studied architecture, gaining his reputation in government circles because of two activities: he helped organize strong Communist movements among his fellow students, and upon graduation he launched into massive projects for the rebuilding of war-ravaged Poland. In the latter field he achieved remarkable results, the one most often commented upon being his reconstruction of whole sections of the city of Lublin and the adding of nearly twenty thousand housing units for war refugees who would otherwise have been homeless.

He was not appreciated by all members of the Polish community, however, because he was so stout a Communist that he could find no place in his heart for religion, and whereas many members of the government decried the Catholic church publicly in order to retain their jobs, then worshipped privately to preserve their Polishness, Szymon Bukowski would have nothing to do with the church, public or private. He believed, as Lenin had repeated so often, quoting Marx, that religion was the opium of the people, and he found his own work of building the new Poland so exciting that he required no intruding opiate. He did, however, keep such views to himself, for he felt that if he fought the battles of building and food, he was not required to fight the church as well.

But he was determined to fight this fellow Buk, whose efforts to stir up the rural population were causing so much concern throughout the country. Farmers saw Buk as the man who would lead them out of the despair in which they were trapped; government saw him as an incipient force threatening the fundamentals of the system. When shipyard workers in Gdansk formed a union which they called Solidarity, that could be considered acceptable, if one wished to stretch a point, for it was a movement within the great tradition of European labor movements. Factory workers in all nations had formed unions, even in old Russia, and Communism had devised procedures for absorbing such unions easily into its system, preempting their good ideas, killing off the bad, and always forestalling any runaway tendencies. The needs of factory workers could be accommodated to the needs of mechanical production.

But when farmers started talking about unions that would control the growing and distributing of foodstuffs, upon which the nation depended day by day, a new and dangerous dimension was being introduced, one without precedent and one which could lead to the most deplorable aberrations. This Lech Walesa, the factory worker in Gdansk, was in no way an enemy of the state; he was a logical outgrowth of the state, and although he might need discipline to keep him in line, his dimensions and his capabilities were known. But Janko Buk, who was creating so much disturbance among the farmers, was unknown; there was nothing in the theory of state socialism which prepared the Communist leaders of Poland to accept a man like Buk, and they were greatly disturbed by his actions.

As the leaders of the party warned Szymon Bukowski when he left Warsaw for this confrontation: "If Lech Walesa causes us to miss the building of one ship, too bad. We can adjust to that and deliver the ship at some later date. But if Janko Buk causes us to lose a substantial portion of even one harvest, this nation will be in profound trouble. You get him straightened out."

The young man to whom this stricture applied now arrived, accompanied by three farmers from surrounding districts. He was thirty-six years old, stockily built like all men of his family, extremely square of face, with a shock of sandy hair and eyes that smiled easily. He had a slight gap between his two big front teeth, but this was offset by their unusual whiteness, which gave him an appealing expression when he gave a wide smile. Like many farmers, he held his elbows out from his body as if ready for any assault which might come at him, but he seemed more stubborn than aggressive.

He was Janko Buk, Janko of the Beech Trees, a name familiar in this village for a thousand years. Some men in his line had been plain Jan, a name of solid virtue; others of a livelier disposition had been called by the affectionate diminutive Janko, or Good Old Jan. He was a responsible farmer, supported by a sturdy country wife and a widowed mother who knew as much about rural life as he.

How had this wonderfully average man with less than a high school education become the spokesman for the farmers of southeastern Poland and by extension, it seemed, all of Poland?

First, he had a strong intelligence capable of seeing that if the industrial unions that comprised Solidarity gained the higher wages to which they were entitled, the cost of things the farmers needed, like machinery and fertilizer, would have to rise. And then, if government kept the prices of food down to prevent riots in the cities, the farmer would inevitably find himself in a bind: "Increased prices on everything we buy, same prices for everything we sell. That leads to ruin." It was really worse than that: "To cover unexpected expenses in the cities, the government is actually lowering what they pay us. We can't live that way."

Because of the tradition in his family, generations of speaking out, including a fiery great-grandmother who had been hanged for refusing to obey nonsensical rules promulgated by the German Nazis in 1939, a father who had probably been executed by the Russian Communists in 1944, and above all, a mother who had defended freedom and decency with a courage that few could have equaled, Janko Buk was more willing to speak out on these matters than most of his fellow farmers, and in those gradual steps which lead simple men from the contemplation of a wrong to discovered truth, to a voicing of complaint, to actual resistance, he had found himself almost accidentally at the head of a vast rural protest against the irrational way the Communist system was managing its farmers, and the more he spoke out, the more clearly other farmers recognized the truth of what he was saying.

So when Janko Buk entered the palace, he brought considerable weight behind him, and the representatives of the government had to treat him with respect. When he came into the meeting room he saw in rapid succession the cups for tea, the doilies beneath them, the bottles of currant sok, the brandy, the cookies, and in the middle of the table the plate of delicious-looking sandwiches, and he was assured that the discussions were to be serious.

He sat opposite Szymon Bukowski and nodded pleasantly. He had never met this high official before but he had heard a great deal about him, and he wondered who should speak first. When Bukowski said nothing, Janko Buk felt no hesitation in plunging right in: "I've always been told, since you became famous, that is, Mr. Minister, that we're related."

"That could well be. I came from these parts."

"My wife thinks that your grandmother and my great-grandmother were the same woman."

"My grandmother Jadwiga was hanged in 1939 for resisting the Nazis."

"Then we are related!" With visible pleasure, Buk stood, reached across the table and shook Bukowski's hand, holding it warmly and strongly in his own.

"That's a good beginning," one of the farmers said, and a member of Bukowski's team agreed: "Token of a good ending."

Bukowski, seeing an opportunity to establish his credentials with the farmers, said: "You know, I was raised in this village. Used to work on your farms. And during the first part of the Nazi occupation I hid in your forest. When peace came I returned to help rebuild this palace . . . worked on this room we're sitting in."

"My family was in Krakow at that time," Buk said. "I'm sorry we missed you."

"So I know your region well, gentlemen. I know your problems."

"I don't think you do," a stern voice from the far left of the table said.

Everyone turned to stare at the speaker, a farmer in his late fifties whose worried countenance spoke even more loudly than his words: "We're caught in a vise, Mr. Minister, high prices for what we buy, low prices for what we sell."

"I understand, and that's why my team has come down to talk with you."

"It isn't talk we need, Mr. Minister." The older farmer spoke with a harshness which surprised some of the Warsaw men. It was obvious that the old days when rural people nodded and agreed with anything the high commissioners said were gone. There was now a contentiousness in this room that was almost frightening. Ten years ago, even two, Szymon Bukowski would have come thumping into this room and said: "That's how it's to be," and that's how it would have been. Had there been even a whisper of protest, he would have indicated either by inflection or outright statement: "Because that's how Big Brother wants it to be." One always said this with a twist of head or shoulder to the east. In those simple days, what Russia wanted is what Poland got. Now it was all different, and both the farmers and the Warsaw men were sparring more with an unknown future than with each other. They were obligated to determine what the relationship between the Polish city and the Polish farm would be, but far more important, they were endeavoring to discover what the logical relationship between the Polish nation as a whole and the Soviet Union ought ostensibly to be. They were a group of administrators and farmers wrestling with a gnawing problem; in reality they were the forerunners of the 1980s and 1990s grappling with one of the most profound problems in the world: how does a Communist dictatorship relax its controls, especially when the collapse of its economic policies demands that such controls be relaxed?

Once the problem was voiced, even inferentially, the embittered farmers knew that they must state their case strongly so as to attain a good bargaining position, and they spoke with a fury the men from Warsaw had never before seen in rural areas:

FIRST FARMER: I cannot pay a hundred zlotys for everything you make me buy from your government retail stores and then accept seventy zlotys from you when I deliver my produce to your wholesale centers. Mr. Minister, that isn't fair.

SECOND FARMER: I don't grow wheat and barley. I grow vegetables which people in the city need right now. Our papers show us your city people standing in line hour after hour for my cucumbers, my turnips, my beans and radishes. And I had to leave my vegetables rot in the ground because your system of purchasing and delivering them has broken down. People are starving and my vegetables are rotting. That's criminal.

THIRD FARMER: Six of us bought a tractor three years ago. Excellent idea. We shared it, with never a problem. Janko Buk was one of us, he'll testify. Now gasoline is high, we understand that, what with the Arabs and America messing around and all. We could adjust to that if we got decent prices for what we grow.

FIRST FARMER: Now wait! Even if you did increase what we got, we still couldn't use that tractor. And do you know why, Mr. Minister? Because we can't get any spare parts.

SECOND FARMER: So do you know what we're doing? We're cannibalizing. We steal parts from everybody else's tractor, then watch our own with guns all night so they can't steal from us. Janko will tell you.

THIRD FARMER: Do you know what I stole last time? One bolt this long. Impossible to buy such a bolt in all of Poland.

FIRST FARMER: I think you know what's happening, Mr. Minister. Our farmers aren't taking our produce to your buying centers. I won't use names, but some farmers' pigs are not going on the national market. They butcher at night, then sneak the meat into Krakow. Sell it door-to-door. Some send their wives to Rzeszow, to sell eggs door-to-door.

THIRD FARMER: My grandfather says it's back the way it was a hundred years ago. No one accepts zlotys any more. They aren't worth a damn, and you know it, Mr. Minister. We barter and trade and sell at night.

SECOND FARMER: We're growing the stuff. We're raising the animals. And our families aren't hungry for something to eat. But the city people will soon begin to starve. And when we can't get any fertilizer or spare parts, we'll starve too.

FIRST FARMER: We're in great trouble, Mr. Minister. The women in my family need new clothes, new shoes. Unless they can find someone who needs our meat and vegetables, there's no way my women can get anything.

THIRD FARMER: Everything seems to be breaking down. Mr. Minister, I think it's the system that's breaking down.

ALL THE FARMERS: Yes! Yes! The whole damned system.

FIRST FARMER: We believe, all of us believe because we've talked about it, if you let us farm in the old way, each man responsible for what he grows and what he sells . . . If he makes a mistake, he suffers. If he works hard and is bright, he prospers. You let us do that, you let us price our goods in relation to what we have to pay for what we buy, we could feed Poland and half of Russia.

SECOND FARMER: In the old days we did. Fifty years ago we did. Ten years ago we did. And we can do it again.

The fusillade continued for more than half an hour, a patient, non-hysterical outlining of proof that Polish agriculture had collapsed. During this time Janko Buk saw no reason to insert his own doleful experiences, for in recent months he had begun to think on a somewhat higher level than mere personal grievance, but if he wanted his statements to be effective, it was necessary that a full account of all grievances be on the table, with a recognition by both sides that they were serious, permanent and apparently incurable. He could afford to wait.

Nor did Szymon Bukowski interrupt. He had learned in recent months that it was prudent to allow dissidents to enjoy the new experience of full complaint before the government official tried to contest each small point. He knew that if he tried to give an answer to the spare-parts problem by itself, he would become totally enmeshed in its details, any one of which could be debated on its peculiar merits, and the discussion would achieve nothing but petty animosity. But if the entire animosity was spewed forth in one great mess, then a sensible man could confute it in an orderly way. So he encouraged them to talk.

FIRST FARMER: Does the government realize that up to forty percent of things grown in this area now filter into the black market?

THIRD FARMER: Not filter. Rush in like the breaking of a dam. Soon it will be seventy percent. And then what happens to orderly life in the cities? Tell me that.

SECOND FARMER: What happens to orderly life on the farm? My wife can't get soap. I can't get tobacco or matches.

FIRST FARMER: I keep speaking about the women in my family; I have to live with them. And they cannot get dresses. Or stockings. Or things at the apothecary's. Damn it, seems to me they can't get anything they need.

THIRD FARMER: Do you men in Warsaw, those of you in command . . . do you realize that your fine plans are falling apart?

Now Bukowski had to speak. Keeping his forefingers to his chin to give the impression that he was thinking deeply, he said: "The government of Poland is going through a woeful deficiency from which we haven't recovered—" One of the farmers started to interrupt, but Bukowski held up his hand: "You spoke. Let me speak. The pricing policy of the oil nations has also damaged us. And for the moment we're having trouble with the international banks to whom we owe large sums, so that this hurts our spare-parts program. We're aware of all this and intend to do something about it."

"When?" some of the farmers said.

"But our nation, as you well know, is undergoing a time of stress—"

"Poland has been under stress for a thousand years," one of the farmers said. "But it always managed to feed itself."

"Stresses of a harsh new kind," Bukowski continued, unflustered by the attacks, which were getting stronger. "We're trying, all across this country, to adjudicate between the claims of the industrial worker and the farmer."

"It's all going to the factory man," the farmer complained.

"For the moment, I grant you, it looks that way. Lech Walesa and his men have won enormous gains—"

"At our expense."

"For the moment, it seems that way."

"It doesn't seem, Mr. Minister," the first farmer snapped. "It is. You have four women who need clothes and other things for the house, and they can't get them, it's not *seems* any longer. It's *are*. We are in desperate trouble."

"Of course you are. That's why we're here. But I assure you that the government has plans—"

Unanimously the farmers hooted at this unfortunate word. Ever since the Russians arrived victoriously in 1944, installing a Communist government which a majority of the Polish people appeared to desire, the farmers of the nation had heard of plans. Originally there had been rumors that all farms in Poland were to be converted forcibly into collectives, following the Russian pattern, but the prudent Polish leaders, well aware of the Pole's hunger for his own bit of land, wisely rejected the collective. Instead, great to-do was made of the fact that "each farmer is to have his own plot, and he will help us to redistribute the fields of the big landowners." So across most of Poland old patterns, under new ownership, were allowed to prevail, and they were wasteful beyond imagination. Each farmer had his collection of long, narrow strips, usually non-contiguous, in conformance to apportionments first made in the Middle Ages. Between one man's holding and another's a wide strip of untilled soil marked the boundaries, thus wasting about eighteen percent of all arable land and making the rational use of tractors difficult.

Of course, in those northern holdings that had been consolidated by the great Prussian Junkers, the Russian collective could be installed, partly for political reasons, partly because there were few intractable Poles on the land to fight it. So some farmers like Janko owned their land, others didn't, but considering all of Poland, nearly ninety-seven percent of the farmland was individually owned, and this the men in the Kremlin did not like.

This dual system might have worked if there had been a rational plan for providing seeds, fertilizer, machinery and ultimate markets, but Communist planners intervened at every point and a horrendous complication ensued, with decisions being made by well-intentioned men like Szymon Bukowski who did not really know enough about the hard-core problems of farming. Slowly, year by year, just as in the Soviet Union, the food-producing capacity of the land diminished until what had once been known as the breadbasket of Europe, a land of waving wheat fields capable of feeding a hundred million, became a land of deficiency.

It was appalling to a sensible man like Janko Buk to see that the planners in Warsaw seemed invariably to choose precisely those plans of action which were guaranteed to diminish the output of the soil. "Don't they want to feed the people?" he often asked his wife and his mother. "Don't they want to feed themselves?" At first he had assumed that the errors stemmed from the fact that the government contained very few experienced farmers; in those days he had supposed that in the manufacturing field the government men, all of whom seemed to have come from that sector, were making sensible decisions, and sometimes he was prone to agree with them: "When they get the factories humming and goods appear everywhere, we'll all be better off. Then we can wrestle with the problems of the farmers. I'm willing to wait."

But now the outspoken leaders of Solidarity were revealing that conditions in the factories were just as chaotic as on the farms, and this was disgraceful. When Buk could buy no spares for the community tractor and it could be kept operating only by stealing from some other farmer, when consumer goods began to disappear from store shelves, when he or his wife had to stand in long lines to buy even the simplest product, then he began to suspect that everything, and not only the farmer's life, had begun to collapse.

At last he was ready to speak. Using the concise sentences he had preferred since his reticent childhood, he said with almost painful slowness: "Mr. Minister, the evidence is on the table. We all accept it. Government is doing everything for the factory worker, nothing for the farmer." This brought assent from the farmers. "I wouldn't object if factory workers got more, so long as they produced more for us."

"That would be all right!" one of the farmers cried.

"Like if my women could get the things they need," the first farmer pressed.

"But from where we stand," Buk said, "it looks as if the factory workers are getting more and producing less. And that puts a cruel burden on us. We pay in two ways. We don't get the money due us, and what money we do get is worthless."

Buk tried to speak precisely, and he used words which two years previously he had not even heard, for his education was proceeding at a gallop. His tough-minded mother had never had formal schooling, but when the Nazi invasion had closed down all institutions, in those darkest hours of the occupation when the Germans were trying to eradicate all Polish learning, she had valiantly conducted a secret school of her own, determined to keep Polish learning alive, and this had forced her to educate herself. She knew a lot and saw to it that her daughter-in-law learned something, too. There were lively discussions in the Buk kitchen, and often the two women lectured Janko so severely that in self-defense he had to master the arts of logical thinking and clear presentation. He was a man trained in that great university of rural Poland with its two colleges: the farm soil and the kitchen argument.

"It seems to me, Mr. Minister," he said slowly, "that your government offers us farmers no protection whatever. You no longer import improved strains of seed. You don't print the instruction books you used to. You take our taxes but you refuse to provide spare parts in return. And you use the police and army to prevent us from selling our food in a free market where we would be clever enough to protect ourselves. Maybe what these men say is true. Maybe your whole system is falling apart."

This persistent charge infuriated Bukowski, for out of a wealth of harsh experience in the bad years of 1939 through 1944 he had concluded intellectually and emotionally that Communism offered Poland infinitely more than any alternative. In the bad years prior to the Great War peasants in this village had kowtowed to the Bukowskis who owned the palace. Children received a pitiful education. People in the city slaved for capitalist owners and participated neither in management nor in profits. The government had been corrupt; it had failed to protect the nation; and it had refused to form an alliance with Soviet Russia, the only country that could protect it. For Szymon Bukowski the arrival of Communism in Poland had signaled the awakening of a bright new day, and he had been proud to be a part of that awakening.

At first he had been merely one student in the new university at Lublin, next a minor member of a Communist study cell, then its leader, and finally, a recognized spokesman for the new system. Even when membership in the party had been less than two million Poles out of a total population of more than thirty million, he had faith that this small fragment contained the leadership that would save Poland. This dedicated six percent of the population knew what the slothful ninety-four percent needed, and was prepared to provide it.

It was decades before he became even a minor part of the leadership, but during that time he was perfecting himself as a Communist, mastering the precepts of Marx and Engels, studying the steps whereby Lenin and Trotsky achieved power and the procedures by which Stalin stabilized it. Szymon Bukowski, at age forty, had been a knowing, devoted Communist and the quality of his thinking attracted those less well trained. Finally the high command recognized his ability and promoted him grudgingly from one level to the next, always testing him, until the day he was made dictator for housing, which was reasonable, since he was an architect, and now of agriculture, which was not, because although he had been reared on a farm and was vaguely familiar with the basic problems, he had never managed land of his own or been in control of even the smallest agricultural process, let alone the complex matters of buying seed, finding fertilizer, and then marketing the results.

Aware of his deficiencies, he had protested: "I am not competent," but the party officials had growled: "Nonsense. A good Communist can do anything." Polish Communism promoted men according to their party loyalty, not their demonstrated ability.

But Bukowski made himself an able administrator, and since the high command had ordered him to placate these farmers and nip this rural uprising, he intended doing so. "You've stated your concerns forcefully, and I understand them. Indeed, I appreciate them, and I concede that you have real problems. On your part, you must concede that I am limited in what adjustments I can offer at this time. Poland faces many crises. Yours is only one, although I agree it's a crucial one . . ."

He continued in this placatory way until one of the farmers asked bluntly: "What can we expect?"

"Well," he said, "you can certainly expect consumer goods to start flowing from the rejuvenated factories—"

"When?"

"How can I be held to a specific date?"

"When can we expect spare parts for our Czechoslovakian tractors?"

"You can be sure the government is looking into that. Most seriously."

"When?"

The tension was broken by a delegate from Warsaw, who cried with almost boyish enthusiasm: "Let's have some of these delicious sandwiches!"

Tea was poured and little glasses were brought for the brandy, but Buk reached for the dark currant juice, which he preferred above all other drinks. However, even as he put his hand out, Bukowski already had the bottle of sok and was pouring himself a large glass.

"Your preference too?" he asked, as he passed the half-empty bottle across the table.

"I love this drink," Buk said. "Tastes like the fields. Like the forest."

"Speaking of the forest," Bukowski said easily. "I see it's visible from these windows."

"It must be," Buk said carefully. "I've not been in this room before. We don't get into the palace much."

Without saying so in words, Bukowski intimated that it would be good if Buk accompanied him to the window that overlooked the forest. There he indicated with the slightest movement of a finger that Buk should look past the cluster of stately beech trees that stood just beyond the village houses.

Since Janko Buk knew well what was in the forest, he looked not at it but at Bukowski, who nodded sagaciously. Then Buk stared into the shadows and saw the sight with which the villagers were so familiar: the glint of sunlight flashing back from metal. "They're still there," he said, and Bukowski replied with considerable firmness: "And there they stay, permanently."

Bukowo was one of three dozen strategically scattered locations in Poland in which powerful concentrations of Russian tanks were kept on steady assignment, threatening none of the nearby villages, menacing none of the cities. They just stayed there, always on the ready, always waiting for that signal from the east which would spring them into action, as had happened in 1956 in Hungary and in 1968 in Czechoslovakia. The soldiers who manned these tanks were highly disciplined and never appeared on the streets of any Polish community; there were no soldier-civilian brawls, no arrogant displays. It was as peaceful an occupation as Europe had ever known, but there the tanks were, immensely powerful objects equipped with immensely powerful armament. One such tank could destroy the entire village of Bukowo in ten minutes, riding down whatever its guns had not pulverized. Fifteen of them could take defenseless Krakow in a day. But they made no show of their power to crush. They just waited.

"They also are a part of our discussion," Bukowski said, and Buk replied: "I know."

When the session resumed, Bukowski acted as if he expected his reminder to Buk to deaden the latter's outcry against the central government, but it did not. Buk said in his quiet way: "We're not fools, Mr. Minister. We know your government is limited in what it can do . . . well, I mean, in what it can permit."

"You're very wise to keep that limitation in mind, Pan Buk."

"We do. We realize that Poland is one part of a much bigger unit. The great bloc of the socialist republics. And we're mindful of our obligation within that bloc. But we're now talking about the management of a food program for a great nation of nearly thirty-six million people. The program is in confusion. Even the food we do grow is not reaching the people who need it."

"We are taking steps—" Bukowski began, but one of the farmers interrupted: "If we say that our baby is taking steps, we suppose that pretty soon he's going to walk, and if he's strong, maybe even run. We no longer have any confidence that your steps will ever lead to walking, let alone running."

"These readjustments take time," Bukowski argued, but the farmers were adamant: "You've had since 1944. And things have grown constantly worse."

Now Bukowski grew angry. He wanted to shout at these clods: "You don't know what you're talking about, you simpletons who have never traveled fifty miles from home. Have you been to Rumania? Poland is ten times better off. East Germany? Poland is superior in all respects. Czechoslovakia—where they're afraid to breathe? Hungary? Even Yugoslavia? And what about Bulgaria? Who in his right mind would trade with Bulgaria?" But as a loyal Communist he could not denigrate the other bloc countries, so he listened in bitterness as the farmers argued.

"I hear Czechoslovakia's much better off for food than we are," one said, but another pointed out: "I'm not so sure about Russia. Why did they stop their people from visiting in Poland? Because they didn't want their citizens to see how much better we ate."

Now Bukowski had to speak: "Poland is a paradise. Everyone else knows it, and you better not forget."

At this, the farmers fell silent, for each knew that of all the Iron Curtain countries, Poland was the one that was relatively free—no heavy police, no army in the streets, and until recently, no rationing of food or clothing. Travelers familiar with other countries within the bloc had liked to play the game "If you didn't live in Poland, which other socialist country would you prefer?" Universally, Bulgaria rested at the bottom; life there was deplorable, beyond rescue. Rumania stood next to the bottom, then East Germany. Czechoslovakia stood in the middle, a land of great promise but soft in spirit. Hungary stood very high, partly because it had braved a massive showdown with the Soviets and survived.

About Yugoslavia the players had to be cautious. One couldn't afford to praise it too highly because it wasn't really a part of the bloc, and to acknowledge that life there was superior, which it was, would be disturbing. People didn't say much about Yugoslavia except in whispers: "That's a gorgeous country." They also used whispers in evaluating Russia: "May God preserve me from being forced to take my vacation there."

This last judgment was shrewd and accurate; the Poles knew what they were talking about. Prior to 1980, Russian tourists had been a familiar sight throughout Poland; they arrived in big buses, stayed severely together under the rigid discipline of a tour director, marveled at the abundance and variety of consumer goods available, and stood gazing in wonder at the displays of flowers. They looked very much like peasants from the eastern part of Poland, good, lively people strong in body, suspicious in mind, and it was obvious that the free, varied life in Poland surprised and made them envious. They were rarely allowed to talk with Poles but they did seem to extend friendship rather than animosity.

Some years back a knowing Pole had summarized it this way: "A Russian coming to Poland is like a Pole traveling to West Germany. He can't understand the freedom and the surplus of food and consumer goods." And that was what the silent farmers were thinking about as they compared their Poland with the other nations.

"Our problem," Bukowski said at last, "is to preserve the great good things we have in Poland. And keep our independence."

One of the farmers burst out laughing. 'It's crazy to talk about our independence when we're free to make no important decisions."

This was moving close to forbidden comment, and Bukowski was about to reprimand the farmer when another remarked: "You think we have trouble in Poland. You ought to spend a winter in Bulgaria!" At this, even Bukowski had to stifle a chuckle.

The recital of grievances continued, and Bukowski felt that it was healthy to allow these rural people who had never before met with a high official to present their complaints before getting down to the real negotiating, and this was not a new tactic devised for this occasion. Discussion had generally remained free and open in Poland, which had never imposed a censorship as rigid as Russia's. Poles tended to say what they thought, and it was only during the first harsh years of Russian domination that they had suffered for doing so. It was not like Czechoslovakia or, God forbid, Bulgaria, where the citizens were terrified and muted.

At the lunch break everyone, even old-hand Bukowski, was startled by the large number of reporters delivered to this little village by the press bus. They had come to report on the talks: London, Paris, Berlin, Rome, Tokyo, Washington and Moscow being represented. Television crews came from most of the nations and double teams from Japan and America. Bukowski, looking toward the Forest of Szczek, saw that the Russian tanks had drawn back, and he was relieved.

Buk spoke no foreign language, but Bukowski could handle German and English, so he stepped forward to offer a résumé of what had been happening, but this did not satisfy the reporters: "We want to hear from the little guy. It's his fight."

Interpreters from among the government people volunteered, but reporters from Paris and Berlin spoke Polish, and they wanted to interrogate Janko Buk directly, so the interpreters were used only to translate Buk's answers to the others, and it became obvious that the newspeople were going to report this meeting as a battle between Buk and Bukowski. BUK VERSUS BUKOWSKI, *The New York Times* would proclaim, and the reporters were right. This was David going up against Goliath.

Buk, who had never before been publicly interviewed even by Polish reporters, showed remarkable self-confidence and restraint in giving his answers. He did not assume the posture of one who had told the government what it must do.

"Could we say," the Paris man asked, "that you explored differences?"

"That would be accurate," Buk said.

"And what were those differences?" a young woman from Berlin asked.

"The problems that you can see all about you," Buk replied.

"Centering on food?" one of the Japanese television people asked.

"We're farmers. Always we center on food."

"And about other shortages?" the Berlin woman pressed.

Buk smiled at her, the gap between his teeth showing attractively. "We men worry about food. Our wives, they worry about shortages in the stores." When this brought chuckles, he added: "But at night we hear about the store shortages too."

Now the Americans began to bore in: "Is it true, Mr. Buk, that you and Minister Bukowski come from this same little village?"

Buk deferred to Bukowski, who said: "We do."

But again the reporters wanted to keep the focus on Buk, so they asked him: "Would it be correct to say he's your cousin?"

Buk looked up at the much taller Bukowski and smiled again. "I never saw this man before today. But I've heard about him all my life. He would be more like my uncle."

"Does he lecture you like Big Uncle?" This was too difficult for the interpreters to handle, not linguistically, for one of them knew the locution well, but no one wished to introduce any word or idea that might represent Russia. The illusion must be maintained that this was a purely Polish debate with no intrusion being made by the Soviet Union.

"What is the exact relationship between you two?" the American asked, and again Buk deferred to Bukowski.

"My grandmother," Bukowski said very carefully, "was Pan Buk's great-grandmother, so he was correct. I am of the generation that would be his uncle." He paused, then left the steps of the palace where the television people had asked them to stand, and walked to a spot from which he could point toward the village. He was not engaged in a game and he wished to bring the interview back to a proper level of sobriety. "The woman we're speaking of was hanged over there in 1939 for grinding her own wheat. My mother, that would be Pan Buk's great-aunt sort of, she was shot against that wall, a few days earlier."

"For what?" the woman from Paris asked in Polish.

"Because she was here when the Nazis arrived," he replied in English.

That ended that line of interrogation. Now a man from Berlin well versed in economics asked: "What solutions do you see to the food shortage, Herr Buk?" and Buk said with great caution: "One, to grow any food at all, we face a grave shortage of fertilizer and spare parts. Two, if we want to increase production, we must have more of everything. Three, to distribute even what we do have, we must change present patterns."

This was a bold, sharp answer, and pencils scribbled rapidly. Both the Japanese and American television men asked if Buk would repeat his three points for their cameras and he said yes, but before doing so he asked that Bukowski appear with him: "Because we're not fighting, you know. We're talking."

So the two Poles with such similar backgrounds and such contrasting positions stood side by side to face the cameras, and after Buk had repeated what he had just said, Bukowski smiled thinly and added his comment: "We're exploring every avenue to relax the present crisis."

"Even a farmers' union?" the Berlin man shouted, and the two Poles merely smiled.

But in their afternoon session both sides began cautiously to explore exactly that question, and Bukowski tried to stamp out the first tentative proposals: "Unions have always been for workers in cities. You can't find a major nation in the world which amounts to anything that allows agricultural unions."

"Maybe it's time," Buk said, and the debate was joined.

Bukowski had been warned by his superiors in Warsaw, who had been warned by *their* superiors in Moscow: "You can make almost any reasonable concession you wish. Prices, schedules, priorities, spare parts, lower rates for agricultural gasoline . . . But under no circumstance should you even discuss a farmers' union. That would imperil the state."

"A rural union," he said with attempted finality, "would be untidy. Difficult to administer. Open to all sorts of fraud. It simply isn't needed."

"But when all us farmers face the same problems, we're going to take the same action whether we have a union or not."

"That's the socialist way," Bukowski said eagerly, "without a union."

"But if we did have a union, our responses would be more sensible, more productive."

"You would gain nothing by a union," Bukowski said with near-contempt.

A Warsaw official who had not yet spoken now did so: "What you would gain, Buk, would be the power to control this nation's food supply, and that cannot be tolerated."

Buk sat with hands folded in front of him on the table. Leaning forward until his chest almost touched his hands, he said: "We will control the food supply whether we have a union or not. You can never make us sow and reap at the rate we did when we were free to find our own markets. You know that's why Russia is starving. With all the power they command, they can't get their farmers to produce two-thirds of what they produced in the old days. And we Poles in 1981 aren't producing two-thirds of what our grandfathers produced, either. And if you allow things to get worse, the food supply will get worse." Leaving his hands folded resolutely on the table, as if they represented his answer, he leaned back.

The fierce confrontation continued all that afternoon, farmers with their backs to the wall defending themselves against a bureaucracy with its back to several walls. But gradually certain definitions did emerge: the government would not allow a union; the farmers demanded one with powers equal to those obtained by factory workers. On that there was a stalemate. But certain concessions were agreed to: the government would make a concentrated drive to find spare parts; the farmers promised not to diminish any further their normal schedules of planting and husbandry.

And then Janko Buk dropped his bombshell. When it had been agreed that he and Bukowski would go before the cameras again and stress the agreements, not the differences, Bukowski said: "We'll resume our discussions tomorrow," and Buk said: "We would like to involve the Bishop of Gorka."

Bukowski stopped dead. His head jerked back and he stared at the farmers. "Yes," they agreed. "We'd like to have the Bishop of Gorka take part."

"He has no concern in this!" Bukowski exploded. "This is an economic problem. This is food and money and oil and machinery."

"It's the welfare of Poland," Buk said stubbornly. "And the church is a third part of Poland. We want the bishop here."

The appearance before the television cameras had to be delayed while Bukowski went to the telephone to consult with Warsaw: "We had everything going smoothly when the clever little bastard threw a hand grenade at us. He wants to involve the Catholic church."

There was a loud rumble in the phone, to which he replied: "That's exactly what I told him. But he still wants to bring in the bishop."

This simple proposal apparently caused as much turmoil in Warsaw as it had in Bukowo, for during five minutes Bukowski did nothing but listen. Then he said meekly: "I think your suggestion is very wise. Yes, yes. Four weeks. Yes."

When he left the phone he reassembled both parties and announced grimly: "The talks will be recessed for four weeks." Everyone wanted to know why, but he stonewalled: "I'll announce it to the press. We'll resume here in four weeks." And when he went before the cameras this time he did not ask Buk to stand beside him. In cold, crisp, bureaucratic tones he delivered an ultimatum: "Our talks have progressed amiably, but both sides feel the need for further study. We'll resume in four weeks." He would say no more and permitted Buk to add nothing, so the world press was free to interpret the impasse as it wished. No reporter came even close to guessing the reason for the break.

Long after the lumbering press bus had started back to Warsaw and the private cars of the lesser Communists had followed, Szymon Bukowski quietly accompanied Janko Buk to the latter's cottage, where he knew he would meet Buk's young wife and an older woman he had known with passionate intensity forty years earlier, not in the way of love-making but in the brutal warfare of life and death. In the early winter of 1941 he had come to this cottage, to this woman and her husband, pleading for help.

When Buk pushed open the door, indicating that Bukowski should enter, he noticed that the commissar was trembling, but then his wife saw them and hurried forward to greet their visitor and he took her hand. Buk's mother stayed behind, hands folded across her apron, standing very still and erect, for she, too, was remembering those distant fateful nights.

Then Bukowski saw her, and he left the younger Buks to stride across the kitchen he had once known so well, and he saw that clean hard face with the dreadful welt from left eye to chin, and he held out his hands, grasped hers and drew her toward him in a long embrace.

"It is many years since you stood in this kitchen at midnight," she said. Then, pulling away, she looked at him admiringly. "You've done wonderful things with your life, Mr. Minister."

"The name is Szymon," he said. "The name was always Szymon."

"You were just a boy when I first knew you," she said.

"Think of it," he said to the younger Buks as he took a chair at the kitchen table. "At seventeen I was in that forest . . . head of a commando . . . had already killed my first Nazi . . . the one who had hanged my grandmother."

He liked what he saw of young Pani Buk: Kazimiera was of that stalwart breed which had always kept the farms of Poland, Lithuania, Ukraine and Russia functioning. She was prepared to serve as wife, mother, cook, seamstress, ox when the plow had to be pulled, and always as the sharp verbal critic. It was to her that he now spoke, as if acknowledging that inside the cottage she was mistress.

"Pani, when I left Warsaw at dawn this morning the women in my building asked me—"

"I know," she said abruptly. "They hoped you could bring home some meat."

"And vegetables." Quickly he added: "I have the zlotys, you know."

Buk's mother broke in: "Zlotys are of no use any more. We can't buy anything with them."

"But I'd leave them anyway. To demonstrate my good will."

"Good will we know you have. I knew your mother, I knew your grandmother. And women like that do not produce poor sons."

They talked for a while of the old days, and tough Biruta began to weep when she recalled that special night when Bukowski had come to this cottage to talk her and her husband into joining his underground unit, then operating out of the Forest of Szczek. "They were heroic days," she said.

"These are heroic days, Biruta."

"How have you managed to mess up this country so abominably?"

"We're not free in Warsaw, you know." And that was all he would concede. "You will let me have some food?"

"Of course. You came here before, begging for food, and we gave it then, didn't we?"

"What can I give you in return?"

"Not zlotys. Szymon, zlotys are no longer worth a damn. But we would like some books about farming . . . for Janko and our young ones."

"Books you shall have," he said. Then he left the cottage and whistled for the driver to bring the government car closer so that its trunk could be packed with items of food no longer obtainable in Warsaw.

II

FROM
THE EAST

IN A.D. 1204, GENGHIS KHAN, SCOURGE OF ASIA, REACHED A straightforward decision. For a score of years he had been trying to discipline the Tatars, that small difficult group of horsemen who lived at the edge of the desert, and sallied forth at unpredictable intervals to upset the Great Khan's plans. Most often they raided grazing lands occupied by the enemies of Genghis, but when such meadows provided unattractive targets, they were just as willing to raid his Mongolia.

Small in number, they were also small in size; even their ponies were smaller than those of the Mongols, but they were an unruly lot, and what they won in rigorous battle they often lost in riotous celebration. They liked to come cascading into an area like the floods of a spring freshet bursting down from snow-capped mountains, sweep everything before them, kill every shepherd or horseman encountered, and drag back to slavery the women and children. They were a devastating force, and when Genghis first encountered them he had said: "These can be the greatest of the lot."

And they would have been had they submitted themselves to his leadership. He was, in these early years of the thirteenth century, incomparably the greatest general in Asia and probably in the world. He was a cruel genius whose simple rule was: "Leave no conquered leader behind who might rally his horsemen." When he subdued an area he killed off all leaders, distributed survivors over vast and differing districts, then galloped off with his booty to the next challenge. Like the Tatars, he destroyed existing orders; unlike them, he established new systems which would endure for centuries.

He had begun by subduing and disseminating all the enemy tribes in Mongolia. He faced little capable opposition when he rampaged through northern China, and by the year 1199 he was supreme in an area reaching from the Pacific Ocean to the Ural Mountains, and then he ran into the Tatars.

The first time he encountered their fierce little horsemen he defeated them, but in the last moments of battle, when they were thoroughly beaten, they somehow slipped away. In the second big battle he thrashed them outrageously, but in the end they managed to regroup. Realizing that he was up against something special, a desert breed that could not be controlled, he sought to make allies of them, and in a series of wild, triumphant battles the Mongol-Tatar forces raged westward to Turkey, slaying, burning, laying waste even the deserts.

But Genghis could never rely upon his Tatars, for at the moment of victory they were likely to go thundering off to sack a city that did not pertain to the major goal, causing the Great Khan to lose an objective which he understood but which they did not. He talked with them, cajoled them, promised them rewards greater than those offered any of his other allies, and in the end they turned against him, not once but three times. The Tatars of central Asia were a force that not even Genghis Khan could hammer into civilized form.

In 1204 he made up his mind. Summoning all the known Tatars in the world to a convocation west of the Gobi and north of the Himalayas, he ordered a line of desert carts to be brought forward and his warriors to apply a simple test: "Any Tatar who stands higher than the axle of that cart is to be slain."

Rigorously the rule was applied. Men, women, girls, lads were stood against the carts, and if the crowns of their heads inched above the hub, they were slaughtered. A few recalcitrants might have remained hidden in gullies and so escaped, but most of the adult Tatars were eliminated, never again to challenge Genghis in battle or disappoint him in peace.

Among the little ones who witnessed the slaughter and survived was a dwarfish fellow named Vuldai, whose age, had it been revealed,

would have automatically caused him to be slain but whose shortened stature kept him below the hub, and the reeducation which the
Mongols forced upon the Tatar children caused great bitterness in his
savage heart. "There never was a Tatar kingdom," the teachers said.
"The Tatars never existed. You are Mongols subservient to the Great
Khan. You will fight the way he teaches you and only when he commands, and after the battles are over, you will behave the way he decides."

Vuldai and the other little ones were taught new words, new gods,
new systems, and in fifteen years the boys became the foremost horsemen in Asia, the girls the ablest women of the steppes. They did learn
the new rules; they did obey the precepts of Genghis; and when he
turned these young battalions loose they accomplished immense conquests. They were the light cavalry of the Mongol horde, men and
women unafraid to dash forward on their small horses, carrying only
some strips of dried meat and a handful of dried beans to sustain
their charge for fifteen or twenty days without returning to camp.

Vuldai and his men did not encumber themselves with the heavy
machines of war which Genghis had learned to use so effectively in
the siege and subjugation of cities: the mangonels, the movable towers, the flamethrowers and the heavy gear for digging tunnels under
fortifications. The Tatars rejected even the arbalests which sped arrows so piercingly; their galloping horsemen were content with spear
and saber and short dagger, and with them they were well-nigh irresistible.

There was one new device which Vuldai did appreciate; it came,
some said, from China; others claimed, from Turkey; but regardless
of derivation, it was most effective when fifteen hundred Tatars had
to defeat seven thousand enemy. It consisted of small kegs of black
powder—not gunpowder—which emitted a sickening, poisonous gas
that could be ignited only when the wind was so directed that it carried the fumes into the faces of the enemy. It did not kill, but it did
ruin battle plans, for while the confused infantry were gasping and
vomiting, Vuldai's cavalry chopped the flanks to pieces, turning the
battle into a rout.

When Genghis died in 1227 his restructured Tatars were the most
formidable fighting force in the world, subsisting on almost nothing,
capable of sweeping forward forty or fifty miles a day, conquering all
that intervened, yet rigorously trained in subordinating their wild forays to the general plan of battle. They were never, under the Khan's

specific orders, used at the center of any attack, only on the flanks, and by habit they customarily found themselves on the right flank, which meant that since most of the Mongol advances were from east to west, the Tatars instinctively drove toward the northwest.

When Genghis was buried, with sheepskins draped over the drums to muffle their mournful beat, his vast empire, continental in size, passed to his lecherous, wine-bibbing, incompetent son Ogodei, forty-two years old, who had the good luck to find in his nephew Batu Khan, grandson of Genghis, a military leader of some ability. Ogodei had wild, drunken visions, Batu the ability to realize them, and in the year 1239 these two learned from travelers who came east from Europe and from spies sent west by the Mongols that the entire continent of Europe, even down to Italy, was ripe for another of those vast explosions which from time to time had come out of Asia.

Ogodei outlined the strategy: "We will attack on two massive flanks. You and I, Batu, will smash into Hungary, which is undefended if we can believe what they tell us. We'll send the Tatars north to smash Poland. Our two arms will meet in Bohemia, then on to the other ocean." Plans no more subtle than this had succeeded eight centuries earlier when Goths and Vandals surged all the way to Rome, and the Mongols were convinced that with their superior horsemanship and tactics, they would succeed again.

The Tatar contingent, on its customary dash to the northwest, would be required to cover enormous distances: campsite to the Caspian Sea a thousand miles, then another thousand crossing the Volga and the Don rivers to that formidable spot where much trouble was to be expected, the fortified city of Kiev on the Dnieper. If Kiev could be subdued—say, seven months of heavy assault—the Tatars would be free to gallop another four hundred miles to Lwow, Lublin and Sandomierz in Poland itself.

Then they would have before them a prize which would justify the manifold dangers of their wild invasion: Golden Krakow would stand awaiting them, with the most beautiful women in Europe to be ravaged, the richest churches to be looted and the finest shops to be emptied and then burned. Krakow was a magnet powerful enough to draw invaders more than two thousand miles, and Vuldai's dark eyes glowed when he visualized it.

At the final planning sessions the leaders of the Mongol horde which would invade Hungary informed two Tatar generals, the brothers Pajdar and Kajdu, that they were to command the thrust into

Poland, and the young men bowed. "God of the Great Distances," the Tatars shouted as they mounted their horses, "lead us to victory!" And in a clatter of lances and a swirl of dust they were off to the far adventure.

The Tatars organized their troops on a basis of tens: a unit of horsemen under a lieutenant, a company of a hundred under a captain, a battalion of a thousand under a colonel, and a tumen of ten thousand under a brigadier. As generals, each of the two young brothers commanded three tumen, that is, thirty thousand horsemen each, or sixty thousand in all, but not all were battle-ready troops, for an immense train followed the Tatar fighters. There were foragers, and horse-tenders, and women to make camp when the warriors regrouped, and children who begged to come along, and spare horses. Not one Tatar in the vast assemblage was on foot. This was, unquestionably, the most mobile force in the world, and one of the most terrifying.

The warriors carried no armor or protection for their horses; defense depended upon evasion and speed. The Tatars appeared to be only an attacking force, but they knew every trick so far devised for protecting themselves and their horses. They liked to divide their force into three segments: the first would attack single file and run into obvious difficulty; in retreat, it would encourage the victorious enemy to thin itself out in swift pursuit, whereupon a hidden second unit would crash in upon the flanks; and when the confusion was at a peak, the third force would dash in to annihilate. The Tatars took few male prisoners.

The two major wings of this assault, the southern Mongols toward Hungary and the northern Tatars toward Poland, achieved larger successes than they had anticipated, so that by the end of 1240 the southern prong was in position to attack the Carpathian Mountains guarding Hungary while the northern closed in upon Kiev, the well-defended fortress city that blocked the approaches to Poland. It seemed to the messengers who moved back and forth between the far-separated arms that the invasion had reached its halting spot and that a year or two might be required for regrouping and a careful assault upon formidable barriers.

"But there is real hope," reported the leaders of the Tatar divisions, "that if we can subdue Kiev within the year, we can gallop into Poland next year and into the heartlands of Europe the year after." Batu Khan, reporting from the borders of Hungary, assured the Tatars that his troops would match that schedule or even improve upon it.

So the attack on Great Kiev, as it was called, began. On a November day the Tatar horde assembled on the left bank of the Dnieper, some ten miles distant from the city, and spies sent out from Kiev reported back: "They resemble no army we have ever seen before. No armor, no machines, no panoply. Just rather small men on rather small horses."

It was cold when the Tatars started to move forward, sixty thousand wiry, eager horsemen coming like a firestorm out of the steppes. They wore thick jackets and had drooping mustaches. They carried lances and daggers. Each man had a small pouch tied to his saddle containing enough thin strips of dried meat to keep him alive for twenty days, but in some ways the most powerful weapon the Tatars carried with them as they rode was a hunger for the spoils they were about to garner and a lust for the women they would soon embrace.

The attack on Kiev turned out to be one of the miracles of contemporary warfare: the Tatars approached at an easy canter, then spurred their horses and simply rode over the defenders. On and on came the terrible horsemen, not shouting or screaming to cause terror, but in irresistible force, shaggy aliens from the heartland of Asia exploding into the mainland of Europe.

The two young generals, Pajdar on the left, Kajdu on the right, led the wild gallop into the city, encouraging the thundering ranks that followed, and before dusk the looting and the screaming began. A city that had considered itself impregnable had collapsed in one day.

The destruction of Kiev was pitiful to see. Noble churches were burned. Streets were corrupted with hundreds of corpses. Any house that looked as if it might contain a single item of unusual value was gutted. And for three days the raping was incessant, and public, and frequently terminated by a score of stabbings with the dagger. Kiev was desolated, leaving the Tatars free to attack Poland a full year ahead of schedule. From the Carpathians, Batu Khan reported a similar unexpected success, and now the messengers between the two groups carried the exultant word that Europe lay defenseless.

In the last cold days of 1240 the Tatars, emboldened by their easy conquest of Kiev, embarked upon an enterprise of great daring. Said

Pajdar: "Let us assemble those warriors with the swiftest horses and the fiercest manner and send them forward to invade as quickly as possible. Speed, speed."

When his wiry little assistant Vuldai asked: "How will the slower horsemen with our supplies catch up?" the daring general replied: "They'll not leave Kiev. They stay here to rebuild the city the way we want it. We gallop on ahead without supplies. Then our men will have to fight, or starve. Every farm we sweep past will give us its pigs and chickens."

"And the loot?"

"Whatever our men can carry."

"And slaves?"

"At four stopping points we'll collect all our captives and send them back to Kiev. But we forge ahead."

The light in Vuldai's eyes as he visualized the endless assault, the unlimited booty, so pleased Pajdar that he said: "You shall lead the southern horsemen. Not many, but very swift. To draw attention while Kajdu and I take the greater mass through the north. We meet at Krakow, then on through what they call the German states."

"My men must start to dry their beef," Vuldai said in proud acknowledgment of his new command, and for six weeks the Tatars took all the beef they could command from the conquered peasants and cut it into strips, which they dried in what sun there was and in the harsh blowing wind. They made little balls of hard cheese from whatever milk they found—cow's, mare's, goat's, ewe's—and by mixing a handful of parched wheat or barley they made a durable, nourishing kind of food which only men with good teeth could manage.

They were particularly careful to salt whatever foodstuffs they dried, knowing that this delectable addition not only helped preserve the food for long periods but also added to its utility when a piece the size of a thumb might have to suffice for three days in the saddle. "A little salt," Vuldai told his men, "is better than a banquet."

By the middle of December the two arms of the assault on Poland were ready, with rude maps showing each the recommended route. Pajdar's men would sweep north through Zhitomir, Chelm and Lublin, crossing the Vistula near Sandomierz; Vuldai's would ravage the lands to the south: Berdichev, Lwow, and Przemysl, negotiating the Vistula well below Sandomierz. They would meet before the gates of Golden Krakow, and when it fell, the men would be awarded seven days for looting and raping.

It was a bold plan, and they knew that if at any point either the Ruthenians (later to be known as Ukrainians) or the Poles managed to mount an effective resistance, their Tatar cavalry, lacking any organized supply, would have to retreat; but if they could gallop from one farm village to the next, bypassing any troublesome cities, they had a fighting chance for success. Speed, savagery, foraging, plunder, the capture of slaves to be marched eastward, that was the daring strategy, and of all the fighting forces then operating throughout the world, the Tatar horsemen formed the one most likely to execute it properly.

It was agreed that Vuldai would start his diversionary sweep to the south seven days ahead of the major force in order to attract the attention of spies. Now, as he rested sideways in his saddle, left leg hanging free, Vuldai was five feet one inch tall and weighed one hundred and eighteen pounds. His hair was close-cropped sides and back; his mustaches were big and drooping. He dressed himself in thick felted trousers, linen shirt and kaftan made from animal skins, and wore a conical fur cap. Tied to his saddle was a kind of thin cape that would be used to fend off rain or snow during storms and the cold when he slept on the bare earth. He carried four weapons, four pounds of dried food, no change of clothing, no medicines, no replenishments of any kind, yet he proposed to ride his horse, and others he would steal along the way, eight hundred miles through nations which should have been prepared to repulse him easily, except for two things: he moved with speed that bedazzled the enemy, and he was prepared to slay anything that threatened to impede him even momentarily. He and his men represented one of the most terrible forces ever let loose upon a civilized world, and he was prepared to devastate that world.

"We go!" he shouted one frosty morning, and his little horsemen headed west.

It was eighty miles from Kiev to Berdichev, and the galloping force covered this distance in two days, but they did not attack the well-fortified city; they swept around it, destroying every outlying settlement and accumulating stores which would carry them safely the two hundred–odd miles to Lwow, where they employed the same tactics.

Their strategy was seen at its best when they approached a small settlement called Polz, a farm village containing some sixty cottages, with an equivalent number of barns and lesser buildings. Two hundred and eighty people lived in or near Polz, clustered about the small, rude castle occupied by the younger son of the magnate who owned sixty other villages of similar size.

When the Tatars' six thousand hungry, excitable horsemen spotted Polz lying ahead, Vuldai ordered his men to ride forward at a slow trot so that their dust could be plainly seen in the village, warning the occupants of what faced them. He then dispatched three horsemen to ride ahead, asking that the villagers surrender all their goods immediately, but when the latter employed delaying tactics, hoping to salvage at least some of their possessions, the three Tatars grew angry and flashed a signal, whereupon the six thousand spurred their horses and came thundering down full force upon the village.

Everything was destroyed. All barns were burned, all houses leveled. Not a living animal escaped, not a pig, not one fowl. During the first mad rush all visible men were slain, some chopped down with swords, most run through with lances. A good many women died too, cut to pieces in the mad onslaught, but when the fury subsided the younger women and the girls were saved for two nights of sporting, then shipped eastward into slavery at what was now the Tatar capital of Kiev. About twenty younger men were saved to service the Tatar horses, but when this job was completed, they were killed one by one, until none was left. A few strong boys were preserved for playful and repulsive games, then marched eastward to join the slaves. And at the conclusion of the two days, there was only death and devastation where Polz and its two hundred eighty citizens had once existed.

But Vuldai and his men had acquired enough food and new horses to sustain them for their gallop to the next village, which would be treated in similar fashion. Cities, because of their walls, escaped these horsemen; no village did.

By 10 January 1241, less than three weeks after having departed from Kiev, Vuldai's men completed their dash across the steppes and realized that their first target, the Vistula River, lay less than a day's ride ahead, with their second target, Golden Krakow, only a short distance beyond. But crossing the river might prove difficult, so Vuldai reined in his rampaging horsemen and sent out two groups of scouts, one to the north to ascertain how Pajdar's army was doing, the other straight ahead to reconnoiter approaches to the river.

The latter moved cautiously, capturing a family of peasants, who informed them that directly ahead lay the huge Forest of Szczek whose far end opened directly on the river, and when the scouts had ridden some miles into the forest and seen the giant beech trees and the oaks, they realized that this would be a splendid hiding area in which to assemble the horsemen. From here the avalanche would be launched to destroy any settlements guarding the river, throwing it open to an easy passage.

Two scouts penetrated the entire depth of the forest, standing finally in a grove of large beech trees from which they could scout the specific obstacles they would face when the time came to cross the Vistula, and they reported back to Vuldai: "A village like the others. Roofs easy to burn. A small castle, wood and stone of no consequence. Easy to burn. To the south, along the bank of the river, a larger castle of stone which can be invested. Wipe these out, and we have a safe passage to the other side of the river, with enough time to build any boats we might need."

So on the morning of 11 January 1241, a date recorded with awe in the chronicles, the six thousand mounted troops of the Tatar leader Vuldai eased themselves quietly into the eastern limits of the Forest of Szczek and started cautiously infiltrating toward the western edge, where the little settlement waited.

One unauthorized person witnessed this passage of the Tatars through the forest. From the village a boy of twelve named Jan was working in the woods gathering fallen branches for his father, also named Jan, but with the additional designation The Woodsman, and he had wandered far to a place which had always enchanted him: a grassy glade hidden among the tall trees which his father tended for the knight who owned them. The area was surprisingly large, a pleasing gap in the forest where birds came and deer and sometimes one of the bears who lived nearby.

Young Jan liked to visit here and rest from his labors, lying on the grass and staring at the open sky, and on this day he was in this position when he heard a clinking sound to the east, and it occurred to him that once again the devil was rattling his chains in the forest to which he had given a name. But when the sound grew closer, appearing to be not devilish but human, he prudently slipped away from the glade and hid himself among the trees.

What he saw astounded him, for out of the trees to the east came two men on horseback, and they were certainly not Poles, for they were dressed in costumes he had not seen before, and their skins were dark, their mustaches long and their eyes cocked curiously. That they were some kind of military men seemed evident from the swords and daggers in their belts, but they rode easily, letting the reins hang slack, and they spoke in low voices as they passed, using words he could not understand.

One thing was clear: they were men ready to strike at anything that surprised them, and when they were gone Jan moved farther back into the shadows lest others follow.

Now solitary horsemen entered the area, always from the east, and they were fascinating to see: small, heavily clothed, darting eyes, each man looking as if he were an inseparable part of his mount. The lone rider would pause, encourage his horse to browse on the good grass, then pass quietly on, leaving the area silent.

But then four or five of the strangers would arrive in unison, and they, too, would graze their horses and talk quietly, then vanish mysteriously into the farther trees.

Now eleven of the little men came through on a determined trot and they did not stop, but six or seven others who filtered through actually dismounted, and Jan saw that they had captured a Polish woodsman who sometimes worked with his father. They threw him to the ground and shouted strange words at him, as if asking questions, and when the woodsman could not reply, they pierced him many times with their daggers, remounted and rode on.

It was then that Jan, staring at the inert body and hearing echoes of the unfamiliar words, realized that these intruders must be the dreaded strangers from the steppes: Mongols! They've come to destroy us all!

He wanted to run westward to his village, but before he could move, large groups of the horsemen passed through the glade, each man reacting in his special way; one dismounted and walked directly toward where Jan was hiding, but at the edge of the glade he stopped to inspect the strange trees whose like he had not seen before. Then he urinated and returned to his horse. But no rider bothered with the dead man in the middle of the glade, for they were accustomed to the death of strangers.

By nightfall more than a thousand warriors had passed close to Jan, and when the stars came out he knew that it was his duty to go quickly and alert his village, but it seemed that all around him the Mongols were camping, and he could move only with extreme caution lest they hear him. Avoiding the trails he customarily followed, he took a long detour, checking with the stars whenever they twinkled through the treetops, and as the night deepened he heard, no matter where he crept, the sound of clinking, warning him that on this night the devil was truly in the forest.

The little settlement which the Tatars were proposing to destroy and which the boy Jan was trying to save was dominated by three Polish families. In Castle Gorka, a shabby stone affair guarding the Vistula, lived a red-haired knight of medium means whose name, Krzysztof, would in western nations have been Christopher, and with the same exalted meaning: *Christo-phoros, the Christ-bearer,* a man of good will dedicated to the service of Our Savior. The ancestors of the present Krzysztof had been placed in this particular castle by the duke himself to serve as frontier guards protecting the eastern advances to the ducal city of Krakow, and through the decades the various knights had served well. Illiterate, and married to the daughters of illiterates, they had occupied their meager castle with only the barest amenities: no forks to eat with, one plate for all things cooked, glass in only a few windows, thin draperies supposed to kill the dampness of the walls, only a few smoking oil lamps to brighten the long nights, heavy old-style armor and not the light new chain, swords of only moderate length and strength, and worst of all, four horses only and not the minimum of thirty which marked an important knight.

But Krzysztof and his ancestors did have three attributes that clothed them in virtue: they loved Jesus and sought to bring his realm into being in Poland; they were brave; and they were loyal to the duke whose preference had lifted their family from the ordinary dregs into knighthood. When Christianity first edged its way tenuously into Poland before the years were counted in thousands, Krzysztof's family had been one of the first to comprehend what the flowing vision of a new world meant, and in subsequent years they had volunteered to fight on behalf of bishops, they had helped build churches and monasteries, and they had supported all the good works of the church. They were Christian in the great good sense of this word and were prepared to live, or fight, or die for their faith.

Their castle, a rough affair built in the year 1060, bespoke no power, for the owners did not control vast lands; they owned some five thousand acres, mostly wooded, and seven rather small villages, but that was all. The fields and the villages had been given to the family in reward for services to the duke, and it was assumed that if the present Krzysztof of Gorka behaved with any distinction, these domains could be enlarged.

The castle stood on a piece of high land that had always borne the name Gorka, and by tradition it was referred to as Castle Gorka, which meant that the owner was known widely as Krzysztof of Gorka, and in the heat of battle, simply as Gorka or Red Head. In the entire settlement, including knights, gentry and peasants, no one carried a last name and no one felt the need of any.

The smaller castle to the north was much older than the one in which the knight lived; records show that it had been in existence as early as A.D. 914, a stubby, tough little affair intended to provide a hiding place for defenders of the river in which they could resist alien sieges until help came from Krakow, and it had served this purpose well. True, it had been burned and nearly destroyed some six or seven times, but it had been a deterrent, so that even if its occupants did perish, they died knowing that they had held up the invaders for precious weeks or even months until defensive forces could gather on the far side of the river. It was a small castle with a giant reputation.

It was now occupied by a family that stood in the same relationship to Krzysztof in the big castle as he did to the duke in Krakow. Zygmunt was a liege of the knight's, by no means a servant but, rather, a man of historic lineage who happened to own almost nothing: he had no land, no villages, no peasants, and worst of all, he had only one horse. He was obliged to report for military duty whenever the knight summoned him, but he was recognized throughout the region as a full-fledged member of the gentry, a man of some distinction whose ancestors had boasted of the same restricted honor.

What he lacked in goods he compensated for with a quality which he exemplified: he was proud, proud of his family, proud of his courage in battle, proud of his piety, proud of his willingness to defend Jesus Christ. A rather stupid man, he walked through the world as if he were a porcupine ready to throw his barbed quills at anyone who even smiled askance; indeed, he was known mockingly to his associates as Jezyk, the hedgehog, the porcupine. Having little but his sense of honor, he wore it like a suit of armor.

The village to which his castle was attached had been known for as long as men could remember as Bukowo, the place of the beech trees, so his official title was Zygmunt of Bukowo, and with his one poor horse he did function as a kind of knight, but a most impoverished one, landless and with little prospect of advancement.

In the village itself, which he and his castle were supposed to protect, three hundred and forty peasants lived in little hovels with earthen floors, no windows, no chimneys and no furniture other than a platform for a bed, a table and a couple of three-legged stools. A few mean pots, some rude equipment to work the fields and never an extra piece of clothing—such was the wealth of the family. Months could pass or sometimes even years without the cooking of a piece of real meat that a man could chew. Over the long grind of life they ate turnips and cracked wheat and thin soup and huge amounts of cabbage in varied forms.

The peasants worked for three masters: Zygmunt in the little castle, Krzysztof in the big castle, and the duke in Krakow, and in some years they would spend three hundred and twenty days working for these masters, forty-two days working for themselves, and three days in idleness at the festive season. They rarely saw money; they tended to die before they reached forty-four; and the only solace they had was poaching a rabbit now and then from the knight's forest and attending comforting services in their little church when some itinerant priest happened by. They spun thread and wove cloth; they threshed grain; they minded numerous geese belonging to the knight; they sang a lot; they fell into bed at sundown and rose an hour before sunup; and they died without ever having moved ten miles from where they were born, unless some marauding enemy captured them as slaves and later set them loose, in which case they invariably returned to Bukowo, for it was known as the finest village along the river, the one with two castles.

Among the villagers there was one stubborn family that had survived every vicissitude, century after century. Its eldest sons were always known as Jan, and because they worked as foresters, sometimes as Jan of the Forest. They were a taciturn lot, clever in the lore of the woods, obedient to the rule of their masters, but occasionally they produced a lad of fiery temperament, gifted in playing pranks and daring in his challenges to authority, and these Jans were always given the affectionate nickname Janko. There had been seven or eight Jankos in village memory and some had been redoubtable. When Ruthenian marauders had penetrated almost to the Vistula, one Janko led a band of village men who drove them back with heavy losses, and from a dead body this Janko had stolen an odd-shaped medal bearing a non-Christian symbol, which the priest wanted to destroy because it was pagan, but which the various Jankos kept hidden beneath one of the walls of their cottage. On the occasions when it was produced, the villagers were convinced that it honored a heathen goddess.

In this generation there was no Janko, nor anything distinctive about the miserably poor family that occupied the cottage. There was Jan the Woodsman; Danuta, his wife, toothless although only twenty-nine; the boy Jan, who loved the forest and was now running through it to spread an alarm; and the girl Moniczka, a lively, pretty lass. Among the four they had only two extra pieces of clothing: a man's jacket, which either of the two Jans could wear to festivals, and a woman's dress, which could be let out or tucked up depending upon whether Danuta or her daughter was to wear it.

It was now an hour before dawn, and when Danuta awakened to make the morning broth she discovered that her son was not sleeping in his accustomed place on the floor and she nudged Moniczka with her foot. The girl jumped up instantly, supposing that she was being summoned to work, but her mother merely asked: "Where's Jan?"

"I thought he was here," the girl said.

"Well, he isn't." Then, with instinctive fear of the unknown, Danuta asked: "Was he here at all?"

Before the girl could answer, there came from the edge of the forest her brother's agonized voice uttering the terrible cry that would awaken the whole village: "Mongols!"

Fifty years had passed since the last intrusion of this dreadful horde, but legends of what it meant were so much a part of daily life that a few fortunate people reacted almost instantaneously and thus saved themselves. Others, terrified by what might happen in the next moments, hesitated or became confused, forgetting promises they had made themselves as to how they would act "when the Mongols came," and these would perish.

Mother Danuta grabbed her shawl with one hand, her daughter with the other, and without even waiting for her son to reach the cottage or for a chance to say goodbye to her husband, who had responsibilities of his own, she dashed for a secret path that led into the heart of the forest and by accident chose the very one that her son was using to leave it. "Save yourself!" she shouted as they passed.

Her husband, reacting to inherited fears, bolted like a frightened deer to the little castle, shouting as he approached "Mongols! Mongols!" and when his panic-filled voice penetrated to the dark halls, Zygmunt knew instantly what he must do. Springing from bed, grabbing what little armor he possessed, he shouted at his wife "Save yourself!" and sped to where his priceless horse was tethered. Leaping to its back, he galloped to the river's edge and goaded the beast to plunge in. As soon as the water was deep enough he slipped out of his saddle, grabbed the horse's tail, and swam with it to the far side, where, as planned, he would meet up with other lesser knights.

Jan, satisfied that he had done all he could to warn the little castle, now dashed along small footpaths to the bigger one, shouting as he drew near "Mongols! Mongols!" whereupon Krzysztof, who was always awake before dawn, appeared at the castle gate urging Jan to hurry inside. As soon as the peasant ran gasping in, the heavy door was clanged shut, to reopen periodically as a group of terrified peasants and two lesser knights from the castle environs clamored for refuge.

Now red-headed Krzysztof demonstrated why his neighbors considered him a man of character. Pacifying everyone and demanding silence, he coldly calculated his position: "Only three fighting knights. Where's Zygmunt?"

"He escaped across the river," Jan reported.

"With his horse?"

"Of course."

"Excellent. We have fifty-five peasants here. Far too many, but what can we do?"

He studied each face as if judging the owner's capacity for heroism, then continued: "We have little water. Damned little food. So we can't survive a long siege." No one groaned, but he did see some jaws drop in fear and he knew that what he said now would be critical. "We have one chance, and it's a good one. We don't know if they're Mongols . . . with machines to knock down castles. Suppose they're really Tatars on an expedition . . . horses only. They'll come raging here, hoping to overwhelm us, but if we kill off the first half dozen, they'll wheel their horses about and gallop off." When some faces brightened, he cried: "To us they must be Tatars. And we must drive them back."

With swift precision he placed his best archers at slits in the wall, directing them not to release their arrows until the Tatars were almost at the gates, and then to shoot three arrows as rapidly as possible: "Don't even aim the last two. Just fire."

"And if the Mongols keep coming?" a farmer asked.

"They are not Mongols!" Krzysztof shouted. "Surely God, seeing our desperate plight, will send us Tatars."

He did his best work on the battlements, where he led most of the male peasants to man the huge piles of boulders he had collected there, year after year. These were to be thrown down with as much force as possible onto the heads of the Tatars: "I trust in God that these great stones will turn them back."

A woman lookout shouted from her topmost position in the tower: "The village is burning." And after only a few minutes she called: "The other castle is burning." And then the fearful report: "Here they come!"

Krzysztof stared at the opening in the forest through which they would appear, and those about him could see that he was praying, and then he saw the first little horsemen with their flowing mustaches and conical fur hats and he knew that he and his defenders had a fighting chance. Falling to his knees before the first arrow sped out from his castle or the first boulder was hurled, he cried for all around him to hear: "Thank you, blessed Lord Jesus, for sending us Tatars without machines," and he began the defense of his fortress.

When Vuldai led his Tatars out from the Forest of Szczek he perceived in one glance that the miserable village of Bukowo was not going to provide much booty, so with a brief flash of his right hand he cried: "Destroy it."

Like an explosion of lava from a volcano, the horsemen swept over the settlement, setting fire to every cottage, slaying every human being they encountered, even killing cattle too old to be herded easily to that night's campsite, wherever it was going to be. Of those Bukowo peasants trapped inside the village, all were slain, even though not one of them had taken arms against the Tatars or tried in any way to oppose them.

When Vuldai found the little castle practically undefended, his men simply broke their way in, slaughtering everyone they caught inside, including the wife and children Zygmunt had abandoned when he swam his horse across the Vistula. Disappointed at the poverty of the goods they uncovered inside the castle, the Tatars took revenge by setting it afire, watching with glee as all things consumable fed the roaring blaze, even the corpses. When the fire subsided, the vigorous little men tore down what walls were left, then urinated on the embers.

The invaders now rode to attack Castle Gorka, but here they encountered a much different situation, for when the first line of horsemen galloped up to the walls they were met by a withering hailstorm of arrows, which killed four men and wounded six others. As these latter lay on the ground, wrestling with arrows that had pierced them, great boulders descended from the battlements, crushing three of the men horribly. And when other riders dashed in to rescue survivors, they, too, were met by arrows and crashing boulders.

When Vuldai approached the castle walls, in the third line of attack, he again perceived the situation quickly, and with another wave of his right hand, cried: "Leave it. We cross the river." And he wheeled his own horse tightly, headed for the steep banks of the Vistula, and scrambled his mount down the shaley slope and into the dark water.

By nightfall his six thousand, somewhat diminished, had reached the western shore, and scouts were already scurrying northward to make contact with the larger army to determine where the two branches should meet to concert their attack on Golden Krakow.

When Krzysztof of Gorka surveyed the pitiful condition of his domain he could have been forgiven had he allowed himself to be submerged in despair, for only his castle remained. His other six villages had been destroyed as completely as Bukowo; his peasants had been slain; the homes of his lesser knights had been devastated and their women killed; and there seemed to be no reasonable strategy by which the terrible scourge of Tatars could be either punished or turned back. Inevitably, Golden Krakow must fall to their torches, but Krzysztof was unwilling to concede this inevitability, and in the perilous days ahead he became the soul and animating spirit of Poland.

He was forty-eight years old, almost an ancient in that time of early death, with no substantial resources of his own except his conviction that knights defended their dukes regardless of circumstances: "We will march to Krakow and save that city from the wild horsemen."

When he studied his position coldly he found little to reassure him: "Nine horses only in my entire territory. Fourteen men who know how to use arms. No food surplus. No help arriving from any quarter. Good! We know we must depend upon ourselves." Running his fingers through his red hair, he laughed, spat on the ground, and renewed his pledge: "We march to Krakow, for the duke will need us."

From the forest he conscripted every man who had escaped slaughter, and found among them the boy Jan whose running shouts had enabled Castle Gorka to prepare its defenses: "You march with me to tend the horses." And when he learned that this lad was the son of that adult Jan who had joined in the boulder-hurling, he cried: "Jan and Jan, that's a good omen. For in the Bible there are many Jans, and they are all men of good report."

With the same enthusiasm he would have shown had he commanded a battalion of well-equipped cavalry, he assembled his fragile troop, then dispatched the older Jan to the far side of the Vistula to locate Zygmunt and any other gentry who had escaped with their horses. His orders were: "You are to come back across the river and assemble at Castle Gorka."

There the expeditionary force was organized, a pitiful rabble of men whose wives and children had been slain, of cavaliers with wretched horses or none, of lancers with no weapons. They comprised about ninety men, if one counted the foot-servants who tagged along and the boy Jan. They set forth immediately for Krakow, hoping to arrive before the Tatars could mount their attack, and when young Jan saw the golden city for the first time, with its splendid towers and walls, and formidable castle and shops with incredible riches, he told his father: "They can never capture such a city," but the woodsman whose eyes were trained to note differences saw quickly that the supposed defenses were more show than reality. He would not allow such walls to be built in the village of Bukowo.

The boy, like his elders, was perplexed by the young duke to whom all present owed allegiance, for although he was sovereign in this part of Poland, he seemed never to know what exactly to do and he alternated between surges of heroic optimism and torments of despair, so that on this day he was prepared to defend the city with his life and on the next he was seeking counsel as to the best way to surrender the town before the Tatars started to burn it. When Jan asked a local soldier about such contradictions, because Krzysztof of Gorka certainly displayed great constancy, the Krakow man explained: "You must excuse the duke. He doesn't know whether Krakow belongs to him or not, or even whether he belongs to Krakow."

This sounded silly, so Jan asked what the man was saying, and the latter replied: "Poor fellow. His friends have put him on our throne five times, but his enemies have kicked him off four times."

"Do they want someone else?" Jan asked.

"No. The people of Krakow don't want to be ruled by anyone."

Jan pondered this during most of one night when he was helping pile logs across the main entrance to the city, and he thought it strange that a big city like Krakow could not govern itself intelligently when a little village like Bukowo could: Our knight tells us what to do and we do it. When the priest comes he tells us how to remain friends with Jesus and we do what he says. Here they have a duke and an archbishop, but nobody obeys.

Next day at noon, when the Tatars were reported on the outskirts to the north, Jan became totally confused, for word flashed through the defenders that the duke, terrified by the prospect of what might happen in the next days, had fled the city completely, taking along two women he liked, with the intention of crossing the mountains into Hungary, where there was peace and where the Tatars never came. In its moment of maximum peril, Krakow was abandoned by its legitimate ruler.

It was curious that no one in the remaining leadership considered even for one moment marching north to engage the Tatars in preventive battle: "They're so swift they'd overwhelm us. The horses of our cavalry are too slow. With Tatars there's nothing to do but hide until they go away."

Krzysztof alone wanted to sally forth, and he believed he had tactics which would neutralize Tatar mobility, but he was forbidden to try. Polish strategy, with the young duke gone, consisted of selecting the largest churches with the stoutest walls and hiding therein as many citizens as possible, then praying that the walls would stand until the Tatars ran out of food or patience.

Four times Krzysztof addressed the knights, pleading with them to take decisive action, but they had no concept of union or strong leadership or concerted movement toward a common goal; they were men of insolent freedom, and the abuse they had showered upon their reasonably capable young duke they also showered upon any one of their own members who threatened to stick his head above the generality. Poles hated strong leadership, and when Krzysztof of Gorka showed signs of exerting it they cut him down.

"You have been given St. Andrew's church with the big cloister," the commanders told him. "Allow as many citizens inside as it will hold, and pray."

On 21 March 1241 red-headed Krzysztof, aware of the disgraceful act he was performing, led his Bukowo men into the nave of the fine old church with the stoutest walls in Krakow, and there they accepted seven hundred residents of the city, including a group of priests who started prayers that the church might be spared. There they remained for three awful days and nights, shivering in terror as they heard the Tatars galloping into the city, where fires began to rage and women scream. They could hear the destruction moving methodically from street to street, until it reached the area of the church itself, crashing at last against the powerful walls. They cringed as they heard great oaken beams come thundering at the gates, and they watched with terror as the gates swayed inward, but at this point Krzysztof and his strongest men rushed forward to support the doors, and they held. When the Tatars tried to set the gates afire, men from aloft poured down precious water, and again the doors were saved, but the screams and the galloping of horses continued throughout the three days.

On the fourth morning, at about the ninth hour, one of Krzysztof's watchmen on the tower shouted: "They're moving off!" and when excited aides rushed up to verify the report, they saw that the Tatars were indeed quitting the city, but they also saw that Golden Krakow of the beautiful towers, this center of light and commerce and religion, had been put to the torch, and when the gates of St. Andrew's were swung open, at noon on 24 March, the survivors walked out in a stupor to see only the charred remains of what had been one of the world's illustrious cities.

Krzysztof of Gorka did not waste time in lamentation; he more than most could appreciate the terrible loss which had occurred here, but he also knew that only a relentless pursuit of the Tatars, an incessant harassment of their flanks, would ever turn them back from their devastating sweep through Christian Europe, and he was grimly determined to provide that harassment.

Collecting all the remnants he could, and turning the governance of the city over to the aides of the absconded duke—for his enemies knew nothing of government except how to overturn it—he marched westward, hoping to encounter other remnants who would coalesce to oppose the Tatars on some battlefield more favorable to the Polish cause.

• • •

The spring of 1241 was one of the darkest periods in Polish history, for the rampaging Tatars had ripped the fledgling nation into shreds. Krakow lay in ruins. The Vistula was closed to river traffic. Fields were left barren and centers of production were burned out. There seemed to be no cohesion anywhere, and deep shadows covered the land.

Krzysztof was faring as poorly as his land. His two best horses had been killed and the ones that remained were not strong, but he did have this fellow Zygmunt of Bukowo, who was proving to be a man of some stability; if you told him to hold a difficult position, he held it. He was not intelligent and could not follow a complex argument, but when his neck muscles tightened and his shoulders squared he could be formidable. There were a few others like him, so with undiminished conviction that the Poles would triumph in the end, Krzysztof led his remnants westward to intermediary battles he knew they could not win.

He mustered a half-hearted stand at Raciborz, where the Poles were almost annihilated by the brilliant horsemanship of General Pajdar and his united forces. Undaunted, he regrouped and retreated stubbornly to the town of Opole, where he fell in with an enormously fat duke named Mieszko Otyly, Mieszko the Obese, who displayed some skill in generalship. With Krzysztof's daring help, the fat one laid a trap for the Tatars as they attempted to cross the Oder River, and the Polish forces might have won their first real victory except that at the height of the battle Mieszko the Obese grew frightened at the magnitude of what was happening and ordered a full retreat. He might have been overly cautious; he might have been downright cowardly; or he might have shown real brilliance in damaging the Tatars and moving off before they could annihilate him. Regardless of what impelled his move, he allowed the Tatars free access to the riverbanks, but he did save his troops for a disorganized retreat to the formidable city of Wroclaw, called Breslau by the Germans, where at last Krzysztof heard some reassuring news.

Wroclaw could be defended, for it, too, stood on the Oder River; it had steep flanks; it already contained a large number of troops; and best of all, it was governed by a remarkable pair: Hedwig, a strong-minded German princess who had come here decades ago to marry a dashing Polish count, now dead; and her able son Henryk

Pobozny, Henry the Pious, a sagacious, just and heroic man whose ambition it was to unite the many shattered dukedoms like Krakow's into one powerful nation. To achieve this, he realized that he must demonstrate his leadership by being the only Polish commander to defeat the Tatars.

When Krzysztof first met Henry the Pious he liked him and saw a chance that here at last was a leader capable of establishing order among the Polish forces and common sense among their captains. Hope began to germinate, but when Krzysztof met Hedwig, whom the years would consecrate as a saint, he was trebly encouraged. She was a rare woman; after she and her husband had produced seven children, she cried "Enough!" and retired to a monastery, from which she continued to give counsel and even rule when her powerful husband was incapacitated.

She was especially likable when she appeared with her son, for his strength and piety were reinforced by her German sagacity, and no part of Poland was better governed than the lands adjacent to Wroclaw. Krzysztof sensed this immediately as he talked with Hedwig and her son, but he was even more impressed by a much different group of Germans who rode in from the Baltic coast.

He saw them first as they approached the north gate of Wroclaw, a company of some four hundred knights, all big, all strong, all blond, all dressed in black, with capacious white surplices covering their armor and proudly displaying the mark of their order: a huge black cross standing out boldly against the white ground. These were the Teutonic Knights, a holy order blessed by the Pope himself and commissioned by him to carry Christianity to the heathen lands facing the Baltic. Each item of their appearance, from their supple chain armor to the arbalests some carried to the grim set of their mouths, announced that here were men ready for battle, and Krzysztof joined the other watchers in cheering their arrival.

They were led by a handsome man in his fifties, Wolfram von Eschl, who, when he approached Hedwig and her son, threw himself before them, grasped the hem of Hedwig's gown, and cried: "We have come to serve Christ in your behalf."

"Rise," she said quietly. "We have great need of you."

In the council directing the defense of Wroclaw, Krzysztof was struck by how similar his own assessments were to those of Von Eschl. Both men believed that Polish troops must meet Tatar mobility by great free movements of their own. Both felt that the place to strike the Tatars was when they attempted to cross the Oder again. And most significant of all, both were convinced that the Poles could win if they kept hacking away remorselessly at the Tatar flanks.

Von Eschl also endeared himself to Krzysztof by saying bluntly: "We must watch this Fat Mieszko. I don't like him, and I fear that if the battle grows fierce . . ." He shrugged his shoulders.

"At Opole he ran away, so don't count on him in your plans," Krzysztof said, but he was concerned with deeper matters. "I'm sure the Tatars know they must subdue Wroclaw or their passage west will be prohibited. They can't afford to bypass us. And they can't sustain a siege. So what we must prepare for is a frontal assault."

To inhibit this, Henry the Pious decided to meet the Tatars a goodly distance east of the city, and there he positioned a major part of his army, with Krzysztof and the Germans on his right flank, and when the two had studied the terrain, Von Eschl said with sober calculation: "I'm not sure we can hold them here. Quite possibly we'll have to fall back into the city."

"But certainly we'll do what damage we can," Krzysztof protested.

"That we will!" the German agreed. "It's like our constant battles with the Lithuanians. Hack away at them whenever you can. Punish them as sorely as you can. But when they outnumber you with better horsemen and more spearmen, let them go past and wait for a better day. But even as they go, cut at their horses, wear them down."

Von Eschl's anticipation of this preliminary battle proved amazingly accurate. The Tatars knew that this time they could not afford to bypass this linchpin in Europe's defenses and they supposed that the best way to take it was by overwhelming the Poles in the first skirmish, and this they did. At their first flight of arrows, which came humming like a flight of deadly birds, Fat Mieszko turned and took his needed brigades with him, leaving a vast empty space into which the Tatars galloped and from which they spread destruction on all sides.

Within less than an hour the battle was over, a total rout, but even so, when Krzysztof and Von Eschl studied the results, they saw cause for hope, glimmering though it was at a far distance. "In this battle," the Teutonic Knight said, "they've tasted real opposition. The fat one fled, true, but you and I made them pay viciously for every horse they stole. You're wondering tonight, Red Head. And I'm wondering. But be damned, the Tatars are beginning to wonder most of all. The next battle, that's when we'll get them."

"Always you say 'the next one,'" Krzysztof said, and Von Eschl, whose ancestors had fought in the Holy Land and Hungary and Prussia and Lithuania, replied: "A soldier lives always for the next battle, because he knows that before it arrives impossible changes can occur in his favor." When the stars came out, he pointed to the defenses of Wroclaw: "Imagine what we'll do to them when they try to attack the city!"

To the surprise of these two tested warriors, the assault on Wroclaw never came, for early next morning Henry the Pious announced that all troops would be withdrawn forty miles to the west, where they would engage the Tatars in a culminating battle around his secondary castle at Legnica. So without firing an arrow, the Tatars took their third ducal city, and as they burned and raped, shouted that now all lay supine before them.

This was not the case. Dowager Hedwig had summoned from all neighboring nations allies to unite in one great effort to repel the invaders, and now the army would comprise not only her son's tested Silesians but also South Germans and Bohemians and a scattering of Frenchmen, and particularly, the huge Teutonic Knights with their blazing white tunics and black crosses. But on 8 April 1241, Krzysztof and Von Eschl were walking through the castle grounds, swearing to one another how each would deport himself the next day, when a massive stone dislodged itself from a cornice and fell only a few feet ahead of the duke.

"It's an omen!" his men shouted, and news spread through the allied camp that God had warned Henry the Pious not to start the battle on the morrow, and that night, when Dowager Hedwig added her pleas that everything wait till a contingent of Hungarian mercenaries arrived from the south, Krzysztof had an opportunity to witness behavior which justified Henry's name of Pious, for the duke said with prayerlike gravity: "Beloved Mother, I cannot wait even one day longer, because great is the misery of my people as they die under the Tatar lash. Therefore I must fight tomorrow, and risk my life, and await death itself if I am fated to die in defense of our Christian faith."

He prayed most of that night, and in the morning he moved as if an aureole placed by God Himself hovered above his head. Inspiring his men as never before, he led them into battle, ten thousand Poles against twenty thousand Tatars, and he came very close to winning an inspired victory, for aides like Krzysztof of Gorka and Wolfram von Eschl ripped at the Tatar flanks, causing terrible disruption, but in the end the miracles which the Poles hoped for favored not them but the Tatars.

It was when the battle hung in the balance that a company of six Tatars rode toward the Polish lines with the wind strongly at their back, carrying aloft a monstrous red banner with an X painted across it. On top of one of the shafts supporting the banner stood the carving of an ugly black head, its chin buried in black hairs, its eyes glaring defiance. When the Tatars reached a point only a hundred paces away, the men began to shake the giant banner with all their might, and immediately this huge black head started to puff out large clouds of smoke which stank so awfully that it nearly knocked the Polish cavalry off their horses, and caused them to choke and even to vomit. And there was confusion everywhere.

At this moment a man rushed from the Tatar lines as if he were a prisoner escaping, and he dashed into the middle of the Polish troops, shouting in good Polish: "Run! Run! All is lost!" And by ill luck this spy ran directly into the section captained by Mieszko the Obese, who became so terrified by the biting smoke and the wild shouts that again he fled the battlefield with all his troops.

With shock and sorrow Krzysztof saw chaos overtake the Polish lines, where a score of leaders were cut down, but there was still a chance to restore reason, so he galloped to where Von Eschl in his white tunic was inflicting real damage on the invaders. But as they fought side by side Krzysztof happened to look across the fray, and saw the Tatars surround the duke, and isolate him, and stab at him many times, and finally sever his head from his body.

In great rage he led his Poles and Von Eschl's Germans in pursuit of the Tatars who carried away the head, but he was frustrated by thousands of fresh Tatar cavalry who now entered the battle, and as day waned, all hope of a Polish victory vanished. But remembering Von Eschl's doctrine that one hacked and chewed at an enemy as long as possible, he did just that, but in time his third horse was killed under him, and he had to pursue his vengeance on foot, for he could not locate young Jan, who was tending the fourth horse.

As he slashed about with his long sword, keeping the Tatars at bay, Zygmunt of Bukowo saw his lord's predicament, dashed through the battle lines, leaped down from his own horse, and shouted: "Sir Knight! You are the one to ride!" Without even pausing to acknowledge the gift, for this was what a liege was expected to do in such circumstances, Krzysztof mounted the new horse and galloped off to join Von Eschl's Teutonic Knights, who were slaughtering Tatars as they attempted to withdraw with booty gathered from Polish corpses.

At dusk the humiliated Poles lifted the headless body of their duke, and a rumor started that the corpse was not the duke's and that he still lived on another part of the battlefield, but Hedwig recognized a scarf she had given him and said: "This is my son," and she directed the men holding the body: "Pull off his left boot," and when this was done everyone saw that the foot had six toes.

Thus died Henryk Pobozny, a man of superpiety who believed that dukes should not run away in moments of danger but should stand and fight for their castles, their people and their God.

When Pajdar and Kajdu, the victorious Tatar generals, surveyed the battlefield their first impression was that they had gained a total triumph, and the latter cried exultantly: "Look at the Polish dead! And we have the duke's head! We'll jam it on the end of a staff and carry it down to Hungary. To show Batu Khan what we've accomplished."

But Vuldai, who had been more personally engaged in the fighting, said: "General, our losses before were never so great. That one with red hair, the other in the flowing white tunic, they fight like devils."

To this Pajdar responded: "The gateway to Europe beckons us. If Batu Khan and his army conquer Hungary, we can ride to where the other ocean flows."

Vuldai saw things differently: "In Wroclaw we had an easy victory but little booty . . . few horses. Today we killed many, but again, where are the horses we need? The food supplies? Each battle becomes more difficult and yields us less."

General Kajdu countered: "It is strange to hear such talk on the night of a great victory. Are you counseling me to retreat?"

Vuldai said honestly: "At this moment, when we count our numbers, can we really call it a victory? If we ride forward another six weeks, we'll meet armies always larger than before . . . and ours will be smaller . . . man by man."

Pajdar snapped: "Speak forthrightly, what do you advise?"

Vuldai, counting the enormous losses in his head, said: "I say go back to Kiev. That's our land. We know it. We can rule there forever, protected by the steppes."

Pajdar, remembering his promises to Batu Khan, asked: "And what about Hungary? Where they'll be waiting for us. For the march together into Europe."

Vuldai said with commendable prescience: "On the night of their great victory in Hungary, they'll be asking these same questions. Believe me."

In some irritation Pajdar asked: "What would you have me do?" But before his subordinate could reply, the general confessed: "Little warrior, your words have meaning." Reaching across his horse's neck, he grasped Vuldai's shoulder: "Tell me straight, what?"

The diminutive horseman, whose courage no man could question, told the brothers: "Half the army turns south over the mountains into Hungary to provide help if they need it, and they will. Half, back to Kiev with our slaves and our booty."

The two brothers indicated that they would stay together, and General Pajdar asked: "Which half of the army will you lead?" and the little captain said: "My heart longs for Kiev . . . and the open steppes," but young Pajdar said: "Mine longs for wherever the next battle is to be."

So it was decided that night that half the Tatar force, under the two fiery generals, would turn south toward the Carpathians, where they would be needed, while the other half, under the command of Vuldai, would deliver the spoils of battle and the slaves to Kiev, where the capital of the Tatar nation would henceforth be.

While the Tatars were adjusting to their victory, Krzysztof and his German friend were assessing their defeat, and Wolfram von Eschl was almost exultant: "We've stopped them. We've struck terror into their hearts."

"We've lost everything," Krzysztof lamented.

"No!" Von Eschl cried excitedly. "We may have lost this battle—"

"We've lost every battle," Krzysztof corrected. "I myself have faced them six times and been defeated six times. Today, worst of all."

"No, no!" Von Eschl said, almost pleadingly. "With every loss we've damaged them more fatally. I hope they continue westward toward the German towns. We'll massacre them!" He stopped, grasped his Polish ally by the wrist, and predicted: "There is no possibility that those men"—and he pointed toward the Tatar camp where General Pajdar and his aide Vuldai were doing their planning—"will dare to continue. They've seen what determined Poles like you can do when your fury is roused." He chuckled at what he was about to say next. "And they've certainly seen what a company of German knights can do with our big horses and strong lances." He came close to flexing his muscles in anticipation of the next battle.

A fugitive thought crept into Krzysztof's battle-weary brain, and he considered some moments before expressing it, for he had not explored its implications, but now he said: "Wolfram, I wish that you and I could continue standing against them."

Without much thinking, Von Eschl said: "My company must return to our Christianizing in the north. We're needed up there." But then the meaning of his friend's comment sank in, and he said: "Germans and Poles should be natural allies. Your countryman Conrad of Mazovia realized this when he invited us into his domain to help him civilize it." He grew enthusiastic: "We Germans could bring you so much. Christianity . . . books for your monks when they learn to read . . . strong government . . . music . . ."

"We have all those things," Krzysztof protested. "Our monks can read. We're Christians now. We've been so for three centuries. And as for music . . ."

"I mean real Christianity," Von Eschl said. "The direct line from the Pope to the head of our Order to men like me handing it over in consecrated form to men like you."

"My great-great-grandfather was already Christian."

"Not really. Poland was never converted in an orderly way. That's what I mean when I say that we Germans could bring you so much."

Krzysztof was not an argumentative man, so he dropped the discussion of Christianity and spoke directly to the problem which concerned him on this night of battle: "I meant that with your skill at arms . . ."

"That we have," Von Eschl said. "And it's yours to call upon at any moment. One day soon we'll have thousands and thousands of our knights along the Baltic, and they'll always be ready to spring to your defense, as we did this time."

"I'm pleased to hear that," Krzysztof said, and with great warmth he clasped Von Eschl's hands, for he had found in this valiant German knight a man upon whom he could rely and he could foresee many future opportunities when they might be fighting side by side. As they said their last goodbyes Krzysztof was almost ready to concede that by dogged resistance the Christian armies had gained a curious kind of victory over the pagans.

• • •

During Vuldai's retreat across ravaged Poland, he issued orders to the conquered people: "From this day on, when Tatars ride in from the east, you are to throw wide your gates, open your barns, herd your cattle before us so we can choose the best, and stand aside while we search your cottages. If you hesitate even one moment, we will burn and pillage and take your women."

In the dreadful years that followed, Golden Krakow would be sacked many times in enforcement of Vuldai's program, and the Poles were bewildered as to why this terrible scourge could not be resisted, but Poland was not alone in its inability to fend off the invincible thrusts coming out of Asia. Hungary also fell. Bohemia was ravaged; Transylvania and Rumania were powerless to halt the rampages; and even the future Russia lay like a stricken caterpillar attacked by legions of ants. It would not be until such time as Europe developed its manufacturing, fighting and governing skills that it would generate the power to withstand the constant eruptions out of Asia.

But it would be precisely in the development of these skills, especially government, that Poland would lag. In the year 1241 all the nations around her were as disorganized as she: the future Germany was a shambles of minor dukedoms; Russia was a vast swampland of petty competitors; France was broken into warring units; Italy would not coalesce for another six hundred years; and England had developed no central tendency around which to unite the various segments of her island.

Thus Poland was by no means unique in her chaos, but she displayed one ominous difference: whereas other European countries were struggling toward some form of central government and were supporting kings determined to impose their will upon fractious barons, Poland seemed determined to tear down any putative leader who showed signs of being able to consolidate the shattered nation. This abhorrence of central power was recent; in the tenth century Poland had been unified and strong enough to send Christianizing missions to the Baltic lands, but in 1138 a king had intentionally partitioned the nation among his three sons, hoping to avert the fratricidal wars of succession so common at that time. Subsequent ducal partitions rendered the country exceptionally divided and weak.

So in those centuries when other peoples were taking their first awkward steps in forging political entities like councils and parliaments upon which future greatness would depend, Poland was frustrating attempts by its sturdy middle class to govern itself, for the nation despised central authority and did everything possible to thwart it.

But there was no nation on earth which prized freedom more. Stubborn men like Krzysztof and Zygmunt in their little castles along the Vistula clung to freedom the way deer in the Forest of Szczek utilized every maneuver to preserve theirs, the way the great dark bear of the same forest fought with claws to stay free. Personal freedom was the lifeblood of Poland, but the supreme irony was that its freedom-loving citizens were not able to develop those governmental forms which would preserve that freedom.

This time the Poles had saved Europe from invasion by eastern barbarians, and in centuries to come they would repeat the sacrifice, but they could not save themselves.

As Vuldai prepared to retreat across the Vistula at Sandomierz on his homeward route through Lublin, he learned from a captive that the big red-headed knight who had wreaked so much havoc at the Battle of Legnica was the same who had repulsed his troops in January at Castle Gorka, only a few miles to the south. Inflamed with desire for revenge, Vuldai turned his army abruptly and headed for the castle, and before long his horde had crossed the Vistula and begun their assault upon the fortress.

With wild and savage grandeur the great destroyers from the east broke down the gates that had once defied them and roared through the rooms, raping and killing. They then piled the castle with limbs from the forest, scattered a pot of oil, and set it ablaze. Every item not stone in this centuries-old building was consumed: roof, ceilings, doorjambs, the bodies of Krzysztof's womenfolk, the corpses of his grandchildren and even the hunting dogs whose throats had been slit vanished in the conflagration. Castle Gorka was no more.

Vuldai then led his men into the Forest of Szczek, which they combed for a last crop of fugitives whom they could carry as slaves to Kiev, and among the beech trees they captured toothless Danuta and her attractive daughter Moniczka, both of whom they raped incessantly.

But this Danuta was a considerable woman, and at the age of twenty-nine she did not fancy spending her days in some savage Tatar camp, so when the speeding army reached Zhitomir, grown careless with its easy victories over undefended villages, she waited till the men who kept her and Moniczka for their pleasure were drunk, and she slit their throats. Appropriating their horses, she and her daughter slipped past the reveling guards and set out across the vast and empty wastes that separated them from the Vistula.

It was many hours before Vuldai learned of their escape, and in his rage he was disposed to send troops to recover them, but when he was reminded of who the fugitives were, and could visualize them, he held his right hand out, twisting it now this way, now that, and he said: "One young and very good, one old and no good. Let them go."

So the Tatars returned to their new capital. They had been gone from late December to mid-June, just about half a year, sixty thousand tumultuous horsemen coming out of the steppes to confront nations that had cities and organized patterns of life. In that time, in addition to what Batu Khan was doing in Hungary, the Tatars had destroyed more than four hundred Polish villages, had ravaged sixteen towns and cities, had gutted and burned nearly a hundred isolated castles, and had slain more than a hundred thousand Poles.

They brought with them from the steppes no new ways of doing things, no inventions, no concepts which would revolutionize life within the lands they conquered. And they took back with them no tangible artifacts which they could use to make their own life better: no process for weaving cloth or putting ideas into written words or building a better wooden plow. They brought nothing and they took nothing.

Yet in exactly this same year Crusaders from Europe were fighting in the Holy Land about Jerusalem, and from that experience they would bring back ideas and artifacts which would revolutionize Europe, and the Saracens among whom they lived and fought would borrow from them concepts innumerable. It was Poland's grief that her visitors were Tatars and not Saracens, that her intercourse was not with cultivated Arabs but with explosive barbarians from the vast Asian deserts.

Explosive? Yes, the Tatars did bring that one thing to Poland, that mysterious poison gas which had so terrified Fat Mieszko. But they did not reveal the formula for its manufacture, so that even this potentially important innovation proved abortive.

If they did not take back things, they did return with something which would in the end prove more meaningful than mere things: the concept of a city, an orderly collection of human beings who could accomplish results that a horde of wandering individuals never could. Remembering Krakow, they established Karakorum, a city of majestic spaces and beautiful constructions. From later raids they would bring back glittering adornments to embellish it, and upon this example, the other cities of central Asia would be fashioned. Rampaging horsemen can conquer; only the city can civilize.

And if they brought one concept home, they left one behind, and this was perhaps the major significance of their invasion. From then on, Poles knew that at almost any time, without reason or provocation, barbarians were free to come storming across their indefensible eastern frontier, and this perilous condition would continue for as long as Poland existed.

Along the Vistula, Vuldai's invasion did have consequences of some importance for the three families of Bukowo. The confusion of dukes who now attempted to rule Poland recognized that in Krzysztof of Gorka they had a champion on whom they could depend, so to help him rebuild his ruined castle and to establish him therein as a bulwark of dependability, they ceded to him tracts of land for which they had little use but which he might make profitable. In this manner he received one town, nine villages and some seven thousand additional peasants whose output would belong principally to him. The deed of grant read:

> I, Duke Boleslaw the Chaste, newly restored to my rightful throne at Krakow, do bestow upon my loyal servant Krzysztof of Castle Gorka, in respect of his innumerable services to me during the recent invasions, lands which pertain to my dukedom. In order to ensure that no other person will be tempted to claim these lands for himself or in any way to convert them to his favor, I have prudently ordered nineteen stones placed firmly in the soil at the places I herein indicate, each stone bearing clearly my initials.

> The first stone, on the banks of the River Vistula near the three oaks. The second stone, placed personally by me at the far end of the village called Minice. The third stone, where the stream Brochocin crosses the footpath leading to the bishop's town of Raszow . . .

All towns and villages and farms within the area marked by my stones belong henceforth to said Krzysztof, except that all persons pertaining to these towns, villages and farms, save only the wine-makers and the priests, are obliged to work for me during six weeks each year, as follows: after the Easter octave, two weeks; after the Whitsuntide octave, two weeks; and before St. Martin's day, again two weeks.

During the summer each adult man must provide five stacks of corn and must cut three cartloads of hay for my use. And whenever I travel in said areas, each village is to provide two carts and two guards. But from this time on, said Krzysztof shall act as judge for the entire area and only in very major cases will any hearings be held in my presence or that of any castellan from Krakow.

Among his new villages was one rather similar to Bukowo in that it also had a small castle, but in this one the knight had been slain by the Tatars while the lady lived, and Krzysztof went to her and said: "Lady Benedykta, it is not the will of God that you should live alone in your castle and I in mine," and she agreed, and the line of Gorka was restored.

At the wedding ceremony, which lasted eleven days, Krzysztof remembered with gratitude the good work performed at various battles by his henchman Zygmunt, and to him he gave Bukowo and its few peasants. At the time this did not seem a generous move, for Bukowo consisted of exactly two reconstructed cottages, but others would be built, and upon that fragile foundation the security of the family of Zygmunt of Bukowo would be established. For the moment he remained a petty knight with only one horse, but that would soon change.

And what of the peasant Jan of the Forest and his son Jan who had behaved so bravely when the Tatars came, what did they receive as a reward for their service and their heroism? Nothing. They were peasants who had belonged to Krzysztof and now to Zygmunt, and it was their duty to serve, whether in peace or war. They did not even get assistance in the rebuilding of their cottage, for where they slept was their affair.

But from an unexpected quarter they did receive benefit from the war and the battles they had engaged in. One morning as they toiled in Zygmunt's fields, for he was a stern master eager to rebuild his fortunes, the boy Jan heard a clinking sound in the forest and for one dreadful moment he thought it was the Tatars returning to pillage, but when he looked more closely he saw to his astonishment that it was his mother Danuta and his pretty sister Moniczka . . . on horses!

Old Jan and young Jan leaped in the air with delight and uttered shouts of joy, but the two women came on in silence, dropping the reins of their horses and leaning forward as if all energy was spent. Through many vicissitudes and many nights of hunger they had ridden more than three hundred miles, and often they had feared that they would never see Bukowo or their men again. They did not weep, or laugh, or cheer, or respond to their men, who did all three, but gravely they descended from their horses. They were home, ready to resume their duties, and the first thing they noticed was that the cottage their men were building needed thatching.

When the village learned that both were pregnant by the Tatars, there was a moment of grief and indecision, but in these years of wild dislocation women were often pawns in the tumultuous movement of peoples, and a little village like Bukowo could consider itself lucky if it received any of its captured women back, so in the end these two were welcomed. Of course, in February of 1242 they did produce bastards, but young ones were so earnestly needed to rebuild the settlement that no disgrace adhered to them. Such events, repeated over the centuries, accounted for the fact that many Poles along the Vistula would have darkened skins and eyes slightly aslant, as if they represented echoes out of Asia.

It was not the two bastards who caused trouble, it was the two horses, because Zygmunt, who took mastery of his new-found peasants seriously, supposed that the horses belonged to him, and he was avid about this, for if he could boast of three, he would move out of the miserable condition he had been in when he had only one. But Danuta could not imagine getting the horses the way she had, cutting men's throats to do it, and then surrendering them, so she refused to yield them to her master.

The argument was carried to Krzysztof himself, and in a solemn hearing convened in Castle Gorka, now with a roof, he listened patiently as his liege Zygmunt tried to establish his claim. At the conclusion the red-headed knight delivered his decision:

"It is unthinkable that a knight, even a minor one like Zygmunt of Bukowo, should have only one horse. Great knights ought to have thirty. But it is also unthinkable that a brave woman like Danuta, whose men tried so valiantly to save this community and who herself captured the two horses and rode them with such difficulty back to our village, should have them taken away from her.

"My decision! The big black horse to Zygmunt, the smaller brown horse to Jan the Forester." (It would never have occurred to him to give it to Danuta.)

So Bukowo was reestablished, and once again its two castles guarded the Vistula, and the number of both its cottages and its inhabitants increased. But to the Tatars, always restless in Kiev, the lure of Golden Krakow was irresistible, and they returned on great foraging expeditions in 1260 and most forcefully in 1287, leveling the village on their way and burning its castles. Each time, the patient Poles rebuilt, for it was ingrained in them to love their land, even though they had not yet found a way to protect it.

They even succeeded in transmuting the hideous invasions into one of the golden legends of European history: during one attack on Krakow the Tatars crept close to the walls at midnight and would have captured the city had not a trumpeter stationed in the watchman's tower sounded a bold call that awakened the defenders. But as he blew a repeat of his warning, eager to alert everyone, a Tatar archer shot him through the throat, silencing him.

Thereafter, every hour on the hour, in the great square in Krakow, a trumpeter from that tower has sent forth the same call. But just as the melody seems about to establish itself, the trumpeting stops. The arrow has struck home.

Since that night seven hundred years ago, thousands, millions have stood in the square and heard the trumpeter of Krakow, and as they listened to his brief, brave warning some have dedicated themselves: "When the Tatars return I must be ready."

III

FROM
THE WEST

I N THE YEAR 1378 A REMARKABLE MARRIAGE CEREMONY TOOK place in Hungary, one which was to have considerable significance for Poland.

The father of the bride was a man of French descent, Louis d'Anjou, who ruled as King of Hungary, and also of Poland, a country he rarely visited. He was a wise king of great personal attractiveness and would be remembered in Hungarian history as Louis the Great and in Poland as Louis the Hungarian. He had three charming daughters, and the later years of his life were preoccupied with finding them husbands and kingdoms of their own.

The bridegroom was a handsome German prince, Wilhelm of Habsburg, who had been reared in Vienna and who gave promise of becoming an excellent king in either Austria, Hungary or, more likely, Poland. He was a good catch for the Anjou family, and King Louis was pleased with the match.

But the radiant star of this marriage was the bride, an adorable princess with an inborn grace, a winsome smile and a beauty which set her apart in whatever crowd she graced. She had a charming habit of looking directly into the eye of anyone to whom she spoke and in this way enchanted kings, cardinals, generals and financiers. She was known widely as one of the choice princesses of Europe, and she was five years old.

The wedding was of course ceremonial, but it was also real, because in conformance with a royal custom followed by various countries, as soon as the bride reached the age of twelve her husband was permitted to exercise his connubial rights, and in this case it was hoped that the princess would have early and numerous pregnancies, for it would be her duty to produce sons.

Her name was Hedwig in German, Jadwiga in Polish, and when her illustrious father died in 1381 it was agreed among the nations that she should inherit the Polish throne. Although only eight, she was old enough to know what this meant, and she assured Wilhelm, of whom she had become desperately fond, that as soon as she reached the age of twelve he would be her consort on the throne.

When she was ten she crossed the Carpathians, entered Poland for the first time, and was crowned king . . . not queen, for the Polish nobles wanted to preserve dynastic links to their original kings. They wished her to be known as their king—the preserver of royal tradition.

As soon as she became king she found herself plunged into dynastic problems which with her premature intelligence she was able to understand, so that when her counselors came to her with the sad news "It is no longer desirable that you be married to Wilhelm of Habsburg" she wept a little, sent a message to Austria that she would always love him, and then listened as the men around her explained why she must marry an extraordinary stranger from the north.

Spokesman for her advisers was a minor nobleman of great mental acuity from the middle reaches of the Vistula, Kazimir of Castle Gorka, a wise man although only in his thirties:

"Majesty, the principal problem of your reign will be how to protect Poland from the power of the Teutonic Knights, who threaten us from the west. Believe me, that is of greater significance than any other difficulty you will face, and you must brood upon it constantly.

"How best to keep the Germans in check? You must operate according to one of the wisest counsels ever given a king: 'He who is the enemy of my enemy is my friend.' For the present, the real enemy of the Teutonic Knights is Lithuania, a good and powerful nation to our north and east. If you can ally yourself with Lithuania, you can forge a great nation powerful enough to hold off the Germans. If you stand alone, you and Poland may both perish.

"Fortunately, Lithuania has now produced a grand duke of great ability and considerable charm. His name is Jagiello, and your counselors advise you, plead with you, to marry him."

"How old is he?" the twelve-year-old king asked, and Kazimir replied: "Thirty-five, but he is young in appearance and vital in performance."

"I am told that he is not a Christian," Jadwiga said, and Kazimir replied: "That is correct, but he has promised that if you will have him, he will become one and will command his entire nation to convert, also." The counselor paused, then said: "Rarely can a young woman convert an entire nation to God's divine guidance simply by marrying the right man."

"I am also told that he is a heathen, with a body all covered with matted hair, like an otter or a bear." The young king blushed.

This was a serious charge, especially the part that she did not voice because of maidenly modesty, for it was rumored throughout the court that Jagiello was not only covered with hair like an elk but was also possessed of sexual organs monstrously large and destined to destroy or kill any woman he mated with.

"Majesty," Kazimir said with a comforting, placid smile on his broad face, "I know your fears. You were to have married a handsome young prince of the Habsburgs. Now we propose to replace him with a hairy barbarian of God knows what disposition. Majesty, I will myself go to Lithuania with two men that you select from your council and we shall ask this Jagiello to take a complete bath in our sight, and we shall report to you honestly what we have seen when he stands naked before us."

Jadwiga agreed that this was a most sensible solution to her problem, so a diplomatic mission consisting of three counselors, eighty horsemen and sixty servants set out from Krakow to journey into Lithuania, where the counselors would request Jagiello to take a full bath in their presence. Sitting not three feet from the carved marble tub, they discovered to their delight that the Lithuanian grand duke was not covered with hair and that his sexual organs were in no wise larger than their own and, as one of the counselors told Kazimir, "Rather smaller, if accurate measurements were made."

They hurried back to Krakow with the joyous news that there was no impediment to the marriage, and after Jadwiga was assured that Jagiello would indeed convert to Christianity and bring his pagan nation to the baptismal font with him, she consented to the marriage. She was thirteen, he thirty-six, and they formed one of the noblest royal couples in Europe.

They gave Poland and Lithuania good government and launched one of the most powerful dynasties in Renaissance Europe. During their reign a great university was founded in Krakow, hospitals were started, and stable forms of government initiated. Lithuania, a country of enormous size—Baltic to Black Sea—was officially Christianized, and Polish influence reached to the doorsteps of Muscovy, the future Russia.

Always Jagiello and Jadwiga kept before them the specter of invasion by the Teutonic Knights, but they knew instinctively that they were not yet strong enough to oppose the terror which the knights visited on the far fringes of their land, and they had to bear the invasions and insults in silence.

"The time will come, Jadwiga," Jagiello promised, "when Poland and Lithuania will rise up against these Germans," but he never predicted when this time was likely to happen. So as Poland made progress in small, carefully considered steps, they watched the Teutonic Knights on their western and northern borders vaulting ahead in military and economic prowess.

In these years Jadwiga became the best-loved king Poland had ever had, a gracious, warm, intelligent woman, wise far beyond her years, gifted in political analysis, and winning in her capacity to convince others of the rightness of what she wanted to do. It was particularly noted by foreign ambassadors to the court at Krakow that she made an ideal partner for Jagiello, and many rumors circulated in Paris, Rome and London that when the proper time came, this amazing Polish-Lithuanian couple intended to take the measure of the Teutonic Knights.

In 1399, at the age of twenty-six, Jadwiga evoked thunderous joy throughout Poland by letting it be known that she was pregnant, and seers predicted as a consequence of many favorable omens that the baby was to be a boy. But the child was stillborn, and shortly thereafter this lovely princess, this regal queen, this king of great ability and fortitude, died, and for some years her widowed husband languished, but starting about 1405, when his equally capable cousin Witold, his successor as Grand Duke of Lithuania, began to show mettle and a willingness to join him in opposing the Germans, Jagiello indicated to those about him that the time was drawing near when the new nation of Poland-Lithuania must take arms against the Teutonic Knights, regardless of the consequences. As he told Witold: "We can no longer bear the humiliation."

But Jagiello was a prudent man, and before launching a major war of defense he desired to know all he could about his powerful enemy, so one day in the winter of 1409, when war clouds began to lower, obscuring the northern skies, he asked his counselor Kazimir of Gorka: "Have we at court someone we could insert into the Amber Road? Someone who would travel quietly to the Baltic and see for himself what the Teutonic Knights are up to?"

"Not at court," Kazimir said, "but I have a liege with a big, dumb face who might serve our purpose. I'm sure no one would take him for a spy, and although he's not quick of mind, he is trustworthy."

"Who is he?" the king asked.

"Pawel of Bukowo."

"I have not heard of him. But if you say—"

"I promise nothing! I've warned you that he's rather stupid, but I assure you he's dependable."

"Send him forth," the king said, and Kazimir left the court and journeyed the relatively short distance to his castle along the Vistula, where he summoned Pawel of Bukowo to meet with him.

This Pawel was a petty nobleman with three horses, a castle that was mostly in ruins and the heavy gait of a farmer. He had almost no neck, sloping shoulders and hands that hung out from his hips. Also, he wore his hair cut straight across his eyebrows, so that he created an appearance that was far from attractive, but if one looked at him carefully, one noticed the shrewd eyes that absorbed most of what occurred about him.

"Pawel," Kazimir asked, "how would you like to buy amber for the king?"

"Why doesn't he buy it himself? There's plenty in Krakow."

Very quietly Kazimir said, looking Pawel directly in the eye: "He would prefer a better quality. Say, from Lembok."

Pawel folded his hands over his belly, rocked back and forth a couple of times, and said: "He wants me to spy on the Teutonic Knights."

"I doubt that he would express it that way, Pawel—"

"Where do I get the money?"

"That will be provided."

"You know what they say, Pan? That not a bead of amber leaves Lembok any more except through the knights' hands."

"We want you to buy it from them. In the end, that is. We want you first to see if you can buy it from the Lithuanians. So that you give the appearance of an honest dishonest trader."

Again Pawel rocked back and forth, assessing this dangerous mission. "And when I do that, the knights arrest me. They drag me off to their castle in Malbork and I get hanged."

"Up to the point of hanging, that's what we want. We want you to be arrested. We want you to see Malbork. But we also want you to come back to us with your story."

Pawel dropped his chin onto his fingertips and studied his master. "How do you propose arranging that?"

"You carry with you a letter from the king himself, authorizing you to buy amber—from the Lithuanians, if possible."

"That guarantees my hanging."

"No, the knights will want to use you to send a message back to the king."

Pawel rose from his chair and moved about the castle room. "They'd see through such nonsense in a minute. The Germans aren't stupid."

"Of course they'll see what we're doing. But they'll also see that King Jagiello wants to establish contact with them."

"Why not send an ambassador? As you did in the past?"

"Too formal. Too weighed down in heavy protocol. When the knights see an ambassador coming, they freeze up. With you, they'll talk."

"Do you want me to do this, Pan?"

"I do."

"Then I'll do it." He rose and moved toward the door. "But I will want Janko to accompany me. He's very resourceful, Janko."

So it was agreed, and the king's letter was composed, and the two suede bags of gold coins were delivered, and on an April morning in 1409 square-faced Pawel of Bukowo started eastward toward the

Amber Road, which led by ship from Constantinople to Odessa, by land to Kiev to Minsk to Wilno to the beautiful seacoast town of Lembok, where precious amber was collected for the bazaars of Persia, India, China and Japan.

When Pawel and his attendant Janko, also of Bukowo, had been on the Road one day, spies hurried northward with reports to the castle at Malbork that two mysterious Poles were on their way to Lembok: "We shall follow them closely and inform you of their doings." But at a stop near the town of Mozyr, Pawel told a Polish spy who was awaiting him: "Inform the king's counselor Kazimir of Gorka that the knights have noticed us and are sending messengers north to keep Malbork informed of our movements."

It must be understood that the Teutonic Knights who crept out of Germany to occupy the Baltic seacoast—which should normally have been a part of Poland—acted under a signed commission of the Pope ordering them to Christianize the pagan lands in that region, so that regardless of how they behaved, they acted with papal authority and the approval of God Himself.

Their Order had been formed near Jerusalem in 1189 by a group of crusading knights from Bremen and Lübeck, and their intentions were the noblest: to provide medical services to Christian soldiers striving to wrest the Holy Land from its infidel possessors. The orotund name they took at their beginning testified to their intentions: "Knights of the Teutonic Order of the Hospital of St. Mary in Jerusalem."

The Order achieved little success, and by 1210 boasted of less than ten members who could move into battle fully armored and mounted. What was more ominous, the Catholic church was beginning to move against the Templars and other orders which had proved difficult to discipline, and it seemed likely that the Teutonic Knights would quietly vanish.

But at this critical moment the Order selected as its Grand Master one of the truly great men of the Middle Ages, Hermann von Salza, who combined piety and managerial ability to a high degree—with more of the latter than the former. In a brilliant move he shifted the Order out of the Holy Land, where they were accomplishing nothing—primarily because it was too far for knights from Germany to travel—and into Hungary, whose savage land awaited Christianity and colonizing. Within fifteen years Von Salza threatened to become more powerful than the King of Hungary, Andreas II, who, with practically no warning, banished the knights from his territories. Homeless, but still possessed of great organizing skill and military prowess, they looked all through Europe for a theater in which to exhibit their abilities, and by the most fortunate chance they heard of a Polish duke who was having trouble managing the pagan barbarians on his northern borders.

In 1226, the year after they were expelled from Hungary, Conrad of Mazovia in northern Poland begged the knights to enter his domain for a brief spell to help him subdue his pagans, and in gratitude for their assistance, he wrote some unfortunate letters that could be interpreted as an invitation to stay permanently and also as a grant of land on which they could build a headquarters from which to Christianize territories that he, Conrad, did not own.

Hermann von Salza had brought his first German knights to Poland in 1226, with the presumed intention of staying a year or two. Nearly two hundred years later they owned most of the Baltic coast, including the lands of the Latvians and Estonians, and showed every intention of soon controlling Lithuania, Poland and much of Russia. Superior in military might, managerial ability and commerce, they excelled in diplomatic relations with the rest of Europe—especially with the papacy—and seemed destined to rule eastern Europe.

Their first Christianizing mission involved the Prussians, a handsome, barbaric, rural group of people who controlled the amber trade along the Baltic. All Europe applauded when the Teutonic Knights brought civilization and the church to these heathens, and it was upon this laudable beginning that the Germans erected their powerful structure.

They Christianized the Prussians in a most effective way: they eliminated them. Dividing the tribes, they dealt with them one by one, driving some into the sea, others into slavery, others into the wastelands of Russia. Those who remained on soil the knights wanted, about half the number, were converted into serfs and forbidden to marry, so that no further Prussian children would be forthcoming; they were to work fifteen hours a day, seven days a week until they died off.

The knights always held the Prussian barbarians in contempt, but when the latter were annihilated, the knights assumed their name and many of their characteristics. In later centuries, when Prussia became a name famous throughout Europe, there was hardly a true Prussian alive.

From this secure base, not very large, the Teutonic Knights launched two campaigns of real brilliance. Avoiding the pitfall which had overtaken early Poland and which would always contaminate its political processes—that of refusing to identify and follow one competent leader—the knights adopted the policy of electing one capable man Grand Master for life and then following his guidance for better or worse. With extraordinary luck, they picked a chain of men who were perhaps not as brilliant as the great Hermann von Salza but certainly as single-minded and as devoted to the Order. Prussia, under the Teutonic Knights, was the best-governed unit in Europe, and not once was there any war of succession, rebellion by contending claimants or uprising by the general population, for with great prudence the knights had replaced the vanished Prussians with loyal Germans imported from the homeland.

Once Prussia was established, a chain of impeccable military campaigns pushed the boundaries of the tiny original grant outward, so that the Teutonic state was fabulously enlarged, with its new areas also filled by German farmers imported from the west. Pomerania was captured, Chelmno Land, Dobrzyn, Samogitia; always the pressure was maintained, the civilized west encroaching upon the savage east.

These military campaigns were an unquestioned success, but it sometimes seemed that the Order's diplomatic triumphs were more fruitful, for the knights repeatedly circulated through the courts of Europe glowing written reports of their extreme piety, their unfailing courage in the face of barbarian enemies, their success in introducing Christianity to alien lands:

> We fight against the savage Lithuanians, the pagan Poles, the heathen Latvians and the Estonians who know not God, and a score of darkened lands between. Especially we war against the Muslim Tatars, a branch of the same infidel nation that controls the Holy Land where we fought for so long. We are the right arm of God, the successful extension of Rome, and all who long to fight for Jerusalem but cannot get there are invited to join this greater crusade at home.

As a consequence of this constant insistence on the virtue of the Germans and the barbarity of all others, a flood of knights from other countries sought to join the Order, and though they were refused full membership, they were granted honorable affiliation, so that when the knights went into battle against a country like Lithuania they had in their ranks young men of noble family from France, England, Luxembourg, Austria, Hungary, Bohemia and the Low Countries, and each man was satisfied that he rode under the banner of Jesus Christ to subdue an inferior civilization and bring it into the glorious fold of the Christian church.

The propaganda campaign was especially vicious against Poland, which had become Christian officially in A.D. 966 and unofficially perhaps fifty years earlier, and it was impossible in this year of 1409 when Krakow had a fine university, a sophisticated court and a strongly entrenched church for Poles to think of themselves as pagan. But that was the report circulated through the knightly circles of Europe, and it was to rescue Poland from darkness that many of the alien knights volunteered to help the Germans.

If one asked a hundred courtiers throughout Europe what the Teutonic Knights did, the answer almost universally would be: "They carry Christianity to pagan lands. They are the right arm of God." And if one asked: "Who are these knights?" the answer would be: "They are ordained priests who have taken the vow of chastity and poverty, and they do only as their leader, the Pope in Rome, commands."

The truth was somewhat different. At Marienburg, not far from Danzig where the Vistula River enters the Baltic Sea, the Teutonic Knights had erected within a semicircle of high brick walls—a river forming the other half of the wall—the most powerful fort in Europe, a magnificent red structure that ran more than three thousand feet from northeast to southwest. It consisted of two great central castles, many-storied and battlemented, and, north and south, two immense walled courtyards filled with administrative buildings. In time of stress, the fortification at Malbork could bring within its protection about ten thousand defenders, with adequate food and cistern water to withstand a siege of months or even years.

This was not a monastery fortress such as one might see at Cluny in France or York in England; this was a tremendous battle station, infinitely rich in possessions and power, and it was ruled by hardheaded men determined to use it as the nucleus of a vast temporal kingdom.

The knights had forewarned the world of their intentions early in their occupancy of the castle. In 1308 the nearby town of Danzig had given trouble, so the knights marched there singing *"Jesu Christo Salvator Mundi"* and killed most of the citizens, about ten thousand in number, replacing them with German immigrants who gave them full allegiance.

It was difficult for the Poles to inform Europe about such matters, because the Teutonic Knights always got their report in first, and also because every settlement in Prussia bore two names, the German and the Polish, and this would continue throughout history, as the following table compiled by a Polish scribe in 1409 testified:

> Its real name is Gdansk but they call it Danzig
> Its real name is Malbork but they call it Marienburg
> Its real name is Pomorze but they call it Pomerania
> Its real name is Klajpeda but they call it Memel
> Its real name is Szczecin but they call it Stettin
> Its real name is Krolewiec but they call it Koenigsberg
> Its real name is River Wisla but they call it Vistula River
> [And so on, for more than a hundred altered place names]

In certain cases the German version was superior; for example, *Marienburg* bespoke a fortress dedicated to Mary the Mother of Jesus from which the teachings of her son were promulgated, while *Malbork* conveyed none of the gentleness of Mary. In a way, of course, this might have been more appropriate, for of a hundred persons residing in the castle at any one time, the distribution was this: Grand Master, one; his immediate council, seven; knights from Germany, twenty; knights from other nations, nine; squires, pages and other assistants to the knights, eighteen; full-fledged priests, three; friars, six; paid soldiers, eight; servants of all kinds, twenty-eight. And if one distributed the gold pieces in the castle coffers among the twenty-nine knights, each would receive more than three thousand pieces, but even this would be deceptive, because the Order maintained numerous subsidiary castles, often of considerable strength, in Prussian towns like Frauenberg (Frombork), Marienwerder (Kwidzyn) and Rastenberg (Ketrzyn), not to mention a dozen lesser ones erected in what had once been Polish towns but which were now occupied by the Order. The fortune of the Order was tremendous, but so were its expenses, and by careful manipulation and the constant watchfulness of the Grand Master, it avoided sending any great tithe to Rome. It was, in fact, a nation unto itself and it intended staying that way, always growing, always encroaching upon the lands of its neighbors.

Said Ulrich von Jungingen, the brilliant Grand Master who controlled the Order in these exciting years: "We are, as we say, the forward arm of God Almighty, but we are also the forward arm of German settlement, and that combination is irresistible." It was upon this powerful state that dumb-looking Pawel of Bukowo was presuming to spy.

He discovered the power of the Teutonic Knights when he left the city of Wilno on his way to the little amber town of Lembok, which lay to the north of the powerful German town of Koenigsberg. From Wilno, the Amber Road passed through villages only recently occupied by the knights, and when he and Janko spent the night at a Lithuanian farmhouse, Pawel learned of their harsh rule.

"We cannot give you good bread," the wife lamented, "because they've broken our quern." And she pointed to the shattered pieces of what had once been her most valued possession: the hand mill, consisting of two flattened stones, the upper of which revolved upon the stationary lower, grinding wheat into flour.

Explained the husband: "The knights have given orders that we must henceforth sell all our wheat to them, at the prices they state. And they've smashed our querns to enforce that law."

Later the wife said: "They're going to allow us to keep our spinning wheels for the time being, because they can't find women to spin for them at Malbork, but they've smashed our looms because only they will be allowed to weave cloth."

"It's about the same with cattle," her husband said. "I had nine, but now I'm allowed only four."

"Did they pay for the five they took?" Pawel asked.

"Pay?" the husband snorted. He stared at Pawel, one farmer to another, and after a while Pawel asked: "What are you going to do?" and the Lithuanian said: "When the word comes, I take my scythe and I help you Poles when you go looking for Germans."

"Who said we were going to do that?" Pawel asked, and both the husband and wife wanted to speak at once. They said that with Witold at the head in Lithuania and his cousin Jagiello ruling Poland, it was obvious that something must happen, and soon. "We can't let the knights gobble up our countries, can we?"

"I know nothing of such things," Pawel said honestly, but he was learning.

At the next village they saw three burned cottages and a woman hanging from a tree, and when Pawel inquired as to what crime she had committed, the Lithuanians told him: "She hid her quern, and the knights caught her grinding illegal grain."

That night three families sat late with the travelers, telling of the terrible repression that had settled over their lives after the knights captured their territory: "Cattle were confiscated. Our mill was burned. Now we must pay to cross the bridge. My sons were taken to Lidzbark to work as servants in their castle. And all trade must pass through their hands."

"Do they leave you any rights?" Pawel asked.

"None. They say we're pagans and that they're doing all this to save our souls. For four generations my fathers were Christian . . ."

"Way to the east," one of the women said, pointing in that direction, "there are still pagans. And because those few remain after Jagiello converted us, the Germans say we're all pagans and that whatever they wish to do is all right, because they're saving us."

Late in the evening one farmer voiced the real complaint of these people: "What hurts more than the loss of the cow is the fact that they treat us with contempt. They treat us like slaves, because we aren't German. And they leave us no hope, because we can never become German, and we see them taking all the good land and moving their farmers onto it, and pretty soon there'll really be no place for us. My farm will go, and his, and his." He halted his recital, clenched his hands, and said: "They treat us with contempt."

After nine days of travel through these newly acquired German territories, Pawel and Janko entered the coastal areas which the knights had held for many years, that chain of beautiful little seaports on which the amber monopoly operated by the knights centered, and Pawel saw at once the superior quality of any place controlled by the Germans. Everything was clean. Order prevailed. The shops were small but they were neat, and people behaved in an organized manner.

As they moved from one seacoast town to the next, always in a northerly direction as if trying to escape the German domination, Pawel became aware of a very large dark-haired knight who seemed always by accident to be traveling in the same direction, and he set Janko the task of determining who this Teuton was. It was not difficult, because the first peasant Janko spoke to in the barbarous mélange of words he had acquired—Polish, German, Lithuanian, Prussian—told him that the impressive knight was Graf Reudiger, commander of the Baltic coastline and enforcer of the amber monopoly, which allowed sales to officials of governments but not to random individuals. When Pawel heard this he smiled, because it was now obvious that Graf Reudiger was trying to catch Pawel circumventing the amber laws, and Pawel was trying to be caught so that he would be hauled off to the legendary castle at Marienburg.

An amusing game developed, with the two Poles asking obvious questions of persons who might be expected to report them to Reudiger, and the big knight trying to look inconspicuous as he trailed them. In this fashion the three came to Lembok, a village of the greatest charm and with the finest amber, and after two days of rest Pawel eased himself into a small building by the clock tower where the amber trade flourished, and there for the first time he saw why it was understandable that an entire roadway across Asia and Europe had been established to trade in this precious substance, more beautiful than silver, more valuable than gold.

The merchant, a German, had on his wooden counter a selection of pieces brought to him over recent days by the Lithuanian fishermen who prowled the shoreline searching for any amber that the waves might wash up and by other Lithuanians who actually mined for deposits laid down long ago. Pawel had no clear idea of what amber was, except that Polish ladies cherished such occasional samples as the knights allowed to filter into that country, and when he was actually permitted to handle a fragment he was surprised by its light weight, soft surface and radiant color.

It did not sparkle harshly, nor was it luminescent when sunlight struck it. A golden brown, it gave forth a soft radiance, but whatever its physical character, it created an impression of worth and loveliness and candlelight. The first piece Pawel handled was opaque, filled, it seemed, by a thousand white bubbles of air, and when Pawel asked about this, the German nodded: "Exactly right! When it formed, it was filled with tiny bubbles, and there they stay, forever."

So Pawel, looking the big dumb peasant with a few gold pieces from his master, asked: "How did it form?" and the German became pleasantly excited; he enjoyed answering that question, for he was the expert.

"Have you ever worked with trees?" he asked. "Good. Have you ever worked with pine trees? The ones that give off sticky substances? Good. That liquid is resin, and when you collect it you can do many things with it."

"But how do you make amber from it?"

The German laughed and jabbed Pawel in the ribs. "You can't make it and I can't make it, but if you put it in sand under the sea for a hundred years . . . two hundred years, it binds itself together and hardens and makes amber."

"You mean that this wonderful thing was once the stuff that makes my hands sticky when I cut a pine tree?"

"Yes! And to prove it, I'm going to show you something extremely precious," and from a little suede pouch he placed on the counter a piece of flawless amber, about the size of a pigeon's egg, completely transparent and with no interior bubbles, colored like the coat of a fawn and hiding in its center perfectly preserved in every detail a single fly with wings extended.

"May I touch it?" Pawel asked, instantly appreciative of its rare form. When he had inspected it from all angles, allowing sunlight to dance past the suspended fly, he asked: "How did you get the fly in there?"

This time the German laughed boisterously. "You think I put it there with my big, heavy fingers? No, my friend. That fly landed on the resin while it was still sticky and it got caught. This was a hundred years ago. And more resin flowed about it, and then the whole thing was left in sand underwater for another hundred years and it became amber." He admired the lovely bead and said: "The fly holds his wings forever ready to soar again the minute the amber lets it go. But it will never let go."

"Is such a piece . . . well, is it valuable?"

"A piece like this? It goes to China, where they appreciate such perfection." And from another pouch he produced a set of beautifully matched nine globelets of golden amber, none with flies, but so radiant in their purity that they formed a kind of halo. "For the Sultan of the Turks," and he spit as he said the infidel words.

Finally he produced the piece which he himself had selected as the nonpareil, the one he had held back until the Pope himself or some great king came by to claim it. It was the size of a small hen's egg and similarly shaped; its color was a soft gray-gold and radiant. Perfectly translucent, it seemed to break ordinary light into myriad colors, and yet it did not shine of itself. Said the German: "It longs to be held by a golden chain below the throat of a beautiful woman."

"What will you do with it?" Pawel asked.

"Wait."

"For what?"

"Just wait."

Pawel took such a liking to this trader, a man who obviously loved his work, that he returned to the center many times, and during one visit the German said: "I suppose you're an official of your government. I suppose you have papers authorizing you to buy."

"Oh, I have!" Pawel lied. That night—with the connivance of Graf Reudiger, who hurried in shortly after each of Pawel's visits—it was arranged that a set of six amber beads would be sold to Pawel. They were extremely beautiful objects, not so large as the special ones set aside for the Sultan, but each matched nicely with the others, as if all were golden-skinned sisters from some remote Asian village.

"They were formed a hundred years ago," the German said, "and they've been waiting for you." Then, as he held them in his hand for the last time, he said: "I sometimes think it must have taken much longer than a hundred years . . . for something like pine resin to make something like this." He was right. It had taken some sixty million years; that insect imprisoned in the other piece was not a fly as Lithuania now knew flies; it was some nameless progenitor that had flown through a pine forest those millions of years ago, and if the amber which held it was indeed more valuable than a similar weight of gold, there was good reason, for amber had a subtle, woodland, sunset beauty that nothing else could match.

After Pawel had wrapped his six beads in linen and then in heavy cloth, he told the dealer: "I shall be very nervous carrying these to Krakow for our king," and the German said with a certain sad cynicism, for he had come to like this stolid Pole who reacted so enthusiastically to the amber: "Yes, you will indeed be nervous." And as soon as Pawel stepped out of the little building beside the clock, servants of Graf Reudiger grabbed him and Janko, and the big knight, now dressed in full regalia with the black cross embroidered on his tunic, stepped from behind a door and said in a loud voice: "You are arrested. For trying to evade the amber laws."

• • •

It was more than a hundred miles from the seaport of Lembok to the capital at Marienburg, and since Pawel was obviously not a full-fledged knight, he was owed no great consideration. He and Janko were allowed to keep their horses but they were lodged wherever Reudiger could find them a bed, and they ate poorly. It took six days to cover the distance, and occasionally the big German knight would ride with them, never abusing them but telling them frankly that at the end of the journey they would doubtless be hanged and their bodies shipped back to Poland—or at least their heads—as a warning to other Poles not to try to breach the Order's monopoly of the amber trade.

Late in the afternoon of the sixth day Graf Reudiger began to spur his horse and commanded the others to do the same, and one of the knaves explained: "He wants to reach Marienburg before night falls," and as the sun was setting, the little company of travelers rounded the side of a hill and saw before them the mighty battlements of Marienburg Castle glowing red, a fortress of such size and strength as to immobilize the courage of any foe who happened to approach it.

Vast, mighty, thick-walled and impregnable, it would stand five hundred years without being taken by siege, both the symbol and the reality of German power in the Baltic states. Pawel, looking at it when it seemed part of the coming night, shuddered to think that within those massive walls he could be imprisoned for the rest of his life, like the fly in amber, or tortured, or even hanged. Janko, less imaginative, compared this tremendous fortress with the scrawny castles he knew along the Vistula, the ones that had been regularly destroyed at fifty-year intervals, and said: "Nobody could ever knock this one down."

They approached it by the eastern gateway, where guards told Reudiger: "You're lucky. Fifteen more minutes . . . closed." And before they left the inspection courtyard, the massive iron gates clanged shut for that night.

With torches they were led through devious pathways which would be difficult for a stranger to follow, and impossible to penetrate if they were defended, and into a walled northern area of staggering size where the heavy shops for the fabrication of swords and armor were located. From here they were led across a wide wooden drawbridge to the massive gateway seven tiers deep, each graced with carved figures, and into the beautifully walled courtyard of the first castle, itself bigger than anything Pawel had seen or heard of in Poland.

They traversed this courtyard without halting and left the first castle altogether, passing through a low archway, easily defended, into the great castle itself, and there Graf Reudiger directed a herald to sound a signal indicating his arrival. Trumpet sounds echoed through the enclosure, bouncing off a dozen walls and making strange melodies, at which a small, heavily ironed doorway in the western wall slowly opened, revealing the tall, severe figure of a knight dressed all in white, except for the black cross upon his breast.

This was Ulrich von Jungingen, brilliant leader, fearless warrior and Grand Master of the Teutonic Knights for the duration of his lifetime. "Brother Reudiger, you have done your job. To the dungeons." Saying no more, he retired.

The dungeons of Marienburg Castle were spacious affairs, larger than most inns and capable of holding more people. They were not composed of individual cells, except for a few reserved for prisoners of major fault, but of huge stone-walled rooms, four of which served a very special purpose: they were packed with large wooden logs which prisoners fed into furnaces that had brick-lined ducts leading to important rooms in the castle. Thus when a single fire raged in the cellar, heat could be delivered to rooms far distant and high above the dungeons.

Pawel and Janko were thrown into one of the lesser compartments, but Pawel complained to the guard that this was improper, since he, Pawel, was a knight and not accustomed to sleeping with peasants. The Germans, taking this complaint seriously, moved him to better quarters, where there was straw upon which he could sleep.

But his nights were wakeful, for he tormented himself with speculating as to what was going to happen to his six amber beads, which Graf Reudiger had rudely taken from him at the time of his arrest, and he conceived the curious idea that his safety, the continuance of his life on earth, depended upon his custodianship of those amber beads. He devised a score of ridiculous plots whereby he might recover them and smuggle them through German lines to Krakow, but he knew they were futile because all depended upon his escaping from this tremendous fortress, and that was not likely.

He could not tell how many days he had been in the dungeon, and it seemed that most of the men who shared it with him had lost sense of time, for they had been there for years: Lithuanian farmers who had tried to avoid delivering their grain to the knights; Poles captured on raids to the south; other Poles caught visiting the city of Danzig; Danish sailors who had attempted to fish the Baltic; and a few Tatar infidels taken on raids into Russia. The dungeons of Marienburg formed a map of German power in the east.

On the sixth or seventh day, when his eyes were accustomed to the gloom, he was dragged forth, allowed to wash, given fresh clothing, and taken to a room where two remarkable men sat awaiting him. The first and tallest was a proper knight, Siegfried von Eschl, forty years old, a traveler to Jerusalem and Rome, scion of an ancient German family occupying various castles along the Rhine, a man devoted to the welfare of the Order and one of its ablest commanders. The second was of a smaller size and a less distinguished bearing, but in some ways he was the more impressive, for he could read and write. He was Priest Anton Grabener of Lübeck, younger brother of a master merchant in the Hanseatic League.

The two indicated that Pawel was to sit on a small chair on the opposite side of the table, facing them, and to answer honestly all questions put to him by Priest Anton, who spoke Polish in addition to Latin, French, Italian and Lithuanian. Since Pawel had been carefully coached in Castle Gorka as to what he must reply when questioned, he was prepared for this interrogation, but to his astonishment it proceeded along lines no one in Krakow could have anticipated:

PRIEST ANTON: Is it true that your King Jagiello is covered with heavy body hair from his neck to his toes?

PAWEL: I've seen him only a few times, but once was when he stayed at Castle Gorka for three days, and I saw no such hair.

PRIEST ANTON: Are his private parts of enormous dimension?

PAWEL: How would I know?

PRIEST ANTON: Is it true that he killed his Queen Jadwiga because she produced in her womb a devil of tremendous size?

PAWEL: No one ever told me that. She died in childbirth, I believe.

PRIEST ANTON: We know she died in childbirth. But why? For what terrible reason?

PAWEL: Many women die in childbirth. My wife's sister—

PRIEST ANTON: Why was no one allowed to see the stillborn? Was it not because of its monstrosity?

PAWEL: I do not know. I heard of no monster.

PRIEST ANTON: Is your King Jagiello known among your people as a pagan?

PAWEL: When he stayed at Castle Gorka, and I was asked to serve as attendant, he certainly joined us in prayers.

PRIEST ANTON: Did he kneel? Did he cross himself?

PAWEL: I suppose—

PRIEST ANTON: We want no supposing. Did he cross himself?

PAWEL *(snapping out the word)*: Yes.

PRIEST ANTON: You are lying, and you can be put to the rack.

PAWEL *(stubbornly)*: I saw him cross himself. On three days I saw him do it.

PRIEST ANTON: Are the Lithuanians who came with him to Krakow, are they not pagans too?

PAWEL: I know none of them.

PRIEST ANTON: Are not the peasants of your village pagans?

PAWEL *(bursting into laughter)*: Our Father Bartosz would give them something to worry about if they tried that.

PRIEST ANTON: In the next village? Aren't they pagans?

PAWEL: Father Bartosz has that village too, and the ones after it and the ones after—

SIEGFRIED VON ESCHL *(breaking in)*: Are there many Tatars in the Polish army?

PAWEL: We fight against the Tatars. They used to burn our village, but now we fight against them.

VON ESCHL: But there are many in your army, are there not?

PAWEL: I've never seen a Tatar, and I don't want to see one.

VON ESCHL: But surely you've heard of Tatars serving in your army?

PAWEL: I've heard only that it's death for a Pole to go to Kiev.

VON ESCHL: Have you been to Kiev?

PAWEL: God forbid, no.

VON ESCHL: How did you get onto the Amber Road?

PAWEL *(breathing more easily, for now the questions would begin on topics whose answers he had memorized)*: I left my village of Bukowo in the month of January, and I rode east for six days, south of Lublin and north of Przemysl—

VON ESCHL *(impatiently)*: Did you not go first to Kiev to meet with the Tatars?

PAWEL: God forbid that I should consort with those devils.

VON ESCHL: Yes, yes. Our own opinion. Then why does your king hire Tatars to fight against the forces of Christendom?

PAWEL: I know of no—

PRIEST ANTON: Have you ever met one Lithuanian who was a true Christian?

PAWEL: I told you—King Jagiello. But you understand, I did not meet him personally, like eating with him. I never claimed that.

PRIEST ANTON: Do not the people of your village consider all Lithuanians pagans?

PAWEL: We don't bother with Lithuanians.

PRIEST ANTON: Your king is a Lithuanian.

PAWEL: We think of him as a Pole, and a damned good one.

PRIEST ANTON: If you use profanity, you can be put to the rack.

PAWEL: I am sorry, Your Reverence, but to tell you the truth, I don't believe I've ever met a Lithuanian.

PRIEST ANTON: When Jagiello was at Castle Gorka, did he ask for fresh pine branches . . . so that he could cast pagan spells?

PAWEL: I heard of nothing such.

On four different occasions Pawel was questioned like this, Priest Anton Grabener hammering at the supposed paganism of King Jagiello, all Lithuanians and most Poles, while Siegfried von Eschl was preoccupied with the presence of Tatars in the Polish forces. Pawel, obviously, knew nothing about either topic, but his apparent innocence merely fortified the suspicion that he was lying to hide the faults of the Polish-Lithuanian confederacy. The questioning was therefore confusing and non-productive.

On the fifth day Von Eschl said with a show of impatience and authority: "We've been questioning you, Pawel, in order to verify facts for an important document which Priest Anton is writing for circulation to the courts of Europe. It must go forth within the week, for couriers are leaving to strengthen our alliances and recruit knights for our crusade. I want the priest to read you three sections of our letter, and I want you to identify anything which might sound dubious or false to you. Proceed with the first."

Von Eschl leaned back, his fingertips forming a little temple at his chin, as the priest, obviously proud of his composition and its irrefutable logic, read the first indictment:

"Know, Sire, that the Lithuanians have never been Christianized, that they are a willful and pagan people, that they live like animals without the blessings of Jesus Christ, and that they constitute a menace to all Christian lands. They must be reduced on the battlefield and brought to a true Christianity.

"Their king, this Jagiello, is known to be a barbarous brute with matted hair covering the entirety of his body and with private parts so much like those of some great horse that he ruptured and killed the saintly Queen Jadwiga, a devout Christian of Hungary. This Jagiello claims to have been baptized, but he makes his claim only to gain the Polish throne, for he remains as pagan as he ever was. On visits to Christian homes he is known to have asked for fresh-cut pine branches so that he might continue his pagan rites and cleanse himself of any Christian influences.

"The Teutonic Knights, right arm of God and personal agency of the Pope in Rome, beseech your help, both in gold and knights to fight alongside of us, for we are determined to convert Lithuania to Christianity and bring it the benefits of civilization."

Von Eschl dropped his hands and asked: "Do you find anything wrong with that?" and Pawel, totally unqualified in Lithuanian affairs, remained silent. "Proceed with the next," Von Eschl said.

"Know, Sire, that one of the most grievous faults of King Jagiello is the irrefutable fact that he employs in the armies he sends against us Tatar regiments composed solely of infidels. Some of the Tatars are pagans from the vast wastelands of Asia, some adherents of Islam, the criminal religion which holds Jerusalem in its grasp, denying access to our Holy Places to all Christians.

"It is disgraceful and an offense in the nostrils of God that a pagan country like Lithuania should employ pagan troops to withstand the pious effort of the Teutonic Knights to bring Christianity to the Baltic coast. We implore you to send us assistance to eradicate this terrible blasphemy, and we inform all true knights in your domain that if they hunger to smite the infidel, which they can no longer do on crusade in the Holy Land, they must come to Marienburg, where we continue the struggle against the infidel and where Christians can once more cross swords with the followers of Muhammad."

"Do you find anything wrong with that part?" Von Eschl asked, and Pawel said truthfully: "I despise Muhammad and the way he keeps

Jerusalem in thrall. If I could, I would go to the Holy Land tomorrow to fight him." Von Eschl nodded and said: "Now listen carefully to this."

"Know, Sire, that the principal reason why the Sacred Order of the Teutonic Knights must pursue defensive warfare in these parts is to bring true Christianity to darkened Poland. Despite what their defenders say, this is not a Christian land. It has never been converted by any saint or bishop or even priest in a direct and honest line from St. Peter to Rome to the Holy German Empire to Krakow. It is a pariah among nations and it must be converted, first by the sword, then by true priests who will bring not only the Bible but also European law and custom to this wilderness.

"The Pole is not like the German or the Frenchman or the Englishman. He is more Asian than European, more animal than man. Only the saving grace which the Teutonic Knights can bring, their superior piety and order, can save Poland, and it is our solemn duty to bring that grace to this moral wilderness.

"As proof of our claim, we cite the fact that Poland willfully chose as its king the pagan Jagiello when it could have taken a proved Christian, Sigismund of Luxembourg, and it forced its saintly Queen Jadwiga, daughter of Louis of France, a devoted Christian, to marry Jagiello instead of Wilhelm of Habsburg, a true Christian to whom she was legally engaged and to whom she had been married since the age of five.

"The only salvation for Poland is for it to fall under German rule, and the Teutonic Knights stand prepared to effect this change if only the courts of Europe will support us and if the knights of Europe rally to our cause."

On hearing this terrible indictment of a land he had known in a much different light, Pawel's neck muscles, which came straight down from his ears to his shoulders, began to stand out like big willow reeds. His face grew red. His hands trembled. And he could imagine no circumstances under which he could accept such condemnation. At the castigation of the Lithuanians he had remained silent, and he had seen no reason to defend the Tatars, whom he had feared since childhood when tales of how they ravaged villages terrified his dreams, but he could in no way approve what he had just heard about his homeland.

"Did you find anything wrong?" Von Eschl repeated, and Pawel said: "It's a pack of lies."

"Be careful," Priest Anton said. "You could be thrown on the rack, you know, for claiming that what the church—"

"We have good bishops in Poland. They preach the word of God. I've heard them. And what you say about them and us is wrong. You say it for some wrong purpose, and you should be ashamed."

They could not bully Pawel into admitting that their condemnation of Poland was accurate, and when they threw him into one of the single cells from which harsh punishment was administered, he sat in darkness, mumbling to himself: "I refuse to say that what he wrote is true." And he was prepared to die for his obstinacy.

But before he could be lashed to the rack, as Priest Anton had directed, he was brought out of his cell, allowed to wash and put on fresh clothes, and taken before the Grand Master himself, who saw in Pawel's presence a chance to promote a scheme which lay close to his heart.

"Brother Pawel," the powerful Grand Master said as they sat with Von Eschl over a quiet lunch, "you are to be set free. You are to take these beautiful amber beads, which you purchased with your funds, to the king in Krakow. And you are to carry a letter from me to him, but first I should like to ask you a series of questions quite different from those my friend here and the scribbling priest asked you."

Pawel bowed, took a healthy bite of the good bread baked by the friars, and waited.

"In your opinion, Pawel, if war came between our Teutonic Knights and Lithuania, would Poland remain neutral?"

"Never. Lithuania and Poland are one nation. With one king."

"That we know, all of us. But matters of national interest do arise. And Poland is a nation quite different from Lithuania. Do you still think she would join the battle?"

In his dark, solitary cell, Pawel of Bukowo, this petty knight with only three horses, had reviewed every word he could remember of the indictment against his homeland, and he had rejected every charge, except maybe the employment of Tatar cavalrymen, about which he knew nothing. And he confirmed his resolve to die rather than to besmirch his nation or its Christian people. Now he was being asked if Poland would betray its major ally.

"Grand Master," he said with proper deference, "it seems to me that what you want Poland to do is stand aside while you destroy Lithuania, so that you can enjoy a free hand later on to destroy Poland."

Ulrich von Jungingen, a master in exactly the kind of diplomacy Pawel was outlining, neither smiled nor frowned. Leaning slightly forward, he asked: "So you think Poland would fight?"

"I know it."

"You gave honest answers, Pan Pawel," Von Jungingen said, and his voluntary use of the Polish honorific proved the sincerity of his evaluation. Now he asked: "If my Order sought an armistice . . . a cessation of all hostilities between us . . . everywhere . . ." He paused to allow the gravity of what he was about to propose to sink in, and when he believed that Pawel understood, he concluded: "If we offered an armistice for one year, would Poland accept?"

"Why not peace for all years?" Pawel asked.

Von Jungingen did not reply. Instead he turned to Von Eschl, tall, straight, keen of mind and brilliant in negotiation, who said very slowly: "Because permanent peace between the Order and pagan countries like Lithuania and Poland is impossible. It is God's will that Christian Germans should bring the glories of civilization to these parts."

"Then why have an armistice, as you call it? Why not war and have done?"

Now the Grand Master spoke, leaning back in the great carved chair which served as his throne: "We propose an armistice now because at certain times each side knows that it is improper to go to war—neither is ready, the issues have not firmed. War at such times would be a sloppy affair . . ."

He hesitated, then leaned far forward until he was almost touching Pawel's hands, and asked with utmost sincerity: "Tell me, does your side really employ Tatar cavalry?"

"I don't know," Pawel said.

"That would be a terribly wrong thing to do," Von Jungingen said. "To use the followers of Muhammad against a Christian army"—his voice dropped several levels—"against an army which fights only to bring civilization to backward countries."

Abruptly he terminated the interview, ordered that Pawel be given fresh clothes, the set of six amber beads and two good horses, one for himself and one for Janko.

But Pawel had grown to love these beads so much, imagining them to have lain under the sea for countless years, that he did not deliver them to King Jagiello in Krakow. He gave them to his lord, Kazimir of Gorka, where they formed the chief treasure of that castle.

Unbelievably, the armistice that Grand Master Ulrich von Jungingen proposed was accepted by Jagiello and his cousin Witold, and for the very reasons that Von Jungingen had outlined: neither side was fully ready for war, and to plunge into one haphazardly might lead to haphazard consequences. The truce was to last from 8 October 1409 until sunset on 24 June 1410, at which time the tremendous battle which had been forming for the past ten years would legally begin.

During this pause no serious effort was made to avert the war, only to postpone it, and for the very good reason that each side vigorously wanted to settle growing animosities. The Teutonic Knights believed that they must pursue with European applause their publicized effort at converting the heathen or they would lose their private goal of building a massive German state which would comprise the Baltic lands, much of Russia and all of Poland. For them, a battle that would crush Lithuania and Poland for half a century was imperative.

It was equally so for Jagiello's two nations, which had witnessed the slow erosion of their lands, as if an insuperable tidal wave from the west were hammering their shores, cutting away Pomerania here, Danzig there, Samogitia on the next wave. As Jagiello told his captains when accepting the armistice: "Next year we either conquer the Crossed Knights or we perish as a nation . . . and as individuals."

He used his respite brilliantly, visiting magnates like Kazimir of Castle Gorka and pleading with them that it would serve their own self-interest to contribute armies to the Polish cause. This begging was necessary because even a king as strong as Jagiello had no real power to make the magnates do anything they did not wish to; they ruled, not he, and if he could not make them see that it was to their advantage to give him an army, he would have none.

But Jagiello's brilliance lay mainly in his ability to persuade, and gradually, from all parts of the chaotic nation, he assembled a force of quite stunning dimensions, one of the largest that had ever operated in this part of Europe. He had Lithuanians in great number, double that amount of Poles, a volunteer battalion from Bohemia, and one group so strange that Pawel of Bukowo, who was sent to enlist it, could not believe his eyes.

The king himself had come to Bukowo with two Lithuanians sent down by his cousin Witold, and he had commissioned his emissaries: "You are to go to Kiev and invite them, pleadingly, to join us, for it is just as much in their interest that we defeat the Order as in ours."

Naturally, Pawel had difficulty conversing with the two Lithuanians, for peoples of the two nations had no common language, but each side had a smattering of words, and on the ride to Kiev, attended by sixteen soldiers, he had an opportunity to learn more about Grand Duke Witold, who was to be of such crucial importance in the forthcoming battle.

"Remarkable man," the Lithuanians said, each one volunteering a broken phrase. "Like a volcano they tell about in Italy. Ten years ago strong ally of the Teutonic Knights. Fight on their side valiantly. Eight years ago, big fight. We declare war against Marienburg. Six years ago, big friends again. Together we fight big battle against the Tatars. Much killing, believe me. Witold a hero, Grand Master himself kisses Witold at Marienburg. Next year German knights steal much of our land. Witold forms alliance with Tatars against Marienburg. But knights very clever. They make peace with Witold and together they fight Tatars again."

"Who is he with this year?" Pawel asked.

"That depends." One of the Lithuanians did not like the sound of this, so he added: "No matter who he fights for, he fights with great valor. He is Witold, champion of all."

When they approached Kiev, Pawel became aware of much movement among the mounted troops guarding the city, and some dozen miles from the outskirts the envoys were in effect arrested by a contingent of cavalry. They were then led by circuitous paths into the city, where they were apparently expected by one of the Tatar leaders with whom Witold had been allied twice and against whom he had warred three times. It was Tughril, a small, wiry, incredibly tough veteran of the steppes and of battlefields reaching from the Black Sea to the Baltic. His official suzerain had been Tamerlane the Great, under whose orders he had attacked Lithuania, but when Tamerlane died, Tughril had found much joy in warring on his own, stealing from the Sultan's convoys at the edge of Constantinople, foraging on the Amber Road, laying siege to Moscow, never winning any great battle, never losing a crippling one.

His left eye seemed not to be fixed, looking now this way, now that, but his right had a piercing quality; it seemed always to be laughing at the insanity of life, and whenever some outrageous proposal was laid before him, his left eye wandered this way and that around the possibilities, while his right stared sternly at the visitor as if to ask: "What gain do I get in this transaction?"

He now stared at the three emissaries from the Polish king: "I can see why your Jagiello wants to battle the Germans, but why should I?"

Pawel had been schooled in the only answer he was to give: "Because there will be much booty . . . much looting."

"Good!" Tughril said, leaning back and stroking his huge mustaches. "How many men do they want me to bring?"

"Ten thousand."

"Impossible. They don't need that many."

"How many can you bring?"

"Can? Can? I can bring the entire city of Kiev if needed. But I will bring about fifteen hundred."

"So few?"

"Each man a warrior. Each man on the fastest horse you've ever seen." He hesitated, desiring to nail down the agreement. "You promise there'll be looting?"

"There will be," Pawel assured him, but one of the Lithuanians warned: "No killing of women and children."

"That happens only under necessity," Tughril said, dismissing the implied criticism of Tatar methods.

"There will be no killing of women," the Lithuanian repeated.

"Not even in the German towns we capture?"

"Not even there."

Tughril shrugged his shoulders as if he had been instructed not to use bowmen against a stone castle; if that was the rule, so be it.

The compact was arranged: Tughril promised that fifteen hundred Tatar horsemen would leave Kiev on the first of May 1410 and arrive in the north one week before 24 June, the day the battle was to begin. The four men embraced, heads were nodded sedately, and the mission was completed, confirmed—that is, unless the Teutonic Knights visited Kiev in the interim, converting the Tatars to their side with the promise that they could loot Polish villages.

When the three travelers reached the separation point, at Zhitomir, the Lithuanians headed north to report to Witold; Pawel, going west to inform Jagiello, had perplexing doubts as to the propriety of enlisting an infidel army in a fight against a Christian king, and he could still hear the voices of the German knights at Marienburg hammering on this very point. It did not seem right. It was a travesty to ally one's self with a Muhammadan in a fight against soldiers of the Pope. But the more he reflected on the matter the more he felt instinctively that in a battle of this magnitude and importance, it was much better to have Tughril fighting for you rather than against you. He was not unhappy with the outcome of his visit to Kiev.

All across Poland, that winter was spent in military husbandry: pikes were given new hafts, swords were sharpened or annealed if they had lost their temper; horses were shod and armor was closely fitted. And the peasant Janko of Bukowo told his wife: "It's time to cut the ash," so together they went into the Forest of Szczek where for some years he had been watching over a young ash tree, now about ten feet tall and three inches thick. At various intervals over a long period of time he had cut deep incisions into the trunk, into which he had inserted rather large pieces of jagged flint, encouraging the ensuing growth of the tree to close upon them, making their bases almost a part of the living tree but allowing their knifelike edges to protrude. Some two dozen of these implantations were now so securely wedded to the ash that nothing could dislodge them, not even the hardest blow against a suit of armor, and when Janko tested each with his thumb and forefinger he found it well rooted.

"I'll cut it first down here," Janko said, "to give me a good knob, then up here for the handle." He asked his wife's opinion, and with her smaller hands she grasped where the handle would be and said: "Maybe it's too thick there," but when he tested it he could find nothing wrong.

It was a solemn moment, deep in the woods, when a man was about to harvest the weapon on which his life would depend, and he could not bring himself to destroy the tree that he had tended for so long. Stepping back, he studied his home-grown war club once more and asked his wife if she really thought he was cutting to the right length. Grabbing the axe from him, she made a big gash at the lower end, then handed him the axe with the assurance: "It will be just right."

From his various villages Kazimir of Castle Gorka assembled a battalion of one hundred and eighty-seven men all told, including himself. He had seventeen gentry of minor category, four or five of whom self-styled themselves as knights, a title few outsiders recognized, about two dozen professional soldiers whom he paid, the rest knaves, farriers, armorers and peasants. One priest, Father Franciszek, completed the roster. Kazimir would allow no women or boys to accompany him, but his definition of the latter category was flexible, for the youngest knave was only thirteen.

They started north in May, like a minute streamlet heading for a distant ocean, but as they moved they accumulated other groups— sixty from this castle, only twenty from that, four hundred from Sandomierz—until by the middle of the month they constituted a vast throng marching slowly, resolutely toward an inevitable battle of tremendous magnitude. And one night as they camped well to the north, Pawel could imagine that in the lands ahead the German knights were doing the same, assembling from the farthest reaches of their territory, and from France and England and Holland as well. Only then did he appreciate what a titanic battle this was to be.

In the second week of June, only eleven days before the armistice was to end, the Polish forces were surprised by the arrival of three Teutonic Knights in full armor and bright trappings. They unfurled a flag of truce and sought to speak with King Jagiello: "The Grand Master proposes that we extend the armistice for three weeks."

"Why?" Jagiello asked, always suspicious that the Germans might seduce Cousin Witold to join them.

"Because knights from the other nations of Europe wish to participate, and we feel that honor should not be denied them."

"Sensible condition," Jagiello said, and the extension was granted.

He did this not out of consideration for the Order, but because he judged that he could use the extra days constructively in aligning his heterogeneous units into a more compact battle array. He was especially insistent that the Tatar cavalrymen be used effectively.

His plan was threatened when Tughril's men did arrive—not the fifteen hundred promised, but only eleven hundred—for they proceeded at once to sack a village, as was their wont, but it turned out to be not a German village but a Lithuanian one, and Witold was enraged. The two leaders had a harsh meeting with Tughril, who looked contritely at Jagiello with one eye, at Witold with the other: "Our men killed no women, as we promised."

"You are to sack nothing till after the battle," Witold said angrily.

"All right! I understand."

On the next day Witold summoned Tughril to a bivouac area, where a branch of his Lithuanian troops had been marshaled, with a stack of tree trunks and planks in the center. Two of Witold's men, hearing about the Tatar sack of their village, had taken it upon themselves to do a little sacking of their own, and it was bad luck that they, too, had struck at a Lithuanian village, not a German one.

"Did you sack the village?" Witold shouted at them.

"Yes."

"Then build your own gallows." And everyone watched in silence as the two men stuck the tree trunks in the ground and fastened crossbars, which they secured with diagonal members. When the gibbets were in order, having been tested by Witold himself, he ordered the men to attach ropes to their necks, after which they were hauled into the air and left kicking.

"That's how we discipline our troops," Witold snapped at the Tatar commander, who said: "You lost two good soldiers that way."

"What would you have done?"

"Forbidden them to share in the looting when we win."

The extended armistice ended at sunset on 4 July 1410, but the battle did not begin on the following day because the two huge armies, like two great beasts on a darkened plain who knew that struggle was inevitable, moved and parried to gain advantage, and the Grand Master, who had been in such situations often before, laid clever traps to trick Jagiello. Deep trenches were dug and covered over with sod on planking intended to break the legs of the Polish cavalry, but crazy-eyed Tughril took one look at the areas from a distance, and because his focus danced back and forth, the camouflage became ridiculously obvious, and he told Jagiello: "Charge your cavalry far to the south, then back up."

On the sixth of July the armies sweated as each tried to outflank the other. On the seventh a heavy rain impeded everyone, but on the eighth the ground dried and it looked for a while as if the Teutonic Knights were going to charge, but Jagiello deftly withdrew to such a distance that the German horses would have been exhausted by the time they reached the Poles.

On July ninth the armies had moved so close together that engagement on the next day was inescapable, and late that afternoon the two generals made characteristic moves. The Grand Master brought his entire force onto open ground so that when dawn came their superior horsemen could sweep with terrible fury at the larger but less skilled body of the Polish-Lithuanian troops. And Jagiello, appreciating the superiority of the Germans, positioned his vast army deep among the trees, where the first charge of Germans could not reach them, for he intended to send his men forth when and how he wished.

As night fell each general prayed, and Von Jungingen asked his aides: "Is it true that no Tatars joined them?" and his spies assured him: "A chieftain named Tughril was supposed to come, but as always, he deserted at the last moment," and Von Jungingen said: "I'm glad. I don't want to face those little fleas. They confuse a battle."

As midnight neared and the fatal day—10 July 1410—began, one could have imagined all Europe holding its breath, for this battle had been so long coming that its tremendous significance was widely understood. And then one of those curious twists of history occurred: the Teutonic Knights positioned their headquarters near the little village of Grunwald, while some three miles distant the Polish commanders slept not in but near to the equally small village of Stebark (Tannenberg), yet in subsequent history the Poles would call this the Battle of Grunwald, after the Teutonic headquarters, while the Germans would name it Tannenberg, after the Polish quarters, but both names would echo with tales of heroism, feats of honor, and dead innumerable.

Since the two villages lay far to the north, and since it was midsummer, the sun rose at about four in the morning, so at half after three Pawel of Bukowo was awakened and, with his serf Janko, was directed to help erect a tented chapel, where shortly after dawn King Jagiello, Witold of the Lithuanians and the other commanders reported for morning devotions.

A slight, misting rain obscured the proposed battlefield and assisted the warriors in that it kept the dust down, but as the commanders entered the chapel they could not keep from casting furtive glances at the terrain, calculating where and how their troops would move on this fateful day.

All the commanders were present except wild Tughril of the Tatars; as a pagan, he felt no need of Christian ritual, but when Jagiello sent for him particularly, dispatching Pawel to relay his request, the tough little horseman shrugged his shoulders, looked this way and that with his wandering eye, and said: "Why not? On a day like this a man needs all the luck he can find," and he marched to the chapel, where Jagiello greeted him with an embrace, standing him in the forefront.

When the priest finished the words of the Mass, ending with Christ's blessing on this great venture, Jagiello spoke: "Brothers, we move this day to end the tyranny which has oppressed our lands. The Teutonic Knights will come against us with the blessing of the church and the cross of Christ upon their bosoms, but they come also clothed in lies. We ride forth with truth as our banner and the deep love of Jesus Christ as our shield. To freedom! To victory!"

Kazimir of Gorka supposed that at the closing of the Mass, Jagiello would bring his cavalry out from the trees and line them up for battle, but the king did nothing of the sort. He talked with his captains, joking with those who seemed nervous, and when Kazimir asked: "When do we move into battle position?" he replied with a broad smile: "We don't."

Jagiello was sixty years old that day, senior to any of his commanders or to any of the enemy leaders, and he had devised a plan which would give him every possible advantage, for his inescapable disadvantages were numerous and could destroy him if he made mistakes or wasted what power he had. The Poles had provided 18,000 knights, 12,000 retainers and 4,000 foot soldiers, to which must be added 11,000 Lithuanians and 1,100 Tatars, for a grand total of about 46,100 troops. But only a precious few were heavy cavalry; most of the Lithuanians were armed with clubs; he had only sixteen cannon; and in almost every respect the allied equipment was inferior to that of the German.

The Teutonic Knights could assemble on this day 21,000 superb heavy cavalrymen, 6,000 massively armed infantry, 5,000 servants trained in battle and armed better than most of the Lithuanians, and about one hundred excellent cannon capable of throwing with tremendous force balls larger than a man's head. In addition, the Germans had the best field leaders in the world, men tested in many battles: Ulrich von Jungingen as Grand Master; Frederick von Wallenrode as Grand Marshal; Kuno von Lichtenstein, one of the finest swordsmen of the century, as Grand Commander; and Albrecht von Schwarzenberg, a marshal serving as Commander of Supply. Each of these men wore a suit of full armor, the chain-link kind and not the massive plate favored by the Poles; each rode a huge horse; each carried a powerful lance which a young knight would not have been able to heft let alone handle; and each wore as a kind of special assurance from God the huge black cross upon the front of his white tunic. Most important, each Teutonic Knight approached battle with the knowledge that his Order had known one smashing victory after another since moving into Prussia.

Outnumbered in bodies, 46,100 Poles and allies to 32,000 Germans, the knights were vastly superior in armor, in horses, in experience and in battlefield leadership. This was to be one of the decisive battles of the world, an immense clash of arms which would determine the history of the Baltic and the destiny of two emerging nations, Poland and Lithuania.

But still King Jagiello did nothing. Five o'clock came and the massed Teutonic Knights could be seen waiting on the horizon, but no Poles opposed them. At six o'clock, when the sun was driving away the mists and making the summer fields oppressively hot, three Polish champions, the heart of the army, came to Kazimir of Gorka, asking him to intercede with them, and together they presented themselves to the king: Zawisza Czarny, Black Zawisza, known on many battlefields as the premier knight of the east; Jan Zyzka, the huge Czech who wielded the heaviest and deadliest sword; Firczyk of Plock, with the massive iron ball at the end of its heavy link chain.

"Your Highness," Zyzka said, "we grow impatient."

"But I do not," the king replied, and then he revealed his strategy: "Let them wait there in the hot sun. Let them wait all morning while we stay here among the cool trees. When they're exhausted by the heat and lack in water, only then do we engage them in battle."

The three powerful champions were not entirely pleased with this strategy, but when the sun grew hotter at six and extremely hot at seven, they began to see the wisdom of their king's plan, for they remained under the trees where cool breezes were blowing.

At half after eight, when the Teutonic Knights were dripping with sweat, Grand Master von Jungingen engaged in a superb maneuver: he detached two of his finest knights, handed each a flowing banner and a handsome long sword, and thus armed, the two men, one showing a black eagle against a golden ground, the other a red griffon rising from a white field, cantered their horses easily across the intervening ground toward where the Poles waited amid the trees.

When their horses rested, about twenty yards from the Poles, one of the heralds cried in a loud voice: "Lithuanians and Poles, Dukes Witold and Jagiello, if you are afraid to come out and fight, our Grand Master sends you these additional weapons." And with contempt the heralds threw their swords point-down into the earth, where they quivered. "Also, you cowardly ones, if you feel you require more room for your maneuvers, the Grand Master says that he will now withdraw our troops one mile to aid you." And at a signal from the other herald, the Teutonic Knights on the distant field did turn about and retreat a full mile.

This insult enraged warriors like Black Zawisza and Jan Zyzka, but Jagiello remained unperturbed and sent one of his aides to recover the swords. Brandishing one, he said: "I accept both your swords and your choice of battleground, but the outcome of this day I entrust to the will of God."

At this challenge the heralds withdrew, gave a signal indicating the failure of their mission, and wheeled their horses to rejoin the monstrous wave of their fellow knights as the latter prepared the charge which would rout the Poles and Lithuanians from their forest and destroy them.

Now Jagiello was ready, and with maneuvers as graceful as the unfolding of a petaled flower, the various groups of knights moved into their assigned positions, each group edging forward to be first in the fray. Trumpets sounded. Cheers rose. And the allied forces waited for the savage charge of the Germans, who came over a slight rise waving their banners and chanting "Christ has risen" as they bore down on the pagans.

In that first moment of battle disaster overtook Jagiello's troops, for with his customary skill the Grand Master had detected where the major weakness in Jagiello's dispositions would probably be, and he had dispatched his foremost cavalry, under the leadership of Kuno von Lichtenstein, crashing into that spot, where the eleven hundred Tatars with their light swift horses abutted the Lithuanians with their light armor.

When Tughril and his lieutenants from the steppes looked up the hill and saw this descending array of giant horses and equally giant Germans—four Germans to every Tatar—he made the only rational decision. He fled. Wheeling his horse before the Germans could get to him, he led his entire complement in undisciplined, chaotic flight. Away from the protecting trees and out onto the gently rolling fields the Tatars galloped, hoping that their speed would save them from the monstrous Germans, and any Tatar who fell even two horse lengths behind was cut down.

Cheering and shouting battle cries, the Teutonic Knights swept on, routing the men from Kiev completely. For more than five miles the chase continued, and whereas more than fifty Tatars were killed, not one Teutonic Knight was even badly wounded. It was as complete a victory as the Germans would gain that day, and it started their part of the battle with a burst of glory.

Of course, when the sweating knights returned from their rout of the Tatars, they were spread out and some were burdened with spoils lifted from dead bodies, and in this careless formation they passed where Grand Duke Witold waited with a contingent of his best Lithuanians, and suddenly the knights were engaged in an entirely different kind of battle.

Now men of roughly comparable strength engaged one another, and the incessant clash of swords was like the rolling of thunder across a field. Lance countered lance, great two-handed swords clove enemies from neck to hip, horses whinnied and went down, throwing their masters under the hoofs of other horses, and a wild, confused and terrible hand battle raged for nearly half an hour, producing no victor. When Kuno von Lichtenstein fought clear and was able to rejoin the Teutonic commanders, he gasped: "The Tatars proved craven, but those damned Lithuanians have learned to fight." When questioned, he said gravely to the Grand Master: "Sire, we can afford no more errors this day. It's going to be fierce battle to the end."

In the third hour the Germans gained a notable advantage and one which came close to ending the battle altogether, and in their favor, for Marcin, the Chamberlain of Krakow, had been awarded the honor of bearing aloft at the heart of battle a big Polish flag marked with the sign of a white eagle, and when the Germans saw this they supposed, sensibly, that King Jagiello must be nearby, fighting at the head of his troops in the European fashion, not realizing that he had stationed himself atop a small hill well to the rear, in the tactic dictated by Genghis Khan and his inheritors.

With enormous courage and determination, a squadron of German knights crashed into Marcin, wounded him, and cast down his flag. In the average battle this would have signaled the defeat of the army to which the flag belonged, and the Germans so interpreted it, with hundreds of knights rushing to kill the fallen king and disperse his immediate entourage.

But this was not an ordinary battle, and when the flag fell Black Zawisza and a remarkable Polish warrior named Florian of Korytnica rushed forward to defend it. Each Polish nobleman had his own heraldic banner—eagle, bear, hawk, Kazimir of Gorka with his castle—but Florian, who loved battle the way some men love wine, had as his insignia a twisted length of human gut, testifying to the fact that even in the remotest part of his intestines, he had never known fear. At his side galloped the mighty Jan Zyzka, and these men not only saved their flag, they drove back the crashing knights and used this event not as an excuse to surrender, as the Germans had anticipated, but to renew the battle.

It was now two in the afternoon, the hottest time of that long, brutal day, and Jagiello's strategy began to show results. The German knights, among the bravest men in the world, had been sweating in the saddle since dawn and some were beginning to tire, especially those who had galloped after the fleeing Tatars. And it was at this precise time that Jagiello released a contingent of his knights who had not yet seen battle, and when these rested warriors joined the fray, the line of German knights was slowly driven back.

But this was exactly what the Grand Master had planned, and waiting until the Poles were extended, he threw in a huge reserve of his own, and these powerful men began to smash the Poles.

The fight was now a general melee, single sword against single sword, one horseman galloping after another and cutting him down from the rear. Like the echo of a vast storm, the sounds of battle rose and fell over the fields of Tannenberg-Grunwald, and the dead fell like wheat stalks cut down by summer hail.

In the individual fighting, the advantage seemed to lie with the Germans, for at this kind of battle they were supreme, but Siegfried von Eschl, perhaps the most astute of the Teutonic Knights, did not entirely like what he saw, and he reported to the Grand Master: "I have ridden everywhere, Sire, and I assure you, the Polish and Lithuanian foot soldiers have not yet been released. Sire, they are lurking somewhere. We must smell them out."

"Good Siegfried, look at the battle. We are winning. At sunset the rabble will have been driven from the field."

"I am afraid, Sire. I am afraid of those damned foot soldiers coming at us from some unexpected quarter."

Von Eschl, a superb tactician, had good reason to be apprehensive, for in the dense woods near the village of Tannenberg, Janko the peasant from Bukowo and two thousand like him had huddled throughout this steaming, explosive day, uttering not a word on pain of death. There they hid beneath the trees, their clubs and scythes and pikes at ready, and three times Janko deemed it right for them to surge forth and cut at passing knights, but always they were held back.

Now it was almost five in the afternoon, and the Germans sensed that before darkness the outcome of this titanic battle would be known, and although they were tired, with many close to exhaustion, their superiority in physical stature, armament and the strength of their horses began to tell.

As Polish fortunes started perceptibly to wane, Firczyk of Plock became a focus of attention. Standing at the center of a circle, his feet planted wide, with massive swings of his oaklike arms he twirled his heavy iron ball about his head, lowering it a few feet whenever a German came into range and smashing the man apart. Horses, knights, foot soldiers, all felt the crashing of this tremendous weapon, and Firczyk was beginning to rally the faltering Poles with his mighty shouts and indomitable courage, when Siegfried von Eschl came on the scene. He watched for some moments the tactics of the big Pole, then dropped dramatically to the ground and rolled forward in four complete circuits of his body, thus escaping the swing of the deadly ball—and found himself face to face with Firczyk. "Page!" the giant warrior bellowed, but before anyone could come to his aid or he was able to slow his swirling ball, Von Eschl drove at him with a dagger, entered his throat above the chain mail, and brought him crashing to the earth. As soon as the terrible ball fell powerless, other knights swarmed upon the bleeding Pole and finished him. The tide of the battle had turned definitely in favor of the Germans.

At this perilous moment King Jagiello from his hillside far to the rear flashed his long-awaited signal, and from the woods the Polish peasants began to emerge, walking gingerly at first, then half-running with their pitiful wooden weapons in the air, and finally surging forward with cries they might have used in hunting bear. They constituted a terrible force, a body of men dug out of the earth and determined to protect that earth. On and on they came, their cries growing louder and higher, until like an all-engulfing dust storm they swept into the heart of the battle.

They moved toward the German flanks like a mass of irresistible ants, on and on and on, falling, dying, shattered by Teutonic power, but never stopping. They hacked and stabbed and pierced; with bare hands they grabbed at rearing horses' hoofs and clutched at wavering knights, and although one mounted knight on a great horse with a long sword could defend himself against eight of the peasants, he could not hold off twenty as they swarmed about him and his horse.

"God who guides us," screamed Kuno of Lichtenstein, "free me of these damned flies!"

Siegfried von Eschl, fresh from his victory over Firczyk, studied the behavior of the peasants and noted something which frightened him. Galloping over to where the Grand Master followed the conduct of the battle, he shouted: "Sire, do you notice that the peasants are leaving a clear path to their left?"

"Accident," Von Jungingen said. "Fall of the land."

"Perhaps not, Sire. I would send our best detachment of cavalry to that spot."

"I see no cause," the Grand Master said, but as he spoke the two German commanders witnessed a most terrifying sight. From the woods that had hidden the peasants through this long day came galloping at full speed the reassembled Tatar regiment, which the Germans thought they had destroyed early that morning.

At their head rode Tughril of Kiev—small, drooping mustache, wild fury in his good eye—shouting for revenge. Behind him came the thousand desert horsemen who had survived the German rout, and they, too, were lusting for a battle in which the odds and the terrain would now favor them. It required about six minutes for the Tatar horde to cover the open ground between their section of the Tannenberg wood and the battle line that had now moved closer to Grunwald, and in that time Von Jungingen, his face ashen and his throat suddenly parched, realized that this was going to be a battle to the death and that his knights might lose. Grasping Von Eschl's arm, he said in hushed voice: "Now comes the time when we defend the cause of Jesus Christ with our own lives." And without hesitation or calling for support, he spurred his horse and dashed directly to the spot where the oncoming Tatars would hit.

It was six in the afternoon, with the sun still blazing hot, when the Tatars smashed into the faltering German lines, and in the ensuing half-hour there was a scene of such savagery that no Teutonic Knight had ever known its equal, not even when he had been the author of it. The infuriated Tatars, burning from the contempt with which the Germans had dismissed them in the morning skirmish, knew no restraint, in either the protection of their own persons or in their attack upon the enemy. Astride their swift horses, they swept into a struggling mass, cut and slashed and killed and sped away. Regrouping at the edge of the entangled battle, they suddenly appeared at some new spot, striking like a bolt of terrible lightning across an empty steppe.

Tughril and some of his men came upon Ulrich von Jungingen and those defending him, and not knowing that this was the Grand Master himself, they fell upon him like a configuration of hawks attacking a wounded eagle and they supposed that they would knock him from his horse and kill him, but with massive swipes of his huge two-handed sword, Von Jungingen drove them off, and displaying a heroism which astonished the Tatars, fought his way clean through their attack, and they galloped off to concentrate on some other foe.

With repetitive force these swift little warriors hacked at the Teutonic Knights, and whenever one of the Germans was thrown from his horse or lamed or left behind, Polish peasants and scythe-swinging Lithuanians swarmed in to slash the stumbling bodies, and three times Janko of Bukowo swung his frightful flint-studded ash tree against a German skull, shattering the bone but leaving the flints unscarred.

Polish horsemen who had been hard pressed at the approaches to Grunwald, where they were trying vainly to attack the German headquarters, took renewed hope when a herald came shouting "The Tatars are back!" and they came roaring against the Germans from the opposite direction.

Slowly, like the remorseless tentacles of a giant octopus, the various bands—Lithuanian, Polish, Bohemian, Russian, Tatar—closed in upon the knights who had so abused them, and when the circle was complete, the slaughter began. Lances, daggers, pikes, scythes, poignards, the hoofbeat of horses, the strangling force of maddened hands, all combined to crush the German power which only one day before had seemed so impregnable.

At the height of the killing, Pawel of Bukowo performed an act which eventually modified sharply the development of his village, his own castle and that of his master, Kazimir of Gorka. It began with a feat of heroism that attracted wild applause from those who witnessed it: ferocious Graf Reudiger, who had led numerous German sorties, was about to lead another which might have rescued many of the Germans, but as he spurred his big horse forward, Pawel, with almost superhuman effort, leaped up behind him and struck at him many times, his dagger hitting only the protective chain armor, until finally, one thrust pierced it and severed the spinal cord.

For several swaying, dreamlike moments dead Reudiger and stub-

born Pawel dashed through the battle astride the panicking animal—
Pawel still stabbing at the body before him, not realizing that it was
already dead—until suddenly the horse reared in terror at the sight
of a peasant coming at it with a pike, pitching the dead German hero
and his bewildered Polish assailant backward onto the earth.

From that ignoble position, with Reudiger's heavy body atop him
and blood streaming from God knew where, Pawel looked up to see
the climax of the battle, for Grand Master Ulrich von Jungingen,
aided by Kuno von Lichtenstein, Von Wallenrode and six of the
bravest knights, was endeavoring to hold off a tumultuous Polish attack, and with their dreadful long swords they were succeeding, until
a group of determined foot soldiers and peasants armed with long
pikes rushed at the Grand Master with such force and in such numbers that he could not repel them all. One point caught him in the
neck just above his armor, another in his face, one in the side of his
head, and a fourth at the left temple. Thus pinioned, he uttered the
cry "Jesus save me!" and perished at a moment when he must have
known that his crusade to crush Poland had failed.

Pawel, still pinioned by Graf Reudiger's corpse, tried to break
free in order to attack Von Lichtenstein, who was battling to break
clear, when he saw rushing to the side of the dead Grand Master a
knight for whom he bore a personal grudge. It was Von Eschl, who
had treated him with such contempt at Marienburg Castle, slim,
fierce-eyed and brave. With a mighty effort Pawel shoved Reudiger's
heavily armored corpse aside, leaped to his feet with blunted dagger
still in his right hand, and rushed toward the German, shouting:
"Von Eschl, it's me!"

He missed and stumbled past the German, but quickly he turned
and with a wild cry leaped forward, flying through the air parallel to
the earth, catching Von Eschl by the knees, dragging him down and
knocking his sword away.

Still shouting for revenge, Pawel drew back his right arm and was
about to drive his dagger deep into the fallen knight's throat, when he
felt his arm gripped powerfully and heard his master's stern voice:
"No, Pawel! Save him for me!" And when Kazimir of Gorka knelt
down beside the two fallen men he said softly, in the heart of battle:
"Siegfried von Eschl, you are my prisoner."

The German looked up into the eyes of his unknown captor and
asked: "Your name, Sir Knight?"

"I am Kazimir of Gorka, and you have two choices. Confess that you are my prisoner and honor-bound to observe that state, or die."

"I accept your capture," the German said.

"I accept your word of honor," Kazimir said. Then, helping Pawel to his feet, he commissioned his man: "You are responsible for this prisoner. With your life you are responsible for him." And during the remainder of the battle Pawel guarded Von Eschl, and when he saw Janko of his village roaring past with a pike wrested from a wounded German he whistled, the familiar sound used often in the Forest of Szczek when the two were hunting wild boar, and Janko joined him, eager to stab the prisoner, but Pawel explained that this one they must keep alive, and so the great Battle of Grunwald, or of Tannenberg if one preferred, ended.

At twenty past seven, when there still remained a half-hour of daylight, Jagiello rode down from his command position and embraced his cousin Witold, who had been the greatest of the allied battle commanders, a man of supreme courage following his years of siding first with the Germans, then with the Poles, then the Russians, then the Tatars, and finally with his own Lithuanians against their mortal enemy. Vytautus the Great, he would be known in subsequent Lithuanian history, savior of the nation.

Together the two leaders, surrounded by their splendid captains, moved across the darkening battlefield, while men who knew the enemy read out the names of the fallen for scribes to indite:

"This is the body of Grand Master Ulrich von Jungingen, died bravely, let his corpse be covered with purple. This is the body of Wallenrode, died at the head of a charge, let his corpse be covered with purple. This is their greatest hero, Kuno von Lichtenstein, died grappling with seven, let him be treated with honor. This is Schwarzenberg, this is the great Graf Reudiger, let them be treated with honor.

"And here we have placed the foreign knights who fought against us because they thought we were pagans who knew not Jesus Christ. This is Jaromir of Prague, none braver, and this is Gabor of Buda, who led the Hungarians with skill, and this is Richard of York, who brought four other Englishmen

with him, and these two are the French brothers Louis and
Francis, knights without reproach. Let them all be buried
with honor."

At dusk, after prayers of victory and thanksgiving, King Jagiello
performed two acts which brought him praise. Assembling some
three dozen Poles who had distinguished themselves in battle—men
like Pawel of Bukowo, who had slain the famous German champion
Graf Reudiger—he asked them to kneel and commissioned them
battlefield knights. And then he went to where the surviving Teutonic
Knights were crowded into a circle guarded by peasants with scythes,
and he asked each Pole who had captured a German to stand forth
and identify his prisoner, and Janko pushed Siegfried von Eschl forward for Kazimir of Gorka to claim, and when captor and captives
were paired, the king said: "You Knights of the Cross fought bravely
today, and you have work to do at home. You are set free, on your
word of honor as knights that you will report to me at Krakow four
months hence on St. Martin's Day. Do you accept the charge?" The
Germans did, and they were set free.

Jagiello next ordered all captured wine barrels to be split open,
lest his troops riot, and Janko, seeing the drink flowing on the ground,
lamented: "The only battleground in history where the blood of the
defeated mingled with the wine of the victors, one loss as great as the
other."

Eighteen thousand Teutonic Knights and their helpers were slain
that day. Of sixty leaders of the Order, more than fifty perished. Of
the foot-soldier Lithuanians who attacked without serious weapons,
more than two-thirds died, and of the eleven hundred Tatars, one
hundred and twenty-six were killed.

It was these Tatars who caused the Battle of Tannenberg to become something of a scandal, because Priest Anton Grabener of Lübeck, who did not participate in the fighting, drafted an emergency
report to all the capitals of Europe informing the courts that the
Teutonic Knights were defeated only because the pagan Jagiello and
his heathen cousin Witold had imported one hundred thousand Tatars, who overwhelmed the defenders of Christianity. Later German
historians would claim that the figure was "two hundred thousand
mad, screaming followers of Islam who killed any Christians they
captured with long-drawn agonizing tortures."

Polish historians, somewhat embarrassed by Jagiello's reliance upon infidel Tatars, insisted that their total number was only two hundred, a substantial difference from the German figures. A Czech commentator on the discrepancy suggested that the Germans could be forgiven their exaggeration because Tughril's eleven hundred screaming little devils must have seemed like two hundred thousand.

In the week prior to St. Martin's Day, 1410, some hundred and thirty Teutonic Knights straggled in to Krakow, where in conformance with their vow, they surrendered themselves for a second time to their Polish captors. Kazimir took Siegfried von Eschl to Castle Gorka and sent Pawel to Germany to arrange for a ransom, and in the castle town of Eschl, along the right bank of the Rhine, Pawel located members of the wealthy family who were eager to ransom their bold nephew from pagan hands.

In the waiting period before Pawel returned with the money, Kazimir the Pole and Siegfried the German had many opportunities to discuss the battle, and it was the latter's freely expressed opinion that the Order's loss at Tannenberg was a loss not only to the Germans but especially to the Poles:

"Your country, Gorka, does not know how to govern itself. Allied with mine, it could form one of the strengths of Europe. We would provide the fighting men, the governors, the scholars; you, the backbone, the wheat, the timber.

"You will never catch up with us, I think. Always you will require the guidance we can provide, and although this time we lost in our effort at civilizing your areas, history will demand that we try again, for under the leadership of Grand Masters like Hermann von Salza and Ulrich von Jungingen we will forge ahead to new accomplishments, while under a king like Jagiello, who is not even a Pole, you can accomplish very little, and what you do, most insecurely."

When Kazimir pointed out that in the recent battle Ulrich von Jungingen appeared to have made several mistakes and Jagiello almost none, Von Eschl asked which side, the victors or the vanquished, stood in better condition right now, and when Kazimir tried to say that Poland did, the German laughed. So Kazimir asked: "Who will be your Grand Master now? Who will lead you to the greatness you foresee?" and Von Eschl gave a surprising reply:

"I know that if my family will not pay the ransom you demand, the Order will, because there was talk that I was to be the next Grand Master. And if I am, and if you continue to have the ear of your king, let us work together as partners, Gorka. Germany and Poland are natural allies. We complement each other in all respects: our leadership in so many areas; your strength in numbers and foodstuffs.

"Also, we have no natural barrier separating us—no great river, no mountains, no impassable swamps. Germany blends naturally into Poland. The division line could be anywhere we set it between us, but I see no reason for a division line at all. Let us be one country, one unit. [And always in these conversations he introduced the phrase which infuriated Kazimir; Von Eschl was powerless to avoid it because he believed it so wholeheartedly.] You see the situation, Gorka. You will always require German guidance."

From these talks, conducted with such frankness, Kazimir deduced that as long as Poland and Germany existed, each would fear the other: Germany would always suspect that indefensible Poland would be a pathway whereby Russian power, when it coalesced, would attempt to invade the German states; and Poland would always fear that its western border would be invaded by Germans whenever they saw an opportunity to use Poland as a buffer against the east.

Von Eschl proved a model prisoner, obedient to every rule his captor laid down, but as soon as the money arrived and he departed, Kazimir hurried to Krakow to report to the king: "The man terrified me. The defeat at Tannenberg taught him nothing. Already he's plotting a return invasion, whenever he feels the Order has recovered its strength."

Jagiello said that such recovery could not take place in fifty years, for all the German leaders were dead: "I saw them on the battlefield. You saw them."

"Sire, I saw the new leaders in my castle. Believe me, our permanent enemy will be the German states. Always we will be attacked from the west."

In the meantime, Kazimir occupied himself by applying the ransom funds that Pawel delivered—a vast sum in those days—to the purchase of huge estates to the north and east, some of them hundreds of miles from the Vistula, and after he had acquired them, people began to speak of him as a magnate, one of the seventy or eighty men of immense power who really controlled Poland. Indeed, before long he was beginning to think of himself and his fellow magnates as Poland.

Pawel did not fare as well, but obedient to the principle that what was good for the master would also probably be good for the servant, he did gain three advantages from the battle in which he had played a heroic part: he had been formally knighted by the king himself and thus promoted from the rank of dubious to acknowledged gentry; he received a second village as a gift of thanks from Kazimir; and he came home with his own plus two captured horses, which, added to the one he had left behind, meant that he was now a respected member of the gentry with four horses.

Janko gained nothing from the battle, although in his own mercurial way he was as brave as either of his lords; it was not to be taken lightly when a man on foot armed with only an ashen stave studded with flint nodules attacked a knight on horseback, and by breaking the horse's leg, caused the knight to tumble so that his skull could be crushed. Such a feat required a special kind of courage, but because Janko was a peasant, supposed to do such things, it went unnoticed.

In fact, the Battle of Grunwald served Janko poorly, for it made him freedom-loving and outspoken and daring, and several times on the long ride home his master Pawel observed to himself: This Janko is going to be difficult to handle. And when the two reached Bukowo, Janko did strut about and talk of his role in the great battle and of how he had spent that waiting day with the Tatars, who were a good lot no matter what the legends of the village said: "I wouldn't mind serving with those Tatars. They know how to have fun."

Infected by the powerful excitement that stay-at-home men often find in wars that introduce them to strange lands, Janko began to experiment with freedom—stealing a chicken now and then, appropriating to his own kitchen fire branches fallen in the forest, and ultimately killing one of Pawel's rabbits.

Some spy informed on him, not only about the rabbit but also about the chicken and the branches and several other offenses which might or might not have happened, and Pawel took advantage of this as an excuse to rid himself of a man he had grown to dislike. Ordering Janko brought before him in the little castle, he found him guilty of numerous crimes, and within twenty minutes of passing judgment, Janko was dragged to the public square, where a rope was suspended from a limb and he was hanged.

IV

FROM
THE NORTH

THE EXCITEMENT AT CASTLE GORKA WAS SO INTENSE THAT Magnate Cyprjan ordered not one but two hogs to be slaughtered, but when the carcasses were hung and he had inspected them he realized that he had more meat than the banquet would need, and in a fit of generosity inspired by the good fortune his daughter was having, he sent for his henchman Lukasz of the little castle at Bukowo. When that petty knight appeared, Cyprjan actually embraced him, which surprised Lukasz exceedingly, for magnates did not customarily embrace their minor gentry.

"Lukasz, I am so pleased this day that I've ordered the butcher to cut away the forequarters of the two hogs for you and Danusia. Make a feast of it in my daughter's honor." When Lukasz bowed, obviously delighted with this unexpected gift of meat, for in his meager quarters this was not often seen, the magnate clapped him on the shoulder, an unheard-of gesture of approval, and said: "Of course, we shall expect you and Danusia at the banquet," and at this vote of confidence Lukasz bowed once more, caught his lord's hand and kissed it.

Then, in a further burst of generosity, Cyprjan said: "And I want you to give the haslet, all of it, to this fellow they call Jan of the Beech Trees. He was most helpful during our last hunt."

So the butcher made two packages, one of the lean but tasty fore-quarters for Lukasz, another of haslet for the peasant Jan, and the lord of Bukowo, as petty a one as lived in all of Poland, rode home with his meat and a sense that he had been honored.

The rich major quarters of the hogs were delivered to the castle kitchens, where an extraordinary woman took charge of them. Twenty years before, Cyprjan had ridden south to the little town of Dukla, where the great Mniszech clan centered, and there he had paid court to Zofia Mniszech, whose famous aunt Maryna had become Czarina of Russia, twice. Zofia had inherited many of the characteristics of her notorious predecessor: headstrong, beautiful in an artless way, daring and extremely capable. At first she had not liked Cyprjan, for he was much too quiet when compared to the robust Mniszech men, those giant brutes whose faces were covered with hair and whose hearts were filled with larceny, but after having rejected him twice, she listened when her uncles told her: "This Cyprjan has so many estates across Poland that he can be a leading magnate, if he wishes, and you're not likely to find a better catch."

"But he is so rigid," she protested. "So proper. He might as well be a Frenchman."

"It will be your job to make him unbend."

"How many estates does he actually have?" shrewd Zofia asked, and she listened attentively as her uncles ticked them off: "He has the very old castle at Gorka, which he honors as his headquarters, and the new castle near Lublin. He has a huge estate with no castle near Przemysl, but his real holdings are east of Lwow, where he has four or five immense estates worked by Ukrainians. Then, as you know, for you've seen them, he has the two small but very nice farms near Warsaw and the two over toward Russia. He is a man of substance, Zofia, and you won't do better."

"Still," as she told her aunt Eulalia, the one who had left her own husband, the Hungarian Bela, "I have dreamed of a man more in the mold of Lubomirski."

"He's taken," Aunt Eulalia said with a sigh, "and what's left for you is Cyprjan."

Reluctantly the headstrong girl had accepted her suitor, and the marriage at Dukla had been a tumultuous affair, nine days of riot, after which Zofia had said farewell to her vigorous family and traveled north to visit her husband's many estates before determining where she would make her permanent home. She had liked the wildness of the Ukrainian fields and the color of their little villages, but she could see that life there would be bleak, for there were no castles and Polish neighbors might sometimes be no nearer than a score of miles.

"I will always want to come here for a season," she assured her young husband, "but let's live somewhere else."

They tried the castle near Lublin, but it was too new and smelled of stonemasonry. "I like Lublin and would always be happy coming here for vacations, but the castle is not inviting. Let's see the farms west of Warsaw."

She found these much to her liking, especially since the great Radziwill family of Lithuania had established a chain of summer homes in that area, and they would be pleasing to visit. But as with the Lwow holdings, the lands contained no residences of note, and she was perplexed as to where she would prefer to live until they traveled south along the Vistula to Castle Gorka, and once she saw its towers nestling beside the river, she fell in love with it. Whenever her family or distinguished visitors from Krakow asked why she had selected this spot above the others, she surprised them with her answer: "Because this fellow Lukasz who lives in the little castle up there is such a remarkable man," and on the spur of the moment she would bundle all her guests into a cart and they would trundle off to see a man whose fame had spread well beyond his little village.

Most visitors, when they first regarded his modest castle from a distance and saw the crumbling tower that had been assaulted by so many raiders, approved of its picturesqueness, saying: "This looks like the Poland my mother spoke of," or "I've always wanted to own a castle just like this," but when they drew closer and saw that the walls, too, were in disrepair, they often modified their judgment: "This place is falling down!"

But once they crossed the filled-in moat and entered the castle grounds, a small area enclosed by walls and marked by trees, they were apt to gasp, for shuffling forward to greet them was a large female bear, who terrified everyone until she drew closer, leaned forward, and planted a slobbery kiss on each visitor's cheek. She would now draw back as if judging the merit of the stranger, then hug him in the most friendly manner and kiss him again.

As soon as the bear decided to let the visitor pass, an otter, long and sinewy, would slither up to give his approval, and then a sly fox would sneak along the path, smelling every footfall, and when at last he sidled up to the stranger and rubbed legs, two huge dogs would come thumping out to jump upon chests and lick faces, at which a pair of tame storks would cackle their delight, and this would bring Lukasz and his wife, Danusia, to the door.

"Welcome to The Ark," Lukasz would shout, and at the sound of his reassuring voice the bear would move behind the visitors and nudge them forward, past the otter and the fox and the giant dogs.

No one who ever visited The Ark of Lukasz and Danusia ever forgot it. Some spoke only of the bear; others, of the otter and the fox playing together; and some, of the tame storks who stalked majestically among the beasts, often nestling their heads on a human shoulder as if to share important secrets.

Zofia Mniszech loved the animals and she would sometimes spend an entire afternoon wrestling with the bear or chasing the sly otter or trying to trap the fox, who eluded her with devilish cunning, waiting until the very last moment before darting away, then coming running back at her with a leaping kiss. She liked it best when she stood at the entranceway and called to the menagerie: "We're going fishing!" Then she and Lukasz would walk in front, with the bear right behind, while the otter and the fox, knowing what lay ahead, jumped and frolicked. The storks marched behind, solemn and almost disapproving, and the two dogs ran to wherever they felt they were needed.

In this way they would descend to the river, where Zofia would take the otter in her arms, and caress it and whisper: "I want some fish for supper." She would then place him on the bank and watch as he dived into the water, disappearing for a moment, then surfacing with some large fish, which he would deposit gracefully and with obvious pride at her feet.

"One more!" she would cry, and off he would go, but this time she would say: "Well done, otter!" and he and the fox would dash back to the walled enclosure which was their home.

Once when the king came to Castle Gorka, and heard that Zofia was absent visiting the menagerie, he cried: "I've always wanted to see that!" so Cyprjan drove him up to Bukowo. When the king entered the courtyard quietly he found the bear lying in a curled-up position, with the otter inside one paw, the fox inside the other; the two dogs were stretched out, their heads pillowed on the bear's flanks, and tired Zofia lay with her head nestled on the bear's neck. And all were sound asleep. The two storks, each standing on one leg, kept guard.

For some moments the king studied the pastoral scene, and then the otter wakened and alerted the others, until one by one the animals came to inspect the newcomer, and when the bear approved, he got behind the king and nudged him forcefully right at Zofia, who was so sleepy she could not recognize who the stranger was.

"I am Jan Kazimir," the king said, and when Zofia rose and curtseyed, the otter, who had grown to love her, stood on his hind legs and kissed her left hand at the instant the king kissed her right.

Later the king asked Lukasz how he was able to tame his animals: "A bear and an otter and a fox? They're never seen together in nature."

"I find them when they're young," Lukasz said, "when they've been deserted, with no mother. I give them my love and they give me theirs." As he said this the bear nestled close to him, and the king could not tell whether she thought Lukasz was her son or her father, but it was clear that she loved him, and then he looked to where Zofia rested, and on her lap he saw the otter and the fox.

It was this Zofia who accepted the hog meat when it reached the kitchen: many chatelaines never saw their kitchens, but Zofia enjoyed not only the hurly-burly of an active cooking place but also the creative things that could be done there, and now she was ready to ensure that the pork would be properly presented to the guests.

She had six cooks, two of whom doubled as waiters, and her instructions were specific: "I want the large cuts to be properly roasted, the heavy skin cut into diamond shapes and studded with caraway, the excess fat to be trimmed away but saved for larding. I want the roast to be seasoned with marjoram and a touch of mace, and as it stands over a slow fire, basted every fifteen minutes with a goose feather dipped one time in butter, the next in beer, the last two times with melted sugar. It must be brought to the table in as large pieces as possible, so that all can see the glazing. And I want to supervise the carving myself, because the knife must cut across the grain, so that the chewing is made easy for those with poor teeth."

It was not difficult to prepare a good roast if instructions were followed, but it required a touch of patient genius to handle the lesser cuts of pork, and since these often proved to be the tastiest, Zofia wanted her cooks to follow the ancient recipes developed by the Mniszechs: "I want the meat to be cut flat, and not lumpy. It is to be well pounded until tender and uniform. Rub it well with garlic and oil, spread it with a generous mixture of onions, sauerkraut and diced apple. Roll it handsomely and tie it with a cord. You know how to watch it while it bakes, basting it with beer and butter.

"I want it served with the best Krakow kasha you have ever made. Soak the kasha in light vinegar, then roast it until each grain is brown and separate and very dry. Then prepare a sauce of eggs and beer and scalded raisins and blanched almonds cut fine, and I want it seasoned as before with pepper and nutmeg and marjoram. Do not stint on the raisins and almonds, for I want each grain of kasha to have its own accompaniment. And you are to serve this great bowl of kasha with eight Easter eggs, brightly colored, around the edges."

Each item of her menus for the three-day visit was supervised in this careful way, and it was proper that she take such pains, because this visitor to Gorka was more important to the welfare of the castle than even the king had been. Chancellor Ossolinski, from the vast estates which stood just across the Vistula, was attached to one of the most powerful and richest magnate families in Poland, and he was bringing his nineteen-year-old son Roman to see if a marriage with sixteen-year-old Barbara was feasible. Cyprjan certainly did not need the wealth of the Ossolinskis, but in the unsettled time that loomed and might continue for the duration of Barbara's life, the Gorka people could profit from the strength and wisdom of the Ossolinskis, which would come to them if the marriage occurred.

Barbara, of course, was offended by all this: "I'm being paraded like a cow at an auction, with everyone looking at me to see if I will give milk."

"You hush such talk!" her father cried. "Girls have to get married, and there's no other way."

"Is he presentable? Has he a chin? Or three ears?"

"Barbara," her father said with considerable insight, "don't you suppose he's asking the same about you? 'Do her eyes bulge? Has she a hump?'" He broke into laughter and dispatched a servant to fetch his wife from the kitchen, and when Zofia came in, protesting that she was needed elsewhere, her husband cut her short: "Where you're needed is right here with us. Barbara's worrying about what your Ossolinski will be like. Three heads maybe. And I wanted her to know that all young people have these apprehensions. Tell her what you had heard about me before I reached Dukla to ask for your hand."

"Oh, that!" She chuckled and sat close to her husband as she said: "All they told me was that this Cyprjan was rich, and of a proper age. That's all I knew. And I began to speculate on what must be wrong with him for him to come so far—all the way to Dukla, when he could have any girl he wanted in Krakow or Warsaw. And all they would tell me was 'If he's from Gorka, he can't be too bad.' And I wondered for days about what *too bad* might cover."

She drew back, studied her now-distinguished husband, and said: "When I met him I saw what they meant. The Mniszech men were big and bold and hairy and very brave and they drank a lot and they showed their love for women by kissing their wives and pinching the wives of other men, and here comes this stick of wood . . . Barbara, we were married six months before I saw him laugh, and I thought: Oh my God, what are they asking me to marry? And what were you thinking all that time, Master Cyprjan?"

He looked at this fiery woman whom he had not understood then, or now, and he confessed: "I was filled with fear, Barbara. I had heard about the Mniszechs . . . uncles to the Czar of Russia . . . brawlers on the frontier . . . difficult men at the king's court. And I tell you, I could not imagine what a Mniszech girl would be like. Halfway to Dukla, I wanted to turn around and run home."

"Why were you going?" Barbara asked.

"Because my very wise father had said: 'Son, we need stronger blood in this damned family.' And look what we got!"

He pointed not to his wife, who was a magnificent woman, but to his daughter, who was a dream of unfolding beauty: long blond hair in braids, dark eyebrows, bright and knowing eyes, an excellent figure, dainty feet, and a kind of rhythm in all she did. At sixteen she was more than eligible to take charge of any Polish castle, except for one fault: she still had a modest opinion of herself and sometimes doubted her ability to move with the magnates or their families.

"I shall be terrified when he appears," she told her parents.

"And so shall we," Zofia confessed. "It's as important for us, Barbara, as it is for you."

In the last two days before the arrival of the barges that would bring the Ossolinskis across the Vistula, Cyprjan summoned everyone from three of his surrounding villages to the castle to tidy up the grounds and sweep the entranceways, trim the trees and clean the stables. He warned Lukasz of Bukowo that the chancellor might want to see the bear and the otter, at which Lukasz said with his normal cunning: "In that case I'd better take my villagers back home to straighten up," and off he went with everyone from Bukowo to work on his menagerie, everyone, that is, except Jan of the Beech Trees, who was kept behind to work on the grounds. When all was polished and the last pruned branches cleared away, Jan went to Cyprjan and said: "My wife and I thank you for the haslet." He dropped to one knee and kissed Cyprjan's hand, at which the magnate bade him rise. "You're an excellent workman, Jan, and I wanted to show my appreciation. Tomorrow, will you brush your clothing and stand here to tend the horses I shall be lending the chancellor?"

"I would be proud to do that," Jan said, and when the barges arrived he was one of forty servants standing by to welcome the visitors.

Young Barbara was not visible when the Ossolinskis, father and son, entered the castle, for she was in an upper room being dressed by an elderly retainer of the Mniszechs who had come north from Dukla, and this old woman was not awed by the visitors, not at all: "Remember when you go down that you're not from Gorka. You're a Mniszech and the blood of great ones flows in your veins. Your great-aunt was Czarina of Russia . . . twice. Your uncle was hetman. And you . . ." She threw her hands to her face, then dabbed at her eyes to stop the tears. "Dear God, was there ever a maiden more lovely than you?"

And Barbara Mniszech of Gorka was exquisite as she prepared to meet the young man who might prove to be her future husband. She was just a little taller than the average girl her age but much more attractive. She had a grace of movement that was winsome and a hesitant smile which captivated. The old woman had dressed her in a long filmy gown that gathered beneath the breasts, put three small flowers in her hair, and tied a delicate gold ribbon about her left wrist. She looked severely unadorned, which the old woman intended as a means of emphasizing her beauty, but Barbara was of no help, for her face was ashen pale with fright.

Twice the old woman pinched her cheeks, to no avail, then slapped her sharply. "Barbara! You must not dream! You are the fairest child in Poland, and if Ossolinski doesn't want you, the King of France himself will come riding here one day and shout: 'Where is this Barbara Mniszech they told me about?' "

But when the girl was ready to descend, with her mother and father waiting at the foot of the stairs to present her to the chancellor and his son, the old woman did not like the three flowers in her hair, and with a rude hand she swept them away: "That's for peasant girls. You're a queen." And from a small chest in an inner room belonging to Zofia, she obtained something that would exactly suit this girl, and her complexion, and her coloring.

It was a golden chain from which were suspended six amber beads of significant size, not perfectly matched but each complementing the other like six individual flowers in a garden, similar but magnificently individual. When the old woman locked the chain behind Barbara's neck and bounced the six pieces of amber up and down so that they fell naturally about her throat, lending a sunlight quality to her appearance, she cried with pleasure: "Barbara, they were made for you! Go forth, Queen of the Sunrise, and may the world greet you with kisses!"

Wearing the amber necklace, the girl left the dressing room and stepped easily to the head of the stairs, and when she looked down she saw with relief that Roman Ossolinski did not have two heads and three ears, and he, looking up, gasped. But it was her mother, Zofia, who was most affected. My God, she said to herself, those beads never looked that good on me! And the chancellor thought: That girl would grace any castle in Poland—and before Barbara had reached the foot of the stairs he had dispatched one of his servants to fetch the diagrams he had brought with him across the river.

As the two powerful magnates stepped forward to greet Barbara, they formed an image of Poland, for their exact likenesses could not have been found in any other country. They were both tall and robust, with heavy bodies enclosed in fine cloth from Turkey or France or Russia, marked especially by long, sweeping coats encrusted with the richest embroidery. They wore boots into the tops of which were tucked white linen trousers, swords which they handled with much ritual and gracefulness, and the invariable mark of their caste: a very long, extremely wide sash which they doubled and wore about their capacious bellies. This sash, a mark of rank, was excessively ornamented, Cyprjan's having been woven in three bold colors, red, green, gold, and studded with silver bolts which made it and him glisten.

But the memorable aspect of the two men came from the extraordinary appearance of their hair: Ossolinski had a copious beard which engulfed his broad face; Cyprjan, no beard but enormous, flowing mustaches which gave him both a noble and a sinister look. Each man had directed his barber to dress his hair in the fashion then popular with the Polish magnates: from cheekbone to almost the top of the head, everything was clean-shaven—temples, sides of the head, most of the crown—except that straight through the middle, from forehead over the top and down to the nape in back, a stretch of thick hair about an inch and a half wide was left.

Once when Barbara was a little girl she saw in a picture book from Germany a drawing of an American Indian whose hair had been cut this way—completely bald except for that running ridge—and she had cried: "Look! They have Papa in the book!" and when her elders came to see, they also exclaimed at the similarity. This strange hair style, coupled with the huge beard of Ossolinski or the wild mustaches of Cyprjan, imparted a sense of exciting barbarism to any assembly of magnates. They were not Frenchmen, nor Spaniards, nor Austrians. They were Poles and proud of it.

At dinner three pleasant things happened. Ossolinski recognized Lukasz's name when introductions were made, and cried with some excitement: "Can I see your otter and your bear?" and Cyprjan was pleased when Lukasz said with a gracefulness not expected: "Sire, they told me when I left that they await your coming!" And the chancellor cried: "Tomorrow at nine! Have them groomed!"

At the seating, Ossolinski halted proceedings to stand and admire the service which Zofia had acquired some years earlier from Paris. It stood on a pedestal in the center of the table, about twice the size of a large melon, and it was constructed of white silver and a very light gold, an intricate sculpture representing the arrival of a Chinese emperor at a pavilion in the middle of a lake. Springs tightly wound in advance moved swans over the golden water and caused drooping willows to drift in the wind, and all was of such an appropriate delicacy that diners had to be captivated by it.

"I have never seen a better service," Ossolinski averred, and then turned to his son and asked: "Have you, Roman?" but the young man was paying attention only to Barbara, whose cheeks now showed a color livelier than that of the amber beads.

Zofia interrupted to announce: "You must choose, roast of pork done in the French style, or roll of pork done Polish style with roasted kasha."

"I will take some of each," Ossolinski said, and at the conclusion of the copious meal, which ended with Hungarian wine and German-style cookies, the chancellor said: "Now may we leave the wonderful service in the center of the table and clear away the rest, because I want to ask Panna Barbara some questions." The girl blushed, not because she was afraid of questioning, for after the good Hungarian wine she was afraid of nothing, but because this was the first time in her life she had been addressed as Panna and it marked a growing up.

When the table was cleared, the chancellor looked directly at Barbara and asked: "Are you interested in building things? In sending life forward?"

"I expect to have children," she said with no embarrassment.

"All women have children," he replied with no embarrassment. "But I mean additional construction? The heavy work of life?" And with that he unfurled two rolls of paper on which architects had done much planning, and to his startled audience he disclosed the wild plans which preoccupied him:

"I am going to build nothing less than the grandest castle in Europe. See! It will have one glorious tower representing the unity of God. It will have these four huge towers, each one— you will forgive me for saying, Cyprjan—larger than your castle here. They represent the four seasons of the year.

"We have inside seven major edifices—living area, guests, warehouses—representing the days of the week. We have twelve corridors for the months of the year and fifty-two separate rooms for the weeks. If you cared to count, you'd find three hundred and sixty-five windows plus this little one here for Leap Year.

"See the mighty bulwarks we plan around the entire, the moat, and the two drawbridges. These steps going down, down, down lead to the subterranean well, which assures us of water during the sieges we can expect, and the interior is large enough to hold three normal villages, with space for the occupants of ten villages plus a good-sized town.

"That is what I propose to build, starting next month, Panna Barbara, and would you like to engage yourself in such a task?"

Pointing at the plans, she said in a low voice, as if apologizing for what she considered her brazenness: "But, Sire, you have no church or chapel inside the walls?" He burst into laughter, shouting: "Cyprjan, by God, your filly's an architect!" And he pointed to a large structure which he had overlooked in his catalogue: "A church bigger than any in this region until you reach Krakow."

He then disclosed the second drawing, showing how the great castle would fit into its countryside, and this had been done as if the castle already existed, so that she could see how the four towers and one spire and the moat and the trees fitted together, and it was a staggering concept, for the artist had sketched beside the walls four men and two cows, and they seemed like specks against that massive structure.

"Can you build it?" Cyprjan asked, and Ossolinski almost shouted: "It's my life's work," and Barbara asked: "What's it to be called?" and Ossolinski replied: "Krzyztopor, the Battle Axe of the Cross."

"That sounds ominous," Barbara said, and he boasted: "We build it to confuse the pagans. It stands there as Christ's axe against all infidels, outside and in." In the silence that followed, for in these years no man knew when the infidels would strike again, the chancellor looked at Barbara and asked quietly: "Would you be interested in helping me to build this great castle?" and she replied: "I would."

When Castle Gorka went to sleep that night it was understood that Barbara Mniszech had agreed to marry Roman Ossolinski, even though neither had spoken a serious word to the other. Early next morning everyone was awakened by the chancellor's merry shout: "We go to see the tame otter!" and immediately after breakfast they all went over to Bukowo, where Zofia called out as they neared the little castle: "Lukasz, dress your bear, for we are here."

When the gate opened, the Ossolinskis were amazed by the bear that trundled over to greet them, but they were astonished to find the otter and the fox playing with the big dogs, biting at their heels, then scampering away when the dogs pretended to snap at them.

They stayed with the animals so long that Lukasz invited them all to stay for lunch. His wife, Danusia, had begun to make meat pierogi from the forequarters of the hogs that Cyprjan had given her, and everyone crowded into the kitchen to watch the final preparation of this admirable dish.

"We find ourselves with meat only rarely," Danusia confessed, "so when we get some I chop it fine." She showed them how with great deftness she sliced the cooked pork, mixing it with spices and shreds of cabbage.

She liked, she explained, to make four different kinds of pierogi at once, "so as to conserve what meat we have," and she displayed the three other fillings: stewed cabbage, roasted kasha with plenty of onion, and the favorite of everyone, extremely acid sauerkraut with mushrooms.

When the four fillings were lined up, she rolled out her dough while Zofia helped, for the Mniszech woman loved such impromptu experiments in the kitchen; it was she who put the salted water on to boil and looked for the two cutters that were so important in the making of this delicacy. She could not find them, and the clutter she made irritated Danusia, who shouted: "Everybody out of here! I'm busy!" But no one left, for Chancellor Ossolinski said: "I want my son to see how this is done."

With the dough flat upon the board and not too thick, Danusia produced from a hidden corner what might be called the jewels of her kitchen, the two pierogi cutters. One was a small circle about four fingers in diameter, and with this she cut out rounds of thin dough, one after another, and as soon as they stood clear upon the board, Zofia and Barbara spooned little mounds of filling in the middle of each round, and then Danusia applied her second instrument, a semicircle of iron whose edge had been curiously cut. It had a heavy wooden handle, and as soon as one of the rounds of dough was properly filled, she deftly folded it in half, pressing the half-moon edges together and crimping them with the tool, so that they formed beautiful puffed-up semicircles of delicious food.

Now the miracle happened. The pierogi at this point were a brownish color of no great appeal, but once they were thrown into the boiling water, the dough was transformed into a lovely translucent covering that revealed the contents inside. "Better yet!" Lukasz cried as he heated fat in a skillet. "When some of them are fried, they're doubly delicious."

So Lukasz of Bukowo, a petty knight with four horses of his own and a ruined castle, fried pierogi for the chancellor of the nation, who could not decide whether he liked the boiled ones better than the fried, or the pork ones better than the cabbage. But finally all agreed that fried or boiled, the pierogi that contained the bitter sauerkraut and the delicate mushrooms were the best.

At the height of the little feast Ossolinski announced: "Panna Barbara has consented to marry my son Roman, and together we shall build the greatest castle in Poland, and everyone will be invited to its christening."

When Jan of the Beech Trees brought the package of haslet home to his wife, Anulka, and she turned back the wrapping and saw that she was to have real meat, and in such unbelievable quantity, she started to cry, for it had been more than a year since she and her husband had eaten anything but cabbage and kasha and beets, with now and then a slab of fat containing no meat whatever, and she could scarcely credit the good luck that had befallen her family.

There it was, in some ways the best part of the hog: the liver, the kidneys, the feet, the heart, the tongue, the brains, the meat still on the head and neck, the sweetbreads—the whole inside and history of the hog, meat so precious that it must be treated with reverence. For a moment she had a fright: "They didn't give us the intestines!" But at the bottom of the package Jan found the long strings of guts, and now she was ready.

First she carefully examined the treasure for whatever choice pieces of meat could be cut, and set them aside, catching every precious drop of blood. She then singed the skin, and carefully cut away the fat that remained close to it. Next she went to the river, where she washed the intestines and singed portions until they gleamed.

She now had three pots boiling, each at its appropriate speed, and had she owned a fourth, she would have kept it busy boiling the kasha. From the fields she gathered the herbs she would need, and after a long day's work she was ready to begin the serious business of making her kielbasa. She carefully seasoned whatever choice meat she had with generous amounts of garlic, pepper, herbs and spices. Then, having tied one end of an intestine with a thread, she took a wooden spoon and carefully fed her mixture into the free opening, pressing it along with her fingers but taking great care never to compress the mixture too tightly lest it burst the skin at later cooking. The whole was then carefully tied into links, which Jan hung in the chimney for smoking. After the kielbasa was properly cured, Anulka would apportion it sparingly, a little piece here, another when the children were good. The fatback was salted and stored in a wooden container. It would be used in the preparation of almost any meal, or eaten with bread to provide nourishment during the long winter months. The blood was mixed with the kasha, spices and onions, spooned carefully into the larger intestines, baked at mealtime, and was called kiszka. The knuckles were cooked with spices and other remaining bones, until even the most minute shred of meat had been loosened, and this became a tangy gelatinous delicacy. Nothing was wasted.

In this prudent way every portion of the Castle Gorka hogs was utilized: the good cuts for the banquet, the tougher ones in Pani Danusia's pierogi, the haslet in Anulka's kielbasa. This good husbandry was symbolic of the rational way in which Poland had organized itself in the year 1646, when magnates, gentry and peasants were about as happy as they had ever been.

The wedding was a joyous affair. It started one Wednesday when peasants from four of Cyprjan's villages arrived, bringing what carts they had, the horses decked in flowers, and each person dressed in the one good garment she or he owned. The peasants wore shoes, which they had carried to the festivities, heavy dark trousers and jackets for the men, brightly colored dresses and headgear for the women. Girls of marriageable age, to which the wedding was a special treat because here they could review the young men of the district, wore particularly attractive skirts, heavily embroidered bodices and scarfs of the brightest color; they moved in groups, laughing and teasing, and seemed at times like little flocks of spring birds chirping with delight.

One village provided a rustic band: an old man with bagpipes, a young man with a fiddle, and a man of middle age with a wooden flute that he himself had carved. They played country tunes with which everyone was familiar: krakowiaks (the dance of Krakow) and chodzonys (a strolling dance) and gonionys (a chasing dance). The musicians, who were occasionally joined by two or three men who performed wonders with the jew's-harp, played incessantly, stopping only when someone slipped them a mug of beer, and this encouraged dancing day and night.

The visiting villagers were housed in various barns on the estate; the largest one was reserved for the dancing, the eating and the general assembling. Here shy young men studied the groups of girls, joshing and pushing each other until one gained the courage to approach them, to be invariably rebuffed with loud squeals and left standing foolishly in the middle of the barn. But as the afternoon waned, each boy somehow subtracted from the groups of girls someone with whom he wished to dance or talk, and then the remaining young women would fall silent for a moment, watching to see how the young man behaved himself.

The peasants were fed from a central kitchen area at which older women prepared feasts from such foods as they had brought with them—cabbages, beets, kasha, onions, a few eggs—but during the first two days there was no meat. For about six hours each day they were supposed to work at tasks set them by the castle, and this they did with generosity and even pleasure, for it was known that beginning with the third day, Friday, the magnate would provide them with meat, or at least fish and chicken, and this was a boon worth working for.

The villagers from Bukowo, who now pertained to Lukasz of the small castle, were brought en masse to Cyprjan's to help with decorating the large castle, and Lukasz came with them to supervise their efforts. As one subservient to Cyprjan, it was prudent for him to perform well, and considering the exalted position of some of the guests, he realized that someone dependable like himself was a necessity.

On Thursday the other gentry who served Cyprjan's extensive holdings began to arrive, mothers, fathers, children, principal servants, and since many of them came from great distances, even from the Ukrainian estates, they had to be housed in the castle itself, except that two of the gentry who were actually Ukrainian and not Polish were sent to the little castle at Bukowo.

Now the pace of festivity increased, and its quality too, because Cyprjan had imported from Krakow two orchestras of skilled musicians who played violins, basses, real flutes, horns and a small drum. One group was Jewish, dressed in their traditional Galician garb: black shoes and white stockings, black pants which came just below the knee, long black coat which came just above the knee, flat hat with wide brim which they wore indoors and out, and beards fancifully cut so that long curls descended about the ears.

"No wedding would be official," Cyprjan said, "without the Catholic priest and the Jewish orchestra," and since the latter would play about eighteen hours a day for the next six days, except on their Sabbath, he had provided a small special cooking area for them in which they could prepare their own dishes in their own traditional ways. Although the Poles did not look kindly on their Jews, who had known Jesus and rejected Him, they did tolerate them and, indeed, expressed pleasure whenever it was announced that a Jewish orchestra would be appearing.

The Jews played good music, sophisticated dances from Hungary and Germany, Ukrainian folk songs of high quality, and at special moments, which they announced to the audience in accented Polish, "music which has come to us from Italy, where it is highly regarded." But mostly they played the excellent Polish music that was being composed throughout Poland and performed in the inns and homes of Warsaw or Krakow. Exciting moments came when they played some fine Jewish dance from Moldavia or Hungary, or from Poland itself, because then the listeners had a sense of the forbidden, or the mysterious, which intensified their pleasure. The musicians did not mingle with the guests, or eat of their food, or drink their beer. They were apart and were content to be so, but they were also a treasured component of the festivities, and they knew it.

With their arrival, serious dancing started within the castle itself and not only in the peasants' barn. Young Barbara, as the bride-to-be, did not dance, nor did she watch the others enjoying themselves; these were critical days for her and she stayed above with the older women, who fitted her with dresses and showed her the linens they were storing in the chests she would take with her to Krzyztopor. But the other visiting maidens between the ages of ten and twenty had a gala time, swaying across the stone floor in pretty dresses and gazing with admiration as young men from other well-born families tested their new shoes in the slower dances.

On Friday there was real commotion, for in the morning the archbishop arrived from Krakow, and he was met by all the local clergy, sixteen of them, who commented on how fine he looked and how well the affairs of the church were progressing under his leadership. He had been to both Rome and Compostela and was a man of substance in the hierarchy. He had known Cyprjan in Krakow and had participated with him in a mission to Lithuania, where a group of clergymen who had been members of the Russian Orthodox church desired to convert to Rome's Uniate church under the dispensation of the Union of Brzesc, 1595. The archbishop had greeted the converting priests with a warmth that pleased Cyprjan, who told the newcomers: "You have left a church wallowing in darkness and joined one gleaming in God's light. You will never regret your decision." Three of them would, of course, because their conservative parishioners out in the distant villages would not understand their apostasy and would shortly slay them.

In the afternoon all the peasants gathered at the riverbank, where a small platform had been erected for the Jewish orchestra and another larger one for Cyprjan, Zofia Mniszech and the bishop; again, Barbara was not to be seen.

Trumpets sounded and there were shouts of "There they come!" and from the west bank of the Vistula three canopied barges decorated with thousands of flowers set out, each with six men rowing and six poling with long shafts that reached the bottom of the river. They came slowly, like faery boats in a dream; the current of the river carried them northward, but the polers fought against this, so that the barges seemed to be moving in a sideways posture. Persons aboard began singing wedding songs, and sound floated over the river, and several fish, disturbed by the unusual procession, leaped into the air as if they, too, were celebrating.

Thus Roman Ossolinski, attended by two hundred, journeyed from Krzyztopor and crossed the Vistula to claim his bride. As his barge, the one in the lead, approached the eastern shore the orchestra broke into joyous music, and the girls who had been coached how to throw their flowers when the chancellor and his family stepped ashore ran to the water's edge, but before the flowers could be thrown, the archbishop stepped forward and blessed the river, the barges upon it and all who had made this journey: "God blesses this day. God blesses Roman Ossolinski, who comes on such a splendid mission. God blesses the union which will ensue." Then five trumpets blasted and the festivities began in earnest.

That Friday night there was a gala banquet served on plates from Paris, each containing enameled scenes of rural life featuring lovers working in the fields while goddesses watched approvingly and birds flew overhead. An orchestra played slow dancing music as forty servants trained for the occasion and dressed in livery supplied them by the master served nine courses, beginning with a delicate white borsch made from soured rye flour and ending three hours later with small pieces of a cake which Zofia herself had made for this opening occasion: a bottom layer of dark-brown walnut cake, an upper layer of golden-yellow almond cake, and over all, a thick layer of orange preserve with chunks of the rind glistening through.

The archbishop, who loved to drink seriously at any banquet, gave a rambling speech in which he avowed that he had never had a better cake to end a meal, to which Chancellor Ossolinski agreed. It was a splendid beginning to a wedding and the guests enjoyed themselves immensely, but Barbara had still not made an appearance.

On Saturday most of the women, including Zofia and Chancellor Ossolinski's wife, went to the kitchen to prepare the ritual bread which would grace the wedding and unite it with the earth. Using only the best grains, the women ground small supplies of symbolic flour: wheat, rye, oats. This they mixed with large amounts of similar flours obtained in the usual way, and ingredients were laid out for the bread-making.

This bread had to be made in specified ways: the salt was blessed; the yeast was taken from special crocks in which it had been carefully nurtured; and the caraway seeds were inspected almost one by one to ensure their purity. When the older women were satisfied that ritual procedures had been observed, they gathered the others and said: "It is time to fetch the bride."

With the two mothers, Zofia Mniszech and Wanda Ossolinska, leading the way and chanting "All men to leave the castle!" the procession of women in their beautiful dresses made its way to Barbara's chamber, while two guards were left along the way to continue chanting "All men to leave the castle!"

They found Barbara sitting with the old nurse, who was in the midst of reminding her once again that the family of Cyprjan and Zofia was no less distinguished than that of the Ossolinskis, whom fate had placed at the top of the ladder at this particular moment, and when the older women stood around the room, one said: "Lady Barbara, it is time now to bake the bread for your beloved," and with the mothers once more in the lead, the splendid procession wound its way back to the kitchen as the women again chanted, "All men to leave the castle."

In the kitchen Barbara went to a special table where ritual ingredients were spread out for the making of dough sufficient for one loaf, and as she mixed them and kneaded the dough the other women did the same, using more ordinary ingredients, for on this gala day they would bake thirty-seven loaves, and as they worked they sang:

"May this marriage be fruitful . . .
May the mouth that eats this bread sing praises . . .
May the womb that this bread nourishes be fruitful . . .

May God be praised in all things . . .
May Jesus Christ be praised . . ."

But before Barbara's loaf could be placed in the oven the archbishop was summoned from among the men waiting in the courtyard, and when he entered the kitchen he knelt before Barbara, saying: "You are to be queen of this household," and then he blessed each of the loaves, uttering a solemn prayer for the happiness of the wedding which this bread was to honor. Into the ovens they were popped, and after Barbara retired to her room, Zofia and Wanda peered into the ovens from time to time, reporting to the others: "The bread is doing well."

That night, when all were seated at the long table with the French plates before them containing nothing, trumpets sounded and the orchestra began playing solemn music, and into the hall came Barbara—dressed in flowing white robes, with a single flower in her hair and the amber necklace about her lovely throat. When she approached the table her attendants withdrew and she stood alone. Walking slowly and with marvelous grace, she went to where the bridegroom sat and kneeled before him, offering on her upturned hands a loaf of the new bread: "I give you the soil of Poland. I give you the grain of Poland. Eat this good bread and be strong. Eat this good bread and be my husband."

At this moment Zofia Mniszech handed a loaf to her husband, Cyprjan, and Wanda Ossolinska honored her husband in the same way, whereupon servants scurried about giving each guest a small piece of the fresh bread. It was eaten not ritually, as in a celebration of Mass, but hungrily, as if this were the substance of Poland upon which all life depended.

Sunday, both for the gentry in the castle and the peasants in the barns, was given over to religious services, so the orchestras were excused until sunset, when a giant feast was served in the castle and the meat from two large roasted pigs was distributed among the peasants. There were songs and dances, and processions and trumpet blasts, while Cyprjan and Ossolinski sat on improvised thrones beaming their general approval.

On Monday, at eleven in the morning, the wedding ceremony was solemnized by the archbishop and three of his priests. He realized that he was joining two of the noblest families of Poland, and two of the richest, and in his brief address to the newly married couple he stressed just this:

"Roman and Barbara, because you come from special families you must accept special obligations. Poland needs your leadership. Poland needs your help in preserving its freedom. Jealous enemies beset us on every side, and we must defend ourselves against them.

"You are building a great castle on the other side of the river, one that will withstand any siege, but you must also build in your hearts a love of Jesus Christ so that you will be ready to defend His freedom, too. The church is the salvation of Poland. Holy Mother Mary is the protectress of our liberties. May you be strong in your defense of both."

That night there were endless celebrations in both castles and in the barns, and there was dancing till morning. The bagpipe-flute-fiddle scraped away with country dances while the Jewish orchestra alternated lively Polish mazurkas with more serious music from Rome and Paris. Barbara, in a lighter dress than the one in which she had been married, danced with every father and son from her father's outlying castles, but when the cock crowed she drew aside, as she had been instructed, and with her mother in front holding a candle, she and all the women in the castle, even the cooks, paraded majestically three times around the dining hall while the men applauded, and then they marched up the great stone stairway to the upper floors, where the bridal chamber, strewn with flowers, awaited.

Now Chancellor Ossolinski lifted a candle, whereupon his son stepped behind him, followed by all the men, and they circled the room, singing "Christ is the bridegroom in heaven, Roman the bridegroom on earth," after which they headed for the stairway, delivering the bridegroom to the chamber. Dawn broke and roosters crowed and men fell into drunken sleep.

Early Tuesday morning all who could be spared were placed in carts and driven the short distance to the Bukowo castle to see for themselves that Lukasz really did have a tame bear, an otter that played with a fox, and two storks, and although the crowd was rather large, Lukasz's animals behaved as if they knew this was a special occasion. The bear moved among the guests, nudging them and pushing them in the chest with one big paw, while the fox darted here and there as if it were his business to greet each guest individually.

To many, it was the two storks that occasioned most comment, for though all had seen these ungainly birds atop their chimneys, few had ever been close enough to inspect their structure or their curious faces; the storks behaved as if they, too, had rarely seen anything as strange as a human being. So the entire morning was spent with the animals, and this became so tiring to the beasts that before the wedding guests departed, the bear was asleep, with the fox and the otter dozing inside her paws.

The next years were among the happiest Cyprjan and Zofia would ever know, for the Ossolinskis proceeded with amazing vigor to the building of Krzyztopor, and when the foundations were dug the enormous place looked even larger than it had on paper. It was tremendous, an entire city within great battlements and protected by those four gaunt towers reaching into the sky. The winding stairway to the hidden well was constructed; the immense chapel was built, finer than many cathedrals; the three hundred and sixty-five windows were installed, and the fifty-two rooms, each an apartment in itself with three or four attendant rooms, were completed.

It was a castle of such strength and magnificence that Cyprjan was proud to think that his daughter was one day to be its chatelaine, and Barbara rose to her responsibilities, applying the lessons she had learned from her tutor while traveling in France with her father, and poring over the books on palaces she had acquired during the year he had served as an ambassador in Italy. She studied the husbandry of the place and how its two hundred servants and groundkeepers and woodsmen were organized and supervised. She grew lovelier each year; motherhood enhanced her charm; and she was becoming known not only in Poland but in surrounding countries as a notable beauty.

At the dedication of the castle and its formal christening as the Battle Axe of the Cross, a Polish poet from the Jagiellonian University at Krakow asked permission to read a poem which he had written in honor of Barbara Ossolinska's famed amber necklace, and he recited a rather heavily constructed but deeply moving evocation of amber's mystery and glory:

> *"Not harsh or brilliant like a challenging diamond,*
> *Nor stained with miners' blood like a throbbing ruby,*
> *Nor brazenly proclaiming its worth like a cube of gold . . .*
> *You are an autumn moon rising over a field of ripened grain."*

The poem, containing three other similar stanzas, occasioned much applause, and various persons asked for copies, so that it became well known and even treasured, but a young French diplomat serving in Krakow considered the poem rather bucolic, and he asked permission to produce a version more in the style of the English poets of the time, whom he admired exceedingly, and on the next night he offered the guests his more graceful version, which he called "A Pretty Conceit in Which My Lady's Amber Is Compared with the Constellation Pleiades":

> *"The Pleiades are seven stars,*
> *But only six are seen.*
> *The seventh is immured by bars,*
> *A sad imprisoned queen.*
>
> *"The Sisters Six glow on your breast,*
> *The fairest ever seen.*
> *The seventh shines beyond the rest,*
> *'Tis you, their heavenly queen."*

He recited his poem with such appropriate delicacy that those about Barbara applauded vigorously, but friends of the Polish poet grumbled: "The Pleiades isn't a constellation by itself," and one man explained: "It's part of Orion, as everyone knows." The Polish poet stared at his defender.

Then, in the year 1648, frightening rumors began reaching both Krzyztopor and Castle Gorka concerning an uprising of Cossacks throughout the Ukrainian territories of Poland, and since Cyprjan had large holdings there, estates vaster than some European principalities, he had to hasten eastward, taking Lukasz and his henchman Jan of the Beech Trees, to stem the trouble before it reached his estates.

They rode at the fastest practical speed for more than two hundred miles, but as they approached the vast empty area east of Lwow they saw the ruins of Polish estates, one after the other, and a sick feeling assaulted Cyprjan, for he could guess what he was going to find when he reached his holdings. Four miles west of the first estate the travelers encountered a Catholic priest who, recognizing Cyprjan, gasped incoherently: "Peaceful . . . your four hundred peasants . . .

the little church . . . the mill . . . and then the Cossacks." They had destroyed everything in one wild protest against the heavy impositions of the Polish landowners and the spiritual tyranny of the Roman Catholic church, since they were loyal only to the Orthodoxy of Constantinople and Moscow.

"All the priests but me . . . slain. All the Jews . . . most of the Poles." When Cyprjan, trembling with rage, asked how he had escaped, the priest said: "A Jew saved me, and then I saved him. We were the only ones who lived." Cyprjan asked where the Jew was, and the priest said: "He went back. The Jews always go back."

It was a time of heartbreak for Cyprjan and sullen rage for Lukasz and Jan, for they saw at each of Cyprjan's five Ukrainian estates only complete desolation and the loss of at least sixty percent of the former population. But the two attendants applauded the determination with which Cyprjan decided to rebuild: "If it takes every zloty we earn along the Vistula and in the north, these estates will be reconstructed. Lukasz, you stay here with Jan and supervise things. I'll send all the gold I can collect."

So the two men from Bukowo were absent from their homes for two years. On the steppes they collected a new group of peasants, who had no other choice but to submit themselves to the custodianship of the magnate Cyprjan. New Jews were imported to operate the stores and the money system, new priests of the Roman faith to rebuild the little churches.

In 1649, in the midst of the rebuilding and before too many goods or houses had accumulated, the Cossacks struck again, killing and burning as before, but Lukasz had anticipated their coming, and he hid himself, Jan, two priests and a Jew who was doing his trading from a cave which he had prudently constructed, and there they waited in darkness until the hurricane passed. After that second sweep, the Cossacks let this part of the Ukraine alone, and a kind of peace was restored, and magnates like Cyprjan dismissed the Cossack incursion as merely one more of the troublesome invasions from the east.

In 1654 an event occurred which at the time seemed much less important than the great Cossack raids but which in the long run proved much more disastrous to the welfare of Poland, for as Lukasz and Jan of the Beech Trees had proved, damage done by the raids could be repaired, but the damage about to be done by this new development would in the long run prove fatal.

The government of Poland had several unique weaknesses that differentiated it from other European nations, making it much less stable than they. First, the magnates dominated the election of the king, but they insisted upon doing so reign-by-reign, lest an inherited dynasty slip into dictatorship. Second, they refused to conduct the election *vivente rege*—that is, while the old king still lived, for fear he might exercise too much influence and throw the election to his son or some other member of his family. Third, the magnates were afraid to elect one of their own number, who might wax too strong and restrict succession to members of his own clan; they strongly preferred to elect foreigners, which inevitably involved them in the dynastic troubles of other nations with which they had no functional affiliation.

At first the elected kings performed like responsible hired managers, and some actually provided excellent custodianship, but the inevitable arrival of weak foreign kings precipitated the decline of the kingdom, for as the papal legate explained in one report to Rome: "It would be much easier for some trivial French nobleman to become King of Poland than for an honest Polish patriot. You see, the magnates are satisfied that if they don't like the Frenchman, they'll be able to kick him out of the country, something they might not be able to do with a native Pole." He might have added that on occasion the voting had ended in such chaos that two different kings were elected, a situation that could be resolved only by civil war.

Electing a foreigner king under such circumstances was bound to be a sorry affair, but even so, it might have worked had not the Poles added a fourth and a fifth complication after the man was elected. Having chosen a Swede or a Saxon or a Hungarian to be their king, they then refused to give him any real power, or any right of taxation, or even the privilege of conscripting a serious army. The king must be kept a figurehead, never a dictator, and what pitiful power he might amass in his self-defense, he could obtain only by cajoling or flattering magnates like the master of Castle Gorka.

Why did Cyprjan behave in this fashion? He was a patriot; without question he was loyal to the concept of a free, strong Poland; he was intelligent and liked to associate with other magnates who were as well-traveled as he, and he listened carefully when they explained what was happening in Italy and England and France. Constantly he speculated on procedures which would prove good for Poland and his family.

And there was the rub! Whenever he voiced this last concern he invariably phrased it: "What's good for my family and Poland." As a great magnate who literally owned more than sixty villages and thousands of peasants, he simply could not visualize any governing entity more important than himself. He was not a vain man, not a poseur, and certainly not one who flaunted his immense wealth, but he was convinced that he was Poland and that every instrument of state power or policy must be judged by one simple criterion: "Is it good for the magnates?" If in the slightest way a suggested change in procedure—such as electing the next king while the old king still lived, to avoid the horrendous interregnums which sometimes left Poland for two or three years without a king while the magnates wrestled over the election—if such a change threatened even the slightest prerogative of the magnates, Cyprjan had to oppose it, which he did, most vigorously. Indeed, he would have taken arms on a day's notice to protect his rights, and he would not have been able to conceive of this as treason, for he thought of himself as markedly superior to the king and much closer to the soul of Poland, for the king would vanish after a brief reign, whereas he, the magnate, would continue forever.

The final monstrosity which the magnates invented to protect what they called their Golden Freedom, and at the same time hamstring both the king and the rising middle gentry, can only be described as insane. Reported the papal legate: "The concept of *liberum veto* must have been devised in hell by a special devil charged with the task of destroying Christian Poland." In 1654, Magnate Cyprjan, through the agency of his slow-witted but honest henchman Lukasz, demonstrated what the *liberum veto* could accomplish in speeding a great nation on its slide to oblivion.

Three times in a row—1587, 1632 and 1648 during the Cossack uprisings—the magnates had elected as their king a member of the Swedish royal family, and this was remarkable because Poland was an intensely Catholic nation while Sweden was just as intensely Lutheran, the most obdurate of the Protestant faiths. True, the various kings imported by Poland had promised that whereas in Sweden they had been Protestant, in Poland they would be Catholic, and they were faithful to this pledge. Up to now, Poland had had no great cause for religious complaint, but there was always confusion and an underlying irrationality. At any moment the apparently Catholic Swedish king might revert to Protestantism, with disastrous consequences.

Magnates like Cyprjan were not at all happy with Jan Kazimir, their present Swedish king, and it was only with the greatest reluctance that they voted him any taxes or army; in 1648 a well-organized Poland should have been able to drive back the Cossacks within three months of frontier fighting, but the confused little army did not like to venture into the frontier, so the Cossacks had been allowed a free hand to burn and plunder.

Now throughout Poland there arose among the lesser gentry, the town burghers, some of the clergy and the farmers who had obtained land, a realization that the current system of government was defective, and there was talk that when the Seym, Poland's parliament, convened in Warsaw, correction would surely be made. Like many other parliaments, Poland's consisted of two houses, Senate and Deputies, and only magnates or their personal representatives or their churchly equals could sit in the first; lesser nobles only, in the second. In addition to passing laws, the Seym acted as the court of last appeal to which any person of noble rank could present his plea for clemency. Of course, townspeople, traders, Jews and peasants could appeal to no one.

Cyprjan, an aloof patriot who did not like personal display and who would have abhorred showing himself arguing in public, deputized Lukasz of Bukowo to sit for him and gave him the strictest instructions as to what he must do and how: "Seym is a silly business. It creates only trouble. You sit there and keep your mouth shut and I'll send you word as to how you're to vote."

When the 1654 Seym had been in session only two of its allotted six weeks, it became clear to the magnates that decisions were being discussed which would strengthen the king, give townsmen privileges they never had before, and weaken the magnates' oppressive grip on the peasants. So Cyprjan, already distressed by his losses in the Ukraine and fearful of any change, which he termed revolution, summoned Lukasz to a meeting with three of the more powerful magnates, who seated him on a chair before them as if he were an unruly schoolboy. They formed a frightening quartet: heads shaved, except for tufts of hair down the middle; great protruding bellies swathed in gold-encrusted sashes; flowing mustaches. And they spoke as roughly as they looked: "Your stupid Seym. Have you gone out of your mind? Everything you propose threatens our position, and that means it threatens Poland."

"We thought that the townsmen—"

"Traders. Men of no substance. Pitiful persons who have been to the university. The townsmen have no rights and they deserve none. Don't speak to us of townsmen."

"We also thought that the peasants—"

"We will tell the peasants what to do. We will protect their interests. The Seym has no concern with peasants."

"But there is a spirit in the air—"

"It is to be extinguished."

"How? It seems very strong."

"It is to be extinguished by revoking every change you have made so far."

"I don't think the Seym would permit that," Lukasz said weakly, for the magnates in their golden coats, brocaded belts and shaved heads were overpowering.

"It is no longer what the Seym wants. It's what we want. What Poland wants."

When Lukasz said nothing, the magnates glared at him, waiting for him to come to his senses, but this did not happen, so Cyprjan, as the owner of the man, said sternly: "Lukasz, everything that the Seym has done will be revoked . . . tomorrow . . . by you."

"Me?" The voice was very small.

"Yes. In the 1652 Seym the patriot Wladyslaw Sicinski, acting under secret orders from the Radziwills, said in a loud voice 'I object!' and this established the good principle that every act of every Seym must have unanimous approval. If even one member objects, the act is rejected. And what is most valuable to us, every other act which Seym has enacted is also rejected. It's as if the Seym had never existed."

"What am I to do?" Lukasz asked, and he received instructions which seemed incomprehensible: "You are to stand up and cry in a loud voice 'I object!' and when you say that, the Seym ends. And everything wrong it's done so far is also canceled."

"But our Seym has four more weeks to run," Lukasz protested feebly.

"Not now it doesn't. Your Seym ends tomorrow."

So when the Seym reconvened, having passed more than a dozen commendable laws which would have strengthened the nation, bringing it into conformity with the powerful nation-states being so painfully forged in England, France, Russia and even America, Lukasz of Bukowo rose from his seat and cried as directed "I object!" and the whole structure collapsed. One little man, voicing the will of one selfish magnate, was able to frustrate the thoughtful efforts of an entire nation to reform itself.

In Seym after Seym, many of the wisest decisions then being made in the world, the equal at least to anything being accomplished in England or France and much like the tentative beginnings in America, were destroyed by the single veto of one man working in the interests of a venal aristocracy. Progress was defeated at each turn by the selfish interests of magnates who preached that they were acting thus to defend their Golden Freedom, and in a sense they were.

They were defending their freedom to neutralize the king; they were defending their freedom to keep the newly built towns subservient to their country areas; they were defending most strongly their freedom to keep their peasants in a state of perpetual serfdom as opposed to the liberties which were being grudgingly won in the western parts of Europe; and they were doing everything reactionary within their power to preserve the advantages they had against the legitimate aspirations of the growing gentry. The Golden Freedom which the magnates defended with every bit of chicanery and power they commanded was the freedom of the few to oppress the many, the freedom of a few grasping magnates to prevent a strong king from arising.

When any essential part of a governing system becomes corrupt, it endangers all parts because it tempts officials to engage in parallel wrong actions, and this inescapable truth became criminally obvious when the magnates took intricate steps to protect the freedoms they obtained through the *liberum veto.* Many magnates began to look outside Poland for support in their efforts to thwart the popular will, and they began to forge alliances with some alien power, accepting bribes and other advantages from Russia, or Sweden, or Austria, or France, or one of the German states in return for voting not in the interests of Poland but of the foreign power that was paying the money. Thus the Radziwills often defended the interests of Russia or Sweden; the Leszczynskis, those of France; and Cyprjan, with a coterie of his friends, those of Austria.

Why would he, with one of the most powerful names in Poland, look outside his native land for leadership, and why to Austria? From childhood he had failed to construct in his mind a vision of Poland united and capable of governing itself. The heroes extolled in his family were the rowdy Mniszechs, the freebooting Radziwills, the self-directed magnates who ventured into the vastness of the Ukraine, hacking out great estates, with thousands of peasants subservient to their whims—they were the prototypical Poles. Never had he visualized the professors at Jagiellonian University as leaders of a nation, not even when he invited them to his castle, and he certainly had no respect for the functionaries who bothered with taxes and the administration of laws. Each Swedish king he had known seemed pettifogging, a Protestant at home, a Catholic in Poland, so that strong central government could not be his ideal, because he had never known it.

On the other hand, he revered the Habsburgs and the resolute way they went about enlarging their territories, decade after decade. He foresaw that one of these days they would encompass outlying principalities like Hungary and Transylvania, and all to the good. He did not actually think that Austria would one day engulf Poland; he was too much a patriot for that, but he did admit that if any outside nation were to do so, it ought to be Austria.

With such rot at the core, the politics of Poland became the most corrupt in Europe, surpassing in venality even that of the Turks in Constantinople, and year by year the Golden Freedom of the magnates meant the weakening and debasement of Poland.

Cardinal Pentucci, the papal legate, wondering how Christian Poland could be saved, reported:

> Now when a bill comes before the Seym the question is not "Will this be good for Poland?" but rather "How does Russia want me to vote on this? Or France? Or Austria?" Because of the corrupt weaknesses that I have spoken of earlier—the election of foreigners, the refusal of the magnates to share their power, and especially the degradation of the Seym with its *liberum veto* and the sale of votes, one might say that Poland has become the plaything of Europe.

Never was this shrewd judgment more applicable than in the chain of years starting in 1655, when Barbara Ossolinska and her husband, Roman, were beginning to make Krzyztopor Castle one of the adornments of Europe.

• • •

"Why would the King of Sweden want to invade Poland?" the legate asked the French ambassador at the latter's palace in Warsaw.

"Because of Sweden's perpetual lust to control the Baltic coastline," the Frenchman replied.

"Can she do it?"

"I think so."

"But will Poland allow her?"

The ambassador considered how best to answer this probing question, and he saw that there were two logical explanations, an easy one pertaining to Poland's military ability, and a most difficult one involving her will power. He decided to tackle the latter first: "Like all nations, Cardinal Pentucci, Poland has wonderful strengths and weaknesses, and they derive from her basic character. But the strangest deficiency, and I've watched the rise and fall of many nations, is her refusal to look northward . . . to the Baltic."

"What do you mean by that?"

The ambassador poured himself and his guest drinks of good French brandy, and said: "I've developed a theory that every nation has a natural territory which it must occupy if it's to fulfill its destiny. At whatever cost, it must reach out and use that space. France has done this. England is doing it rather well with her recent alliances with Wales and Scotland. On some appropriate day your Italy will do it, and Germany is already in the painful process."

"I see what you mean about nations with natural boundaries. But what about Poland, which has none?"

"There you're wrong! East and west you're right. Poor Poland has no natural limits. But in the other directions she does. South with the Carpathians. And most important, north with the Baltic Sea. To fulfill her destiny she must, in my opinion, control her proper share of that coastline."

"Yes, yes," the legate said reflectively. "Her great river the Vistula does empty into the Baltic. Danzig does control all her trade. The fish her people love so much do reach her in the fishing boats of other nations."

"Don't you see, Cardinal? If she allowed the Teutonic Knights in the past, or Sweden now, or Germany in the future to dominate her Baltic coastline, she's sure to be strangled. Yet she does nothing to avoid it. Time and again, she backs away from her own destiny."

"Would she have the power to halt Sweden now, even if she did have the will?"

"Bluntly, no. Poland's allowed herself to become incredibly weak. Her magnates will permit no army, afraid it might become an agency of the king."

"Is he as foolish as he seems?"

"Jan Kazimir is deceptive, Cardinal Pentucci. As the Catholic King of Poland, he's rather good. A real patriot. But as a secret Protestant trying to gain the throne of Sweden . . . It's a pitiful confusion."

"He's been baptized a Catholic, you know," the legate said. "And I believe he's a rather good one."

"But as a member of the Swedish royal family, he dreams of becoming King of Sweden, and obviously the Swedes will permit none of that."

"Is he really so ill-advised?"

"He's worse. He not only dreams of becoming King of Sweden. He takes overt steps to achieve it."

"And so the legitimate King of Sweden . . . His cousin or something? He must oppose. And is that where the threatened invasion springs from?"

"The king ruling in Sweden is like all other kings, Your Eminence. One-third avarice. One-third stupidity. One-third sheer brilliance in protecting his interests."

"And if this complex man, this Charles X Gustavus, proceeds with his plan to invade, will he conquer Poland?"

"I have advised my king that Sweden will crush Poland within a matter of months."

The two men pondered this for some minutes, after which the legate said: "Is it not strange that a small country like Sweden, with so few people and such little wealth, can presume to conquer a great nation like Poland, superior in so many ways?"

"It isn't strange if the small nation is well governed and holds together, while the big nation is poorly governed and flies apart."

"Does government mean so much?"

"It means everything."

"But what about spirit? Will? Faith?"

"Without an army, what are they?"

"A great deal, sometimes. What army has our Pope? He has only faith and will."

"That's why he rules the world of faith, and kings rule the world of power and wealth."

"I cannot believe that a Catholic Poland will surrender so easily to a Protestant Sweden."

"Now there," said the Frenchman, "you begin to face the real problem. Poland by itself could exist, and nicely. But when, through its unfortunate kings, it becomes involved in the dynastic disputes of neighboring countries . . . then it falls into peril. And if you add religious warfare as well, the whole thing falls into chaos. Have you heard what the Swedish king has boasted in a letter to Oliver Cromwell? 'When I finish with Poland, there will not be a papist in the land.'"

"Alas! Another Lutheran fanatic to deal with! Poor Poland." But even as he issued this lament, he thought of certain Polish leaders he had met who did not fit the description of irresponsibility the ambassador was drawing: "I know this man Cyprjan of Gorka, and I truly doubt that he could ever bring himself to betray either Poland or his king."

"Cyprjan is one of the finest," the ambassador conceded. "And I've heard good reports of this other magnate, Lubomirski."

"Yes, yes. If the nation had enough like them, it would have a chance of survival," the legate said with an echo of hope in his voice.

"But the good are so few and the weak so many," the Frenchman said, at which the legate nodded. "In Rome the same."

With extraordinary perception the Frenchman had anticipated exactly what happened when the dynamic Swedes struck the lethargic and leaderless Poles, but not even he could have foreseen the speed with which the invaders triumphed, nor the collapse that overcame Poland's army, her civic will and the leadership of her magnates.

On 21 July 1655 the Swedish armies, led personally by their energetic king, burst into Poland, and a brief four days later the Polish armies began to cave in. On 18 August the great Lithuanian magnate Radziwill hastened forward to surrender all his part of the Polish kingdom, and by the first of September, Swedish troops had overrun the entire nation. Rarely had a major nation collapsed with such great speed and such little effort to protect itself.

What the French ambassador had not been able to predict was the ferocity with which the Protestant victors treated the Catholic losers. Cities, towns and villages were destroyed in maniacal fury. Churches, guildhalls, shops and farmhouses were sacked and burned. Priests and nuns, burghers and Jewish traders, housewives and farmers defending their possessions were slain in terrible numbers, whole communities being erased in fire and fury. No invader had ever behaved with more savage contempt than the Swedes who overran Poland.

During the last days of that dreadful summer the Swedish forces approached the formidable castle of Krzyztopor standing on its slight rise and surrounded by its wide, secure moat. The Ossolinskis, surveying their water and food supplies, satisfied themselves that their mighty fortress could withstand any siege, so when the chancellor suggested that perhaps Barbara might want to flee to Krakow, she refused the offer.

"This is my castle," she said, displaying the fortitude which had marked both her father's and her mother's families. She was at the height of her beauty that summer, a stately woman of extraordinary charm who had schooled herself in the various subjects necessary to be a good manager: she could read and write; she had traveled to France and Italy; she patronized musicians and artists, so that songs were written to her and portraits painted; and she had a nice feel for politics, assessing accurately the grievous errors made by the magnates with whom her various families associated. She was a voice of the new Poland, the one that might come into being after this Swedish deluge had subsided, and she intended to make Krzyztopor Castle a focal point of that revival.

The immediate problem was simple: "We must resist the Swedes and allow them nothing. Roman, you must ensure that the guards do their duty, and do it well."

Such warnings from the chatelaine were not necessary, for everyone within the castle walls was determined to save this castle for the important years that lay ahead.

Had this been the year 1241 when the Tatars were attacking this area, or the year 1410 when the Teutonic Knights were rampaging, the castle could have withstood a siege of better than a year and repulsed all invaders, but this was 1655, when mighty new cannon were available and when moats however wide afforded little protection.

The Swedish king marched to Krzyztopor, took one look at the massive walls, and told his generals: "Wait till we can haul in the cannon," and when those great gray monsters were lined up, all facing the northern wall, the bombardment began, and the Swedes could see that the entire wall would be breached at more than a dozen spots, through which as many Swedes as wished could enter. Krzyztopor was doomed. Almost before its hearthstones were properly heated, it was to be destroyed.

Inside the castle the Ossolinskis listened with mounting horror as the cannonade broke down their wall, and when it became evident that the fortress must fall, Roman suggested that he approach the Swedes with a white flag, seeking safe passage for Barbara and the other women, but she would not permit this: "My fate is linked with that of my castle."

Through two horrible days she watched the protecting wall crumble, disintegrate as if it had been built by children, and as night fell on the second day she realized that before noon on the following day her castle would be overrun by northern barbarians, and she began to put her life in order.

She went to the large church inside the walls and prayed. She then talked with the older of the two priests and asked him to bless her, whereupon she talked with her three children, trying to instill in them the courage which she possessed. After that she visited the castle kitchens, reassuring the women that the Swedes would do them no harm, and then, as if the Swedes were guests who were coming for a few weeks, she went automatically to the linen chests to assure herself that all was properly arranged, and when she saw the neat stacks assembled at such heavy cost of money and her effort she broke into tears, and where no one could see her grief she cried: "This was to have been a center of light for a hundred years." Looking up at the vaulted ceiling, she lamented: "We built you with such care . . . such love. Oh God! This can't perish. Surely, they'll not break down this beautiful thing we built."

But even as she uttered this hope, she knew it was vain, for in her despair she had uncovered a profound truth: "We built the wrong castle, in the wrong century, to protect ourselves against the wrong enemy, the wrong kind of warfare. Dear God, what fools we were."

Then, ashamed of her temporary weakness, she went in search of her husband, determined to lend him what support she could, and he told her: "Barbara, we'll resist as long as possible, then surrender with honor and throw ourselves upon their mercy."

There was to be no mercy. As Barbara had anticipated, the Swedes broke through the final defenses at about ten in the morning and began the systematic destruction of the castle and all things within it. Roman Ossolinski and his wife were slain in the first onslaught. Their children were killed and the women in the kitchen and the two priests and all the defenders. No one escaped the terrible fury of the soldiers who had been defied for three days.

And then the sack of Krzyztopor began. Every item of even the remotest value was carried out into the huge central courtyard: food supplies, the chalices from the chapel, the brocades from the walls, the furniture, the chests, the dresses, the ceremonial robes of the priests. All corners of the castle were stripped and laid bare.

Carts commandeered from surrounding villages before they were burned were hauled in through the tall gates and loaded with treasures of Krzyztopor and sent on their way to Stockholm. Most precious were the books taken from the castle and the personal records, for these represented the lifeblood of a nation. Most valuable was a golden chain from which were suspended six lovely globelets of flawless amber, ripped from the corpse of the beautiful lady who had once ruled this castle. They were placed within a paper folder, then wrapped in canvas and tucked into a corner of Wagon 307, where they would rest securely until they reached Sweden.

In the closing days of that fateful year, 1655, Swedish forces reached the Vistula, where they went totally berserk, throwing down the walls of Castle Gorka and killing all the women and children. The village of Bukowo they burned, leveling every cottage and killing more than half the peasants, but they saved their most hideous behavior for the smaller castle, where Danusia, wife of the absent Lukasz, tried to herd together her tame animals and explain to the invaders . . .

One soldier lunged at Danusia with his lance and pierced her above the heart, whereupon two others lanced her from the side. The tame bear, seeing her drop to the ground, ambled over to comfort her, but the soldiers intercepted it and speared it numerous times. The otter, of course, tried to protect the bear, and was slain. Then the red fox hurried up to help the otter, and it was speared. Finally the storks flew down, as was their custom when guests came, and they were clubbed to death. Then the castle was set ablaze, becoming a funeral pyre for all the creatures who had once shared so much love.

So the three women who had kept their homes such warm refuges were slain by the Swedes: Anulka, who made the spicy kielbasa; Danusia, who baked the best pierogi; and Zofia Mniszech, who kept a huge kitchen bustling—all were murdered. Why had their men proved powerless to defend them?

When the great debacle began and other craven magnates turned traitor, rushing to the side of the Swedish king, Cyprjan and his liege Lukasz stood firm. With the field hand Jan of the Beech Trees along, they formed the nucleus of a small personal army that retreated from one indefensible position to another, until they came finally to the heavy-walled monastery of Czestochowa in the west.

Here a devout group of priests and monks manned the shrine that contained Poland's most precious religious relic, a time-darkened Byzantine painting of the Virgin Mother holding her infant son, the famous Virgin of Czestochowa, adored by the faithful. Here the patriots of Poland would make their final stand against the ruthless invader.

When Cyprjan of Gorka marched his pitifully small group into the monastery, the prospects of holding it against the cannon that had destroyed Krzyztopor seemed minimal, but all inside the walls were determined to offer as stout a defense as possible, and Cyprjan found himself in charge of the east wall, which was where the Swedes would probably concentrate their attack.

On 18 November 1655 the invaders began the assault, expecting to gain an easy victory over the unarmed monks, but two surprises awaited them. The clerics defending the monastery proved most resourceful in repelling attacks, and the walls, rebuilt and strengthened many times through the centuries, showed remarkable resistance to the cannonades. And if a hole was hammered through, Cyprjan's men repaired it quickly. This siege was going to be much different from the easy victory at Krzyztopor.

On 1 December the Swedes were no closer to winning than they had been two weeks before, but their two heavy cannon were damaging the walls, and if this continued indefinitely, the tide of battle would have to flow their way, so on 5 December, Cyprjan and some other daring spirits began contemplating the possibility of knocking out the cannon: "We could sneak sacks of gunpowder to the sites, stack them around the cannon, and blow them up."

"What do we do with the Swedes guarding them?" a friar asked.

"Kill them," Cyprjan said, and when some of his listeners blanched, he said: "I will do this thing, I and my men."

He did not ask for volunteers; he told Lukasz, Jan and six of his other peasants: "We will creep out tonight," and they had to follow.

They left the monastery at about eleven o'clock on a cold, blustery night when the Swedish guards would be having a difficult time keeping warm. Moving with extreme caution, they crept down a gully that carried rain water away from the walls, came upon a dozing guard, whom Cyprjan himself strangled, and then to the protected embankment on which the two cannon rested.

For more than fifteen minutes they huddled close to it, speaking no words but surveying the situation, and when each of the nine knew exactly what he must do in the next blazing moments, they swarmed upon the cannon, killed the guards, piled their sacks of powder, and retreated to light the fuse. It required about a minute and forty seconds for the tiny flame to negotiate the length of fuse, and during this awful suspense Swedish soldiers, alerted by the killings, began running toward the embankment, and Cyprjan heard himself praying, "Beloved God, delay them!" They were not delayed, for with loud cries they burst into the emplacement, but the writhing fuse reached there first, and with a tremendous explosion the two cannon and the fifteen running Swedes were shattered and tossed high in the air.

On Christmas Day the infuriated Swedes mounted a massive attack, which was repulsed by the iron-willed monks, so during the night of 26 December the enemy began to withdraw. Three days later the only sign that the Swedes had ever been there was the extensive damage to the eastern wall and the blackened scar where the two major cannon had been.

On that day the sacred image of the Virgin, black and radiant and victorious, was paraded through the monastery grounds and across the battlefield outside the gates, for her triumph had been complete. The faltering courage of Poland was revived and men began to see some hope that their homeland, ravaged though it was, might be rescued.

After their defense of Czestochowa the three widowers—Cyprjan, Lukasz and Jan—from the destroyed village of Bukowo allied themselves with similarly devastated patriots who vowed that Poland must not perish.

They formed a tatterdemalion army, lacking in food, clothing and arms, but they did occasionally gain some small victory by harassing the Swedes in night forays and daring ambuscades. However, the enemy was powerful and cleverly led, so that the Poles were forced to retreat more than they advanced, and by late March of 1656 this particular band of irregulars had been practically driven out of Poland proper.

They withdrew from one vantage point to the next, always breathing hard, always short of supplies and, what was worst of all, facing each week some new enemy whose troops were fresh. This week they had to stand off rampaging Cossacks; next week the King of Sweden himself led the charge against them—and always they were defeated, but always they tired the enemy and made him wonder when this dreadful war, which had once seemed so easy, would end.

Sometimes at night during these fugitive years when there had been little food and no comfort, Cyprjan would awaken with a sense of strangulation at his throat. He would bolt upright, gasping for air, and in the darkness he would wrestle with the specters that haunted him and all of Poland: the devastation of the land, the endless killing of the people, the burning of the villages. But then his images would become more personal, and he would see his lovely daughter slain in her castle, and the hideous death of Zofia Mniszech, and then he would see Lukasz's tame bear, riddled with lances they said, and he would begin to tremble as he thought of all that lost wonder, and he would cross the boards where they were trying to sleep that night and rouse Lukasz from his sleep: "I was thinking of your bear, Lukasz, and the pierogi Danusia used to make." The men would remain silent for a while, and then Cyprjan would vow: "By God, Lukasz, they'll be avenged." But when he was in his bed again, the choking would return and he could not sleep.

Once when they were camped near Lwow, the major city of the Ukrainian area in which he held his largest estates, he came upon another man of some importance who also could not sleep. It was the king himself, Jan Kazimir, tortured by the calamities that beset his kingdom, and he wanted to talk, but not with Cyprjan and not even with Lukasz, the petty knight, but with Jan of the Beech Trees.

"What is it like," he asked in the spring darkness. "As a peasant, how do you live?"

"We get up at dawn," Jan began.

"As I do," the king said.

"And we work all day, and at sunset we go to bed."

"What do you eat?"

"Cabbage, beets, we grind our own flour."

"I mean, what meats?"

"We never eat meat. Well, at Easter, maybe one chicken."

"And what do you work at, Jan?"

"Whatever the master tells us. Then six weeks each year for the duke. And three weeks for you."

"What do you work at?"

"We till the fields. We sow the grain. We harvest. And then we go to bed."

The king could scarcely believe what he was being told, and all through the night he interrogated Jan, even demanding to know how he got his clothes, who assisted his wife in childbirth, what medicines he used, and this led to a peculiarly meaningful exchange.

"Jan, tell me again, what do you do when you fall sick?"

"We die."

Two days later the king informed Cyprjan that he wanted him, Lukasz and especially Jan to be present in the cathedral at Lwow, where in front of a treasured portrait of the Virgin Mary he was going to make an important statement, and when the four tattered magnates were assembled, and the seventeen lesser nobles and the hundred peasants and the townsmen and even the Jews, he made this pledge:

> "When with grief in my heart I hear of the oppression which our peasants suffer and I see the tears with which they pray for relief, I think, Blessed Mother of God, that it is your Son, a just and merciful judge, who has been punishing my kingdom with pestilences, wars and other failures, and I know in my heart that we, and all of us here, have been guilty.

> "Therefore, I promise and vow that after peace has been restored, I will do my best to prevent further misfortunes, and I promise now on bended knee before you that I will free our peasants from all unjust burdens and hardships. Help me, Merciful Lady and Queen, enlist on my behalf the grace of your Son to help me fulfill this vow, which I make willingly before my magnates, my people and my peasants."

Lukasz and Jan were impressed by this Vow of Lwow, but Cyprjan and the magnates whispered knowingly: "Clever thing for the king to tell his troops when the war is going badly. But when we win we can force him to rescind."

. . .

In the dark weeks that followed, there was little talk of winning, for a series of new blows struck the poor country, almost destroying the will of men like Cyprjan and Lukasz to continue their fight. From the west the newly powerful state of Brandenburg, scenting a chance to make a kill, came roaring in with many troops and guns to tear off its share of Poland. From the east the Cossacks, seeing their traditional enemy about to be dismembered, launched an attack to seize the Ukraine. In Lithuania the Radziwills, satisfied that the union with Poland could not survive, volunteered to build a new Lithuania under Swedish protection, and most dreadful of all, from the turbulent state of Transylvania in the south a man of terrible power, Gyorgy Rakoczy, marched his troops to pick off his share of the spoils. Like hungry wolves on a stormy wasteland who turn to attack one of their own who has been wounded, the nations gathered to dismember Poland.

By a grotesque coincidence the King of Sweden assembled the leaders of these predators at the ruined castle of Krzyztopor, where in the desecrated chapel he brought in tables and chairs and sleeping arrangements for the generals and their advisers. And there, in the only part of the great fortress that still had a roof, the victors met to divide the spoils. The ruiners met amidst the ruins.

The King of Sweden and Rakoczy dominated the proceedings, of course, but it was the political adviser who accompanied the Brandenburg generals who exerted the subtlest influence. He was Wolfgang von Eschl, a tall, thin, clean-shaven man of icy intellect whose ancestors had been familiar with Polish problems, and once the gross details of who was to receive what had been agreed upon, he more or less took command, his penetrating questions and crisp decisions introducing structure into the discussion.

RADZIWILL: We seek a free Lithuania protected by Sweden.

VON ESCHL: I doubt that guarantees will ever signify much in this part of Europe. Each state must be viable within its own integrity.

KING OF SWEDEN: Are you questioning our intentions?

VON ESCHL: No, your power. It seems great now, almost unopposable. But it cannot remain that way for long.

KING OF SWEDEN: What will subdue it?

VON ESCHL: Time. Russia.

KING OF SWEDEN: We will handle Russia, when the time comes.

VON ESCHL: No one will handle Russia. You will accommodate yourself to Russia as we will have to, and all the others here.

COSSACK: We will never surrender to Russia.

VON ESCHL: You most of all.

RAKOCZY: What will you do to help Transylvania if the Turks decide to attack us?

VON ESCHL: Nothing.

RAKOCZY: Is that true, Sire?

KING OF SWEDEN: We have no fight with Turkey.

RAKOCZY: But I do.

VON ESCHL: Then you must protect yourself. We're giving you most of southern Poland. Use it creatively to build protection.

RAKOCZY: But we can protect ourselves only if we all stand together.

VON ESCHL: We stand together on this day to partition Poland. After that's done, each must protect himself.

RAKOCZY: Are we not building a grand alliance?

VON ESCHL: No.

KING OF SWEDEN: Let us agree, then. Sweden will take all the Baltic coast down to Danzig. The Germans get all the west, including as much of Silesia as they wish. You Cossacks get a free hand in the Ukraine. Rakoczy gets all of southern Poland. And Radziwill gets his free Lithuania. Shall we leave a small central area around Warsaw for the Poles themselves?

VON ESCHL: A nation which cannot defend itself has no right to exist.

RAKOCZY: I agree. Remove Poland from the map. Move all our borders in till they meet.

VON ESCHL: Excellent proposal. Poland will always require leadership from outside, and the German states are prepared to provide it.

From the day that the roof had been placed atop the castle at Krzyztopor, bats had inhabited the rafters, and as this fateful day drew to a close, they began to stir themselves and waken for the night. One by one they left their hiding places, circled through the near-deserted church and flew out for their foraging. They created a stir with their wings and an interruption with their soft stutters, as if they were discussing the decisions of that day, but after a while they were gone and the resolutions continued.

KING OF SWEDEN: We have the nation subdued except for one small trouble spot. That difficult town of Zamosc on the eastern frontier. I suppose you'll all join me in subduing it?

RAKOCZY: I must attend to Krakow. I intend making it a secondary capital, you know.

VON ESCHL: The Germans will not fight that far east.

KING OF SWEDEN: You Cossacks will. It's on your doorstep.

COSSACK: I led our siege of Zamosc in 1648. Forty days, and they knocked us back. We have no taste for Zamosc, because we consider it a Polish town.

KING OF SWEDEN: Don't you see that as long as it stands free—

COSSACK: We have no interest in Zamosc. None whatever.

KING OF SWEDEN: Then you agree with me that we ought to leave a small free Poland at the center?

VON ESCHL: There is no justification for a free Poland of any size, any character. You must listen to me. If we allow any kind of Poland to exist, we shall have only trouble with her. The Poles are a most difficult people, most stubborn. They can't govern themselves and they don't allow anyone else to govern them. They must be removed from the face of Europe, and the German states will discharge their responsibilities in achieving this. But you men must do your duty, too. Zamosc must be reduced by you Swedes. Eliminated. Rakoczy says he will capture Warsaw. The Cossacks will do their duty, I'm sure. And Radziwill can be depended upon. Gentlemen, there must be no hesitation now. This troublesome sore must be cauterized . . . deeply . . . permanently. Is it agreed?

ALL: It is agreed.

Gyorgy Rakoczy discharged his obligation brilliantly, but with a brutality Poland had not witnessed hitherto; even the Tatar invasions of 1241 had been gentle compared to the savage devastation wrought by the Transylvanians. The slaughter was so terrible that one priest wrote afterward:

It seemed that they were determined to kill even the stones, for they spat on them and urinated on them and burned them with fire. People were killed thoughtlessly, not in anger but because they were there. I saw them kill eleven nuns for no reason whatever, and scores of children. They killed pigs and chickens in the same way, and there was nothing of value they overlooked. One man in our town had a gold tooth, which they cut out of his mouth before they killed him, hacking and jabbing with their daggers.

Oh God, I cried in the midst of the devastation, why have You
permitted this in a Poland which has always cherished You?
Where shall I live now, with my church burned, my village
destroyed, my town in ashes and all my parishioners dead?

The lament of this priest was in no way hyperbole. In these awful
years the population of Poland dropped from ten million to six million, which meant that in every town and village four people out of
ten were killed. Farms were ravaged; cattle were slain; every item
of value was stolen; every human process by which people live together in some kind of reasonable order was disrupted. In a hundred
churches, only five or six priests survived to say the Mass, and in
those same churches not a piece of golden ornament or silver remained. And in the towns all the buildings in which the elders met,
and the councillors, were leveled.

The tempestuous success of the allied armies had one curious consequence: the few Polish defenders were compressed ever more tightly
into the eastern corridor, where, with their backs to the wall, they
determined that the decisive battle, the one that would end everything, would be fought in the vicinity of Zamosc, that remarkable
walled city built in one year by one man with his own funds and his
own driving energy. He was the Magnate Zamoyski, wise before his
time, a patriot of glowing character who had visualized the necessity
of some permanent fortified city on the frontier—a city that would
be defensible against Russians, Turks, Cossacks, Hungarians, Swedes,
all of whom would at one time or another seek to subdue it, all of
whom would fail.

When Cyprjan's raggle-taggle troops were still fifteen miles south
of the town, he told them: "You are not about to enter a fort. This is
a real town, and a most beautiful one. It was built by an Italian architect who gave it a chain of lovely arcades cool in summer, protecting
in winter. I love Zamosc and would like to end my days sitting in the
grand square, drinking a little wine and watching the girls as they do
their shopping. My daughter Barbara . . ." As he visualized her passing through Zamosc and stopping at the Italian arcade, tears came to
his eyes. Now there was no Barbara, there was no Zofia Mniszech,
there was no Castle Gorka—there was nothing but the human resolve not to allow this fearful drift to continue any longer.

"Men," he said, "when we reach Zamosc, there is nothing more. We stop them here, or we . . ." He said: "We stop them here."

Very soberly his men marched inside the walls of Zamosc, where many like them had gathered, and whereas the fortifications were not immensely thick—not half as thick as those at Krzyztopor—they encompassed the entire town, so that the town itself and all within became the fort, with human will power forming an extra chain of bastions immensely more resistant than the walls of Krzyztopor.

"Here we have a fighting chance," Cyprjan assured his men, and because of his leadership they were not terrified in early November when the King of Sweden moved his entire force before the walls to begin the methodical bombardment. The first rain of cannonballs frightened the inhabitants, but Cyprjan ran amongst them with heartening news: "The Cossacks are not participating! Rakoczy's men are not here! We face no Germans! We can hold them off!"

When it became apparent that the king had not brought enough cannon to reduce the walls, the defenders actually made two sorties, one led by Lukasz of Bukowo, which damaged the besiegers considerably, and in the following weeks the Swedes became apprehensive about their chances of ever breaking down the walls of Zamosc.

The day came when the King of Sweden realized that he must lose this battle, and with it, his opportunity to erase Poland from the map of Europe. The stubborn resistance of men like Cyprjan of Gorka, when all was lost, when there was not a chance of victory, had weakened the coalition and dissipated its force. Even the Swedish army, incomparably the best in Europe at that time, was worn down by the years of war. The only sensible thing to do was withdraw and return to Sweden.

As the retreat started, a terrible climax to the war occurred, for a large detachment of Swedes became confused, or received wrong instructions, for they found themselves without heavy armor and were easily surrounded by Poles streaming out of the town in a victorious chase, and so embittered were the Polish troops, who had seen their villages destroyed and their women slaughtered, that a furious battle ensued in which the Swedes were annihilated.

It was never known how it started, but some Polish peasant, blood-red with anger, cried to a partner: "They swallowed our gold coins to keep them from their officers," and these two men began to rip open the bellies of the dead Swedes, and in the intestines of the very first man they gutted they found two Austrian thalers, and word spread like fire among the troops, and a general gutting of the corpses began. It was in this horrible scene that Jan of the Beech Trees, whose family had been cremated in the sack of Bukowo, found himself four large pieces of gold, which he gave to his master Lukasz, and it would be this wealth wrenched from the gut of Sweden that would enable Lukasz to build a new home along the Vistula.

In these hectic years, magnates like Cyprjan slowly became aware of a redoubtable man named Jerzy Lubomirski, who had the gift of associating with himself patriots of the most diverse quality—other magnates, gentry, Jewish merchants, burghers from the towns, peasants and mercenary troops—and with this rabble he began to win battle after battle against superior troops of the Swedish-German-Transylvanian coalition. Lubomirski became a name to utter with respect, and Cyprjan remembered that as a girl, Zofia had been in love with him. Others informed him that Lubomirski had suffered fearfully at the hands of the enemy: "From his castle at Wisnicz the Swedes carried away one hundred and fifty-two wagons of paintings, jewelry and furniture. Rakoczy's men burned his castle at Rzeszow. And the Germans destroyed two of his biggest castles up north. He is a man of vengeance."

When the siege of Zamosc ended with the Swedish troops in retreat, this Lubomirski conceived the daring idea of defeating Rakoczy's forces not by a frontal assault, which the Poles would surely lose, but rather by a foray into Rakoczy's own backyard, and with Cyprjan's help he assembled a wild and rugged army that marched right out of Poland and into the heart of Transylvania, where they created so much havoc that the fearsome Rakoczy had to scurry back to protect his national interests.

Too late! Lubomirski, displaying unusual talent as a general, continued to destroy Transylvanian property and at the same time evade bloodthirsty Rakoczy. Indeed, Lubomirski left Transylvania in such shambles that the Turks from the south, to restore order in what was essentially their territory, would ultimately have to invade it and kill the terrible Rakoczy as no longer useful to their cause.

So in the autumn of 1658 the widowers Cyprjan, Lukasz and Jan came slowly and painfully back to Bukowo, where the two castles stood in ruins and the village consisted of one cottage rebuilt by an enterprising peasant who had tilled his field for winter planting.

Cyprjan, surveying the desolation, listened to reports from his various outlying towns and villages. All were destroyed, and Lukasz, standing with him, started to weep, but Cyprjan consoled him, telling those about him: "A Pole is a man born with a sword in his right hand, a brick in his left. When the battle is over, he starts to rebuild."

And rebuild they did: Castle Gorka, upon the old foundations but with improved conveniences; the village itself, with cottages in the time-honored tradition; and for Lukasz, not the little castle, which was now beyond repair, but a big, strong house halfway between a farmhouse and a minor mansion. Poland's left hand was doing excellent work.

Of course, the men needed wives to inhabit their new homes and lend them grace, and prudent Jan of the Beech Trees was the first to solve his problem. Stolidly he walked from village to village, inquiring as to whether any widows had been left by the war, and finally he found a woman of thirty, but she was frighteningly pretty and he surmised that he would never be able to hold her, so he passed on. In the third village, and not one belonging to either Lukasz or Cyprjan, he found Alusia, a fine woman left with two children whom the Swedes had not slain, and within ten minutes of meeting her he asked if she and the children would consent to live with him: "I work hard and I'll build you a sturdy cottage." Since she had no better prospects at the moment, nor the likelihood of any in the future, she accepted, and the four started walking home, the two children shying away from Jan, the stranger who was now their father.

Jan's life, even with his new wife and children, was modified in no way by the generous oath the king had made in the Lwow cathedral. No reforms of any kind were instituted; indeed, the peasants found themselves burdened with extra obligations, less time for themselves, and the impossibility of finding even a chicken at Easter. The king had wanted to respect his pledge, but the magnates had warned him: "The war devastated our estates so sorely that we must have more work from our peasants, not less," and they spoke so forcefully, Jan Kazimir realized that if he opposed them he would be booted out altogether, so he did nothing.

Lukasz solved his marriage problem in much the same way as Jan, except that instead of visiting villages, he rode from one small castle to the next, inquiring as to the fortunes of war, and in several he met men like himself who had survived but whose families had not. At Baranow, down the river, he found such a member of the gentry, a man older than himself, who said that he believed two sisters had survived in a small town near Tarnobrzeg, so they mounted their horses and rode to this town, and it did indeed contain two sisters who desperately needed husbands of quality, but there was some discussion as to which sister should marry which man, and Lukasz proposed a simple solution. They would put two beans in a hat, one white and one black, and the older sister would draw—black for Lukasz, white for the Baranow man—and this seemed the only practical solution; since none of the four could read, written ballots were impossible.

The drawing took place and Lukasz was won by Zosienka, the younger sister, who was not unhappy with her award. "Do you like animals?" Lukasz asked, and when she said she did, he told her that he had found a baby bear in the Forest of Szczek, at which she chuckled: "Oh, you're the man who had the bear and the otter! I'd love to have an otter!" and he explained: "Otters aren't so easy, but we'll find something to play with the bear."

Cyprjan's problem was solved in an equally practical way. Many fine estates were in such ruin that their owners, lacking money, had no chance of restoring them, and others had been owned by men and women slain in the carnage, so that magnates like Cyprjan, whose other estates yielded a little income, were in a position to extend their holdings.

There was such an estate abutting the roadway that ran from Lublin to Zamosc. It took its name from a village of exceptional attractiveness called Lubon, a word which carried an implication of *love* or *loveliness* or *a thing to be cherished,* but cynics averred that it meant only *a kind of sweet plum.* At any rate, it had a castle of distinction, and as soon as Cyprjan saw it and realized its nearness to Zamosc, a town which now had extra meaning for him, he decided to buy it. But when he approached the owner, Halka, he found her to be an attractive widow with a daughter of about the age Barbara had been when she married Ossolinski, so instead of offering to buy the estate and its castle, he proposed to Halka and married her, knowing that together with her daughter they could restore the line of Gorka.

But shortly after their marriage he ceased using the name *Gorka* and was never again referred to in that way. The change occurred because the papal legate who had spoken so well of him to the French ambassador did the same in his reports to Rome, so the Pope announced that he was "conferring upon Cyprjan of Gorka, who had defended the Faith so valiantly at both Czestochowa and Zamosc, the title of Count," and out of his love for his new bride he took the name *Lubonski*. Henceforth the master of Castle Gorka would be Count Lubonski.

So the rebuilding of homes and families in the Bukowo district prospered, but there were some losses that could never be restored, not even if the survivors carried bricks in both hands. When the Swedes had retreated from Poland in 1657 they took with them 2,183 wagonloads of old books, the maps, the paintings from the castles, the gold and silver work from the cathedrals, the furniture, the family heirlooms, the accumulation of centuries of good living. The culture of Sweden would be nurtured by the heritage of Poland.

Fortunately, this grand historical record passed into the hands of people who appreciated and protected it. Items of significance were catalogued, so that in subsequent years, anyone wanting to study Polish history could go to Swedish museums and libraries.

The golden necklace bearing the six amber droplets was not lost. In its paper folder, wrapped inside the canvas cloth, it remained in Wagon 307 of the Krzyztopor hoard till it reached Sweden, and may now be seen—in all the beauty it possessed back in 1409 when it was first assembled and in 1655 when it was taken from the corpse of Barbara Ossolinska—as it sleeps in its velvet case in a Stockholm museum.

V

FROM
THE SOUTH

SELDOM IN THE LONG HISTORY OF HUMAN EFFORT DID ANY NAtion recover so swiftly from disaster. In 1658, Poland lay prostrate following the terrible destruction visited upon her by the Swedes, the Germans and the Transylvanians, but in January of 1683 representatives of five European governments convened in Warsaw, begging for Polish help to protect Christianity from a dark cloud of terror which threatened from the south.

Germany, France, the Papal States, Hungary and, most of all, Austria pleaded with the Poles for help: "Without your assistance, and soon, Europe will be overrun by the most terrible menace that has ever threatened it. Please, please, spring to our assistance. Lead the great crusade which alone can save us."

The danger was real, and of quite a new dimension: Turkey was on the march, having already consumed Greece, Bulgaria, Rumania and much of Hungary, and wherever the Sultan's victorious army triumphed, the losers who were lucky enough to survive faced a harsh choice: convert to Islam or suffer vast disabilities. Only rarely did the Muslims massacre whole populations for religious reasons; they preferred to keep them alive as slaves, producing Janissaries for the army and trade goods for taxation, but life for a Christian under Muslim rule was harsh.

Europe trembled, for it saw that unless unprecedented action was taken, the key city of Vienna must fall to the Turks before the year was out, and whereas the Germans and the Austrians were willing to resist with what armed force they had, they realized that they would be ineffective without Polish strength and leadership. So the very nations which only a short while before had been endeavoring to destroy Poland now came to her begging for assistance.

What had ignited this transformation? And more important, how could a nation with almost no army suddenly find itself with one of the best?

Four factors explained the miracle. First, the good-hearted but confused Swede serving as King of Poland, the bumbling Jan Kazimir, had the good sense to quit; finding himself hamstrung by venal magnates and frustrated by the *liberum veto,* he abdicated. Second, after a painful gap without any king, and a furious struggle by various foreign powers to elect men favorable to them, the Seym chose a pathetic Polish incompetent, who had the good sense to die rather promptly. Third, after another perilous interregnum and a brutal fight between French and Austrian aspirants, much the better man won, and he happened to be from the French camp. Fourth, and most significant of all, the victor, Jan Sobieski, was in the process of proving that he was one of the most active kings Poland would have.

He was an extraordinary man, fifty-four years old and most curiously shaped, with a large head, an enormous belly and small feet. "He is," reported a French observer, "a perfect oval which from a distance looks like a very large egg stood on the small end." A man of gargantuan appetites, explosive rages and piercing perceptions, he might have ended poorly had he not had the great good fortune to marry a brilliant Frenchwoman who had one of the most cupidinous natures in history. Rumored to be the illegitimate daughter of Louis XIV's queen, she believed that no married couple ever had enough money and that any king was worth double what the state allowed him. Repeatedly this Marysienka, always calculating possible advantages, warned her husband: "Look at what happened to the two before you. Jan Kazimir kicked out. The other one persecuted to his grave by the magnates who would give him nothing. Take advantage of things while you have the chance."

Together Sobieski and his queen sold every office in the land; if a clergyman threatened to give trouble, they arranged to have him made a cardinal, then charged him for the favor. Nothing was granted without cash in advance, and before long these two had estates, palaces and jewels worth fifty million in modern currency, and the queen had her own secret security fund in cash of more than five million.

But they gave good value. With the lithe quickness of a leopard Jan Sobieski sprang from one corner of his nation to another, driving back this attacker or that, and in doing so, had four times faced large Turkish armies, winning thrice. During that time he put together a formidable army, spearheaded by a cavalry unit unlike any that Europe had ever seen before.

To begin with: the hussars were excellent horsemen, and they backed this up by first-class work with the long lance, the short sword and, if necessary, the dagger. Pride of unit made them especially fearsome when they charged into a battle line from a distance, for they rode with terrible precision, their lances evenly leveled and inescapable. But what made them unique was that as they charged they wore riveted to the back of their armor a curious lyre-shaped metal-and-leather construction, which seemed to come out of their backs and rise two or three feet higher than their heads. To it was attached in a beautiful fanlike design some three dozen large turkey or eagle feathers whose purpose was mysterious. Wrote one German knight who had faced their charge at a battle near Szczecin, which he referred to as Stettin, its German spelling:

> Like all my fellows, I had heard of the fierce Polish hussars, and like them I supposed that their quality lay in the discipline of their charge and the uniformity of their work with the long lance, but when I first saw them approaching in battle array, coming at me from the crest of a hill, I was astounded by their appearance. Each man seemed to come with a halo about his head, like a Madonna in some Italian painting. The feathers made a wonderful sight, but I asked as we prepared for battle: "What are the feathers for?" Because they obviously were real feathers, and feathers cannot serve as armor, not in any way possible.

> Then, as they drew near, galloping in the wind, the feathers began to mourn, or to chant like old women at a funeral or like witches at a false Sabbath, and then to shriek as the wind tore through them. I got frightened by the weird sound and the hellish echoes, but my horse became terrified. He reared and whinnied and I could not control him, and the effect on

the other German horses was the same, so that by the time the Polish hussars reached our battle line, all was in confusion.

I can state without fear or apology: The Polish cavalry did not defeat us in fair battle. They sang us to death with those damned feathers.

It was these hussars that Europe now wanted for its protection against Islam, and no plea was too undignified for the other nations to make: "Sire, without your aid the Star and Crescent will fly over Paris," and there was much truth to this, because the Turks already controlled the Danube, occupied Budapest, and were on the march to Vienna, which would surely capitulate long before autumn unless Poland sprang to the rescue.

But Poland's insane way of choosing its kings had created a difficult problem. France spent huge sums to bribe magnates in favor of Sobieski—Germany, Austria and Russia doing the same to support a Habsburg—and the contest had become quite ugly, with hardly a magnate uncontaminated by foreign gold. In the end, Sobieski had won, but he and everyone else knew that he did so as a lackey of the French.

Where did the complications arise? In European politics France always supported Turkey against her mortal enemy Austria, and Germany supported Austria against her mortal enemy the Turks. It was preposterous, in many ways, for these nations now to ask Sobieski to ignore his patron France and ally himself with his enemy Austria, and the pleas would not have succeeded without the presence of a very old cardinal of the Catholic church, dispatched personally by the Pope.

He was Cardinal Pentucci, the papal legate who had watched so closely and with such keen, knowing eye the debacle of 1655, and he had now come back to Warsaw with an urgent request from the Pope himself and with stubborn persuasive powers of his own. In the general meetings he offered merely ritual remarks, which might have been expected, to the effect that the continuance of Christianity itself depended upon what Poland did now, but in private he was crisp and canny and to the point:

"Jan, child of God, if you do not help us, the church will suffer and perhaps even vanish, but you already know that. I must remind you that Poland also will vanish, and most cruelly. If you think the Turkish occupation of Hungary is brutal, with the mass slayings and the appropriations, think of what it will be like if Turkey invades Poland.

"They will remember the humiliating defeats you have visited upon them, at Podhajce in 1667 before you were king, at Chocim in 1673, which qualified you to become king, and at Zurawno in 1676 after you were king. Sultan Muhammad IV remembers every one of those defeats, and he will be avenged in strange and terrible ways.

"Jan, child of God, you are like a hunter deep in the woods who has attacked a bear but not slain him. You may wish to retire from further battle, but the bear will not allow it. You have aroused him and he will fight with you until one of you perishes. You have aroused Turkey and you are not free to stop the battle now. If you do, and if Vienna falls, Krakow will be next, and then Warsaw, and we shall never see Poland again."

This was sage counsel, for when Vienna fell, say, at the middle of August, the Turks would surely bring their Tatar subsidiaries across the Carpathians and into the flatlands of Poland, where they would be encouraged to desolate the country one final time. If Germany and France were threatened by the vast Turkish sweep, Poland had cause to fear that she would be eliminated permanently.

Sobieski, much sobered by the hard advice of the old cardinal, met with the military men who had accompanied the diplomats to Warsaw, and they told him a doleful story:

"Sultan Muhammad has given his Grand Vizier Kara Mustafa the green cord, and you know what that means. Capture Vienna or strangle yourself. So it will be a siege to the death, ours or his.

"Hungarian spies who have watched the Turks marching through that country report that Kara Mustafa wears the green cord about his neck day and night, so that all subordinates who speak with him will know the gravity of the undertaking.

"He brings with him an army of three hundred thousand, including the best engineers, the best cannoneers, and what is most important, the very best sappers in the world. Vienna is a walled city now, but when those Turkish sappers finish digging tunnels under the walls and into the heart of the city itself, and then explode enormous charges of gunpowder, Vienna will be blown apart.

"Our job is simple, Sobieski. We must rush to Vienna to neutralize Kara Mustafa's three hundred thousand, and we must do it before his engineers break down the walls, or his cannoneers knock down all the buildings, or his sappers blow the whole place to hell. And only you can lead us, for our Germans and Austrians have never defeated the Turks, and you have done so, three times."

When Sobieski asked whether the other forces would accept him as their general, he was assured that the Duke of Lorraine, who would be in charge of the Austrian forces, was most eager to cooperate, and that Prince Waldeck, who would be leading the German contingents, had told Emperor Leopold of Austria: "Without Sobieski and his hussars, we have no hope."

Assured on this delicate point, because fighting a battle as part of a coalition had to be one of the most difficult of all military operations and not to be attempted if even one of the partners was disgruntled, he then asked about the relative strengths of the contending armies, and received a more balanced report: "It is true that Kara Mustafa did leave Turkey with about three hundred thousand men, but at least half of them were not fighting soldiers. Did you know he brings whole tents filled with houris? Our soldiers could have some pleasure with them if we win."

"We shall win," Sobieski said. "What are our strengths?"

"Austria can provide twenty-three thousand. We Germans will have at least twenty-eight thousand. They tell me you might bring as many as thirty-four thousand." When Sobieski frowned at the disparity of his troops compared to the Turks', his informant reassured him: "Sire, by the time Kara Mustafa gets his horde to Vienna, it will have diminished to half the size. We have a chance."

"That leaves an army of a hundred and fifty thousand, roughly twice our size," Sobieski said. "But of the real army, two-thirds are forced conscripts from captured lands, and who knows how they will fight when they have to face our hussars and the German pikemen? And twenty thousand will be the Tatars on one of the wings, and not even Kara Mustafa himself can predict what they will do. So it comes down to eighty-five thousand of our proved troops, and about the same number of theirs." He broke into a robust laugh. "Gentlemen, I have never faced the Turks when their army was not three times the size of mine."

"How did you win?" the emissary of the Duke of Lorraine asked, and Sobieski replied: "Speed. Those blessed hussars of mine, singing across the battlefield. And one thing more. Although the Turks always outnumbered us, I never permitted all their force to congregate at one time. They are a terrible foe, one of the worst ever to be let loose on Europe, but they can be defeated."

"And you think we can save Vienna?"

"We must save it, and we shall, to preserve Christianity in the world."

At the end of the meeting he learned one thing which pleased him: "You know, Sobieski, that you already have a Polish army in Vienna."

"I did not know."

"Yes. Lubomirski is inside the walls there with three thousand of the best. And he promises that when you attack from the outside, he will attack from inside and there will be a happy reunion."

"I would always be proud to cooperate with Lubomirski. His family knows how to fight."

Those meetings with the papal legate and the Austro-German generals took place in January 1683, and during the next three months, while Kara Mustafa and his Islamic warriors crept closer and closer to Vienna, details of the treaty that would govern the coalition were painfully hammered out. When Gyor in Hungary fell to the Turks, and Petronell in Austria, death rattles could be heard issuing from Vienna, and the allies speeded negotiations.

On the last day of March 1683 a grand defensive alliance was agreed upon by Austria and Poland, with King Jan Sobieski promising to march at the proper time to the rescue of Vienna. On the first day of April, with Cardinal Pentucci blessing the holy occasion, formal papers were signed in Warsaw by which Poland, a devastated land only twenty-five years earlier, volunteered to stand forth as the champion of Christian Europe. It was a resurgence that no one would have dared predict.

When the convocation broke up, with each group of emissaries about to head for its own beleaguered country and with Cardinal Pentucci in tears of gratitude for what had been accomplished, Sobieski told his allies: "It will take me till mid-August to assemble my army. But I will do it. You, in the meantime, must assure that Vienna withstands the siege. I will send a messenger to Lubomirski to encourage him with a promise that I shall soon be at his side."

But even when faced with this dire predicament, with the fate of European civilization in the balance, the Polish Seym was incapable of behaving in a responsible manner. Only two years before, when Poland itself was threatened by a Turkish invasion, one deputy, a man named Przyjemski, who had accepted one thousand pieces of gold from the Hohenzollerns, who wanted to disadvantage the French, stood in the Seym and cried "I object!" and the entire defense structure had been destroyed. When one of Sobieski's men asked: "Why didn't someone shoot him?" he was told: "The magnates insist upon their Golden Freedom, which is far more important to them than what the king wants."

Now Sobieski encountered more of the same opposition, with the danger that at any moment some magnate in the pay of some foreign government with a special interest in the continued subordination of Poland might rise and cry "I object!" and there might go the whole alliance against the Turks. So the king moved cautiously, talking privately with first this magnate, then the next, and obtaining from each a promise of troops and tax support for the crusade that was about to set forth.

He encountered major opposition from a source which surprised him. Count Lubonski of Gorka, now a slim, austere patriarch in his seventies, with his protruding belly long gone but his golden sash still in view, was reluctant to follow Sobieski's leadership. Always faithful to Austrian interests, and always dreaming of a Habsburg on the throne of Poland, Lubonski had opposed Sobieski's election move vigorously and in the years 1674–1683 had worked consistently against the king and his French advisers in support of any move that would strengthen Austria. As one of the richest men in Poland, he never accepted outright money bribes from the Habsburgs, and they never offered them because they knew they didn't need to, but he did accept other favors, like excessive honors at the Habsburg court when he visited Vienna and vague promises that a position of enormous power would be his whenever an Austrian was elected king.

Magnates like Lubonski had already precipitated the abdication of one king, the Swede Jan Kazimir, and had been on the verge of doing the same with his pitiful successor, when the latter died, so it was natural that after a taste of Sobieski they decided to depose him, and in this struggle Lubonski had taken the lead. The movement failed because Poland realized that Sobieski was the only man who could protect the nation, but the animosity between the two men continued.

Now, however, things were changed. Sobieski needed the support of Lubonski and his private army, and Lubonski found himself obligated to help Austria, whose interests he had always defended. It was a strange meeting that occurred in Krakow after Sobieski had sent a personal envoy to Gorka, imploring Lubonski to meet with him. They met as equals, a powerful king who already sensed the great things he might accomplish in building a stronger Poland and a better Europe, and a most powerful magnate who wanted no change except the union of Poland and Austria under a Habsburg king. Enemies the two men were, yet each knew he needed the other, and it was Sobieski's brilliance which solved the dilemma.

"Lubonski!" he cried as he rose ponderously from his chair, projecting his great bulk forward to accord the old count the deference he merited. "I need your help so badly."

"I think all patriots stand ready to help, Sire."

"In your case I have a special need . . ."

"You may have my army. I shall ride at its head."

"I knew that," Sobieski said, almost dismissing the offer. "What I require from you is difficult and daring."

"I am ready," the tall, stiff nobleman replied.

"I remember you as the man who blew up the two big Swedish guns at Czestochowa."

"We did indeed destroy them."

"And one of the heroes at the siege of Zamosc."

"We drove them back that time."

"Many claim that it was at Zamosc that you broke the back of Charles X Gustavus and sent him reeling homeward."

"Someone had to do it."

"But most of all, Pan Cyprjan, I think of you as a papal count, a man ordained to defend Christianity."

Still erect, still refusing to seek the comfort of a waiting chair, the old man said: "I would be proud if I were so considered."

"And it is in that capacity that I seek your help—your personal help."

"I've said my army would join you."

Again the king dismissed the offer: "I don't want your army—Oh, of course I do. I hoped for it and felt sure I'd be allowed to have it. What I really want is you."

"You have me. Poland is endangered, and you have me."

"I want you to slip into Vienna, to meet with Lubomirski. To find out what the prospects are. And most important, to scout the route to the city. The route we will follow when we march there this summer."

This was a most dangerous assignment, and both men knew it. Capture would probably mean death, but there was a good chance that Lubonski's elevated position might induce the Turks to treat him either as a diplomatic envoy or as a subject for extreme ransom. And if the mission did succeed, and if Lubonski could return with the needed information, it could mean a significant difference.

"I will go," he said, and now Sobieski pulled him down to a chair beside him and shouted for beer with which to celebrate this pact.

Before the servants could bring it, the king snatched an Italian book he had been consulting and showed Lubonski a handsomely engraved plate of a snarling lion, the astrological sign under which he, Sobieski, had been born. Jabbing at a paragraph beneath the lion, the king said laughingly: "You magnates have a poor opinion of me, and a worse of my French wife. I know you call me avaricious, and stubborn, and poorly advised. But read what the stars say about me." And he shoved the almanac at Lubonski, who could see that someone had added to the printed page a notation in ink, but what the words said he was unable to decipher: "I can read French and German, Your Majesty, but not Italian."

Showing no displeasure, Sobieski took back the book and with an impulsive gesture of friendship drew Lubonski close. "I added this in my own hand. 'Jan Sobieski, born 17 August 1629 under the protection of Leo.' Now here is what I wanted you to read, and when you hear it, you must tell your friends how the stars assess me." And with obvious pride and satisfaction he read:

"The man of important position born under this sign will be good, pious, righteous, honorable, faithful, serene, pleasant, discreet, charitable, peace-loving, kind, sincere in all his friendships, clever, brave, honorable, of cautious audacity, hot-tempered when his honor is impugned, very alert to grasp meanings before others, and with a remarkable memory. Without the regular offices of Venus he falls easily into distemper."

Hammering at the almanac with his fist, he cried: "By God, they got it all right, and that's worth noting, since they never met me in person." Then he nudged Lubonski and said: "They were also right about the Venus business. If I do not lie with a lady four nights a week, I grow nervous. How about you?"

"That seems a long time ago."

Sobieski roared: "When I'm ninety I'll have three different women a week. But for the present, my French wife— God, Lubonski, she's adorable. I could not live a day without that dear woman."

At this moment the servants, three of them, appeared with flagons of beer and a plate of country cookies, which Sobieski wolfed down, three at a time, cramming them into his mouth so roughly that crumbs spread across his capacious lap, from which he brushed them with a huge, darting hand. Lifting his flagon, which held nearly a quart, he cried: "To our wives! To the green cord that Kara Mustafa wears about his neck. May he have occasion to draw it tight before this summer is over."

The impending war with Turkey exerted curious effects upon the three old veterans who lived at Bukowo. Count Lubonski, aged seventy-three, felt it his duty as a papal count to undertake the dangerous mission to Vienna and later to lead his private army into battle. These were extraordinary decisions, and his age alone would have excused him from either, but to avoid his responsibilities never occurred to him. All his life he had volunteered to serve where needed, and if King Jan Sobieski had mentioned two of his major contributions— Czestochowa and Zamosc—he overlooked three others: the defense of the Ukraine against Cossack invaders, the raid into Transylvania to punish Rakoczy, and his service on the western front when German troops tried to take the best grain fields of Poland.

He was not by nature a warrior; he showed no command ability, but the times had required him to be a dogged, brave, willing soldier, and this he had trained himself to be; since eleven wars occurred during his adult years, it would have been difficult to escape soldiering.

Like all the nobility, he felt that a man of his position was degraded if he had to move about on foot, so he had always been a cavalryman, and even at the siege of Zamosc when he made a sortie he did so on horseback.

He maintained a stable of forty-eight horses with carriages in proportion, and although he did not at his age qualify to ride with the winged hussars, he did form, wherever he was, a reliable part of the ordinary cavalry that performed so well. So in a spiritual sense as a good Catholic and in a military sense as a fine horseman, he was ready for war.

But in his private life he was not. His second wife, Halka, had brought with her an attractive daughter whom Lubonski adopted eagerly, spending almost two years endeavoring to find her a suitable husband; with Halka's help he finally settled on one of the young Lubomirskis, nephew of the general who had performed so well during the war, but after the marriage, which united two of the great families, the young couple moved to one of the eleven Lubomirski castles and Cyprjan saw them infrequently, a fact which distressed him.

Belatedly, Halka had given him two sons who showed signs of being true Lubonskis: conservative, patriotic, Austrian in their sympathies as if one could never be merely a Pole; devoutly Catholic; and while not brilliantly intellectual, learned in their alphabet and figuring. They were fine lads, and before long they would reach the age at which their father would go searching the better castles and palaces for brides.

He therefore wished to stay home, at Gorka, surrounded by people he knew, and cared for by servants who had been with him for many decades. He felt no threat of death, for his health was excellent and his mind alert, but he had reached those years when spare time ought to be allocated to the furtherance of his family interests. Halka was a lovely wife, similar in many respects to Zofia Mniszech, but since she came from only a modest family with one castle and sixteen horses, she lacked the bargaining power that Lubonski had. He was needed at home, but he was also needed in Vienna, and the latter obligation superseded.

When he announced that on his mission he would take Lukasz of Bukowo, the old animal-lover was delighted. He was sixty-two years old, still hearty and still adept at finding orphan animals and teaching them to live with others not of their kind. He had a bear now, a male, but he had never been able to replace that wonderful otter slain by the Swedes. In its place he had a small deer, a female who loved the red fox that completed the coterie of wild animals. He had no storks now, they were most difficult to tame, but in their place he had a splendid egret who stalked about the place like a hetman with a gold baton. And of course he kept two large dogs, who often seemed bewildered by the diversity of wildlife with which they had to share their quarters.

In place of the castle courtyard in which the original animals had lived, this group occupied an area between the manor house, if anything so rude could be called such, and the farm buildings. It was enclosed by a wicker fence which the deer could leap over if it wished, or the fox penetrate or the bear knock down, but they were happy within their voluntary cage and did not stray even if the gate was left open.

The manor house, erected in 1660, was a poor thing when compared to the stately country houses of England, France or Spain, but Lukasz preferred it to the drafty old castle whose ruins grew more picturesque each year. It had two low stories, the lower built of stone and plastered over, the upper of wood and heavily shingled with cuttings from the forest. Windows were small and scarce, walls thick to repel future invaders, and the chimney large so that storks could nest. The house was distinguished at one corner by a small onion-shaped tower in the Russian style, and considered as a unit, it was a heavy, dark, secure and reasonably comfortable residence.

Lukasz was about as happy with his new home and his new set of animals as he had been with the old, and he was certainly as happy with his new wife, the girl Zosienka, whom he had won at the drawing of the beans. Zosienka had produced two excellent children, who played with the Lubonski boys and who showed a real love for the river. One summer when Lukasz put together a tremendous raft of logs carefully chosen from the Forest of Szczek, he had permitted his son to ride it with him all the way down the Vistula past Warsaw and Plock to Gdansk, where they supervised the loading of valuable logs onto a freighter bound for London.

It had been a rewarding journey, with the sun so far north that there was scarcely any night, and as the great raft drifted silently past this town or that, Lukasz told the boy of events associated with the area. At Plock, for example, he told about the famous hero Firczyk who had swung his massive iron ball at the Battle of Grunwald, holding the German knights back until one crept beneath the swinging ball and stabbed him. At Torun he showed where Nicholas Copernicus had studied the stars, and when the raft went past the place at which vast Malbork Castle lay somewhat to the east, he told of the time their great-great-great-great-great-great-great-great-grandfather had been imprisoned there because he had tried to buy an amber necklace.

How marvelous that trip had been! So if he was content with his animals, and his wife, and his children, what inspired him to shout when the count invited him to risk the trip to Vienna: "I'd like that!"?

The problem was one which assails many families, in all societies and all nations. Zosienka, lovely as she was and hard-working too, had one grievous fault. She had a brother named Piotr, and despite all the benefits that Lukasz had provided the young man, all the doors he had opened for him, Piotr remained a problem. Four times he had bungled arrangements that Lukasz had made for his marriage to some appropriate girl, and twice he had failed spectacularly in positions Lukasz had found for him, once with Count Lubonski himself, and now it was clear that Lukasz and his wife were burdened with the young man.

He was known as Brat Piotr, Brother Piotr, for he had joined the fraternity of monks who served at Czestochowa, but this did by no means remove him as a burden from his Bukowo relatives. He always needed extra money, or clothes, or recommendations for an advantage of one kind or other. Twice he had been dismissed from the order as unsuitable—he was a tall, ungainly man who would wander off, not on any particular mission, just off—and only special pleas from Lukasz and Count Lubonski enabled him to win reinstatement. During the periods when he was allowed to leave the monastery, he invariably came to Bukowo, where he would appear suddenly at dusk, opening the gate and whistling to the bear and perhaps playing with the animals a good hour before he bothered to inform his sister that he was there. The children loved him, as did the fox and the deer, but Lukasz and his wife were distressed to the point of pain by his irresponsibility and by the fact that at age forty-five he still behaved as if he were eleven, walking in the forest with the children and even climbing trees with them.

Lukasz would be damned content to get away from Brat Piotr for a while.

The case with Jan of the Beech Trees was quite different. His life had been one of incessant labor, inadequate food and repeated wars. If Count Lubonski had served Poland with distinction during these troubled years, leading in battle and counseling with the king, Jan had served with no less distinction. When the castles were torn down, he rebuilt them. When a raft of valuable logs must be assembled for the float downriver to Gdansk, he cut them. When the village of Bukowo was destroyed by Swedes or Cossacks or Transylvanians or Germans, he had always helped the other men rebuild their cottages. And when the fields needed plowing or the crops harvesting, Jan had done the work.

He had started at the age of three, back in 1626, and he had not stopped for fifty-seven years. In his own home he had never known a wooden floor, only earthen; he had never had a window in his cottage; he had never had a chimney to carry away the smoke. He had eaten meat so rarely that he could savor a good bite of chicken for nine months, and he had never had more than two pairs of pants at a time, the good one lasting for twenty or thirty years. Now he was tired. His life, spent so honorably, was drawing to a close, and sometimes he wished that he could just for one season—summer or winter, he didn't care which—be left alone to rest in the sun.

The population of Poland had increased since the Swedish war and was now about nine million, which meant that there were some three million peasant men like Jan who had spent or would spend their lives in the kind of remorseless labor he had performed, and around them the strength and the greatness of Poland was built.

Obviously, in these days of near-exhaustion Jan occasionally thought of death, and the word held little fear for him. He saw it as a form of release, a final benediction for work well done. He loved his wife, Alusia; she had proved a far better helpmate than he could have expected and he worried now and then about leaving her, but he knew that she was resourceful, and with four older children upon whom she might rely, she was not going to be destitute the way many peasant widows were. But the principal reason why he faced approaching death with equanimity was that his youngest son, whom they called Janko, was such a delight. Blond, good-looking, quick in his movements where Jan himself had been slow, gentle in manner and bright in his ability to understand rapidly, he was a pleasure to have about the cottage, and at fifteen he was as able as any of the men in the village. He was the kind of son who made a father happy, and old Jan was not loath to think that when he did die, young Janko would take over the cottage. That he would be generous with his mother, Jan never doubted.

Indeed, the boy had only one fault. On the occasions when Brat Piotr left the monastery at Czestochowa and appeared at the mansion in Bukowo to visit with his sister and brother-in-law, Janko displayed an immoderate desire to be with the friar, listening to his improbable yarns and strolling with him among the beech trees.

"You must stay clear of Brat Piotr," both his mother and his father warned. "That one is no good, no good at all." They told their son what Lukasz from the big house had himself said about his wife's brother: "Our red fox is more dependable than Piotr." But no amount of harsh counsel dissuaded the boy from showing his affection, and even his regard, for the tall, gangling, grinning friar.

They formed an interesting pair as they headed for the forest or explored along the riverbank—Piotr, in his monk's garb and his big, flapping shoes, loose-limbed and all out of joint, a grown man who had never matured, and Janko, marvelously average and proper in all things. Walking together, the boy was silent and attentive, the friar animated, waving his hands, bobbing his angular head, and pointing out the mysteries they encountered on their brief journeys.

"That's where some family of rabbits lives, surely," Piotr would say, and they would stop to investigate. Or at the river he would notice where birds had walked and they would speculate on where those birds had spent their winter: "Not around here, surely. Too cold."

They were fascinated by the storks, those ungainly creatures that looked so much like Piotr himself, and he proposed the extraordinary theory that because they were so thin, they needed little heat and so spent their winters at the North Pole. Janko thought this unlikely, and when he argued against the theory, Piotr shrugged his shoulders and said: "You may be right."

But on the matter of historic battles which had been fought along the Vistula he admitted no rebuttal. He could see Tatars as they came dashing out of the forest, or Swedes as they burned the castles, or Hungarians when they arrived in strength, and often he told Janko: "I was destined by Almighty God to be a great warrior, a hussar I think, with the feathers singing about my ears and me on a white horse dashing through Russian and Turkish and German lines." On several occasions, when they were on flat land, he would bestride his imaginary charger, wave his long arms, and set his lance for the Tatars coming out of the woods. And off he would go, flapping his arms and whistling to imitate the feathers. At such times he frightened Janko, who supposed that Piotr would do the same with the enemy—if he ever got himself a horse, and a suit of armor, and a horseshoe of feathers over his head.

The simple fact was that Brat Piotr was fun. His unbounded imagination inspired others, not the leaders of the monastery, to be sure, and certainly not his brother-in-law Lukasz, but all the younger monks and the lads like Janko.

"I'm always glad," old Jan told his wife, "when Piotr leaves. He is not good for the boy," but Alusia replied: "All work isn't good for him, either."

They were engaged in this mild argument one April morning when their lord, Lukasz from the mansion, appeared, bubbling with good news: "Jan! We're going to Vienna!"

Jan, two years younger than Lukasz by the calendar, fifty years older when the burdens of time were considered, said: "Vienna's too far."

"No! The king himself has ordered Count Lubonski to represent him on an important mission. And the count ordered me to help him, and now I'm ordering you to help me. We leave on Thursday."

"Are you sure you want me? I won't be of much help."

"Jan, we've been in all the battles together. I trust you." And the two old men reflected on the endless warfare they had known, and Lukasz, with obvious enthusiasm, told Alusia: "One night at Czestochowa we crept out, Jan and me, and we blew up the Swedish guns. You never heard such a bang when they exploded. And in Transylvania one morning just Jan and me, we captured an entire village, and do you remember how terrified we were when we realized that no Polish troops were behind us?"

Their lives had been one unbroken battle conducted over the face of eastern Europe, with interludes now and then for the rebuilding of their homes, which some new enemy would destroy, and they had good reason to believe that this would be the nature of life in Poland for as far into the future as they could imagine. Now the battleground was Vienna, a new one, but the enemy was Turkey, an old one.

"On Thursday we ride west to Krakow, where we'll meet the king, then over the mountains to Vienna."

All his life Jan had been obedient to the orders of those who owned him and he was obedient now: "Thursday morning, I'll be ready." But after Lukasz left, it became apparent to Alusia that her tired old husband was not prepared for this lengthy and dangerous trip, and when he failed to rise early the next day she knew that something was seriously wrong. She sent for the women who advised on such matters, but by the time they reached the cottage Jan was out of bed and packing the small amount of gear he would be taking with him: his good knife for hand-to-hand battle if that became necessary, a stout cudgel he had raised in the forest—an ash tree into which he had imbedded jagged chunks of iron while the tree was still growing, so that the spikes became an integral part of the club—and a pair of rude leather shoes for use in the mountains.

It was a pitiful collection to represent a lifetime of labor, but that is what he had, and in the past it had served him well.

However, at noon on Wednesday the old man had no appetite for his turnips and kasha, and by sunset it was quite clear that he was not going to rise next morning from his bed, so Alusia sent Janko running to the mansion to inform Lukasz that Jan of the Beech Trees was far too sick to leave for Vienna, or for anywhere else. This news displeased the master, who came himself to the cottage to ascertain what the true situation was, and just as he entered the low door, his face ascowl, the old man gasped, tried to rise on his left elbow, and fell back dead.

At that moment there was a commotion in the village square, and those about the deathbed heard young Janko shouting: "Here comes Brat Piotr!" and indeed it was the lanky friar, and when disgruntled Lukasz left the cottage, saddened only because he had lost a man who had served him so well, he saw Jan's brother-in-law ambling along with children at his heels, and on the spur of the moment he cried: "Piotr! We leave for Vienna in the morning!" and the friar's face became brighter and wider than the setting sun's: "Ah! What a glorious adventure! Vienna?" But immediately he became practical: "Do I get a horse?" Satisfied on this point, he then asked: "Do I get arms?" And when he learned that he would be given a lance, he grasped Janko's hands and jumped up and down like a wooden doll on a string: "I'm going to war! I'm to be a knight!"

From the village of Bukowo to the imperial city of Vienna was a distance of two hundred and eighty miles, and in the last days of April and the first of May in the year 1683 the land was as filled with beauty as it had ever been. The route of the travelers—the elderly count, the petty nobleman and the rather ridiculous friar, accompanied by a small detachment of soldiers who tended the extra horses—took them west to the ancient town of Cieszyn, which everyone called *Chzn,* as if it contained no vowels. This fine town, which guarded the area's only low pass through the mountains, had a tumbling river coming down the middle. The emissaries bought what provisions they would be needing on the ride to Vienna, packing their bags with the good sausages made there and the hard black bread filled with caraway.

On a bright spring morning they moved into Moravia, that gentle flower garden of eastern Europe, and slowly made their way along a roadway which had been used for a thousand years and by a hundred thousand adventurers. Lipnik, Olomouc, Brno and Nikolsburg appeared where expected and with the friendly reception accorded any potential ally who promised assistance against the Turks, whose armies moved closer week by week.

Among the people it was a tense, uneasy season, but with the land it was a time of glory, as if it wanted to remind its owners of what a paradise they had. Lukasz and Piotr were enchanted by the grape arbors; north of the Carpathians, grapes could not be grown, and their mouths watered to think of what those vines would be producing in September if the Turks allowed these grapes to mature. They were equally preoccupied with Moravia's specialty, the vast fields covered with poles along which sturdy strings had been stretched and up which grew the hops with which much of Europe flavored its beer.

And since all Poles loved flowers as much as they did music, the travelers were awed by the richness of the blooms that covered the Moravian hillsides. This was a land of plenty, and Lukasz asked the count: "How does it happen that Moravia is not joined to Poland, or the other way around?" and Lubonski answered correctly: "The Czechs and Moravians are such stubborn Protestants that no good can come from them."

"Are the people of Vienna Protestant too?"

"No, thank God. They acknowledge the true church, which is why Jan Sobieski must come here to save them." And Lukasz said with some enthusiasm: "This Moravia is well worth saving."

From Nikolsburg the travelers dropped due south toward Vienna, but as they rode they were met by Austrian soldiers who demanded to know their reason for being on the road at a time when Turkish forces might appear at any moment, and when Count Lubonski explained that they came with assurances from King Jan Sobieski, the troops were delighted and began cheering, for they knew that by themselves alone they could never repel the Turks.

Lubonski and his unusual team were to be taken directly into the city, but since they could not reach it before gates were closed for the night, they camped at dusk some miles north, and in the morning they were awed by an experience which not even Warsaw or Krakow, grand as they were, could provide. Over flat land they approached the Danube River, and as they crossed it on a ferry they could see for themselves how broad and swift it was, how magnificent a river. When they landed on the south bank they assumed they were in Vienna.

Instead, they were in a large cluster of outlying villages, and from the way the defenses of the city were being hastily constructed, it was obvious that all this valuable territory was going to be surrendered when the Turks mounted their siege. "Are you giving this up?" Lubonski asked in amazement.

"We have no other choice," one of the soldiers said. "There," he said as he pointed directly ahead, over arid land that contained not a single structure, to where the walls of the great city rose. "There, inside those walls is where we make our stand."

Not one of the Poles could have visualized what a remarkable thing had been done at Vienna, since they had supposed it was going to be like any of the cities they had seen in their wars. But not at all. For a distance of about half a mile from the stout walls of the inner city, every building had been eliminated. There was not a shed, not a barn, not even the meanest house in which an invader could take refuge as he crept closer to the walls. Vienna was surrounded by a broad strip of emptiness in which a blade of grass became conspicuous and a mark of landscape. What was equally important, where this flat empty land joined the walls, a glacis had been constructed, a sloping, stone-covered, perfectly smooth rise, up which any attacker would have to scramble, finding no toehold or handhold as he crawled into the muzzles of the waiting guns. To subdue Vienna was not going to be easy.

The walls of the city, which completely encircled it, contained a dozen or so major towers, beautifully interlocked so that the firing from one covered the approaches of the other, and some two dozen smaller towers that supported the majors. In addition, an enormous canal had been dug—a river in itself, really—bringing an arm of the Danube right up to the city walls on the north and east, forming a moat of enormous width and depth.

But when Lubonski and his men entered the city itself they were struck by how small it was, and Lukasz, who noted such things, said: "Two-thirds of Vienna lies outside the walls, and that's to be surrendered. It's this small central nut that counts, but it will face hell when the Turks surround it."

Before noon on their first day inside the walls, they met Hieronim Lubomirski, relative of the great Jerzy Lubomirski of Wisnicz, under whom Lubonski and Lukasz had invaded Transylvania in 1657. Like his predecessor, he was a daring man, commander of three thousand Poles who had come to the defense of Vienna more than a year ago. From the moment the visitors started talking with him they were assured that he intended staying at his post regardless of what happened to the city.

But he was not hopeful. As he conducted his fellow Poles through the city, he pointed out its manifest weaknesses. Once when a carriage passed bearing some important personage to the palace, he said: "Before the summer is out, we'll be eating those horses."

"Is food so short?" Lubonski asked.

"Space for storing it properly is."

"You'll have plenty of water, with that arm of the Danube."

"It stops outside the walls. First thing Kara Mustafa will do is deny us that water."

"Is he an able general?"

"He's a Köprülü. Those Albanian bastards who've given the Turks such able leadership."

"I believe he's not a Köprülü himself," Lubonski corrected. "He's married to the sister of the great Köprülü who died a few years back."

"One and the same. They're a tremendous family, with victories from Venice to Kiev. And Kara Mustafa intends to improve the family record."

"Can he capture the city?" Lubonski asked, and General Lubomirski stopped his inspection, turned to face the two Polish noblemen, and said with grave emphasis: "If we are restricted to our present forces, Kara Mustafa will subdue Vienna by the middle of July. Men like me will be slaughtered. Everything of value will be taken from the city. The people will be allowed to live, most of them, but they'll have to convert to Islam. The churches will become mosques, and the city will be used as a great base from which to subdue the rest of Europe."

"But these walls? The excellent glacis? The moats? Do they count for nothing?"

Lubonski asked these agitating questions as they were entering a small, beautiful street near the cathedral, Anna Gasse it was called, and at the far end, where a broader street intruded, they halted before a fine old house on which, set into the wall facing the street, there was a handsomely carved stone bearing the legend:

ANNA GASSE

22

1648

Lubomirski indicated the house and said: "Don't those walls seem solid?" With his knuckle he tapped the carved stone, which returned no echo.

"They look strong," Lubonski said.

Then Lubomirski did a strange thing. Standing close to the wall, he hammered with his heel on the surface of the roadway and said: "Down there is where the Turks will defeat us," and when Lukasz asked: "What do you mean?" he explained: "They have the best sappers in the world, and on the day the siege begins Kara Mustafa will take one look at our walls, and especially at the glacis at the end of that open space, and he'll tell his men: 'It is impossible for us to march up to the walls and reduce them,' so he will put his sappers to work."

"But how can they get to the walls?" Lukasz asked. "To undermine them?"

"They will start far, far out there, even beyond the empty space, and they will dig like swift moles under all that protected area, right under it, and they will come up three feet below the cellar of this house"—and again he thumped on the roadway with his boot—"and they will pile enormous sacks of powder right under this house, and one day in mid-July they will ignite the whole damned thing . . . this house and that and that . . . and into our city they'll swarm and massacre us all."

Very carefully Lubonski looked about him, and when he was satisfied that no Austrian soldiers or officials were listening, he asked: "What about our leadership?"

"I think Emperor Leopold will scamper out of the city with his women at the first threat. He always does. But this Rüdiger von Star-hemberg, who will be left in command, is a very dependable man. If Poland and Germany fail to send help, and Vienna falls, as it would have to, I expect Von Starhemberg to be standing beside me when the Turks come rushing in. I would be appalled if he wasn't." He hesitated, shook his head, and added: "It would be unthinkable for him to desert me."

When they returned to Lubomirski's headquarters, Lubonski bored in with the question which had immediate import: "Will the other allies send troops to help?" and now the general became downright enthusiastic: "Duke Charles of Lorraine is as dependable as the rising of the sun. He promises to bring twenty-three thousand additional Austrians from all parts of the country, and I assure you he will. Prince Waldeck of the German states will bring us at least twenty-eight thousand. Bavarians, Thuringians, Saxons and Swabians. He's a grand general, and I trust him. Now please tell me what Sobieski will do."

Lubonski felt, and correctly, that the safety of Vienna and Europe depended upon what happened in the next few months, and he believed that a man as brave as Lubomirski deserved a completely honest statement: "Sobieski has promised thirty-four thousand and the Seym has authorized this number."

"Splendid! With that reinforcement we have a chance."

"But as you know, promises on paper, sworn to on word of honor, do shrink when a final count is made."

"What will the Polish thirty-four thousand shrink to?"

"I'd be happy if we mount twenty-six thousand."

"I'd be happy to receive them."

"With them, do we have a chance?"

"It becomes a race." With his expressive hands he indicated compass directions. "Will Sobieski and the Poles reach here from the north before Kara Mustafa's sappers blow us to hell from the south?" He paused to allow the gravity of his remark to sink in, then asked bluntly: "Tell me honestly. When is the earliest that Sobieski can leave Krakow?"

"August fifteenth."

"Good God!" Lubomirski gasped. "That may be too late."

"But he will come in great strength . . . and with his winged hussars . . . and with the knowledge on both sides that he has already defeated the Turks three times."

Lubomirski studied this response, and made small strategic patterns with his hands, as if he were disposing his troops. "We will have a fighting chance to hold out. Not good. We'll be eating the horses before long. But we will have a chance . . . if you hurry."

In the remaining weeks of May and June, all the hurrying was done by the Turks pressing in from the east and south. They won a significant victory at Gyor, then routed General Lubomirski's Polish volunteers at Bratislava, and on the thirteenth of July approached Vienna with an army that had originally contained about 300,000 men, including even servants and muleteers, but which now had some 115,000 who could be called fighting units.

They were an extraordinary army representing an extraordinary state. Turkey, whose center of power continued to be Constantinople, was governed by Sultan Muhammad IV, who had ascended the throne at the age of six. This meant, of course, that the extensive empire had to be governed by a regency, in this case one person, the boy's mother, one of those terrible, remorseless women more capable of ruling than most of the men with whom she had to deal.

After watching the grandeur of Turkey decline through the ineptness of her assistants, she had started to promote from rank to rank a man of notable ability, the Albanian Köprülü whose freedom from the palace intrigue of the capital kept him relatively able to govern in an honest manner. And from a nation near dissolution from bad government, he had built an empire that reached from Italy east to Russia, from Persia north to Hungary, encompassing such European nations as Greece, Macedonia, Albania and Bulgaria.

The Sultan, meanwhile, had seemed to be concerned only with his own interests: women and hunting. To assuage the former hunger he had enormous seraglios, but even when they were crammed with the most delightful houris from eleven nations, his principal joy continued to be hunting. He had extensive preserves throughout Europe, each area larger than Belgium or Holland, in which only he was allowed to hunt. On one historic occasion he dragooned ten thousand Christian inhabitants of an area to serve as his bearers over a period of three weeks, during which he shot or shot at several thousand deer, bear and buffalo. In one part of Bulgaria his Christian slaves served as custodians for a herd of eleven thousand buffalo, which were reserved for him.

The various Köprülüs responsible for governing the empire had adopted a simple policy: "Keep the idiot happy, for as long as he lives, we live." In the days of rapid expansion this tactic worked, for they managed exceedingly well and captured fortresses which the Christians had deemed impregnable; whole nations fell into the Turkish grip and the possibility of further conquests seemed endless. But starting in 1681 this irresponsible Sultan began to see that as his troops pressed forward on significant cities like Vienna, Christian retaliation would become inescapable, so he began to caution Kara Mustafa, his grand vizier of the moment: "Take all of Hungary. It's a miserable land unable to govern itself. And take Poland too, if you will, because it has no future. But do not try to capture Vienna, because if you do, you will arouse the sleeping dragons."

Kara Mustafa, eager to emulate or surpass his predecessors who had marched all the way to Venice, would not listen. "If I can hold together my army, and if I can have enough Tatars on my left flank to harry whatever enemy we encounter, I can take Vienna and all of Austria."

Muhammad was insistent: "I foresee real danger if you try."

But still Kara Mustafa would not listen. "Since you ascended the throne in 1648, decisions of war and peace have been made by my family. Let it continue that way, and Turkey will rule Europe."

Muhammad, now forty-one and surprisingly knowledgeable despite his preoccupation with women and hunting, became angry with his grand vizier for treating him like a child, and to the tremendous surprise of his court, he stepped forward and handed Kara Mustafa a green silk cord, very strong and more than two arms in length: "Go to Vienna, besiege it, but if you fail, you are to hang yourself."

In accordance with ancient tradition, while the Sultan and his court watched, the grand vizier tied the green cord into a running knot and passed the noose over his head, tightening it when it reached his neck. From that day on, during the march through Hungary, and the battle at Bratislava, and the exciting approach to Vienna itself, Kara Mustafa never removed the silken cord from around his neck, and if General Lubomirski inside the walls was apprehensive about the forthcoming battle, so was Mustafa, for each man knew that this was a battle to the death.

The Sultan, for his part, decided to support his army by a display of austerity at home. From his several harems he dismissed battalions of his best concubines. In seven different countries he closed down many of his hunting establishments, turning the land over to peasants. And most important of all to a confirmed huntsman, from his many stables he released nearly nine hundred of his favorite horses to the military. He did not make himself destitute, however, for he did keep an impressive selection of the most attractive women, nine of the best hunting areas and about four hundred choice horses, and in the years 1682 and 1683, as the battle for Vienna approached, he continued to enjoy himself, but he often paused to speculate on how Kara Mustafa and his green cord were doing.

By early August, when he had assembled what expeditionary force he was going to be able to collect, King Jan Sobieski already knew that Vienna was completely surrounded by Turkish troops and that a siege of the most brutal efficiency was under way. On the fifteenth of July, the day after the attack began, General Lubomirski had asked a brave assistant to see if he could slip through the Turkish lines with an urgent message for Sobieski, and this man, riding at top speed, informed the Poles as to what was happening at Vienna:

> "The siege began at dawn on the fourteenth. Trumpets sounded and three horsemen from the Turkish side cantered easily across the empty land leading to the city walls, set up a small catapult and threw numerous rocks into the center of Vienna. Each bore a message: 'Surrender now and you will be saved. Open your gates, turn your churches over to us and lay down your arms, and no one will be killed. If you resist the Will of Allah, your leaders, and all of them, will be slain. Able men and women will be sold into slavery. You will be allowed no rights of worship, and your mighty walls will be thrown down. Fight and you die! Surrender and you live!'"

When Sobieski interrogated him regarding military details, the man said: "On the north and east, where the arm of the Danube protects us, large concentrations of Turkish soldiers are blocking any movement in or out of the city. On the south huge arrays of cannon already bombard us night and day. And to the west, from which the greatest trouble will come, sappers already work at digging tunnels to deliver gunpowder under the walls."

"How long did Lubomirski estimate the forces inside the city could resist?"

"You must reach Vienna before the end of August."

"That I cannot do," Sobieski said with heaviness of spirit.

"Then the city is doomed."

Gravely Sobieski walked back and forth, a huge man whose monstrous unruly mustache made his head look even larger than it was. "We must rely upon two miracles. Those in Vienna shall resist the siege until September. Those of us outside must reach there in time to save them." He raised his large arms to heaven and cried: "Blessed Virgin of Czestochowa, allow us those miracles."

When all was in readiness at Krakow he delayed departure for four days to allow him time to journey to that shrine of the Virgin, where in the company of his advisers, including Count Lubonski, he prayed before the Black Madonna, and as he rose from his knees, a priest attached to the shrine presented him with a reproduction of the painting which one of the monks had done. It was about two hands high, one hand and a half wide and was suspended from a heavy gold chain, which the priest passed over the king's head, so that the painting came down over Sobieski's chest, hanging like a small plate of armor.

The incident moved the king deeply, and placing his left hand reverently upon the painting he asked for his sword, which he raised in his right hand until it pointed to heaven, and cried in a loud voice: "Poles! It has always been our duty to defend the Christianity of Europe from the threat of its barbarian enemies. Tomorrow we ride forth once more to hurl back the infidel. May God ride with us."

On the trip back to Krakow he told Lubonski: "Old man, it is not necessary for you to repeat this long and dangerous journey. You've served Poland well. Go home and pray for us."

But Lubonski could not accept this advice. "It seems I have spent my life fighting the enemies of my homeland. But the greatest battle was saved for the end. If we lose Vienna to enemies of God, we lose all." And Sobieski, imbued with religious fervor, understood this attitude and said: "Come along, old man. You'll be the best warrior we have."

So Lubonski sent Brat Piotr, the friar from Czestochowa, galloping to Bukowo to fetch Lukasz, but when those two reported to Krakow ready for the forced march into Austria, Lubonski saw that they had brought with them young Janko from the village, and he protested: "We want no boys on such a venture," but Piotr replied: "He is the son of Jan who served with you in all the battles, and he is ready."

"Bring him along," Lubonski said, and next morning, 11 August 1683, the king and his army rode forth, as Cardinal Pentucci cried when he blessed them, "to save the world."

Not even the king knew how large his army was, for although he had promised the coalition 34,000 Polish troops, he had reason to believe that the honest number had to be smaller than 30,000, but how much smaller he could only guess. It was not that his clerks were careless; they handed him carefully compiled lists that showed a specific total: *In all, 29,516 men under arms.*

This precise figure, so neatly presented, was worthless, because each unit commander reported many more men and horses than they had in order to draw down excess stores, which he then sold for his personal profit. So when Sobieski marched toward Vienna he did not know whether he had 27,000 troops or 26,000, and in reporting to his fellow generals he would use either figure, knowing that regardless of what he said he would be wrong. But of course their figures would be wrong, too, and for identical reasons.

As they moved west toward the mountain pass at Cieszyn, they formed an amazing spectacle: the winged hussars in front, the cavalry made up of magnates and the lesser gentry, a horde of foot soldiers, a much larger horde of servants like Brat Piotr and Janko, and about a thousand wagons carrying the goods that would be needed. In the rear, utilizing most of the spare horses, came the hundred and twenty huge cannon which Sobieski hoped would offset those of the Turks. It was an act of considerable will power even to think of transporting such an army at great speed across mountains and rivers, but actually, it was an act of faith.

They did not follow the leisurely route which Lubonski and Lukasz had taken on their expedition into Austria, but rather a direct line to the towns of Brno and Hollabrunn, where the Austrian and German generals participating in the battle would meet them, and as they marched, always at maximum speed, Brat Piotr, with Janko at his side, began to strike friendships with the noblemen who formed the contingent of winged hussars. He was at their camp every evening, pestering them about their horses, their special lances, and especially that halo of turkey and eagle feathers they wore about their heads when they rode into battle.

"Could I see how the feathers are attached?" he asked on the fifth night, when the riders had become accustomed to him. They allowed him to inspect the contraption which held the tall feathers in place, and he studied every aspect of it, explaining it most imperfectly to Janko.

Some evenings later, when camp was struck early—about eight, when there was still plenty of daylight—Piotr prevailed upon one of the hussars to let him try on the piece of armor to which the crown of feathers was riveted. When he felt the armor on his body and could see from the corner of his eye the feathers rising above his head, he called to Janko: "Fetch me a horse," and once astride it, he began brandishing an imaginary lance and dashing back and forth over the campground, shouting in a high-pitched voice: "I am a winged hussar. Stand back, you infidels."

At one point, his long legs kicking at his mount, his elbows flapping and his dark-brown monk's garb flying in the wind, he came roaring down upon Janko, who would have been ridden over had he not leaped into a ditch: "You are dead, foul Turk! Lie there in your blood!" Back and forth the wildly excited friar galloped, his feathers making a mournful sound in the dusk, and when slowly he brought his horse back to where the owner of the gear stood laughing, he was most reluctant to surrender it. Fondly he patted the armor, avowing that it was as fine as any he had ever seen, and with care he straightened each of the feathers.

"You must be proud to wear such a uniform," Piotr said, and the hussar replied: "I am."

Now each night when halt was called, Brat Piotr mingled with the hussars, borrowing armor first from this one, then from that, and he galloped so fervently over the campgrounds, his arms and legs extended in strange directions, that the hussars began calling him The Flying Friar, for he looked like those pictures in German books showing goblins and other strange beings flying through the air at night. But always when he finished his ride he would seek out Janko: "I used to think that being master of a great monastery was the best a man could hope for, but I would rather be a hussar with feathers singing about my ears, fighting for the will of God against the infidel. That I would very strongly like to be."

On 31 August, when it was doubtful that Vienna could much longer withstand the dreadful siege being mounted by Kara Mustafa, Jan Sobieski rode into the small town of Hollabrunn, northwest of Vienna and only a short distance from the Danube River, which the army would have to cross before it could engage the Turks, and there he met for the first time with two of the finest gentlemen of Europe.

The meeting could have been terribly embarrassing. Back in 1674, when Sobieski was elected king through French support, his principal opponent had been Duke Charles of Lorraine, a Habsburg for whom Austria was buying votes scandalously. The contest had been keen, with many believing that Duke Charles would win, but in the end the French poured in huge sums, bought magnates right and left, and secured the victory for Sobieski. Now the former antagonists must work together not only as allies but as generals sharing a difficult command.

Another reason for likely failure was that the generals, all of them, must devise a workable plan under which three disparate armies, which followed different systems and had not even a common language, could do battle against a force immensely larger than their own. When the three leaders, accompanied by their staffs, met for the first time in a poorly lit room in an inn at Hollabrunn, there was a moment of extreme tension, for on the rustic table confronting them lay the jeweled baton, about thirty inches long, which would be carried by the commander in chief, and no one knew who that would be.

King Jan looked at the splendid baton with narrow, conniving eyes; he was a vain man who might demand the baton as a kingly right. Duke Charles, stiff and proper, represented the host nation, which gave him a substantial claim. And watchers could see the German Prince Waldeck eying the baton with real desire; he was not only contributing the largest number of troops but he was also a proud, able warrior. This meeting could end in disaster.

However, it started well, for the moment Duke Charles saw his mighty adversary for the kingship of Poland, he stepped forward and embraced Sobieski: "You are welcome, Sire, you are twice welcome!" And then Prince Waldeck kissed Sobieski's hand, crying for all to hear: "We have waited desperately for your troops. Thank God you have come."

Now the three generals hesitated, and the watchers could not anticipate how the problem of the baton was to be settled. Then the Duke of Lorraine placed one delicate forefinger on the emblem, and immediately Waldeck did the same, and slowly, gravely they pushed the baton to where Sobieski stood. When he realized that he was to serve as commander in chief of all the armies, he lifted the baton, kissed it, and said: "It shall be my duty to bring us victory," and the watchers cheered.

But when they sat down to a frugal dinner, each man knowing

that a great battle and possible death waited only a few days away and a few miles distant, a difficulty of the most dangerous kind arose, at first only a raised eyebrow, but, potentially a disaster that could destroy the alliance.

Sobieski, as commander in chief, sketched on paper provided by Duke Charles the plan of battle. "We are three armies, all twenty miles west of Vienna. How we march to that city and in what formation may determine the outcome of the battle. There is an easy route, the left flank along the Danube. There is a very difficult route, the right flank through the high hills of the Vienna Woods. And there is a route half-easy, half-difficult, down the center."

The generals—some dozen of them—nodded agreement, for they had studied this terrain.

"What I propose is that we Poles take the extremely difficult right flank through the mountains and the woods. We have the men and horses to haul our cannon across the ravines." All favored this gallant proposal, but now they leaned forward to catch the next decision, the important one. "I think, strongly, that Prince Waldeck and his Germans, who have not fought in this kind of terrain before, should assume the left flank, along the Danube." Then, very quickly, before there could be the protest which he was sure would arise, he snapped out: "And the Austrians will come down the center." Some of the generals gasped, and when two started to exclaim, he knew he was in trouble.

For several centuries the armies of Europe, when marching to battle, had observed a convention which stated that the right flank constituted the position of highest honor, and in the present situation all agreed that Sobieski had priority in that claim. He was a king, he was commander in chief, and he had repeatedly proven his ability. But the position of second honor was always the left flank, while traditionally, the weakest force or the one led by a general with dubious reputation occupied the center, from which he could not run away, since the two flanks led by heroes would hem him in.

In an army composed of troops from one nation only, it was a simple matter for the king or commander to assign the center position to his weakest general, and the latter had to accept because he usually realized that he *was* the weakest. But in a coalition when national honor was at stake, the leader of that coalition incurred a grave risk when he assigned the troops of one nation, in this instance Austria, to the center.

"Sire!" a lesser Austrian general cried. "It would be a requirement which the Duke of Lorraine could not accept, to occupy the center."

"He cannot!" several other irate Austrians agreed, whereupon Sobieski appealed to the duke, praying that the latter would graciously accept, but Charles was a man of the most sensitive pride, and he said with no embarrassment: "As leader of the forces of the host country, it would be highly improper of me to place my troops in the center."

A tense silence filled the little room in which these men were plotting strategies which would determine the fate of many nations, and all hung in the balance until Sobieski performed an act that won him the enthusiastic support of all; he left his place at the head of the table, walked ponderously to where Prince Waldeck sat, and bowed low before him, his massive belly seeming to touch the floor. "Honored Prince, I have just made an unforgivable mistake. I overlooked the honor of a great champion. Duke Charles has every claim on the left flank, and I beg you to accept the center." Before Waldeck could respond, the king said: "To you will go the honor of facing Kara Mustafa himself. For in the Turkish line of battle the center is the place of honor." And then, still afraid of Waldeck's reaction, he continued: "I know what I speak about, Prince, because in my battles against the Turks, I always chose the center so that I could get to their commander myself."

While Sobieski remained in his supplicating position, the German generals conferred, and in the end Prince Waldeck said, with obvious sincerity: "This battle will be big enough for any position to be one of honor. I accept your placement."

A sigh filled the room, and when Sobieski was back in his chair he asked: "And what do we know about the Turkish position?" Now Duke Charles assumed command. "As you just said, Kara Mustafa in the center, and a very dangerous opponent he is. But I do believe he has already committed a fatal error. He has split his troops. About forty percent of the best remain preoccupied with besieging Vienna. Only sixty percent have been moved into the battle line to oppose us."

The generals engaged in vigorous discussion of this critical mistake; they could not comprehend how a military man as successful as Kara Mustafa could allow it, and when they were satisfied that he had indeed made it and was persisting in it, they agreed that this opened a chance for victory.

"And where will the twenty thousand Tatar horsemen be?" Sobieski asked.

Duke Charles rubbed his chin and said: "Now, there we have a problem. They are far removed, on the Turkish left flank. This means that when you come through the Vienna Woods, Poland, you will have to face first the ravines in the hills, then the Turkish cavalry when you break through, and always the threat of the Tatar attack on your flank, each footfall of the way."

"Where exactly are they camped?"

"Here. From where they can strike at your flank, no matter where you are."

"Well," Sobieski said, "we fight on two fronts. East against the Turks, south against the Tatars. Pray God they don't both hit us at the same time."

"They will," the duke said, and Sobieski nodded; he had faced joint enemies before. But now he asked: "Who is leading the Tatars?" and the duke replied: "Khan Murad," at which Sobieski frowned. "The best. I've fought him twice. The best."

Count Lubonski asked: "And how is General Lubomirski, inside the city?"

"It's very difficult for us to receive messages from inside," the Duke of Lorraine said. "A few daring souls sneak out between the Turkish lines. They say the city's starving. Starhemberg is valiant, no doubt about it. And Lubomirski is a pillar of strength."

"And Emperor Leopold?" Lubonski asked.

The duke looked away, unwilling to answer that difficult question, but a lesser Austrian general did, allowing no inflection of any kind to creep into his voice: "When danger threatened, Emperor Leopold and his women fled the capital, heading for Linz, a hundred miles west of here. With him he took six thousand of our best troops." No one spoke, so after a while the general added: "He pointed out that in a time when disaster threatened a nation, it was important that the emperor be kept safe so that he could ensure guidance . . . if the battle was lost."

"I understand that feeling," Sobieski said generously, but he could not approve the cowardice; as King of Poland he had volunteered to march more than two hundred miles to anticipate trouble and strangle it before it could injure his country.

At this solemn moment Prince Waldeck said: "We face a bad terrain and a terrible foe. But the salvation of a great city depends upon us, and the preservation of Christianity. May God allow us to be valiant." And on this prayer the remarkable meeting at Hollabrunn broke up. Three vain and strong-minded men had met, judged one another, and formed an alliance which would not be broken, regardless of the adversity which threatened it.

On the morning after he was created commander in chief, Jan Sobieski launched his remorseless attack on the Turks besieging the city, and although his three armies were still twenty miles away from the battleground, they began to take those effective steps which would qualify them for victory. Duke Charles, with his 23,000 Austrians, moved slowly down the right bank of the Danube, exercising care lest he get too far ahead of his allies, who had to traverse much more difficult terrain, and in proper time he established his headquarters at Klosterneuburg, not far from the Turkish front lines. Prince Waldeck, with his 28,000 Germans, hacked his way through moderately difficult areas to reach a point from which he would be able, on the day of battle, to thrust directly at Kara Mustafa's center.

Jan Sobieski and his Poles had an infinitely more difficult task; first he had to move from Hollabrunn, over low and marshy land, to a point opposite the Danube town of Tulln, and there he had to assemble pontoon bridges which would lift his troops across the river and onto the side of the Danube where the Turks waited. This required four agonizing days, on each of which he expected Khan Murad and his Tatar horsemen to attack. "If they hit us when we're on the river, they win," he told his generals, but for some incomprehensible reason of their own the Tatars did not strike. Scouts reported that all twenty thousand were waiting in a camp only a few miles distant.

Once across the Danube, the real struggle began, because according to plan, the Poles were required to march well south from Tulln, then turn sharply east through the lovely and historic Vienna Woods, an area of low mountains, rolling hills and occasional small streams.

Mountains worry generals and horses; they terrify peasants, who know that horses are too valuable to be used hauling cannon up steep slopes, and therefore it would be they, using ropes and skids, who would do the work. Now Janko learned what warfare was, because he and eighteen men older than himself were assigned to one rope, another two dozen to a second rope, and three dozen to the job of turning the heavy wheels by hand, grabbing first one spoke, then the next as the cannon made its way slowly up the hills.

It was murderous work, from the fourth of September to the tenth, and on two occasions, as they struggled in the fiercely hot summer sun, they saw on the crests of hills to their right bands of Tatar horsemen who kept track of their progress. When these men from the steppes would strike, no one could guess, but if they did so now, when the entire Polish flank was exposed, they could create havoc.

As he slaved over the cannon with Janko, Piotr, sweating and swearing in his monk's garb as he hauled on the ropes, advised: "Only the hussars know how to make war, Janko. They don't waste their horses on work like this." At dusk he was too exhausted to seek out the cavalry encampment, but at dawn he had to go back to the cannon.

It was brutal work, and it succeeded only because Kara Mustafa refused to believe his Tatar scouts when they reported that the Poles were dragging their cannon right over the mountains. It was inconceivable to him, accustomed as he was to orderly battle in which one army approached the other on flat ground, that Sobieski could move an entire army across terrain as rugged as the Vienna Woods and come out on the right flank prepared for battle. And as to the possibility that the Poles would bring cannon and hussars through such forests—he dismissed the idea.

So inch by inch, while the Austrians and the Germans waited in their prepared camps, Sobieski's men crept through the grassy woodlands, watching always for the attack of the Tatars who could have destroyed them so easily.

On 10 September, Janko and Piotr, straining at their ropes, reached the crest of the final hill, and when they looked eastward they sighted something that both horrified and enchanted them. Before the walls of Vienna, and for as far as their eyes would carry, were the tents and the guns and the emplacements of the huge Turkish army, dug in and waiting. Piotr gasped: "It's like a field of flowers. They're everywhere." But Janko looked in silence, realizing that within the next days he and the other peasants, armed only with clubs and knives, would be expected to march through that vast assembly of tents and battle the men now waiting in them. It was an awesome moment, and the boy appreciated its gravity.

The Poles spent the next day making their way down the steep slopes and onto the level ground on which the battle would be conducted, and now Piotr and his men had to tie their ropes to the rear of their cannon, and work just as hard to keep it from running down the hill as they had done to drag it up.

When the fearful passage was completed, the Polish forces assumed battle formation, still waiting for the Tatar strike—which never came. "Khan Murad must be mad to have allowed us to come down that final slope unopposed," Sobieski said as he reviewed the disposition of his troops. "But for that favor we thank Almighty God. Now if Murad strikes, we can repel him."

The roles of the men from Bukowo were clearly understood: Count Lubonski would ride not with the hussars, for they were a special force, but with the gentry's cavalry. He would be supported on horseback by Lukasz, a man of proven heroism. Brat Piotr would march with the foot soldiers, brandishing a pike. And Janko would tend the extra horses, which he would keep close to Lubonski in case either the count or Lukasz might need a remount. All four would be in the location of greatest honor, the right flank of the right flank. "May God permit us to deport ourselves with bravery," Lubonski said as he explained their responsibilities.

On the evening before battle Supreme Commander Sobieski, surveying the field from the courtyard of a church high on a hill, told his associates three things: "Kara Mustafa continues to divide his forces, half at the walls, half here. Our flanks will harass the Turks badly, but we must depend upon you Germans to punish the main body. And although our Polish position is strong, with our cannon in place, we are still vulnerable on our right flank, for the Tatar cavalry is waiting until we get stretched out. We shall have to watch carefully."

Duke Charles asked when Sobieski intended to release his winged hussars, and the king said regretfully: "We've scouted the land in front of us, and it's too uneven for a major cavalry charge. The Turks have cut trenches across it. But once we get past that, about four in the afternoon, I'll set them free."

"How long do you expect the battle to last?" the German prince asked, and Sobieski said with great caution: "No battle of this size can be decided in a single day. But by the night of the second day, if God supports us, we shall have a victory." And the generals prayed.

While Sobieski and his generals were planning their attack on the Turkish camp, Kara Mustafa was urging his men, sometimes with whips and hangings, to speed the capture of Vienna. If the sappers could place their charges beneath the walls and at various spots throughout the city and explode them before the coalition forces could strike from the west, his Janissaries would be able to storm into the city and capture it before the battle even began. His sappers were so skilled in their work—engineers from France, Germany, Italy and Hungary—that the ground underneath the city was beginning to resemble a honeycomb, and his experts assured him that the explosions would become possible sometime around the middle of September, less than a week away. On his crucial gamble, Kara Mustafa seemed to have won, and as he moved about, always wearing his green silk cord, he exuded confidence.

Certainly those inside the city were aware of the likelihood of its fall. General Lubomirski, endeavoring to maintain discipline among his starving Polish troops, tried not to hear the sounds of the sappers underfoot, and once when he was inspecting conditions in Anna Gasse and came upon the beautiful small house at Number 22, he shuddered when he heard the distinct sounds of Turkish engineers chipping away the last bits of earth before the gunpowder was installed.

For three weeks he had eaten nothing but horsemeat, and very little of that, and good water was more precious than wine. More than a month had passed since either he or his soldiers had seen any vegetables, and nights were sometimes made unbearable by the cries of hungry children. Rarely had a major city been so completely isolated as Vienna was now, but rarely had one been besieged by such a formidable force.

"If Sobieski said he was coming by mid-September," Lubomirski assured his troops, "he will be here," and with this daily encouragement the Poles became one of the mainstays of the city. Accustomed to meager rations, they managed the deprivations better than most, and their unflagging courage heartened the citizens. But major credit was also due the stalwart deportment of Von Starhemberg, who consistently turned down Kara Mustafa's repeated demands for capitulation: "We will all die here, in defense of a city we love." And when the Muslims tied messages to the rocks they were catapulting into the city, he did not endeavor to censor them; instead he read them personally to crowds that gathered: "Mustafa promises that if we surrender, all Christians will be allowed to remain Christian, without let or hindrance." Whenever he read this promise he paused, then shouted: "Ask the Greeks what that promise means. Ask the Bulgarians. Ask the Thracians, the Albanians." Then he would pause dramatically and cry: "How do the people of Vienna reply to that invitation?" And men planted in the starving crowd would shout "No!"

But the digging continued and soon the city must explode.

Another general besides Sobieski and Lubomirski was also perplexed by Kara Mustafa's obstinate refusal to take troops away from the walls so that the army facing the coalition might be strengthened, and that was Khan Murad, who had fretted for some months at the sorry misuse to which his gifted Tatars were being put. Hidden in a camp far to the south as if they were pariahs, not used in any of the assaults on the city, and now forbidden to attack Sobieski's exposed flank, the Tatars had justification for deeming themselves insulted by the Turks, but this had often happened in the past and Khan Murad was familiar with such treatment.

Now, however, such insolence had become more than a matter of pride to a valued ally; the misuse of the Tatars threatened the success of the whole enterprise, and Khan Murad was not disposed to see his Tatars defeated in some pitched battle when by clever thrust and parry they could have so harried the enemy that the set battle would never take place.

So Khan Murad left his camp, accompanied by two subordinates, determined to confront Kara Mustafa, but as he rode he saw two things which infuriated him: coming down the slopes, which he could have attacked so easily, was the Polish army, unimpeded except by the difficulty of the terrain; and spread out in the battle camp of the Turks were countless tents of lavish construction and elaborate adornment. He was ashamed of this army of which he was a fighting part.

Turning away from the Poles, who were being allowed such an easy progress to the battle, he focused on the tents of the minor viziers, so luxurious that they seemed more suitable for a parade ground at some provincial capital where gallant horsemen and well-groomed women assembled than for a battlefield. One tent in particular offended him; austere on the outside, it carried near the flap of the entrance a small green embroidery signifying that it belonged to a man of rank, and since the day was warm the flap was thrown back, and Khan Murad could see inside the three beautiful women garbed in silken robes as if attending a picnic, and the ornate decorations that crowded the interior walls of the tent: Horrible! He must have spent more on that tent than I spend on my whole army.

There were a hundred such tents, each with some refinement that the others lacked: portable bathtubs, mirrors from Bordeaux, huge hampers of figs and dates, boxes of rare clothing for the women who tagged along, and gold and silver ornaments beyond counting. Some tents, like the one with the green emblem, had walls half covered with ceremonial scimitars encrusted in gold and precious stones, and some had marshals' batons heavy with diamonds and rubies, the mark of the Sultan's approval. These tents represented a concentration of wealth such as Khan Murad could scarcely imagine, and he was outraged.

When he was finally allowed to see Kara Mustafa he spoke abruptly, avoiding the usual courtesies, even though he was aware that by doing so he endangered his life: "Grand Vizier, you place us in jeopardy by keeping your forces divided."

Fingering the green cord which gave weight to what he was about to say, the vizier nodded: "It must seem so to you."

"And you kept us from attacking the Poles as they came across the hills, where we could have destroyed them."

"You will destroy them when the battle starts."

"And I remember well when the Sultan himself advised you not to attack Vienna, that it would cause the nations to unite against us. At that time I spoke in his support. You have done a foolish thing, Kara Mustafa, in coming to Vienna. And now you seem determined to lose our battle. I am distressed to participate in such decisions."

Only rarely in any tenure did any grand vizier have to listen to such words, and almost always the person who spoke them was beheaded, and Khan Murad must have appreciated the grave danger in which he had placed himself, for when he saw the vizier's face grow red and his hands tremble, he could guess that when the battle ended he faced execution, so he said harshly: "And do not think to slay me, Kara Mustafa, when the battle is over, for I shall not be here."

And before the startled grand vizier could respond, the Tatar chieftain was gone from the great tent in which the meeting had occurred, and from the congregation of lesser tents, and from the whole battle area itself. In disgust he rode across empty land to the segregated spot to which his Tatars had been assigned, and he summoned his commanders.

"We ride!" he shouted, and they shouted back "Against the Poles?" and he cried "No."

He led them away from the battlefield, and from the besieged city, and from Austria completely. He led them across Hungary and through the glens of Transylvania and through the Ukraine and across eastern Russia, until they reached once more the steppes of central Asia, where they were absorbed by that endless landscape. Never again would Polish armies be required to fight against or with the Tatars.

At half after three on the morning of 12 September 1683, Jan Sobieski rose, prayed, and placed about his neck the portrait of the Virgin of Czestochowa. In the growing daylight he surveyed the vast battlefield on which his three armies would perform during the next two days, and the magnitude of the Turkish camp might have appalled him had he not been inwardly convinced that his troops could subdue it. The 25,000 tents glowed in the dawn, the 50,000 carts stood like ramparts; the 80,000 Janissaries and spahis in this part of the army looked like ants, and the 60,000 horses moved uneasily as if they knew a battle was about to begin.

"We shall cut them this way and that," Sobieski told his subordinates, and his heralds announced the start of battle.

In the first hour the Germans under Prince Waldeck performed heroically, for as Sobieski had promised, they were the ones who encountered the main force of the Turkish army, and they did so over terrain that was forbidding: vineyards, each one protected by low stone walls behind which the Turks lay hidden. But Waldeck used his small cannon with good effect, blasting a wall to rubble, then sending in his men with lances and bayonets.

Because the Poles on the right flank had to move much farther than either the Germans or the Austrians, it was the latter under the Duke of Lorraine who next made contact with Kara Mustafa's troops, and they performed excellently, moving with studied force over their flatter terrain: stand-fire-charge, stand-fire-charge, yard by yard they kept moving forward, and Sobieski was so pleased with their rugged determination that he sent a messenger to congratulate them.

And now, on the right, the Poles at last reached the Turkish lines and began a systematic assault different from either the Germans' or the Austrians'. Once they started moving forward, they kept coming vigorously until something like a stone fence or a barn stopped them. Then they milled about in seeming disarray until they regained forward movement, when they overwhelmed the Turks. Now the three armies were moving forward in unison.

However, Kara Mustafa was not impotent, and whenever he spotted a weakness in the allied line, or a flank exposed, he sent his men dashing to that spot, and with the skill they had acquired in many battles, they knew just how to wreck the allies' plans. By nine in the morning Austrians on the left, Germans in the center and Poles on the right were well bogged down, and a general melee ensued, in which hand-to-hand fighting predominated.

This continued for two hours, and the Duke of Lorraine became so disconcerted by the lack of forward movement that he dispatched a messenger to Sobieski: "When will you send the hussars forward?" and Sobieski had to reply: "As of now the terrain will not permit it, but as soon as we break through . . ."

To test the terrain, and especially how far the grape fields and the stone fences continued before flat ground became available, he asked for a volunteer cavalry force—not his precious hussars, who must be held in reserve for the critical moments—to penetrate the enemy lines and bring back a scouting report. Count Lubonski cried: "I shall lead!" and horsemen formed about him. Sobieski, himself fifty-four years old, knew that the count was far too old for such a venture, but he also knew that the leadership of such a man would prove invaluable in a dangerous mission like this, so he brought his right hand up to the edge of his fur shako in a salute of honor: "God ride with you!"

At the head of his detachment, Lubonski started his horse at a slow pace, then spurred it to a brisk trot, and when the Turkish lines were close he jabbed his horse with his heels, set his short lance at the ready, and led the charge into the heart of the enemy force. Dodging and twisting both his horse and his own body in the saddle, he succeeded in getting three-fourths of his horsemen into the rear area of the Turkish camp, back among the tents, and there he found the flat ground the remainder of the cavalry would need, so with a wild cry he wheeled about and led his men back through the exact part of the line they had penetrated.

There they went! Their steeds leaped over the low fences and cleared the ditches. They galloped straight for an obstacle, then veered cleverly away, man and horse swaying in the bright sunlight. They swept through the vineyards, knocked down the Janissaries, gained open ground between the combat lines, and galloped back to the Polish headquarters, where old Count Lubonski saluted his king and said: "Four hundred yards, Sire, and we are free."

It was a fearful four hundred yards. From one in the afternoon till nearly five the three armies moved forward almost inch by inch, for when the Turks realized that their tents were being threatened, their valued homes for the past two years, they stiffened their resistance, and with Kara Mustafa always in the thickest of the battle, for he was exceedingly brave, they confronted the coalition.

It was now apparent to the three generals that they would have to be lucky if they were to traverse the final four hundred yards before nightfall, camp uneasily there, and resume the battle in the morning when the cavalry could be used, but at this critical juncture the lesser cavalry, composed of petty noblemen like Lukasz of Bukowo, began to break through here and there, so that Sobieski, as the day began to die, saw a chance not only to cover the four hundred yards but also to gain a solid footing on the level ground for his night's camp, and he gave the signal for all his Polish troops to make a supreme effort during one last hour, and this they did.

No one, in later analysis, could recall where the break came, but it was probably not along the Polish front at all. Waldeck's Germans, seeing the Polish effort, emulated it, and because Kara Mustafa had rushed troops to stop the Poles, he had to leave the center sector weakened, allowing the Swabians and Thuringians to rip a great hole in his lines. Almost immediately the Austrians did the same, and immediately thereafter the Poles cracked their line, and in one roaring sweep the entire allied line surged forward, traversing the last of the bad terrain.

It was five in the afternoon when this fortunate development crowned the allied effort, and both Lorraine and Waldeck sent messengers to Sobieski congratulating him on having obtained a solid base from which to launch the next day's attack, but when the Polish king saw for himself the wonderfully flat land his troops now occupied, and when he saw disorder among the Turkish troops, who were retreating hastily to their tent area, a flash of vision like a bolt of summer lightning possessed him, and he cried: "We can finish this battle tonight!" And with a mental vitality equal to his enormous physical size he barked out a dozen orders: "Hussars to the front! Every man in every unit who has a horse, to the ready! Along the entire line, when my cannon fires, charge and carry to the walls of Vienna if we can!"

The three armies at that moment were about six miles from Vienna, the first five were level land, the last one was the denuded area leading to the glacis and the wall itself, so once an immense cavalry charge got started, it was not unreasonable to believe that it could go a great distance. There would be three thousand winged hussars in the lead, followed by some five thousand superior cavalry, backed up by thirteen thousand fighters on horseback, mostly petty noblemen and farmers with no military training but long experience with horses and self-defense. There had probably never been, in European warfare, a cavalry charge of this magnitude.

It was twenty minutes past five, on a day when the sun would set at half after six, when Jan Sobieski gave the order to charge, and like some boundless autumn wind chasing dried leaves, the twenty thousand horsemen spurred their mounts to a gallop and bore down on the disorganized Turks. For only ten minutes did the outcome of the charge hang in the balance; during that time Kara Mustafa, with the green cord growing tighter about his throat, performed heroically, endeavoring in vain to rally his troops. Some remained faithful to him, many did not, and he realized that all was lost when at the height of the enemy attack he saw his own troops begin to loot the tents of their officers.

"You!" he shouted at some Bulgarian slaves who were ripping apart a tent valued at eight hundred gold pieces, and when his command had no effect, he shrugged his shoulders in a pathetic admission of despair and told his own bodyguard: "Take what you can," and a general looting proceeded, not by the Germans or the Poles, but by his own men.

The looting had one tragic outcome which no one could have anticipated. Count Lubonski, austere and brave and straight in the saddle at age seventy-three, kept his horse in the van, and with his modified lance, for he no longer had the strength of arm to master a long one, he accomplished much, sending Turkish soldiers scattering. He was ably supported by Lukasz, who rode at his left, and by Brat Piotr and the boy Janko, who kept not far behind with the extra horses.

But as the quartet from Bukowo entered the tent area, where the confusion was greatest, Piotr saw that a young hussar had been slain by a Turkish cannon shot, and his left leg was still in the stirrup, his precious circle of feathers broken in the dust, so on the spur of the moment the friar reined in his horse, leaped down, and tried to tend the fallen hussar. A moment's inspection proved the young Pole was dead, but there was his armored vest, his halo of feathers, so with breathless delight Piotr stripped him, placed the armor about his own chest, adjusted the crown of feathers, discarded his own rather ordinary mount, and leaped upon the dead hussar's beautiful beast.

Feathers waving, long legs kicking, Piotr galloped forward to join the charge, shouting as he came: "Make way for the hussars!" And with no lance or any other kind of weapon, he started chasing Turks.

It took him only a few moments to catch up with Count Lubonski, and the feathers, the flailing legs, the stretch of friar's garb flowing behind, made such a ridiculous figure, even Lubonski had to laugh. Young Janko, now at the count's side, was captivated by the idea that the man he liked so much had at last attained his life's desire, and, thoughtlessly, he left the count and joined the *soi-disant* hussar.

Together the two roared through the rear guard of the retreating Turks, dashing in and out among the canopied tents, and accomplishing nothing except the exhilaration of the ride.

The metal-and-leather frame to which the feathers of the winged hussar were attached had been broken when its former owner pitched to the ground, and now as Piotr rode with it about his ears the left half tore partially loose, dropped down, and began to flap about the horse's left eye, so that instead of terrifying enemy horses, as intended, the feathers now annoyed the hussar's horse, who began to run under its own direction, hoping to break free of the pestilential flapping.

Piotr, never a first-class horseman, found himself unable to control the runaway horse, so he resorted to the coward's only defense: leaning far forward, he grabbed the horse's neck, and with feet dangling, robe flying behind and the good half of the feathered halo still about his right ear, he roared through the Turkish camp, astonishing both the Poles and the Turks. Janko, endeavoring to keep close, shouted encouragement: "Hold on, Piotr! You're a hussar now."

And as the pair galloped, causing as much consternation among their own troops as among the enemy, Piotr caught a glimpse out of the corner of his eye of a special tent, austere on the outside, but with a small green medallion by the flap and a glimpse of richness inside, and although he looked the fool astride that horse, he was not a fool, and with almost superhuman effort he stopped the horse, wheeled it about, and brought it to a halt before the tent, where he hastily dismounted, and when Janko stood beside him, peering inside, their mouths gaped at the wonders which stood revealed.

The tragedy of this affair did not pertain to the adventures of Piotr and Janko, but to the exposed position in which their desertion left Count Lubonski, for now he had only Lukasz to support him, and no spare horses, for they had vanished with the deserters. Even this might have proved acceptable had not Lukasz suddenly noticed something which stunned and delighted him.

Lubonski's charge, always headed for the strongest concentration of enemy forces, had carried them into one of the rear areas where the Turks guarded the animals needed in their stupendous enterprise, and at first Lukasz saw only strings of camels chewing sideways as if there were no battle, and herds of buffalo brought along for their meat, but in an enclosed area he also saw some two hundred of the best Arabian horses, and as a fly-by-night Polish nobleman who had never owned more than five horses, he was mesmerized by the richness of his find, and without making a moral choice, he drifted away from Lubonski and started selecting the two dozen Arabians that he would claim as his booty when this day ended.

Cyprjan Lubonski, now alone and like any courageous warrior in the van of his troops, rode on for some minutes before he realized that no one supported him, and when he did discover his predicament he considered, briefly, wheeling about and seeking help, but he rejected this, for he supposed that others, perhaps even the winged hussars, would soon overtake him, and at a slowed pace he continued to move forward. As he did, he came upon a contingent of special troops who had remained loyal to Kara Mustafa in this moment of disaster, and when they saw the lone Polish horseman, erect and bewildered in his saddle and with only a short lance, they fell upon him with great fury.

One struck him in the throat, bringing blood to his mouth. Another cut at his head, and hot blood blinded his left eye. One spear entered at his right knee and penetrated upward to the hip, but still he maintained control of his horse, trying to escape. The Turks were relentless, and with cries of triumph they moved in close, hacking at him with their scimitars, slashing his arms and legs. Finally, one spahi leveled a great lance at Lubonski's gut, rode forward with speed and pierced him through, knocking him from his horse and breaking his neck bones.

Still the old man did not faint or die. With only the broken shaft of his lance he tried to fend off his attackers, but when he had to lower his bleeding right arm, foot soldiers stabbed him many times. Cyprjan Lubonski died as he would have wished, not in the saddle but almost, and facing till the end the enemies of Christianity.

The tremendous battle should have taken two days, but it ended in one. A French engineer, working for pay with the Turks, saw the general rout and shouted to his European friends: "This is a real *sauve qui peut,*" then led the desertion of the foreigners.

The people starving inside Vienna became aware at dusk that the Turkish threat was ended, and they began surging through the city gates, running toward the tethered buffalo, which they began to butcher on the spot.

General Lubomirski, too, left the walled city, seeking King Jan Sobieski, and when they met in the growing darkness, Lubomirski so thin he seemed like a shadow, the two men wept.

Kara Mustafa, resisting the efforts of his loyal troops to drag him safely from the battlefield, cried that he wanted to die here, but they insisted upon surrounding him, and saving his life so that he could later strangle himself with the green cord at some rear headquarters like Sofia or Edirne.

Prince Waldeck sought neither Sobieski nor Lorraine; he was appalled at the cruel fighting his Germans had been required to do that day, and as he sat exhausted in a captured Turkish tent he told his assistants: "Never speak to me of where the place of honor is, left flank, right flank. The place of honor is where the enemy hits hardest, and today it was the center."

The first thing Duke Charles did when it became apparent that the victory would be won this day was to dispatch two messengers to Linz with a reassuring message for the Austrian king: "Leopold, Sire, it is now safe to return to Vienna." The duke realized that it was important to have the king on hand, in person, lest the Pole Sobieski garner all the honors, with consequences that might prove embarrassing.

Lukasz spent that night guarding his twenty-four Arabians, and when a group of Polish soldiers passed he tried to commandeer some of them to help him protect his booty, but they ignored him. However, when some of the French deserters came by, he accosted them, and glad to find refuge for the night, they stayed with him.

In the tent with the green blazon Brat Piotr and young Janko were bedazzled, for the interior was rich beyond anything they had ever imagined, and the friar assured the boy: "Not even the treasury at Czestochowa, where the Virgin keeps her brocaded robes, has anything like this."

Closing the flap quickly to prevent others from seeing the shimmering wealth, they moved about in the gloom, noting the encrusted daggers richly bejeweled, the carpets woven with gold and silver threads, the open bags of thalers, the sumptuous fabrics. Suddenly there came a terrifying scream from Janko.

Poking into a small room within a room, he had come upon a fallen body from which had gushed an inordinate amount of blood, and when Piotr hurried to his side, he saw the corpse of an exceedingly beautiful young woman, one of the legendary Circassian slaves so highly prized by the Turks, and he told Janko: "I think her owner must have killed her himself. To keep her from being molested by the victors. She was probably a Christian, and we must say a prayer for her deliverance."

Janko could not pray. He was sickened by what he saw, for whoever had killed the beautiful girl had tried to chop off her head, but had failed; it now lay at such a grotesque angle from the torso that Janko turned away from the sight, and while Piotr prayed over the corpse of what had indeed been a Christian slave, Janko stepped outside the tent and vomited.

As he raised his head, two Polish soldiers came roistering down the passageway between the tents, and seeing Janko, asked him what was going on. Before the boy could respond, Piotr, sensing danger and the possible loss of this immensely valuable find, rushed out, made the sign of the cross, and cried: "King Jan Sobieski." This sudden combination of piety and political power confused the soldiers, and after a prolonged consultation, during which Piotr explained that the king personally had placed him there to protect the royal booty, the two soldiers decided to help him guard it.

"If you do that," Piotr assured them, "the king will reward you when we return to Krakow."

So the guard was mounted, and all during the night whenever intruders tried to ravage this tent, Piotr reared up before them, crossed himself once or twice, and said in a loud voice: "King Jan Sobieski."

Sometime after midnight Janko told Piotr: "I want to fix the dead lady," and he left the others, returning to the little room which had made him so violently sick only a few hours before, and tenderly he straightened out the exquisite fawn-colored dress and draped the voluminous cloth, which weighed almost nothing, so that folds covered the bloodstained areas. Then, his heart beating as if it might explode, he knelt down and placed his two hands tenderly about the girl's head, moving it slowly until it resumed its proper angle in relation to her torso. Then he sat in the darkness at her feet, as if she merited a guard of honor, and he was still there when dawn broke.

"Now!" Piotr cried when the sun was up. "Your job is to find Lukasz." And he sent the boy out to search the area, and in time Janko found his master and one Frenchman guarding the twenty-four Arabian horses. He started to take Lukasz aside to whisper about the treasure he and Piotr had found, but Lukasz said: "The man knows no Polish," and he listened with his mouth agape as the boy spoke.

Lukasz, sixty-two years old and a veteran of a dozen wars from which he had brought home almost nothing, sat down and studied his position. He already had in his possession, more or less securely, twenty-four of the best horses he had ever seen, and with them he could start a stud at Bukowo. It would require some careful managing to get the horses home, but with the help of Brat Piotr, Janko and the Frenchman this might be done.

But if what the boy said was true, and it was not improbable, then the more important booty might be that tent, and to transport it and its contents home would require wagons, so he told Janko: "Find me three carts. Get them to the tent immediately."

"How?"

"That's your task. But first, lead me to the tent."

Tying the horses one to the other, Lukasz and the Frenchman and Janko led them to where Piotr waited with his two soldiers, and when the friar heard approaching footsteps he rushed to the flap, threw it back just far enough for him to exit, and shouted: "King Jan Sobieski," but when he saw it was his brother-in-law Lukasz, he cried: "God has smiled upon us!"

Janko took the two soldiers and scouted the demolished camp area for wagons and the horses to draw them, but at first they found nothing. Then, turning a corner, they came upon a storage area that contained at least two thousand carts, and carefully selecting ones which looked as if they might survive a journey of several hundred miles, they commandeered a set of horses and drove back to the tent.

Lukasz was staggered by the sumptuousness of the tent, especially by the incredibly valuable fabric from which it was constructed—drab on the outside, flashing with precious metals and jewels on the inside, but he was also impressed by the luxury with which the owner had gone to battle: "What time did he have for fighting, Piotr, tell me that? A golden basin for washing his hands. A big tub of what looks like marble for bathing himself. Fifty cloths for drying. This basket of figs and dates and dried plums. The bags of Austrian money. And those little swords decorated with rubies. My God, Piotr, one of those swords . . ."

"The trick will be to get them home," the friar warned, and many times that day he had to make his sign of the cross, most reverently, and cry: "King Jan Sobieski."

Janko faced his own problem: he wanted to make sure that the slain girl was buried. The camp contained so many corpses that one more scarcely mattered, but when he saw how the townspeople of Vienna, free at last to move about, were vandalizing the bodies, he crept into the tent, carefully picked up the slave girl and carried her to a grassy bank, where with a stick and his two hands he dug a shallow grave. He collected some rocks, which he piled over it, and although he could find no wood with which to form a cross, he used his digging stick to draw a rude one in the dust, for he had convinced himself that she must have been a Christian. He then crossed himself and returned to the treasure-filled tent, where he suddenly burst into tears and remained unconsoled while Lukasz and Piotr plotted how they might get their three wagons home.

That day, the thirteenth, when Sobieski had expected to be in the midst of battle, he rode in triumph through the battered streets of Vienna, a flopping, misshapen man dressed in royal purple and wearing a large Russian-style fur shako that seemed on the point of falling off his pumpkinlike head. He was not accompanied by either the Duke of Lorraine or Prince Waldeck, for they were fearful that if they appeared on the streets before King Leopold had time to get back, they might be severely disciplined, and indeed the reception Sobieski received as the savior of Vienna did infuriate the emperor, who was already designing a grandiose monument which would proclaim him to have been the salvation of the city.

When Leopold finally arrived he expressed no gratitude to the Polish troops who had come so far to rescue his city, nor would he review the winged hussars whose whistling flight had started the rout of the Turkish armies. He rebuffed Sobieski, paid no tribute to General Lubomirski, whose fortitude during the bleak days had been heroic, and refused permission for the erection of any statue, ever, to Sobieski. He authorized two for himself, and perhaps he was sagacious in what he did, however ridiculous it might have seemed, for if the dead Count Lubonski had always envied Austria, siding with her in every contest between the nations, it could only have been because the Habsburgs gave the country excellent leadership. When the long welfare of Austria was considered, it was much more important that the Habsburg Leopold be remembered as the victor of Vienna rather than the intruder Sobieski, who would not be able to found a dynasty even in Poland.

Now the hard work began. Lukasz Bukowski, as he would be known after his exploits in this battle, had to transport three heavily loaded wagons and twenty-four Arabian horses—six stallions and eighteen mares—two hundred and eighty miles to his village. He would be threatened at every step of the way by voracious Poles who would seek to grab their share of the loot, and by the streams which had to be forded, and by the mountain passes to be negotiated. The returning army, which had not lost an excessive number of men thanks to the brilliant manner in which Sobieski had used it, contained about twenty-two thousand men, and each one was now a potential enemy of Lukasz Bukowski.

To help him in his difficult task he had his undependable brother-in-law, the peasant serf Janko, the French engineer and the two soldiers Brat Piotr had conscripted. They had arms, but so did everyone else.

The little expeditionary force left Austria in good style and completed half of Moravia with the loss of only one horse; two men from Lublin made off with it one midnight.

They were approaching the mountain pass at Cieszyn, which would take them into Poland, when disaster struck . . . twice. One evening just after sunset a small group of cavalrymen returning to the walled city of Zamosc dashed in among the Arabians and made off with five of the best, taking time to ensure that they had one stallion and four mares. Lukasz trembled with rage when he learned of it, and he wanted his five assistants to storm after the thieves and recover the horses, but Piotr simply stared at him and asked: "Brother, have you gone mad?"

That was all. Piotr would not allow anyone even to track the stolen horses, let alone try to recover them, for he knew the raiders were armed and bound by no law.

Piotr was undergoing curious changes as this foray into Austria ended. He had seen great battle; he had ridden as a hussar, although a rather dubious one; he had helped defeat an enemy of Jesus Christ; and he was half a year older. He realized the futility of much that mankind did, and he sometimes speculated on what honor meant when a man as stalwart as Count Lubonski could end the way he did, alone and pierced by sabers, and he grieved over the insulting way King Jan Sobieski had been treated by the city he saved. Then, too, although he had behaved in a more constrained manner than young Janko, he had been deeply shaken by the beheading of the Circassian slave, and as he rode north he reflected often on the strangeness that must have characterized her life. Where had she been born? Who captured her for what slave market? The man who bought her had obviously loved her deeply, for he had killed her—or tried to—rather than have her fall into the hands of others. No fabric in that tent had been more precious or more beautifully made than the simple gown she wore. Piotr knew nothing of women, but he supposed that had he lived an ordinary life, like his brother-in-law Lukasz, he might have loved a woman like that dead girl, and he thought kindly of young Janko for having buried her properly.

He was reflecting on these matters when the Frenchman raised a cry, and all the Lukasz party ran to where the trouble was. Too late! An army contingent on its way back to Warsaw, a rough lot, had boldly swept in and stolen an entire wagon, and were now so far in the distance that overtaking them was impossible. One-third of the treasure was gone, but when Lukasz, blinded by tears, surveyed what remained, he said several times: "Thank God, they didn't get the tent!" And Piotr began to realize that his brother-in-law valued the ornate tent more highly than any of its contents. The eighteen remaining Arabians first, then the tent, then the jeweled scimitars.

When they reached Krakow the two soldiers and the Frenchman

supposed that Brat Piotr was going to turn his cargo over to King Jan Sobieski, whose property he had proclaimed it so often to be, but it became quickly clear that Lukasz Bukowski intended marching right past the king's palace and on to his home village of Bukowo, and the men began to complain.

Lukasz faced this dangerous situation head-on, for he knew he required their help now more than ever, for as the army dispersed, the various contingents became in effect freebooters capable of almost anything. So he and Piotr assembled the three men: "We shall be taking the king's treasure to our village, where the dead count's family must get his share. Then the king gets his. Europe is in turmoil and so is Poland. You men know nothing of what is happening at your homes. Stay with us in Bukowo and we will give you a little piece of land and a cottage and local girls from whom to choose a wife. You can have a good life with us, and the new Count Lubonski will be just as fine a man as the old. You saw what he could do."

So these clever conspirators delivered the two wagons and the eighteen Arabians to Bukowo, where they formed the basis of the Bukowski wealth and prestige, for Lukasz was no longer a poor nobleman with only five horses. Now he had eighteen Arabians and the nine regulars that had hauled the wagons and the riders north, and he was at last a man to reckon with.

But as they approached Bukowo and saw looming on the horizon the towers of Castle Gorka, both Lukasz and Piotr were overcome with remorse over the fact that they had deserted their knight in battle and been the agency of his death. So as soon as the wagons were safely delivered to Lukasz's mansion, and the treasure safely stored in his rooms, he and Piotr selected one beautifully decorated small dagger—one six-hundredth of the total—and ceremoniously delivered it to Countess Halka Lubonska, with a heartbreaking account of how they had stood with her husband in the fatal moments when eighteen Turkish Janissaries had ambushed them, and of how the three had fought almost clear of their assailants when Lubonski's horse had stumbled, killing him instantly.

"We did manage to hold off his attackers," Lukasz said with tears in his eyes, "until we could recover his body, which we buried with honors on the battlefield. Piotr himself said the prayers." As a token of the affection in which they held the old count, they wanted Halka to have a memento of the fight: "Your husband captured it from a Turkish general just before he was slain."

But when the two heroes returned to Bukowo village Lukasz faced an accounting which stunned him, for Piotr forced his way, uninvited, into the room where the treasure was being kept, and when Lukasz demanded sternly: "What are you doing here?" the friar said: "I have come for God's share."

"What?"

"Brother Lukasz, you have stolen this treasure from King Jan. You have stolen it from the soldiers who helped us bring it here. And you have stolen it from the widow of Count Lubonski. But you cannot steal it from God, who has protected us in this venture."

Trembling, Lukasz asked: "What do you intend?"

"We are going to divide this treasure, half for God, half for you."

"And what are you going to do with God's share?"

"Give it as a votive to Czestochowa."

Lukasz broke into relieved laughter. "You must be insane. The monks there don't need this."

"You are right," Piotr agreed. "They don't need it, but the safety of their monastery does. Remember how it stood off the Swedes and saved Poland? It needs strengthening against the next siege." He saw that his avaricious brother-in-law was not impressed, so he said quietly, but with unmistakable conviction: "If you do not give God His share, He will strike you dead. And if He doesn't, I will."

Lukasz looked at his stupid brother-in-law, this scarecrow of a man, and saw that he meant what he was saying. "You would . . ."

"I will kill you, Lukasz, and publish to the world how you behaved in the battle."

So the two men sat in the room and divided the spoils, this to God, this to Lukasz, and from time to time the latter would protest his share and lift a piece from God's pile into his: "God doesn't need anything that rich," and Piotr allowed this, for as he said: "God never objects to a little stealing."

The treasure was delivered to Czestochowa by the two brothers, and the priests in charge of the shrine were astounded by what Brat Piotr had achieved, for like Lukasz, they had underestimated both his intelligence and his piety.

In the centuries to come, architects' diagrams of the great monastery in which the Black Madonna rested would show a set of formidable bastions protecting the compass points of the fortress, and each carried the name of the man who in reverence had paid for it: Lubomirski, Potocki, Czartoryski and, one of the most reverent, Bukowski.

So in the grand distribution of spoils from the legendary victory of the Poles over the Turks at Vienna, each participant received something. Poland received a spiritual boon of dubious and temporary value—respect among nations for her valor in defending Christianity—and two practical gifts of long-lasting value. Coffee had not been known in the country before, but when Sobieski's soldiers brought samples home it quickly became the national drink; and potatoes were welcomed not only as a tasty alternative to kasha but also as the staple food of the peasant. The Virgin of Czestochowa, who fought on the bosom of King Jan Sobieski, received a new defense system. Count Lubonski won a hero's death and a small bejeweled scimitar for his widow. Lukasz Bukowski came home with a name, eighteen Arabian horses and a room full of treasure. Brat Piotr was promoted to a position of some distinction in his order. The Frenchman and the two soldiers received wives, cottages and small plots of land in the village. And the peasant Janko, as always, received nothing, for it had been his duty to go where his owner directed and do as he was told. He did, of course, remember for the rest of his life the Circassian slave girl whom he had buried.

VI

THE GOLDEN FREEDOM

LEGEND IS REPLETE WITH INSTANCES OF HOW MARS, THE GOD of war, influences the history of nations, and never more instructively than in the case of Poland. Incessant war with Tatars, Teutons and Turks—it sometimes seemed as if Poland were the special province of Mars.

But Venus, the goddess of love, can also play a major role in the destiny of nations, and once more Poland is a good example. It was Jadwiga, the heavenly Hungarian, whose love for Jagiello, the barbarous Lithuanian, inspired him to develop the courage and the skill to win the Battle of Grunwald. The last two kings of the original Polish line, Zygmunt I, who ascended the throne in 1506, and his son Zygmunt II—who in 1529, at age nine, was elected king to rule jointly with his father—experienced unfortunate first marriages and magnificent second ones. The father had the great good luck in 1518 to import Bona Sforza of the famous Italian family; she brought with her flowers, music, painting, good table manners and a fierce intuition where the defense of royal prerogative was concerned. The son made an important dynastic marriage with the daughter of the Habsburg emperor, only to find that his child bride was a hopeless epileptic; when she died prematurely he fell under the spell of two powerful Radziwill brothers who, fortunately, had a sister Barbara of great beauty, and they maneuvered her so that in 1547, Zigmunt could not escape falling in love. Thus he found himself a charming, passionate, knowing assistant who helped him stand off the pressures of the other magnates, but not of the Radziwills.

King Jan Sobieski owed an enormous debt to his French divorcée, the conniving Marie-Louise, known to her admirers as Marysienka, who took him when he was merely another magnate and converted him into a magisterial king with a personal fortune of eighty million. But in no instance was the power of Venus greater than in 1757, when in two towns not far from Bukowo two of the ablest families Poland was to produce combined for the moment in daring enterprises which changed the destiny of the country.

At Pulawy, a lovely little town some distance to the north on the right bank of the Vistula, the tenacious Czartoryskis, who had never attained the political power to which their intelligence entitled them, were developing through study, travel, thoughtful analysis and exceptional instinct a vision of a greater Poland. It was to be led by a strong king who would found a dynasty in which elections dominated by alien powers would no longer be permitted. It would have a properly elected Seym exercising the same functions as the English Parliament; people living in towns would at last be entitled to vote and own land, and serfs owned by rich people would be set free.

The Czartoryski brothers had a sister Konstancja, who married a man of insignificant background, a Poniatowski, with whom she produced six handsome, clever and enterprising sons. One of them, Michal, would be placed in the priesthood, where with his uncles' goading he would become primate of all Poland. His younger brother, Stanislaw August, was earmarked for an even more exalted position, King of Poland, and groomed with meticulous care for the throne. The uncles felt that as king he could sponsor their reforms and coax Poland into the family of respectable nations. In brutally frank discussions with their young protégé they said: "If you do become king, your first job will be to produce sons who will inherit the crown after you, and their sons after them, so that never again shall we elect foreigners, who do us only damage." Since he was an ambitious young fellow, he listened.

The Czartoryskis were not powerful enough to achieve this exalted goal by themselves, but they had the support of an equally remarkable family, also late to acquire conspicuous power, the Zamoyskis, who had built with their own funds the walled city of Zamosc, so important in Polish history. From decade to decade power seemed to flow toward the Czartoryskis and Zamoyskis, and always the two great clans kept in tandem, striving mutually for a better, saner Poland. They were supported by many—the powerful Potockis and sometimes the intelligent branch of the Radziwills—but the leadership came from them.

They were opposed by many, too—the Lubomirskis, the Lubonskis and invariably the neanderthal Mniszechs of Dukla—but as the 1750s waned, it began to look as if the Czartoryskis with their splendid tier of Poniatowski nephews were destined to triumph, and Poland's chances for a modern state never looked brighter.

In this year of 1757 the studious Czartoryskis decided that if Stanislaw was ever to become king, he had better learn kingly manners, and they arranged for him to be sent to St. Petersburg to catch a taste of court life. He arrived there one snowy day, a twenty-five-year-old handsome diplomat with good manners and a command of French, German and Russian; within a week of his arrival he had attracted the serious attention of a headstrong, beautiful German noblewoman, Sophia Anhalt-Zerbst, who would be known to history under a more glamorous name, and within the second week he was in bed with her.

They enjoyed a passionate love affair: sleigh rides over frosted fields, with wolves howling in the forest; a duel in military barracks; concerts at court; and when spring came, endless bucolic picnics. Young Sophia obtained from this flattering attention a strengthening of her ego; Poniatowski gained notoriety as her Polish lover, a young man of enormous promise, and it was here in the Russian court that he was first publicly mentioned as a possibility for the Polish throne. "With Russian help," Sophia said several times, "you could become king."

"And how would I get Russian help?" he asked.

"Through me," she replied.

"You're a German," he said.

"I intend to be a Russian," she said with a grimness he had not observed when they were in bed.

The possibility that she might help him to the throne burgeoned spectacularly in 1762 when the tough old Empress of Russia, Elizabeth, the daughter of Peter the Great, died. This meant that by a series of improbable events, Sophia Anhalt-Zerbst's pitiful husband, Peter, became czar, in which position he proved himself as incompetent as he had been in bed. His brief rule of 185 days was so inept, so totally chaotic that Sophia had to take steps to protect her interests. Rallying about her a group of officers, many of whom had shared her favors, she proclaimed herself Empress and Autocrat of all the Russias; as Catherine the Great she would rule for thirty-four tumultuous years. Eight days after her self-coronation her husband was found murdered.

Young Poniatowski trembled with excitement as these events unfolded, and imagined himself Catherine's new consort—in Russia, husband of the czarina; in Poland, king—and he made plans along these lines. But Catherine had moved far beyond her interest in this rustic Pole; she was now so enamored of an authentic count, Grigorii Orlov, that poor Poniatowski became an embarrassment; he was hustled out of Russia without wife or crown.

However, his ambitious uncles in Pulawy did not intend to allow this unique opportunity for family advancement to slip through their fingers. Intimate friendship with a czarina, even though it had evaporated, was negotiable, and they sent emissaries to St. Petersburg outlining the advantages which would accrue to Russia if Catherine threw her considerable support to Stanislaw: "If he is not elected King of Poland, some German or Austrian will be, greatly to your loss. If you help him to the throne, you will have bought yourself a constant ally."

Catherine repaid her former lover in a most dramatic way. When the Saxon king died, last of a pathetic chain of bumblers, the magnates of historic and distinguished lineage like the Lubonskis and Radziwills refused to allow upstarts like the Czartoryskis and Zamoyskis to put one of their members on the throne; as so often before, the Polish magnates would much rather see a weak German or Frenchman or Portuguese as king than a strong Pole, and they made it clear that young Poniatowski was not acceptable. He and his family seemed to have lost their bold gamble.

But Catherine was unwilling to see her one-time favorite abused, especially when he might prove to be of service to her in the future, so after a disgracefully protracted interregnum, in which five nations pressed large sums of money upon the voting magnates, she told her advisers: "We cannot maintain a festering Poland on our doorstep." As a reward for Poniatowski's love, she dispatched a full Russian army to the place in Poland where the magnates were conducting their circus. Surrounding the voting area, the Russians let it be known that Catherine insisted upon the election of Poniatowski and that if any magnates refused to abide by her wishes, they would be shot. In this crude and even brutal manner, Poland elected the king who would prove to be her last.

So Stanislaw August ascended the throne thinking that Catherine had awarded it to him because she still loved him, and he told his uncles: "With her support we can achieve all we dreamed of. A bright new day has dawned for Poland."

He miscalculated dreadfully. Catherine, watching the debacle in Warsaw from her command post in St. Petersburg, chuckled with the knowledge that she had solved her Polish problem so easily: "Poniatowski will prove a miserable king. He has the heart of a poet. He proved that many times. But he's weak. He knows not his own mind. He will be despised by the senior magnates because he's so obviously *nouveau riche*. And in the end he will destroy the nation he loves."

"What will happen to Poland?" an adviser named Fyodor Kuprin asked.

"It will break into a thousand pieces," Catherine said. "And you are to be there when it happens, my dear Kuprin. To pick up our share of the pieces." When he bowed obediently, she added: "Go there quickly, Kuprin, and encourage it to fall apart."

It can be seen from this peculiar chain of events that Venus proved as adroit as Mars in altering the destiny of nations, but the scandalous affair with Catherine the Great represented only half the goddess' intervention, with the second episode the more interesting. The Czartoryski uncles recommended that in order to reinforce the concept of dynasty, with members of the family inheriting the throne perpetually, it would be prudent for King Stanislaw August to marry one of the Czartoryski girls, a somewhat heavy, gawky young woman his own age named Izabella. She was not from one of the historic families, nor was she what even her friends could call a beauty; what was worse, she was already spoken of in the Pulawy district as a young woman with a sharp mind of her own.

The uncles made the embarrassing mistake of spreading the rumor—"The king is going to marry Izabella"—and there was even speculation as to when the wedding was to be. But the king, having known the splendor of the Russian court and the excitement of a love affair with a czarina, could not imagine himself wedded to a drab like Izabella, and he rejected her: "Too plain. Too lacking in courtly graces." He chose instead a woman with a lineage more distinguished, a face more standard and a mind more vapid, with tragic consequences which would become apparent only thirty years later.

In the year 1771, after Catherine the Great had done everything possible to weaken Poland and prevent King Stanislaw August from instituting the reforms the Czartoryski-Zamoyski cabal proposed, a strategy in which she was supported by Prussia and Austria, it became apparent to Poland's neighbors and to Europe generally that the amorphous nation surrounded by great powers was no longer viable. Prussian diplomats sent messages to Russia: "As long as Poland is allowed to exist, she will form a danger spot between us," and Russian diplomats wrote to Austria: "The time approaches when we should settle the Polish question lest it become a bone of contention between us," and Austria sent a *démarche* to Prussia: "If you and Russia are prepared to settle the Polish question once and for all, we will join you."

What animosity did these three powers have toward Poland? There were religious differences—Poland was devoutly Roman Catholic; Russia was Orthodox Catholic, with all the bitterness which that implied; and Prussia was Lutheran—but even such fundamental contrasts had rarely caused open breaks. Economically the interests of the four nations interlocked and provided no cause for warfare or invasion. Dynastic struggles would be eliminated with the establishment of a Czartoryski-Poniatowski ruling family, and since each of the adjoining nations had conspicuously larger armies than Poland's, she posed no military threat.

But even so, the danger she represented to the others was real, and each of the great powers sensed it. Poland loved freedom; it was a restricted freedom, to be sure, and it applied only to the very rich, but nevertheless it was freedom. Specifically, every incident in Polish history testified to the nation's determination to avoid autocracy and dictatorship. King Jan Sobieski had been a noble king, no doubt about it, and he had saved Poland, but the nation did not want his inept son inheriting the throne. Nor did Poland want to spend its good money supporting a large army which might, like the armies of ancient Rome and modern Turkey, become the agents of repression.

Very rich people—in all nations—can be divided into two categories; those with brains and those without. Those with brains make a great effort to hold on to every penny they have while preaching to the general population that freedom and dignity and patriotism are possible only under their protection; in this way they elicit the support of the very people they hold in subjection. The magnates of Poland used this tactic brilliantly, preaching loudly: "The most insignificant member of the gentry with one horse and sword is the equal of the most powerful magnate in his castle," while at the same time depriving landless gentry of almost all rights and treating them with contempt. The peasant was kept happy by being assured that it was the magnate who defended Christianity. The townsman, who was allowed no rights whatever, was reminded: "It is the magnate who protects your freedom and your shop." And all were told repeatedly: "If the magnate is left free to accumulate his great wealth, you can be sure that some of it will sift down to you."

Rich people without brains, such as those in France who were heading blindly into a revolutionary debacle, saw no reason to defend themselves with words and built no philosophical justification for their position of privilege. "Let them eat cake" would soon be their response to demands for freedom. No Polish magnate, in public, ever uttered such inflammatory words, although Janusz Radziwill, father-in-law of Count Lubonski, did one day proclaim during a drinking bout at Castle Gorka: "The petty gentry, those who clutter the palaces of the magnates, jumping at every command, they're nothing but horse manure. And the peasants whom some of our fools worry about, they're the ugly little beetles that burrow in the dung." But such opinions were kept to the privacy of the great halls, where they were believed and acted upon.

And yet, despite all its cynicism, Poland was a democracy; it did know freedom, and its gentry were both more numerous than in any other nation of the time and more involved in the rights of government. It was the nation's misfortune to espouse these relative freedoms at the precise time when her three neighbors were developing the most powerful autocracies Europe had known for a thousand years. The Habsburgs in Austria, the Hohenzollerns in Prussia and the Romanoffs in Russia were perfecting techniques which would keep them in dictatorial power for more than a century, constantly enlarging their prerogatives at the expense of the burgher and the peasant. At the precise time when good-hearted King Stanislaw August was honestly attempting to improve the lot of his peasants, Catherine was depriving hers of what few privileges they had, and she would not stop until ninety-seven percent had been driven into the most abject serfdom. To Russia, which was enforcing such a cruel dictatorship, it was offensive for neighboring Poland to strive to build a workable democracy, for if the Polish worker attained even the slightest freedom, it might encourage the Russian to attempt the same, and that could not be tolerated. Poland must be crushed.

Adroitly Catherine enlisted Prussia and Austria in her plan, and together they devised a program in which the internal weaknesses of Poland could be cleverly used to destroy her, and in the winter of 1771 three foreign diplomats convened at the Granicki palace in Warsaw to ensure that destruction.

"Poland's grief," said the Prussian minister, addressing the committee that would decide how the country should be divided, "is that no other nation can take her seriously."

"Quite right," the Austrian ambassador agreed. "Three times now they've elected two different kings at the same time, and the ultimate winner had to be decided by warfare. Preposterous."

"One would think," said the Russian agent, Fyodor Kuprin, "that they would have learned from our history. One of the worst things that can happen to a nation is an interregnum. That fearful period when no one knows who is to be the next king."

"With every election Poland has that," the Prussian said. "We would never permit it in our country."

"I disagree with you, sir, on your basic point," the Austrian ambassador said reflectively. "Poland could have survived dual kings the way Rome survived two Popes. And could have weathered the interregnums. Other nations have. But no country could exist for long with the *liberum veto*. The day that started, Poland was doomed."

"No," said the Russian. "She could have survived even that monstrous wrong if she had defended herself." Turning to the German, he asked, "How big is Prussia? I mean in people?"

"Two and a half million."

"And you support an army of a hundred and forty thousand."

"We do. At great cost, but we do."

"And what is the population of Poland?"

"About twelve million," said the Austrian.

"But has an army of only eighteen thousand."

"In truth," said the Prussian, who knew about such matters, "it's an army of eleven thousand. They tell the king it's eighteen thousand

and he pays for eighteen thousand, but there is so much deception and falsification." The minister shook his head. "In Prussia they would all be shot."

"They do our work for us," the Austrian said, and then, without philosophical preparation of any kind, he asked bluntly: "Are we to partition the entire country, so that nothing remains . . ."

The German laughed, a thin-lipped, grudging laugh, more in contempt than jollity: "You know what my king once said of Poland? 'Let us eat it as we would an artichoke, leaf by leaf.' I no longer subscribe to that. Let us with one stroke finish this pitiful country, each of us taking his just share."

"No," said Fyodor Kuprin, who had a clever, devious mind. "Russia wants a truncated Poland to stand forever, no strength of her own and subservient to whatever we three decide, but existing." He paused, either to find the right French words to explain his position or to allow time for the others to appreciate the gravity of what he was about to say. "We feel it would be best to retain something called Poland as a permanent buffer between Russia and Germany, between Russia and Austria."

The German representative was a tall, thin man skilled in negotiation, Baron Ottokar von Eschl, whose family had served the German states for centuries and who had acquired from his hard-thinking ancestors a distinct vision of what eastern Europe should be. Only forty-one years old, he had many reasons to believe that Poland would never be viable, regardless of how much land the present partition allowed her. "There is no need in the future history of Europe for an entity called Poland. If we offer a partial solution now in 1771, we shall have to come back in 1781 and finish it, and if we offer another partial in 1781, we will be called back to our task in 1791. Let us erase the foolishness now, once and forever."

He found no support for this daring proposal: Kuprin adhered to his belief that eastern Europe needed Poland as a buffer, and to Von Eschl's surprise, the Austrian ambassador said that he would have moral qualms about eliminating a free nation entirely.

Von Eschl was sharp in his rejection of that timorous attitude: "Prussia is Lutheran. Russia is Orthodox. Only Austria is Roman Catholic, and I think, sir, that that colors your attitude."

"It certainly does!" the Austrian agreed with surprising enthusiasm. "Poland is a Christian country deserving of Christian rights."

"So you will carve off a small piece for Austria—" Von Eschl began, but Kuprin interrupted: "Not so small, either," and Von Eschl concluded: "You'll take some but not all?"

"I think that represents a significant moral difference," the Austrian said, but Von Eschl was still reluctant to concede that Prussia's proposal had failed: "Is it settled, then? Austria and Russia refuse to allow total elimination?"

However, when those two plenipotentiaries nodded, he acquiesced with a graciousness he did not often display: "So be it. A partial cutting away. But in years to come, please remember what I prophesied this day. We three will return to this table, and sooner than you imagine, to complete our task. Poland is doomed, but we allow her a short breathing space before the death rattle sets in." Amiably he rose, shook hands with his colleagues, and said brightly: "Let's bring out the maps."

This meeting, which would initiate the dismemberment of Poland, took place in the very heart of Warsaw, in the Granicki palace, and when the large oak table was cleared and Von Eschl had spread his carefully drawn map, the others gasped, for the Prussian cartographers had awarded themselves all of western Poland including Warsaw, with the huge expanses of the east going to Russia and an insultingly small section in the south to Austria. No entity called Poland remained. But before the others could point out that this total elimination was precisely what they had rejected, Von Eschl crumpled his map and threw it on the floor, saying with a cold smile: "Obviously, that's not what we want . . . at this time."

When Kuprin revealed Russia's map, both Von Eschl and the Austrian ambassador were visibly surprised, for the area to be absorbed by Russia was astonishingly small, not much larger than what would be given to Austria, but as the three men studied the map, Von Eschl began to appreciate the cleverness of Russia's proposal. "You win Poland's sympathy by taking little, but from your foothold, you intend to dominate all."

Kuprin smiled. He was fifty years old, a man who had served on many delicate missions and who knew that he could not hoodwink this clever Prussian. "To dominate what's left of Poland? Isn't that what we all aspire to?"

The three plotters interrupted their map study to discuss this interesting point, each disclosing what plans his nation had for the disciplining of Poland, but after a few exchanges Von Eschl said with some impatience: "Let us see the Austrian map," and when it was spread on the table, he saw that to a marked degree it resembled Russia's.

"Did you compare plans?" he asked, and when each denied any complicity, he shrugged and said: "Prussia is defeated. My map is useless, so we shall conform yours and yours."

For two days these brilliant men sat in the Polish palace and divided Poland, each with considerable knowledge of the terrains under debate, each with a clear view of what ought to be done. Von Eschl fought for all the lands that had ever been held by the Teutonic Knights back in the fourteenth century; Austria, for the rich farmlands east of Krakow; and Russia, for the low flatlands that would provide an easy entrance into Europe. If one granted that Poland had to be partitioned because of her inability to govern herself, the partition devised by those neighbors was not impractical. Each received what it felt it needed, and a central core as large as France remained for the Poles to play with in their game of Golden Freedom.

As the diplomats folded their maps, each duplicating the lines on the others, Von Eschl said: "Our major weapon in the years ahead, gentlemen, will be the phrase that the Poles themselves invented. The Golden Freedom. Everything we do to keep Poland off balance, everything we do to strangle it in preparation for the final partition, let us do in the name of Golden Freedom. We will become the champions of Poland's freedom. We will defend her rights against the revolutionaries. When we send our armies to Warsaw, and we will, let us always do so waving the flag of Golden Freedom."

"Why do you propose that?" the Austrian asked, for his nation had less intimate experience with day-to-day political maneuvering in Poland than either of the other two.

"We have in our hands a subtle control," Von Eschl explained. "If we cry to the world 'We are doing thus-and-so to protect Polish freedom,' we will be permitted great latitude. We must show ourselves always to be the champions of freedom. Freedom this, freedom that. Our hearts bleed for freedom."

"To what devious purpose?" the Austrian asked.

"No deviousness whatever," Von Eschl replied sanctimoniously. "We really shall protect Polish freedom—the freedom of a nation's few wealthy magnates to destroy the whole. The great families must remain free to terminate one Seym after another with the *liberum veto*. They must continue to own the serfs and control their labor. Let them continue to prevent townsmen from ever owning land. Let them remain free to oppose the king in any sensible move he tries to make. Gentlemen, by preserving such freedoms, we shall encourage Poland to strangle herself, and we shall divide the corpse without our marching battalions' ever firing a shot."

"Can we rely upon the magnates to commit such folly?" the Austrian asked, and the Russian Kuprin replied: "You can depend on them to do almost anything stupid that you can devise."

At this point the conspirators engaged in a negotiation so shocking that they felt compelled to lower their voices. In the heart of Warsaw, which stood at the heart of Poland, they discussed which Polish leader was in the secure pay of which foreign power, and the precise degree to which this patriot could be depended upon to betray his country.

"You Russians," said Von Eschl, "have the Mniszechs tucked away in your hunting bag. And the Granickis."

"We ought to have," Kuprin said, "considering how much money we spend on them every year. But you Germans do the same with your Pasek."

"And we get just as loyal service from him as you do from Mniszech."

"We have only two solid supporters," the Austrian ambassador confessed, "but they are sterling. Count Lubonski of Gorka, to whom we make no payments whatever, and the younger Prince Lubomirski, to whom we pay a great deal."

"Why do you give Lubonski nothing?" Von Eschl asked. "He's your strongest voice in the Seym."

"Lubonski visualizes himself as a patriot," the Austrian said. "He acts on our behalf because his family has always been strongly pro-Habsburg." Smiling, he added: "The traitor you win by conviction is always a better bargain than the one you hire."

"But sometimes," Von Eschl said, "the paid spy works harder. We pay Radziwill handsomely, and from him we get excellent results."

"Excuse me," Kuprin said. "It's Russia that pays Radziwill. And a great deal, too."

"You must mean another Radziwill," Von Eschl said. "I'm speaking of Janusz Radziwill, of Lithuania."

After briefly consulting his papers, Kuprin said: "So am I. Janusz Radziwill, whose daughter Anna is married to Austria's Count Lubonski."

"That Radziwill?" the Austrian ambassador cried, consulting his own list. "We're paying him . . . and rather generously, Janusz Radziwill, father-in-law of Count Laskarz Lubonski, of Gorka. He came to us himself with a most interesting proposal—came to me personally—and he's been in our pay ever since."

The three diplomats fell silent, conjuring up pictures of Janusz Radziwill, sixty-two years old, slight of build, clean-shaven in the French style, sharp-eyed, quick of speech and deft of manner, a nobleman at home in any court . . .

"Remember," Von Eschl said, "Radziwill spent two months in Paris three years ago, and in several close negotiations he seemed to us to favor France's position much more heartily than he did ours."

"You must also remember," Kuprin reminded the others, "that France and Turkey are always allies, and we know for a fact that Janusz Radziwill accepted large gifts from the Sultan for a favorable vote on the Ukraine settlement." He broke into a hearty laugh, for it appeared that this Radziwill, one of the more impecunious ones, had managed to place himself in the paid service of five different countries.

The men then proceeded to analyze which other magnates were receiving substantial funds from France, from Turkey and especially from Saxony, whose ruling family had occupied the Polish throne for more than sixty years and aspired to return. When the impressive list was completed, showing the apportionment of magnates among the competing countries, the Austrian ambassador asked: "Is there no one to be considered honest?" and Von Eschl replied: "The Czartoryskis and the Zamoyskis . . . they're the ones we must fear."

"They're new to the ranks of the magnates," Kuprin said. "Too young to have been corrupted."

"But they seem to side with Russia these days," Von Eschl complained.

"They're like honest Lubonski," Kuprin said. "He votes always for Austria because he believes in the Habsburgs . . . without pay. The Czartoryskis and the Zamoyskis vote for Russia because they honestly believe that only our Catherine, whom we are beginning to call Great, can save Poland."

"Does nobody vote for Poland?" the Austrian asked.

"Nobody with any sense," Von Eschl said. "Because if he had sense, he would know as we do that Poland is doomed."

"It might survive another ten years," Kuprin said. Then, pointing to the pile of maps, he asked: "Are those boundaries agreed upon?"

"For the time being," Von Eschl said, and the First Partition of Poland, the one of 1772, was under way.

Not everyone in what had once been Poland was unhappy with the new distribution of territory; some who were now within the Russian empire preferred their new masters and the Orthodox religion practiced there; some who found themselves in Prussia respected the stern order of that nation and its rigorous leadership; and a good many in southern Poland were finding it easy to accommodate to Austrian rule.

Most of the people living about the village of Bukowo actually preferred the new regime, and in this response they were led by their count, Laskarz Lubonski, who proclaimed: "At last we have reason in the saddle and the prospect of an easy canter through the remainder of this century." He personally supervised the transfer of land titles from Polish law to Austrian, and encouraged his people to learn German so that they could cooperate with the new government.

As a reward for his services in helping to bring this huge area of Poland under Habsburg rule, he was offered a position with the new government, but declined: "I can serve you better by staying here at home and seeing that things move easily." Nor would he accept any money payment for his leadership on behalf of the Habsburgs, but he was pleased when Vienna verified the title Rome had given him and added one of her own: he was now Baron Lubonski of the Austrian nobility, but he continued to use the older title of Count.

When he studied the new map of the area, he saw with interest that whereas Poland had previously contained about 300,000 square miles, making it much larger than any other European nation except Russia, it now contained only 200,000, but this proportion did not maintain where population was concerned, because there the drop was from 12,000,000 to a mere 6,500,000. The salient facts about the partition were that Russia gained a geographical entrance to the heart of Poland, Prussia picked up a few points of great strategic importance, while Austria, which had not sought partition in the first place, acquired a large helping of the best lands and the most productive people.

Lubonski's castle at Gorka stood at the extreme northern edge of the Austrian territories, so that his Bukowo holdings represented a kind of frontier fortress, and he was pleased to find that Zamosc was similarly situated: "We are the keys to northern safety. Vienna will have to treat us considerately." But he did not voice his sore disappointment over the fact that his major castle, Lubon, remained not in the new Austria but in the old Poland; the dividing line ran two miles south of it.

"It's a blessing!" dapper Janusz Radziwill cried when he visited his son-in-law. "Look, Lubonski, if you have your major estates in Austria, you possess great leverage in Vienna, and if you have three or four estates in what is still Poland, you can also operate in Warsaw. I would like that."

He asked Lubonski to spread a map of his estates, and when the large free-hand paper was before him he picked out almost avariciously the fourteen large holdings of the Lubonskis: "Gorka and Przemysl, here at the northern edge of Austria. That's good placement. Lubon and Ostroleka in old Poland, along with the three smaller ones. Two west of Torun in Prussia, and we can't predict what will happen to them. And the five really big ones in the Ukraine. They're the ones that will safeguard your income, Lubonski."

Always eager to know the most intimate details, Radziwill continued: "How many villages do you own, Lubonski?" and the count replied that he thought it must be about two hundred: "But many of them are in the Ukraine, and they don't amount to much."

"How many serfs?" Radziwill persisted, and Lubonski estimated that counting the rather substantial population of his six real towns, he might have as many as a hundred and thirty thousand: "But many of them are toothless infants at one end, toothless old people at the other."

Radziwill was pleased at the position in which his daughter and her husband found themselves. "You have castles in four countries, counting the little one that's now in Russia, so you can exercise a voice in four governments. I've always preferred doing that, because then you can protect yourself."

"No," Lubonski said, "I'm a man of one country. I wish it could be Poland, but that seems impossible. So I shall be quite content to be an Austrian."

"Lubonski . . ." his visitor began, but then he directed his attention to his pretty daughter. "Anna, I charge you. Do not let your husband sever his ties with Poland. Events of enormous importance will develop there, and a clever man— Look, with Russia, Prussia and Austria all fighting for the spoils, a clever man . . . he could accomplish almost anything."

"Where will you be during the squabbles?" Lubonski asked.

"Well, I have that little place in Warsaw and I keep the family manor in Lithuania, and I've been living in St. Petersburg a lot. What I wanted to learn from you, Lubonski, is whether I could use the castle at Lubon. It would keep me close to Austrian interests."

"You would always be welcome, Father," Anna said, and with sudden emotion she crossed the room to kiss her ebullient parent. He was returning home from Paris and Vienna, and this opportunity to see Anna and her two-year-old son, Roman, had proved enticing.

"I don't know what will happen to Poland," Radziwill said. "I'm sixty-three and I've had the feeling several times that I might die before it's settled."

"Don't say that!" his daughter protested. "Our family lives to old ages."

"I'm worried about those Czartoryskis and Zamoyskis . . . their radical views. You've heard what they're proposing next? To allow townspeople to vote, and own land, and even sit in the Seym."

"Would that be so wrong?" Anna asked.

Her father looked at her in astonishment. "The heart of the world is the honest landowner, like Lubonski here. He knows what's good for the nation, what's best for the peasants. The man who lives in town is a bloodsucker, or a sniveling priest, or a Jew. In the long history of the world, no decent idea ever came from a town. Anna, believe me, when townspeople in their dismal shops get the right to vote, the world as we treasured it is doomed."

"But can so few continue to keep power from so many?"

"That's what history is. The efforts of men like your uncles and Lubonski's sainted father, Onufry, to keep things as they are. Do you remember how he behaved when the king sent him to Torun to look into that wretched affair when the ten Protestant burghers refused to convert to Catholicism, even when the students at the Jesuit school begged them to do so? Onufry didn't waste words or pictures. As judge, he asked them twice 'Will you accept the true religion?' and when they said 'No,' you remember what he did? I was there at the time, fifteen years old, and saw it all. For the third time he asked 'Will you accept?' and when they said 'No' again, he gave one simple command: 'Chop off their heads.' And they chopped them off with me watching, and we had very little trouble with Protestants after that."

"I have always been ashamed of what my father did that day," Lubonski said. "It is the only blemish of its kind on our history, and it grieves me to think that my family was involved."

"It settled things," Radziwill said. "Some of my family were dissenters, you may remember, and I suspect that some of them are secret Masons now, but, by God, after those heads rolled in the sand at Torun we heard very little about it."

"Whose side will you support, Janusz, if things go poorly for Poland?" the count asked, and his father-in-law replied: "If they go poorly? My dear son, they're bound to go poorly, and I suppose, as always, you'll back Austria."

"I will. Because the Habsburgs bring order. And you?"

"I had some very interesting talks in Paris. You know, Lubonski, they're terrified of Prussia. They believe our interests are best served through Russia. I incline that way myself."

"But you just asked us for the Lubon castle, so that you could be near Austria."

"I certainly can't guess at this point how things are going to go."

"You just said you thought Russia."

Radziwill looked at his son-in-law in disbelief. "Lubonski, a game of vast dimension is being played, old France and new Russia opposed to old Austria and new Prussia. Who in this room is wise enough to predict how that game will go? If you're intelligent, Lubonski, you'll put in appearances at your castles in each of the countries. Listen, and test, and judge, and be prepared always to jump in the right direction."

"Is that what you're going to do, Janusz?"

"That's what I've always done. That's why I have two beautiful daughters married to men with castles, and two handsome sons married to women with castles." He laughed at this felicitous summary of his life, then scowled. "Anna, twice in our conversations today you sounded as if you were defending the rights of townspeople. What's got into this child, Lubonski?"

"She's been talking with this fellow Bukowski . . . at the manor house in the village."

"Command her to stop," Radziwill said, but the count reminded him: "You warned me at our wedding: 'Son, remember one thing. No man has ever been born brave enough to give orders to a Radziwill woman.'"

• • •

Lubonski had been correct in assuming that his wife's surprising inclination toward republicanism as opposed to the Golden Freedom of the magnates stemmed from her casual associations with Tytus Bukowski, who occupied the manor house in the village. She had met him occasionally at the castle when he came to discuss political matters with her husband, and during the next dozen years she had continued to move about the area with that intellectual and social restlessness which had always characterized the best Radziwills.

At such times she often asked Tytus what he thought of how Austria was governing her section of Poland: "Doesn't it seem to you that they treat us as merely another remote colony?" And he would remind her that although he did live in the Austrian sector, subject to its laws, his more important responsibility was to serve in the Warsaw Seym as protector of Count Lubonski's interests in free Poland. It was an insane system, made worse by the fact that Lubonski worked diligently to bring all of remaining Poland under Austrian rule. Poles conspired to destroy Poland.

In recent years things had not gone well with the Bukowski family; indeed, things had never gone particularly well. The substantial fortune which one ancestor had filched from the Vienna expedition against the Turks had been quickly dissipated in the stables for the Arabian horses that accompanied the fortune and in dowries for daughters whose young husbands quickly squandered them. In only one decade after the Battle of Vienna, the Bukowskis had already fallen back to what they had always been: very poor gentry with an honorable history and some horses. Now, in 1785, their manor house needed major repairs and their fields improvements, but the stolid owners went their careless ways, with conditions along the Vistula continuing much as they had done for the past seven centuries.

There was, however, one notable change. Tytus Bukowski, for reasons which not even he could have explained, had begun to speculate on the nature of Polish history, especially as it compared with the development of surrounding countries about which he heard many accounts, and he saw that each of Poland's neighbors had strong central governments, and regular taxation, and armies which increased in size, while Poland did not.

More specifically, when he watched the Seym, of which he was now an important member, he realized that almost everything he was ordered to do by Count Lubonski, Prince Lubomirski and the powerful Granickis and Mniszechs was helpful only to them and extremely hurtful to the nation as a whole. Tytus was not a revolutionary, but he did believe that the time had come when people who lived in towns—some of the best people in Poland, he judged—must be given the right to own land, to vote, and even to take their rightful place in the legislative bodies. Jews he was willing to exclude because they denied Christ and the primacy of Rome, which any good Pole subscribed to, and he was not yet certain what he thought about freedom for peasants, since he owned three villages, and to give peasants rights might mean financial loss, but even in this case he was beginning to see that a prospering society required much more freedom for serfs than Poland now allowed.

One spring morning Countess Lubonska asked him about these matters: "Tytus, when you meet with the Seym in Warsaw, what will be your feeling about greater freedom for the townspeople?"

When the countess first asked such questions he had temporized, for he suspected she might be a spy sent to test him on behalf of the magnates, but with the passage of time he found that she was much like himself: a person trying to visualize a new Poland, and he grew to trust her. "I think the time has come, Countess, when we must have a union of strong men in the towns with strong men in the countryside."

"You've heard what my father says? 'Townsmen are like horse piss. Smelly, noisy and good for absolutely nothing.'"

"That was the old view, Countess. But if Poland wants to protect itself . . ."

"Would you allow your daughter to marry a townsman?"

"I'm nobility, Countess. Poor but noble. My family has always married with its own kind."

"So you have the same opinion as my father?"

"I do not." He leaned against a stone fence that separated the castle grounds from those of the village, and said very carefully, choosing each word for its exact meaning: "Countess, you must prepare your husband, and his friends, for what I believe the Seym is going to do if it is ever allowed to meet again."

"It will do what it's told," Anna Radziwill said, as if she were one of her fighting uncles.

"I think . . . that such days . . . are ended." As soon as he uttered these portentous words, both he and Anna appreciated their profound significance, for they constituted a revolutionary challenge and she wanted to know its dimensions. Perching herself upon the fence, she asked bluntly: "And what will your Seym attempt to do?"

"Have you listened to your magnates, Countess? Have you just listened to what they say when they meet in your castle?"

"They talk a lot of bombast, but I think all men do." She laughed, a beautiful, free-spirited woman approaching fifty, amused by the contradictions of Polish life, whether in the Austrian segment or the free, and with a finger that contained two rings she pointed at Tytus and said: "Right now, Bukowski, you're talking bombast, aren't you?"

"I must respectfully contradict you, Countess. I am the voice of the future, not of bombast."

"Tell me about the future, Tytus."

"Let's take three magnates. In old Poland, where I work. One takes his orders from Prussia because it's growing. One takes his orders from Russia because it's big. And one listens to Austria because it's well governed."

"It's always been that way," Countess Lubonska said, smiling. "You speak as if there were something unusual."

"There is. At a time when Poland needs everyone joined together in a great effort, the first magnate despises everyone in the town—the burghers, the shopkeepers, the Jews, the priests, the artisans. They're all cut off—permanently—from Polish life." With both hands waving in the air, he made broad exclusionary gestures. "The second magnate hates peasants—will grant them no freedoms at all, not even land."

"Who's left for the third magnate to despise?" the countess asked.

Bringing his hands back to his chest, he tapped himself with his fingertips: "Me. The little nobleman with few horses . . . few villages . . . few peasants."

"Oh, they don't despise you, Bukowski. I'm sure my husband doesn't despise you. If he did, he wouldn't use you as his voice in the Seym, would he?"

"He uses and despises," Bukowski said, dropping his voice on the last word as if to end that line of argument.

"Yes, there are degrees," she conceded. Flicking her dress so that its folds fell attractively over the stones on which she sat, she said: "My father . . . well, you're right about him. He despises all your three groups. He sees Poland as the fief of about sixty families—the only ones in his opinion who count." She brought her hands to her face to hide the broad smile; then she dropped them to look bewitchingly at her husband's factotum. "Tytus, when I was about eighteen my father took me aside, sat me in a chair, and showed me a small sheet of paper on which he had written seven names. I can see them yet, in order, starting with Radziwill. Then: Lubomirski, Lubonski, Potocki, Ossolinski, Mniszech, Granicki. They were the families from which I must select my husband, for in his opinion no others existed."

"How were they numbered?" Tytus asked.

"A combination of ancient power and modern wealth. The Granickis were newcomers, but they were damned rich. The Mniszechs were of Czech derivation but they were damned powerful. Ossolinski and Lubonski were both ancient and rich, and Lubomirski, of course, was best of all."

"Then why did he place the Radziwills first?"

"Because we are first."

"Weren't the Czartoryskis and Zamoyskis already rather rich and powerful?"

"Father had them on his list—over to one side, with a note above them: 'If things go poorly.'"

"Meaning?"

"That if I couldn't catch a Lubomirski or one of the rich Radziwills . . . You know, of course, that our branch of the Radziwills . . . we had damned little. That's why my father has had to be so . . ." She thought for a long time as to how best she might characterize her conniving parent, and she smiled as she visualized him in his long overcoat darting here and there as his probing nose smelled out possibilities. No appropriate word came, and in the end she said in a kind of defeat: "That's why Father has had to be so flexible."

"Was it easy, catching a Lubonski?"

"From the moment I saw Laskarz, and I think that from the moment he saw me . . . because I was not ugly when I was young . . ." She kicked at the stone wall with the heel of her left boot, then asked in real anxiety: "Oh, Tytus, what's going to happen to Poland?"

One day in 1786 they carried this question to the count, who laughed at their fears, citing an old truism: "Anarchy is the salvation of Poland. We have always thrived on chaos."

"But if we can't defend ourselves?" his wife asked.

"Our strategy is to be so obviously weak that no neighbor will feel it necessary to attack us."

"It seems to me," Bukowski said, "that in 1772 our neighbors attacked us rather severely. They stole half our citizens."

"That was a readjustment," Lubonski argued, "and I think you'll agree we're better off now than we were then."

"People are beginning to take seriously the proposals of the Czartoryskis," Tytus warned, and the countess jumped to his support: "Yes, I've heard much good said about their plans."

Now the count dropped his easy rebuttals, for he had heard even some of his associates discussing seriously the proposed reforms, and he simply could not fathom why a man in his senses would even listen to them, let alone accord them attention. "I want you to hear, one by one, the incredible things they're suggesting. First, abolition of the *liberum veto,* the agency with which we protect our rights. Second, the Seym to serve for two years instead of six weeks, and God knows what would happen then. Third, townsmen to have the vote. Fourth, banishing landless gentry from the Seym on the grounds that they vote always for the magnates who pay their bills. Fifth, an end to private armies like ours and the installation of a strong central army, which would threaten our freedoms. Sixth, peasants to be given their own land, at our expense. Seventh, additional power to the king, who would soon dictate to the magnates. Eighth, hereditary king rather than free election by the magnates and the gentry."

As he listed these demands, his voice grew more and more grave, until at last it was a mournful rumble, as if he were lamenting the passage of an era, and he looked soberly at his listeners to impress upon them the revolutionary nature of these proposals. But then he brightened. "This was before your time in the Seym, Tytus, but when the patriots awakened to what was happening, we sprang to action. Lubomirski, myself, Granicki, Mniszech . . . there were other good men too, but we led the way in defense of the motherland."

"What did you do?" the countess asked.

"We proposed our own series of bills, the ones that would preserve freedom. First, the king to be elected, preferably from among foreign nominees, by us magnates. That would protect us from dictators and hereditary domination. Second, continuance forever of the *liberum veto,* which is the protection of the few against the pressure of the many. Third, the ancient right of any magnate to renounce allegiance to the king, if the king persists in error. Fourth, land ownership and office occupancy reserved exclusively for magnates and their supportive gentry. Fifth, landowners' control of peasants to be continued and strengthened."

"Who won?" the countess asked.

"For the moment, reason prevailed and we won. But revolutionaries like Czartoryski refuse to surrender, and if we ever have a Seym again, you can be sure they'll be back with their radical reforms."

In 1788, to everyone's astonishment, the Seym was permitted to open a session which many predicted would be a turning point in Polish history, and they were right, because the sober, well-educated men who met this time were deeply aware of the fact that the salvation of their country depended upon the decisions they were about to make, and they approached their task with prayers and a proper gravity.

Historically, Seyms were supposed to meet only in alternate years and then for just six weeks. This one lasted four glorious and rewarding years that saw one after another of the restrictive old privileges swept away: the *liberum veto* was abolished, meaning that henceforth Poland's parliament would operate like those of other nations, on the majority principle; townsmen were allowed to own land; the more onerous impositions on the peasants were removed, but of course serfdom was continued, since even reformers could not visualize Poland without it; the Catholic church was deprived of its vast land holdings but was justly compensated; and most important of all, the town businessmen were invited into the halls of government.

On 3 May 1791 a new constitution evolved out of this revolutionary four-year Seym. It was recognized as the best in Europe and the equal of what had recently been promulgated in America; philosophers hailed it as an architect's drawing for a modern nation. With one gigantic leap, Poland left the Middle Ages and catapulted herself into the front rank of governments. The Czartoryskis had defeated the Lubonskis.

But in Prussia and Russia the new plan activated alarms of terror, for the rulers of those autocracies properly evaluated it as a mortal blow to their dictatorships. In Berlin the King of Prussia summoned Baron von Eschl and stormed: "Your partition in 1772 was supposed to have forestalled such nonsense. If this new constitution is allowed to function even one year, it will spread havoc in the German states. Everyone will be demanding similar freedoms."

"We must start a war to disrupt things," Von Eschl proposed.

"That we'll do, but first you get yourself to Warsaw and repair the damage your leniency allowed."

"Are you willing, Sire, to support me if we erase Poland altogether this time?"

"Wipe it out."

"Even if Austria refuses to come along?"

"We're in a better position if she doesn't. I want you to occupy everything we need—Warsaw . . . Krakow . . . Lublin . . . all the way to Brest-Litovsk."

"Russia and Austria might combine against us."

"That's a risk we must take. But Poland is to be eliminated. It has no excuse for existence." And with this harsh directive, Von Eschl made his way to Warsaw.

In Moscow the Empress Catherine was even more disturbed, and at a session with her councillors she enunciated, without being aware that she was doing so, the policy that would henceforth govern Russian-Polish relations: "Whenever the people of Poland enjoy a better life than those in Russia, we are in mortal danger. At such times Poland must be held down." After the meeting she held private counsel with Fyodor Kuprin: "My dearest little adviser, things have gone sadly wrong in Poland. Hurry there and make corrections."

"Total dismemberment this time?"

The question posed the most severe difficulties for Catherine, and she attacked it circuitously: "I intended that my old friend Poniatowski should vacillate, for I knew he was weak. But I never expected him to be this weak. When those men laid that new constitution before him, he should have shot them all. Since he refused to do the job, we'll have to do it for him."

"Then you do mean total dismemberment?"

"I wish I did, my treasured little guide, but we must keep one consideration always in the forefront. We are not strong enough right now to engage in war with Prussia. Sadly, we must temporize. And what we must prevent more than anything else is a situation in which Prussia grabs most of Poland and sits on our front doorstep, growling to be let in to Moscow."

"What must I do?"

"Cut Poland to pieces. Great slices off here and there. But leave a central core, because for the present we need it as protection against Prussia."

"You hand me a most difficult assignment. Kill, but not quite."

She rose and kissed him, this strange little man who had served the Romanoffs so dutifully, chopping off heads for Empress Anna, ripping out tongues for Empress Elizabeth, subjugating Cossacks for Czar Peter, and now destroying nations for Catherine. "We do one thing at a time, little friend, but I assure you that before the years pass, you and I will finish with Poland forever. Now off to Warsaw."

While the two diplomats were moving into position for their assault on the Polish nation, pamphleteers in both Berlin and St. Petersburg started sending out messages to all the courts and journals of opinion in Europe, one from autocratic Russia sounding the tone that would prevail:

> It is sickening to all who love freedom to learn in dispatches from Warsaw how the freedom which the people of Poland once enjoyed is being trampled underfoot by the same kind of revolutionary excess which has darkened France with the blood of its best citizens. In Poland the rights of man have long been protected by an admirable system known as the Golden Freedom, under which kings and peasants alike, knights and townsmen, equally enjoyed the benefits of benign rule, and under which the precepts of Christianity were observed.

> Now the historic Golden Freedom which made Poland a leader among nations is being swept away. Radical reforms strike at the very heart of a free nation, threatening to make it a nation of slaves, and this the liberty-loving nations of the world must not permit. It is the duty of all to rise up and warn the tyrants of Warsaw that the family of nations will not allow this desecration to go forward. It is our duty to halt it and to restore to a strong and beautiful nation the freedom it has always enjoyed.

When Baron von Eschl reached Warsaw he became the leading spokesman for all who were defending Poland's freedom, and he rallied around him magnates like old Janusz Radziwill, now eighty-three but still persuasive in argument, and the Paseks, who carried weight with the distant magnates who maintained their own armies. Von Eschl's heart bled, almost literally many Poles thought, for the good of Poland, and on his extensive trips into the eastern portion of the truncated country he noted the location of all castles and the means by which they attempted to defend themselves.

He was a brilliant, forceful debater, and whenever he met with magnates, for he refused to deal with anyone of lower position, he stressed one overwhelming fact: "Gentlemen, always bear in mind what happened in the aftermath of 1772. The Prussian government did not confiscate a single estate owned by your brothers. No Polish magnate lost a square of land to us. But what happened where Russia took over? You know better than I. Kleofas Granicki, a true friend of Russia's through the years, two of his largest estates near Vitebsk ripped from him and given to Russian generals who now call themselves noblemen . . . at Granicki's expense. If you side with Russia, all your precious freedoms will be lost. If you side with Prussia, your estates and your freedoms alike will be protected."

In this manner Von Eschl won over to his side many of the leaders of Poland, but Fyodor Kuprin was not idle. He met often with his Prussian counterpart, compared notes with him, and smiled when Poles suggested to them that their countries might soon be at war with each other over how to divide Poland. That some kind of further partition threatened, everyone acknowledged, but the form it might take, with Austria not participating, was uncertain.

In Tytus Bukowski's mind several pressing questions arose. "Why," he asked patriots like himself, "do we allow these two foreigners to parade about Warsaw plotting the war that might destroy us?" To this he received no sensible answer, except that King Stanislaw August was too weak to discipline them. Tytus also asked: "How will this nation continue to exist if even more territory is stolen from us?" The answer to this was a universal "We'll get by somehow." His third question was more persistent, and he directed it to almost every Pole he met: "What can you and I do to prevent the tragedy that looms?"

He even asked this question of Countess Lubonska during one of his visits home when the Seym was not in session, and she responded gloomily: "I'm terribly afraid a great theft is under way, Tytus. Let's discuss this with the count."

When Tytus presented Lubonski with his evidences of Prussian and Russian duplicity, he found the count reconciled to whatever evil might happen. "Your Seym has gone too far too fast. Any one of the reforms might have been palatable. I have nothing against townsmen owning a little land. But taken altogether . . . it's inescapable that Russia should react unfavorably."

"But you've always sided with Austria," the countess said. "If what Tytus reports is true, there could be a partition between Prussia and Russia alone. Poland could even disappear."

"Now that's ridiculous," the count said. "Poland will always be needed where it is. If it didn't already exist, Russia and Prussia would have to invent it."

"As a Habsburg man," Tytus asked, "are you happy to see Austria excluded?"

"Such things are of little moment, Tytus. Poland will always be there, and if a few miles are chopped off for Prussia and a few for Russia, no great harm is done."

He ordered refreshments and then heard that his son and Bukowski's were tending horses at the stables, and he sent for them, and when the young men appeared—Roman Lubonski, aged twenty-two, tall and extremely shy, and Feliks Bukowski, a year younger and a slender, healthy fellow—he asked them to join the discussion, for he was eager to have his son learn the workings of Polish politics, and this meant that young Bukowski must, too, for in a sense, well-adjusted Feliks was a planned companion for the self-consciously diffident Roman.

"Tytus has been telling us that things looked dark at Warsaw. Explain to the boys." And Tytus gave a brief summary of the ominous slide which he and his friends in the Seym had witnessed, concluding: "It looks like war."

"Should it come," the count said, "we have no part in it . . . no interest in it. Do you understand that, young men?"

"I should think we'd all be very interested," Feliks said.

"I agree," his father said hastily, without considering what effect such opposition to the count's opinion might have. To his relief, Lubonski did not lose his temper: "All we're discussing is a little trimming of the fat. Russia wants a few miles that Poland doesn't need. Prussia wants her share. And there's no more to it. To start a war over such inconsequentials would be folly. Don't you agree, Tytus?" And this time Tytus nodded.

But when Bukowski and his son were back at their own home the discussion was quite different, for Tytus said: "I'm a Pole, Feliks, and so are you. What happens up there concerns me and I hope to God it concerns you . . . always."

"The count says we're Austrians now. But the countess tells me on the sly: 'You're Polish and always will be.' I asked her if she was Polish too, and she said: 'Forever.'"

Tytus led his son to a window, and as if to lend emphasis to what he was about to say, pointed toward the river: "As long as the Vistula flows, it waters the soul of Poland."

"What can be done if Russia and Prussia attack?" the young man asked.

"Nothing," his father said in a frank admission of the futility that oppressed him. "But the time will come, Feliks, and be attentive to recognize it when it does come, when patriots will arise and sweep Austrians out of our lands, and Germans out of the west, and Russians out of the east."

"Are you sure?" Feliks asked.

"As sure as a man can be. Poland will be Poland again."

"When?"

Tytus slumped in a chair and pondered that most difficult of questions, and when he had weighed all possibilities, he felt that he must speak honestly with his son: "I fear there will be another great retreat, and then perhaps another. It's even possible that our lovely neighbors will gobble us up completely. For a time. Maybe even for a long time, because they're powerful and we're weak." He rose from his chair, and again he and his son looked down at the great river which had always commanded so much of their family's life, and his voice was strong as he said: "As long as the Vistula flows, Poland will be Poland."

Two weeks later a most fatuous debate erupted in the Seym, proving that even a patriot like Tytus Bukowski could behave like a child when some matter of truly Polish concern had to be handled. This one involved horses.

A deputy with experience in both Russia and Prussia addressed the parliament with some vigor:

> "I have visited five foreign nations in my day, and being of a military cast of mind, I have invariably studied the armies of the lands I've been in. And I want to assure you gentlemen that we in Poland are committing a terrible mistake, which must be corrected if this nation is to preserve its existence.

> "Listen to these figures. In the Prussian army the foot soldiers who fight the battles and take the land constitute sixty-eight

percent; cavalry who dash about for show, thirty-two percent. [Here there was a wild upheaval as cavalry officers in the Seym demanded a retraction, which the speaker was forced to give.] I meant no aspersion on our proudest branch of service.

"In Russia the proportion is sixty-nine to thirty-one in favor of the foot soldier. In Austria, which has always been partial to cavalry and losing important battles, something closer to sixty to forty. [Here again there was rioting and a demand for another apology, this time not only to the cavalry but to Austrian heroism.] In France, so far as we can ascertain during the revolution, seventy to thirty, and in England, where they fight with heroic courage to win their battles, which they seem always to do, seventy-two infantry to twenty-eight cavalry.

"And what is the proportion in Poland? Foot soldiers who do the fighting, twenty-nine percent; and cavalry who—[Cries of *Careful. Retract. Retract.* And a general disturbance in which Delegate Tytus Bukowski, who loved horses, challenged the speaker to a duel. Unperturbed, the critic continued.] So we must ask ourselves whether in our new army, which the Seym has so courageously authorized, we intend to have the infantry fighting or the cavalry parading."

The debate, so forthrightly presented, fell quite out of hand, and it was the general opinion of all the delegates, save those who had traveled abroad or studied military history, that no Polish gentleman worthy of that distinguished name would go into battle on foot; it had never been done and it never would be. Orators reminded the Seym of the gallant Polish knights who had ridden into battle at Grunwald in 1410 and of the even more dashing, daring winged cavalry who had defeated the Turks in Vienna in 1683.

"The honor of Poland has always ridden astride some great horse, and it always will," cried a Lubomirski appointee, and Tytus Bukowski, speaking for Count Lubonski, said: "The Polish infantry is a rabble of peasants armed with clubs, and no gentleman would have anything to do with it." At the conclusion of a fiery oration defending the horse, he renewed his challenge to the delegate who had opened this subject, but the acting chairman, a clergyman, prevailed upon him to withdraw it, which he did in a phrase which circulated approvingly throughout the castles of Poland: "As long as Poland has a well-trained cavalry, she will remain free, and if the day ever comes when she relies on the foot soldier, she will march to her surrender."

But when in the summer of 1792 a group of magnates begged Czarina Catherine to send in an army to protect their Golden Freedom from the nihilistic reforms proposed by the Seym, and when the ardent defenders of the horse saw that the Russians came with few cavalry and many foot soldiers, who occupied and held on to territory, even men like Tytus Bukowski had to confess their error, for the new-style Russian army was irresistible. And when shortly thereafter Prussian armies of comparable composition began to win great victories in the west, Polish reformers saw that their cause was doomed; by the beginning of 1793 all was lost.

Tytus did not hurry back to the sanctuary in Austrian Poland to which he was entitled. Circumstances had converted him into a patriot; with like-minded friends, he had given Poland one of the finest constitutions in the world, one of the best forms of government, guaranteeing freedom for all within a workable future, and he could not stand idly by and see this noble vision perish.

Count Lubonski, aware, from things his wife had disclosed, that Tytus might stay with the reformers, saw to it that the two young men—his son and Bukowski's—did not bolt off to join him; he kept them tight within his castle and was careful to censor what news reached them. They were fine lads, he thought, better educated by far than he had been at their age, and although Roman did seem rather slow at times and reticent to state his opinions, when he did so they proved surprisingly sound. He had his mother's brilliance of insight, his father's tremendous stability, and the count could visualize him performing well at the court in Vienna. "He could easily become the governor general of Polish Austria," Lubonski told his wife, "and I like the way in which young Bukowski helps him in this developing period. We must look out for young Feliks and assist him when we can, because I'm afraid his father is irresponsible."

Tytus Bukowski was proving his lack of stability rather spectacularly. Gathering about him eighteen members of the Seym, he organized a cavalry unit and placed it at the disposal of the general defending Warsaw, but the Polish effort was so chaotic, compared to the steady pressure of the Prussians from the west and the Russians from the east, that not even the valiant efforts of the patriots accomplished anything, and a general debacle ensued.

The army was defeated. The traitorous magnates who had invited Catherine in to devastate the country she had once given to her bedfellow Poniatowski fled the country. Prussia and Russia occupied the entire nation, or as much of it as they cared to. And tall, austere Baron von Eschl and short, clever Fyodor Kuprin met as before to draw the new lines.

When Bukowski saw the map he choked with despair. This was not the nibbling away of which Count Lubonski had spoken so cavalierly; this was wholesale, callous, brutal dismembering of a great and Christian state. For no moral cause whatever, except a desire to crush a liberal nation whose leaders were charting new courses to freedom, Prussia and Russia had castrated Poland in defense of their Golden Freedom. All the good works of the years from 1772 to 1793 were scorned and discarded by outsiders before the insiders had a chance to make them function. It was one of the crudest destructions in history and one of the least warranted, the more remarkable in that no foreign state protested. A sovereign nation was raped while the trading nations loaded their ships and spoke of freedom of the seas, and religious leaders spoke of moral responsibility and justice.

The more Bukowski studied the map, the deeper became his despair. Russia was taking a vast expanse from Vitebsk to Minsk, and Prussia was doing the same, from Poznan almost to the gates of Warsaw. "My God!" Tytus cried when he saw the pitiful remnant, an elongated strip with no logical basis for existence. "How do they expect us to live?" And he was so outraged that he stormed into the quarters where his improvised cavalry unit was berthed and persuaded a group of men like himself to make protest against this crime. They mounted their horses, brandished what informal weapons they could find, and started out at a slow canter to attack the Granicki palace, where the Prussian and Russian diplomats were meeting to refine the boundaries of the lands they were stealing. As they reached Senatorska, the wide avenue leading to the royal castle and the palace, they spurred their horses to a faster pace, but when the time came to leave Senatorska and head for the palace, a detachment of Prussian guards intercepted them, the German commander shouting: "Halt! It is forbidden!"

Bukowski, in the lead, refused to slow his horse; instead he spurred it, so that he and the horse leaped right past the Germans, with others following.

At this moment Baron von Eschl, hearing the disturbance, came to the front door of the palace, and comprehending immediately what was happening, he screamed in his high, quavering voice: "Fire on them!" This brought the Prussian guards to their senses, and kneeling in the snow, they took aim and brought Bukowski down, four bullets through his back. When his horse stumbled, other horses fell, and there was a general massacre.

When the fusillade stopped, all Polish horsemen having been gunned down, Von Eschl walked over to the commander and said: "You'd better shoot them all again. We need no heroes." And as he watched, the officer went to each of the prostrate bodies and put a bullet through the temple. No such *coup de grâce* was needed for Tytus Bukowski, for he had died at the first volley.

As soon as Count Lubonski learned that his factotum had been killed in the disturbances attendant upon the Second Partition, he dispatched a messenger to the manor house at Bukowo with a request that the inheritor of the Bukowski estate report to him at once.

Selecting one of the Arabian horses for which the manor was noted—and which kept it plagued by nagging debts—Feliks rode slowly south to Castle Gorka, where he presented himself to the count, who in this time of sorrow would be his adviser and in a sense his commander, for he still practically owned the Bukowskis and their estate.

"Feliks!" the count cried as he hurried forward to greet the young man. "I am saddened by news which has reached me from the north."

As he and his wife feared, the young man had already heard of the shooting and was distraught, and Countess Lubonska tried to console him: "Your father died a hero, and in a heroic cause." The count, hearing these dubious words, wanted to growl "He died a damned fool opposing the inevitable," but he kept his silence, for he liked young Bukowski and wanted him to adjust quickly to his loss.

Feliks was twenty-two years old, and unlike most of the Bukowskis, was slight of build, blond-haired and generally attractive. He had a quick mind, a rarity in his rather stodgy family, and a keen interest in all things Polish, but in this tragic time he was obviously confused and not yet aware that he was now in charge of his family's fortunes.

"Sit down, Feliks, while I call my son," said the count as he poured the young man a glass of Hungarian wine. Lubonski, fifty-six years

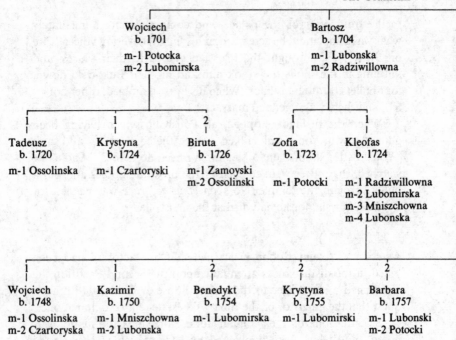

The Granickis

old and at the height of his considerable powers, fumbled among his papers while they were waiting, and when the tall young nobleman appeared, Lubonski cried: "Good! Now we can study the map."

"Why?" Roman asked.

"Because there's a new world to be mastered . . . a new Poland to be understood . . . and because it's needful that each of you find a wife."

Roman blushed. "I have not thought about a wife," he said, and his father snapped: "Young men rarely do . . . at least not in the right way." Then, unfurling a map, he added: "This time, though, we shall all go about it in the right way," and with the young men standing behind him he began to piece out the grand tour they would be starting three days from then. But before he indicated the first stop he looked up at them, smiled warmly, and said: "What we shall be doing, the three of us, is searching out the beautiful young ladies of Poland." Then he added almost sadly: "But of course, with the new changes, most of them won't be in Poland any longer."

With long, delicate fingers, almost the hallmark of his family, he indicated a castle only a short distance to the north: "We'll go first to

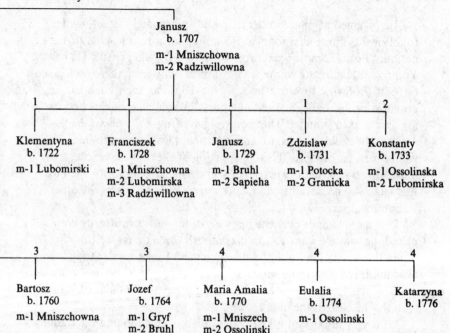

of Radzyn Castle

Janusz
b. 1707

m-1 Mniszchowna
m-2 Radziwillowna

1	1	1	1	2
Klementyna b. 1722 m-1 Lubomirski	Franciszek b. 1728 m-1 Mniszchowna m-2 Lubomirska m-3 Radziwillowna	Janusz b. 1729 m-1 Bruhl m-2 Sapieha	Zdzislaw b. 1731 m-1 Potocka m-2 Granicka	Konstanty b. 1733 m-1 Ossolinska m-2 Lubomirska

3	3	4	4	4
Bartosz b. 1760 m-1 Mniszchowna	Jozef b. 1764 m-1 Gryf m-2 Bruhl	Maria Amalia b. 1770 m-1 Mniszech m-2 Ossolinski	Eulalia b. 1774 m-1 Ossolinski	Katarzyna b. 1776

Baranow of the Leszczynskis, one of our noblest families, then up to that troublesome spot, Pulawy, to see what the great Czartoryskis plan to do with what's left of Poland, then over to my favorite city, Zamosc of the equally powerful Zamoyskis."

Here he lifted his hand from the map and asked the two young men to sit down while he addressed them. "It is important, it is crucially important, that you see and understand these two new families—Czartoryski, Zamoyski. They represent dangerous forces in our society against which you must protect both yourselves and the nation. They're charming people. They're able. And I am the first to admit that they've done some good things. But they represent a terrible threat to the welfare of Poland, and they must be opposed in whatever they attempt."

"Isn't King Stanislaw August a Czartoryski?" Roman asked.

"He is. His mother was sister to the two powerful brothers, so it's a family to be reckoned with."

"Then why do you dislike them?" his son asked.

"Because they represent all that's revolutionary . . . all that might destroy what's left of the Golden Freedom that made Poland great."

He resumed his place at the map and summoned the young men to follow his finger as it roamed the immense eastern reaches of the nation: "From Zamosc we'll drop down to Granicki's castle. He has a daughter Katarzyna whom we must meet. And from there we'll go far east of Lwow to our estates in the Ukraine, then back to the grandest of all, Lancut, where the great Lubomirska has invited us for six weeks in summer. That you will never forget. I believe she has a niece who seeks a husband, and if either of you can catch her, you will be fortunate indeed. Then the portion of the tour that excites me most, down to Dukla, where the Mniszechs have a glorious child, Elzbieta, who needs a husband, and over to Wisnicz, where the other Lubomirskis have two daughters awaiting us."

Placing his hands over the map as if the tour were already completed, he said: "I want you to accomplish three things on this trip. Study the new Poland to estimate its chances for survival. Study the old families to determine which of them will survive. And find yourselves wives. The countess has something to say on that matter," and with this he cleared the desk for her.

"It is very important for each of you young men to find the right wife." Looking boldly at her son, she said: "Roman, you must find a girl who will help you at the court in Vienna. With the right wife, anything will be possible. Money you do not need, but as my father will assure you, for he's never had any, it is never harmful. Feliks, you have a name and a fortune to make . . . an estate to build. Your family has reached a point where the next marriage will be crucial, and you must consider the matter most carefully."

As she spoke of the importance in Polish life of making the right alliances, by which she meant important to the magnates who in her opinion constituted Polish life, she asked one of her servants to fetch the pasted-together sheets of paper she had been preparing in her room, and when the first of these was spread upon the table she instructed the young men: "One of your most important stops will be at the Granicki castle. A newish family of no historic distinction, but extremely wealthy because of the brilliant marriages the three brothers made in the last generation and the even more excellent ones Kleofas has made during my lifetime. The man is exceptional, and you can learn from him the intricacies of the marriage game." Almost proudly she pointed to his remarkable record, commenting upon each element as she went.

"You must notice carefully several things, Roman and Feliks. The

Granickis have always lived on dangerous land in dangerous times. Their men have gone repeatedly to battle, so that many of them have had two wives or husbands, with the mighty Kleofas wearing out his fourth right now. His first wife was my aunt, Grazyna. The second important fact is that these Granickis always had large families, and in building a dynasty, a girl baby is just as valuable as a boy. Look at some of the excellent alliances those girls achieved. But the fact that supersedes all others, and the one my father drilled into me— You know, my brothers and sisters made quite wonderful marriages, but even back in the old days when our Barbara married King Zygmunt the Second, the Radziwills have always married well.

"What was I saying? Oh, yes . . . the vital fact is that the Granickis in their many marriages have done well. Look at that parade of distinguished names. Ossolinski of the millions. Czartoryski of the power. And always here and there a Lubomirski to lend wealth and elegance. You know, even when one of the children strayed a little to marry into an upstart family like the German Bruhls, they chose one with new power and new money."

The countess looked admiringly at the impeccable record of the Granickis, and with a kind of reverence, as if she were blessing them, placed her fingertips on the genealogy and said: "To a family like this, it doesn't really matter what happens to Poland. It's the family that continues." Then, as if to share with them the pragmatic lore which had kept the Radziwills strong through all vicissitudes, she told them: "Even when you've found your first wife, keep watching, because the probabilities are that one of these days you'll need a second, and in our family it was often the second marriage that proved significant." With that powerful Radziwill forefinger, which in centuries past had so often spotted the good alliance, she pointed to the tenth child of Kleofas: "Katarzyna Granicka. She'll be seventeen this year and well worth anybody's attention."

Even if the two young men had not participated, this tour would have been an important one for Count Lubonski, who had not visited his Ukrainian estates for several years and realized that decisions of some importance were required there, since, under the new partition, one of them now lay in Russian territory. So when he rode out of his castle grounds it was at the head of a considerable equipage: thirty servants, six wagons, two carriages, forty-four horses, two tents, a complete kitchen, a barber, a traveling laundry and seven members of the Lubonski private army.

But his major interest on the trip was not his various estates, which would be visited in turn, but the introduction of his two young men into the niceties and the history of Polish life, and as the group approached each new stop he summarized the importance of the family they were about to meet. When the beautiful low towers of Baranow became visible he said: "This is an excellent place to start, for it reminds us of what love can achieve. From this little castle Maria Leszczynska left to become Queen of France . . . Louis XV . . . He had a score of mistresses at the same time, some of them quite famous, I think, and we Poles didn't approve. But he always came back to Leszczynska, for she was the woman he loved and the mother of his children. Imagine, from this small place."

For some days they kept toward the riverbank as it traveled north to the lovely village of Pulawy, and on the evening when they were close enough to see the roofs of the various palaces, the count decided to pitch camp in an area from which they could look down at this formidable spot where so many decisions affecting Poland were being made: "These next days could prove the most instructive on our tour. The Czartoryskis are relentlessly striving to make their family the hereditary kings of Poland—through the line of Poniatowski—and each year their efforts grow bolder. You'll find no girls here available for marriage. They're being saved for alliances which can strengthen their claim to the crown."

When servants brought the evening meal the count laughed and told the young men: "Perhaps I'm jealous of those brilliant plotters down there. You must judge for yourselves. Listen to them. They're a clever lot, and although I despise their revolutionary politics, I have to admire the way they've magnified the power of their family. We could all learn from them."

Pulawy was a revelation to the young men, for its great mansions were filled with scintillating members of the family, Czartoryskis and Poniatowskis alike, and it seemed to the visitors that all of them had learned degrees from Padua, or Geneva, or Oxford, or the Sorbonne. They were a dazzling lot, and one entire wing of the palace in which the travelers stayed was filled with artists and musicians from Italy and France. The library in this palace alone contained thousands of books, and Feliks learned that in a large building nearby this influential family conducted what amounted to an informal university.

But the young women of the Czartoryski family overawed both Roman and Feliks, who found many to be attractive but all to be of an intellectual level that was forbidding, and young Roman said one night to his father: "They educate the daughters just as they do the sons," and Lubonski said: "A dangerous process. Never marry a Czartoryska."

At Pulawy discussion turned sooner or later to politics, and on the last evening one of the Czartoryski men confronted Count Lubonski with a sheet of paper and a question which lay at the heart of Polish life: "Laskarz, tell me one thing. Why do you and your old-style friends still seek to revive the *liberum veto*?"

"Because the major problem of any free government is how to protect the responsible few from the pressures of the irresponsible many. Plato knew that. So did Cicero."

"But look at these figures. Under King Augustus II, eighteen Seyms met, but only eight were allowed to enact any legislation."

"I'm sure the other ten deserved to die."

"Under King Augustus III, fourteen Seyms met and only one was allowed to function. Your people halted all the rest."

"And saved Poland from a flood of bad laws."

"In later years nine tried to meet, and all nine were broken up by your men. How can a nation govern itself under such circumstances?"

"We used the veto to prevent wrong decisions, Czartoryski, and our courage saved men like you from your own folly."

"Are you . . . you handful of magnates . . . are you wise enough to make all the rules for Poland?"

"We are, because only we know the value of freedom."

"Lubonski, talk sense! Your creatures may have broken up a Seym now and then to protect your freedom, not Poland's, but what about those that were broken up with the money of some foreign power, to protect their interests, not Poland's?"

"That never happened."

Coldly, bitterly, the facts were set forth: "In 1730 France paid the Bishop of Smolen sixty thousand livres to negate all the good work that the Seym had accomplished. A few years later Russia paid Granicki forty thousand rubles to do the same for it. Not long ago Prussia paid Pasek fifteen thousand ducats. And God knows how many thalers Austria paid her agents in the Seym to render it futile."

Lubonski ignored this terrible indictment, turning instead to one of his and Poland's strongest points: "Look at it this way, Czartoryski. What is the biggest complaint we have right now from our neighbors? That their peasants are flooding into Poland, depriving their owners of valuable property. And why do they come to us like an unending plague of locusts? Because they know that Poland is free and their homelands are not."

From Pulawy—memories of which lingered even as they headed eastward, for in this little village men discussed matters which gnawed at the soul—the travelers proceeded to two of the major Lubonski estates, the mansion at Ostroleka and the name-castle at Lubon, where only agricultural business was conducted. But when they resumed their journey, there was much exciting talk about the approaching halt at the walled town of Zamosc, where the other radical family centered, the noble Zamoyskis. "I do not like them," the count said as they approached the town, "but at various crises in our history some Zamoyski has stepped forward to save the nation, so we owe them respect. Of course," he added sardonically, "when the danger passed we found that somehow or other the Zamoyski in question had acquired seven more villages and two thousand more serfs. They own most of this part of Poland."

They stayed eight days with this powerful clan, one much ruder than the cultivated Czartoryskis, but just as Feliks was about to relegate the Zamoyskis to a lower stratum, he learned that two men in the family had been rectors of Italian universities. "They're different," the count explained when they were alone one night. "I would never want you to marry a Zamoyska . . . far too unreliable . . . new ideas all the time. But I think that in a time of crisis like this, they should be listened to." Laughing, he added: "What I'm advising is, listen to the men but don't look at the women."

His counsel was unneeded. There were three Zamoyski girls of marriageable age, but it was painfully obvious that each considered the two young men much too bucolic and uninformed, and what conversation there was centered on the recent partition and was carried on by the elders.

"Do you think there will be another?" Lubonski asked.

"Without question," Zamoyski said. "Prussia and Russia are rapacious, so for us it's merely a question of 'Will they bring Austria in this time?' and if they do, 'Where will we wind up, in Austria or Russia?'"

"What is your thinking?"

"Well, I know you're an Austrian at heart, Lubonski, and I know you feel that Habsburg rule is on the whole congenial, but I tend to think that the future lies with Russia. More excitement . . . more energy . . . more . . . You'll laugh at this, but I see Russia as having more poetry and music, and any nation which has them in abundance lasts a long time. I hear damned little singing in Austria."

Lubonski could not accept this: "Wait! Wait! Vienna has the greatest musicians in the world—the operas, the symphonies, the little groups."

"Paid music, yes," Zamoyski agreed, "but the music of the soul, no."

"If there is another partition, where do you suppose Zamosc . . . your castles and mine, that is, where will they land?"

"I . . . think . . ." He paused a long time, obviously not happy with his alternatives. "I . . . suppose . . . Austria."

"I'm relieved," Lubonski said, and the wise old man who had charted the Zamoyski course for many years nodded: "I was sure you would be. Will you be moving to Vienna?"

"I doubt it," Lubonski said. "You know they've made me a baron there. But I'm sure my son here will in due course. As soon as he's married . . . after he finds his bride, that is."

In the awkward pause Zamoyski made no attempt to propose one of his granddaughters, for he knew that none would want to ally herself with these reactionary rural men, and two days later the visitors departed, with Roman and Feliks expressing no regrets.

They were excited by the prospects of the next stop, for there they would meet for the first time the mighty Granicki family, including the legendary Kleofas of the four wives and ten children. As they approached the huge, stumpy, thick-walled Radzyn Castle that had withstood half a dozen sieges, Lubonski told them: "You saw my wife's chart. I have nothing to add except that Kleofas has always been strongly in the pay of the Russians, so let's not speak well of Austria."

But minutes after they met him, huge, bulky, head-shaven Kleofas growled from beneath his monstrous mustaches: "By God, Lubonski, I wish my estates had fallen into Austrian hands rather than Russian. You were damned lucky. Catherine has stolen two of my best lands from me and I'm worried sick trying to protect my other two from her rapacity."

The young men liked Kleofas from the moment they saw him; he was an epitome of the old Poland, for he dressed in the style of the 1400s in long, sweeping cloaks covered with embroidery and chains, and he talked in that style too, with many round oaths and recollections of battle. Six of his children were sharing the castle with him at the moment, each in his or her own suite of gusty rooms adorned with wall hangings from the past, and one of them was the unmarried daughter Katarzyna, seventeen and charming in her various costumes, also in the style of the 1400s. She was the daughter of Kleofas' fourth wife, a Luḃonska who had the grace which characterized that family and who had passed it along to Katarzyna.

As soon as Feliks saw her he was enchanted, for she was a delightful young woman, her hair in long braids, her smile unusually free and warm. There was, however, a distraction: in the castle at this moment was a young member of the Lubomirski family who had been studying in both Geneva and Paris. He was a year older than Roman, which made him two years older than Feliks and infinitely older in charm and learning. His name was Ryszard—Richard he called himself when traveling abroad—and it was obvious that since he had come to court the charming Katarzyna, Feliks was not going to stand much chance.

But there was a major reversal during the first dinner at the castle, an affair for thirty, because young Lubomirski appeared in the French style of dress rather than the old Polish style favored by the Granickis, and from the moment he entered the large room with the glistening mirrors there was trouble. Kleofas roared: "Who brings women's clothes into this castle?" and young Ryszard affected not to have heard the gibe. This amused Kleofas, and he bellowed to his wife: "Jadwiga, we have an extra woman for dinner tonight." At this the various wives snickered behind fists held to their mouths, whereupon Kleofas shouted: "Let's see what she wears underneath!" And before his wife could halt him, the huge man had leaped from his chair, grabbed Lubomirski from behind, and started shouting for his sons to help him strip away the offensive French clothing.

Two of the Granickis joined their father, who despite the screams of his women ripped away Lubomirski's jacket and shirt and trousers, leaving him in the skimpiest possible covering. "Now," roared the head of the Granickis, "we have a true Pole at our table."

Feliks could not keep from staring at his rival and wondering what he would do in such a situation, and he was astonished at how Lubomirski handled it. Flushed, but showing no anger whatever, he resumed his seat at the big table, reached for his glass of wine and half-toasted each of his aggressors, then sat back waiting to be served. Old Kleofas watched the performance, again leaped from his chair, ripped down a drapery from one of the windows, threw it about the bare shoulders of his guest and embraced him, kissing him on both cheeks. "By God, you're a true Lubomirski. You'll get the first cut of lamb." And onto the young man's plate he heaped a large slab of meat.

Now for the first time Katarzyna spoke, sharply, directly at her father: "I have told Ryszard that I am like the women of the Czartoryski and Zamoyski families. I will marry no man who continues to dress in the old style."

"Then you will never get married," Kleofas roared, "for I will have no son in this castle who wears French clothing!"

"Good!" Katarzyna snapped, her eyes blazing. "You can fit me for a nun tomorrow."

Kleofas reached over, slapped a chunk of lamb on her plate and growled: "Eat it and keep quiet." Then he burst into loud laughter, pointing with his carving knife at young Lubomirski: "By God, he looks like a Roman senator, but at least he don't look French."

By the time the visit ended, Feliks Bukowski was hopelessly in love with Katarzyna, and the thought of leaving her in the castle with a competitor as attractive as Lubomirski depressed him, but when the Lubonski caravan was preparing to start eastward toward the endless expanse of the Ukraine, Kleofas surprised everyone by announcing that he was moving his own visit forward and would be traveling with them as far as Lwow. To the delight of Feliks, he said also that Katarzyna would go with him, for it was time that she saw her eastern estates.

It was an extraordinary convocation that Kleofas Granicki put together for his regal passage: a hundred and sixty horsemen, tents galore, kitchens, a priest, a tutor for his daughter, and enough servants to staff a major hotel. A German traveler seeing the departure from Radzyn wrote: "Granicki has two hundred and thirteen separate stalls for his horses and eleven books. He knows the name of every horse but the title of no book."

What made the procession memorable was that on his visits to his Ukrainian estates—through marriage he had acquired half a dozen in the other parts of Poland—Kleofas dressed all his horsemen in Tatar costume, and when they reached the great plains he liked to have them charge, shouting and firing their guns and yelling battle cries as they approached any village. It made a brave show, and often he rode along at the forefront, his flowing mustaches making him look like a Tatar on a rampage. Of course, he had terrified the villagers in the old days, and in several cases peasants had fired at him to protect their homes, thinking the invasion a real one. Now members of his entourage slipped ahead to warn the people on the lonely wastelands: "Kleofas Granicki is riding again. Lots of noise but no real bullets." And when he galloped up to the edges of the villages, women were apt to be waiting there with their children to see the crazy magnate.

The last snow of winter covered the ground when the Granicki-Lubonski expedition approached the ancient town of Przemysl, and once the San River was crossed, Feliks was astounded by what this amazing Kleofas did next: from the direction of Lwow came a camel corps of sixty riders, also in Tatar uniform, also firing their guns and shouting battle cries. They were the honor guard of the Granickis for entry into the Ukraine, and during the entire visit this corps would ride with them.

The slow, wonder-filled journey from Przemysl to Lwow, over the flat and glistening snow, was one that Feliks would never forget; Katarzyna rode with him sometimes, she on her camel, he on his, and occasionally they would urge their stately beasts well ahead of the others. He would imagine himself and this delectable girl riding forever into the vast distances, and when Katarzyna asked: "Would you be willing to wear modern clothes?" he interpreted it almost as a proposal of marriage.

The land was almost as enchanting as the girl, an incredible sweep of emptiness dotted here and there with small villages populated by Ukrainian peasants who existed at the starvation level, then some town of modest size filled with intruding Polish merchants and Jews and Roman Catholic priests who scarcely dared move out among the Orthodox Ukrainians. When the snow was fresh, it was like crystal, stretching forever; and when it started to melt, it revealed a million little flowers, gold and blue and red and bright yellow, all smiling at the sun and the passers-by.

Six of the camel riders formed a small band featuring Ukrainian balalaikas, and at unexpected times the men broke into songs that all the riders knew, and then the steppes echoed with joyousness, and once on such an occasion a village loomed on the horizon, and the camel corps broke into a run, with Katarzyna and Feliks amongst them, and they dashed at the village, singing and firing their rifles and wheeling the camels about as if it were some great attack, and the peasant mothers told their children: "Here comes that wild Pole again," and the entire village joined the singing.

In Lwow, Granicki owned a small palace which he used only for such visits—once every two or three years—and for six starry days the young people said their goodbyes; Roman told his father that Katarzyna was about the most attractive girl he had ever met, and when Lubonski relayed this important information to Granicki, the old man growled: "I'm afraid Lubomirski with the French clothes has settled the matter." The count did not inform his son of the probable engagement, and he certainly did not tell Feliks, who was not to be considered a competitor, but he did say to Kleofas: "Things often change, old friend, as you and I know."

"Damned well we know," Kleofas roared. "Remember when I wooed your cousin? She snapped: 'An old man who's already had three wives! Begone!' So I smashed her across the ear and said: 'No one tells me *begone*,' and we had quite a tussle. She was going to shoot me with my own gun, but in the end she considered the matter and accepted me, and we've had three beautiful daughters."

"The loveliest is Katarzyna."

"No," Granicki corrected. "The loveliest is always the one who hasn't found her husband yet. For the moment that's Katarzyna."

"Will she marry the Lubomirski boy?"

"I think so."

"I think maybe not," Lubonski said.

They parted in the morning, Granicki heading northward toward his estates now in Russian hands, Lubonski eastward toward his vast Ukrainian holdings. And when the camel corps started to move through the flower-strewn steppes, with the horsemen and the wagons trailing behind, and old Kleofas and his lovely daughter bringing up the rear, Feliks felt his heart bursting. For the first time in his life he was truly in love.

Without the Tatar charges on little villages, and without the camels to divert attention, the Lubonski group assumed a more honest character, and now Feliks and Roman could study the real Ukraine, that mysterious land which lay between Russia and Poland, between Europe and Asia, and the more deeply the caravan penetrated this always-conquered but forever-unconquered land, the more the young men respected it. They were therefore in a receptive mind when they approached at last the village of Polz, the largest of the Lubonski holdings in this area.

It was a low, flat village of small cottages built of many inexpensive substances—wood, wattles, mud—and it contained only one building of significance, a small wooden church with two onion-bulb steeples painted in red and blue. The nearby manor house was also of one story, but its walls were stone and it rambled over a substantial area in order to provide rooms for the many attendants who accompanied the count on his periodic visits. The factotum, a man named Grabski, occupied a cottage indistinguishable from the others except for the multitude of flowers which surrounded it whenever the snow melted.

The young men were fortunate to see Polz at this time of year, for Easter was at hand, not the real one, which had come while they were en route, but the more lively Orthodox one when the Ukrainian year reached a climax and young women wore their best while their mothers counted eggs to ensure that there would be enough for the decorating geniuses produced by every village, none better than in Polz. After the long snows of winter, and the shivering nights, the earth seemed to burst with new life at Easter, as if the year were just beginning, as it had in the old calendar.

Roman and Feliks had an interesting introduction to the daily life of Polz, for on the morning of their second day in the village a young Ukrainian of about their own age appeared at the manor house to seek a beneficence from the count, who sat himself in a chair with high back and heavy arms, waiting to hear the applicant's plea: "Your Excellence, I want to get married."

"Have you found yourself a good girl?"

"Yes, Benedykta, the cobbler's daughter."

"Does she wish to marry you?"

"She does, Excellence, and she hopes we may have the cottage that old Natasha occupied."

"Is Natasha dead?"

"No, her mind left her . . . during the coldest part of the winter."

"It may come back."

"It might, Excellence, but now she lives with my aunt and her cottage is empty. I beseech Your Excellence . . ."

"Let me think about this. Return in four days."

It was clear to Feliks that Count Lubonski had decided within the first moments to allow the young man to marry Benedykta, and to have the cottage too, and the postponement was to remind the young fellow and his intended bride that the power in such matters rested with the count, who owned them, and their cottages, and their land.

On the third morning Feliks was walking in the village when he saw the young suitor and they spoke, the Ukrainian using a few words of Polish, Feliks a few of Ukrainian, and the former asked: "Would you honor me by greeting my intended?" and Feliks nodded, whereupon he was led to a cottage near the edge of the village, its walls decorated gaily and its flowerbeds in bloom.

"Benedykta!" the young man called, and a most beautiful girl came to the low door, slim of waist, her flaxen hair in braids, a wide smile on her wide face, and a kind of poetic lilt in how she held her head and moved her hands. Feliks thought he had never before seen a girl who so completely expressed the joy of being young and beautiful and in love, and he noticed especially that her quilted dress, tight at the waist and flaring out below her knees, was made not of ordinary cloth but of a felted material ornamented with tufts sewn to it, and bright bits of metal, and many areas of singing color.

How fortunate this fellow is, Feliks said to himself as he stepped forward to meet Benedykta, but to his surprise the Ukrainian showed disappointment and asked the girl: "Where's Benedykta?" and before she could reply he told Feliks: "This is her sister, Nadzha," and Feliks felt an actual burden lift from his heart.

He spent much of his time during the next days at this cottage, so beautiful on the outside, so meager and forbidding inside. It had no floor other than the earth, no furniture other than the table, the beds and the three-legged stools, and nothing much else except the bench on which the father mended shoes, yet it was one of the wealthier homes in the village and a center of much delight, for the two daughters were beautiful, and there was bread, and the parents had their teeth.

Nadzha accompanied her sister to the manor house on the morning when the latter and her young man stood before Count Lubonski to receive his formal permission to marry and occupy the old woman's cottage, and the sisters formed a lovely pair, Benedykta slightly taller, Nadzha slightly more animated. "I am sure this is to be a good marriage," the count said as he left his big chair to kiss the intended bride.

The girls also appeared together when on the Saturday before

Easter they brought to the manor house the seven decorated eggs which their family had presented there each Easter since history began; when the count was in attendance they delivered them to him, singing an old song as they bowed before him with these gifts of elegant and intricate beauty: the eggs of Easter were the sonnets and the symphonies of the Ukraine, and those prepared in the cobbler's house were among the most honored:

> *"I bring these eggs*
> *As Melchior brought myrrh.*
> *They are the gifts*
> *That Jesus played with*
> * In the manger . . ."*

The girls' voices blended nicely, and they bowed together as if studiously trained, so that even Pan Grabski, who was not a happy man and who disliked Ukrainians, admitted openly to everyone: "The cobbler's daughters bring the best eggs and the brightest smiles."

By Saturday afternoon, when all the required eggs had been delivered, seven by seven, the large room in the manor house resembled a field of flowers, or a jeweler's shop, for the decorated eggs, each a work of superlative art, shone in the shadows: red and green and blue and gold and a dazzling black that made the other colors dance. Each family had its own preferred designs, several hundred to choose from, and each colored its eggs according to secrets long protected, but in the end the total collection from the village formed a kind of hymn to nature and to God, a subtle and magnificent blending of a small fragile thing and the longing of human beings to create something of beauty.

Feliks was awed by the Easter eggs of the Ukraine and pleased by the imaginative use to which Count Lubonski put them. On Easter Monday, at nine in the morning, he allowed the children of Polz to gather at his grounds, about which his servants had hidden the eggs provided by the parents, and at the firing of a gun the little ones were free to run where they wished in search of the colored eggs, but Lubonski held in his personal reserve about four dozen, which he himself distributed to the children who were too small to find any for themselves. Mothers and fathers beamed at the benevolence of their count.

After the rigors of Lent were relaxed, the village held a dance at which the cobbler's daughter and her young man were feasted, and it lasted three riotous days, during which the fiddle, the flute and the tambor were constantly at work, one player after another assuming responsibility for the music-making.

Here for the first time Feliks and Roman saw the robust, artistic dancing of the Ukrainian peasant, so much more earthy and vigorous than that of their homeland, and Feliks in particular noticed the enticing manner in which Nadzha twirled to cause her heavy dress to flare out parallel to the floor while she flashed her pretty eyes this way and that as her head turned in the echoing air. She was delectable, the essence of a young woman flirting, whispering, laughing to the young men of her village: "Here I am, Nadzha the cobbler's daughter, Nadzha the beautiful dancer."

Feliks Bukowski was dangerously attracted to her, for after he had danced with her several times at the extended party, and the fiddle and flute fell silent, he walked with her along the edges of the village, and although he was himself responsible for the peasants of three similar villages in Poland, it was only through her that he learned what village life meant, and the grave obligations he undertook when he presumed to direct it.

"We girls are beautiful for a few years," Nadzha said one day in a remarkable confession. "Then the five babies come, and we grow fat, and we lose a tooth here and there, and"—she pointed to the women moving through her village—"at twenty-seven we're old women and the felted skirts are put away. At thirty-eight we're dead, and our husbands find themselves a second bride, and the dancing begins again. And it is like this forever."

As the days passed, with Lubonski inspecting all things and holding long meetings with Grabski over the accounts, Feliks and Nadzha wandered farther and farther from the village, until at last they reached that grove of birch trees by the small stream where, like others before them, they were hidden from sight, and they allowed the full springtime flood of passion to sweep over them. Nadzha, even though she appreciated the ignominy that would result if she became pregnant, could not reject this fleeting opportunity for love with a sensitive man, even though he was Polish.

Her older sister was more prudent: "Oh, Nadzha, you're doing a terrible thing. No man in this village will have you when he leaves."

"I do not care," she cried defiantly, glancing at her mother as she tended her chores.

Benedykta—miraculously safe in her own marriage, for often,

she had observed, it was the most beautiful girls who had the greatest difficulty in landing a man—brought her mother into the argument: "Nadzha is destroying herself. Speak to her."

"Time destroys us," the old woman said, and she left it at that.

"He will leave you," Benedykta predicted. "And with a baby, no doubt. And then where in God's hell will you be?"

But Feliks did not propose to leave this impeccable girl, so much more sincere than Katarzyna Granicka, with whom he had been so deeply in love three weeks before, and as he pondered what to do, it occurred to him for the first time that magnates like the count and gentry like himself had family names—Lubonski, Granicki, Bukowski—whereas peasants, who were just as vital and important to the land, had none. Nadzha, the most exciting and challenging woman he had ever met, was nameless, and when she died, having borne her five children, she and all memories of her would perish from human record and from her corner of the steppes.

Then he had an idea. Reporting to Lubonski early one morning, he said: "Grabski is not happy here, and I can see you're not happy with Grabski. Why not let me be your factor for the Ukraine? Here and the three other estates. I could earn you—"

"Feliks!" the count broke in peremptorily. "The most terrible thing a young man in your position could possibly do, I mean even worse than murder, is to accept a job as factotum, for anybody, anywhere, under any conditions."

"But why? I can count. I can manage."

"Once you retreat from being real gentry, however mean, and become a manager, you announce to the world that you have surrendered ambition, that you are of the fifth category—as disgraceful as if you were in trade, or lending money like a Jew."

"You mean . . . I can never work?"

"Of course you can work. For the king . . . for the Austrian emperor . . . for the church if you have the vocation . . . or for the cavalry. But never as the manager of someone's estates. That contaminates you . . . demotes you from the ranks of gentry."

When Feliks started to explain that he could reorganize the Lubonski estates and produce real income, the count said gently: "I know very well what's causing this insanity. You've fallen in love with some girl in the village and you imagine yourself—" He broke off that line of reasoning and added harshly: "Whoever she is, she can't read. She knows nothing. She has one dress. She's Orthodox, with all the corruption that implies. And in ten years she'll be old and fat and lazy, and then where in hell will you be, saddled with such a wife?"

He rose and stamped about the room. "Where is your undying love for that little Granicki girl? You could have had a magnate's daughter . . . and you set your heart on some Ukrainian peasant. I'm disgusted with you." And he would say no more.

Feliks kept to his room the rest of that long day, angered and embittered by the count's behavior and deeply tormented by the problem of the Ukrainian peasants, who labored so diligently and received so little, but even in those troubled hours he did not yet equate the plight of the Ukrainian serf with that of his own peasants. Nadzha's mournful summary described the peasants of Polz, not of Bukowo.

After a sleepless night he rose early and walked through the quiet village to the cobbler's cottage, where he knocked on the wooden door, polished and waxed for Easter, and called out that he wished to speak with Nadzha. To his surprise, it was Benedykta who opened the door, and she said grimly: "Nadzha's gone. She's gone for good."

"Why?" Feliks cried, pain echoing in his voice.

"Grabski came yesterday in the afternoon. He took her to the manor house, to see you I supposed. But it wasn't that. The count told her that she must leave this village forever . . . that she no longer had a place here. And Grabski brought her back and told us all: 'If she sleeps here this night, you lose your cottage and your cobbler's bench and this girl's wedding will be forbidden,' meaning me."

"What happened?"

"We wrapped her a little bundle—her felted dress, her sewing—and she started to walk to some village not belonging to the count."

"Where did she go?"

"Who knows?" As she said this, Benedykta drew back into the protection of her dark cottage. "You did this, you know. Now go away. Leave us, or I shall lose my intended too."

Feliks ran to the stables attached to the manor and leaped upon a horse already saddled and intended for the count's morning ride. Spurring it cruelly, he galloped out to the road that Nadzha must have taken, calling for her vainly as he went. It was a narrow pathway, hardly a road, but it led through flowered glades and out into the immensity of the Ukrainian steppe, and when he reached a spot from which the village could no longer be seen, or any other habitation, he realized that Nadzha must have followed some other route into her exile, and he leaned down upon his horse's head and wept.

The first four days of the journey back to Poland were a solemn affair, because the count was openly displeased by the behavior of his young protégé and would not speak with him, but Roman was more kindly disposed and it was now that the two young men drew closer together.

"She was beautiful," Roman said.

"Have you ever known love?" Feliks asked. "I mean real love with a wonderful girl?"

"Oh, no!" Roman said quickly.

"Are you going to marry Katarzyna Granicka?"

"Oh, no!" They rode in silence, after which Roman said tentatively: "I thought you were in love with Katarzyna . . . the camel rides, I mean . . . and she did kiss you goodbye."

"I was in love with her," Feliks said, sitting sideways in his saddle so he could speak more easily. "I think anyone would find himself in love with her."

"I think I was . . . in a way," Roman said, but then he blushed so furiously that Feliks dared not question him further.

On the sixth day, when they had passed Przemysl, the count resumed the instruction of his young charges: "In the morning we shall arrive at Lancut, and riders have informed me that the Princess Lubomirska is already there for her summer visit. She's an extraordinary woman and deserves your fullest respect."

He told them that she had been born Izabella Czartoryska of the great family at Pulawy. "She's about my age, a little older maybe, and has become a handsome woman." Realizing that this must sound odd to the young men, as if she had not been a handsome girl, he added: "On one point you must remain silent, even if she touches upon it. As a young girl she was supposed to marry Stanislaw Poniatowski, who became king, but he refused her . . . said she was too ugly. The wound never healed, and even though she married the best of the Lubomirskis and inherited their many castles, she has borne the scar and has worked day and night to drive Poniatowski from his throne. She is his mortal enemy, and before this century is out she will have her revenge."

"Is she an ugly woman?" Feliks asked.

"Heavens, no! In European courts she is known as a beauty, but I find that European courts use that word for any woman with four towns, sixty-three villages, a hundred and forty-five thousand serfs and nineteen castles."

"Has she so much?" Feliks asked, and Lubonski said: "More."

They broke camp at seven and made an easy ride to Lancut, a vast establishment with which the count was familiar but which stunned the young men, for its size and grandeur exceeded even what they had been told. A tall iron fence, its segments imported from Prague, enclosed a park the size of a large town, in the center of which, surrounded by a broad, deep moat and perched on a man-made hillock, rose what had once been a walled castle of enormous strength but which had recently been converted into an Italian-style palazzo with the original castle buried somewhere within it.

Its main entrance, set in a three-storied pink-and-white wall, and flanked by two tall towers with onion-bulb tops in the Russian style, was an ornately carved doorway which would have graced a cathedral, composed as it was of four concentric arches, each handsomely carved with allegorical marble figures. Its roof was a bright pink, and the same color was used in the nine or ten very large buildings on the palace grounds: the orangerie, the games house, the music hall, the little Greek-and-Roman museum and the huge stables. The lawn, which was kept meticulously trimmed by forty-seven scythe-wielding peasants who worked incessantly, was enormous; truly, one could not see the end of it, so far did it reach, broken here and there by lakes and fountains and running streams.

One of the towers was completely covered with pale-green ivy, which made it appear to be very old, like some castle along the Rhine; the other, of gleaming white marble, seemed as if it had been built a month ago. And everywhere Feliks looked he saw the tall, noble, varied trees of Lancut: pines from Norway, cedars imported from Lebanon, poplars shipped in from Lombardy, oak trees from England, clusters of birches from Russia and specimens of all the strong trees from Poland itself.

Lancut was a feast to the eye, all parts in perfect balance, but the construction which gave it distinction, and notoriety throughout Europe, was the central palace. It contained three hundred and sixty rooms, a resplendent art gallery with works by Rubens, Correggio, Watteau, Fragonard and a dazzling sculpture by Canova, a library unequaled in Poland, and a host of affectionate little refinements: one room incorporating frescoes imported from Pompeii, another with the best art of China, and a third furnished with the rarest treasures ever allowed to leave Persia. As it stood in the summer sunlight that morning in 1793, it represented a treasure of incalculable dimension, accumulated by the Lubomirskis over many generations.

During their first day in the palace the young men did not even meet its mistress; she was in another wing of ninety-seven rooms attended by eighty servants, where she might stay secluded for a week at a time, but on the second day she came forth to meet her interesting new guests; she had thirty-one staying with her at the time, but the Lubonskis were special.

Feliks was awed when he saw her, a rather stout, handsomely gowned woman of sixty, with bluish-white hair studded with diamonds, an ample bosom decorated with a single gold medal, and the warmest, most ingratiating smile he had ever seen on a woman of such distinction.

"My dear Lubonski, give me a kiss and tell me which of these divine young gods bears your name." Then she clutched Roman to her, crying in her imperative voice: "You are to stay with me forever." To Feliks she extended her hand, and when he stared at it she said heartily: "You stupid peasant. You're supposed to kiss it, but that's a silly French custom." And before he knew what was happening, she grasped him in a huge embrace and kissed him on both cheeks. Then, pushing him away, she said: "Lubonski, you must tell me accurately who this young god is."

"He is gentry going back to the time of the Tatar invasions. He fought at Legnica . . . with my ancestor at Grunwald . . . with Jan Sobieski at Vienna . . . and against the deluge at Czestochowa."

"He sounds as if he might be older than the Lubomirskis, and even older than my family, the Czartoryskis."

Roman, remembering how his mother had downgraded the Czartoryskis, winked at Feliks and thought to himself: It depends on who grades our families, doesn't it?

"But family age means little these days. The important thing, is he rich?"

"Like a thousand others, Princess, he fought but he did not save. He is impoverished, and like my son, he comes seeking a bride, but unlike my son, he must find a wealthy one."

Feliks thought he might faint from the embarrassment of such talk, but Lubomirska, as she was invariably called by those who did not know her personally, smiled at him generously and warmly. Taking his hands in hers, she said: "A young knight's major responsibility is to serve his lord. His second is to find a rich wife, and we shall find you one, young knight."

She told them that she would be having a formal dinner at eight that night and that she would appreciate it if they would dress in the old style, to which the count replied: "There is no other style in which I could dress," to which she replied: "You are the conservator of old Poland, the one that dies a little more each day."

The dinner was a limited affair, only forty-eight in the huge room and only one silver service in the center of the table: a sculpture from Verona showing the many-towered town of San Gimignano under siege, with little soldiers moving to and fro as the silver springs unwound. Thirty men were in attendance, and the brilliance of their costumes made the room glitter. About half wore the ancient Polish dress: tight trousers barely visible under long coats richly ornamented, ruffs at the neck, great wide sashes about the waist, ends hanging to the calf, and various gold chains from which hung medals and remembrances of past heroics. But several, who like Lubonski could boast of ancestors who fought at Vienna against the Turks, affected Oriental costumes marked by gold and silver crescents, Persian-type gowns rather than coats, and delicately embroidered fabrics rather than furs. These Orientalists avoided flashy jewels, a mere diamond here or there, and they tended to wear their hair a little longer than those in ancient costume. Three men, each one a diplomat, wore the modern French dress, made by English tailors in Vienna or Berlin, with exquisite silken fabrics, tight white breeches and silvered shoes.

Roman and Feliks, of course, wore the old Polish dress, and on their slim youthful bodies it looked superlative, the costume of those intended by divine grace to command and rule and make decisions of significance.

The eighteen women dressed in a variety of styles, borrowed mainly from Vienna and Paris, and their expensive dresses complemented the men's costumes, their wealth of diamonds and pearls and rubies showing well against either the Oriental dress of men like Lubonski or the more austere perfection of the diplomats' modern wear.

Feliks was seated next to a French lady in her forties, referred to as Mam'selle, who served as Lubomirska's secretary but not her confidante, and this woman liked to talk, so that during this gala evening and on the days following he learned much about his hostess:

"Lubomirska is probably the grandest woman in the world today. Here. Read this. It appeared in a German newspaper. Wolfgang von Goethe said, and you can see it right here. I'll read it for you: 'I remained an extra week in Weimar so that I could converse further with the Princess Lubomirska, who must be the most intelligent, witty and perceptive woman God has made in this century.'

"In Paris, where I met her, she was the constant companion of two brilliant Americans, Benjamin Franklin, whom she loved and I thought might marry, and Thomas Jefferson, younger and more revolutionary, God forbid. They adored her and brought their problems to her almost daily.

"She has nineteen castles like this one, and she endeavors to visit each one at least once every two years. For many years she has employed three teams of architects, mostly Italian and Dutch, to refinish and improve her castles. Each team moves from one to another, working at each about two years. She is constantly building, because she says that if One as powerful as God could afford to spend a whole week at His building, she can afford to spend a year or two at hers.

"She keeps, I believe, about a hundred and sixty servants here, not counting the gardeners or the stablemen, and they work at their jobs all year. But she is able to come here for only about four weeks in the summer, and in many years, as you might guess, she doesn't get here at all. But she loves to travel . . . is on the go constantly . . . and has erected along all the major routes she uses, from one castle to the next, little homes—four rooms for her, two for the servants who live there the year round. She has some forty of these, I suppose, all over Poland, and years might slip by without her using this one or that one, but there it waits, always ready for her if she chances to pass by."

By the end of the first enchanting week Feliks realized that it would require far more than six weeks for him to plumb the richness and the wonder of Lancut, but the greatest richness resided in the princess herself, and he was delighted to discover that she enjoyed talking with him, but he was also intelligent enough to know that she found pleasure in doing so because he was so naïve, so uninstructed.

"My husband was a dear man, Feliks, but the Lubomirskis, God bless them, usually are. He was a gentleman, and it was through him that I inherited sixteen of my castles. I am especially proud of being a Czartoryska, and if what Goethe said of me is true, it's because of the grinding education my father made me master. 'Learn languages, you little idiot,' he shouted at me. 'You aren't going to stay in Pulawy all your life.' What languages do you speak, Feliks?"

When he revealed how impoverished he was, she lamented: "Half your life gone . . . totally wasted. How can you ever be governor of Galicia if you can't speak good German in Vienna? You know I spoke English to Franklin and Jefferson."

"Who are they?"

To his surprise, she grasped him to her bosom and held his head against her throat for some moments. "Blessed God, I wish I had a son like you," and while she still embraced him she said: "All the energy I spend in building, and no one of either Lubomirski or Czartoryski to leave my empire to when I die. It is very painful, Feliks."

During the ensuing weeks she kept Feliks close to her, instructing him in the ways of Polish society, and sometimes as she did so she spoke of the king: "How miserable he must be in that petty castle of his, watching his kingdom evaporate before his eyes. He was given the world to command . . . and will lose it all." Feliks could see her mouth grow tense as she told him vengefully: "He started with so much . . . to end with so little. I with so little . . . to end with so much." It was obvious that she hated the king, but Feliks, obedient to Lubonski's command, made no comment, nor did he tell Roman of his conversations with the great woman.

Each day he spent in Roman Lubonski's company he liked him more; the young man was not at all slow-witted, as some had said, nor was he indifferent to evidences about him. He was merely quiet, thoughtful. "Lubomirska frightens me, but then all women do, even my mother." He laughed quietly, then corrected himself: "Especially my mother. She wants me to become some important figure and pesters me constantly with the fact that to do so, I must first find the right wife." He looked sideways at Feliks and said hesitantly: "You're in love with Lubomirska, aren't you?"

Feliks was. Like many ambitious young men before him, he had been swept away by his first acquaintance with a truly grand woman, for he could imagine the tremendous difference such a helpmeet would make, and this discovery encouraged him to compare his first two boyish loves with this dynamic, mature one: "When Katarzyna Granicka and I rode across the steppe on our camels, I wished the world would go on like that forever, and when Nadzha was banished from her village, I knew my heart was breaking. But now that I see Lubomirska . . . You know, Roman, I think you're in love with her, too."

"Have you ever watched a summer storm thundering down the Vistula from the mountains? How it sweeps everything before it? Even the small boats that aren't tied securely? Lubomirska is like that. I'm terrified of her, she's so powerful."

During the third week of their stay, Lubomirska imported from Krakow a company of some three dozen musicians, who would perform at the palace for three weeks: the best Jewish orchestra from that city, fourteen men in knee pants, black stockings and shoes, long black coats, flat hats and copious hair about their faces; six German soloists who knew Mozart and Handel; and sixteen other singers who could serve either as chorus or as soloists in a variety of forms.

Now the palace was filled with music, and Feliks would sit in the splendid rooms in which it was played, his head back, his eyes following the ornate stucco work which decorated the ceilings: cupids and angels and lions and tigers, all without bodies, white-faced and staring down at the listeners. And there were times when the German soloists departed and the robust Polish singers took over with folk songs from Krakow; then Lancut would ring with scores of voices joined together in a festival of song.

At the conclusion of one such concert, Lubomirska obviously wanted to talk with Feliks, and this gave him an opportunity to ask questions which had begun to gnaw at his conscience: "Is it true, what Mam'selle told me, that you have nineteen castles like this one?"

"That is true."

"And that you keep three teams of architects busy, year after year?"

"We Czartoryskis are builders, Feliks. We find a corner of empty Poland and we build something on it."

"But sometimes you don't visit one of your castles for years on end."

"One must also visit Paris and Vienna. And Rome and Venice. Have you ever been to those places?"

"Roman's been to Vienna. He says it was a little city of great charm, hiding within gigantic walls."

"Sometimes walls save a city. Would to God we'd had walls of some kind around Poland, we might have saved it."

"Is it true that you own more than a hundred and fifty thousand peasants?"

"Who knows?"

"Will they be set free . . . I mean one of these days? The baron said at dinner that they were set free in France and England."

"Did your father tell you such things, Feliks?"

"He taught me about them."

"And such thinking got him killed, didn't it? I wish you'd fetch Roman."

When the two young men sat with her in the gallery crowded with the marble statues of Greek and Roman heroes, including numerous Caesars, she told them: "The most dangerous thing a young man can do when he's trying to sort out the world is to apply a situation in one country to some other where it doesn't apply. In your lifetimes you'll hear many rumbles from France, and they may prove quite exciting, but not one of them applies to Poland. France is France, and her peasants are to be set free with pikes and staves in their hands, killing their betters. Poland is Poland, divided into three and soon I think to disappear forever because of our stupid king."

Feliks could not restrain the question which fermented: "Why do you despise the king?"

Without hesitating, this great woman who should have been Poniatowski's queen said: "I despise any man who could have become something powerful, and failed. If events crush him the way Hamlet and Macbeth were overwhelmed . . . all right. Or if evil forces bring him down the way Othello fell . . . all right again. But to fail because of one's own temerity . . ."

"What is temerity?" Feliks asked, but she ignored him. Turning to Roman, she grabbed his two hands and shook them vigorously. "If you, young man, could be an officer of the Habsburg court in Vienna and fail to grasp the opportunity, or to perform well if you do grasp it . . ." She thrust his hands away. "I will be watching from heaven, and I'll be ashamed of you."

But Feliks persisted: "Will your peasants be set free?" and she replied evasively: "Wolfgang von Goethe was the most brilliant man I ever met, master of the universe. But Ben Franklin was the wisest, master of the human soul. I never liked Tom Jefferson much—too revolutionary, too scientific and inhuman. And each one of these exceptional men told me that for the present, some kind of serfdom was inescapable: slavery in America, peasants in Poland. If America thinks it can end its slavery, it will perish. The day when serfs are set free in Poland, it will perish."

"Seems to me," Feliks said, "it's already perishing."

"I mean the real Poland ... the countryside ... what you see here, whether it's ruled by Austria or Russia, it goes on and on."

"Will Lancut go on and on?" Feliks asked, and now she grasped his two hands, saying sternly: "You ask dangerous questions, young man, and if you persist, you will end in an Austrian prison or a Russian mine. With France in flames and America inviting others to mimic her revolution, the rulers of these parts are not going to be lenient with radical young men whose radical fathers had to be gunned down in the streets of Warsaw to prevent revolt."

At the height of the musical festivities, when more than sixty guests crowded the castle bedrooms, two horsemen galloped in from the east with the exciting news that Kleofas Granicki was riding west with his camels at the whirlwind conclusion of his investigations in the Ukraine; in addition to this information, they handed Lubomirska a written message, which she crumpled with joy, shouting: "Yes! Yes!" And for the rest of that day there was vast excitement at the palace, with the hundred and fifty servants dashing about inside and the forty-seven gardeners raking the lawns outside and gathering huge garlands of summer flowers. Three teams of rural musicians were sent for—bagpipes, fiddle, drum—and the many cooks were put to baking.

Lubomirska would not reveal what had been in Granicki's note, but on the morning of the next day, when the wild man arrived at the head of six cameleers firing their rifles, Feliks and the others watched with amazement and delight as a team of eight gaily decorated camels drew a huge, improvised wagon through the palace gates, bearing inside a young couple who were obviously to be married at Lancut.

It was the lovely Katarzyna Granicka and the handsome, witty young Ryszard Lubomirski, who had been denuded at Radzyn Castle. They formed an imposing pair, she seventeen, he twenty-three, inheritors of power and wealth, and Feliks was not the least bit envious. Years and years ago, it seemed, he had loved Katarzyna for one reverberating spring when flowers filled the steppe, but now he was so infinitely older and wiser that she seemed like an unformed little girl whom he wished well.

To Roman he said, as the couple passed in their flower-packed wagon: "I thought you would marry her," to which young Lubonski replied: "Two years from now I would."

As was fitting in such surroundings, the wedding was a sumptuous affair, but it was also the occasion for an unusual performance to surprise and amuse the guests. The groom was a relative not of Lubomirska herself, for she was not of his family, but of her dead husband's, and thus it was proper for him to borrow Lancut palace as the site for his festivities. At the big dinner on the evening prior to the wedding, when Katarzyna was not allowed to be present, young Lubomirski appeared in old-style Polish dress. "I wear this in honor of my father-in-law, Kleofas, and out of respect for his ideals." He bowed low toward where the old warrior was sitting, then to the astonishment of all, he began to undress, right where he stood, and when he was down to the briefest possible underclothes he whistled for his servant, who brought in a stack of French-style dress, and ceremoniously he donned one item after another until he stood forth a handsome young fellow who would have been at home in either Paris or London.

Gravely he lifted from the floor the old dress, placing each piece on the extended arms of his servant, and when the pile was complete he turned to Kleofas and said: "From tomorrow on I must obey your daughter's wishes." And he again bowed low.

It was in the noisy conversation which followed this daring act that Feliks Bukowski first heard the name of Tadeusz Kosciuszko; Kleofas Granicki was bellowing: "I heard from St. Petersburg that our young hero Kosciuszko is making an ass of himself in Paris."

"Not surprising," Lubomirska said. "He was totally corrupted in America."

"What's he up to?" an Austrian baron asked.

Kleofas had imperfect reports: "He's fighting, of course . . . he's always fighting for some cause or other. He supports the revolution and may even be a general in it."

"That poor fool," Lubomirska said with real sorrow. "He comes from a good family, you know. Was desolated by the First Partition in 1772. Went to America . . . fell in with men like Tom Jefferson, whom I never liked—"

The Austrian baron, an officer in the Habsburg cavalry, interrupted: "We had strong reports of him as General Washington's right-hand man—engineering, fortifications, things like that."

"Can the American experiment last long?" Granicki asked.

"No," the Austrian said, and in this manner Kosciuszko was dismissed.

At the end of the sixth week of the Lubonski visit, Princess Lubomirska started her servants on the task of packing for her departure; she would move on to her great castle at Wisnicz, which she had not visited during the past three years and where one hundred and sixty servants and thirty-eight gardeners awaited her arrival. The last concerts were given—sixteen separate arias from Mozart operas, backed by the entire chorus—and a last tour of the ninety major European paintings was made, with Lubomirska herself explaining to the two young men why this artist was first class and that one not. The endless flower vases were wrapped in cloth and stored, and the machines that delivered water to the nine spouting fountains were halted.

There were tears as different groups of the sixty guests departed, and special ones when the Lubonskis went: "My dearest Count, give the Mniszechs my love. Roman and Feliks, find yourselves good wives. Goodbye, goodbye, and may we remember this glorious summer when the music played." She walked with them to where they mounted their horses and pulled each man down for a farewell kiss, for she suspected that she might not return to Lancut for several years, her problems at the rebuilding of her other castles and palaces requiring her attention.

The Lubonski company rode diligently in a southwesterly direction for several days, making far less progress than before, since now they were entering the low foothills of the Carpathian Mountains, but as the first cold winds of autumn struck at them from the south, they came to the ancient town of Dukla guarding the passes into Hungary.

The young men were almost disappointed in what they found, for the ancestral seat of the mighty Mniszech clan was a shabby affair, neither bold and big like the Granicki castle nor sumptuous like

Lancut. It was a frontier fortress occupied by defenders of the frontier, and as such it had importance, for as Count Lubonski warned his charges when they rode up to the gloomy affair: "Without the Mniszechs down here wrestling with Hungary and Russia, there'd have been no Poland." And he reminded them that Cyprjan Lubonski, the first to wear the title *Count,* had been vastly aided by his youthful marriage to Zofia Mniszech, who had more or less established the style of the Lubonskis and had mothered the unforgettable Barbara who perished in the fall of Krzyztopor: "The Mniszechs are a notable family, and if their young Elzbieta is as lovely as they say, we will have made a good journey."

Alas, Elzbieta was not in residence; she had traveled with her father, Ignacy, to a remote castle on the Hungarian frontier, where the Lubonskis were invited to follow after due rest at Dukla. Obviously the young men, excited by reports of Elzbieta's beauty and liveliness, were disappointed, but the enforced layover in Dukla turned out to be one of the high points of their journey, for they fell into the hands of an extraordinary Mniszech woman, Urszula, widow of a great warrior, who told stories of her family with all the ardor and joy that Sophocles and Aeschylus had shown when telling of the House of Atreus. She was in her sixties that autumn, and for five enchanted weeks she narrated wild and glowing accounts of what the Mniszechs had done when they wandered into Poland out of the Czech lands, of how they had battled bears with their hands, and fought against the Russians, and then with the Russians against the Tatars, but always, to the delight of the young men, she returned to stories featuring the young women of the clan, whom she referred to in the feminine form of their name, *Mniszchowna,* and she pronounced this with such mystery, clothing the women in romances so alluring, that Roman and Feliks had to conclude: A Mniszchowna must be irresistible.

"In 1589, Jerzy Mniszech and his wife, Jadwiga, who was born a Tarlowna, gave birth to a beautiful child they christened Maryna, and she grew to become the fairest young woman of these mountains. Her fame was widespread and men drew portraits of her. One fell into the hands of the youth who was to be the Czar of Russia, Dmitri by name, although there were some who called him False Dmitri because his claim to the throne was contested by Boris Godunov.

"This Dmitri, always seeking the throne, came here to Dukla, lured by the portrait he had seen of Maryna, and in this little town Maryna's uncles and brothers and men of the Tarlows schemed to make him czar, and believe it or not, they succeeded, and he became Czar of All the Russias, and in grand ceremonies at Krakow, attended by kings and princes from Europe, he married our Maryna, and she became czarina, at the age of fifteen.

"Short happiness. There was an evil Russian called Prince Shuiski who wanted to be czar, so after less than two years he assassinated Dmitri, and our poor Maryna was left a defenseless widow in Moscow. But a beautiful woman is never truly defenseless if she uses her head, which our Maryna did. She found another young prince, also named Dmitri, who also claimed to be czar, the first Dmitri having been little less than a fraud.

"So our Maryna married this second Dmitri, and for the second time she reigned as czarina, but this one, too, was assassinated, so that Prince Shuiski regained the throne, but if I remember right, he was also assassinated. Ugly things happen in Russia."

"What happened to Maryna?" Feliks asked, and Urszula's eyes glowed with delight at what she must report next:

"Alone, widowed, heartbroken with grief, Maryna met a Cossack hetman and ran away with him into the steppes of Russia, where together they planned a big rebellion, but it never amounted to much. As I recall, they were captured by the real czar's army, a Romanoff I think, and Maryna and her Cossack were taken back to Moscow and beheaded publicly. But she was a true Mniszech and spat at them from her scaffold."

That night Count Lubonski told his charges: "Much of what she said was true, you know. Maryna was czarina twice, and I think she did run away with the Cossack, but I doubt she was beheaded."

"What else was false?" Feliks asked.

"Her beauty. I've seen portraits of her, from that time, and she had two rather big warts. Also, she was quite small. When the czar's soldiers tried to arrest her the first time, she huddled down and hid herself under the skirts of her nurse."

"You spoiled the story," Roman protested, and his father said: "I believed it when my mother, who had Mniszech blood, told it to me. You choose what part you want to accept, because in essence it's true."

Urszula never mentioned a Mniszech woman without assuring her listeners that the subject of her tale was extraordinarily beautiful, so that Roman and Feliks came to accept this as an essential characteristic of the family.

"I was living, you know, when Ludwika, the daughter of Josef Mniszech and a different Tarlowna, married Josef Potocki, and you must keep these names straight, for another Potocki, not a very nice one, comes along later. Ludwika was the most beautiful girl in these parts and painters drew portraits of her which show her to be quite heavenly, a word I use with careful meaning.

"The young couple went to live at the big castle north of Przemysl, I always forget the name, and one day when Ludwika was in the bell tower, though why she was there I could never understand, a horseman came dashing into the courtyard, which is as big as all of Dukla, crying: 'The young master is killed. He fell from his horse and is killed!' With a scream of despair Ludwika threw herself from the bell tower and died.

"Now, at midnight when there's a full moon, she stalks the towers of Krasiczyn, I remember the name now, dressed in flowing robes and mourning the death of her beloved. The ugly part of this beautiful story is that Josef Potocki wasn't dead at all. He rode back home as good as you or me, buried his wife, and promptly married an Ossolinska, I believe it was, and she and he lived in the castle very happily, I'm told."

Count Lubonski said with some pride: "I believe our castle at Gorka is the only one in Poland that doesn't have a female ghost in a filmy gown walking the battlements at midnight. Lubonski women are too clever to waste their time that way. If you ask me, they probably stay close to heaven, listening to good music and drinking mead."

"But was her story true?" Roman asked.

"They were real people. We passed by their castle on our way to Lwow."

"I should like to believe it was true," Roman said, and his father replied: "I'm quite pleased with you on this trip, Roman. Young men ought to believe—in the Crucifixion, in the goodness of ancient Athens, in Charlemagne's ability. Such fixed bases help you to sort things out."

"That's the second time you've used that phrase," Roman said, and his father replied: "I've spent my life trying to sort things out."

"Have you succeeded?"

"No. I've lived in an age of disaster. And I came here to Dukla to talk about it with Ignacy Mniszech. I'm terribly disappointed about his absence, and I think we should move west to catch him at Niedzica."

"I'd like to stay here. These tales captivate me." And Feliks said that he, too, was enjoying himself, so they lingered, hoping each day that Elzbieta would return, and it was fortunate that they did, for this enabled them to hear from Urszula a harrowing tale of events that had occurred in the last generation of Mniszechs:

"Jerzy August, who was the brother of that Ludwika who threw herself from the bell tower at the castle, he took his second wife, a rich and powerful German girl named Maria Amalia Bruhl, of the great Bruhl family that came into Poland with our Saxon kings, amassing huge fortunes from the careless Poles.

"Well, Maria Amalia was like a bolt of lightning. I knew her well and was terrified by her. German this and German that, but beautiful and able. She had a daughter Jozefa of my age, and I adored her. Intelligent, she could read before any of us. Traveled to Italy and could sing like a bird. I was in this room when her parents announced that she was to marry the most dashing man in the countryside, Szczesny Potocki, and there was great feasting, I can tell you, for this was a match made in heaven. Mniszech money and Potocki lands.

"But before the wedding could take place, this bastard man Szczesny falls in love with a rather attractive daughter of a minor gentry, Gertruda Komorowska, miles and miles inferior to our Jozefina. He married her, insulting all of Dukla, and he got her pregnant, very big pregnant I was told.

"This was not the kind of insult that we Mniszechs would tolerate, and especially when Maria Amalia Bruhl with German stubbornness was involved. So one night when pregnant Gertruda was returning home in a sleigh, a gang of Cossacks hired by Maria Amalia dashed out, stopped the horses, dragged the pregnant wife onto the snow, strangled her, cut off her head, and pitched her body into the San River. That taught her to steal a husband intended for the Mniszechs."

Roman, obsessed by the history of this violent family, asked what followed, and the old woman rocked back and forth, savoring the gory details of an affair in which she had participated:

"Mniszech men, indebted to the Cossacks, gave their leader, Berezow, one of their villages in the Ukraine and two thousand extra serfs. His son became Count Berezowski and married one of the Potocki girls. But the interesting part is that the same Mniszech men forced the disgraceful Szczesny Potocki to marry our Jozefina, as originally intended, and Maria Amalia told him at the wedding that if he ever mistreated her, she herself would strangle him.

"Well, the Komorowskis were pretty distressed by this whole affair, as you might imagine . . . their beautiful daughter strangled by a bunch of Cossacks and she with child. They brought suit in the Krakow courts for revenge, but the Mniszechs were too powerful. Our side bought off the judges, my husband delivering the money, and the Komorowskis were told in effect to go to hell.

"The Komorowskis were not powerless, and although they were not of senior category, they were gentry, so one night three of their young men, I knew them all, crept into the home of Szczesny Potocki and killed our Jozefina. Killed her dead.

"Maria Amalia Bruhl thought for a while that maybe Potocki himself had killed her, and she warned him: 'If you ever remarry, you dog, I will personally strangle your wife.' I think this scared him, for he never remarried. Instead he took up with a beautiful Greek dancer named Zofya and they are very happy, I'm told."

Roman was entranced by this story, but Feliks expressed some doubts, which infuriated Urszula, who took him by the hand and led him, with Roman following, to a roughly built but imposing stone church, Santa Maria Magdalena, which dominated Dukla's central square. In its largest chapel she sat Feliks down on a bench from which he could study a professionally carved sarcophagus which stood against a wall. On its base of black marble reposed the gleaming white recumbent statue of Countess Maria Amalia Mniszchowa, dead at the age of thirty-six, the mother of four children. Across her placid face drifted a benign Christian smile.

"There lies one of the most powerful women I was ever to know," Urszula said. "Harsh at times but very capable."

"Is Elzbieta like her?" Roman asked, and Urszula replied: "All Mniszech women are like her."

The journey from Dukla well west to Niedzica was an experience totally different from any the young men had previously experienced, for the rugged pathway traversed turbulent mountain streams, gorges and small mountains which at times seemed impassable. Feliks, noting with growing interest the altered terrain, told Roman one evening as the sun sank behind hills: "Old Urszula's yarns were a good preparation for land like this," to which Roman snapped: "They weren't yarns. They happened." And it was he who now rode ahead to catch the first glimpse of each new and exciting vista.

Roman was in this preferred position when they entered a picturesque gorge, which apparently was going to run deep into the mountains, and he signaled for Feliks to join him, so that together the two young men led the way into terrain which offered constant surprises: now a sheer wall, now a tumbling rapids in the river whose bank they were following. A local guide employed by the count to lead them through the forbidding land told the young men: "Any merchant traveling from Budapest to Krakow must pass along this route, so bandits have always infested our area. They're still here today, even though the Austrian government tries to control them. If we didn't have soldiers with us, whsssst! Out of those hills they'd come and cut our throats."

Hoping that bandits would attack, so that gunfire would explode about them, the explorers hurried ahead, and as they rounded a bend in the tumbling river Roman cried: "There they are!" and in the distance, perched on two massive hills, one to the north of the river, the other to the south, rose the twin castles of Niedzica, forming a unique and stunning sight. Had these castles stood in some accessible spot, they would have been famous throughout Europe; hidden away in this remote gorge, they were legends spoken of with respect by all who had actually enjoyed their hospitality.

The Lubonski party rode for half a day with the castles in view, and when they were so close that Roman thought a human voice would alert the inhabitants, the guide discharged a volley, at which men appeared on the ramparts of the southern castle to fire back, and a lively set of echoes reverberated through the gorge, and after a while people began to emerge from the castle, a great train of them, men and women alike, and as they proceeded down a steep footpath to the river's edge, both of the young men thought: Elzbieta Mniszech is among them, and they began to strain their eyes for a sight of her.

Since the pathway up the gorge had followed the north bank of the river, the travelers would have to use a ferry to reach the Niedzica castle on the south, and as they rode up to a rude departure area, four shallow skiffs poled by mountaineers in heavy felt jackets started across the river to fetch them. As soon as the count and his two young charges stepped gingerly into the first skiff, there was much gunfire and shouting from the castle side, and as the skiffs were brought to shore, Roman and Feliks stared at their waiting hosts, who now crowded the landing area.

"That's Ignacy Mniszech," Lubonski told them, pointing to a huge man with long mustaches and head completely shaved, dressed in the old style, "and that smaller man in green-and-gold jacket is Horvath Janos, the Hungarian who owns the castle. And remember that they give their last names first, so don't call him Pan Horvath." There were four other large men with heads shaved almost clean, and a larger number dressed in the distinctive fashion of Hungary. Halfway up the stairs leading to the castle waited sixteen soldiers in green uniforms, and far beyond them, some hundred feet higher, began the castle walls.

And then the young suitors saw standing in the shadow of Ignacy his daughter Elzbieta, twenty years old, dressed in a Hungarian peasant costume adorned with heavy braid and wearing big clumsy fur

boots. Like most of the Mniszechs, she had dark hair and fair complexion, and as soon as the young men identified her, they both saw
her as the next in line of heroic and romantic Mniszech women, but
that was perplexing because this one looked as if she was gentle and
soft-spoken. When she became aware that the visitors were staring at
her, she withdrew behind her father.

A confused bustle developed as the Hungarian gentlemen reached
down to help the visitors disembark over the frail, narrow boards
that were thrown out from shore to the edges of the skiffs, and when
one of Lubonski's men slipped into the water, not deeply, there were
cheers. Ignacy himself reached out to grab for Roman, and after he
pulled the young man safely ashore he gave him a huge bear hug and
a kiss on the forehead: "Welcome to Niedzica, young man, and this
is my daughter Elzbieta."

Not shyly, for she was a mature woman, but with a lovely reserve,
Elzbieta extended her two hands and grasped Roman's, and later
when she did the same with Feliks that young man realized as if in a
blinding flash that he was at last in love. Katarzyna Granicka had
been attractive in the general way that all young women are, and
Nadzha the Ukrainian without a name had been deeply moving, and
the great Lubomirska had been a kind of stimulation, but Elzbieta
Mniszech was the culmination of a long journey, and he knew that as
long as he lived he would love no other. In his instantaneous infatua-
tion, and perhaps not so instantaneous, for it had been kindled by the
preparatory legends of old Urszula, he quite forgot that the more
important Roman Lubonski was also looking for a wife and that
Roman had been as deeply affected as he.

The next days were enchanted, for this Niedzica castle contained
seven round towers, each topped with battlements from which one
could look down upon the gorge or across to the northern castle,
standing upon its own rocky prominence, and occasionally one
could see a caravan of horses slowly following the river on its way to
Krakow, and once as Roman and Feliks watched, Elzbieta came to
stand with them at the top of the highest tower. "Right there"—she
pointed—"is where the robbers strike if the merchants are caught in
the gorge at night."

"Have you ever seen it happen?" Feliks asked.

"No, it comes in the dark, the attack. But it did happen one night
while we were sleeping. Two Austrian Jews left dead."

Like her great-aunt Urszula, she was a storyteller, and her account of things that had happened in these twin castles kept the young men bewitched, for she spoke in a soft voice, allowing it to rise in excitement as she approached important climaxes:

"My uncle said that these twin castles, remote though they are, summarize Polish history. When the Tatars swept the land in 1241, the frightened Duke of Krakow fled here for hiding. And have you ever heard of Jadwiga, the glorious Hungarian princess who married Jagiello? When she entered Poland to become our queen . . . here's where she slept on her first night in our country.

"Our last Swedish king, Jan Kazimir, came hiding here during the Deluge, and my uncle thinks it was here that the grand Jerzy Lubomirski hid the royal treasury when the Swedes conquered everything. One of the False Dmitris hid here, too, before he became czar, and the famous robber-peasant Kostka led his revolution from these castles.

"When I first saw the castles I thought: My God, this is the end of the world. But it was often the center. And now here we are, at the end or the center, who knows?"

When snow fell, the area became a silent wonderland, with deer moving down from the hills and ice immobilizing the skiffs. Then everyone stayed in the great halls, with fires crackling and stories echoing. Ignacy Mniszech dominated whatever was under way, a huge opinionated man, his head glistening in the firelight, his mustaches threatening anyone who disagreed with him: "By God, it would be better for us all if Russia took over what's left, and the part Austria has, too. Catherine knows how to rule."

Feliks noted that at such moments, without ever raising his own voice, Count Lubonski resisted Ignacy's arguments: "I think we'll find, in the long run, that Austria is going to govern its part of Poland much better than either of the others."

When Ignacy stormed, his voice growing louder and louder, Lubonski patiently rebutted his arguments, and when he was alone with the young men he reminded them: "The Mniszechs have always been in the pay of Russia. He has to say what he does."

Ignacy looked at his best one snowy day when someone suggested a bear hunt in the nearby hills. "Aren't bears asleep now?" Feliks asked, at which Mniszech bellowed: "They are, and it'll be our job to wake them up."

When the hunt was organized—enough gentry and soldiers to storm a castle—Elzbieta announced that she would join it, and at first her father said angrily that she should stay home with the cooks and be damned, but when she persisted, he awakened to the fact that she was eager to be with the young men, to observe how they behaved, and he gave her a huge hug, crying: "If you get your pretty face clawed, that's your fault." Feliks said quickly: "We'll protect her, Pan Ignacy," and the leader of the hunt roared: "You better!"

Feliks could still not understand how there could be a bear hunt when there were no bears, but when they were far into the woods and up the side of a mountain, Ignacy called for the brands, and when they were well lighted and throwing smoke, he climbed into several dangerous spots from which he thrust the brands into caves that might contain hibernating bears, and after three disappointments, which left his hands and one side of his face scratched, he found a cave which he judged to be especially promising. Calling for more brands, he stuffed their smoking ends into the entrance, and after a while he shouted: "By God, a bear!"

And from the cave, sleepy and distraught, emerged a large brown bear who took one look at Mniszech and retreated in terror, but his cave-refuge was now so filled with smoke that he could not enter it, so in desperation he shied away from Mniszech and started lumbering through the sparse and leafless woods. With wild shouts, armed men loosed their dogs and started in pursuit, with Roman and Feliks making a way for Elzbieta, who reveled in the chase.

For about a mile the bear kept ahead of his pursuers, but he was emaciated from his long sleep without food, and in the end he tired so pitifully that the dogs had an easy time with him, sinking their sharp teeth into his flanks, and with four of the dogs tormenting him in this way and making any further progress impossible, the weak creature turned to face his encircling enemies. With wide swipes of first one forepaw and then the other, he punished some of the dogs, sending them away with agonized yelps and bleeding faces, but always the men moved closer, and in the end Ignacy lunged forward with a long pike, transfixing the bear with a mortal thrust. Feliks felt sick at his stomach and showed it.

He did not perform well, either, on the night soldiers trapped two

bandits as they attacked peddlers moving from Hungary into Poland, for when the heavily garbed robbers were dragged into the castle, their pockets still crammed with the goods they had stolen,
soldiers were encouraged to beat them, and Feliks protested: "They
killed no one."

"They probably killed those two Jews last month," Mniszech
stormed, and the beatings continued, to Feliks' disgust.

He was ill-prepared for what happened at dawn. Bugles sounded
and everyone in the castle assembled in the large square subtended by
the towers, where a rude platform had been erected, hastily rather
than sturdily. It wobbled when one of the soldiers with an axe
mounted, and when the first of the robbers was shoved onto it the
props almost fell. "Hold them up!" Mniszech cried, and three soldiers were assigned to each pole to keep it steady.

They failed, and when the man with the axe tried to chop off the
head of the first robber, the neck moved and he bungled the job horribly. The second robber, aware that he was going to be treated the
same way, stared in horror as the axe came down the third ineffectual
time, and fainted.

Feliks almost did the same, but he steeled himself to look as the
inert body of the second robber was lifted onto the rickety platform,
where the man with the axe prepared to decapitate him. "Do it right,"
Mniszech bellowed, "or you're next." Since it was entirely possible
that this threat might be carried out, the executioner's hands trembled visibly, but with two powerful and ill-directed blows he managed
to sever the head. Feliks could watch no longer, a fact which Elzbieta
noted with approval, for she, too, had turned away.

In the week after Christmas, Feliks showed to excellent advantage, for all in the castle journeyed to a small town nearby, where
snow in the narrow streets had been packed flat by the feet of many
peasants and where teams of swift horses had been harnessed to
sleighs of an extraordinary nature. They were so narrow that only
one person, always an unmarried girl, could find a place to sit. The
runners were waxed and razor-sharp, extending in back as a kind of
platform from which the driver, always an unmarried young man,
would direct the horses with long reins and an even longer whip of
extreme flexibility made in France.

The ride through the narrow streets was not a race, because two
sleighs could not run side by side, but it was nevertheless a test of
competitive skill, because each driver whipped his horses to their top

speed, with the girl hanging on desperately and forbidden to scream, regardless of what happened. Often the tiny sleighs, little more than a foot wide, upset, throwing the girl into a snowbank, and sometimes horses in the following sleighs had to leap over her; this was a discredit to her driver, who must keep his sleigh upright no matter what.

Roman Lubonski flatly refused to engage in this perilous sport, for once he had seen a girl disfigured, and his father did not press him to change his mind, for such rides were a Cossack invention and a fallback to more primitive society, but Feliks, seeing a chance to have Elzbieta as his partner, jumped forward to volunteer, and he was given a sleigh with the painted name *Firebird,* and on its narrow seat he placed Elzbieta, assuring her they would win this competition.

Heart galloping like his horses, Feliks whipped his team into the narrow streets, kept them roaring around the corners, waved to the watchers, and headed for the critical passage in which two sudden turns were required. "Hold on!" he warned Elzbieta, and with a skill that astonished the mountain people, who were unaware of his love for horses, he negotiated the dangerous twists and brought his narrow sled and its precious cargo safely home.

The crowd applauded and Roman ran up to shake Feliks' hand, but he was prevented from doing so by Elzbieta, who reached up at this moment to give her driver a triumphal kiss. "We did it!" she cried. "It was so wonderful, the frightening curves." Again she kissed him, but then she saw Roman, and grasping his hand, she said: "Roman, I'd have fallen off if he hadn't warned, just at the bad part, 'Hold on!'" Together the three walked back to where Mniszech and the count waited to applaud them.

Two days after New Year's, men whom Feliks had not seen before and whom Roman did not know either, arrived at Niedzica from two different directions. From Vienna came Count von Starhemberg, descendant of that brave Austrian who had helped defend Vienna against the Turks; the twin castles and all the territory around them were now Austrian property, and Feliks supposed that he had come to inspect it. He was a young man with a sense of command, and Feliks guessed that he was intended for some superior post in the Habsburg government.

The other man was more perplexing: Baron Ottokar von Eschl of Prussia, in his sixties, reserved and proper, and impatient with the normal social niceties. When Elzbieta was presented to him he barely acknowledged her, and he ignored completely her two suitors, for obviously he wished to get down to business after his long and tiring journey to this remote spot. But what that business was, Feliks could not guess.

At the large dinner that launched the unusual meeting, with snow swirling about the parapets and the fires crackling, Von Eschl attracted the young men's attention by speaking almost disrespectfully to Count Lubonski: "Why can't you Poles discipline this fool Kosciuszko? If he continues, he's going to make serious trouble."

"We hold him in no regard, Baron," Lubonski said with obvious conviction.

"But if he keeps talking over your heads . . . exciting the peasants—"

Mniszech broke in: "If the peasants make one move, we'll crush them the way Catherine crushed hers." And no more was said.

During the following days, while Mniszech and Lubonski met long hours with the two visitors, Feliks Bukowski was left alone to ponder the various shreds of information he had gathered on this disturbing trip, because if his four love affairs had been disorienting, his experience with the problems of Poland had been catastrophic. He was, he always remembered, the son of a man who had given his life to preserve Polish freedom, and Feliks knew precisely what his father's definition of freedom had been: "Feliks, the time has come when we must move like France and England and America. The freedom of fifteen great families to dictate in all fields isn't good enough any longer. Men should own land. They should work for themselves, not for some castle, and they should pay taxes to the government, not to some damned fool like Przamowski."

Feliks would never forget Przamowski, of the petty gentry in a nearby village. By every device known in Poland he extracted labor and money from his serfs, charging them duties, which the Bukowskis never did. Przamowski had his own grinding mill, which his peasants must use for an exorbitant fee, and his own brewery, which his serfs had to patronize. One hot summer a peasant in one of Przamowski's cottages refused to buy his ration of beer because neither he nor his wife liked it, so Przamowski came screaming to the cottage: "You owe me for three gallons!" And when the peasant said: "But we don't drink beer," Przamowski in a rage poured the beer on the ground at the man's doorstep. "Now, goddamn you, you have your beer and I want my zlotys," and the man had to pay.

Feliks could not shake out of his mind his memories of Lancut palace, the endless rooms used a few weeks every other year, the battalions of servants, the gardeners picking at individual pieces of grass, the eighteen other palaces and the teams of architects perfecting them for visitors who never came. He could see that row of sixty faces about the long table, the faces of men and women who had used Poland to their private advantage, and he began to wonder what the phrase Golden Freedom really meant.

At first he had been disposed to accept Granicki's judgment that Poland had known greatness only because the magnates ruled it well, but he knew that those days were gone, flames flickering in the wind, and that now new solutions were required. Because he held Count Lubonski in such high regard, he had once been prepared to believe that all magnates were like him, but now that he was seeing others at close quarters, he began to suspect that they had always been a robust, thieving, self-centered lot who had given Poland not good government but one of the poorest in Europe. They were eager to defend their country against powerless robbers who lurked in river gorges, but extremely loath to protect it against real robbers like Prussia and Russia, who were invited to conduct their depredations openly.

He had no clear concept at this time of who Tadeusz Kosciuszko might be, but the several things he had heard about the man excited him: he was a patriot who opposed the partitions; he had acquired fresh new ideas in France and America; and he seemed to support the kind of freedom for which Tytus had died. "I think I would like Kosciuszko," he told Roman, and the young man replied: "Better not tell Father so."

But the day after Feliks formulated these tentative evaluations the men at table spent more than an hour extolling the Golden Freedom, and they made such a good case that Feliks was confused. Count Lubonski reminded his listeners: "When France was burning the Albigensian heretics, no fire was ever lit in Poland. When England crucified Jews, they lived free in Poland. When religious wars swept over Germany, one horrible decimation after another, Poland remained a bastion of freedom. My father, may God grant him respite, did authorize the beheadings at Torun, but even he was ashamed and they were never repeated. Freedom did mean freedom for all."

"It was a remarkable contribution to European government," Baron von Eschl agreed. "A nation without a large standing army. A parliament in which the freedom of the intellectual few was protected against the rule of the mob. The constant cultivation of the best families, who ruled with supreme wisdom. Small wonder Russia and Austria and Prussia have always rallied to protect that freedom."

"When I studied Polish history at the time Austria gained these territories," Von Starhemberg said, "I concluded that Poland offered the finest democracy since ancient Athens. The people ruled, not the king. You allowed no dictatorship, no savage rule. In its day your Golden Freedom lit a beacon for the world, and that's why Vienna has always been first to protect it."

On and on the encomiums went, until Feliks gained the impression that it must have been Poles who had organized the two partitions, because obviously Austria, Prussia and Russia had fought constantly to defend her.

But one afternoon when he was looking for Elzbieta, who was spending more and more of her time with Roman, he passed an open door and heard the four men—Von Eschl, Von Starhemberg, Mniszech and Lubonski—arguing heatedly, and like any inquisitive young man, he lingered. Mniszech was saying: "Tyodor Kuprin came to me at my estate in west Russia and assured me that his Catherine was now reconciled to terminating Poland. Wiping it out altogether and forever."

"Will she back Prussia if we make the first move?"

"She will if Austria joins us."

"We cannot trust a vague promise like that," Von Eschl said, at which Mniszech flared: "Are you doubting my word?" and Von Eschl said: "I am doubting Catherine's. She has lied to us too often in the past."

Feliks could not follow what was said next, for everyone spoke at once, but finally Von Eschl's cold, clear voice, always cutting to the heart of the matter, asked: "Von Starhemberg, tell us in the simplest possible terms, will Austria join us in a final partition?"

Before the Viennese count could reply, Lubonski said in a voice so low that Feliks could scarcely hear him: "Horvath Janos assured me on the day I came that he had representations from Vienna promising immediate military support if Russia and Prussia chose to make a final move."

"And you have Catherine's and Kuprin's promise that Russia is ready to take the leap."

Von Eschl said: "Throw that door shut. Someone might overhear us, and I do not want Horvath to know what we're deciding." And the door was slammed.

• • •

In great confusion of spirit Feliks dropped his speculation about Poland's freedom and directed his whole attention to the courtship of Elzbieta Mniszech; for two weeks Roman had enjoyed a fairly free field, but Feliks now proved himself a formidable contestant. He was not shy; he spoke well; each day he was acquiring additional sophistication, and although he was somewhat shorter than Roman, he was more pleasing in overall appearance. He was also infatuated with Elzbieta and had reason to believe that she was attracted to him.

Twice she referred to the sleigh ride at which he had performed so ably and several times she allowed herself to be trapped in corners of the castle, where they kissed passionately. Once when they lingered there for the better part of an hour, caressing each other, she broke into tears. "Oh, Feliks, you're going to be a man any girl would be proud of."

He did not know how to interpret this, but the more he talked with her the more convinced he became that she was a rare creature: beautiful, compassionate, gifted in four languages, and wise. For one rich and glorious week he imagined himself married to her, and when he wakened from this dream he found her waiting for him in a corridor leading to one of the battlements, and they went out into the wintry air, where snow made the mountains and the gorges one gleaming beauty. Rarely could young people have been in love in a setting more conducive to wild feelings and bold imaginings, for the entire world seemed to lie at their feet.

"I am going to ask Pan Ignacy for your hand," Feliks said, whereupon Elzbieta kissed him ardently, but then she began to tremble as if the cold had attacked her, and he asked if she wished to leave the exposed spot and the whistling winds.

"Oh, no!" she cried, clutching at his arm. "It's . . . well, we don't know what Father will say."

"I think he likes me."

"He does. He's told me so."

"He did?"

"But I think . . . I'm afraid, that is . . . I think he has hoped I would marry Roman."

Once she uttered this fear, Feliks understood how real it was; Count Lubonski had come to Niedzica not only to discuss Poland's future with the executioners but also to find a family alliance for his diffident son Roman, and with the Granicki girl already married, Elzbieta became not only an attractive prospect but perhaps the sole one. Roman, with his distinctive lineage as a real magnate, was a formidable opponent and Feliks thought it best to confront the situation openly: "Are you in love with Roman?"

"I'm in love with you, surely you know that."

"Will you marry me?" he blurted out.

She blushed, held his hand tightly, and then kissed him as they leaned against the battlement. Very carefully she said: "I think, Feliks, you had better let me speak to Father about that."

"It's my duty to speak," he said, feeling the ardor of her hand loosen into fear. "It's always the man's duty."

"The Mniszechs are different," she warned. "If Father is angered . . ."

"I would not be afraid," he said with sharp finality, and she shrugged her shoulders and said: "Speak to him, then." So they descended from the tower to seek him out, and from the manner in which she stayed close to Feliks, it was apparent that she intended supporting him in his supplication.

They found Ignacy in deep consultation with Baron von Eschl, the two men leaning over a map and drawing lines which now and then they scrubbed out, and although Feliks was loath to interrupt, Elzbieta went right up to her father, saying: "Can we speak with you, please?" Von Eschl smiled coldly, as if he could guess what they wished to speak about, for he had been watching the young people and knew fairly accurately what had been happening. Folding the map four times and placing a heavy book upon it, he left the room.

"Father, we wish to ask you a question," Elzbieta said, reaching out for her lover's hand to lend him support, but as Feliks stepped forward to make his speech, Ignacy Mniszech moved forward too, and he seemed enormous, a giant that leaned forward like the cliffs of a river gorge, with a stare so intense that Feliks feared he might lash out with his huge fists.

Instead, his huge face broke into a warm, compassionate smile, and before Feliks could utter a word, he felt his two hands being caught in Ignacy's and clasped with passionate warmth. "You were wise to come to me, Feliks. It's what a gentleman should do, and I appreciate your courtesy." Dropping the hands, he threw a bearlike paw about the young man's shoulders and eased him out of the room without allowing him to have said one sentence, and as soon as the couple were at the door they could hear him bellowing: "Von Eschl! Find the Austrian and let's get back to work."

"I think he accepted the idea," Feliks said hopefully as he led Elzbieta along the stony corridors of this historic castle, and she agreed with him: "There's hope."

"But he said nothing," Feliks reflected, and with these words he could feel Elzbieta grow curiously distant, a sensation which intensified when they met Roman coming in from a morning hunt. In some unstated way she had dissociated herself from Feliks and moved closer to Roman, and it was then that Feliks began to suspect that there might be some arrangement between his two friends and between Elzbieta and her father, so that words between the latter pair had been unnecessary.

Seeing this excellent girl in morning light, detached from him as it were, he realized what an exceptional person she was, how exquisitely ordained to be a wife: she was lively and brave, as she had shown at the sleigh ride; she was warm and affectionate, as her kisses had amply demonstrated; and she had strong character, as when she summoned her father from his work with the German baron; and she was as beautiful as a fawn in early summer when every meadow is an invitation to leaping and exploring. Elzbieta, he whispered to himself, if the answer is no, I think I shall die.

Ignacy Mniszech himself went into the kitchen to supervise preparation of the soup, a task at which he spent most of that day, absenting himself from the noontime meal so that he could avoid responding to Bukowski's implied proposal of marriage. He spent that time slaughtering a young pig and carefully catching all its blood in a ewer, which he brought back to the kitchen, where he added vinegar and salt to the blood and set the ewer aside.

Asking the cooks for what meat stock they had, he added to it bits of cooked pork and chicken, two large handfuls of chopped vegetables, three heavy soupbones and six large dried mushrooms that he and his daughter had gathered that autumn.

"Prunes!" he called, and cooks hurried up with a large handful. "Cherries!" and they came with a cupful of dried delicacies, which he tossed into the brew.

He tended the soup all afternoon, tasting it now and then and soliciting advice from his professionals: "I want this to be the best.

More salt, do you think?" When it was done to everyone's approval, a distinguished golden Polish soup, he stirred in a large helping of crumbled honey cake to bind the various elements together.

"An excellent soup," he said before the evening meal, and when he heard the guests assembling in the dining hall he divided his soup into two portions, one extremely large, the other so small that it would serve only one person, and into this latter helping he stirred the dark blood and vinegar, keeping it over the fire until it turned an ebon black.

"Dinner!" he shouted as he left the kitchen, and behind him came four servants bearing soup bowls for the guests, who sniffed approvingly as their rich portions of amber-colored soup were placed before them. Ignacy took the final bowl from the fourth servant and walked silently, ceremoniously to where Feliks Bukowski sat. Deftly, using both his big hands, he placed the bowl of black soup before the impetuous suitor, and when Feliks looked down at it and saw the terrible blackness he knew that his proposal of marriage had been rejected, and so did everyone else at the table.

Convention required that he make no comment, betray no emotion. Like a soldier assigned to hateful duty, he ate his black soup, cruelly aware that the soup of the others was a rich golden brown, and after Feliks had finished his bitter dish, Ignacy Mniszech, big and bald and brazen, rose and announced to his guests: "On this day my daughter Elzbieta is announcing her engagement to Roman Lubonski, son of my dear friend—Count Lubonski in Poland, Baron Lubonski in Austria. Wedding's to be at the Mniszech palace in Warsaw, and you are all to attend."

Now convention required that Feliks, his black soup obediently consumed, felicitate the engaged couple, which he did with solemn grace, raising his glass and speaking in a voice from which emotion had been excised: "May you enjoy unending happiness." But when he resumed his seat and looked dispassionately at the guests, a terrible confusion of images hovered about the long oaken table: the sleepy bear routed from his wintry cave became Poland, driven to extremity by the hunters converging upon her; the first robber whose head had to be hacked off with many blows became the map over which the other executioners pored; and lovely Elzbieta, the fairest girl he would ever know, climbed onto the narrow sleigh, holding Roman Lubonski by a silken string as if she were playing with him.

Then the images dissolved and he realized that he had been used

both at the Granickis' and now at the Mniszechs' as a foil: the spirited young man whose courtship of the castle princesses would
awaken the interest and the jealousy of the future count. He had
prepared the way for Roman; his kisses had alerted Elzbieta to the
important task at hand, a union of Mniszech and Lubonski.

Ignacy was speaking: "A century and a half ago Zofia Mniszech
left Dukla to marry Cyprjan Lubonski, one of the happiest alliances
in our family history. Inspired by Zofia, Count Cyprjan went on to
defend Czestochowa against the Swedes and Vienna against the
Turks. May this marriage with our Elzbieta encourage Count Roman,
in his time, to similar braveries." The guests cheered and started to
discuss their preparations for the wedding in Warsaw, and Feliks
learned with dismay that the procession would not visit the grandest
of the Lubomirski walled castles, the one at Wisnicz, on the way
home. He remembered that this branch of the family had two marriageable daughters and was eager to see them on the chance that he,
too, might take home a bride, but when he asked: "Shall we not halt
at Wisnicz?" Count Lubonski said abruptly: "We have much work to
complete in Warsaw," and Feliks thought: He found a bride for his
son, so to hell with me.

The Lubonski-Mniszech wedding had to be speeded, or Warsaw
might disappear as the capital of a nation which no longer existed.
The precise timing of Poland's demise would depend upon the plans
of the Romanoffs in Russia, the Hohenzollerns in Prussia and the
Habsburgs in Vienna, but the design was so remorselessly set—like
Lubonski's and Mniszech's design for the marriage of their children—
that no reversal was possible. Poland's future and Feliks Bukowski's
hopes were doomed.

Count Lubonski was so pleased with the way Feliks had functioned
in the courtship of his son Roman—exciting Roman's interest in Elzbieta and more or less goading him into proposing to the Mniszech
girl—that he insisted upon Feliks' attending the wedding. Following
a three-week layover at Castle Gorka, the grand expedition was assembled again, with an entourage of seventy, and started for the
capital.

As before, the riders left Austrian Poland and crossed the border
unimpeded into old Poland, but this time there was a major difference: Feliks was taking with him his peasant Jan of the Beech Trees, a

man slightly older than himself and one very wise in rural ways. This Jan had also been pondering many of the questions which had assaulted his master during the latter's tour of luxurious palaces; he, too, wondered why his village should have been organized for the benefit of only one man, Count Lubonski, who happened to be a gentle soul but one without any feeling whatever for his peasants, and very little, so far as Jan could discern, for his various gentry like Bukowski. Jan had never seen a really sumptuous establishment like Lancut, but he had worked often at Castle Gorka and could see the vast difference between how a count lived, with his fifty horses and forty servants, and how his peasants lived, with meat once a year, a new suit of clothes once every ten years, little medicine and less education.

Therefore, when, on the way north, Feliks dropped a word here or there concerning Poland and its future, Jan listened carefully, and gradually became aware that his master was concerned about many of the problems that troubled him, and after they had passed Pulawy, where the Czartoryskis had expressed vivid hopes for a new Poland in which even peasants would have rights, Jan felt bold enough to ask: "When will these good things begin to happen?" and Feliks had to confess: "Never. I think that soon there will be no Poland." And for many miles, as ice thinned in the beautiful valley of the Vistula, these two discussed the impending fate of what had once been their homeland, and Feliks laid forth his anxiety:

> "I think Poland will be destroyed by her protectors. I think that in these days, when we're building a fine new state marked by real freedom and not the Golden Freedom of a few, we will be engulfed by a new deluge and erased forever. The other nations hate us not because we're backward but because we lead the procession. Every good thing we do imperils them and they will have to strike us down."

Jan, lacking Bukowski's education and sophistication, could not appreciate much of his master's thinking but he certainly comprehended the basic argument, which he expressed forcibly in his own terms:

> "It isn't right, Pan Feliks, that I should work so hard and get so little. The Austrian king takes two weeks. The bishop takes two weeks. Count Lubonski takes six weeks. And you yourself take most of the rest. A man from Krakow came running through

our village while you were gone, looking over his shoulder for the police, who followed after him three days later. He told us: 'A general named Kosciuszko will bring an army to free the peasants. Be ready to join him when he comes.' I think, Pan Feliks, that if he comes, I will join him."

Discussion along these dangerous lines halted as they approached Warsaw, and many local citizens who watched the colorful parade, with its men in ancient costume and its horses caparisoned in the old style—seventy of them to attend one bridegroom—must have thought that they were witnessing a funeral procession honoring the burial of past custom, for this kind of display was now rarely seen in the capital, which was apprehensive about its very existence.

The expedition entered the city on a broad thoroughfare that had always been known under the curious name of Krakow Suburb, since it had formed in even the oldest times the initial stage of the highway leading to that southern city. As they traversed this boulevard they could see the imposing palaces of the Radziwills and the Czartoryskis, but as they approached the center of the beautiful city they came on that fine street Senatorska, where the Lubonski palace, a modest affair of marble and pyracantha bushes thirty feet high, stood beside the Lubomirski palace, a tremendous affair, and across from the stately Mniszech home, the most severe and imposing of them all. When Feliks saw the latter palace, where Elzbieta would be waiting for her wedding, he felt his heart contract, and he wanted to dash across the muddied roadway and throw himself at her feet, pleading with her to reconsider. Instead, even as he looked longingly at the Mniszech palace, he entered the portals of Count Lubonski's Warsaw home.

Although it appeared modest when seen from Senatorska Street, each of its three fine stories had thirty rooms, more or less, and this was customary in the homes of the leading magnates, for they liked to have in their Warsaw complement a dozen or so of the penurious gentry beholden to them, and these petty knights brought with them their wives and children, so that a palace might have as permanent guests some sixty or seventy persons, each of whom was obligated to serve the owner when he put in an appearance at the capital. In time of war, of course, the men would be called on to serve in the count's private army, fighting on whichever side the magnate had elected to support.

Feliks had settled into his modest room, for he had no wife to justify an apartment, for only a few minutes when a messenger from the palace next door arrived with a summons: "The Princess Lubomirska invites you to join her in a visit of inspection to the Palais Princesse," and when Feliks asked what that might be, the messenger smiled broadly and said: "You'll see."

Feliks was delighted to see Lubomirska again and was honored when she stepped forward almost eagerly to kiss him on the cheek. She was in her Warsaw costume now, fur decorating her dress, with jewels in her silvery hair and an imperious and condescending smile on her lips. "I have such a delightful surprise for you, Feliks. Climb into my carriage."

She directed her driver to go eastward on Senatorska toward the castle, where her arch-enemy King Stanislaw August still reigned, as she said, "clinging on by his fingernails," but when the six horses were almost entering the castle compound, the driver pulled them smartly to the left, and Lubomirska with her young companion entered that most charming of the Polish streets, Miodowa, the Street of Sweet Nectar. Not big and broad, like Senatorska, nor obviously important, like Krakow Suburb, it ran for only one very long block, but it contained some of the loveliest buildings in Warsaw, churches and bishops' palaces and the residences of those new millionaires who mattered in the city now.

As they rode, Lubomirska explained to Feliks who lived where and who commanded what authority, but as her carriage approached the end of Miodowa she gripped his arm and cried with the pleasure of a little girl: "See what the Mniszechs have done for their child!" And on a plot of ground newly landscaped with the shrubs and flowers of spring, she showed him what was already called the Palais Princesse, a little marble building of exquisite taste, sitting back from the street, each window, each decoration balanced by another, as charming a small palace as all of Europe could provide.

"What a beautiful wedding present for a beautiful child!" she cried as she pointed out its various perfections. "Quick, we must slip inside."

The hurried building of the *palais,* which would always be called by its French name, had muddied Miodowa so that Lubomirska's coachman had to carry her to the entrance and then come back for Feliks lest he muddy his boots. Once at the doorway to the *palais,* Lubomirska assumed command, and with grand gestures, entered the little jewel and started describing its quiet glories: "See how everything balances, a room here, a room there, the piano here where it will echo well, the harp over here where we'll be able to see the player."

She led him to each of the floors, expostulating on what a superb job "those heavy peasants, those bearded Mniszechs" had done, and in a small room on the third floor they found Elzbieta sewing on a piece of gold-threaded fabric. "Darling child! No one told me you were here!" Lubomirska engulfed the bride-to-be in her arms, then pushed her toward Feliks with a gracious introduction: "This is my young friend Feliks Bukowski, who pertains to Count Lubonski, your new father-in-law."

Neither Elzbieta nor Feliks acknowledged any previous acquaintanceship; they bowed; he took her hand gravely when she extended it and said: "I wish you much happiness, Panna Elzbieta."

"As do I!" Lubomirska cried enthusiastically, kissing her robustly, and with that they withdrew, but when the visitors had descended to the second floor, where they inspected a barely furnished salon, Feliks fell into a chair, covered his face with his hands, and sobbed. Lubomirska, unable to guess what had assailed her young friend, drew a chair beside him and took his hands. "What is it, Feliks?" And he burst forth with an account of his love for Elzbieta, and their sleigh ride, and their kisses on the battlements of the frontier castle.

"Pani Izabella, what shall I do? She is my life."

"And she should be. I would to God that I were she, at her age, with her beauty." She gripped his hands tightly and said with a kind of grim determination: "I was, too. I really was, Feliks. Maybe not with her striking beauty, but at seventeen, when I was supposed to marry Poniatowski, I was an important young woman with a strong mind and a good character." He could feel her hands tightening about his as she said: "And I was scorned as few girls ever have been. Now I move from palace to palace, from country to country, and watch that silly man who scorned me slip down and down to an infamous conclusion."

She dropped his hands and sat with hers folded severely in her lap. "I could have saved him, Feliks. Jan Sobieski was a great king because he had a great wife, that Frenchwoman. Stanislaw Poniatowski could have been a great king if he'd had character and support. But he doomed himself when he elected easier routes."

She left her chair and displayed profound distress as she stamped about the room. "He doomed himself, and I shall do everything within my power to speed that doom. He is strangling in his castle over there, and where is Catherine to help him now?" She laughed. "Help him? She leads the three eagles who attack his liver."

"Why do you hate him so?" Feliks asked when the storm subsided. "I don't hate Elzbieta. I seem to love her even more."

"You're not a Czartoryski," she said. "I am, and I am cursed with tremendous pride."

"Are you working with the others . . . to destroy Poland, I mean?"

"What others?"

"At Niedzica, in Hungary . . . they gathered like vultures. Mniszech for Russia, Lubonski for Austria, Baron von Eschl for Prussia . . ."

"Were they at Niedzica?"

"They were. For two weeks at least."

"And had they maps?"

"They did."

"And you guessed what they were up to?"

"I did. Count von Starhemberg came up from Vienna to speed things."

"And what did you think, little spy, that they were doing?"

"They were preparing the final assault on Poland."

"That is exactly what they were doing, little spy. You're a clever lad, and now we must take the necessary steps to protect your future in this time of change."

She drew her chair close to his and said: "I love a lad who can weep for a lost lady. Feliks, we must find you a wife." Before he could respond, she said with that striking realism which marked all she did: "We must find you a wife with money, Feliks. All you have to offer is a good appearance and a respectable name. To that you must add money if you are to survive in the new Poland."

"The Mniszechs laughed at me when I wanted to marry Elzbieta. Ignacy himself served me the black soup."

She astonished him by saying bluntly: "So also would I, had you come courting my daughter. No magnate of serious importance is going to accept you into his family. Poland has a thousand lads like you, young, good-looking, two horses and a historic name. Feliks, in the grand design you are nothing, and you had better realize that cruel fact."

He gasped at the severity of her analysis, but when she hammered at him: "Do you acknowledge that what I say is true?" he had to answer: "Yes. But what shall I do?"

"Money is everything. And how shall you find money?" As she uttered this harsh summary of his situation she indicated with a sweep of her right hand the immense sums the Mniszechs must have spent to build this little *palais,* this flawless salon. "Feliks, tell me, where are you going to find the money?" Again she intercepted his answer: "Only by marriage to the daughter of some rich merchant."

When he protested that he had no desire to humiliate himself by marrying a townsperson, she became impatient: "Whom are you to choose, Pan Feliks? You can't marry into a magnate's family. And you mustn't just drift along, marrying the daughter of some petty gentry as impoverished as yourself. Your fathers always did that, and where did it get them?"

This brutal question had only one answer; Bukowski men had never made brilliant marriages, and as a consequence they lived in penury, obligated to do whatever the various Counts Lubonski directed, and it looked as if they must do so interminably unless Feliks could find himself a girl with money.

In the gathering darkness the Princess Lubomirska instructed the young man she had once said she wished were her son: "There is in Warsaw a wealthy merchant of tested character. I like him, always have. His name is Orzelski and he has a daughter of your age named Eulalia. He is rich enough to hope for her marriage with a young man of nobility. You're poor enough to hope for marriage with an heiress. I think we should visit this Orzelski." And without allowing Feliks to object, she led him down the stairs of the Palais Princesse, which would now hold his beloved, and out to her waiting carriage, where she was again lifted over the mud. "We shall go to Orzelski's."

Gustaw Orzelski conducted a large establishment that imported goods from St. Petersburg, Paris, Vienna and London, sending in return the lumber and wheat of Poland, and since he had served as banker for many of those with whom he conducted his negotiations, he had been able to amass a respectable fortune. Princess Lubomirska, of course, had met him only at his place of business, a large and handsome store on a street parallel to Miodowa, and it was there that she went with Feliks.

"This is my dear and trusted young friend Feliks Bukowski, of good family, who has come to court your daughter." Orzelski, now in his fifties, bowed low to the princess and offered a respectful but limited nod to Feliks. Then, with the boldness which characterized Lubomirska in all her negotiations, she said: "I think we three should drive directly to your home, Orzelski, because these things do not wait."

"But it wouldn't be fair to Eulalia . . ."

"Send your carriage on ahead. Right now. To warn her. You ride with us." And it was she who dispatched the Orzelski footmen with instructions that Panna Eulalia was to present herself within the quarter-hour in her own drawing room.

During the tense ride to the Orzelski home, a large house but not a palace, on Krakow Suburb, Lubomirska spoke forcefully: "I think God must have ordained it that my Feliks should meet your Eulalia. These two young people need each other . . . desperately . . . a union made in heaven."

"But, Princess, I've just met this young man, and he hasn't even seen my daughter."

"True, but sometimes things are arranged in heaven, and this is one of them." She would allow no further discussion. "What a splendid little palace the Mniszechs have put together for their daughter. Have you seen it, Orzelski?" He said that he had supplied the furniture from Paris: "And very good it was, too. Also the crystal hangings in the salon."

"I didn't notice them," Lubomirska said.

"For good reason. We don't install them till tomorrow."

When they reached the Orzelski home the two men were perspiring, one more nervous than the other, and as Eulalia moved forward to greet them Princess Lubomirska understood why, for as she was to write to a confidante: "The unfortunate girl stepped clumsily at us, fat and red and positively oafish, and my heart wept for Feliks, but she was the only young woman available with the proper amount of money, so we had to accelerate things lest she fall into the hands of another."

It was a painful meeting, Eulalia blushing like a wounded beet, Feliks barely able to hide his shocking disappointment, and Orzelski obviously dismayed to realize that he and Eulalia were not to find with Lubomirska's help a member of the magnate class, to which they had rather fatuously aspired. Tea was served in the English manner, with china from France, and Eulalia played rather more heavily on the piano than her Viennese professor would have approved. There was no mother, she having died some years previously, but there was a younger daughter as florid and awkward as her sister.

It was a doleful meeting and Lubomirska knew it, so when the two girls were excused, with Eulalia almost bolting from the room, she became angry and sat the two men before her as if they were schoolchildren:

"You, Orzelski, are disappointed that you are unable to find a young man from a family of greater distinction. You, Feliks, behaved shamefully, showing your disappointment in not finding a rich girl of greater beauty. Who are you, pray tell me honestly, Pan Feliks, to demand anything? What have you accomplished either in acts or wealth that entitles you? I am disgusted with you, that you should humiliate a young girl in that brutal way. I am disgusted with you!

"My dear friends, both of you. Families are like birds in the sky. Yours, Orzelski, is flying upward . . . wealth . . . respect . . . hopes. Yours, Bukowski, is swooping downward . . . no money . . . no propects . . . only honor . . . historic pride. [Here she moved her now-heavy arms beautifully in the air, making crisscrossing patterns.] You are caught in a moment when your two paths cross, one brief moment in infinity. Orzelski, Bukowski occupying the same fragment of the heavens. You will never cross paths again. You will never again share this mystical moment.

"Now I want you to listen. Orzelski, if you marry your daughter to this young man, you gain esteem and the possibility of his promotion to almost any position in the government, whatever it's to be. Bukowski, if you marry this wealthy girl, your son can aspire to the daughter of a major family and his son might marry the daughter of a magnate. This is a golden opportunity for each of you.

"Feliks, I want you to go right now to whatever room Panna Eulalia sits in, crying her heart out, and I want you to ask her if she will walk with you tomorrow, and you are to smile, and kiss her hand, and tell her that you shall await tomorrow with joy . . . with joy, do you hear?"

She pushed him from the room and sat talking with Orzelski about his last purchasing trip into Russia and about how he would conduct himself if Poland were ultimately destroyed; he judged that whoever took over would require business affiliations, and he was prepared to provide them.

Feliks did walk with Eulalia the next day, and before the week was out he and Eulalia met with Orzelski and Princess Lubomirska, who said: "When a young man like Bukowski has no father, he having died with great heroism in a ridiculous cause, some older person must serve as parent, and I am proud to do so. I want the wedding to be held in my palace, for I have grown to love this young fellow and wish him well."

It was arranged that the Mniszech-Lubonski wedding would take place on Tuesday and the Orzelski-Bukowski on Thursday, and they were the highlights of the fading winter season, one brighter and more lavish than the other, and fortunately, Princess Lubomirska was never told of the curious behavior of her protégé on the night of his wedding, but it was known among her servants:

> "The wedding ended in our palace at three, and a procession of sixty horses led Bukowski and his bride to her home on Krakow Suburb, where one must suppose the marriage was consummated, but toward three in the morning he was seen leaving the Orzelski house and walking, without a hat, through the mud and snow to Miodowa, where he stood silent in the street, staring at the new Palais Princesse. He was there at dawn, just staring at the *palais,* when Pan Orzelski himself came and without saying a word led the young man back home."

That very afternoon Jan of the Beech Trees came to the Orzelski home with secret information that an officer of the cavalry wished to see Feliks, immediately, so the confused young man allowed himself to be taken to a coffeehouse near the cathedral where a group of fiery young men were speaking in hushed voices, which often rose into daring cries: "Kosciuszko has appeared on the streets of Krakow, back from France and America, and he says that Poland can defend herself."

"Is he to be trusted?"

"None better. A true patriot."

"How old is he?"

"Nearly fifty, I suppose."

"Too old! Too old! He'll start something, then quit at the first cannon fire."

"Not Kosciuszko."

"Has he a chance? I mean a serious possibility?"

"We can win!"

Feliks was impressed by the structure of this group: three sons of magnates, half a dozen lesser gentry like himself, four or five sons of merchants like Orzelski, and a handful of students from no discernible background. Seven were cavalry officers, the most eager of the lot, and all were of the opinion that patriots must move south immediately to support what appeared to be a major uprising.

The only question Feliks voiced was one of the most profound: "Whom are we fighting against?" and one of the leaders said: "Against them all."

He learned, however, that the real battle, if one developed, would be against Russia, whose Empress Catherine was uttering bold threats. "Can we defeat Russia?" one of the cavalrymen asked, and another answered: "Prussia will move in to help us, you can be sure." Feliks, having overheard the conversations at Niedzica, was not at all sure.

But during the next week excitement in Warsaw grew, especially when one of Kosciuszko's personal lieutenants slipped into the city to enlist volunteers in what he described as "our great crusade." Feliks was inclined to join those who that day started to move south, but as a new husband with the responsibility of introducing his bride to her country home at Bukowo, he felt an obligation to return south with Count Lubonski rather than with the revolutionaries, and on the long ride home when he asked the count what he thought of men like Kosciuszko, the answer was: "A man of good family, but a renegade. Picked up rotten ideas in America and especially France. Poland, no matter how it splits, will always be a country of peasants down there and magnates up here, and if you apply your new money wisely, Feliks, you can become a magnate one of these days . . . not soon, but quite possibly."

"What will happen to Kosciuszko?"

"Forget that name! He's a flash. He'll march out of Krakow, and if the Russians don't destroy him, the Prussians will."

"His people think the Prussians will rush to aid him."

Lubonski broke into laughter. "How ridiculous can you get, Feliks? It's Prussia that's determined to annihilate us." He paused.

"And maybe with good cause. Maybe it will be better for us all when Poland quietly vanishes."

"Do you believe that?" Feliks asked in obvious astonishment.

"Of course! Feliks, don't you see that with your new funds, Warsaw is your enemy! It's Warsaw that talks about liberties for the peasants . . . land for the townspeople . . . seats in the Seym for Jews, even . . . Once we allow that festering sore to be eradicated, Russia and Austria and Prussia will surely protect interests like yours and mine."

When Feliks started to ask: "But is there not a general sense of—" Lubonski halted him: "I'll tell you what the general sense is— revolution. And it has got to be stamped out. Men like you and me will soon be fighting against Kosciuszko, not for him."

On the second of April 1794, word reached Bukowo that General Kosciuszko—he held that title in the armies of three nations: France, America, Poland—had marched from Krakow at the head of two battalions and twelve heavy guns, and on the very next day Jan of the Beech Trees rushed into the manor house, where Eulalia was beginning to supervise things, with even more disturbing news: "General Tormasov of Russia is marching with a big army toward Raclawice just across the Vistula." And on the fifth of April messengers sweating with excitement crossed the river: "Kosciuszko has won a great victory. Routed the Russians completely."

Now the contrast between Count Lubonski, defender of the old freedoms, and his liege Bukowski, aspirer toward the new, became irreconcilable, because the former summoned his private army to support the Russians, while the latter, attended by his peasant Buk, opted to join Kosciuszko, and though neither Lubonski nor Bukowski would have fired upon the other personally, each considered the other a traitor to Poland's cause and hoped that the traitor's side would perish.

In a small boat Feliks and Jan poled themselves across the river on 6 May 1794, the master armed with two guns, the serf with a mowing scythe and a length of metal-studded ash tree. When they landed on

the far shore, they were greeted with exciting news: "General Kosciuszko himself is going to meet with us."

"Where?" Feliks asked.

"Here at Polaniec," the men said, and they were correct.

One of the crucial events in Polish history was destined to occur
only a few miles from Bukowo at the ancient market village of Polaniec, and all that night patriots discussed the first great victory at
Raclawice and those still to come as the Russian forces of General
Tormasov and his Polish allies—among them, Count Lubonski—
were driven out of both old Poland and the territories stolen in the
two partitions. It was a night glowing with the sparks of triumph, but
it did not compare with what was to happen on the following day.

It was about a mile from the riverbank, near which the men had
camped, to the tree-lined field where the general was to meet a large
assembly of local citizens, hoping to enroll them in his crusade; he
was especially eager to entice men of substance like Bukowski from
the Austrian territories, and all that morning little boats from the occupied zone slipped across the river bringing new conscripts to the
cause.

Symbolically, Feliks and Jan, master and serf, walked together up
the gentle hill from the river and along the beautiful country road
leading to Polaniec, joining a growing crowd, each man armed in his
own peculiar way but most with scythes, which they were prepared to
use against Russian guns. They came at last to the field, where several
thousand irregular troops, themselves variously armed, marshaled
the newcomers into orderly units well scattered over the area.

At noon a wild shout of victory arose from the troops, for Kosciuszko himself was coming up the slight rise, and what caused the
shouting was the fact that he was wearing, for the first time in this
campaign, the heavy white felted peasant's jacket popular in Krakow.
"He's one of us," shouted the men with scythes, and the orderliness
which the troops had tried to enforce broke down as men from everywhere rushed forward to greet their hero.

Forty-eight and in the glory years of his life, he looked a veritable
hero. Not tall, not robust, he was spiritually commanding, a handsome, compact man with an almost angelic clean-shaven face framed
in copious hair which came to his shoulders. He wore his usual uniform with the air of a patrician, which he was, and his peasant's cloak
with an easy informality that made him one of the people. Most of
all, he was a leader, for when the rest of Poland lay sunk in chaos,

betrayal and despair, he alone had stepped forward with a promise that the nation could be freed, and with his early victories against almost insuperable odds, had proved his claim to the spot prepared for him. Without dismounting, he launched into his oration:

"Men of Poland! With few, we proved that we can triumph and bring real freedom to our imperiled land. With many, we shall drive the invaders from our fields, reunite our severed parts, and establish a new nation founded on justice.

"I speak especially to you men with scythes and clubs who fought as your ancestors did against the Teutonic Knights at Grunwald. When victory comes, you are to know a freedom you have never known before, and as of this moment your liberation begins.

"Peasants of Poland, you are free! Peasants of Poland, you have all the rights other men have, and I shall name them. The land you have worked so faithfully can never be taken away from you by your landlord. The forests you have tended shall be your forests too, and everything that grows therein you, too, shall share, the wood and rabbits and the deer. The days of labor which you have given your magnates and gentry shall be diminished by three-quarters. Where last year you worked eight months for them, you shall now work two.

"We form a new partnership in Poland, and we form it now, the master and the peasant side by side, rejoicing in new freedoms, new liberties for all."

The proclamation was so sensational that it sent shivers up men's spines and giddiness to their heads; few of Kosciuszko's listeners could assimilate it entirely, but one landholder, who stood to lose much under the new rules, cried with remarkable insight: "Hooray! France and America have come to Poland!" And the air was filled with waving scythes.

From his horse, General Kosciuszko reached out and grabbed one of the scythes and demonstrated how it was to be used in battle: "From the most ancient times farmers have used the scythe to mow their grain. Look, it forms a letter L, long handle, short cutting edge. If you carry it into battle that way, nothing can be achieved, because the Russians aren't going to stand there waiting for you to come close and cut them down." Men who had already been in battle laughed. "No! What you must do is this." And deftly he untied the little ropes which bound the blade to the haft, then retied them in a way to hold the long, sharp blade as a forward extension of the handle, transforming it into a pike eight or nine feet long. Stabbing and jabbing with his new weapon, Kosciuszko cried: "The weapon of freedom." Then, touching his peasant's cloak, he added: "The uniform of freedom!" and his rude army bellowed its approval.

Bukowski and his serf Jan did not return home; they were caught up in the frenzy and would remain so for the duration of this amazing effort. They marched with Kosciuszko toward a small town west of Sandomierz where a Russian detachment was garrisoned, and with the scythe-men rushing forward, impervious to gunfire and the roar of cannon, they overwhelmed the enemy. In this battle, which lasted only forty minutes, Feliks captured two fine Russian horses, and thinking to reestablish the old tradition, he took one to Jan of the Beech Trees, saying: "Jan, hold this for me in case I need him in battle," and to his astonishment, Jan said: "I fight on my own, and you on your own," and he would not tend his master's horse as his ancestors had faithfully done for seven centuries. Feliks solved the problem by finding a young lad to serve as his squire, but now he had to pay money for this service.

Some of the gentry were outraged by Kosciuszko's revolutionary idea that peasants could be set free, and after they experienced the kind of rebellion which Feliks had seen with Jan, they muttered protests: "This can never work in Poland. Peasants are born to serve, and the harder they work for us, the more content they are."

"They're cattle, really," one landowner said.

"I did not say that," a protestor said. "I asked Bishop Proszynski about that very topic, and he told me firmly: 'The peasant has a soul. He is a real human being, but he was born to work and needs no alphabet or books.' Kosciuszko is terribly wrong in thinking he can give them freedom."

Some of the disenchanted asked to speak with the general, who kept himself open to all, and after he had listened to their complaint that Polish peasants were different from French or American, he said firmly: "I have been forced to travel much. I've seen many lands. And I've learned one thing. All men are alike in the eyes of God. All are entitled to the same freedoms."

"But the Polish peasant . . ."

"Is exactly the same as the French peasant, who is exactly the same as the French nobleman."

"Could the French peasant appreciate a good wine?"

"I have seen them do so . . . when they invaded the master's cellars with guns and torches."

"Aren't you preaching revolution against the gentry?"

"I am trying to avoid revolution against the gentry. Come my way, dear friends, and you will save Poland. You'll create a much better society, believe me."

The more Feliks saw of Kosciuszko, the more he admired him.

"This man is all of one piece," he told the dissidents. "He treats his horse with the same respect he treats me, and I've seen him treat my peasant Jan with the same respect he treats his horse. And he can laugh at himself."

One night at the campfire before a morning battle with a Russian army, Kosciuszko sat with his cavalrymen, smoke from the embers wreathing his handsome head. "I knew a lot of trouble with General Washington, maybe the best man on earth these days. He made fun of my name, said no one could pronounce it or even remember it. Recommended that I change it to Kook. I grew angry and told him: 'Look here, General, my name has the same number of letters as yours, and the same number of syllables, too. It's *Kosh-choosh-ko*, and anyone with an education ought to be able to say that,' but he continued to pronounce it in four syllables *Koss-eee-yoú-sko* and sometimes even *Ko-shuń-ko*, so I stopped trying to educate him."

"Was he a good general?" Feliks asked.

"He was a lucky one, and that's even better."

"How, lucky?"

"About fifteen times when I served with him the English could have killed us dead had they attacked at the moment. Always they hesitated, allowed us to regroup, or bring up reinforcements, and I call that luck."

"May the same luck attend us," an older man said, and Kosciuszko replied: "It is for that we pray."

During one waiting period, when it looked as if the rebels were going to drive the Russians clear out of all the Polands, old and new, Feliks and Jan slipped away, crossed the Vistula, and sneaked back into their homes, where Feliks saw with amazement the many good things that Eulalia had done in his absence, and he noticed that when his wife was dressed as a rural housewife rather than as a Warsaw belle, she could be quite handsome, the kind of woman Princess Lubomirska must have been when King Stanislaw August, the young Poniatowski, rejected her. It was rewarding to talk with her, for she loved to explain in detail what exactly she had been doing: "I decided that the stables should have windows, and in the village I found this man with remarkable skills as a carpenter, so I paid him to—"

"You paid him?"

"Yes. Your general's proclamation at Polaniec reached here and the peasants believe they are free."

"But . . ."

"I see no great problem, Feliks. We pay them a little. They work harder. We earn more. And everybody's better off."

She was still, as Lubomirska had so harshly described her: "fat and red and positively oafish," but she was also pregnant, and this gave her an appealing dignity, and since her father had supervised her education, she had accumulated ideas from the books in three languages which she had brought with her to the manor house. Eulalia Bukowska was exciting to be with, for she had already adjusted to the new world that was coming and saw a score of ways by which she could use it to her husband's advantage.

"Win the battles and hurry home," she told Feliks as he prepared to rejoin Kosciuszko for the inevitable confrontation with the Russians at the gates of Warsaw, but before that crucial battle could be joined, a Russian general of supreme talent arrived in Poland to replace all those who had allowed Kosciuszko to outsmart them. He was Aleksandr Vasilievich Suvorov, a scrawny, ill-tempered sixty-five-year-old military genius who had spent half his life battling the enemies of Catherine the Great on distant fields and half-battling the Russian establishment, which despised him for his unorthodox behavior. He was a remorseless adversary, and when he appeared on the scene the Russian backbone stiffened.

The showdown battle occurred at the village of Maciejowice, some distance south of Warsaw, and in the early stages Kosciuszko's extremely brave peasants with their scythes created their customary havoc with the Russian lines, wave after wave of pike-wielding serfs simply smothering the czarina's troops, but in the end the discipline of a professional army tipped the balance. In one cruel charge—three hundred Polish peasants armed only with clubs against eight hundred Russian riflemen—Jan of the Beech Trees was shot four times through the chest and head, his dream of freedom ending on a grassy mound.

Kosciuszko, wounded, was captured and taken to a Russian prison, but he had encouraged some of the younger officers to escape northward to oppose Suvorov in his attack upon Warsaw. Feliks Bukowski was one of these, and in October, when the first snows were already falling, he slipped into the city, riding one horse and leading another. As he went down Krakow Suburb and turned into Senatorska, thinking to announce himself to Lubomirska, he saw Miodowa, the Street of Sweet Nectar, and turned abruptly into it, riding slowly toward the Palais Princesse, where his beloved lived in her little marble mansion.

He reined in his mount, and for some minutes stood quietly, his two horses gladly resting from their long march, and after a while children gathered, asking him about the battles, and he told them that General Kosciuszko was lost and that the battle for freedom was imperiled. They asked him where he had got his horses, and he explained that they had been captured from the Russians. They wanted to know the horses' names, and he told them "Czar and Czarina," and one little boy yelled "They're both men horses," and he said "I must have the names wrong."

The noise in the street attracted attention from within the marble *palais,* and a stern footman appeared to caution silence: "The young mistress is gravely ill and deserves quiet."

"Who? Who?" Feliks cried.

"Pani Lubonska, the Mniszech mistress," the footman said. "She delivered her son and he does well, but she herself is endangered."

Feliks leaped from his horse, throwing the reins to the boy who had noticed that both horses were male, and shouted: "I must see her."

"That you cannot do," the footman protested, and when Feliks brushed past him, dashing toward the door, the footman began to bellow, making far more noise than the one he came to silence: "Master! Master!"

At the entrance to the *palais,* Roman Lubonski intercepted him: "Feliks! From where?"

"From the battlefield. Kosciuszko's lost."

"I expected that," the young nobleman said; he had not joined his father's army opposing the revolution, but spiritually he had supported the Russians, and was pleased to know that the rebels had suffered a major defeat.

"I want to see Elzbieta," Feliks said, at which Roman began to weep: "You cannot. Not even I am allowed . . ."

"Is she so ill?"

"Gravely." And Roman retreated into the *palais,* closing the door behind him and shutting Feliks, his companion of many years, off from any contact.

For two days Feliks stood watch in Miodowa; he slept spasmodically at Lubomirska's palace, talking with her in brief interchanges and learning that she reveled in the approach of Suvorov and the imminent termination of Poniatowski's kingship. Once Feliks said: "The poor king, Suvorov attacking him from the outside, you trying to bring him down from the inside." She replied: "He surrendered his crown the moment it was placed on his noble brow, for it did not fit. He had no concept of what it signified. And his cowardice before Catherine disqualified him. It has been thirty years of unceasing surrender and it's time we terminated it."

One morning she told Feliks: "I'm as bad as Poniatowski. I ought to have you arrested as a traitor—a Kosciuszko man . . . freeing the peasants and all that rubbish. But I love you, Feliks . . . By the way, how's the little Orzelska, though God knows she's not so little."

"She's bigger now, Pani. She's pregnant."

"Thank God! That's what matters, Feliks. A family, a farm, a cradle, obedience up and down—that's the soul of Poland and now you're a part of it."

"Your nineteen castles, Pani? Should you be allowed to keep so many?"

"Poland needs leadership, Feliks. Only the magnates can give it. And besides, I rebuilt my castles and palaces, and no one else would."

"Your hundred and fifty thousand peasants—the ones you own. Kosciuszko told me—"

"Kosciuszko is a fool, and he will die in a Russian prison. The basic Poland will never change."

She encouraged him to see the Mniszech girl, and on the third day he went boldly to the door of the Palais Princesse and demanded entrance. There was a scuffle, during which he forced his way in. Dashing upstairs, he threw open door after door until he located the sickroom, barging in just before Roman Lubonski could stop him.

"Elzbieta!" he cried, rushing toward her, but when he saw her dreadful pallor he realized that she was near death, and he halted some feet from her bed, standing with his head bowed.

She was even more beautiful than he had remembered—a young girl on a sleigh, a young woman cheering the bear hunters on their trip into the mountains, a young bride kneeling before the priests, and now a young mother approaching death. He did not speak, but his heart called her name, this splendid Mniszech woman who stood in the grand line of czarinas and murderesses and ghostly figures dressed in white on castle turrets. Oh, Elzbieta, it was worth a lifetime to have kissed you once.

Tears like the river at Niedzica rushing through the gorge came from his eyes, and after a while, without ever having spoken to the dying girl or without her having been aware that he had been in her room, he allowed Roman Lubonski to lead him away. All that day he stood in Miodowa, and at dusk, when bells inside the Palais Princesse began to toll her passing, he bowed his head and even his body, as if the weight of centuries lay upon him.

The end of Kosciuszko's insurrection came with a force so terrible that all Europe shuddered. It was never known for sure who gave the order for the Pacification of Praga, or in what form General Suvorov received it; it was suspected that Catherine delivered it in person, but some believed that Fyodor Kuprin wrote it out as part of his grand design for the Final Partition: "You must teach these Polish pigs a lesson." No better agent for such a lesson than Suvorov could have been found, for on 1 November 1794 he threw his massive Russian army around the suburb of Praga on the right bank of the Vistula opposite Warsaw, where a last remnant of some 14,000 Polish patriots, including Feliks Bukowski, had assembled to try to protect the capital. Praga also contained about 10,000 civilians who were doing what they could to support the defenders of their little settlement.

Against these Poles, Suvorov had brought up an army of nearly 40,000 professionals, and when the battle for Praga started he told them: "No mercy. No prisoners. We must teach these pigs a lesson."

The siege lasted only three days, the first, second and third of November, for on the fourth the Russians broke through, and then the terrible slaughter began. Of the 14,000 Polish troops, only 4,000 escaped to flee across the Vistula; the rest were gunned down, mercilessly. Those who tried to surrender were shot as they raised their hands in the air. Thousands more were bayoneted when they sought to submit. Those who tried to resist were clubbed to death with rifle butts. Groups of twenty and thirty Russians would chase down an alley after one Polish soldier and stomp him to death when they caught him. And the only ones who survived within the city were those few like Feliks who hid themselves in cellars until the fury passed.

But it was the ruthless slaughter of the civilian population which stunned Europe, because Suvorov's men rampaged through Praga, shooting everyone who moved and stabbing those who didn't. Knifings, beheadings, shootings, castrations, rape and then piercing became the rule. It is said of such horrible affairs that "the gutters ran with blood," but that is ridiculous; however, in Praga blood did drip into the gutters, staining them forever with the hideous vengeance of the Russians.

On the evening of the last day, a roving patrol of Russian soldiers heard a noise in a cellar, and when they inspected they uncovered Feliks Bukowski, two Polish peasants with scythes, and a woman whose infant child had made the noise. With the savage sweep of a rifle butt they silenced the child forever, and with two bayonets they slew the mother. The sight of the peasants with scythes infuriated them so that they stabbed each of the two men a score of times, and then, recognizing Feliks as a member of the gentry who may have encouraged insurrection against Catherine's power, they kicked him to death, their heavy boots breaking most of his bones.

The dream of real freedom was ended. The sham of Golden Freedom was restored.

In early 1795, Baron von Eschl and Fyodor Kuprin met for the last time in the Granicki palace in conquered Warsaw, and now they were assisted by Count von Starhemberg from Vienna. With cold efficiency the three victors restudied the map already agreed upon at Niedzica, and only slight variations had to be made in the boundary lines that separated the territories of the three partitioning countries.

Poland vanished, the new lands of Russia, Prussia and Austria meeting at a point not far from Brzesc Litewski, which the rest of the world would know as Brest-Litovsk. Each of the conquerors acquired lands he had long lusted after: Austria gaining Lublin and Pulawy; Russia picking up the Ukrainian estates owned by magnates like Lubonski and Granicki.

There was no justification for this terrible rape of a free land. Such nations as Switzerland had long been encouraged to exist as buffers between larger powers, and there was no reason why Poland should have been denied this privilege, except that she had committed two fatal errors: she had evolved no way to defend herself with a stable government, regular taxation and a dependable army; and in her weakness she had endeavored to initiate freedoms which threatened the autocracies which surrounded her. Had her neighbors been England, France and America instead of Russia, Prussia and Austria, she would surely have been permitted to exist, for the innovations she was proposing were merely extensions of what that first trio had already accepted. To be both weak and daring is for a nation an impossibility.

But it was what Baron von Eschl proposed during the final meeting that would shock the world when it was revealed; for many years his memorandum was unknown in foreign capitals, for it was not allowed to circulate, and there would always be some who would deny that it was ever promulgated, but it had been:

> It is the wish of my King, who is supported by the Empress of Russia, that from this day henceforth the word *Poland* never be used in any official document or spoken in any government circle. In our several portions every effort must be made to stamp out the language, the history and the observations.

> If a nation does not exist, the name does not exist, and we must never allow either to revive again. We have been patient. We have been compassionate. And we have been just. But as of this day a new order rules in eastern Europe, a final solution has been reached.

With remarkable speed, peace and adjustment came to Bukowo. Jan of the Beech Trees was dead, but his widow would mind the fields until her son could assume charge. Their welfare deteriorated savagely, for with the defeat of General Kosciuszko and the imposition of foreign rule, rich landowners were encouraged to convert the hours their serfs owed them into cash taxes, which meant that Jan's son now owed Lubonski not forty weeks of hard labor but a hundred and ten zlotys, which he could accumulate only by many hours of additional labor at wages established by the count. Life for the peasants of Bukowo became increasingly brutal, reverting to the days of 1250, but at the same time the Lubonskis grew richer, and soon they rivaled the wealthiest families of Spain or England.

Eulalia Bukowska was left a widow with a child about to be born, but she had grown to like the old manor house of Bukowo, appreciating what could be done with it if her dowry was wisely spent; her plans were both artistic and sensible, but they came to naught, because her father spirited her back to the new Warsaw, now in German hands, where his business was flourishing. In the city he found her a new husband, a member of the gentry slightly more elevated than Feliks had been, and as Lubomirska had predicted, his grandson would be eligible for membership in that gentry. So the Bukowskis lost all the Orzelski millions and the manor house reverted to its unkempt meanness. Ownership passed to Feliks' younger brother, who suffered for some years because it was remembered that Feliks had participated in the insurrection.

For Tadeusz Kosciuszko, immured in a Russian jail, the disappearance of Poland brought dramatic consequences: Catherine the Great, near death and seeing no possibility of further danger from the Polish hero, stayed the execution which he had expected, and at her death he was reprieved completely. Seeking voluntary exile in France, he refused an exalted appointment from Napoleon, whom at an early point he had interpreted correctly as a tyrant, and as the years rolled round he lived to see himself avidly sought after by the Russian czars as their representative and intermediary in government for their Polish holdings. But he, like the two Bukowskis, loved freedom as a tangible entity; it was good to be free, and it was good to bring freedom to others. So he chose exile in Switzerland, and one of the last acts this great man performed was to set free a group of slaves he had been awarded in America. General Suvorov, on the other hand, was rewarded for his famed Pacification of Praga by being given two thousand serfs as his personal property, some of them coming from the estate Count Lubonski held at Polz in the Ukraine, and he showed no signs at all of freeing any of them.

The Lubonskis fared well under the new regimes, receiving additional estates and privileges as a reward for the army they had contributed to the alliance. They prospered politically, too, for when the Habsburgs realized that they had all of Galicia, and a good deal more, securely in their grasp, they looked about for reliable Polish leaders to rule the area, and Count Laskarz Lubonski was remembered for his long and faithful services. Appointed governor of the area he had been so instrumental in bringing into the Austrian fold, he took immediate steps to ensure that his son Roman would one day be appointed to the Vienna cabinet itself.

But before this became practical, it was essential that Roman find a second wife, and especially one who had the potential for forwarding his career. There was an ugly little byplay with the Mniszechs, who insisted that title to the Palais Princesse, which, after all, they had built for their daughter, revert to their family, but Count Lubonski argued in the courts, with a battery of lawyers from Berlin, that under Polish law title had passed to the husband at the moment of marriage, and a bench of three judges, who took bribes from both families, decided finally in favor of the Lubonskis, who had paid the most. Palais Princesse, retaining its lovely name, was now the Warsaw seat of Roman Lubonski, who would soon be Count Lubonski of Vienna.

Selection of his next bride took a curious turn, for one summer's day his mother, the present Countess Lubonska, appeared alone at Lubomirska's palace with a startling proposal: "Princess, I've been thinking about many things—Europe, Russia, especially the Habsburgs in Vienna. And if my son is to pick his way intelligently through the traps I can see looming ahead, he's got to have a clever wife. My husband has never trusted your family—'Those damned Czartoryskis!' he calls you, always stirring things up. But as I grow older I see that the perfect wife for my son would be some able Czartoryski girl—someone exactly like yourself, as you were fifty years ago. Are there any?"

Lubomirska was flattered; it had always been her task to keep track of the marriageable children in her extended family, so it was easy for her to rattle off four names of girls who were showing real promise: "You need someone who knows languages. Russian for the future. French for the past. German for power and English for common sense. Of course, she'd have to have Polish for singing."

"How many do you speak?"

"Those five plus Italian. But she should also have had experience in the good schools of Switzerland, Italy and either France or England. Forget those of Germany, they train only policemen. Above all, as you Radziwills know, she must be clever."

"And attractive."

"If she's all the rest, she'll be attractive. My nephew Karolek at

Pulawy has exactly the girl you seek, and may you be lucky enough to find her before someone else does." That evening she dispatched a rider to Pulawy with a simple message: "In the case of Moniczka, do absolutely nothing until the Count and Countess Lubonski arrive." And next day the Lubonskis traveled south to Castle Gorka to pick up their grieving son Roman for a casual visit to the great Czartoryski families at Pulawy, where a marriage was arranged.

The final days of King Stanislaw August were mournful. During the siege of Warsaw his brother Michal Poniatowski, Poland's leading Catholic clergyman and her primate, had been so eager to escape capture by revolutionaries that he wrote a secret letter to the King of Prussia, advising him how best to capture the city. Unfortunately, his message fell into the hands of Kosciuszko's men, who were so outraged by it that they threatened to hang him. The distraught king, thinking only of his throne, presented his brother with a terrible edict: "Hang yourself, for if you wait for them to do it, the scandal will destroy the throne." Michal had obeyed, but his suicide accomplished nothing, for soon thereafter both the throne and the nation collapsed.

Stanislaw August, no longer a ruling king, became an embarrassment to the victorious powers, who solved his case rather neatly: he was taken to Russia as a kind of state prisoner, and although he repeatedly petitioned his former bedfellow, Catherine the Great, for mercy, she refused to grant it or even to see him. Having found many lovers she liked better, she allowed him to rot in his comfortable prison, and there, in 1798, he died, an exile, a rejected lover, the unwitting architect of his nation's suicide.

VII

MAZURKA

TWO DAYS BEFORE CHRISTMAS IN THE YEAR 1895 THE SPACIOUS steamboat that plied the Danube between Vienna and Budapest arrived at the former city in early afternoon, bringing with it a tall, slim man in his mid-forties. Since he was a nobleman and a member of the emperor's cabinet, he was given special treatment; when the steamer docked in the canal, which had been dug to bring an arm of the Danube right into the heart of the city, all lesser passengers had to wait until this austere gentleman debarked into the cold, wintry town, his massive fur coat drawn tightly about him as protection from the snow which drifted down.

He was Count Andrzej Lubonski, Minister of Minorities, whose mission to conciliate the Hungarian agitators had succeeded so conspicuously that he could expect commendation when he reported to the emperor. Hungarians were not easy to deal with; they demanded all and conceded nothing, but he had to respect their furious patriotism and would tonight give public evidence of that respect.

Waiting for him on the quay were two liveried servants, one driving a curtained carriage drawn by two handsome gray Lippizaners, the other a footman who handled luggage and then rode perched beside the driver. Policemen monitoring the arrival area recognized the count's carriage and gave it deference; other would-be politicians from the lesser provinces of the empire, places like Croatia and Tyrol, sometimes tried to make a splash when they came to Vienna, acquiring for themselves a team of four or six dazzling white Lippizaners, but such men were quickly perceived as being *nouveau,* a French word much used in the capital, and were ridiculed.

Count Lubonski, with one of the richest holdings in the Austrian section of Poland, could have afforded sixteen Lippizaners had he so desired, but he felt that such display was best left to the royal family; he would be content to have his sober-gray carriage drawn by sober-gray Lippizaners, but he did have four matched teams.

Acknowledging no one, he moved quickly from the gangplank to his carriage, where he said simply: "Ringstrasse." The footman busied himself with adjusting the bearskin robe that would protect Lubonski from the cold, then scrambled to his perch, and the carriage was on its way.

It proceeded along the quayside for some distance, then left the Danube Canal, turning into that glorious chain of boulevards which encircled the ancient heart of the city. Thirty-eight years before, in 1857, the Emperor Franz Josef had decreed that the walls of Vienna, which had protected it so valiantly in centuries past, should be torn down, with the empty glacis which then separated the fortifications from the encroaching suburbs to be converted into a number of wide, tree-lined avenues, on each side of which were the great buildings of government. It had required nearly a quarter of a century to complete this grandiose plan, and some historians had objected to the demolition of walls which reached back almost a thousand years.

"Let us retain in Europe one noble city which illustrates how our ancestors lived," these antiquarians argued. "Let the new Vienna proliferate on the other side of the glacis, and keep our walls as the symbol of our city's history."

The emperor would not listen, and although Vienna lost an awesome medieval monument, it gained as noble a series of boulevards as the world provided. "Paris has better," some travelers claimed, but the French ones, named after Napoleon's marshals, were not so intimately connected with the heart of their city, nor did they have that sequence of majestic buildings.

On its Ring stood the great museums, the votive churches, the university, the theater, the Rathaus, the buildings of parliament and the stately opera. When Count Lubonski drove past these solid monuments he felt that he was at the center of the world, and he always rededicated himself to his assigned task of keeping the multiple minorities which comprised the Austrian Empire placated within the intricate system.

Lubonski dealt constantly with members of some forty different national minorities: the able Hungarians, who were almost the majority; the fractious Croatians; the Italians, whom no one could discipline; the Rumanians, thirsting for their freedom; the Transylvanians, caught in a vise between more powerful groups; the Bohemians, keeping Prague in uproar; the Slovaks, insisting upon their own entity; the Wends; the Ruthenians; the Slovenes; the Montenegrin fragment; the Bosnians; the Germans of Silesia, who felt themselves oppressed; the agitators from Bukovina, from Temesvar, from Teschen, from Carniola and the Trentino. And always, in the back of his mind, the special problems of the Poles, who occupied Galicia; they were in some respects the strongest, ablest members of this amorphous empire, and he had been chosen for this difficult assignment of keeping all in balance primarily because he was a Pole.

The emperor had advised his councillors: "Lubonski is a Pole, and they're damned difficult, but he's also a gentleman. Vast estates. I'm told he keeps ten thousand Ukrainians on his fields. He'll understand minority problems." Several of his German advisers had counseled against bringing a Pole into the highest levels of what was still essentially a German government, Austrian style: "We've made concessions to the Hungarians, and we're no stronger for it. We've granted the Czechs and Slovaks what they wanted, and if we promote this Lubonski . . ."

As with the tearing down of the ancient walls, the emperor had his way, and the Pole Lubonski was brought into the government. It was a sagacious move, for every complaining faction of the empire now felt that with a Pole in charge of their affairs, they would get at least a decent hearing: "For is he not himself a member of a client state, like us?"

With a gloved hand, the count slid back a glass partition separating him from the coachman. "Karl Peter, if Bukowski is at his coffeehouse, I should like to speak with him."

"Yes, Excellency."

The carriage continued along the Ring past the university, then pulled into the garden of a fine old building housing one of the better coffeehouses of the city—Landtmann's, a brocaded, chandeliered refuge where hot chocolate, European newspapers and gossip were provided. Karl Peter, going to the entrance hat in hand, inquired of the doorman: "Is Herr Bukowski, the young Pole, is he in attendance?"

"He is," the doorman said, pointing to a blue-and-cream fiacre whose public driver dozed while his fare disported himself inside. "That's the one he always hires."

"Please to advise him that Count Lubonski would like to speak with him. In the count's carriage."

At the mention of this respected name the doorman drew himself up to a haughty position, nodded toward the carriage, whose curtains were still drawn, and hurried inside the coffeehouse. In a moment he appeared with a young man of slight build, trim mustache and well-pressed, modish suit. In his hurry to report to the count, the young fellow had merely thrown about his shoulders an overcoat made of English wool, and with bare head he half-ran toward the carriage, whose door opened invitingly as he approached.

"Come in, Wiktor," a voice said, and with one continuous, graceful movement the young man entered the carriage and took a seat opposite the count.

"How was Budapest?" he asked.

"As always. Music good. Food very good. Countesses the most beautiful in Europe. Politics . . ." He shrugged his slim shoulders. "As always, the worst in Europe."

"Can I be of service, Excellency?" Wiktor Bukowski did not work in Count Lubonski's ministry; he held a minor position in the Ministry of Agriculture, where he was appreciated as an expert on horses, but as a young Pole new to the capital, he naturally fell under the supervision of the count, who utilized him now and then on farming matters and instructed him in the ways of the imperial city.

"The emperor had a message awaiting me when the Budapest boat docked. Seems there's a gentleman from the Banat with an urgent problem."

"I've met him, Excellency. Man named Pilic. He's stopping at Sacher's."

Lubonski frowned. It had been his experience that self-important agitators from the provinces always stopped at Sacher's Hotel near the opera and took their sweets at Demel's near the Hofburg, and more frequently than he cared to remember, these enthusiastic patriots had tried to lure him to one of those establishments for discussions of pressing problems. It had become a matter of pride with him never to have entered either the hotel or the pastry shop: "They are for visitors, not for those who do the work of empire."

He could visualize this Herr Pilic from the Banat. "You don't have to describe him, Wiktor. Small, thin man. Heavy suit made from Rumanian wool. Leans forward when he speaks. Has moist hands when he greets you. Thinks he's in heaven because he's in Vienna. But desperately wants to take Banat out of the empire." He shook his head dolefully. "I really do not care to see him."

"I'm afraid you must, Excellency. He's come a long distance."

Lubonski sighed. Everyone who wished to see him in Vienna had come a long distance, because that was the nature of the Austrian Empire. It was a very long, dusty train ride to Croatia, much longer to the remote corners of Transylvania, and in some ways the longest of all from Vienna to Prague, which was not distant in miles but infinitely separated in ideas.

The Banat of Temesvar was a small territory wedged into a corner by Rumania, Hungary, Transylvania, Serbia and Croatia, abused by all, defended by none. Herr Pilic, judging by his name, was probably of Rumanian descent and had come, no doubt, to complain against his Hungarian oppressors. His mission must be serious, for the emperor himself had directed Lubonski to listen to his protests.

"Fetch him to my house," Lubonski said. "Half after six, sharp."

"Yes, Excellency. You would not care to stop by his hotel right now?"

Lubonski did not change his expression. "I do not stop by hotels." And he kicked open the door, indicating that Bukowski was dismissed, but before the younger man could leave, the count reached for his arm and said warmly: "The countess and I will be expecting you tonight, after the concert."

"I shall be honored. I shall be deeply honored, Excellency." And while Bukowski returned to the warmth of Landtmann's and his London newspaper, Lubonski directed his coachmen to take him home.

Now he pulled aside the curtain on the right-hand side of his carriage, for he was approaching that string of noble buildings which made the Ring so distinctive, and he wanted to see them. As he passed them he experienced once more that inner warmth which suffused him when he reflected that he played a major role in the governance of this city and the empire which it represented. As a Pole he missed the Vistula, and his castle, and his vast estates in Galicia, and the winter visits to Warsaw, but in Vienna there were compensations, and now he approached one of them.

For after his Lippizaners, noticed favorably by all who appreciated good horses, had drawn him past the splendid museums, they reached the opera, that crystal-pure little heart of the city, loved by all who loved Vienna, and there they turned north into Kärntnerstrasse, and for the first time in his journey from the boat Lubonski saw ahead of him the noble spire of St. Stephen's Cathedral, seven hundred years old and the beaconlike center of the city.

A light snow had begun to fall, throwing a blanket of silver over the ancient church, and Lubonski directed Karl Peter to halt the carriage so that he might savor this lovely sight. Then, with a knock on the partition, he indicated that the coachmen should proceed. They drove only four short blocks, then turned right into a small, distinguished, almost private thoroughfare labeled on the corner *Annagasse*. Had it been a wide street, it would have been called Annastrasse; its present name signified an alley or a very narrow street, and this it was.

It contained, close to the cathedral, some of the finest small houses in Vienna, three- and four-story affairs, severe in façade, soberly austere in the courtyard, interiors often magnificent in their muted splendor. With quiet satisfaction Lubonski checked off the houses in his alley, visualizing the notable families that lived therein, and finally, at the end of the row, on the right-hand side, he came to a modest house, its front occupying every available inch of sidewalk, its stone plaque proclaiming in the style used two centuries before, when street names were not jumbled together:

ANNA GASSE

22

1648

It had been an old house when King Jan Sobieski marched down from Krakow to save the city from the Turks, and under its cellar there was still a deep cavern dug by the Turkish sappers who had planned to blow up the city with their huge deposits of gunpowder.

Now came the moment that Lubonski relished whenever he returned from a trip to Hungary or Bohemia or Croatia. Karl Peter rang a bell attached to the carriage. Servants inside the house ran to the two huge gates, swinging them aside. The horses left Annagasse and drew the carriage inside, where a very large square, not visible from the street, was paved with blocks of oak rather than stone, the purpose being to muffle the sounds of hoofbeats.

Many Viennese houses and minor palaces had such courtyards, with twenty or thirty rooms wrapping around the area, but what distinguished Lubonski's 22 Annagasse was the wall that faced the visitor when he entered, for during the past hundred years servants had carefully pruned a huge pyracantha bush into a magnificent espalier which bifurcated beautifully left and right as if drawn by some master designer. One set of branches outlined the windows of the first floor, another emphasized the second floor, and a third, high against the wall, crept under the windows of the fourth floor.

Even in late spring, when the plant seemed rather drab, it provided a grand design, but in autumn and winter, when it produced a multitude of bright orange berries, it was a thing of splendor. Now, at Christmas, with light snow festooning the leaves and the berries, it was stunning, and the count stood in the courtyard for some minutes, appraising it and thinking of how fortunate he was that his great-grandfather had bought this perfect place years ago when the Lubonski part of Poland first fell under Austrian control. His family had owned this house for more than a century; his servants had brought this pyracantha to its present state of perfection; and he sometimes thought that it was this sturdy plant whose roots tied him so strongly to Vienna.

Leaving the courtyard, he hurried inside, ran upstairs, greeted his wife, Katarzyna, and called for a bath. "I'm to meet some dismal fellow from Temesvar. Yes, here. Then we go to the concert. And I hope you've invited the musicians for dinner afterward."

His wife, a daughter of the great Zamoyski family whose estates since 1815 had been in Russia, enjoyed sitting on a stool in the bathroom while her husband bathed, for then she knew that she could command his unbroken attention, and now she smiled at him and asked if his meetings had prospered in Budapest.

"Famously. If I weren't a Pole, I'd enjoy being a Hungarian. Robbers both."

"Who's the man from Temesvar?"

"A Herr Pilic. Rumanian, I judge."

"But why here?"

"He's stopping at Sacher's, and I refuse to conduct business in hotels." He paused. "You remember, I'm to wear my Hungarian uniform tonight. To show that in Vienna, I pay them the same respect I do in Budapest."

Lubonski, like all members of the imperial cabinet, owned twenty-odd different resplendent uniforms. Some pertained to historic Austrian regiments, but more than half were gold-and-silver-and-bronze-decorated uniforms of foreign governments: Russian, German, French, English and one dazzling affair from Italy. It was international courtesy for an Austrian official to appear in the uniform of any visiting king or prince, and Lubonski always honored this convention, except that he was ill at ease in the Italian uniform, since the northern section of Italy had so recently broken away from Austria.

More important, in view of his particular responsibilities, were the eight or nine gaudy uniforms of the various components of the empire; if he entertained Polish officials, he customarily donned Polish dress; Bohemians were honored by seeing him in their national costume; and Slovaks were similarly respected. Patrician in all aspects, he graced any uniform he wore, but the one which gave him solid pleasure was the Hungarian.

As he left his tub his wife withdrew, leaving the dressing of her husband to his servant, and this man toweled his master, powdered his feet, attended his hair, and led him to where a gorgeous assembly of clothing, medals, daggers and swords awaited.

When his underpants were adjusted, the valet doing the work, he slipped into the skintight suede trousers, then the knee-length woolen socks that would fold down over the calf-length elk-leather boots from Bohemia. He chose a lightweight silk blouse, subtly embroidered in pale-red and blue designs, with a silver clasp at the high ribbed collar. His jacket was of Hungarian peasant pattern, heavily brocaded and rather florid when compared to the tasteful blouse. He wore a cap made in Budapest, a tricorn affair topped by egret feathers, and about his shoulders he draped a leopard skin, beautifully finished and fastened with three silver frogs.

Resplendent as he was, he was not yet fully costumed, for a wide sash pulled everything together, whereupon his valet slipped into the stocking of his left leg a sheathed dagger ten inches long, while into the folds of the sash Lubonski himself fastened a long sword with a gold-and-silver handle.

He presented a dashing figure when all parts were given last-minute adjustments by the valet, who said admiringly: "The emperor himself will applaud you this night."

He received a less enthusiastic welcome from Herr Pilic when he entered the drawing room at six-thirty: "My God, Your Excellency! I came all the way to Vienna to protest against the Hungarians, and here you are, a Hungarian nobleman."

Lubonski enjoyed such sallies and explained: "Yesterday in Budapest, I gave the Hungarians nothing they wanted. Tonight in Vienna, I give them this." He pointed to his shimmering uniform, then asked politely: "And what can I give you, Herr Pilic?"

"The Hungarians, they treat us like peasants."

"Sit down, please." Lubonski ordered wine, but told the butler: "No tokay, please. Herr Pilic does not enjoy things Hungarian."

"What I don't like," Pilic said, "is the way in which the Hungarians abuse your imperial government. Your Excellency, they take everything from you and give nothing to us."

Lubonski chuckled. "No one has ever said it better, Herr Pilic. The Hungarians badger us day and night for what they call their freedoms. Heavens, they run the empire. But always they want more. Yet they treat their own minorities like swine. Slovaks come to me crying complaints about them. Rumanians, Transylvanians, Croats, Slavonians . . . it's always the same: 'The damned Hungarians are persecuting us.' What can the emperor do? Tell me, please."

"The Banat of Temesvar must be an independent unit within the empire."

Lubonski called for an atlas, and when its large pages were unfolded he pointed to the Banat, a mere speck within the vast complexity of Austria's responsibility: "Herr Pilic, look for yourself. What you ask is an impossibility. We can't fragment this great empire."

When Pilic started to remonstrate, Lubonski stopped him. Pointing now to huge Galicia, many times the size of the Banat, he said: "Look at my Poland. A huge territory. But we exist within the empire."

"You don't have Hungarians on your necks."

"True." The count leaned back, keeping the atlas on his knees, and said in the most conciliatory way: "Pilic, share with me your honest thoughts. I need your counsel. What do you think should be done?"

"May I speak frankly?"

"You've come very far to waste your time, otherwise."

Without waiting for the servant, Pilic poured himself a large drink, gulped a good portion of it, and said: "A confederation. Each natural nation on its own. The Banat. Croatia. Bohemia. Carniola. Hungary off to itself." When he saw Lubonski frowning he added quickly: "Poland too. Poland a nation of its own."

Lubonski showed no change of expression, for he suspected that Herr Pilic might have been sent by his German enemies within the government to test his loyalty. Ringing for the servant to pour additional drinks, he said quietly: "So far as I know, there is no outcry for a Polish state. Or for one in Carniola. Or Bohemia."

"There is great unrest in Bohemia, Excellency. You must know that."

"One out of ten thousand does not constitute great unrest, Herr Pilic."

"If he is the right one, he does."

"I am not aware of any great demand for a separate state in the Banat."

"But you must be aware of our anger over the oppression we suffer from the Hungarians. They are not easy people to live with, Excellency. You know that. They are hell to live under."

"Would the Rumanians be any better masters? Or the Slovaks?"

"Why must we have any masters?"

Lubonski pondered this difficult question, so common in the empire these days, and replied gently: "Because that is the way God has ordained this part of Europe." And he placed his left hand on the map so that it covered most of the Austrian Empire.

"When you dress like a Hungarian, Excellency, you talk like one."

"Tonight I am Hungarian."

"So my visit is a waste of time?"

"No!" Lubonski cried, throwing the atlas aside and rising to his feet. "Herr Pilic, you shall meet all my subordinates. Right after Christmas. And they shall listen to your complaints, and if justice is required, you will get it."

With his leopard skin falling gracefully over his tunic, the count placed his arm about his visitor's shoulders and walked him to the door, assuring him as he went that he had arranged this extraordinary meeting in his home because the emperor himself had requested it. "The Banat of Temesvar may be small, Herr Pilic, but it is never lost in our conscience."

"It's an honor to talk with someone who knows where it is."

"And now I must help my wife prepare for the concert."

"May the music echo with the sounds of Christmas," Pilic said as he went down to the courtyard, where a surprise awaited him.

"I've asked my coachman to return you to your hotel," Lubonski said, and he watched with real pleasure as the little man climbed into the exquisite carriage and settled back against the cushions as the two gray Lippizaners clip-clopped their way upon the oaken blocks that softened the sound of their going.

The gala Christmas concert was held in a theater that seated more than a thousand, but for the first part of the evening the guests looked less at the stage than at the imperial box, where the Emperor Franz Josef sat. The emperor—sixty-five years old, with heavy white sideburns and mustache—was married to one of the most glamorous women in Europe, and one of the most neurotic. Empress Elizabeth, a German of the House of Wittelsbach, had lived with young Franz Josef long enough to bear him three daughters and a son, but had then sought refuge from the intense boredom of the court by traveling incessantly—Greece, Italy, France, England—by building a vast palace for herself on the island of Corfu, by attaching to herself a series of what she called "my attendants"—a Greek professor, an English hunting gentleman, an impecunious teacher—and by writing impassioned letters to other men under one of her pseudonyms: Gabrielle, the Countess von Hohenembs, Mrs. Nicholson.

No other supreme emperor in history had ever been so poorly served by his wife as Franz Josef. Empress Elizabeth's behavior was a scandal and her lavish expenditure of public funds a threat to the monarchy, but Franz Josef could do nothing to discipline her. Instead, he sought refuge in a bizarre way: a forty-year alliance with one of the most ordinary mistresses an emperor had ever selected, and on this night she was visible to the Viennese public.

Kamarina Schratt, deserted wife of a minor Hungarian landowner, had made herself into a popular actress in comic roles. Not pretty, not gifted, not blessed with any unusual talent, she had developed a rowdy style of comedy which exactly suited her bubbly personality and her rather plump form. She was, in fact, an Austrian hausfrau converted into a most ordinary actress, and it was because of her commonplace appearance and behavior that the emperor had chosen her as his companion and confidante.

This was reasonable, since Franz Josef, this all-powerful emperor of a sprawling empire which embraced all of central Europe, was himself a most ordinary man. He read no books, appreciated none of the great plays then available in Vienna, understood no music except German military marches, and failed even to comprehend the vast political movements which agitated his empire. Unable to control his beautiful empress, who saw him only a few days each year when she returned to Vienna from her interminable travels with other men, he found consolation with Frau Schratt, but in what precise way, not even the intimates of the court could say.

"Is the little Schratt his mistress?" a Bohemian politician asked Count Lubonski during a painful set of negotiations. It was customary in Vienna to use the phrase "the little Uspanski" or "the little Kraus" to refer to any reasonably presentable young woman who was unattached: it depersonalized her, making her fair game for the men of the city.

"The little Schratt? Who knows? I certainly don't," Lubonski said, and when on another occasion Wiktor Bukowski asked the same question, Lubonski reprimanded him: "It is not proper for a man your age to inquire into such matters."

On this evening Frau Schratt had come into the concert hall with the emperor, but she was not seated in his box, for that honor was reserved for the absent empress, but in a nearby box occupied by two noble families from the countryside west of Vienna. The buxom little actress refrained from looking at the emperor and he kept his eyes on the stage, but the pair caused great excitement among the Christmas gathering.

The program was in that heroic mold made popular in Beethoven's day, when an evening's entertainment might consist of two or three symphonies, a concerto or maybe two, improvisations by the pianist and perhaps a half-dozen songs. The Viennese loved music, and on this night they would enjoy a substantial treat.

A conductor well known in Berlin would lead the local orchestra in Beethoven's Eighth Symphony, a jolly, holiday affair, after which a Berlin pianist would join the orchestra to present Mozart's delectable Piano Concerto No. 21 in C major, K. 467. After an intermission, a group of singers from Munich would offer Brahms' glorious *Liebeslieder Waltzes,* with the Berlin pianist and one from Vienna as dual accompanists. Then the same singers with their pianists would venture a radical presentation: Gustav Mahler's *Songs of a Wayfarer,* scored not for contralto as originally composed, but for a quartet. Then would come a second intermission, after which a young Polish pianist from Paris, Krystyna Szprot, would offer a selection of pieces by the Polish composer Frederic Chopin. As the program, embellished with angels and Christmas ornaments, explained: "Mlle. Szprot will announce her selections from the stage."

When the Count and Countess Lubonski came down the aisle to their seats—as a conservative Pole working among Germans who distrusted him, he deemed it imprudent to take a box in which he would be conspicuous—his quick eye saw several things: the emperor had none of his family with him; the little Schratt was properly off to one side; young Wiktor Bukowski was in place, properly dressed, in the seat next to his; and Herr Pilic from the Banat of Temesvar had purchased himself a seat with other visitors from protesting provinces.

He also saw that the hall was resplendent in the Viennese style: glittering uniforms like his own, which often made the Austrian officers more beautiful than their women; at the last three European competitions Austrian uniforms had won first prizes for color, for design and for overall grandeur, but the military men wearing them had won medals for nothing. In its last four wars the Austrian army had been humiliated.

When the orchestra was seated, the Berlin conductor walked stiffly onstage, bowed to the emperor, then to the other boxes, and finally to the orchestra itself, and with a quick flash of his baton, sent the players into Beethoven's rollicking little masterwork, composed not far from where the musicians sat. The orchestra did not play the music, they danced through it, appreciating the fact that no other symphony in the repertoire would have fitted so perfectly the mood of this Christmas season.

But just when Lubonski was most attentive to the masterful way in which Beethoven was bringing his little gallop to a pleasing conclusion, he felt Bukowski nudging him; the young man was pointing to the imperial box, where the emperor had fallen asleep.

"Keep your eyes on the stage!" the count said in sharp rebuke, and by the time the German conductor reached the final coda Franz Josef was awake.

Bukowski, a difficult young man to repress, said as six husky stage personnel pushed a large piano into position: "If that thing ever started slipping . . ."

"It's their job to see it doesn't," Lubonski said. "Do you know the Mozart they're playing?"

"No. But I've heard both the Brahms songs and the Mahler. I'm waiting for them."

"You'll soon hear some splendid music, Wiktor. Listen carefully."

Bukowski was not much impressed with the first movement of the concerto and judged that the German pianist did not strike the piano keys hard enough; in fact, his mind wandered and he began to scout the various boxes to see which of Vienna's beautiful young ladies were in attendance, and at one point, when the piano and orchestra were marching through some undistinguished routines, he again nudged Lubonski and whispered: "That box next to the little Schratt? Who has it tonight?"

Lubonski was irritated by the interruption, but he was also interested in who might be attending in official capacity, and he followed Bukowski's discreet pointing. "That's the American ambassador. A boor, but extremely rich. From Chicago, I believe."

"And is that his daughter?"

"I suppose so," Lubonski said without looking. He loved this Mozart concerto and had picked it out on his piano to the extent that he could follow the music, but Bukowski, interested as he should have been in attractive young women, stared at the American box and tried to deduce what kind of person the ambassador's daughter might be: She could be his niece. Or just a visitor. Not what you'd call pretty. But striking. Yes, striking, and I'll wager that gown came from Paris, not Chicago.

He was engaged in such assessments when the first movement of the concerto ended with an agitated succession of sounds and a coda of some brilliance. "Wasn't that inspiring?" Lubonski asked, and the young man said: "One of the best, Your Excellency."

And then, as he still gazed at the American box, the orchestra began the second movement with a soft but very marked waltz beat 1-2-3, 1-2-3 in the winds, horns and cellos, atop which came the violins in a theme so delicate and lambent that he turned his full attention to the stage, where that obsessive 1-2-3 continued, with the violins producing an even more enchanting melody. Then, when he was not noticing the piano, that instrument broke in gently with its own statement of ravishing melody.

"Oh!" he whispered, but Lubonski did not hear. He was captivated by the elegance exhibited onstage: waltz beat, violin melody, piano statement, all fused into one of the miracles of music, a perfect harmony of composition and performance. This second movement of Concerto No. 21 was one of the most ingratiating ever composed, and Vienna accepted it warmly on this festive night. But Bukowski noticed that the emperor was again asleep. However, when he sought to point this out to Lubonski, the box was empty. Franz Josef had slipped away from this boring fiddling, as he called it, and after a decent interval Frau Schratt followed.

They would return to the palace, where in the emperor's private quarters she would make him a cup of hot chocolate and talk to him as he munched biscuits and warmed himself, after which he would be in bed by nine, for in the morning he must be up at four, reading carefully every report placed before him, making brief notes on the margins, altering nothing, commanding nothing, just working his way through another day at the head of his vast empire.

During the intermission Count Lubonski wanted to talk about the scintillating Mozart and the magical manner in which the three parts of the second movement were held in balance, but Bukowski was eager to see if he could manage in some way or other an introduction to the American ambassador and his entourage. He failed, but when the concert resumed he found a gratification he could not explain from the fact that the ambassador's daughter or niece was still in attendance.

The *Liebeslieder Waltzes* of Johannes Brahms had been written in Vienna for Vienna: to the lively accompaniment of two pianos a mixed quartet sang of the joys and despairs of love. Both Bukowski and his count knew these songs, so very popular in the city, and each had certain selections he preferred; Lubonski regarded the lovely apostrophe to the Danube, *"Am Donaustrande,"* a perfect evocation of the city in which he spent most of his time these days, and he was especially fond of the song to the little bird, *"Ein kleiner hübscher Vogel,"* for it reminded him of the pleasures he had known in the Vienna Woods in which the bird lived.

Bukowski, for his part, liked the cry of the tenor and baritone as they sang of their love for women in general, *"O die Frauen, O die Frauen."* This was a song which he himself might have sung, for he was fearfully confused about women; he cherished them, dreamed of them, wondered which one he would marry and whether she would agree to live half the year in Vienna, the rest in his rather gloomy half-mansion on the Vistula. During the twelve months of 1894 he thought he had been desperately in love six times, with six totally different young women, two Austrians, two Poles, one Hungarian and the niece of an English lord to whom he had never spoken, and this year had been no better.

Now he closed his eyes, allowing the rich sounds to flow over him with their heavy burden of longing, their promise of ultimate fulfillment, and the blending of the four voices, the extreme manliness of the baritone, the feminine apotheosis of the soprano, seemed to him the most powerful statement of sexuality he had ever heard. The vanished emperor was forgotten, the bright uniforms, the glitter of the boxes, the shimmering quality of the concert hall, all were gone and he was in some timeless setting. *"O die Frauen!"* he whispered.

"Hush!" Lubonski snapped, poking him sharply with an elbow. The count liked Bukowski, for the young Pole showed promise of becoming an excellent official, qualified to hold some important position in the Austrian government. A man of significance, especially a minority official like Lubonski, had to be careful whom he sponsored, because many young Poles had made asses of themselves in the capital. They'd proved themselves provincial yokels, bringing scorn upon all Poles, and until a young fellow had been tested, there was no way of predicting how he would meet the challenge of a great city like Vienna. A man could be of some significance in Krakow, yet prove himself a fool when posed against sophisticated Germans and Frenchmen.

Bukowski looked promising. He spoke German, French and some English, knew how to dress, flattered women easily and made small conversation with their husbands. But the real Bukowski had yet to show himself, and Lubonski would prudently mark time before pressing the imperial government to promote him.

The young fellow was unaware of the count's speculations, for the two women singers were uniting in a song which tore at his heart:

"A bird will fly afar
*   Seeking the proper glade.*
So a woman must find a man
*   Before her life can flourish."*

He was convinced that this was true, and he wondered when the seeking woman would find him, so that her life could blossom. Where was she? How did one locate the woman?

When applause for the singers ended, Lubonski told Bukowski

and the countess: "This next is rather daring, you know. Mahler, whom you met at the opera, wrote these wayfaring songs for solo voice. Now four are singing them, but you know . . ." He paused to nod to Herr Pilic, who had moved so as to attract Lubonski's attention. "You know that Mahler later borrowed the songs to use as the base for his first symphony."

"And very good it was," Bukowski offered.

"If you like Jewish music. The songs won't be light and dancing like Brahms, I can tell you that."

After only a brief pause the singers rearranged themselves and the two pianists began a slow and mournful theme, to which the voices soon added a lament, but now the spirit changed, and a broad swelling movement developed, in which Bukowski could visualize himself striding over bleak, empty spaces . . . alone. In the rich sadness of late youth he indulged his passion for romanticism, spurred on by the changing, driving imagery of the Mahler songs. Count Lubonski had been right; this music had little to do with Brahms, or Beethoven either, yet it was passionately Viennese, the almost majestic inheritor of the great tradition.

"It's very Jewish," Lubonski whispered to his wife, "but I must say I like it."

Throughout the cycle the two pianos and the four voices created an increasing sensation of persons lost in vast expanses, wandering forever toward some goal undefined and never to be realized. It was music for the year 1895, on a snowy night, in central Europe.

There is the key! Bukowski thought. I'm on the plains of Poland, Russian Poland that I saw once from the train. It's my land, my Poland, and I've never really seen it or been part of it.

Now his music-driven footsteps became longer, for he was striding toward something, toward a homeland which he had never appreciated when living in Bukowo as a child. As the music swirled about him, its marvelous minor harmonies inflamed his imagination, and he became for a moment the romantic Pole lost in a vast horizon.

"Do you like what they've done?" Lubonski asked. "The four voices, I mean?" When he looked at his young friend he realized that Bukowski was not in the concert hall but adrift in some wandering fantasy land, where a young man should sometimes be.

It was in this dreamlike state that Bukowski wandered through the salon of the theater during the second intermission, and at some distance from the bar, where servants in red uniform were pouring champagne, he encountered the American ambassador and the two women who could be presumed to be his wife and daughter. Lacking an introduction, Wiktor could not speak to them, but to his delight the young woman said to him in French: "It's very daring, the four voices I mean," and he replied in English: "Very powerful statement, is it not, yes?"

"You speak English!" the young woman said, reaching for the older woman's arm. "Mother, this young man speaks English."

"The newspapers, I mean from London, one reads them, you know."

"And what do you do?" the American woman asked forthrightly.

"Wiktor Bukowski, to your service, Ministry of Agriculture," he said. "And my sponsor, Count Lubonski of Minorities, told me that you were the American ambassador's family, yes?"

"Yes," the older woman said. "Where did Oscar go?" Looking around for her husband, she said, "Well, he's missing. This is my daughter, Marjorie."

"Miss . . ."

"I'm sorry. I'm Mrs. Trilling. This is Marjorie Trilling."

"I saw you enjoying the Mahler," the girl said, and Bukowski blushed like a schoolboy who had been complimented, deeming it incredible that this young woman from a foreign land should have noticed him particularly.

"You are beware that Mahler used these songs in his symphony?"

"Aware," the girl corrected with no embarrassment, and she did it so forthrightly that Wiktor was not affronted.

"I speak French a little better," he said, and she replied in French: "I knew about the Mahler. We played his symphony in our orchestra."

"You played?" he asked.

"Flute," she said, but before he could ask what orchestra, she was summoned by her father, who led his women back to the third part of the concert.

The six husky men had taken away the two heavy pianos used to accompany the singers, replacing them with a much frailer instrument with glowing ebony sides, and to it came a small, delicate young woman who wore a white dress with a beltline just below her breasts and whose black hair was adorned by a single silver clasp. She seemed much too small to manage the piano, but when she bent over to adjust the seat, she did so with such authority that it was obvious she was in command. Then, still bent forward, she smiled at the audience and said in French: "I must reach the pedals, you know."

When the laughter stopped she said, again in French: "Tonight I am proud to play for you selections from our great Polish pianist Frederic Chopin." From various quarters in the audience, marking areas where Poles sat, came murmurs of approval, at which she repeated her announcement, this time in halting German. Some applauded.

She proceeded to outline her program: "First I shall play the Ballade in G minor, Opus 23, then a few waltzes, and a lovely scherzo . . ." When she said this last word, Bukowski felt the count snap to attention and heard him whisper something to his wife, but the young man was diverted when the pianist said with great charm: "And I shall conclude with music that we pianists like very much, the études."

Seating herself carefully at the piano, adjusting her filmy white dress and testing her reach to the keys, she paused a long moment as if for the audience to appreciate how small she was and how large the task she was undertaking. Then suddenly she darted forth her hands and struck those five lovely notes which comprised the opening theme. She played with such alternating force and delicacy that the audience made no sound, listening intently to the flow of Chopin's beautifully contrived composition.

Bukowski, who intuitively preferred the opening orchestral selections to the singing, and the singing to piano solos, listened respectfully, proud that a Polish artist was playing music by a Polish composer, but not really involving himself in it. And even when Mlle. Szprot came to those faerylike arabesques that decorated the middle portion of the ballade, he remained detached, continuing so when she reached the thunderous closing passages.

"The little one can play," Lubonski whispered as the ballade came to a conclusion in which the five opening notes reappeared in force, then drifted gently away in the same melancholy which had characterized the Mahler songs.

The audience applauded loudly, more for the charm of the artist than for the skill of the composer, and like a practiced little flirt, Mlle. Szprot bowed gracefully and placed her hands over her lips as if she wanted to express her thanks but did not dare speak.

She played seven short waltzes with the delicate touch that one would have expected: extremely feminine, obviously light, almost inconsequential, but with such inventiveness as to make them proper ornaments for any Christmas celebration. Bukowski liked them, but realized that they were music on a much less intense plane than either the Beethoven or the Mozart.

Indeed, he was about to dismiss Chopin as a transparent lesser artist when Mlle. Szprot brought her waltzes to a graceful conclusion, full of arabesques and adornments, after which she left the piano, came forward toward the edge of the stage and said, first in French, then in Polish: "This is Christmas and I bring to my Polish friends a special present. First a group of seven mazurkas, the wonderful music that only Chopin could have written, and then . . ."

Again Bukowski felt Lubonski stiffen, and turned toward him as the count grasped his arm almost in apprehension. "And then I shall play for you the music we Poles have always loved at Christmas, the Scherzo in B minor." As she said this, Lubonski gave a muffled cry of delight, gripped Wiktor's arm even more tightly, and whispered: "I knew she would play it!"

It was a much different Krystyna Szprot who returned to the piano. Grimly, forcefully, as if she must make an important statement for all Poles living in exile, whether in Paris or the capitals of captivity like St. Petersburg, Berlin or Vienna, she attacked the mazurkas, those curious and terrifyingly inventive compositions which only a Pole could have written. The mazurka had begun as a kind of peasant square dance, much loved by Chopin when he was a boy living in the country, but in his creative hands it became a work of masterful overtone and implication. One English critic, marveling at the effects Chopin achieved with the form, said: "He took cobwebs of Italian moonlight, French elegance and German romanticism, mixing them all with Polish heroics, making of them something to which the Polish heart responds."

On this night that judgment was accurate, for when the Poles in the audience heard the famous rhythm of the mazurka, the same three-quarter construction as a waltz but with a much different beat, their hearts seemed to expand, as if some special and great musician were playing solely for them. No other nation had such music, and no other composer had used the country idiom so effectively. Bukowski was especially moved by a brief mazurka consisting of 1-2-3 repeated four times in a minor key; when he heard it he felt himself back on the banks of the Vistula.

But when Mlle. Szprot announced that she would conclude with the two mazurkas she particularly liked, he suspected that these might be something special and he listened with added attention, hearing in the first as gently modeled and poetic a piece of music as Chopin was to write; and in the second, a poem of broken rhythms, minor chords and subtle harmonics. The man who wrote this music, Bukowski concluded, was no ordinary genius.

Count Lubonski listened to the mazurkas with his head bowed, as if he wished no one to see how profoundly the music was affecting him, but this apparently was not the case, for when the great Polish dances came to an end he gripped Bukowski's arm again and whispered almost with joy: "Now we shall hear something! Do you know this scherzo?"

"No."

"You will."

At the first crashing chords of the Scherzo in B minor, Opus 20, several Poles in the audience began to applaud, but Bukowski could ascertain nothing unusual in the music; it seemed more chaotic and disorganized than the mazurkas, but as it progressed he began to hear chords of great distinction, as if they knew they were presaging something of importance, and he noticed that Lubonski tensed whenever these particular chords were struck. But then the music degenerated into mere frenzy and he lost its thread.

Then, however, after the most careful preparation the chords reappeared, very gently, very softly, transposing to a new key, after which came a long pause, and then the beginning of a theme even more ravishing than that used earlier by Mozart. It was perfection, and several Poles began humming in accompaniment, for it was a Christmas cradle song dating back a thousand years, an authentic voice of people to whom the coming of winter had been a time of starvation and terror and hope. At the start of the second statement of the theme, Bukowski heard the count and countess whispering softly:

"Lulaj-że, Jezuniu, moja perełko . . ."
(Rockabye, little Jesus, my little pearl . . .)

Bukowski, whose grandmother had sung this to him, sat with hands clenched, tears forming in his eyes, and he was actually relieved when Mlle. Szprot began pounding the piano in a recapitulation of the earlier frenzied wandering, but even as she did so, he began to hear those premonitory chords which assured him that the cradle song would appear one last time. It came, but in a much distorted form, as if to say that even Christmas passes.

Drained of emotion, Bukowski did not applaud at the conclusion of the scherzo. On this festive night he had frolicked with Beethoven, rejoiced with one of the best things Mozart ever wrote, sung of love with Brahms, and wandered over dark plains with Mahler. He had also peered into the soul of Poland, and he was much disturbed. He therefore looked with detachment when Mlle. Szprot came forward to announce her last segment: "Some people consider Frederic Chopin not too manly. I'll conclude with some of his more vigorous études."

She marched back to her piano like a little soldier, stopped, reflected, then said: "I am playing tonight on a Pleyel piano. One that Chopin once used in this city." And with that she slammed herself down on the stool, stamped her right foot on the pedal, and launched into seven of the strongest études, those strange pieces of music lacking in melody or poetic form but filled with the inherent power of the piano. But when one had accepted them as merely the exercises of a brilliant keyboard artist, they unexpectedly erupted into passages of extremely moving music, and when played by a contentious little Polish woman eager to display the full range of her favorite composer, they could be explosive.

She had arranged her selection with care. First a pair of quiet, intricate exercises that contributed only virtuosity, then two much appreciated by other musicians, the "Aeolian Harp" in A flat major, Opus 25, No. 1, and the "Butterfly" in G flat major, Opus 25, No. 9.

Bukowski did not know enough about the piano to appreciate the first four études, and since they featured no memorable melody, he listened quietly and without feeling obligated to respond, even though both composer and artist were fellow Poles. But when the pianist leaped into the "Revolutionary Étude" in C minor, Opus 10, No. 9, he could visualize his ancestor dashing into battle with Tadeusz Kosciuszko a hundred years earlier, for this was music right from the heart of Polish history, a fiery challenge, a call to patriotism—and he responded.

He was therefore in an unsettled frame of mind when she paused after the conclusion of the "Revolutionary," took a deep breath, and crashed out the eight powerful notes which constituted the structure of "Winter Wind" in A minor, Opus 25, No. 11. Still, he was not impressed, for it seemed too repetitive, the eight minor notes being first offered in a very loud version, then in a whisper, then in a host of variations, and he had about concluded that this very long concert had effectively ended with the earlier Chopin, when Mlle. Szprot began to play the last étude Chopin had written.

At first it signified little, some agitated arpeggios serving as a capstone to the evening, but then, to his amazement, he heard another set of deep chords beginning to evolve, once more predicting something of majesty. Then it came, a sequence of thirteen of the most wonderful chords he had ever heard. Perhaps no one else in that large hall even noticed them, and certainly none could interpret them as he did, but across the years of desolation and despair, the exile Chopin spoke to the exile Bukowski, and the world was turned upside down.

This last étude was not long, only two and a half minutes, but when the great chords appeared again, amid the wild fireworks, Bukowski could only sit limp in his seat. He did not applaud. He did not cheer when the pianist reappeared to bow and accept bouquets, nor did he rise when the Lubonskis did. He had been overwhelmed by a night which had struck him with fury, but the more significant episodes were only beginning.

When he left the theater, still bedazed, he found Count Lubonski's four carriages, each with its Lippizaners handsomely combed, and he remembered that it was his assignment to fetch the Munich singers to the reception being held at 22 Annagasse, so he told the driver of his carriage to pull aside and wait while he sought the musicians, and when he had them together, he bundled them into bear rugs for the journey through the cold Viennese night. To reach the count's residence they had to cross the city, and as the carriage swayed through the streets lightly covered with snow, Wiktor had an opportunity to talk with the Germans, and when he told them how much he had enjoyed the two duets *"O die Frauen"* and "A bird will fly afar" the singers were pleased with his knowledge of their work, and the two men began to sing their apostrophe to women, with Wiktor and the two women joining in, so that the carriage was filled with music. Then the women began their song about the necessity of finding a good man before happiness could be attained, and at the conclusion Bukowski asked: "Do you think that's true? That every woman must seek till she finds her man?" and the soprano said with disgust: "All men are donkeys," to which the contralto agreed heartily.

"Now wait!" the tenor protested, whereupon the soprano snapped: "And you in particular." The tenor tried to defend himself, but the contralto attacked him savagely, whereupon the soprano began to weep, drawing off into her corner, and Bukowski was perplexed. Onstage the four singers had appeared so handsome, so intertwined in their responsibilities that to think of them now engaged in some quarrel not explained was deflating. He judged that all of the singers were older than himself, in their thirties at least, and he supposed that they were married, in pairings he would never know about, and in his already disturbed mood he felt profoundly sorry for them.

"Was it pleasing?" he asked in German. "To sing the Mahler in four voices?"

"Frankly, it was disgraceful," the baritone said, and now he withdrew into his corner and conversation ended.

But Bukowski wanted to discuss this exciting concert: "Did you happen to notice those great chords in the last étude?"

"The what?" the tenor asked.

"Chopin's last étude."

"We weren't listening," the tenor said.

When the carriage pulled into the Lubonski courtyard and the singers saw the beautiful pyracantha, lit by six lanterns, they chattered noisily about the orange berries, the snow and the joy of being in Vienna. However, when they preceded Bukowski up the stairs to the main floor where the reception was to be held, a Viennese newspaperman said to Bukowski: "Four second-class voices. You'd never get the first-class to leave Munich at Christmas." Wiktor then learned that they were sailing next day to Budapest, and for a moment as they disappeared ahead of him he saw them as Mahler's wanderers, lost like himself on the plains of Europe.

The large room in which the Lubonskis entertained opened onto three others, so that 22 Annagasse provided an almost regal reception area and was decorated accordingly, with marble statues from Greece, red-and-gold curtains, small boughs fresh-cut from woodlands and many gilded chairs. In the center of the main wall stood a grand piano, for with the Polish nobility no evening was complete without music, and when the guests were assembled an important-looking, heavy man went to the piano, but not to play.

He was Herr Dr. Henzzler, leading music critic with a Berlin newspaper, and he said: "Count and Countess, ladies and gentlemen, artists of the evening, the city of Vienna has been a most gracious hostess, and all of us from Berlin thank you. We thank you for a most German Christmas."

Bukowski thought this an inappropriate and even ungracious statement, as if Germans held a monopoly on the holiday, but before he could develop this line of thinking his attention was diverted from Herr Dr. Henzzler to Krystyna Szprot, who appeared in a different dress, one which made her look even more elfin and delightful. A group of men quickly surrounded her, but he elbowed his way through and was paying his respects when Henzzler announced: "To complete our evening, Herr Limbrecht, one of Berlin's greatest, whom you heard interpret the Mozart so magnificently, will perform for us Beethoven's immortal *Appassionata,* after which Fräulein Szprot will play something by Chopin."

Bukowski winced at the comparison: "The immortal *Appassionata* and something by Chopin," and he watched Henzzler with distaste as the self-important critic showed pianist Limbrecht to the stool, as if he, Henzzler, were the host and in charge of this gala evening. In fact, Bukowski was so irritated by everything that had happened in the salon since his arrival that he scarcely heard the very good rendition of the Beethoven.

During the playing he moved close to Mlle. Szprot, who at one point whispered in French: "Are you Polish?" and he replied in that language: "I certainly am," and a fellowship manifested itself not only in her approving smile but in the fact that she reached out and grasped his hand momentarily, sending wild shivers up his spine. But when he attempted to hold her hand, she pushed him off and indicated with a toss of her pretty head that he must listen to the *Appassionata,* which was now moving into the slow and profoundly disturbing middle segment. Seeing Bukowski's disappointment at her rejection, she said in Polish: "He plays very well," and he whispered back: "But not as good as you."

When the Beethoven ended, to an enthusiastic applause led by Count Lubonski, Herr Dr. Henzzler returned to the piano to announce: "And now we shall have a divertissement by Fräulein Szprot and her fellow countryman Chopin."

Moving like a grand duchess to the piano, Krystyna Szprot stuck her jaw forward and announced in German: "I shall be playing the greatest sonata of recent history, B flat minor, Opus 35." She glared at the Berlin critic and plunged directly, and with a certain heaviness, into the Chopin masterpiece, but after the preliminary flights of tentative music were passed, she reached the wonderfully inventive passages in which the piano was made to sing in unaccustomed rhythms and exult in broken harmonies.

The audience separated itself into two halves: those Germans and Austrians who longed for the heavy, unbroken beat of the Mozart-Beethoven style, in which all parts were under control, with the music moving forward in orderly progression, as it should; and the Poles and French and some of the empire's minorities who responded to the more Slavic-Gallic improvisations of Chopin. No one was indifferent or perched in the middle. In Vienna you liked either Beethoven or Chopin and you defended your preference.

Lubonski and Bukowski, men from the Vistula, adopted Chopin and thrilled as the pianist gave him a majestic reading, subduing any effeminate tendency that some critics noted and making his music march with grandeur within a great tradition. With Beethoven, Lubonski thought during the energetic second movement, the piano was a kind of orchestra on four legs; with Chopin, it was an eagle soaring free.

But now Mlle. Szprot came to the third movement, that extraordinary funeral march which tore the human soul apart, reminding it of things dark and gravelike, and everyone in the salon paid close attention, for this was music just beyond the perimeter of what music could accomplish. The pianist seemed incredibly petite and wispily human as her deft hands played this heroic composition, but the effect was spoiled when she darted into the curious final movement, a brief minute and a third of confused chords that seemed to have no relationship whatever to the sonata as a whole, and certainly no contact at all with the stately funeral march.

She had played this strange passage defiantly, hammering out the ugly chords with great passion, then leaping to her feet as if to challenge the world to say anything against Chopin or his music.

Herr Dr. Henzzler was ready: "It illustrates what I've always said. Your Chopin is admirably fitted for rather delicate drawing-room fantasies. But in a big hall like tonight, or with the traditional sonata form . . . nothing."

"I beg your pardon," came a voice in stern German. It was Wiktor Bukowski, not known as a music critic. "Are you saying that Frederic Chopin cannot compose?"

"Not at all!" Henzzler said with heavy emphasis. "A little waltz, yes. What you call a mazurka, yes. But I think you will agree . . ." He turned and reached for Krystyna Szprot's hand, drawing her back to the piano. "Please, Fräulein, play the last movement of your little sonata again."

Abashed by this sudden command, she sat down and ripped off almost angrily the series which lasted for eighty seconds, of mixed chords and broken rhythms, after which Henzzler threw up his hands and asked: "Now, who can make anything of that?"

"I can," she cried in French. "Some great man has lived a fine life, as in the first two movements. He's buried with the admiration of the world, as in the third. And in the fourth, the mourners hurry away from the grave, talking and drinking and belching and laughing lest their hearts break."

There was silence in the huge room, broken when Count Lubonski started to say: "Ladies—" He was interrupted by Herr Dr. Henzzler, whose professional dignity had been offended by this snippet of a Polish refugee from Paris. Striding to the piano, he commanded Herr Limbrecht to take the stool and play themes as he directed: "Now listen to what a proper sonata is. The opening, please," and Limbrecht dutifully played the first theme of the *Appassionata,* after which Henzzler stated: "Everything must march in order. First theme, development. Second theme, development. Contrast, coda and a nice conclusion." He nodded approvingly as Limbrecht banged out the illustrations.

"The second movement? Slow, dignified, not too much development, or it grows tedious. Show them, Limbrecht," and the visiting pianist complied. "Now the third movement, and there can be only three, the law of the sonata says that. We want a strong theme but not elaboration, or we overshadow the first movement, which is the important one."

He explained how in the classical sonata all things were kept in balance, all things in order, arriving on time as they had always done, with nothing helter-skelter. That was the way Beethoven and Mozart had done it, as Herr Limbrecht so ably demonstrated.

"But your Chopin," he said, almost with contempt. "What does he do?" He beckoned to Krystyna Szprot, drew her to the piano again, and directed her to give him the broken, scattered themes of the first movement: "Who can grasp anything of such chaos?" He held an equally low opinion of the second movement, but as she played the somber theme of the funeral march he said sternly: "It's the middle movement that should be slow. Not the third. Never the third. And listen, the theme is too important for a last movement. And listen to the second theme. Much too powerful."

He then directed his pianist to play a few bars of the final movement, after which he gave his pronouncement: "Nobody in this world could make anything of that jumble. Our pretty pianist attempted an explanation, but that was literature, not music. No," he said, dismissing her, "I think we must agree that Chopin knew nothing about the sonata."

From the rear of the big room came a loud voice, quivering with rage: "And I think we can agree that you, Herr Dr. Henzzler, are a pig's ass."

It was Wiktor Bukowski, unable to bear the humiliation visited upon his countrywoman and her Polish composer. Breaking through the crowd, he ran from one woman to another, crying: "Have you a glove?" and when he was offered none, he snatched a large napkin from one of the tables on which the supper would be served, and with this waving in his right hand, he rushed at Herr Dr. Henzzler and slapped him across the face with it: "Beckmesser, I challenge you to a duel!"

Henzzler brushed the napkin away and started to ask: "What have I—" but the enraged Bukowski shouted: "You've insulted this lady. You've insulted the memory of a great musician. And you've insulted Poland. Name your seconds."

Henzzler, who was accustomed to conducting his vendettas in the columns of his newspaper, had not the slightest intention of accepting or even acknowledging this young fellow's preposterous challenge. "Come," he said to his German musicians, "we're not wanted here," and he stalked toward the door, followed by the two pianists and the man who had conducted the orchestra. But the four singers, having seen the food that was about to be served, did not wish to leave without something solid to eat; they could not dine heavily before a concert lest their diaphragms constrict, and now they were extremely hungry.

"Come!" Henzzler commanded, and the two men obeyed, lest he castigate them in the Berlin press, and they prevailed upon the contralto to follow, but the soprano, the one who had wept after telling Bukowski that all men were donkeys, refused to leave before being fed, and when Bukowski saw her defiance he broke away from the men who were restraining him and ran to her, clasping her hands and bringing them to his lips. "Madame, you are heroic."

Henzzler had seen enough disgraceful behavior this night, so he grasped the soprano's arm and pulled her out into the hall, where he turned to the crowded room and delivered his final judgment: "You Poles have Chopin, a manufacturer of confections. We Germans have real musicians, Beethoven, Brahms, Schubert . . ." He hesitated, then added with great contempt: "Not to mention Johann Sebastian Bach." And he was gone.

Count Lubonski, standing apart and watching the offended Germans leave, was worried. A fracas like this must be reported to the emperor, who was doing his futile best to placate the hot-headed young Kaiser Wilhelm, who had ascended to the German throne before his character had formed, and there could be repercussions, except that one lucky aspect of the affair might clothe it in humor rather than tragedy. Very clearly, at the climax of the fray, young Bukowski had chosen a most fortunate name: Beckmesser. By equating the insufferable Herr Dr. Henzzler with the comic villain of Wagner's *Die Meistersinger von Nürnberg,* Bukowski had given the brawl a broadly humorous coloration, and Lubonski was relieved to see that his guests were already laughing at the young Pole and repeating: "Beckmesser, I challenge you!" By tomorrow afternoon all Vienna, the city being the gossip center it was, would be chuckling over the discomfiture of the pompous Herr Dr. Henzzler, and perhaps even the emperor himself would laugh when Frau Schratt explained Beckmesser during their early-morning breakfast at which she cooked sausages for him.

Now waiters appeared with huge trays of food—French, German, Austrian, Hungarian, Polish—with wines from the first three countries. In his dashing Hungarian uniform the count moved from table to table, greeting his guests and apologizing for the disturbance, about which they continued to laugh.

When the feast ended he rose at his table and said: "No one could have performed better this night than our guest from Paris, Krystyna Szprot. But I wonder if she would grace us with a repeat of that wonderful scherzo, so that we might sing with her and announce Christmas properly?"

The guests applauded, and Bukowski, aflame with emotion, leaped to his feet and escorted the beautiful artist to the big piano, where she said in French: "It is an honor to bring the country fields of Poland into the heart of this magnificent city." And when she played the magic chords presaging the coming of the lullaby, everyone rose and all the Poles sang:

"Lulaj-że, Jezuniu, moja perełko,
Lulaj-że, Jezuniu, me pieścidełko . . ."
(Rockabye, little Jesus, my little pearl,
Rockabye, little Jesus, my sweet little one . . .)

But when the scherzo ended, with no applause and many tears, Bukowski, who had remained close to the piano, said almost pleadingly: "Mademoiselle Szprot, I was deeply moved by your playing of the last étude." And she looked up with melting eyes and said: "If you liked that, you're a true musician."

Following Krystyna Szprot's little additional concert, a professional Viennese pianist was brought forward to play for those guests who wished to dance, and a series of local waltzes filled the salon while men in gala uniform whirled about with women in silvery dress. It was quite beautiful, but toward two in the morning Lubonski announced that still another pianist, a Pole this time, would play mazurkas for dancing and that he and the countess and their Polish friends would remind the other guests how to perform this delightful dance, popular in much of Europe.

So the room was cleared even more than for the waltzes, and the mazurka began: bold country music from the piano; a 1-2-3 beat with a marked rubato on the second note; men on one side, women on the other; graceful patterns; swift exchange of partners; lively steps; much masculine posturing; much feminine coquetry.

Because she no longer had to play for the guests, Krystyna was free to dance, and on several occasions Wiktor Bukowski maneuvered to be her partner, so that she had to know that he was captivated by her, and she in turn liked him for his Polish manliness and the bold manner in which he had sprung to her defense. It was a heady mazurka they danced that night, the gold-and-silver brocades of the room quivering with the excitement.

At one point in the dancing, when Countess Lubonska was instructing a visitor from Moravia in how he must manage his feet to do the mazurka properly, the lines became entangled and Bukowski found to his embarrassment that he was at the center of a trio of beautiful women, unable to decide who his proper partner should be: there was the countess, a member of the Zamoyski family powerful in Polish history; there was a charming unmarried Viennese girl, daughter of a banker; and there was Panna Krystyna Szprot, the exile from Paris; and they each moved toward him as their partner.

"I have ruined the dance!" he moaned, not knowing which way to turn.

"The mazurka can do that sometimes," the countess said, laughing. And as the snow fell on the espaliered pyracantha and dawn approached over the Danube, the Polish exiles danced.

In the western part of Vienna, well beyond the Ringstrasse and not far from where the new railway station was to be built, there was a flat, spacious open area known by the curious name of Die Schmelz. For decades it had been used as a parade ground for military maneuvers and equestrian displays, and during recent years had been the site of festive gatherings between Christmas and New Year's. In 1895, when a springlike sun had dispersed the snow clouds, the army decided upon a gala to honor some event or other in the life of their perdurable emperor. The empress, of course, would not be present; she was in Greece, trying to sell the enormous palace she had built on Corfu only a few years before at a cost of millions.

Those who frequented the cafés looked forward eagerly to the event because it was rumored that the young Polish nobleman who had challenged the insufferable Herr Dr. Henzzler over his love for a lady pianist would be riding, and it was said that since he was an excellent horseman, the affair might be exciting.

Wiktor Bukowski had been invited to ride in the formal exhibition and to participate as well in the informal races, and there was a good chance that he would do well. When he reported to the ministry in Vienna, he had brought down from his establishment at Bukowo three of his best horses, Arabians strengthened by Polish stock, and they were regarded as the equal of any of the Austrian steeds.

Bukowski lived about as far north of St. Stephen's Cathedral as Count Lubonski lived south, but in a much more modest fashion. Concordiaplatz was a stolid paved square rimmed with handsome, conservative five-story buildings whose character was invariable. On the ground floor, small and expensive shops. On the first floor, known as the *Nobeletage,* the owner's family. On the second floor, the occupant who paid the most rent. On the third floor, some once-rich widow with her sister from the country. And on the top floor, reached by four flights of tiring stone steps, a large, almost impoverished family or collection of families. In the basement, of course, dark and often damp, lived the servants.

Bukowski rented the second floor, two of the rooms being assigned to his Polish servant Buk, who had come with him from the Vistula. The other six were sparely decorated and rather gloomy in their general effect. On the nights when he entertained, he instructed Buk to fill the big main room with flowers, polish the piano, which came with the apartment, and to use many lights in an effort to achieve a sense of gaiety and even grandeur, both of which escaped him.

His three horses lived rather better than he. They were stabled on the north side of the Danube Canal, only a few blocks from where he lived, and were exercised by an Austrian who loved horses and recognized these as exemplars. Bukowski did not use his horses in the city, reserving them for times when either he or his friends wanted to take a canter through the parks or in the Prater, which lay not far away. Slight of build, erect posture, he made a good figure upon his favorite mount, Mustafa, named after the famous Turkish general who had conducted the siege of Vienna in 1683 and from whom an earlier Bukowski had acquired the horses that had formed the basis for the Bukowo line.

In the city, Wiktor utilized a public fiacre, but he did it with such consistency, riding in it to work every morning, then relying upon it to carry him to Landtmann's coffeehouse in the afternoon, and to whatever affair he might be engaged in at night, that what was normally a public conveyance became in effect his private carriage. The driver was a dour Serbian who viewed his employer impersonally, disliking him because he was a Pole, respecting him because he paid promptly.

Wiktor Bukowski was not a wealthy man, but he did have a small, steady income from his Vistula estate, plus a gratifying salary from his ministry, so he lived well. Had he been willing to dispense with his horses, he could have converted his bleak and mournful rooms into one of the finer bachelor quarters in the city, but this he refused to do: "A Polish nobleman without horses? Intolerable."

He continued in his rather depressing quarters because at age twenty-seven he supposed that some day he would encounter the young woman who would change his life, and he would leave to her the furnishing of his rooms. Also, there was the reasonable chance that the woman who entered his life might be wealthy, with a house of her own, a palace perhaps, in which case he would abandon

Concordiaplatz—just walk out and leave it, but of course he would take his three horses to her stable, to be cared for by her footmen.

His great pleasure, which he indulged almost every day, was visiting Landtmann's, sitting in a brocaded booth, talking with friends, reading either the Paris or London papers, holding them conspicuously so that others could see that he had mastered languages, and having the café's famous hot chocolate. He did not like coffee, finding it too acrid, and since he exercised rather vigorously with his horses, he did not have to worry about gaining weight from the chocolate and the small sandwiches which Landtmann's provided. Prudently, he did not indulge in sweet cakes or pastries. Nor did he read books.

Into a life like this a public gala at Die Schmelz came like a burst of winter sunshine, and on the day after Christmas he directed Buk to have the horses in top condition for the exhibition. Twice he went to the stables to apply saddle soap to his leather fittings and polish the silver chains. The horses were curried, their hoofs blackened and their nails trimmed. They and their master would be ready.

But when he reached the coffeehouse this afternoon he found a young Austrian awaiting him with a message that Krystyna Szprot was playing that afternoon for a few friends and would be pleased if Pan Bukowski would attend. As soon as he heard these magical words, the chords of the Christmas scherzo began to resound in his head, and with great anticipation he called for his fiacre and invited the young Austrian to join him on the ride to the house at which Panna Szprot would be playing. And as he left the coffeehouse he could hear that whispering so sweet to a young man unsure of himself: "That's Bukowski. The Polish nobleman who challenged the German. Over love for a lady pianist. Gallant devil."

Krystyna had been staying with the other artists in a small and dismal hotel, but with the departure of the German singers, she was free to find her own quarters and had moved in with some young Polish students, at whose apartment she was going to play. It lay well beyond the Ring in the vicinity of the university, Alserstrasse, where students sought inexpensive quarters.

The apartment, shared by two couples, did have a piano, and when Wiktor arrived Krystyna was seated at it, running through some Chopin waltzes for which she apparently had little regard. After listening for some minutes, Wiktor went to her and said in English: "I am he who spoke for you . . . other night."

"I know," she replied in French. "My champion."

"Would you be so very kind," he asked in his good German so that the others could hear, "to explain for me how the chords progress in the first part of the scherzo? So that we know the lullaby is coming?"

"That would be interesting!" one of the students cried, and several gathered about the piano, but Krystyna gave her attention only to Wiktor, as if she had already formed an interest in him which she would explain at some later time.

Although Wiktor could not understand fully the words she used, he certainly grasped the musical meaning of her illustration, and was enchanted by the tricks Chopin had used to lead listeners like him into the exact trap intended: "He uses a chromatic progression, inserting chords of great importance which alert you to the coming of a significant passage. Listen, dominant to dominant by three simple stages. How beautiful! And now a seventh, half a tone higher. C sharp, this is E, G, an added seventh, then this aching half-tone higher, now back to B major. And now . . ."

With the subtlest artistry she drifted like a delicate cloud into the heavenly notes of the Christmas carol. But she played only a few notes, then crashed the keys in a dissonance and said sternly: "Let's go over it again. What you must know is that Chopin uses not a single note by accident. He is leading us along by the nose, as if we were children." And she repeated her instruction, but at the crucial point in the progression Wiktor cried: "Stop! There's the magic. How does he do it?"

Pleased that a fellow Pole had penetrated to the heart of the scherzo, Krystyna went back to the beginning, repeating her analysis.

"Does he use the same . . ." Wiktor hesitated for the right word in German, and Krystyna helped him in Polish: "The same strategy?"

"Yes. Does he do the same in the last étude?"

"The one you liked so much?"

Wiktor smiled with pleasure. "You remember?"

"About music I remember everything. No, Pan Wiktor, the process is not similar. The last étude is sheer power." She turned toward the students: "That damn-fool German said that Chopin was good for salon divertissements. Soft. Vague. Till Bukowski here slapped him in the face with a glove. It was a napkin, really. But listen to this, which I played that night on purpose to stifle such rumors."

She launched into a titanic rendition of the final étude, striking the great chords with such force that the room trembled, running the blizzard of arpeggios until it seemed as if they must engulf all Vienna. When the brief, tempestuous piece ended she turned to Wiktor and said gently: "I will explain it, but I'm not sure you would understand. It's very technical, you know." Then she smiled at him as if the sun were reappearing after a storm. "Chopin tricks us all the time, the little magician."

Playing the étude very softly, she spoke along with the notes: "He adds a sixth, a seventh and an eighth to produce the new chord you like so much. And from it emerge the thirteen great bass chords. It's a harmonic variation, really. C minor to C major, then subtly back to C minor and here an A flat major. And the great chords appear first in the right hand, not the left. Then they thunder over to left, with everything becoming C major."

As Wiktor stood silent she asked for some paper and a pencil, and with exquisite script she wrote out the thirteen notes which made the étude so powerful. "You can play them on your own piano. C to set the stage. Then C, B, E flat, C. Then C, B flat, A flat, B flat. And the last chain B flat, A flat, F, A flat. And there you are." She showed him how to pick out the single notes, and on the third repetition he had them mastered.

"Now you can play Chopin," she said with impish delight, leaving the piano and going to where beer and sausages were being served.

Wiktor followed her and said, with quivering emotion, while she stuffed a very large sausage into her mouth: "Panna Krystyna, will you do me the honor of occupying my carriage at the gala tomorrow?" Before she could answer, he added: "It's not my carriage, really. It's a fiacre, but I hire it all the time."

"I would be delighted," she said between bites. "But what is the gala?"

He explained that he would be riding against the best Austrian officers at Die Schmelz, and she said quickly: "But if you're off riding, I'll be alone. May I bring Karl and Steffi to keep me company?" With her mug of beer she indicated two students, who stepped slightly forward to introduce themselves. They did not look quite like the kind of people he would have invited, but Krystyna Szprot was so delectable that if he could acquire her only with them, he must agree: "Please join us."

At seven in the morning Buk took the three Arabians out to the parade grounds where hundreds of other horses, equally polished

and groomed, awaited their riders, who arrived, like Count Lubonski
and Wiktor Bukowski, in private carriages or hired fiacres. By eleven
the grounds were filled with some of the most colorful uniforms in
Europe, and at noon the emperor himself arrived in a red-and-gold
barouche, from which he prepared to review the opening parade of
his regiments.

Wiktor, as a civilian, did not participate in this exhibition, but he
and Krystyna watched with pleasure as the units marched past, military bands blaring German tunes and marshals on horseback patrol-
ling the parade. It was the Austrian Empire at its most magnificent,
and if the wars that ravaged central Europe could only have been
fought on such parade grounds and by such troops in neat array,
Austria would surely be the most powerful nation on earth.

"Look at them!" Karl said scornfully from the back seat of the
fiacre. "They haven't won a battle in forty years."

"Is your uncle there?" Steffi asked.

"He's the fat one on the horse."

"Which horse?"

"The borrowed one."

Buk came up to advise his master that the riding exhibition was
about to begin, so Wiktor begged Krystyna to excuse him, took from
a box at the rear of the fiacre a plumed hat, and walked crisply to
where the horses were tethered. Buk had the best of the three, Mustafa, ready, but Wiktor said: "We'll save him for the race. I've got to
win the race."

He chose instead the horse of middle quality, a most handsome
beast who responded well to commands regardless of how they were
delivered: a pressed knee, a shift of Wiktor's hips, the shadow of a
whip, a change in voice. This mare had lived so long with her owner
that she had become an extension of his existence, and if any civilian
was going to have a chance to compete equally with the fine horsemen of the cavalry units, Wiktor Bukowski on this mare was such a
man.

If Emperor Franz Josef had dozed through most of the musical
concert, he certainly stayed awake at the exhibition of horsemanship.
In his youth, many decades ago, he had been an excellent horseman,
and the portraits of himself that he liked best were those in which
German and Italian painters had depicted him astride one of his
large horses. Then he looked truly imperial.

Now he sat in his barouche, accompanied by two barons with

their baronesses, covered with medals that shone in the sunlight. He was an impressive man, not given to fat, still erect, still captivated by any display of uniform and plume and glittering sword. A more brilliant man could not have held his vast empire together, but he in his bumbling way showed himself so ordinary that he did not evoke great envy.

"Who's the gentleman there who rides so well?" he asked, and his equerry said: "The Polish nobleman Bukowski who challenged the German critic to a duel over a pretty pianist."

Franz Josef frowned; the incident had been pejoratively reported in the Berlin press, as the embassy there had informed him. But Bukowski seemed to be an interesting person: "Isn't he the one with the Arabian stud? Up in Galicia somewhere?"

"The same."

Franz Josef said nothing, and the equerry signaled for the competition to begin.

Teams of four riders from the various regiments displayed remarkable skill in maneuvering their mounts through displays rigidly prescribed, and not all were officers from cavalry regiments, since army regiments also took pride in having members who were fine horsemen, but on this bright, sunny day it was the cavalry units that triumphed, and the winning four had trained their horses to kneel before the emperor as he bestowed the first prizes. Clearly, the best team had won.

Now came the competitions for individual riders, and since civilians were admitted to certain of the events, there was a kind of disarray, for they were not in military uniform and this detracted from their general appearance, but when Wiktor Bukowski appeared on his fine mare, he in the uniform of a Polish magnate glorious in fur and shako, the horse in polished silver fittings, he created a stir, and patrons in the carriages told one another that this was the Polish nobleman who had behaved with such gallantry a few nights before. Even Lubonski, who had feared some kind of reprisal because of his protégé's misbehavior, observed with pleasure the fine impression Wiktor was making. "He could marry anyone he wished, that one," he told his wife, and she agreed.

The competition had been arranged so that each rider had maximum opportunity to display his horsemanship: turns, leaps, gallops, twists, obedience and general deportment. Half the contest depended on the horse, half on the man who rode it, and nearly a dozen notable cavalrymen preceded Bukowski in the trials, but when he rode forth, he quickly became the crowd's favorite, and there were both gasps and cheers as he led his horse through the intricate tests, concluding with a wild, mad dash in which he seemed an ancient warrior on upland plains.

He won. And while the crowd cheered he brought his horse to the imperial site, but he did not ask the beast to kneel or bow. Horse and man stood proud in the wintry sunlight and accepted the prize.

"Are you Bukowski from the Vistula?" Franz Josef asked.

"I come from the northernmost of your villages, Your Majesty," Bukowski said, and this would be reported in the press. It wasn't exactly true. Several villages in western Moravia were slightly more northern, but only by a few miles. Wiktor Bukowski would be proclaimed as his emperor's northernmost subject, a superb horseman and a man of gallantry.

In the race, which he had planned to win with Mustafa, he had the great good fortune to lose to a popular cavalry major. For a Pole to have won two events would have been too much, but he was called back to the imperial presence for a silver medal and additional encomiums.

When he returned to his own fiacre he found Krystyna excited by his performance and eager to grant him a victor's kiss, but on the ride back to the city center the two students asked Wiktor how he could justify such a preposterous display, and to his surprise, Krystyna agreed with them when he tried to explain. She felt the exhibitionism quite brazen at a time when citizens in various corners of the empire lacked food.

Karl said: "It makes one wonder if the empire can continue."

"What ever do you mean?" Wiktor asked, and Steffi replied: "Your Poland, for example. Broken into three parts, no one of them well-governed."

Bukowski was stunned by such remarks. Poles in Vienna sometimes thought about the partition of their country, and occasionally in dark corners they whispered about it to friends, but it would be unthinkable, for example, to raise the question with a minister of government like Count Lubonski. And since he, Wiktor Bukowski, might conceivably be such a minister one day, he, too, must refuse to countenance such talk. "It has been agreed among the powers that Poland should be divided, and you must admit that of the three parts, the Austrian is much the best-governed, thanks principally to patriots like Lubonski."

The others fell silent, but when the fiacre, at the end of a long line of carriages returning to the city, reached the Ringstrasse, the two students said they would alight, which left Wiktor seated alone with Krystyna. Trembling so much that his hands showed his nervousness, he took a deep breath and asked: "Panna Krystyna, would you consent to dining with me tonight . . . at my rooms?"

"I would be delighted," she said so quickly that he could only gasp. Calling to the dour Serbian driver, he directed him to Concordiaplatz, where he told the man to wait while he hurried the pianist up the wide, curving stone stairs. Almost thrusting her into the big gloomy room, he said: "See, I, too, have a piano," and with that, he rushed down the stairs to ask the driver to go to several stores and purchase the ingredients for a dinner, hurried down to the basement to instruct a maidservant how to prepare the food when it arrived, and then ran back upstairs.

"Well!" he said breathlessly. "This room could use a woman's touch."

"Exactly what I was thinking," Krystyna said, and shrugging, she went to the piano and began half-playing, half-strumming some Parisian music-hall songs. "They do wonders with an accordion," she said, and with a skill that astonished Bukowski she struck the piano in a rhythmic way which simulated the effects of an accordion.

"I love Paris," she said. Then she struck a series of discordant notes. "But my heart yearns for Warsaw."

"Why don't you live there?"

"Forbidden. The Russians will not allow me to return."

"Why not?" Wiktor sat beside her on the piano bench and gazed at her distraught face, seeing for the first time some of the tempestuousness that plagued her.

"I said some things about Polish music. That our Moniuszko was better than any music being composed in St. Petersburg or Vienna."

"Do you believe that?"

"Of course! That's why I said it."

"And you were exiled?"

"By the police. I can't go back." She hesitated, then shrugged her shoulders and added: "Well, it was Moniuszko . . . and other issues."

He said: "You like things Polish, don't you?"

"I am all things Polish. I play Chopin to proclaim my attitudes to the world."

"But you do play other composers?"

She turned to face him. "I am very good at other composers."

"Like Mozart?" He paused. "What I mean . . . when the Germans played the Mozart concerto the other night. I thought that slow movement was . . . well . . . exquisite."

Krystyna turned back to the keyboard and with great poetic feeling played the piano portion of the slow movement, that sigh of autumn wind passing through a forest of golden leaves. It was quite thrilling, the way she played it, and Wiktor asked: "What I mean, do you think the lullaby in Chopin's scherzo . . . well . . . is as good as the Mozart?"

Now she played the lullaby, that flawless composition, so perfect for its setting within the larger piece of music, and for a while she passed back and forth between these two splendid works, and she was allowing her fingers to drift when Wiktor caught her by the shoulders and kissed her fervently.

"I liked that," she said forthrightly, and by some magic gesture, or by the passion of her next embrace, she let him know that she intended spending the night with him, here in this barren set of rooms.

When they stopped kissing she resumed playing the two themes and said: "The Mozart is very good. Perhaps as good as music can be. But it's mechanical. It could be anything—German, Moravian, French, even Chinese. Mozart sets the engine in motion and it chugs along. Very little heart." With heavy, mechanical beat she played the wonderful theme, then slipped easily into the Chopin, with its hesitations, tremblings, delicate nuances. "Chopin could be only Poland. No machinery animates him. It's impossible to predict where he's going."

Boldly she contrasted the two great themes, then laughed, kissed Wiktor, and delivered her opinion: "I like Mozart very much. Love him, in fact. But I revere Chopin, and all Poles should, for he recorded our heartbeats."

She stayed with Wiktor for three holiday nights and two days, and they were an experience far beyond anything he had hoped for, or ever imagined. She was a vivid, energetic little person, half-woman, half-child, and she made love as if it were the second half of a concert, the culmination of all that she had been preparing for.

"You're a wonderful man, Wiktor," she told him during the second night, and he was elated at the thought that this established artist could find him attractive, even though when with his horses or on parade he knew himself to be quite dashing. That was public, this was private, and he could not reconcile the two. But on the second day he received quite a jolt when he came back to Concordiaplatz from a visit to his offices to find that Krystyna had moved into his staid apartment two young couples who were seeking lodging in Vienna. How exactly she had met them he never discovered, nor where their permanent homes might be; all he knew was that they were vigorously against the Austrian government because it oppressed Slovenes in some place beyond the Danube. He asked Krystyna if she had ever been there, and she replied: "No need to go. We're all brothers."

When she left him, after the third night, he was quite bewildered. He was in love with this mercurial little genius, but he was also perplexed by her unorthodox behavior, and the very fact that she had stayed with him so willingly, almost without his asking, made him suspicious of her motives. Also, the bold way in which she had used his quarters had come close to offending him. He did not like her friends and supposed that if he knew her acquaintances in Paris, he would dislike them too.

His confusion was not diminished when a carriage drawn by two Lippizaners came to Concordiaplatz with a messenger who directed Wiktor Bukowski to report at once to Count Lubonski at 22 Annagasse.

When he hurried up to the reception room he found the count and countess awaiting him, rather grim in bearing, and the former launched directly into the problem: "Wiktor, the secret police have been here this morning. Reporting on your behavior since the Christmas concert." Glancing at a typed report, he droned: "You insulted an official guest of the Austrian government, challenging him to a duel. You did well at Die Schmelz, but then you visited 119 Alserstrasse, a notorious center for radical activity against His Majesty's government. You took into your quarters Krystyna Szprot of Paris, a political exile from Warsaw and an avowed enemy of the Russian government, with whom we have peaceful relations. Not content with that, you brought into your home two men and two women who have been agitating in Slovenian territories, and you are in the gravest danger of being declared an enemy of the state."

Bukowski was aghast, but before he could speak, the countess, whose illustrious family had weathered a dozen major storms of Polish politics, said: "Wiktor, what you must do, at your age . . . It's really quite important, Wiktor. Find a respectable young lady of good family, get married and settle down."

He was too confused to speak, so Lubonski took over: "The daughter of the American ambassador, Miss Trilling, let me know that she would be pleased to meet you again. I've invited her to our little reception tonight. Please appear in your best presentation."

The countess laughed. She was the daughter of powerful men and women, those who had built with their fortunes the entire city of Zamosc and from it had helped govern Poland in its good days. "What Andrzej means is wear respectable clothes and respectable manners." She paused to allow these suggestions to sink in, then added: "You have no great family fortune, Wiktor. Only two villages and a strong, clean name. Your only hope in this world is to marry well. And radical pianists from Paris do not qualify. The daughters of extremely rich ambassadors do. Please be prompt."

But when he returned to his quarters at Concordiaplatz he found that Krystyna had forced her way in, and had brought her belongings as if intending to stay indefinitely. She was a much different woman from the one he thought he knew: pianist no more, she revealed herself to be a dedicated revolutionary, and the force of her comment stunned Wiktor: "Heroic Poles have been combatting our oppressors for a century, and it's now time for you to join the battle. Do you even know what's been happening?" She drew back, studied the handsome young boulevardier, and said scornfully: "You, a man of your ability, wasting your time at the Austrian court when you could be in Paris helping to push forward our revolution."

"I discharge serious responsibilities right here."

"But the real struggle? Are you aware of it?"

"Not really."

"Then it's time you learned." And sitting him down, she recited that chain of events which Poles like her kept in their memories like a rosary, these gallant men and women on the battlements, always praying that some lucky stroke would come along to revitalize their captive nation and enable it to repel the invaders:

"When Napoleon marched through Poland with his soaring
promises of freedom, no one else in Europe had assisted him
the way my great-grandfather did, and thousands like him.
We were willing to fight the entire Russian army, and we did.

"In 1831 my great-grandfather was with the Warsaw corps that revolted, and we kept the tyrants on their toes for two years. My great-grandfather fled to Paris with Chopin and Mickiewicz. That's why I was born there, because my great-grandfather was a hero.

"In 1844 we supported the weavers in their pitiful bid for freedom and a decent wage. In 1846, more revolution. In 1848, fires all over Poland, and we almost triumphed that time. How many of us died then? And in 1863 we launched our great war against Russia—yes, outright war. As soon as the gunfire started, my father, God bless him, he came right back to do his part. Escaped Siberia by a hair. Secret police trailing him wherever he went. We almost did it that time."

"You keep saying *we*," Wiktor said, awed by the young woman's fury, and she replied: "I was part of every revolution," and he said: "You weren't even born," and she said: "And I shall be part of every move that occurs after my death, because Poland will never surrender. People like me will never surrender, and you must be one of us."

"I have my duties here," he repeated, as if that justified everything, and she was about to excoriate him; instead she leaped up, gave him a passionate kiss, and said: "Wiktor, I wouldn't be here if I didn't love you. So Polish, so handsome, so stupid." Before he could express hurt she caught him by the hands and cried: "Let's go to the reception and watch the old order dying on its feet." He was so enamored of her, so irritated by the condescension of the Lubonskis, lecturing him as if he were an ignorant peasant, that despite the dangers Krystyna Szprot represented, he dressed in his most flamboyant Polish costume, sent Buk to fetch the Serbian and his fiacre, and proudly led the beautiful young revolutionary into the Annagasse palace . . . twenty minutes late.

Bowing grimly to the countess, whose face was livid, he nodded to the American girl and introduced Krystyna to half a dozen dignified persons who had not attended her concert. It was a chilly beginning, but Andrzej Lubonski had not advanced to level of minister without having mastered the art of diplomacy, so he accepted the affront and made both Wiktor Bukowski and his talented mistress welcome. The accounting would come later; he would see to that.

After dinner some of the guests, learning that Mlle. Szprot was an accomplished pianist, asked if she would honor them with a few selections, and after a polite demurral, she allowed herself to be escorted to the piano, where she played a series of lively numbers by Offenbach and then a potpourri from *Die Fledermaus,* which, she explained "had been first presented over twenty years ago in Vienna."

The audience was charmed, but both Wiktor and the count realized that she was laughing at them, and the latter said coldly: "Perhaps Mlle. Szprot would favor us with something a little more classical?" When the audience responded enthusiastically, she said in her halting German: "What I like best, the mazurkas of my Chopin." And with great skill she played a selection, moving from the easy ballroom measures to those intricate, broken-patterned ones which bespoke the very essence of the dance, as if the composer had been seeking music not for a man and woman but for the dance itself.

When she reached a conclusion she said in French: "I should like to end with a composition which has come to mean much to me," and she started the étude "Winter Wind," with its eight grand notes and tornadolike arpeggios, and this, of course, led to the last étude, the one that captured Bukowski's imagination, and when the mysterious thirteen chords approached, he leaped beside the piano and cried: "I have composed a poem to this music, a poem of my homeland." And with sturdy voice he chanted the thirteen syllables:

> *"Home!*
> *The fields are green,*
> *The woods are clean,*
> *My soul serene . . ."*

Krystyna, startled, stopped her playing to look at him: "Wiktor! You're a poet!" and at that same moment the young nobleman dropped to his knees before her. "Krystyna!" he cried in French. "Will you marry me?"

Before she could say anything, three young men in overcoats broke into the room, rushed to the piano, grabbed her, and hurried her out a side door.

"They're after you!" some of the guests heard the men say as they spirited her away, but they were unable to share this knowledge with the other guests, because now four policemen came into the salon demanding of the count to know where the revolutionary Krystyna Szprot was hiding.

Lubonski, who had arranged this charade, pointed to the door through which the conspirators had fled, and out ran the four policemen, banging their way as they went. Wiktor Bukowski, still on his knees at the vacated piano, looked up at the guests as if to ascertain what kind of bomb had exploded in his face, and he saw the American girl in white dress and pale-pink jewels smiling at him. No, not smiling. She was laughing . . . quietly . . . with amusement rather than ridicule.

This triple notoriety—duel, riding championship, public proposal to a beautiful revolutionary—made Wiktor Bukowski a personage in two centers. The secret police began looking into his precedents and found him to be exactly as represented: a rather confused Polish provincial who had oscillated among seven different women of seven sharply contrasting natures, but who had never harmed either them, himself or the empire. When his summary was read, it created the portrait of a rather impulsive fellow who bore watching lest he be duped by those more clever, but German investigators dispatched to check on his Bukowo behavior reported: "He is no more stupid than your average romantic Polish landowner who has never been away from his estates."

The second group of Viennese now interested in Wiktor were the marriageable young women, and their investigations, often more perceptive than those of the police, showed him to be a real nobleman, though in distinctly limited circumstances, a young man of gallant instincts, a dancer of more than average ability, a fellow with a good singing voice and a man who wore his clothes well. They learned also that he lived alone in a rather large apartment in Concordiaplatz, and that if there was any young man in Vienna who ought to have a wife, it was he.

He therefore became a three-week social sensation, with liveried messengers stopping by Concordiaplatz and Landtmann's with invitations, but the most intriguing came from the coachman at the American Embassy. Miss Marjorie Trilling, whose parents occupied one of the minor palaces among the nobility of the Schwarzenberg Quarter, wondered if Mr. Bukowski would care to join her family at a small celebration. He would, and when his fiacre drove up to the gracious palace, small but elegantly designed, he felt that a new life was beginning for him.

Mr. and Mrs. Trilling were unusually gracious in receiving him, and the ambassador said: "We watched you at Die Schmelz. Superb."

"And you, sir," Wiktor said in English, "is it that you are also a horseman?"

"Heavens, no! But Marjorie is."

When he shook hands with the clean-looking, strong-bodied young woman, four years younger than he, he noticed that she was just a mite taller, so he stood slightly on his toes. "Your excellency father says that you like to ride, perhaps . . ."

"I'd love to. No city in the world has finer parks than Vienna."

"Could it be that you have seen our Prater, yes?"

"No, but I should like to."

"Then I believe it could be arranged, on a day which I do not work . . ."

"You have a regular job?" she asked in French.

He noticed that Miss Trilling bored right in with her questions.

"Oh, yes!" he replied in English. "All the Poles in Vienna have jobs, even a man as excellency as Count Lubonski."

"Do you know him? In Poland, I mean?"

"Of course. His palace is next to mine." But as soon as he said this he observed how the words had affected Miss Trilling, so he took her arm and said quickly in French: "But you understand, his is a real palace. Well, not like this, all marble and gold. A real palace Polish style. Mine is . . ." He paused in embarrassment. "No one in his sensible mind would call where I live a palace."

"Is it very old?"

"My castle? Maybe the year 1000 after Christ." And again he tried to be honest: "But it was ruined in 1200 after Christ. Each year one more rock tumbles down from the walls. My family lives in a house near the castle."

"Is it old?"

Wiktor had never pondered that question. His home certainly looked old and he supposed that it had been erected first in those painful years following the Tatar invasion, but he was sure it must have been destroyed when the Ukrainian Cossacks swept across the land and certainly when the Swedish Protestants came surging in from the north. He summarized the history of his home in words calculated to inflame the imagination of any young American: "It was built, I think, in 1214 or 1215 and burned by a dozen invaders. But always it was rebuilt on the same spot, looking over . . . Or is it overlooking?"

"Overlooking. You mean overlooking the castle ruins?"

"No. Overlooking the Vistula."

"And what is the Vistula?" she asked, but before he could master his astonishment at her ignorance she cried: "Stupid me! Of course, I studied that with the man who tutored Father when he got his appointment to Vienna. The Vistula is Poland's Danube." In some embarrassment she stopped. "We were instructed never to use the word *Poland*, but it is Poland, isn't it?"

"It is," he said gravely, "and one day you must to see it."

"I would like to. And I would like to ride with you in the Prater, too."

This was not to be, because when Wiktor rode back to Concordiaplatz that night he found awaiting him the tall, thin young man who had shared his fiacre at the riding exhibition, and he brought a neatly written letter from Paris:

Dearest Wiktor,

   Come at once to Paris where all who truly love Poland and yearn for its freedom congregate against the day when that freedom comes. We need you and I long for you. Together we could do so much.

   Your dearest,
   Krystyna

"I've read the letter," the young man said. "You must go, really you must." And for two days Bukowski's head was in a whirl, for he visualized himself in Paris with this exciting artist. He saw himself in bed with her in some small set of rooms, or carrying her music as she played in London and Munich and Rome. But mostly he saw himself in love with her, involved in the problems of real living and not drifting through the routine of a minor job in a minor ministry in an empire he really did not like.

Then the chords of the last étude came crashing at him, bringing his own words back to haunt him:

Home!
The fields are green,
The woods are clean,
My soul serene . . .

He wanted to be in Poland, to be a part of Poland, to see his land once more united as in the old days. He was, in brief, one of the thousands of Poles homesick for a way of life that had vanished, and responding to that seductive sequence of nostalgic chords, he seriously considered chucking everything and heading for Paris.

He was halted in this folly by Count Lubonski, to whom the secret police had brought a copy of Krystyna Szprot's letter, and he more than most could appreciate the turmoil this epistle must have ignited in the heart of his young countryman, for he had seen many exiles from the Russian part of Poland commit themselves to stupid actions when caught up in emotional crises. He therefore dispatched one of his carriages to Concordiaplatz, and when Bukowski stood before him in the large reception room he said simply: "Wiktor, the police have shown me a copy of Mlle. Szprot's letter from Paris. Come, sit over here."

He talked for a long time with the hot-headed young man, sharing with him incidents in his own life, and then he asked one of the servants to fetch the countess, and when she saw the letter she folded it, tapped it against her teeth, and said: "It's exactly the kind of letter Andrzej once received from a great actress in Berlin. All young men should receive such letters, Wiktor, but they should never act upon them."

"What should I do?"

The count answered: "I've sent my man to pack your things. You're not to return to your rooms. You're catching the night train to Krakow, and I want you to spend the winter months at Bukowo, reminding yourself of what life is to be like. In March, come back to Vienna and find yourself a wife."

"But my man, Janko Buk . . . My horses?"

"Buk will be on the train. We're moving your horses to my stables. Wiktor, this is a major crisis in your life. Face it, conquer it, come back and do your job, and I believe that one day you could succeed me as a chief of ministry."

Countess Lubonska agreed with this: "Vienna will always want to keep one Pole in high position, and it might as well be you, Wiktor." She kissed him as he left the great room, a young man in total confusion.

At the train station he suffered one bad moment, for as he sought Buk and the count's man who held his tickets he found himself in a queue of animated travelers heading for a train labeled MUNICH-STRASBOURG-PARIS, and for one heady moment he felt like staying with these lively people all the way to Paris and to freedom. But

Janko Buk caught sight of him and pulled him away to the proper queue VIENNA-BRNO-KRAKOW-WARSAW, where he obediently went aboard.

The train consisted of four types of carriages: a luxurious first class, a clean and spacious second class, a wooden-bench third class, and three large, bare wagons for conveying the passengers' goods. Wiktor proceeded directly to his first-class accommodations, where he consumed an immense meal, and then, despondent, went to sleep.

Janko Buk found himself a preferred corner seat on one of the wooden benches, where he could rest either sideways against the window or back against the seat. From a cloth bundle he produced rolls, cheese and a half-bottle of wine, which he offered to the man sitting across from him. The man was a Czech going only as far as Brno, a congenial workman who produced a bottle of his own, and after the drinks were shared, with each man deeming his the better, they fell to talking.

The Czech had been discharged from his position as doorman at one of the ministries because he championed the cause of a fiery young Czech revolutionary, Tómaš Masaryk, who was arguing for a free nation consisting of Bohemia, Moravia and, perhaps, even Slovakia. But he himself wanted no part of Slovakia because he had found Slovaks to be crooks, thieves and murderers.

"What will you do in Brno?" Buk asked in German.

"What a man always does, survive somehow. Maybe go to Prague and work for Masaryk."

"Who would pay you?"

"Who knows?"

In response to the Czech's careful questioning, Buk explained that his master, an admirable young man, was being sent home for general misbehavior: "He challenged a stupid German to a duel."

"We'll drink to that!" the Czech said. "I like your young fellow immediately."

"Then at the big riding exhibition he defeated all the Austrian officers."

"We'll drink to that too. I'd like to work for your master."

"Then he fell on his knees at a public gathering and proposed to a young artist from Paris and she turned out to be a Polish revolutionary, fighting for freedom from Russia."

"By God, let's go see your master, for he's my kind of man."

The men were stopped as they tried to pass through the second-class carriages, but the conductor, seeing their jovial inebriation and dismissing it as a normal frolic, spoke no harsh words: "Your place is back there, and if you don't return quickly, your good seats will be taken." So they went back and resumed their conversation.

"Are you married?" Buk asked.

"No, but I'm thinking seriously. A man ought to have children."

"My own thoughts," Buk said, and he confided that in his village of Bukowo there was this hard-working girl Jadwiga: "She's two years or maybe three older than me, but she's very pretty and she can work like a horse. If we could get ourselves a piece of land . . ."

"Not possible in Bohemia. How about Galicia?"

"Almost impossible, but I notice that every year some peasant grabs on to a piece, here or there, this way or that."

"What will happen to your fine young master?"

"The count's man told me—"

"What count?" The Czech allowed nothing to pass.

"Count Lubonski."

"You mean the minister? He's a very powerful man. He used to come to our offices and we all stepped when he appeared."

"His man told me that Bukowski, that's my master, he'd be in exile a few months till he got his head screwed back on."

"Have you ever noticed?" the Czech asked. "You and me, we get fired, it's for good. Starve, you miserable bastard. But a nobleman gets fired, three weeks he has a better job."

When the Czech left the train at Brno, Janko settled back against the wall to catch what sleep he could, but the clatter of the wheels kept him awake and he thought patiently and seriously about his problems. He was twenty-six years old, healthy, strong. He did not like serving as a groom in Vienna, for although he loved horses and was adept at handling them, he felt a great affinity for the land and wished to be associated with it: I could be a good forester, maybe a better farmer, or maybe a farmer who also took care of horses at the big house.

But most of all he wanted a piece of land which he could call his own, something that he could till and seed and reap, something from which he could subtract a corner for the building of his own cottage—two rooms, no more—which he could pass on to his son and he to his son, the way the Lubonskis and the Bukowskis passed along their lands. For one shining moment, as the train moved north toward the

Polish border, Janko Buk visualized a world in which every man owned his land and cottage, but he could imagine no system which would permit him to acquire his.

Since the year 830 the men and women of the Buk line had belonged to other men and women of the Bukowski line, who in turn had been subservient to the men and women of the Lubonski line, who were subservient, by God, to no one, except that they had mismanaged things so sorely that they were now subservient to the Emperor Franz Josef, and you better keep that firmly in mind. Things changed for the Lubonskis and to a lesser degree for the Bukowskis, but for the Buks they never changed.

However, the concept of passing a farm and a cottage on to one's sons encouraged Janko to consider seriously his possible relations with this girl Jadwiga, as fine a woman as any of the villages along the Vistula provided. She was the daughter of a widow, which was bad, because that could mean that her husband might have to support not only a wife but also a mother-in-law, and this was a real possibility, because if the old woman could no longer farm the master's land constructively, she would be thrown out of her cottage, and then what?

On the other hand, not many men caught themselves wives as capable as Jadwiga. Besides, she had a free and easy smile, as if she had made her peace with the world and with the fools that inhabited it. Watching her swing along a lane, bringing the geese home at the end of day, or chasing across the meadows to fetch a wandering cow, was to see grace and beauty, and Janko had reason to believe that she would always retain these qualities. She was, in village parlance, a good woman, and he knew for a fact that she had already refused proposals of marriage from men not worthy of her.

So by the time the train approached Krakow, where wagons would be waiting to carry the travelers on to Bukowo, Janko Buk had pretty much made up his mind to court Jadwiga seriously and in due course to propose marriage, whether he had a cottage of his own or not, whether he owned the land he sought or not: A man can't wait forever to have children.

And then he fell to wondering about his master, and he had one simple wish: He's as generous a master as a man could have. I only wish he'd find a good Polish woman, someone at a palace like Lancut or Gorka who has lots of money, and he could stay here with his horses and not go back to Vienna . . . He laughed as he reflected on this: Maybe he wants to go back to Vienna. Maybe it's only me that wants to stay home.

On the ride from Krakow to the village, Wiktor sat with his groom and revealed that he did indeed want to get back to Vienna as soon as his informal exile permitted: "There is so much to be done. So many people to see."

"There's lots to be done at Bukowo," Janko said.

"I know. The roads. The buildings. And we do need a barn for the horses."

"Why not stay home?"

"Money. Janko, we have no extra money but what my salary gives us. At Bukowo, I know a hundred things that need doing, but I haven't one spare crown."

"There must be a lot of girls in the big houses . . . looking for husbands."

"It's not like the old days. I'm told that then you could travel to sixteen houses and find fifteen wives."

"Isn't it a pity Lubonski has no daughter."

Wiktor looked at his groom, aware that this conversation had become too personal, but he liked the frank peasant, and concluded: "I've often wished that the countess had given birth to a daughter." As he said this they were riding past the great and gloomy castle of Gorka, a place that would never again know the levity of the old days when the Counts Lubonski held court here; now they languished in Vienna. They had that splendid little half-palace at 22 Annagasse, but they languished nevertheless, and Bukowski knew it, for that was the destiny which awaited him.

At the Bukowski home he found things much as he had left them after his parents' death. Auntie Bukowska, no immediate relative but a reliable woman imported from a distant branch of the family, remained in charge, as she had for a dozen years. Her daughter Miroslawa was six now, a quiet, large-eyed child who gave no trouble. The horses were poorly stabled and the fields were not as carefully tended as they had been when Auntie's husband had served as steward of the two villages. Rents were sometimes not collected, but the cumbersome system did go creakingly forward, providing Wiktor with just enough surplus to pay for his apartment in Vienna and the care of his three horses.

It never would have occurred to Bukowski or to Lubonski, not even to Janko Buk himself, that if he had been placed in charge of the estate, it would have flourished, yielding surpluses for all. To make such a radical change would have been totally impossible; stewards were freedmen of the towns, or sometimes the third or fourth sons of the gentry, who in their amiable ways ran the great estates into the ground. Peasants were not stewards. For one thing, few of them could write or keep figures.

And so things settled into the old ruts: the estate languished, the peasants walked somberly to their distant fields, and church bells rang, and once or twice a year the villages erupted into robust celebrations when some young couple were married or some old man was buried. At the Bukowski house young Wiktor drew plans for a stable that would be built some day, looked idly at the estate books he could not understand, and pined for the excitements of Vienna. Using lesser horses from his stud, he rode across his fields and talked with his peasants, encouraging them to make whatever improvements they deemed best. He also visited with the priest who served these territories, and sometimes fished in the Vistula. He was invited to several big houses in the Russian part of Poland and even to a mournful celebration organized by a branch of the once-great Mniszech family at the Palais Princesse in Warsaw, but he did not care to display himself in his banishment.

There was one significant change in his routine. Auntie Bukowska had discussed it with him in tedious detail: "I can't go on climbing the stairs, and little Miroslawa is too young to be of real help, so we must hire another girl while you're here. It's only sensible, and to that I'm sure you'll agree."

She had noticed that the girl Jadwiga might be a likely servant: "She's big and strong and rather intelligent, I think. We can get by with paying her almost nothing, and she can care for all the upper rooms." She asked Wiktor if he wanted to check as to the girl's appropriateness, but he said simply: "If she satisfies you, she satisfies me."

She did indeed. With nothing better to occupy his mind, he began talking with this strong-willed peasant girl and found her frank and firm: "Master, my mother is an old woman now and we must find some way for her to live."

"You have your cottage."

"But it will be taken away."

"I'll speak to the steward."

Jadwiga noticed that he was always *going* to do things, but never *did* them, and in this he contrasted very unfavorably with the young man who had begun courting her. Janko Buk said on Monday that he had been thinking about doing something to improve the fields that were not even his, and on Tuesday he did it. But she enjoyed talking with Bukowski, and liked to listen to his colorful stories of Vienna.

One morning, as he came out of his way to watch her at work, she asked bluntly: "Why haven't you found yourself a wife?" and he asked: "How old are you, Jadzia?" and she told him: "A year older than you and ten years wiser," and he laughed: "I think you're right."

"You haven't heard my question. Why no wife?"

He threw his hands wide, indicating his estate: "A man like me, with no prospects and only two villages. I need a rich wife, I really do."

"Cast a net and catch one," she advised him. "North of the line, in Russia . . ."

"And you? Why no husband?"

"I've had men courting me. Plenty. But I have no mind to work my life out for a man who accomplishes nothing. Born in a filthy hut. Die in a filthy hut."

"You should go to Vienna, Jadzia."

"Born in a filthy corner. Die in a filthy corner. Here at least we breathe clean air."

Day after day they talked like this, a nobleman preoccupied with his horses, a peasant woman seeing with terrible clarity the years ahead, and one morning when he had dispatched Auntie to the village, he pulled Jadwiga into an unused room and began to fondle her, aware that she was resisting him with a cynical knowledge of exactly what compelled him: his ennui, his pride in his position of ownership, his longing for the city. And in the end she allowed him to force her onto a bed when with a flick of her powerful right arm she could have knocked him across the room.

It was harsh love-making overlaid with a hundred complex motivations, and in the numerous repetitions which followed, so that even Auntie must have known what was happening with her new servant, the compulsions never changed: Wiktor needed a diversion to make his banishment palatable; Jadwiga welcomed this brief vision of a new world during this cold, dreary winter when snow was deep upon the fields.

During one protracted love-making she replied imprudently, in answer to his endless questions about her life: "Before all this happened I thought I might take your Janko Buk as my husband," and he answered with equal imprudence: "Wonderful man. If you were to marry him—when I'm gone, that is—maybe I'd find him a farm . . ."

"You mean, his own land?"

"No, I didn't mean that at all. But maybe . . ."

Without his being aware of it, Jadwiga now crossed his path with peculiar frequency, and one morning in March, as spring thaws began, she told him: "I think I'm pregnant."

"Ridiculous. You can't be."

"And why not? You're a powerful man . . ."

Any attention he might have paid to this critical matter was diverted by a telegram dispatched from Vienna: YOU ARE NEEDED AT YOUR MINISTRY THE EMPEROR AGREES TO YOUR RETURN LUBONSKI.

Rushing about to pack his belongings for what he suspected might be a long and important stay, he had little time to discuss Jadwiga's problems. "You'll manage something. Girls always do."

She asked only one question: "Are you taking Janko with you?"

"Of course. Someone has to tend the horses."

"And who will tend me?"

"You'll manage something."

There were only three cities in Europe in which a man twenty-eight years old who felt his chances slipping away should be in love: Rome, where the proper patronage could always accomplish miracles; London, where there was always a chance to marry money; and Vienna, where the games of love and power were constantly under way. Wiktor Bukowski was allowed one last chance to operate in the imperial city, and he did so masterfully.

Instructing Janko Buk to keep his three horses always at the ready and his Serbian fiacre driver to be at hand almost constantly, he purchased two new suits from a London tailor on the Kärntnerstrasse and had his tailor refurbish his two Polish national costumes. Thus armed, he laid serious siege to the affections of the American heiress, Miss Marjorie Trilling of Chicago.

He went first to a German-Austrian bank to ascertain what Oscar Trilling's position was in the Chicago commercial world, and found it to be even more dazzling than he had been told: "The ambassador's family has been engaged in railroads, land, cattle, forests and all other aspects of settling the vast American West. He has only one daughter, a secure position with both the Republican and Democratic leaderships, and a personal worth estimated at well over nine million dollars American." It was reasonable to suppose that such a man might bestow at least a third of that fortune on his daughter while he was still alive, and much more at his death. Miss Trilling was an enticing opportunity.

He took her riding in the Prater; he took her to the Burgtheater, where *Hedda Gabler* was disturbing the citizens, and to *A Woman of No Importance,* which was delighting them. They visited the great museums, especially ones showing the Breughels and the relics of the Napoleonic wars. And always they attended concerts, listening with respect to the works of Beethoven and Schubert, with curiosity to those of the local wonders Mahler and Bruckner, with condescension to the peasant harmonies of the Czechs Dvorak and Smetana.

When Wiktor asked how Miss Trilling had acquired so much knowledge of music, she resumed an earlier explanation which had been interrupted: "I attended a distinguished college in America, Oberlin, where music was important."

"You went to college?" He had never before met a woman who had done so.

"Of course. So did my mother."

He was not sure that he liked the idea of women attending college, or becoming doctors, while the prospect of their actually playing in orchestras, as Marjorie said she had, was almost repulsive: "Don't all the men stare without listening to the music?"

"Men always stare," she said, "and women appreciate it."

In return for his courtesies, she introduced him to the social world of the embassies, inviting him to formal teas at Sacher's Hotel and to informal ones with young men and women from other embassies who convened at Demel's pastry shop for monstrous desserts, always *"mit Schlag,"* the heavy whipped cream from the Vienna countryside. There were dances, receptions, riding exhibitions and occasionally a glimpse of the old emperor, who supervised everything as if he were the burgomaster of a small village.

Wiktor, enchanted by this participation in a life he had not previously known, became a fashionable host, inviting the embassy people to Landtmann's or to private rooms at Sacher's, and one morning he told Janko Buk: "Hire me a carriage to which you can harness our two lesser horses, and find out which is the best road to the hills behind Grinzing." There, where the Vienna Woods began, he took Marjorie riding, and while Buk fished they engaged in amorous dalliance so prolonged that each participant realized the attachment had become more than a passing adventure.

"I wish I could see the Vistula," Marjorie said as they drove dreamily homeward.

"You can!" Wiktor cried with real excitement. "You get aboard a train, go easily to Krakow, and drivers meet you for the ride to Bukowo."

"I would require a chaperone," she said.

"Let's find one."

They drove to 22 Annagasse, where they talked frankly with the countess, who was delighted with the progress of their courtship. "I will go with you myself and you can stay with me at Gorka. Or it might be even better if your mother accompanied you." While they waited she dashed off notes to the Lubonski estates at Lwow and Gorka, then wrote a cordial invitation to Marjorie's mother.

Once the Lubonskis decided to do something, they moved with force; next day the count called upon Ambassador Trilling and said: "I'll vouch for this fellow Bukowski. Known his family for six centuries. Always poor as church mice. Always men of great dignity. And they have the best Arab stud in the empire."

"What about the revolutionary little pianist? Quite a scandal, you know."

"I better than most. It was I who called in the secret police . . . but only after she was safely away."

"Was he . . . compromised? I mean, with the government?"

"Exactly the kind of hearty escapade a young man with spirit . . . Wiktor's first class."

So an excursion to the Austrian portion of Poland was arranged, with Countess Lubonska making the decisions: "You'll stop first at our estates near Lwow. Then the Potockis who now occupy Lancut will entertain you, after which their people will carry you on to Gorka, where I shall be waiting to receive you. From there it's a little jump to Bukowo and you will have seen the best, except that I shall myself take you on to the town built by my family, Zamosc, the heart of all that's good in Russian Poland."

Mrs. Trilling, who like her husband had studied Austrian history and geography, said: "You keep speaking of Lwow. I've never seen it on any map."

"That's our old Polish name. They call it Lemberg now."

Departure was set for mid-May, when Galicia would be at its loveliest, but during the last week in April, Wiktor Bukowski, who had every reason to hope that the journey would end with his public engagement to the ambassador's daughter, received a nasty shock. Auntie Bukowska sent him a peremptory letter:

> The girl Jadwiga is pregnant and threatens to cause immense trouble unless you find some solution. Your proposed plans for a visit at this time would prove disastrous and must be canceled. More important, advise me immediately what I am to do about Jadwiga.

How miserable it was to have built, with great care and planning, a structure of importance, only to watch it come apart because of some trivial accident. Why had he dallied with this servant? Why had he not detected in her forthright and even brazen conversation the seeds of trouble? And what in hell to do now?

His rescue came from an unbelievable quarter. The girl Jadwiga, having heard about the master's passionate wooing of the American, for all Bukowo was aware of what was happening, had sent a peasant to Vienna with a message for the master's groom. Fortified with this knowledge, Buk walked across the bridge over the Danube Canal and presented himself unannounced in Concordiaplatz.

"I think I might be of help to you, sir."

"In what way?" the irritated and distracted young man asked.

"In the matter of Jadwiga." When Wiktor gasped, unable to make any sensible response, Janko pressed on: "If her condition becomes known, sir, it could bring ruin to your design."

"What are you speaking of?" Bukowski thundered.

"I've been driving you and the American girl into the woods. Do you think I'm stupid? Do you think I don't know what game you're playing?" Without being invited, he took a chair.

"Who told you to sit in my presence?"

Ignoring the question, Janko continued: "One word of this, as you know, and the American girl and her parents . . ." He made a peasant sign for a bird flying away.

Bukowski was sweating. This oaf had done two things to him by this visit: he had terrified him with a crystal-clear vision of disaster, and he had somehow suggested that it could be avoided. Licking his dry lips, Bukowski poured himself a drink and asked Buk if he would have one, too.

"Please," the peasant said.

"Now what brings you here? Blackmail? I'll have you shot."

"Pan Bukowski, don't talk like a damned fool. Obviously I come to help."

"Thank God!" the frightened man cried.

"I like you. You've been a good master, and I could never say otherwise."

"What can we do?"

"Good. Now you're talking like a sensible man. Pan Bukowski, for several years now I've been wanting to marry Jadwiga—"

"You'd marry her?" Wiktor cried, leaping from his chair to pour his savior another drink.

"I would have married her three years ago," Janko said very slowly.

"Why didn't you?"

"Because we . . . had . . . no . . . land."

Silence. In some irritation Bukowski looked away: These damned peasants, always trying to filch a man's land, land he's held for a thousand years.

It was important, Janko thought, that Bukowski make the next statement, so he calmly sipped his drink, staring all the while at the distraught young man, whose eyes came back to his from time to time. Ageless, rooted deep in the soil he had never owned, Janko Buk kept staring at his master who controlled the land he had never used wisely. Finally the master broke.

"What did you have in mind?"

"Jadwiga sent me a drawing."

"So it was her plotting?"

"I'm sure you weren't wholly at fault, Pan. As the priest always says, 'No girl can become pregnant if she keeps her knees together.'"

Bukowski took the carefully drawn map, with every trail and cottage clearly delineated. "Your girl can draw, that I'll say."

"For the present," Buk said, "she's your girl."

"This area that's marked? Is that what you think you need?"

"And the cottage. It's marked too."

"And if I give you these . . ."

"And that little corner of the forest. I marked that. I want the fallen branches and the rabbits from that corner."

"And if I say no?" Bukowski asked, deeply disturbed by the arrogance of his groom.

With great care Janko now said what he had known would have to be said: "Pan Bukowski, with the American ambassador, you're playing for millions. I'm playing only for a small field, a decent cottage and a corner of the forest my family has tended for a thousand years. Think about it."

Silence, much more powerful than before, much more shot through with the meaning of life and the accumulated wisdom of history. Millions against a few fallen branches, a few rabbits in a winter's stew.

The tension became so great that neither man dared break that silence. Bukowski hated his groom for trying to drive such a bargain in such a shameful cause; Janko Buk hated himself for having allowed himself to become engaged in such a negotiation. But each man was fighting for his life, for all the values he had accumulated beside the Vistula in past centuries. One of the old Bukowskis had warned his family: "The day peasants get their own land, that day Poland crumbles." And the Buks who had tended the land and guarded the forests from enemies innumerable had always whispered: "The only man who prospers in this country is the magnate, the priest, the Jew or the peasant who grabs hold of a little land."

Bukowskis in time past had owned the Buks, had hanged them for infractions, had forced them to fight wars, and had taken everything they produced, and it was insufferable that now a Buk should sit here making demands. Wiktor was unable to respond. His tongue clung to the roof of his mouth and he could not speak.

Finally Janko rose, went to the wine bottle, came back to where Wiktor sat and refilled his glass. Then he poured a fresh drink for himself. Raising his glass, he said softly: "Pan Bukowski, we can each do a great thing for the other. I shall leave Vienna tomorrow and marry Jadwiga before the baby comes. And I'll tell Bogdan that his big cottage is now mine and my small one his, for his wife is dead and his children gone. I'll not fence off my corner of the forest, but you and I will know it's mine, and when you marry and rebuild Bukowo as it should be with your new money, you'll go to the lawyer and sign the paper stating that the corner of the forest and the field and the cottage are mine."

He extended his hand, and Bukowski, still unable to speak, took it.

• • •

During the first leg of the journey to Lwow, Mrs. Trilling enjoyed the experience even more than her daughter, because the train traversed almost the whole of Hungary, and she was able to see for the first time large areas of territory for which her husband was technically responsible. She made notes about the agriculture east of Budapest and looked forward with wonder as they approached the Carpathian Mountains, which would mark the separation of Hungary from the Austrian province of Galicia. As the wife of an important official accredited to the Austrian court, she was careful to avoid the word *Poland,* for legally it no longer existed, and it would have been offensive to the emperor to imply in any way that he did not own now and forever the lands that had once been Polish.

Her daughter Marjorie felt no such constraint. It was obvious to her, and she knew it must be to her mother, too, that she was making this visit to determine whether or not she wished to marry a delightful, somewhat flighty, definitely impecunious Polish nobleman, and before she could give a final answer, she felt that she must see his land and evaluate where he had come from and what his character might be in relation to his homeland.

She was desperately eager to see what had once been Poland, and she did not intend to call it Galicia, so at dusk, when the long, slow train started up the winding slopes of the Carpathians and it became obvious that entrance into Poland would occur late at night or perhaps even at dawn, she told her mother: "I shan't go to bed tonight. I must see Wiktor's land as it opens up before me."

Mrs. Trilling thought this completely sensible: "I'd do the same at your age, Marjorie. But I'm not your age, so you'll excuse me."

As she prepared for the bed in her private drawing room she reflected with some amusement on the situation which faced her family, and she was wise enough to see certain preposterous aspects of this journey. This was the age when scores of newly rich American families brought their daughters to Europe to find titled husbands who would add luster to the social circles of New York, Chicago and Boston. President Grant's daughter had caught a titled gentleman in Turkey or somewhere, as had the daughters of railroad tycoons, wheat millionaires, packing-house magnates and the owners of trolley-car franchises.

But each of them, Mrs. Trilling reminded herself as she laughed at herself in the mirror, purchased idle young men with real titles. Count this, Lord that, the Duke of something else, and even a Prince or two. Wiktor, God bless him, has a family which has been ennobled for a thousand years longer than most of them, but he bears no title. What folly!

Prior to their departure, Count Lubonski had briefed the Trillings: "Poland confers no titles. Our family got ours through merit, plus a little judicious bribery, two centuries ago, from the Papal States. The Radziwills got theirs on the cheap from Lithuania. I believe Leszczynski got his, also through purchase, from the Holy Roman Empire. And others, I suspect, have just given themselves whatever titles they thought appropriate. Your young fellow Bukowski could have had any title his ancestors might have been willing to purchase, but he's in the tradition of the great Mniszech family, with which mine has often been affiliated. They scorned titles and wound up with estates larger than Belgium."

Mrs. Trilling was no snob. Her social position in Chicago was so secure that she felt no need for a titled daughter to display at receptions, and she was prepared for Marjorie to marry young Bukowski if love developed between them and if Marjorie responded to what the girl called "the Polish experience." It would be disgraceful, Mrs. Trilling thought, for a girl with such a problem to spend the hours asleep when her train carried her for the first time into the fabled lands which might prove to be her future home.

"God bless you out there," she said aloud as she went to bed.

The young couple had moved into a salon car with very wide windows, where servants offered drinks and small refreshments through the night, and there they watched the Carpathians loom out of the darkness when the train's bright lights pierced ahead. At midnight the train halted for about an hour, during which Wiktor and Marjorie walked in the spring air, asking the workmen how far ahead the border of Poland might be, and the men responded: "Galicia, five miles up."

They were a long five miles along a tortuous roadbed flanked by dense evergreens, and then—with no fanfare, no stopping for passport control—the train edged into Poland, and a perplexed Bukowski whispered with an echo of fatality: "Well, we're here," and Marjorie could feel that he was trembling.

"What is it, Wiktor?" she asked in English. "Aren't you pleased?"

And in that language he confessed: "It's become a confusion, Poland. One knows not what to think of it."

Later, when the train had carefully climbed down the escarpment and dawn had broken over the vast plains south of Lwow, Marjorie experienced a sensation of wonder, for the land was so enormous, so empty that she knew nothing with which to compare it. In time, the train crossed a river whose signboard evoked childhood memories: "We used to memorize that river in grade school. West to east. 'The Dniester, the Dnieper and the Don.' Who could have dreamed that I would one day see the Dniester?"

The short run from the river to Lwow was a revelation to the Trilling women, for the few villages seemed pitifully poor, the land tremendous in its isolation, but when they neared the city they saw repeated signs of energy and affluence. They did not remain long in Lwow, but changed immediately to a smaller train that carried them eastward toward the Russian border. At a remote station, which looked incredibly forlorn, they detrained for a line of horse-drawn carriages that awaited them, and over the empty plains, which had once been devastated by Tatars coming to burn Krakow, they rode to the eastern frontier of the Austrian Empire.

Toward dusk on a beautiful spring day they came at last to one of Count Lubonski's estates, where the manager had some two hundred Ukrainian peasants in colorful dress waiting to welcome the visitors from America. Many knew where Chicago was; members of their families had emigrated there.

There could have been for Marjorie Trilling no entrance into Poland more appropriate, for she grasped at once the mystery and the magnificence of this land which she was contemplating as her home. She saw the poverty, but also the warmth, of the Galician villages. She saw the efficient manner in which the estate was run, but also the virtual serfdom under which the Ukrainian peasants lived. She saw the lack of farm machinery, but also the rich yield of the winter crops now being harvested. Always there was the contrast: the rigid control of the church, the spiritual freedom of people who knew freedom of no other kind.

"This is an amazing land," she told Wiktor on the third day.

"Do you like it? So far?"

"It frightens me."

Mrs. Trilling said that it frightened her, too, but she told her daughter what the countess had said when planning this extraordinary trip: "'I shall start you at our estates near Lwow, and there you will see the essential Poland. Then to Lancut to see regal Poland. Then to Gorka to see how an average noble family lives, the Lubonskis. Then to Bukowo to see . . .'" Mrs. Trilling did not repeat what the countess had actually said: "To see where Marjorie may be living one day." Instead she edited the sentence: "'To see where our dear Wiktor lives. And then to my town of Zamosc . . .'" The countess had said: "To be married, if such is God's will, in the church where I was married so very happily." Mrs. Trilling said nothing descriptive about Zamosc.

After five confusing, soul-twisting days on the Russian frontier, the party boarded a creaking, protesting train which took them westward to the keystone city of Przemysl, where the emperor had a huge fortress that guarded his eastern territories. The Trillings stayed at the fort as guests of the commandant, and more than a dozen young officers from all parts of the empire paid court to the charming American heiress, giving her good opportunity to compare her possible intended with other young men his age. She told her mother: "Wiktor excels all of them. In dancing. In conversation. In looks," and her mother replied: "I can't argue with that. I like your young man more every day."

Wiktor was appearing at great advantage, and when the Przemysl commandant, having heard of Bukowski's triumph at Die Schmelz, suggested a riding competition, Marjorie cried: "Wiktor will be glad to participate, if someone will lend him a horse," and the commandant said: "He can have my best." Since the commandant had brought seven horses with him to this farthest outpost where there was little but riding to provide excitement, Wiktor had a rich choice and he selected well.

Marjorie noticed that he was a much different rider from the one who had competed so graciously and with almost Hungarian charm in the capital of Austria. Now he was on his home terrain, a native Pole challenging the entire Austrian contingent, and he rode with desperation, as if this were not a race but a statement about the honor of his land. With grim effort he succeeded, and the Austrian officers, believing that this had been a mere sporting competition and not a test of empire, congratulated him on winning.

There were balls each night, with lovely Polish girls from Przemysl supplementing the dozen or so wives of the senior officers, and Mrs.

Trilling danced almost as much as her daughter. It was as gallant a visit as the two American women had ever spent, exceeding the best nights in Chicago or even the gala affairs in Vienna. It was romantic Austria at its best: young men from good families serving their allotted time extremely far from the capital in a fortress which might be attacked at any time from almost any quarter. Turks, Tatars, Russians, Ukrainians, Hungarians had all besieged Przemysl at one time or another; one year it had fallen, the next it had withstood the attackers; twice there had been general massacres; more often, there had been ringing of cathedral bells as the besiegers withdrew in humiliation.

There was a hill in Przemysl from which one could look down upon the winding river that encircled the town, and on the last day the commandant and seven of his officers invited Mrs. Trilling and her party there for a picnic in the French style, with much wine and fruit and sausage omelets, and a band of Jewish musicians to play tunes of the region. When the commandant sat alone with Mrs. Trilling he told her: "You could marry your daughter to any one of fifteen of my officers. All from the finest families. Starhemberg an offspring of the man who helped Sobieski defend Vienna against the Turks."

"Marjorie's a bit of what we call a tomboy . . ."

"I know the word well. I served in England as attaché. She's an adorable tomboy, and if I were twenty years younger . . ."

"She'd like it, being stationed here at your fortress for a while."

"We like it. This tests a man. You'd be surprised at how many we ship back to Vienna. Can't take it. The loneliness. The Cossacks raiding the frontier, with never an open fight. But I love it, Madame Ambassador, and if your daughter decides . . ."

"Decides what?"

"Count Lubonski telegraphed me: 'If you like young Bukowski, allow him to show himself to good effect. If you dislike him, encourage him to make an ass of himself.' Andrzej Lubonski and I served in the same regiment, you know."

"Tell me, how was a Polish count accepted in an Austrian regiment? I mean, aren't they always second class?"

"Yes," the commandant replied without diverting his gaze. "They are always second class—unless they prove themselves to be first class."

"And Bukowski?"

"First class, I think. A rider like that, with manners like that, I'd be pleased to have him in my regiment."

Early the next morning six carriages drew up to the fortress, each with four horses, and the Trilling women were introduced to the grandeur of rural Poland. The carriages were luxurious; the horses were beautifully groomed and reined with leather tooled in silver. They were from the famous stables of Count Potocki, whose ancestor had married the only daughter of the great Lubomirska of Lancut. The tremendous palace was now his and he proposed to entertain the Americans in style.

It was about fifty miles to Lancut, and the coachmen had been instructed to drive moderately, with an overnight stop at a house which Count Potocki had ordered built especially for this occasion, so in late afternoon when a spring sun flooded the recumbent landscape the carriages pulled into a road which had been built only seven days before and up to a fine country house which had been finished only yesterday. The peasants who toiled on the old Lubomirski estate had not had new cottages for two centuries; the American visitors had an entire new mansion, which they would occupy for one night.

And they enjoyed it! Bukowski, who had himself never seen Lancut, sat before the fire, regaling the women with legends of its ancient grandeur: "It has three hundred and sixty rooms, a collection of famous European art." But the courier leading them to the palace interrupted: "The Potockis added much when they took over. A new theater better than most in Paris, and those marvelous new galleries filled with Polish portraits. And have you heard about our huge stables where our horses are treated like princelings? We have fifty-five exquisite carriages, you know, and only one built in Poland. The rest? Vienna, Berlin, Paris." Smugly he added: "The Potockis have not been idle, you know."

By departure time Marjorie was dizzy with images of grandeur: "You mean, she had nineteen palaces like the one we're to see?"

"You must remember," Wiktor said, "she was Poland. Even when it was divided, totally, she was still Poland."

The road now passed through large forests whose tall trees blotted out the sun, and when the carriages halted for a noonday picnic beneath the pines, and the white cloths were spread and foods from all parts of Europe were uncovered, the manager of their journey said: "These are the Lancut forests. They've never been harvested." Marjorie told her mother: "We've never seen lovelier land. It's so rich, we mustn't drop even one seed or whole fields will sprout with olives or Italian grapes." And wherever they looked they saw Lancut fields and Lancut peasants.

They arrived at the castle at about five in the afternoon, when the sun was at its highest, and in its golden glow they saw the turrets, and the broad lawns, and the dozen smaller buildings, each the size of a minor palace. It was the tremendous stables that captured Bukowski's attention, and he went to inspect them while the women went forward to greet Count Potocki, who welcomed them to what he called "the modest domicile of my family."

They were led to a suite of eleven rooms, with two London-style bathrooms as modern as one might have found in New York. Everything suggested wealth unimaginable: Marjorie's room was decorated with three major Italian paintings from the best period of the Renaissance, and the floor coverings on which she walked had been woven of small-knot silk in Samarkand.

At dinner, in the grand hall, a table which could have seated eighty had been neatly partitioned off with a dozen flowerpots so that it became a comfortable dining area for thirty, who ate off gold plates while eleven musicians played Mozart.

"Count Potocki," Wiktor said with some daring, "please, if you will, advise our guests that only a few in Galicia live like this, and not the Lubonskis or the Bukowskis."

The Trillings received six days of such hospitality, capped by an entertainment by singers imported from Krakow who offered a concert version of Stanislaw Moniuszko's excellent opera *The Haunted Manor*. As Marjorie sat in the Lancut theater, with ninety seats, built into the heart of the palace, she told the other guests: "This opera is better than anything we've been hearing in Vienna," and Wiktor suffered a twinge of regret, because Krystyna Szprot had told him that her banishment from Russian Poland had come from her expressing such an opinion. She was right, he thought. This is better than Strauss or Lehar. But because it's Polish, it never gets a hearing.

Next morning Count Potocki took Wiktor aside and counseled him: "Forget all others. Marry this American. She's not beautiful in the Vienna way, but she's charming and will make you a damned good wife."

"She likes your Lancut, yes. But will she accept my Bukowo?"

"She's a romantic, Wiktor. And such women are capable of anything."

"Sometimes I'm afraid of her."

"I married a Radziwillowna." To a fellow Pole he used the feminine form of the name. "She's much like your American. And I've been afraid of her ever since."

"Could it succeed, do you think?"

"If you show her your ruined castle, which I admire immensely, and if you indicate that she can rebuild your mansion . . ."

"It's not a mansion, sir."

"You must make her see it as one, because if she does, she'll marry you. And you could be very happy with a girl like that." He paused. "I've certainly been happy with my Radziwillowna."

The count drove them to the railway station, where they boarded a train, unbelievably slow, which would carry them to their destination, a day's ride away. To their delight, Countess Katarzyna was waiting there with a convoy of carriages, and after many kisses the entourage started for lonely Castle Gorka, which had guarded the Vistula for so many centuries.

When Marjorie saw it, standing bleak against the skyline, she cried: "This is what I've always imagined," but Wiktor was at her elbow, reminding her in French: "This is not my castle. Not by a wide margin." She started to reply: "This would be far too grand for us," but she thought better of such a statement and ended: "Far too ancient for any American."

Countess Lubonska was a much more congenial hostess than the people at Lancut had been; she organized picnics and a boating on the Vistula and carriage trips to small towns where interesting fabrics were woven. And always she attended to the preferences of the two Trilling women, sharing with them all the secrets she had collected while serving as chatelaine of this old and sometimes drafty castle.

It was obvious that she loved the place, for no corner was too trivial for her to display: "From these parapets one of Andrzej's ancestors saw the Tatars coming on their second or third invasion. He brought everyone inside the walls, and although his people nearly died of starvation and lack of water, he held the devils off. He didn't defeat them in battle, but he did frustrate them, and sometimes that's just as good." Then she said something quite undiplomatic: "In Vienna the Germans often try to humiliate my husband, but he's a crafty one, and he feigns not to understand what they're up to, until he gets a chance to sink in the knife." She made a slashing gesture, then added: "The emperor appreciates Andrzej as one of his soundest men."

"My husband says the same," Mrs. Trilling confided.

"What does he say about that one?" and she pointed down to where Wiktor was testing a horse.

"Oscar is a very practical man, Countess. He says the history of a daughter is a drama in three acts. One: from age three to nineteen you will kill any man who touches her. Two: from age twenty to twenty-five you hope that one at least of the young men nosing around will prove satisfactory. Three: from age twenty-six on you pray that any man at all, even a train robber, will take her off your hands. Marjorie is twenty-three and my husband no longer dreams of a perfect husband. Just an acceptable one."

"I like your husband more and more."

"So do I."

"But in Vienna we see many splendid American girls like your Marjorie . . . and she is splendid, I've watched her. We see them make the most appalling marriages. Any young fellow with a title, no matter how insignificant."

"Are you saying that Bukowski . . ."

"I'm saying that if you two don't grab him, I'm sure you'll accept someone terribly worse. I've known him all his life . . . his ruined castle just down the river. You could do infinitely worse, Mrs. Trilling."

"I suppose you know he's . . ." In some embarrassment she hesitated.

"Marrying her for her money? Mrs. Trilling, we teach our sons to do that. How do you suppose the Potockis got hold of Lancut, that fairy-tale castle? A handsome son with few prospects married the daughter of the great Lubomirska. And how did they cement their fortune? Another handsome son married one of the most powerful Radziwill daughters. And how will young Bukowski save his estate? By marrying your daughter."

When Mrs. Trilling started to protest, the countess cut her short: "Wiktor Bukowski is extraordinarily thoughtful of his horses, and one can hardly say anything better about a young Pole."

Countess Lubonska did not go with them when they made the short trip to Bukowo, but she had not, so far as the Trillings learned, made any plans for returning to Vienna, and they supposed that she intended waiting at the castle until Count Lubonski arrived there on his summer vacation. But she did send the young people off with what amounted to her blessing: "Have a splendid visit at Bukowo, Marjorie. It could be a very congenial place."

It was midmorning when they approached the castle ruins from the south, and when Marjorie saw them, gaunt and broken from centuries of abuse, she clutched Wiktor's hand. "It's magnificent. It's Lord Byron at his best. Mazeppa might have ridden to this castle." She studied it for several minutes, then said: "No, this is where Taras Bulba came."

Now the bad moment that Wiktor had feared approached, for the carriages proceeded beyond the castle ruins to the rise from which the Bukowski house would first be visible, and he realized that Marjorie and her mother must view it in comparison with the fine Lubonski home east of Lwow, or the military quarters in Przemysl, or the glories of Lancut, or the ancient stability of Castle Gorka, which they had just left, and he was humiliated.

Leaping from his carriage and running ahead, he called for the driver of the first carriage to halt, and when he reached the Trilling women he said: "At the top of this rise you will see my house. It is not a castle. God knows, it is not a castle."

Marjorie, having heard from Countess Lubonska what she must expect at Bukowo, touched her mother's hand and said: "Wait here. Wiktor and I will walk the rest of the way."

They walked in silence, she not fully prepared for what she was about to see, he mortally afraid that when she did see it, she would laugh. Though the rise was not steep, they both held back, so that the journey required some minutes, but at last they reached the spot from which they simply had to look ahead at the rambling house and the ramshackle barn in which the prized horses were kept, and it was pitiful: the home of a disadvantaged Polish nobleman who had little to commend him except his ancient and unsullied lineage, his love of horses.

They looked for a moment, each seeing the house as it truly was, and then Marjorie took his left hand in both of hers: "With my help we can make Lubonski's castle look like a barn."

"We?"

"Yes." And in the six halted carriages the other travelers could see the couple embracing, tentatively at first, and then with great enthusiasm.

· · ·

Countess Lubonska now disclosed the reason why she had refrained from returning to Vienna. Appearing one morning at Bukowo, where Auntie Bukowska was delighted to be serving as hostess to a real countess, she assembled everyone concerned and announced: "The wedding's to be held in the old family church at Zamosc, where Andrzej and I were married. I've telegraphed Vienna, and my husband and the ambassador are leaving at once for Krakow."

"How will we get to Zamosc?" Wiktor asked, and the countess said: "The way we always have. By the old roads." She had already spoken to her own coachmen, who were now in the village talking with Janko Buk, who would lead the Bukowski carriages.

"But isn't Zamosc in Russian Poland?" Mrs. Trilling asked.

"It is, but we've telegraphed St. Petersburg and they'll be sending diplomatic officials from Lublin."

"I'm not Catholic, you know," Marjorie said.

"And who counts that a difference? To drive through the little country roads will be exciting. To be married in an old walled city will be more exciting. Child, it's like a fairy story."

"It is," Marjorie said, pleased by what the countess was proposing, awed by its international, interfaith complexity.

When the two dignitaries from Vienna arrived, serious plans were devised, with the imposing countess making all decisions: "The Lubonskis will take four carriages, the Bukowskis four."

"We have only two," Wiktor said.

"You'll have two of ours," the countess replied. She then said that she and the count would be taking seven servants, three of whom would tend the Trillings, and that Wiktor should bring four for himself and Auntie Bukowska. And without serious consultation she nominated the maid Jadwiga Buk, not yet big with child, to head the Bukowski servants.

"It'll be eighty miles," she said, "so I've corresponded with four families en route. We'll be taken a little out of our way, but who cares? You have a wedding like this only once in a century."

Although Mrs. Trilling was fatigued by even the discussion of such a venture, her husband was pleased at the prospect of having his daughter married under such romantic circumstances. "The Russians have been most accommodating in this affair. Their ambassador in Vienna assured me that every courtesy would be extended."

When the trip started, with eight carriages in line and extra horses trailing behind, Ambassador Trilling and Count Lubonski rode together, discussing political problems of the empire, while their wives followed in the next carriage, speculating on the social politics of the capital. Obedient to rural superstition, the countess refused permission for Wiktor and Marjorie to travel to their wedding in the same carriage, so during the four days the Polish bridegroom rode with Auntie while Marjorie shared a carriage with her maid, Jadwiga, wife of the man who was driving, and this could have been tedious, because Jadwiga had only a few rudimentary words of German and English, while Marjorie was not advanced in her dogged study of Polish. But each woman found her deficiency only a limited drawback, because each was determined to master the other's language.

Jadwiga was an excellent teacher, alert and inventive. She spoke with exaggerated sign language, and often their carriage rollicked with laughter as the two young women used words and gestures and facial expressions to convey meanings. Jadwiga explained how in their village the opinions of only two men mattered: "The priest . . . long robe . . . flat hat . . . long sermons . . . eat free at every cottage. The master . . . good man . . . no money . . . now lots of money . . . horses, always horses . . . maybe build house new."

She explained that she was pregnant. Her husband was the coachman. Yes, they had a cottage and a field about as big as that one. Good crops. No money, but maybe now some money.

In answer to Marjorie's question, Jadwiga said that she hoped her child would be a girl. "Poland, not many want girls . . . girls grow stronger every year . . . men sometimes weaker . . . a girl is like the oak tree."

"I think so, too," Marjorie said with many noddings of her head. "Look at the countess. At a party in Vienna"—and she indicated the ballroom, the musicians playing, the excellent food—"Count Lubonski seems the important one . . ." and she became a minister of the government. "But at Gorka"—and she showed the castle rising by the river—"the countess tells what to do."

Jadwiga said: "You will tell Wiktor." When Marjorie demurred, the servant said: "Wiktor, he needs someone to tell him. He knows nothing to tell." And she depicted him on horseback, chasing over the fields.

At the close of the first day the pilgrims halted at the country place of the last magnate on Austrian soil, and it was a robust hunting lodge filled with the horned heads of animals shot by the owner and artifacts many centuries old. The magnate himself had not been able to join the party but had sent eleven servants to make the place comfortable, and although it was already spring, they had three fires blazing and meat upon the spits.

In the morning the countess proposed that Marjorie ride with her, since the maid spoke no English or French, but Marjorie surprised her hostess by insisting: "I'll ride with Jadwiga again. She's teaching me Polish."

On this day Jadwiga, still using her hands and her smile, told Marjorie that after the marriage she would like to serve as her maid, and later she explained why: "If I have a daughter . . . to read . . . to write . . . I wish that she can read and write."

"Can't you read?" She took from her belongings a book in French and handed it to the servant. "You . . . these words . . . nothing?"

"Nothing."

"Of course your daughter will learn to read. Auntie Bukowska has a daughter. Five or six now . . ."

"Good girl . . . very gentle . . . name Miroslawa . . . she reads."

"She'll teach your daughter. They can learn together."

Jadwiga frowned. "Priest"—and she gave a vivid description of the village dictator—"priest says no women to learn."

Marjorie was not going to be trapped into any protest against a church with which she would have to live. As an Illinois Protestant she was already apprehensive about being married by a Catholic clergyman, but the countess had assured her that this was a formality easily accepted: "Besides, at Zamosc the ritual will be in Latin and Russian, and who understands either?"

"We will teach your daughter to read," Marjorie promised.

At about four o'clock on the second day they crossed the border into Russia; there was no guard, no customs officer, no soldiers, simply a rudely lettered sign which warned travelers to report to the police at the next town. As they entered this great empire, stretching from Warsaw across two continents to the Pacific, the travelers were variously affected: the Trilling women were awed and asked that the carriages be halted so that they could alight and savor this historic moment; Bukowski was appalled by the poverty allowed and even sponsored by the Russian government in what had once been prosperous Poland; and Ambassador Trilling asked Count Lubonski what Slavic Russia's attitude was going to be if Austria made a move to annex Slavic Bosnia and Herzegovina, as some predicted might happen.

Lubonski scowled. "Under no circumstances should Austria reach out for additional territories that would give her only more minorities to placate."

"But she will try to grab them, won't she?" the American pressed, but Lubonski refused to answer.

On the last night before reaching Zamosc, the eight carriages halted at a small castle on the outskirts of a town bearing the incredible name Szczebrzeszyn, and the countess had fun teaching the American women how to pronounce it. Following the lesson, as the fireplace crackled and the wine was soft, she told the Americans how one of her ancestors—"the Zamoyskis, not the Lubonskis, remember"—had come in the year 1580 to open fields and said, "Here we will build the city," and with his own funds had imported Italian architects, who built a city for twenty thousand citizens: "Every house was owned by Zamoyski, every laborer worked for him."

They rose early so as to make entry in good light, and when the carriages at last reached the huge central square surrounded by arcaded houses such as might be found in Bologna, Marjorie cried: "Mother, it's like the Campo in Siena," and it was, except that it showed a northern touch. The surrounding houses were square and made of solid stone; and each seemed to have been built by the same hand, which was the case. The town walls were thick enough to have withstood eleven sieges and looked as if they were ready for eleven more. But the most ingratiating aspect was the gloriously ugly central palace.

Tall, massive, it looked as if some inspired Italian had wrestled with the northern landscape and lost. Its proportions were wrong: its tower blended with nothing in the huge square; its windows were jammed together impossibly; and the final effect was of a pile of massive stones not yet assembled into a real building. But even as Marjorie laughed, she saw to the left the very old church in which she would be married, and it looked as if it had been placed there by God Himself, so perfect was its appearance.

She wanted very much to see how the church looked on the inside, but the countess restrained her: "Bad luck!"

The party of Russian officials, who had come down from Lublin to the north, saw the Lubonski group and hurried across the great square to greet them; they were led by the son of the grand duke who governed Russian Poland, and he was gracious in his welcome. He appreciated the fact that Ambassador Trilling had come so far; he was pleased that Minister Lubonski was gracing the affair; and he was delighted to meet the countess and Madame Ambassador; but his real charm was reserved for Marjorie, whom he invited to be his companion at dinner.

It was an affair which only the son of a Russian grand duke could have arranged, for it seemed as if the entire population of Zamosc was engaged. Many of the townspeople remembered that it had been a Zamoyski who had built this fortress on the frontier, and they were honored to have a member of that distinguished family choose their town for this occasion; others of lower caste wanted to see the visitors from America, for they had relatives who had emigrated there to escape the gnawing poverty of these Russian lands.

Some eighty residents of the area attended the dinner; some hundred and eighty townsmen and peasants worked to make it possible—and when the exhausting affair was over and the nineteen Jewish musicians had gone home, Marjorie asked her mother, on the last night of her spinsterhood: "Can this go on much longer? I mean the extravagant wealth? The grinding poverty we saw in the countryside?"

"Nothing can go on forever," Mrs. Trilling replied. She, too, had attended Oberlin College in Ohio and had absorbed its liberal cast. "Now go to sleep and don't talk politics on your wedding eve."

Suddenly Marjorie broke into tears. "It was gorgeous. It was simply gorgeous. A wedding party that no one . . ." She clasped her arms across her breast and shivered. "But the contrast is too much to absorb. I wonder if I'm capable . . ."

"We make ourselves capable, Marjorie." Her mother pulled her onto the bed and sat beside her. "I was the daughter of a farmer. All he ever read was the almanac. How could I possibly have prepared myself for Vienna? For a grand duke's reception like this in Zamosc, a town I never heard of? Marjorie, we make ourselves capable, and if you don't, I'll be forever ashamed of you."

"But in a fortress city like this I hear the sound of drums."

"That's why they made it a fortress."

The wedding was held at ten in the morning, before three Russian priests, and it seemed as if all Zamosc was at the church, for the countess had arranged for twelve little girls to scatter flowers and eighteen others to sing as Marjorie came down the aisle on the arm of her father. The Russian diplomats occupied the major seats, Auntie Bukowska the place of honor to the right. Countess Lubonska was not visible, for she was stage-managing everything, and when sixteen young officers in full uniform, Russian and Austrian, marched out to accompany Wiktor, the ancient church was filled with music and flowers and brightness.

But when Marjorie received her wedding certificate she was not pleased: "It's in Russian! And I had dreamed of learning Polish from my own certificate." Countess Lubonska consoled her: "Zamosc is Russian now. I feel the contradiction as much as you." But she would say no more, and she halted Marjorie when the latter tried to protest further.

The first days of Marjorie's marriage to Bukowski were more pleasant than she had anticipated. Wiktor was proving to be considerate and warm-hearted, a young man without any conspicuous fault, but after she had been in residence at Bukowo for two weeks, with her parents down the river at Castle Gorka with the Lubonskis, she stumbled upon two aspects of her future life which rather disturbed her.

The first came as the result of a picnic excursion organized by the indefatigable countess, who seemed never to enjoy herself unless six or eight carriages were involved. "My dear child, you simply must see Krzyztopor. It's magnificent and played a major role in my husband's history . . . that is, the history of his family." And she prevailed upon the count to relate the story of Barbara Lubonska and the building of the Ossolinski castle.

He related the tragic affair with quiet simplicity: "She was, by all accounts, the most beautiful child our family had ever produced, and she married the son of the richest magnate in the country. For her he built the finest castle ever seen in Poland, and they enjoyed it for seven years. Then Swedes came down and destroyed it, and killed Barbara and her husband and her children, then came here to knock down my castle and burn Bukowski's—and the land was desolate."

"You must see Krzyztopor," the countess said, "to understand Poland."

So a traditional Countess Lubonska excursion was planned, with six carriages this time ferried across the Vistula for the relatively short ride to the castle ruins, and once again Janko Buk drove the Bukowski carriage, with Jadwiga attending the new mistress.

It was a pleasurable ride up the left bank of the Vistula as compared to that somber journey through the stricken Russian areas leading to Zamosc, for in the Austrian section the fields were rich and the prosperity obvious, but toward dusk the Americans saw looming ahead the gaping ruins of what once had been a tremendous castle. It was staggering in size, many times bigger than Gorka or even the better castles around Vienna, and although most of the walls were now heaps of rubble, enough remained standing to create the impression that armed knights could come riding out at any moment.

"We'll camp here tonight," the countess said, and her servants began pitching tents and preparing a country supper.

They spent that night discussing castles and the incursions which had destroyed them, and Marjorie found it impossible to go to her bed, for she felt correctly that she was at last catching an insight into the heart of Poland, that vanished land which somehow refused to vanish, and under the stars her father took her aside to reassure her: "Marjo, darling, you can have as much money as you need to rebuild Bukowo. Your mother and I can see that you're going to be very happy here. We're buying for ourselves, after the ambassadorship ends, a small but very comfortable place on Annagasse, not far from the Lubonskis. They found it for us, across the little street from where they are. You and Wiktor can have it whenever you like, so between the two places . . . But, Marjorie, rebuild Bukowo. Make it something we'll all be proud of."

Marjorie kissed her father ardently. "You dear! I've already told Wiktor to start. The workmen arrived yesterday and I saw them spreading their tools."

But when the excursion to Krzyztopor ended three days later, Marjorie found that the twenty workmen Wiktor had hired were executing plans not for the house but for new stables, which would cost $180,000, and she realized for the first time that her husband was going to remain exactly what he was when she first met him: a young Polish nobleman with no money of his own, no common sense, and a great love for horses. When the stables were completed and the horses properly housed, there would be time to work on the Bukowo mansion.

Her second discovery involved a situation inherently more significant but also more easily dismissed; Wiktor's shallowness would be a lifelong problem, but what she now learned about him was, she trusted, a one-time thing.

It evolved from her determination to learn Polish, and this meant that she would be spending more time with Jadwiga Buk, and when Auntie Bukowska saw that the two women were forming more than the mere acquaintance customary between a mistress and a servant, she felt that a stop must be put to it, out of deference to the Bukowski reputation.

She spoke no English and Marjorie was still totally deficient in Polish, but each woman had acquired a few kitchen words, and with these and agitated gestures Auntie tackled the problem of informing the mistress: "Jadwiga . . . no."

"I like her."

"Not good." Auntie conveyed this meaning in six or seven different ways, but each of the maid's disqualifications was some characteristic that Marjorie especially appreciated, like her outspokenness, her lack of humility, so that Auntie was driven back and back until the truth had to be told.

Puffing out her own belly and patting it to indicate Jadwiga's pregnancy, she started to tell Marjorie how that pregnancy came to be, when the American woman interrupted: "It's good. Baby born, study with your daughter Miroslawa."

When Auntie deciphered this startling news and realized what profane thing the mistress was saying—that Jadwiga's child would learn to read, and with Miroslawa—she became downright terrified at the revolution which threatened, and she cried loudly and with gestures that could not be misinterpreted: "Baby in belly. Whose? Not Buk. Bukowski."

Marjorie looked at the housekeeper and tried not to understand what the woman was saying, but Auntie's graphic repetitions made ignorance impossible, and finally she had to ask: "The baby? Wiktor's?" and Auntie replied with stubborn satisfaction: "Yes."

Marjorie went to her room and sat by the window, looking out at the castle ruins and the Vistula beyond, and she saw for the first time that in a human life there were many ruins which remained, giving the landscape meaning, and that like the great river, life flowed on, coming out of the mountains, seeking the ocean of which it was a part. And everything one did entailed the creation of ruins and involved one in the implacable movement of the ongoing river.

She heard a sound at the courtyard door and Auntie's voice raised to a high pitch, and she remembered that Jadwiga was supposed to come at eleven for a language lesson, and Marjorie very much wanted to inspect her in this new light, so she ran downstairs and interrupted the scene: "Come in, Jadwiga."

"She knows!" Auntie shouted in Polish, but who knew and what, Marjorie could not decipher.

She led Jadwiga upstairs to the study room, and they talked in their horribly broken manner, Marjorie awakened to the fact that whereas she was learning very little Polish, Jadwiga was becoming rather skilled in acquiring a workable English vocabulary. And then Marjorie realized what an average lesson was like: she would ask Jadwiga the Polish name for something and the girl would give a quick answer, followed by patient questioning: "How you say in English?" Jadwiga was teaching Marjorie ten minutes in the hour, but Marjorie was teaching Jadwiga forty or fifty minutes, and in a perverse way the American girl was pleased that if her husband had to have an affair before their marriage, and with a servant at that, it was reassuring that he had at least picked an intelligent girl.

When the lesson ended and Jadwiga left, Marjorie found herself quite perplexed, especially when Auntie stormed back with garbled information as to how Jadwiga and her husband had maneuvered to get their new cottage, their field and their corner of the forest. This information was so complex that Marjorie could not digest it all, but there was evidence that it must be accurate, so she asked for a carriage and Buk to drive it, and off she went to talk with the countess, who seemed by far the most knowledgeable person in these parts, and to that sagacious woman she spread forth the entire situation.

Katarzyna Zamoyska had not reached the age of forty without having observed many such escapades in her own robust family and in that of her husband's. "I find nothing unusual. No murders. No infants slain at night. No treason, with man and woman fleeing across the border. Marjorie, I see no problem that ought to concern you."

"In my own house . . ."

"She doesn't have to be in your house. You keep her there, as your maid, from what you tell me."

"I like her. She's a bold, intelligent woman, and I like her."

"But wouldn't you agree that if you continue keeping her, your husband might . . ."

"I've wondered about that."

"Wiktor Bukowski is one of the luckiest men alive, Marjorie. You came along to save his life . . . in numerous ways. He was doomed to be just another habitué of the coffeehouses. You made a man of him, and he knows it. I'd gamble that he appreciates this and will never touch her again. But if you insist upon having her in the house . . ."

"You think it's folly?"

"Of the worst sort."

"But the child?"

"In Poland, children come and go."

"But this child . . . of a good mother . . ."

"They come and go, Marjorie."

On the drive back she sat hunched up in a corner of the carriage, staring at Buk as he drove the horses, and she wondered by what tricks he had connived at getting possession of the best cottage and a field of his own, and her mind began to construct so many possibilities, none more exciting than actuality, that she grew almost to approve of this clever peasant. Her grandfather, in dealing with the New York bankers who tried to destroy him, had been much like Janko Buk, and although she admitted the wisdom of what the countess had advised, she felt that in losing Janko and his clever wife, she was suffering a real deprivation. But they would not accompany the Bukowskis back to Vienna; Wiktor could jolly well find himself another groom and she would look elsewhere for her language instruction.

Without Jadwiga, her learning of Polish lagged; she found the language much more difficult than French or German, and Wiktor was of little help. Eager to improve his English, he rarely spoke to her in his native tongue, and when she implored him to do so, he told her: "Most of our life will be spent in Vienna, so you will have little need for Polish."

She startled him by voicing openly for the first time a conclusion she had reached after much thoughtful assessment: "Poland will be united again before we die."

"You mustn't talk like that. You saw what happened to the Polish pianist from Paris who talked like that. Whisk! Out of the country!"

"Countess Lubonska told me that you came very close to eloping with her. Running away to join the revolution."

"I was in love with her. I was in love with twenty-six different girls, I think, till you came along."

"Weren't you in love with her ideas?"

"No," he lied. "Austria's our attachment for as long as man can see."

"I don't believe that at all. One day we'll sell the house Father's buying in Vienna and live here . . . and maybe in Warsaw, too, as the capital of a free nation."

Wiktor laughed. "I don't think you should study Polish any longer. You're beginning to believe what you read. And in Poland that can be dangerous."

She had indeed made limited progress in learning the language and recalled with amusement that day in Vienna when she had been confronted by the formidable Polish names on the written itinerary which Countess Lubonska had prepared for her, listing the places they would visit on their way to Bukowo. She well remembered the terror she felt when seeing for the first time names like Przemysl and Rzeszow, and how she had turned to Wiktor for help.

"Look at this," she said petulantly, pointing to Przemysl. "How in the world do you pronounce it?"

"Quite simple," he said, repeating it several times. *"Shemish."*

"Now wait! You can't tell me that with all those letters, it comes out Shemish."

"It does. You can hear for yourself. Shemish."

"What happens to the P at the beginning and the L at the end?"

"In strict accuracy, it ought to be P'shemish'l, and if you listen with extra attention you may hear the muffled P and the final L. But mostly we just say Shemish." He broke into laughter, and Marjorie thought he was ridiculing her. Not at all: "I was remembering how much trouble it gives the Austrian officers who speak only German. They go home to their families and announce proudly, 'I've been appointed lieutenant commander of our big base at Przemysl,' and however he pronounces it, that first time becomes the accepted name in that man's family. Shemish he never says." He laughed again. "How would you say it, Marjo?"

"Per-zem-y-sil," she said firmly, "just as God intended it to be pronounced."

"Never try to reason things out in Poland," he said reassuringly. "Just accept it as Shemish," but she resolved to avoid the word whenever possible.

She was shocked when she endeavored to unravel the mystery of the Winesooth palace, which both Countess Lubonska and Wiktor referred to repeatedly, for when she tried to find it on the maps given her, she failed.

"Where is Winesooth?" she had asked Wiktor, and he had said rather sharply: "On the map, where else?"

"But where on the map? Clearly, it's not on mine."

"It's got to be," he snapped, grabbing the map from her, then jabbing at it with his finger. "Right there, where it should be."

"But that says Lancut," she protested, and when Wiktor looked again at the map he repeated: "It's right here, where I said."

"But where you point . . . it's Lancut."

For a long, perplexed moment Wiktor had looked at the map, then at his intended bride, and it was as if someone had lit a light in his face. "Darling, this *is* Winesooth."

"Are you teasing me?"

"No!" he said emphatically, pointing to the letters *Lancut.* "That's Winesooth. That's how we pronounce it."

"Oh, Wiktor!"

"Look for yourself. The L is pronounced W, the A isn't like your A, sort of an I, which makes a *Wine.* Our C is really a TZ. And we give the final T a kind of Th sound. So it comes out *Wine-tzooth.*"

She stared at her two maps, each of which clearly showed Lancut as the site of the palace; the word even carried a minute drawing of battlements to prove the point, but now she knew the name was really Winetzooth. Looking up, she had said: "I'm so glad you've proved you love me, Wiktor." She had slammed the books shut. "Because otherwise I'd think you were trying to drive me crazy."

When it seemed that she would never master this difficult language, she had faced two alternatives: she could surrender in despair or she could laugh at herself and try anew. Having been an honors graduate at Oberlin, she chose the latter, and drew up a small poster which she attached to the mirror in her dressing room:

ALWAYS REMEMBER
POLISH IS EASY

C is pronounced TZ, TS	BRZ is pronounced BZHE
Ę is pronounced EN	ICZ is pronounced EETCH
J is pronounced Y	RZE is pronounced ZHE
Ł is pronounced W	SZCZ is pronounced SHTCH
W is pronounced V	STRZY is pronounced STCHI

Łodz = Woodge
Rzeszow = Zheshoov
Szczorz = Shtchoozh
Pszczyna = Pshtchina
Szczebrzeszyn = Shtchehbzhehshin

And the name of that dear little gardener Vahtzwaff is really spelled Waclaw

And with this guide constantly before her, she continued her struggle with the language, reminding herself when progress was slow: I shall make myself Polish. For I am marrying the land as well as the man. And in this resolve she never wavered.

Wiktor had proved an understanding husband, and one morning he appeared at breakfast like a little boy with a big secret: "No, I shall tell you nothing. Except that you're to climb into that carriage out there and ride with me to Krakow." And in that romantic old city he mysteriously placed her aboard the train to Warsaw, and when they reached that Russian capital he hired a fiacre, which took them to the offices of a German estate agent, who was most pleased to see them: "Madame Bukowska, what a surprise we have for you. And since it is a very fine day, we're not going to hire a carriage, but we three are going to walk down Miodowa and feast your eyes."

He led Marjorie and Wiktor out into the street leading to the lovely residential Miodowa, and conducted them to a spot from which they could see the exquisite Palais Princesse built by the Mniszechs a century before as a wedding present to their daughter Elzbieta at the time of her marriage to Roman Lubonski. On the very spot at which they stopped, dreamy young Feliks Bukowski had wept his heart out prior to enlisting in the crusade of Tadeusz Kosciuszko. All Bukowskis since 1794 had entangled in their memories visualizations of this delicate palace with the beautiful marble façade.

"That little building set back from the street," Marjorie said, indicating the *palais*. "That's quite lovely."

"It's yours," the agent said in German. "Your husband bought it for you two weeks ago."

"You didn't come to Warsaw," Marjorie said, turning to Wiktor. "You never saw this building."

"I've seen it all my life," he said, and then he said no more. He did not want her to know that he had bought it not for her, but for himself, to assuage an old grief which had been handed down in his family from generation to generation. And when they entered the little palace, the brightest gem in all Miodowa, he felt as if old scores had been settled, for several pieces of furniture were ones that Elzbieta Mniszech herself had purchased before her death.

Their stay in Warsaw had another fortunate outcome. The German estate agent introduced Marjorie to a German art dealer whose family had maintained a salon in the city for three generations, and this erudite man told her that he knew of various canvases which she ought to buy for the little Mniszech palace on Miodowa, but she surprised him by saying: "The Palais Princesse is decorated precisely as we would like it, but we're building a more important place in Austrian Galicia and we'd be interested in certain things for it."

He told her that Krakow had produced a very fine painter, a man named Jan Matejko, who painted enormous canvases much in the style of a Venetian painter named Paolo Veronese. "I know Veronese's work," she said crisply.

"You do? How fortunate! How very fortunate. I have an uncle in Berlin, a great scholar, really, and he controls a number of Italian works you really must see."

"I'd prefer to see the Matejko, if he's Polish."

"Indeed. There is in Warsaw at this minute a grand canvas he did. *Jan Sobieski on the Route to Vienna*. It's not the famous battle scene, but much better, in my opinion."

"How large is it?"

The dealer was reluctant to tell how huge the thing was, but when he consulted his notes and stepped off the enormous distances, Marjorie cried: "Exactly what I've been looking for." Then, having betrayed her interest, she added: "If the price is reasonable. So let's talk price first."

"You haven't seen the painting."

"In Vienna, I saw several fine photographs of Matejko's *Battle of Grunwald.* I thought him a gentleman's Peter Breughel."

"Oh, madame. You know art."

"I should like to see *Jan Sobieski on the Route to Vienna.* You know, my husband's ancestor rode with the king."

The canvas was as big as the man had said, as fine as Marjorie had anticipated, for in it she could imagine Bukowski's great-great-something setting forth on the adventure which had brought him his horses and the Turkish jewels with which he had built the house they were now rebuilding.

And then the dealer had another good idea: "Have you ever heard of the Russian-Polish painter Jozef Brandt? He's very good, and he has a canvas almost the same size as the Matejko, *The Defense of Czestochowa,* and if—"

"The same ancestor fought there."

"Madame, you must have the Jozef Brandt," and when she saw it, and visualized it hanging opposite the Matejko, she knew that the Bukowski mansion would be well regarded by all who loved Poland, as she now did.

It was, however, a purchase she made from the uncle in Berlin which played a crucial role in the history of Bukowo; it was the portrait of an Englishwoman by Hans Holbein, and it was hung in her bedroom along with a small Correggio study of *Leda and the Swan.* For her husband's room she bought a Rembrandt *Polish Rabbi* and a Jan Steen *Topers at an Inn.* For the small reception room she acquired a Philip Wouwerman *Horsemen on a Hill,* but for the garden room facing the forest, she bought an extraordinary canvas, a green-and-blue-and-white study of water lilies by a Frenchman whose work she had seen in Paris, Claude Monet. When Wiktor saw a photograph of the painting he told his wife he disliked it intensely, and he barely relented when she assured him that it would stay in the garden room, where only their intimate friends would see it: "It's my intimate friends whose good opinion I want to keep."

By the time they left Bukowo for Vienna, the mansion was well under way, with the canvases waiting in a Krakow warehouse and furniture being shipped from various centers. On the train to the capital Marjorie calculated that she had spent of her father's dowry more than a million dollars, including the stables, which were now costing some $197,000—far more than all the canvases.

The two Bukowskis were equally happy: Wiktor with the decent home for his horses, Marjorie with the paintings which she believed were rather good.

It was a much different Marjorie who returned to Vienna that autumn, for her stay in the country and her visit to Warsaw had converted her into a passionate defender of things Polish, and she now looked at the Austrian Empire from within, as it were. She startled Count Lubonski with some of her observations and embarrassed her father with her intensifying republican ideas, for he was by nature a defender of royal prerogatives and a champion of empire. In fact, he intuitively felt that England, Austria, Germany and, perhaps, even Russia had systems of government superior to that of the United States, and any talk of Polish or Hungarian separatism irritated him.

But he sympathized with Marjorie when she came home one day when Count Lubonski was visiting and demanded: "Why in this great city of Vienna, crawling with statues, is there no monument to Jan Sobieski, the Polish king who saved the place from becoming Muslim?" When Lubonski said that he thought there was a small statue somewhere, she stormed: "I've just come from the new military museum. It's a grand place, really, with displays of Napoleon and white statues of all the military leaders. It's disgraceful, too. They have monuments to frightened lieutenants who led an army of seventeen horsemen, but not a word about Sobieski, who led a combined army of seventy-eight thousand. It's shameful."

Lubonski explained: "Germans—and you must always remember that Austrians are essentially German—have always had a low opinion of Poles. They see us as the savage hinterland between significant Germany and great Russia. Germans don't dare to condescend to Russia, which is an empire of magnificent strength. So they vent their contempt on us."

"But why should Austria do the same?" Trilling asked, and the count replied: "Because she has territories much more interesting, she thinks, than ours. Hungary is a very exciting land. Transylvania is challenging. Moravia and Bohemia are first-rate centers. Very few Austrians ever get to their part of Poland, so they ignore it."

It seemed to Marjorie that Count Lubonski made every excuse possible for his government. "He's more Austrian than Pole," she told her husband, and Wiktor said: "I've noticed that. And I was on the path to becoming just like him—servant of the emperor, defending everything he did." He walked up and down the big room at Concordiaplatz, stroking his mustache and pondering whether to discuss his plans openly with his wife. Finally he confided: "Marjo, would you think ill of me if I resigned my position in the ministry?"

"I think it would be wonderful, Wiktor. Let's go home to Poland and really work."

"I don't mean to leave Vienna. This is where things happen."

"But they will be happening in Poland, believe me."

"I wouldn't want to miss the music . . . and the theater."

"And the coffeehouse."

"As a matter of fact, yes. I like to keep up with the world."

"But we're to have our own theater at Bukowo . . ."

"For family theatricals . . . recitations . . . and one piano."

"One piano can do wonders, sometimes. Remember?" And she began to hum the grand theme from the last étude, and soon they were singing together the words that Wiktor had composed:

"Home!
The fields are green,
The woods are clean,
My soul serene . . ."

He took her by the hands and said: "We'll live in Bukowo part of the year, and in Warsaw, too. But the capital of Galicia will always be Vienna, so we'll keep this apartment until your father goes home. Then we'll move into Annagasse." And this delightful scheme of existence was agreed upon.

The week after Wiktor's resignation from the ministry, the Bukowskis had an opportunity to savor Vienna at its best, for Count Lubonski gave a rather large party at 22 Annagasse. For entertainment he had acquired the services of a string quartet that had given concerts in Paris and London, and tonight they were augmented by a powerful double bass and three wind instruments: horn, clarinet and bassoon.

They were to offer a miniature concert, a delightful piece of music composed in Vienna: Franz Schubert's Octet in F for Strings and Winds, Opus 166, and this interesting combination of instruments enabled the listeners to follow the various themes as they appeared, sometimes in the violins, at other times in the distinctive horn or bassoon. It was the acme of Viennese music—deft, inventive, light but with serious intentions—and as it unfolded in six unusually long movements, Wiktor whispered to his wife: "This is what I could never bear to lose," and she nodded, for it was the most congenial music she had heard since coming to Europe—not heavily significant like Beethoven or Bruckner, and not of the very highest quality like the best of Brahms, but gentle and singing and delectable, the song of Vienna.

The long fourth movement was a theme and variations, and here Schubert had outdone himself, for with the different colorations available, he took a theme that was good to begin with, then embroidered it with variations so inventive that Marjorie almost clapped her hands with joy. "It's so exciting to hear how he brings the strands together—each instrument off on its own, then all of a sudden . . ."

But the significant moment of the evening was one in which she did not participate, for when the long octet came to a triumphant conclusion Count Lubonski remembered some paper work he must attend to, and he retired temporarily to a small room in the rear of the establishment where he maintained a study, and he was working there when the countess told Wiktor: "Go fetch my husband. The German and Russian ambassadors want to leave."

So Wiktor wandered through the spacious rooms until a maid directed him to the study, and when he entered he surprised the count. "Excuse me," he apologized, "but the countess . . ."

"That's all right," Lubonski said, and then he saw his young friend staring at a series of four carefully drawn maps which he kept on his wall. They depicted the dismemberment of Poland in 1772, 1793 and 1795. The fourth, labeled 1815–?, showed what once had been Poland, now dissipated among the partitioning powers—Russia, Germany, Austria—a nation vanished from the earth.

Lubonski said: "I'm sorry you saw that, Wiktor. It was not intended . . ."

"Do you dream of a reunited Poland?"

"Every day of my life I look at those maps and ask 'When?' "

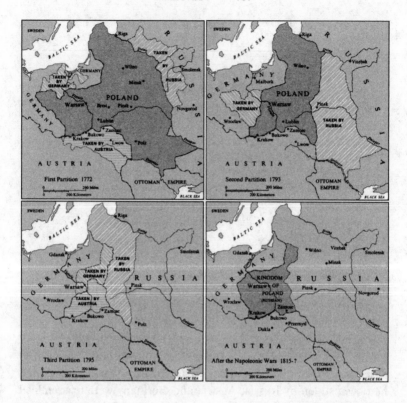

VIII

SHATTERED
DREAMS

I N 1918, AT THE CLOSE OF WHAT WAS THEN CALLED THE GREAT
War, Poland reappeared on the map of Europe after an enforced
absence of one hundred and twenty-three years. Various parts that
had been stolen by Russia, Austria and Germany were reassembled
by the victorious Allies, and with throbbing excitement an old-new
nation resumed its stumbling, heroic course through history.

Count Andrzej Lubonski, now sixty-eight years old and a wid-
ower, no longer an official in the dismembered Austrian Empire,
gladly moved his headquarters from the little semi-palace at 22 Annagasse in Vienna to his family's castle at Gorka. He was in Warsaw
a good deal of the time, advising the Polish government in the area
on which he had concentrated while a senior member of the imperial
Austrian government: how to deal with minorities. He had, in fact,
merely transferred his seat of operations from Vienna to Warsaw, and
he judged that his tasks had not become simplified in the change, for
whereas Austria had grappled with its forty minorities, some, like the
Hungarians and Czechs, of nation size, Poland wrestled with its half-
dozen dissident groups, each with its own inflammable nationalist
aspirations.

To the east the Ukrainians of Galicia yearned for a nation of
their own and for freedom from both Russia and Poland; they were

agitators of masterful power but they lacked any central government or the ability to form one; they were a people adrift, dreaming of freedom but ignoring the basic steps by which it might be obtained. Lubonski, much of whose life had been spent on his Ukrainian estates, prayed that some kind of Polish-Ukrainian union might be effected for the time being, acknowledging that within half a century the Ukraine would acquire enough skill in self-government to strike out on its own. But he also knew that if these wild, undisciplined Cossacks sought to establish a nation now, when they were in reality a hundred and fifty warring principalities, each with its own self-important ataman, they were doomed to disintegration and swift absorption by some better-disciplined neighbor.

"The only hope for the Ukraine," he told his neighbors the Bukowskis, "is a temporary alliance with Poland and Lithuania. Anything else is suicide."

But the Lithuanians to the north presented a special problem. For centuries Lithuania and Poland had formed a union that dominated eastern Europe, a nation of vast size and great accomplishment. In 1410, Lithuanian armies had joined with Polish to repel the Teutonic Knights at the Battle of Grunwald; Lithuanian nobles had been chosen to occupy the throne of Poland; Poland's greatest poet, Adam Mickiewicz, was a Lithuanian, as was the present national leader, Jozef Pilsudski; and most intellectual Lithuanians had been educated in Polish, the language in which they best expressed themselves.

Thus there was every reason in the world for the Lithuanians and Poles to resume their ancient alliance, and one very good reason why this might prove impossible; the Lithuanians longed for their own nation, minute though it must be, and almost no important leaders called for union with Poland, for they realized that in such an association, Lithuanian culture would be submerged by Polish.

"Sickness has possessed them," Lubonski said, "that terrible sickness we saw attacking the Austrian Empire. Each little group dreams of its own sovereignty. Each will attain it, some way or other, and in the end, each will perish." He confided to Wiktor Bukowski that he was just as afraid of Poland's future as he was of Lithuania's and the Ukraine's: "Unless we unite with those two countries to save them, we may not save ourselves. Russia and Germany will always want to absorb us, and we will exist in a state of peril."

When Bukowski reminded him of that night in Vienna when he

had inadvertently disclosed his continuing dream for Polish freedom, he laughed and confided: "Tonight I'm exactly like the Croats and Slovaks who used to pester me. I have my freedom, but I'm terrified by its potentials."

In the north Poland had a most uneasy border. The angry state of Prussia was now divided into two parts by the Polish Corridor, and Gdansk had become the so-called Free City of Danzig, yearning to unite openly with Prussia. Only the superpatriot believed that this arrangement could continue indefinitely.

In the west Poland had acquired much of Silesia, but the citizens living in those former German areas were not happy; and to the south the Poles endeavored to wrest the little province of Cieszyn away from the new nation of Czechoslovakia, which called it Teschen; what the real composition of Cieszyn was, insofar as the national allegiance of its citizens, no one could say, and privately Lubonski thought that the disputed area should be yielded to Czechoslovakia.

Within the nation itself there were the Jews, a substantial minority of the total population, about ten percent, highest in Europe. Jewish influx had begun in the eleventh century, when many flooded in to escape persecution elsewhere. Here they were given the right to own land, conduct business, and preserve their unique culture. At one time they operated the Royal Mint, and in all cities they began to form the nucleus of an emerging middle class, something desperately needed in Poland.

Through succeeding centuries Polish kings extended protection to Jews fleeing other lands, and in what was a pluralistic and tolerant climate Jewish life thrived as nowhere else in Europe. The lives of Jews and Poles meshed together, despite inescapable divisions created by religious differences and language barriers.

But during the partition Jews fell under the rule of foreign powers that were openly and sometimes savagely anti-Semitic in their official policies. During an entire century excesses against Jews were orchestrated by the occupying powers, and pogroms, often officially sponsored, flourished. Inevitably, some Poles were raised in a climate which encouraged religious prejudice.

Now, in these exciting years when Poland was reestablishing her independence, large numbers of poor Orthodox Jews—especially those from little towns and villages—found themselves thrust into a new political environment alien to them and with which they felt no affinity. Failing to shout for Polish regeneration, they aroused suspicions among the Polish nationalists who were shouting.

Count Lubonski never shared in suspicion of the Jews, for he had lived through the disgraceful anti-Semitism of Vienna in the 1890s. He had known the flamboyant anti-Jewish mayor Karl Lueger, and had watched the skill with which he utilized racial prejudice to advance his career. Repelled by such abuse of power, Lubonski sometimes feared that some of his neighbors in Poland were awaiting their own Karl Lueger to lead the Poles in a drive to cleanse the nation of Jews and Jewish influences, and he was determined to forestall such movement if possible.

"They've given me a massive job," the slim white-haired man told the Bukowskis, "but I shall leave the Jews and the Germans to others. My task is to persuade Lithuania and the Ukraine to join us in a union which will stabilize this part of Europe." And he unfolded a map, which he kept with him at all times, and showed how sensible his plan was: "From the shores of the Baltic to Kiev on the Dnieper River, from a safe border with Germany to a safe border with Russia, such a union could protect itself for the rest of this century."

"With the hatred that would have to be submerged," Bukowski asked, "could such a marriage be arranged?"

"It has to be," Lubonski said, with fire flashing from his wise old eyes. Then he took his younger friend by the arm and said: "That night you spoke of . . . in Annagasse when you penetrated my secret and saw my four maps. Well, the miracle I longed for then has come to pass, a true act of God. So now I'm calling for a new one"—and he touched the map—"and I believe it, too, has a chance, if God is listening."

Wiktor Bukowski was now fifty years old and his palace did, as his American wife, Marjorie, had once predicted, "make Lubonski's castle look like a barn." It consisted of a beautifully designed capital U, with the open end facing the Vistula and giving a fine view both of that river and of the ancient castle ruins to the south. It contained three stories, really, but the first was mostly underground, with only narrow windows showing. The two wings which formed the legs of the U were handsomely proportioned and faced with marble from an Austrian quarry; between them ran a fine dual driveway cutting deep into the building, so that the carriages of visitors, and now their automobiles, could come to the main entrance in one direction, deposit their guests and drive off in the other. For nine months each year the soil in between was filled with flowers, and these were the only external adornments, except that in each of the wing façades was a niche in which stood a marble statue from Italy.

There were no towers, no baroque curlicues, no unnecessary excrescences, only the lovely mass and balance of the building itself, with the huge eastern wing a major palace in itself. There was, however, to the north and nicely balancing the living quarters, a stately building longer than the widest extension of the palace; this housed the stables in which Wiktor Bukowski kept his forty Arabian horses and his thirty-six black carriages and sleighs. By good luck, plus a little rearrangement of the façade by the Italian architect who had done the palace, the building fitted perfectly the grand design of the area, while the semi-formal gardens which linked it to the palace made the Bukowski estate, with its three notable features—castle ruins, palace, stables—one of the most congenial in all Poland.

But it was the palace itself which guests remembered most, for the contents of its seventy rooms were nicely varied. Most impressive was the great hall, with Matejko's massive *Jan Sobieski on the Route to Vienna* on one wall and Jozef Brandt's *The Defense of Czestochowa* facing it; many visitors from Paris, London and New York would gaze at the paintings with awe: "We did not know that Poland produced such excellent art." And Marjorie Bukowska would say with pride: "I didn't know it, either, till I married Wiktor. But these, I think, are as good in their way as Paolo Veronese."

Some of the better-educated guests preferred the more standard works of Rembrandt, Holbein and Correggio and said so; the men almost always elected the Jan Steen or Philips Wouwerman because of the homely treatment of familiar subjects; in these days almost no one commented on the Claude Monet *Water Lilies,* but Marjorie confided to certain of her European friends that she was beginning to prefer it above all her other paintings.

To her surprise, she found that many of her guests spent most of their casual time in a long gallery on the first floor, where the half-windows threw little light on the extraordinary assembly of Polish paintings she had gathered from all corners of the nation. There were thirty-one of them and they could all have been painted by the same inadequate artist, except that a knowing viewer would quickly detect that the costumes worn by the ferocious men came from widely separated periods of Polish history.

The paintings were all about eight feet tall, three and a half feet wide and heavily framed. Invariably they showed some Polish nobleman in full regalia, staring fiercely out of the past as he dictated to the Seym, or tyrannized his Ukrainian peasants, or led a rebellion against some hapless king. About half the portraits showed men with their heads shaved either totally or with a two-inch strip of hair left down the middle, but all of them displayed as a major feature the magnate wearing a very wide band or sash about his ample waist, the ends trailing down his left leg.

What especially appealed to the visitors were the plaques, all done in Polish and French by the same elegant sign painter in Sandomierz, giving interesting details about the subjects:

> This Radziwill engineered the marriage of his beautiful sister Barbara to Zygmunt II August, King 1548–1572, the son of Queen Bona Sforza, the beautiful Italian whose efforts to enhance the power of the throne evoked so much antagonism among the magnates that they led an uprising against her, The Hen's War of 1537.

By no trick or inference did the American chatelaine imply that any of the thirty-one worthies was related to the Bukowskis, but the long spread of time covered by the portraits—1487–1799—and the wild adventures attributed to the men depicted encouraged the viewer to believe that some, at least, had touched the Bukowski family in times past.

The portrait that attracted most attention was Number 27, which showed a glaring tyrant with a head completely shaved, a monstrous mustache, massive eyebrows and a huge beard which reached down to the eight-inch-wide gold-studded sash that held his enormous belly. Viewers at once accepted him as the epitome of the Polish magnate, but what they remembered long after the image had paled was the brief history on the plaque:

> Zdzislaw Mniszech, 1545–1619, Magnate of Dukla and seventy other towns, a wise and powerful ruler famous as the uncle of extremely beautiful Maryna Mniszech, 1590?–1614, whom he maneuvered into the arms of the False Dmitri who took her as his bride while striving to attain the Czardom. In June 1605 Dmitri became Czar of All the Russias and Maryna his Czarina, an arrangement which lasted until May 1606,

when Vasili Shuisky had Dmitri assassinated so that he could himself ascend the throne. Shuisky ruled only briefly, 1606–1610, and died in 1612, probably of poison. Maryna is said to have died of a broken heart at the age of twenty-four.

The part of the Bukowski palace that Marjorie preferred was the theater on the third floor, for it was a gem of 1896 architecture, a spacious stage with full equipment for giving a three-act opera, but with red-and-gold armchair seats for only fifty-seven spectators. The proscenium provided space for nine marble busts honoring the immortal musicians and playwrights whose work might conceivably be displayed here. In keeping with Marjorie's special feeling for music, there were five musicians: Beethoven, Bach, Verdi, Wagner, Meyerbeer. The four dramatists were: Molière, Calderón, Shakespeare and Goethe.

Visitors were sometimes surprised to find Giacomo Meyerbeer in this distinguished grouping, and several Polish guests pointed out that he was really Jakob Liebmann Meyer Beer, whose relatives had once inhabited the Polish ghettos, but Marjorie rebuffed them: "I don't care if he is Jewish. The closest I have ever been to heaven was when Enrico Caruso stood on my stage and sang 'Ô Paradis' from Meyerbeer's *L'Africaine*. And I know others who share that opinion."

Many of the world's great singers had been lured to Bukowo to give recitals for an audience of thirty or forty; Pani Bukowska paid them generously from the immense Trilling fortune monitored by three Chicago banks, and when superlative artists like Caruso or Luisa Tetrazzini appeared, all seats were filled and standees were invited to line the walls.

Actors also came to Bukowo en route from St. Petersburg, in the old days, to Berlin; Sarah Bernhardt had come twice to give monologues from her greatest successes, including three deathbed scenes, the best of which was from *La Dame aux Camélias*. Poland's own Helena Modrzejewska, who when she became the favorite of Europe and America shortened her name to Modjeska, had made her last appearance anywhere in the world on this stage in early 1909. She was sixty-nine then, a frail elderly woman, but when she essayed the role of Schiller's Princess Eboli, the doomed Spanish woman whom Verdi was to immortalize in *Don Carlos,* her wavering voice filled the little theater with the mood of tragedy.

Occasionally some troupe would pass through from Moscow to Paris, and Pani Bukowska would hire the entire ensemble, if not too numerous, to detour to her palace for three or four nights of entertainment, and guests would come from Krakow and Lwow and Lublin and Przemysl to enjoy a major treat. William Gillette played *Secret Service* here, and when Sir Henry Irving gave *Othello* with only five players, the Moor, Desdemona, Emilia, Iago and Cassio, the mob scenes were scarcely missed.

One major change had occurred in the palace since those days in 1896 when Marjorie Trilling first envisaged what could be done with this fine setting on the Vistula: Auntie Bukowska was dead, and the firm grace with which she had ruled the decrepit mansion was deeply missed by all who had borne her sharp criticisms. Her place was taken by her daughter Miroslawa, now a tall, shy spinster of twenty-eight who governed the forty servants and ten gardeners but who otherwise kept pretty much to herself. She was essentially an attractive woman, somewhat too thin, a little more austere than required, but she had good features, strong teeth and eyes that saw far and deep.

She read a great deal, and from contacts with certain professors at the Jagiellonian University in Krakow who visited the palace to enjoy the entertainments, she had been directed to books which had moved her deeply, works on politics and the nature of a good society. Step by step, and without being aware of what was happening to her, she had in 1910 become a Positivist, a person who believed that Poland could be saved by the application of hard work, by allegiance to traditional values, and by the exercise of constant pressure on the three occupying governments—Russia, Austria and Germany—until all civil rights were obtained and assured.

It would have been difficult to ascertain which of these three ideals she subscribed to most ardently, for sometimes the Positivists were a confused lot. They had surrendered all romantic dreams of revolution as their pathway to freedom, for they had seen only disaster come from this; on the other hand, they did not preach a supine gradualism, which most often became defeatism. What they trusted was the persistent development of basic rights that could not be repressed, and they were willing to devote their lives to the genesis and protection of such rights.

Miroslawa, however, was developing her own interpretations, and during the year 1913, when Austria faced a crisis because of her arrogant annexation of Bosnia and Herzegovina, two territories she did not need and could not govern, she awakened to the fact that only the universal disruption of a world war could create the climate from which a free Poland could evolve, and during these hectic fifteen months from May 1913 to August 1914 this tall, quiet woman moved about the Bukowski palace awaiting Armageddon, and when it came, with Austrian troops rushing through the village on their way to the eastern front, and then Russian troops surging through in their great victory over the always hapless Austrians, and then the brutal Hungarians marching north to drive the Russians back, she watched dispassionately the tides of war, aware that it mattered little who won so long as all were losers, for in the disruption of total defeat, new things long dreamed of by her Positivists would come to pass. In brief, she had become a philosophical anarchist, even though for her the throwing of a bomb would have been impossible.

But she retained many old loyalties, and she did want the Bukowski palace to survive, because it was a center of humanity, a good, decent place. And although she refused to admit her next concern even to herself at night, she did hope that Seweryn Buk, the bastard son of Wiktor Bukowski and the maid Jadwiga Buk, would survive the various battles which raged about her so furiously.

Seweryn was several years younger than Miroslawa and he had spoken to her only a few times, but as a boy of seven he had been encouraged by her to learn his letters, and throughout his uneasy youth he had been vaguely aware of her helping her mother in the palace, reading her books under trees in the garden, or riding out on the better horses from the stables. One day, when he was fifteen, she had stopped to hold a long conversation with him, telling him for certain what he had previously heard only as a rumor: "You're a Bukowski, just like me. You have a right to the name, to a good education. You could even attend the university at Krakow and become a leader like Wincenty Witos."

The ideas had come too swiftly for Seweryn to digest: that he was a Bukowski, that he might become a flaming revolutionary spokesman like Witos, that this woman of the gentry cared what he became.

He asked his hard-working mother: "Am I really a Bukowski?" and for a while she sat silent, saying at last: "Call your father." When Janko came in from the fields, which he tended so assiduously, she said bluntly: "The boy desires to know if he's a Bukowski," and Janko slapped his much-loved son on the back and said: "You sure are."

With little embarrassment the two peasant parents informed their son of the conditions of his birth, and of how it had enabled them to acquire the good fields they now owned, the cottage they enjoyed and, above all, the corner of the forest which was theirs and no one else's. Janko spoke with a certain defiance, Jadwiga with intense passion: "You brought this family all its goodness, Seweryn, and you will inherit it as if you were our only son. I hope your brothers Jan and Benedykt will get an education and work elsewhere." When the boy tried to speak, his father interrupted him: "Seweryn, before you came we lived like animals. No floor. No chimney. Smoke destroyed the eyes. No fields of our own. No fallen limbs to feed the fire. We were slaves, six days a week working for the mansion, tilling our own plot of vegetables after dark." He gripped his son's knee as if he would break it. "We've never told you these things because we didn't want to burden you, but you were born into a terrible world, Seweryn, and your mother made it a little better for you, and for your brothers, and for all of us." The matter took an important turn two days later when Miroslawa came to the Buk cottage with an astonishing proposal: "Seweryn is a Bukowski, of that there can be no doubt. And as a member of that family, I want him to take his rightful name."

"This is craziness," Jadwiga said promptly, determined to forestall public scandal, which would accomplish nothing. She was a powerful woman who tended the beehives from which her family earned most of its surplus cash, and she knew at once that what Miroslawa was proposing bordered on the ridiculous; it was an idea of equality she had picked up from those professors at the university.

When Miroslawa took her concern to the young priest at Gorka, Father Barski, the prelate was aghast at her presumption. "Fifteen years ago an event happened in your village which has been absorbed, digested, accepted. Whether the right things were done, I can't say, Panna Bukowska, but I think you must agree that a workable solution was found. Don't disturb it at this late point."

"But he is a legitimate member of my family," Miroslawa insisted. "He has rights. An education . . ."

"You utter three grave errors. He is not legitimate. Legally he is not a member of your family. And as a peasant, which he is, he has no right whatever to an education. Believe me, let him stay where he is, as he is."

She next visited a lawyer in Sandomierz to ascertain whether she could adopt Seweryn and thus give him her name, but at this immodest proposal, from a woman in her twenties, the lawyer laughed. "Panna Bukowska, what you propose might work in a radical country like France or someplace like America, where they have no traditions at all, but this is Poland. And through the years, with the help of our church, we've established certain customs and rules for dealing with bastards. Trust me, they're the right rules, and if you try to upset them with your modern ideas, you will create only tragedy. Now go home and forget this nonsense." She went home but she did not forget.

This is how things stood on the right bank of the Vistula, with almost everyone accounted for: Auntie Bukowska and the grand Countess Lubonska, nee Zamoyska, both dead and sorely missed; Count Lubonski endeavoring to forge a union of three such disparate nations as Poland, Lithuania and the Ukraine; Pani Marjorie Bukowska entertaining famous artists in her palace; Jadwiga and Janko Buk improving their fields with the help of their sons; the spinster Miroslawa Bukowska looking after the housekeeping at the Bukowski palace and dreaming about the future of Poland; and the young priest Father Barski watching over everything with his cautious Catholic eye. And Wiktor Bukowski—what of him? He led the relaxed, aimless life of the Polish country gentleman, tramping his estate, kicking a clod of earth now and then, and accomplishing nothing. Even though Poland had regained nationhood, he had only the vaguest understanding of who was ruling the country or what was happening in the surrounding countries. Deprived of the newspapers he used to enjoy at Landtmann's coffeehouse, and no longer involved in the governance of the Austro-Hungarian Empire, he sometimes felt that the world was slipping away from him and wondered what he might do to catch up.

Having turned over the management of his estate to a factotum from Warsaw, he rarely saw any of his peasants in the fields, and the palace itself was run most elegantly by Marjorie and Miroslawa. He did spend time at his stables, but even there, most decisions were made by the six grooms who tended the Arabians and the elegant carriages. He enjoyed most of all riding one of his spirited steeds up the riverbank to Castle Gorka, where he chatted with Count Lubonski if he was in residence, but he admitted he could not follow the tedious divagations of Lithuanian and Ukrainian politics. He doubted that common sense could ever be knocked into those heads and he suspected that it didn't make much difference one way or another.

Since those heady days in Vienna when he first listened seriously to the music of Chopin, he had remained devoted to the works of this great Pole, but he could never become excited by his wife's constant importation of actors and actresses for her theater. Nevertheless, he did indulge her passion and went out of his way to be polite to her theater people, who sometimes remained at the palace for a week or more after their performances. When they did, he took them for rides in his black carriages and, in recent years, in his two Packard cars imported from America. Unlike some of the magnates, he did not like to drive automobiles and was content when a guest volunteered to do so.

He did, however, enjoy arranging excursions to places like the old Lubomirski palace at Lancut or the Austrian fortress at Przemysl, for then he could show his visitors other aspects of Polish history. He loved his country and was proud of its achievements, and was pleased when occasion came for any visit to Warsaw, for then he and his wife ensconced themselves in the charming little Palais Princesse on Miodowa Street to entertain the grand families of the new Poland.

With the dissolution of the Austrian Empire, the Lubonskis and the Bukowskis, like other Polish officials, found no further reason to spend the better part of each year in Vienna, so the families had sold their holdings in that city, and the evening galas in Annagasse were no more. Wiktor missed Vienna, sometimes most desperately, but Marjorie did not. "I've become a Pole, and Warsaw is twice as interesting to me as Vienna ever was. Anyway," she explained to her new friends, "the victors in the last war have made it a capital without a country, and who wants to waste time in such a place?"

What Wiktor really did was follow his wife around Poland, around Europe and around the United States. Like all Poles, he loved Paris, for it symbolized the civilized aspects of man's nature, and it also reminded him of Krystyna Szprot, the little pianist who had burst into his life with such incandescent power a quarter of a century ago. Through the journals he had followed her career; "The Voice of Poland" they called her, and once, in New York, he and Marjorie had attended one of her concerts; at that time she was still championing Chopin and Polish nationalism and was still forbidden by the Russians to enter Poland.

He was reserved in his judgments of the United States, and as a

Polish nobleman, was offended by the Poles he was forced to meet in Chicago and Detroit: "They're nothing but Galician peasants transported across the Atlantic. Some of them can't read." He felt that they would all be better off if they went back home, returned to their villages, and allowed the Polish gentry to look after them as in times past. He was not a believer in democracy and feared that America must run into difficulty if it persisted in its undisciplined ways.

He had the same apprehensions about Poland, for he saw that with the breakup of the feudal estates and the minimizing of the gentry, the nation was losing its direction: "A man like Count Lubonski knew how to hold his estates together, and I didn't do too poorly. Now? Anyone with fifty zlotys considers himself a leader, and where will it get us?"

In 1919, Wiktor Bukowski had no occupation, no burning interests, no commitment to anything in Poland or Europe, and no continuing concern except that payments would arrive regularly from the bankers in Chicago who handled the Trilling fortune. The old ambassador had seen to it in his will that the money could not be alienated from the United States or fall into the hands of his son-in-law, "that Polish fellow."

So Wiktor drifted amiably along, an avatar of the eighteenth-century Polish nobleman, happiest when he was with his horses, most impressive when dressed in national costume and riding some handsome beast across the plains of eastern Europe.

Who was not accounted for in this review of the Vistula settlement? The two most important members of the two leading families.

Walerian Lubonski, aged thirty-one and heir to the title and estates of Castle Gorka, was in London perfecting his English and his understanding of the British system of government. Since it was assumed by members of his father's group that Polish democracy would incorporate the best aspects of British self-rule, mastery of English was obligatory, and young Lubonski was proving an able student, both of the language and the politics. For him the old count had great hopes.

Ludwik Bukowski, on the other hand, at the age of nineteen showed no specific aptitude for anything except self-indulgence. At the beginning of the war his mother had wanted to whisk him off to Chicago, where her relatives could oversee his education at the University of Chicago, or preferably to Yale, but Wiktor had put his foot down: "I refuse to have a son of mine attend some second-rate institution with no sense of history or culture." So Wiktor had employed tutors from Vienna to teach the lad French, which had always been the preferred language of the Polish nobility, and when peace came in 1918, he had slipped his son into Paris, where he was now supposed to be attending the Sorbonne. Actually, he was drifting casually into various ateliers where he dabbled in the appreciation of art; for politics he had no curiosity whatever, listening with equal inattention to republicans, royalists and revolutionaries without developing the skimpiest understanding of their competing strengths and weaknesses.

These two were symbolic of the young men who would determine the future of Poland, but for the present cycle they would not be on the scene; as always, the history of this strange and marvelous land would be determined in large part by what happened outside its borders.

The two were alike in most respects; each was clean-shaven, handsome, wealthy, arrogant and of greater than average intelligence; each was emotionally supportive of things Polish and proud of that inheritance; each was eager to assume leadership, Lubonski in politics, Bukowski as a social luminary, and each had the capacity to do so. But there was one salient difference. Lubonski, like his ancestors, was a man of stern character; Bukowski was not—so that each month the future count spent in London intensified his character, while Bukowski's dawdling in Paris weakened his.

In the decades ahead—the 1940s, for example—Poland would be governed by this combination of historic strength and inherited weakness.

One day toward the close of 1919, when all the world seemed to be in flux as it tested its new boundaries, Marjorie Bukowska announced that she had succeeded in arranging a true gala of Polish music: "I've invited many guests from Krakow and Lwow and two artists you won't believe." When Wiktor pestered her for details, she refused to divulge her plans, and even when visitors began to arrive from the two southern cities, she still refused to share her secret.

The Bukowski palace had thirty-one guest bedrooms, but in her enthusiasm for this exceptional affair, Marjorie had invited more

people than could be accommodated, so she arranged for the over-
flow to be housed at the Lubonski castle, and the count considered
this fortunate because he was at that moment entertaining two distinguished visitors who would profit from meeting a wide selection of
Polish citizens.

Witold Jurgela, a clever professor from Wilno, was head of the
Lithuanian delegation with whom Lubonski was negotiating regarding the future of eastern Europe, and Taras Vondrachuk, a wealthy
farmer from near Kiev, was leader of the Ukrainians. The three men
had agreed to meet privately at Castle Gorka to unravel various proposals, and Pani Bukowska's musical gala would be a welcome diversion from their difficult haggling over boundary lines and innate
rights.

Most of the guests had arrived at either the Bukowski palace or
the Lubonski castle by Friday noon, and lavish luncheons along with
the best wines were offered, and small string ensembles played local
airs. But at three it was announced that a chauffeured car from Rzeszow would reach Bukowo within the half-hour and Pani Bukowska
hoped that all her guests would be in attendance; another car would
arrive from Krakow toward five, and it, too, would contain a surprise. So it was with increasing excitement that everyone began to
cluster about the looped driveway that gave entrance to the Bukowski
palace.

"I have no more idea than you," Wiktor told the guests. "This is
an American plot," and he was as stimulated as the others by the
mystery.

At half after three one of the black Packards was seen passing the
castle ruins and approaching the palace; a few moments later it entered the long driveway leading to the pillared entrance, and when it
drew to a halt the people began to clap, for out stepped a man of
handsome appearance and great international distinction. It was Ignacy Jan Paderewski, the famous pianist who had been chosen to
serve as prime minister of the new nation, a man of fifty-nine with all
the honors the nations of the world could provide.

Although he normally avoided such private parties as beneath the
dignity of a prime minister, he had in this case made a concession to
Marjorie because of the repeated hospitalities she had accorded him
during his arduous years of politicking for Poland in America and
Europe. He cherished the Bukowskis as loyal Poles, "the wife more

than the husband," he teased, and in the waning days of his leadership of the nation he was pleased to be with them.

When Marjorie stood proudly beside him she announced, "During the next three days the Maestro will play for us occasionally," whereupon everyone cheered, but the reception was somewhat dampened by the premature arrival of the second Packard. It brought from Krakow another pianist of distinction, who on seeing the great Paderewski, dashed across the lawn ignoring everyone to plant a kiss upon his forehead.

It was Krystyna Szprot, herself a well-known spokesman for Poland in the various capitals of Europe. Her reputation as a patriot was unblemished: exile by the czars, arrests by the secret police of both Russian and Austrian Poland, attacks from apologists in the pay of all three occupying powers, and wherever she went, unflinching testimony to the ultimate freedom of Poland.

She was forty-nine now, a short, dynamic woman with graying hair and a little more weight about her middle than when Wiktor Bukowski had first met her that winter in Vienna. She had never played in concert with Paderewski and was considered several levels below him in reputation, but the old hero was delighted to hoist her in the air and give her three mustachioed kisses, for he recognized her as a great patriot who had reinforced the work he had done in the days when Poland fought for her liberation.

At seven those staying at Castle Gorka arrived, along with Count Lubonski and his two distinguished political visitors, and there came a gracious moment when Prime Minister Paderewski stepped forward to greet them. At the introduction Lubonski remembered that whereas his guest was certainly Witold Jurgela, his first name took quite a different form in Lithuanian, for it was that of his country's outstanding hero. So Lubonski said: "This is Vytautas Jurgela, of Wilno," and Paderewski replied instantly: "A descendant, I see, of the great Vytautas who led the fight against the Teutonic Knights at Grunwald." Then he turned to the Ukrainian Vondrachuk and said: "And this huge fellow, I'm sure he's one of Mazepa's hetmen."

When the laughter subsided he said: "It would be quite improper for me as prime minister to intrude upon your political discussions. I'm here only as a pianist, and as a friend of the dear lady who is going to insist that I play for you. I hope you like banging on the piano."

As the four men stood together in that felicitous moment, Marjorie thought: How handsome these Slavs can be! What a noble race! The Ukrainian standing there like a great mountain of gold. Paderewski slight but with the power of volcanoes about to erupt, what a strong face he has. And dear old Lubonski, tall and straight as a Roman senator, a man of rectitude. And I like that Lithuanian professor. He could be teaching at Yale or Chicago.

Then, perforce, she looked past the four prominent men to where her husband stood, chatting with Krystyna Szprot, and she had to contrast the great men's dignity of mind and bearing with Wiktor's boulevard charm: the London suit just a little too tight so as to display his build, the mustache a little too waxed, the smile much too forced, the gallantry quite proper for 1880 but not for 1919. How I wish that man of mine would do something significant, that dear, lovable, wasted man. Now, as she stared at him, he was charming the ladies, and doing it in his best Viennese manner.

The fifty-seven chairs of the little theater were quickly occupied when the two pianists indicated that they would be pleased to play several short numbers before dinner, and Miroslawa Bukowska supervised the placing of extra chairs along the walls, then showed the remaining guests where they might stand. The theater had a small balcony seating sixteen, and here she took her place inconspicuously, indicating with an almost imperceptible shrug of her right shoulder where the peasant Seweryn Buk might hide himself behind some statuary; she had deemed it important to his education that the young man hear the great music about to be played.

From the apron of the stage containing the two Steinways which the Bukowskis had imported from America, Marjorie announced: "Maestro Paderewski has agreed to honor us with a rendition of what we all consider his major composition, Variations and Fugue in E flat minor, Opus 23. The Maestro wrote this in . . ." She hesitated, looked at Paderewski, who was adjusting himself to the Steinway, and asked, "When did you write it, Maestro?" and Paderewski shrugged his shoulders.

"Nineteen hundred three," volunteered a voice from the audience, and Paderewski said in French: "That's as good a year as any other," and the audience laughed.

The piece, which was indeed Paderewski's masterwork, started with a bold, bare sequence of seven notes that established the theme upon which twenty wildly differing variations would be constructed. It was not a congenial theme or one that could be whistled, and certainly it sounded nothing like Chopin, but it was strong and magisterial, like Poland itself, and as the enchanting variations progressed, now happy, now sad, now in a minor key, now in a major, but always surging with power, Marjorie thought: The great man placed the history of Poland into this composition. He knew what he was doing. And she wondered why these excellent variations had not won the approval of the public; the only time she had ever heard them played was when Paderewski himself had placed them hesitantly in one of his programs in Boston; then the audience sat quietly, listening respectfully while it waited for the real music of Chopin or Schumann or Liszt.

Now Paderewski hunched his shoulders and launched into the grand fugue which ended the composition, and again Marjorie was astounded by the virtuosity of the piece; she wondered if there was any major piano music she loved as much as this, perhaps Liszt's Sonata in B minor and maybe the Chopin sonata which contained the funeral march, but these variations of Paderewski would rank high, and she hoped that he would one day record them for the new talking machines.

It was difficult to assess how the audience felt about the composition. Count Lubonski and his distinguished guests sat stony-faced; some of the music professors from Krakow and Lwow seemed to be following each note, but betrayed no reaction; and the general audience was, to use a word that had just crossed her mind, respectful. But as she turned to inspect the little balcony, she saw tucked in behind one of the white marble statues the surprising figure of the peasant Seweryn Buk, his eyes riveted upon the piano as though his ears were straining to hear every note. At first she supposed that Wiktor had invited the young man for what might well be one of Paderewski's last concerts ever in these parts, but then she saw Miroslawa Bukowska sitting prim and impassive, hair pulled back, as she, too, followed each note. She must have invited him, she said to herself. Part of the education she insists upon giving him.

Her attention left the balcony as Paderewski almost sprang into the furious yet controlled finale to his fugue, and as all the notes tumbled into position, creating a grand effect, she began to applaud, and even before the composition ended triumphantly, the audience was on its feet cheering. They loved this man. They were proud of his international honors. And they liked his bold way with music. But most of all they revered him for the persistence he had displayed in America in the years 1916, 1917 and 1918, when, on the strength of his own integrity, he was able to prevail upon President Woodrow Wilson to include in his famous Fourteen Points the memorable Paragraph Thirteen, which read: "An independent Poland with access to the sea and under international guarantee." As he stood beside the piano, bowing repeatedly, he was not only the prime minister of Poland but also its regenerator, and Marjorie had tears in her eyes as she reflected on the rumors now afloat that he would soon be deposed because of his inability to compromise with the various stubborn leaders of stubborn factions. It's like old Poland, she told herself. The magnates tearing down the king, always unwilling to accept any sensible leadership.

Count Lubonski, clapping with restraint, looked at Paderewski with gentle compassion. Whispering to his Lithuanian and Ukrainian guests, he confided: "The man's pretty well run his course. We're told he'll be quitting Poland shortly."

"That will be bad for all of us," Vondrachuk whispered back. "It could mean war, you know, if your hotheads like Pilsudski gain a free hand."

"There will not be war," Lubonski insisted. "None of us, not you, not you, not me, could support a new war so soon after the old one."

"Then keep your pianist in Warsaw," Vondrachuk advised.

Paderewski, having offered the group the best music of which he was capable, walked to the wings of the little stage and brought forth Krystyna Szprot, dressed as always in a white dress with the embroidered waistline coming just below her breasts. She was still an enchanting figure, with a beguiling way of enlisting the sympathies of her audience: "For the master of this house, whom I once knew in Vienna, I shall play two études of Frederic Chopin, and I must tell you that he wrote some wonderful words to this music, words which have stayed with me for a quarter of a century, for they said verbally what I have tried to say musically, that Poland will always survive."

The audience cheered, whereupon Wiktor rose to bow, but Marjorie noticed that Krystyna went carefully to the second piano and not the one that Paderewski had used; that was his and she would allow no other hands to touch it. Then, with her powerful fingers,

Krystyna started to hammer out the eight notes of "Winter Wind," that haunting composition which alternated the wild fury of a Polish storm with mournful echoes of the soil, and it seemed that she was too small to play this music, except that under her command, it soared from the piano.

Then, subtly, she proceeded to the final étude, and a chill went down Wiktor's back as those wonderful chords began to echo through the theater, wandering ones at first and then the thirteen which had once moved him so deeply and which he had carried with him for so many years. It was as if he were himself a tautly drawn string that reverberated harmonically with this music, and he almost choked with emotion as he recalled the revolutionary words which had miraculously come true:

> Home!
> The fields are green,
> The woods are clean,
> My soul serene . . .

One could scarcely believe that Poland had attained the freedom of which this song had prophetically dreamed, but it had happened through the efforts of men like Paderewski and Lubonski and of women like Krystyna Szprot and Marjorie Trilling of Chicago. It was a miracle, and he was overcome.

Krystyna now told the audience: "Maestro Paderewski and I will give two formal concerts on the next two nights, so I don't want to play anything heavy in this brief introduction. But I think you might enjoy a selection from Chopin's mazurkas." The people applauded, and she delighted them with a dozen of these intriguing little dances.

Dinner was served for sixty-six in the grand banquet hall lined with mirrors at each end and the two gigantic paintings along the main walls. It was a lavish affair, with fifty-three waiters who served silently from gold and silver platters, and all was overseen by Miroslawa Bukowska, who did not eat with the guests but watched from various vantage points. Four different wines were served by six butlers, one of whom was Seweryn Buk, dressed like the others in a sergeant's dark-gray, light-blue uniform.

After dinner, when the red-and-gold-brocaded chairs were pushed back along the walls, Lubonski suggested that Paderewski and Bukowski join him in an informal session with the delegates, but the prime minister deemed it best to avoid direct participation in the negotiations, so he accompanied Madame Bukowska to a salon, where they enjoyed tea and whiskey with the guests.

This left Lubonski and his neighbor Bukowski to talk with the Lithuanian and the Ukrainian, and the four continued their discussion till three in the morning. Taras Vondrachuk, whose grandfather had been a Dnieper Cossack in rebellion against the czar, established the tone of the argument:

> "We Ukrainians have got to think, Count Lubonski, that you Poles wish to talk about a possible union of our lands only so that you magnates can win back your estates in courts of law, and lord it over us in the future as you did in the past. The union you propose would be everything for Poland, nothing for Ukraine. And even so, it would be nothing for the people of Poland, everything for you magnates."

To this, Lubonski replied: "Do you think that in three hundred years we've learned nothing?" and both the Lithuanian and the Ukrainian said eagerly: "That's exactly what we think."

Lubonski then reminded them that for thirty-two years, from 1885 to 1917, he had served in Austria's Ministry for Minorities, and did they not suppose that during that time he had learned about the inalienable rights of minorities, to which they replied: "You, yes. But Poland, no."

Toward midnight Witold Jurgela, an extremely bright fellow with two years of study in Germany, took from his pocket a small piece of paper. "Lubonski, undoubtedly you know your fellow Pole landowner Gustaw Prazmowski."

The count threw up his hands and cried: "Don't speak to me about that scoundrel," but the Lithuanian negotiator proceeded:

> "In Vilnius [which was how he pronounced the name of the city the Poles called Wilno] we had an opportunity to observe how Prazmowski dealt with people for whom he had little respect, namely, us Lithuanians, and I have here the notes I made one day when he was being especially offensive: 'As a friend treacherous, as an enemy venomous. Able in all things, reliable in nothing. Uses words to obscure truth and truth to obstruct justice. Bathed in self-pity, he envies everyone who does better than he. A cruel master, a contentious equal and

a craven subordinate. Has a lust for property and an aversion to working for it. Worst of all, his petty, screwed-up face and narrow suspicious eyes constantly betray his confused inner passions. He is a man to be avoided, for he can never be trusted.' "

Carefully Jurgela folded his condemnatory document, returned it to his pocket, and asked: "Do you seriously recommend that we Lithuanians trust our security to people like him?"

Without blanching at this savage description of a type of frontier Pole with whom other nations were familiar, Lubonski asked quietly: "Do you describe me in those phrases . . . when you discuss our meetings with your superiors in Wilno?"

"You're an Austrian, Lubonski, no longer a Pole."

Vondrachuk joined in support of his colleague: "Count, do you remember an agent you employed to run your estates east of Lwow? Man named Szypowski? A raging tyrant, worse than the man Witold described. And he was your man, Lubonski, working under your orders."

"In my employ, Vondrachuk, not under my orders."

"The supreme drawback to your proposal of a three nation union, Lubonski, is that both Lithuania and Ukraine have seen your magnates in action. All those graspers want is to reclaim their lost estates, their lost serfs. Justice is not in them, and you know it."

As always, Lubonski retreated to his maps, spreading before the men a large one which encompassed the region that lay between Berlin and Moscow, and with ice-hard logic he began to speak, indicating every area as he did:

"Let's start with facts we can all accept. Poland, lost in this sea of steppe and forest, a land with no natural boundaries east, north or west, is an orphan. Caught between Russia and Germany, it can exist only briefly unless it makes friends and establishes some kind of self-defense union with other powers.

"Our most propitious union would be with what we now call Czechoslovakia, but three things make this impossible. First, the Carpathian Mountains restrict normal discourse. Second, Czech leadership is stubbornly Protestant, we just as stubbornly Catholic. Third, we're engaging in near-war with them over Cieszyn, so that peaceful discussions are not possible.

Any dream of a Czech-Pole or Hungarian-Pole or Czech-Hungarian-Pole union is unattainable, and will never come to pass, to the detriment of us all.

"So that leaves only some kind of reinstitution of the ancient patterns, the ones that served us so well in the past. Lithuania-Poland-Ukraine, united in one grand confederation which can sustain itself. I beg you to forget past differences between us and devote your energies to the only solution which will allow us to survive."

When Jurgela protested: "There's no quarrel between the Ukrainians and the Lithuanians, it's only with both of us against you domineering Poles," Lubonski replied: "You have no Lithuanian-Ukrainian quarrel because you have no common borders. You fight with us because we touch you and are available for the fight. Believe me, gentlemen, if you were neighbors, you would fight each other just as much as you fight us. But now we seek a new order, when fighting between neighbors falls out of fashion."

At this point Bukowski indicated that he wished to leave the discussion, but did not reveal why: he desperately wanted to talk with Krystyna Szprot and learn how she had spent the years since that night when he proposed to her in Vienna, but as he moved toward the door Count Lubonski almost commanded him to stay: "In the next round of talks on the merger of our three nations, I shall request you as my aide, Wiktor. You must familiarize yourself with the problems." And with that the four men settled down to deal with the real problems which would face their peoples in the decades ahead. Lubonski was free to use advanced concepts because both Jurgela and Vondrachuk had always spoken Polish as their language of learning and external commerce, regardless of what they spoke at home; so he spelled out the difficulties:

"I'm an old man now, and I've spent my life grappling with problems of nationalism, and it has become increasingly clear to me that a body of people needs two conditions before it can graduate into nationhood.

"The first requirement is the easiest defined. A coherent land mass big enough to survive as a unit, occupied by people similar enough to have common interests and numerous enough to constitute a viable economy. On these criteria we three fare rather well. The total land mass would be enormous and of enormous importance, much bigger than any existing European nation. And the people are reasonably homogeneous, three different home languages, one common language for intercourse.

"The population is big enough, too. Lithuania, perhaps three million; Poland, twenty-seven; the Ukraine, twenty, and depending upon boundaries, maybe as much as thirty million. Again, we're bigger than any existing European nation."

"But not Russia," Vondrachuk broke in, to which Lubonski countered: "I never think of Russia as European." Now, as he reached the difficult part of his argument, he rose and moved about the room which Marjorie Bukowska had decorated with such elegance: the Holbein portrait on one wall, a suit of armor against another, a large Polish tapestry covering a third:

"The second requirement is not so easy. To justify becoming a nation, the land and the people must have produced a unifying culture. [Both Jurgela and Vondrachuk began to protest that their people did possess a culture, as of course they did, but Lubonski was thinking on a higher plane.] By culture I do not mean folklore, cooking patterns or nationalistic myths. I mean music which all respond to. I mean architecture which constructs buildings of spatial and utilitarian importance. I mean conscious poetry, not doggerel. I mean great novels which generate and define a people's aspirations. And above all, I mean the creation of a philosophy which will underlie all acts passed by your parliaments, all utterances made by your teachers and professors.

"Gentlemen, the accumulation of such a culture requires time and the dedication of men and women who know what they're doing. [Here he paused, almost afraid to make his next statement. Then, walking briskly back to face his visitors, he spoke.] You Ukrainians have not had time to build such a culture, and if you try to establish a state of your own with inadequate foundations, it will collapse. Vondrachuk, I assure you, it will collapse, probably within ten years, because you lack the cohesive background upon which to build. You lack the music, the architecture, the beautiful town squares, the great novels. I concede, the poetry you have, thanks to one man who would understand what I'm saying, your fellow Shevchenko, who almost single-handedly gave the Ukraine a soul."

Vondrachuk could not suppress his indignation: "Why do you always say *the* Ukraine? You don't refer to Poland as *the* Poland." But Count Lubonski interrupted: "One does, however, refer to The Hague." Now Vondrachuk instinctively reverted to his native language to express his deep convictions: "But *Ukraina* is a nation! It's true, Pan Lubonski, we may be lacking in cultural refinements. By preference, we do not even use titles in our forms of address. And Shevchenko is only a beginning . . . a taste of freedom. Your point may be well taken geographically, but Poland will never permit us to grow as a nation and we refuse to continue to be subservient to the whims of Polish magnates."

"Vondrachuk, you cannot make it alone. You can only exist as one of three. But let me continue.

"As for Lithuania, I'm afraid it's too small in its present state. Not enough people. Not enough land. Not enough commerce. You have the history and the common interests, Jurgela, but you will never be able to exist for very long as a free nation. Either Germany will engulf you from the south or Russia will gobble you up from the east. There is no hope."

To this gloomy prediction Witold Jurgela had to protest, and he made a vivid defense of Lithuanian patriotism and culture, pointing to the antiquity of both and to the noble traditions of the past, when Lithuania was the master nation in this part of the world, more powerful than Russia, more extensive than Poland. The room sang with echoes of Lithuanian deeds and a present yearning for a reestablished sovereignty.

Lubonski allowed the flood of rhetoric to pass on, then said quietly: "In the Austrian Empire forty units like yours, Jurgela, constructed justifications for their freedom—"

"And many got it," Vondrachuk interrupted. "Czechoslovakia, Hungary, the Yugoslavs and you Poles."

"The more important question will be: How many will retain it? Even the big ones. As for the infants . . ." With sadness and concealed contempt he rattled off the names of tiny units whose patriots had pestered him with their claims: "Bosnia, Slovakia, the Banat of Temesvar, Transylvania." He put his hands to his head and almost moaned; then he returned to his map and pointed to the tiny area of Cieszyn, a short distance southwest of Krakow: "We cannot even settle among ourselves the disposition of this tiny corner. We are seriously considering a major war to determine its destiny."

Now Jurgela took possession of the map, and with delicate strokes of his right forefinger he outlined what he proposed as four new nations which would cluster on the western flank of Russia: "Up here, Finland, a very cohesive group of people. Here, Estonia with its own language. Here Latvia, very solid patriots. And down here, free once more, the Republic of Lithuania with its own historic culture . . ."

He was about to say more, when Lubonski with an extended left hand covered that entire section of the map, erasing it from sight: "In one week Russia would envelop you all, and we would never hear of you again." Then he slapped his right hand over the proposed Ukrainian state: "And you, too, Vondrachuk, would vanish."

It was Jurgela, trained in debate, who countered this devastating prediction: "And what about you, Lubonski? Do you consider yourself invulnerable?"

Lubonski lifted his hands, freeing the satellites for their brief days of glory, then pointed with left and right forefingers to his own endangered country: "Poland is the most vulnerable of all, because whenever either Germany or Russia seeks to move, each nation will have to settle with Poland first . . ." With devastating thrusts of his fingers he slashed at his exposed country, indicating ancient enemies in new dress as their armies whipped across the flatlands of Poland.

"I sometimes think, gentlemen, that Poland needs you far more than you need us, because if we unite in a strong three-part republic, we can protect ourselves. If we go separately, we perish."

It was Vondrachuk—grandson of an ataman, a man whose Cossack father had commanded seven villages, deeming himself greater than the King of Spain and willing to fight to the death against the Cossack who commanded eight neighboring villages—who spoke the words that ended this long discussion:

"The time comes in the history of a people when they believe they're ready for freedom . . . for nationhood. When that moment arrives, anyone who opposes the public will is swept aside. We Ukrainians are convinced that our time for nationhood has arrived, and we don't need your music and architecture and philosophy to justify us. We've done that with our swords, our horses, our conquest of the steppe. We are a nation, and we require no instruction from Poland, who has been our timeless enemy. You go your way, we'll go ours, and I pray we can have peace between us."

"I understand we're to meet at Brest-Litovsk," Lubonski said, using out of respect to his visitors their name for Brzesc Litewski. "Let us each review his positions before that final meeting."

But as Bukowski watched the three negotiators separate he felt no assurance that when they did meet again, their individual animosities would be altered: Lubonski, the proud Pole who had stood in the halls of the mighty and who now fought to reverse centuries of history; Professor Jurgela, who felt the blood of the entire Lithuanian nation, past and future, coursing through his veins, and who was determined to revive eras of greatness; and tough, uneducated but very wise Taras Vondrachuk—named after one of Ukraine's legendary revolutionaries—battling to establish a nation which lacked books or buildings or any memory of self-government, and never doubting that will power, plus swift horses and the Greek Catholic religion, would be sufficient base for a modern state.

"It should be very interesting at Brzesc Litewski," Bukowski told his wife when he awakened her at half after three in the morning.

"Did you accomplish anything?" she asked.

"What could one accomplish with a dumb Lithuanian and a stupid Ukrainian?" he asked.

At the first of their two concerts Paderewski insisted that Krystyna Szprot open the evening, and this she did with a sparkling selection of mazurkas, after which he said enthusiastically: "We could have had no better opening. Real Polish music. Now I shall follow with an equal number of polonaises." When the applause died down he stood beside his piano and said in a voice resonant with patriotism and love of land: "You are to imagine the king's court in Krakow. All the nobles have gathered in their traditional dress—furs for the men, jewels for the ladies. A march forms. See, they come in stately fashion, arms akimbo, they bow, they turn, they disappear down that aisle and out that door. The eye fills with tears at the majestic march of the Polish patriots."

Like many in the audience, he wiped his eyes, then sat at the piano and launched into the first of the eleven polonaises he would play that night. How melodic they were, how surprising in their changes of rhythm, how infused with the essence of a vanished Poland suddenly revived.

"And now," he said at the conclusion of one of the deft promenades, "we come to music I love." When he began the hushed notes of the longest and perhaps most impressive of the polonaises, Number Five in F sharp minor, Opus 44, a few people clapped, and instead of rebuking them, he turned and smiled, nodding his head in agreement. Those who had applauded knew that midway through this piece the music would drop to a heavenly whisper, one of the subtlest of Chopin's inventions, and when this happened one could hear a sigh echoing across the theater, as if the people of the new Poland were joining with those forgotten promenaders of the old.

But Paderewski did not propose to end his concert on any such note of nostalgia, for when this difficult and lovely music ended he stepped to the apron of the stage and said: "In those heartbreak years when I wandered the world an exile, visiting capitals and pleading for Poland's freedom, it was customary for Polish pianists playing abroad always to include in our program the two wonderful polonaises of Opus 40, for we believed they summarized our history, first the glorious past, then the prolonged agony of defeat. That's the order in which Chopin wrote them, for he had known both the glory and the despair.

"But tonight, when we have won our freedom, and hereafter whenever I play, I shall reverse the order. First the tragic years in C minor." Bowing his head over the keyboard, as if this music were too painful to begin, he finally started that exquisite threnody, that long lament for lost dreams, and rarely had a piano seemed so intimate a part of a nation. With deft skill he brought the sorrowful notes to a conclusion, keeping his head bowed long after the final chord.

Then, with almost savage joy, he struck the triumphant notes of the A major, which many called the "Military," and with this burst of patriotism, written when Chopin was at his loneliest, the little theater rang with cheers, and Marjorie Bukowska's pleas for quiet went unheeded, nor did Paderewski object, for this was a night of celebration. When he ended, there were more cheers and applause, not only for his performance but also for his years of noble service, which he acknowledged with two sentences: "We have won so much. Let us strive to keep it."

On the second night the two pianists offered as a joint encore a more or less impromptu offering of some Brahms waltzes, during which Paderewski stopped the music twice to instruct Krystyna in how a passage should be handled. The first time she nodded demurely, changed her approach, and followed him through that particular waltz, but at his second bit of instruction she demurred: "It will sound much better if we play it as written," and she ran through a passage of difficult transition. Then she rose, turned to the audience and asked them: "Now, doesn't that seem more like a waltz?" When the audience applauded, Paderewski also rose, walked over to Krystyna and kissed her. Then, with his powerful right hand, he swatted her on the bottom: "Now we shall play it my way," and they did.

Since Jurgela and Vondrachuk suspected that their host at the castle, Count Lubonski, had brought them to the Bukowski palace to impress them with the accomplishments of Polish culture as opposed to the bleakness of their own, they had resisted appreciating the great artistry of these two pianists, but on their final night their hostess presented a program which anyone anywhere in the world would enjoy, for it was felicity itself in bright costume, youthful vivacity and joyous singing; to men born and bred in Slavic lands, it would be especially endearing.

A troupe of nine singers in full costume had come by train from Krakow with their own pianist, first violinist and conductor. Assembling two different groups of highly skilled local Jewish players who had mastered everything from polkas to Beethoven, the visitors had formed an orchestra, and now, after two rehearsals, were prepared to offer a simplified version of Stanislaw Moniuszko's delightful opera *The Haunted Manor.* As the leading tenor explained: "It may seem just a bit confused at first, but bear with us. Because when I and the other soloists are not singing our lead roles, we shall become the chorus, and at that time we will put on these caps, so when you see me in this cap you are to forget that I am the hero and tell yourself: 'Look, there's another villager.'"

When Marjorie heard the music with which she was now familiar, she thought again of its high quality; the solos were as good as any being offered by Smetana in Vienna or Glinka in Moscow, and when the basso profundo sang his aria she judged it, accurately, "to be as good as Colline's apostrophe to his overcoat in *La Bohème.*" It was glorious music, ideally suited to the ornate little theater, and the nine singers presented it with just the proper make-believe.

There came a moment in the action when the father of the two girls who were seeking husbands stepped forward to describe what it was he sought in a man who might enter his family, and the aria, written in the 1860s while Poland was still in bondage, had been used as a device to describe the ideal revolutionary Pole—such a man as Count Lubonski, biding his time in Vienna, or a woman like Krystyna Szprot, living in exile but breathing wherever she went the message of ultimate freedom. It was a splendid aria, deeply loved by Poles every-where, and as the baritone enunciated the meaningful words, all in the audience who had fought for Poland's resurgence compared them-selves with the father's description of the ideal citizen and calculated how far they had fallen below the target. Andrzej Lubonski wiped his eyes and remembered how his valiant Zamoyski wife had worked so resolutely during the long years in Vienna, dying before freedom was attained but assured even on her deathbed that it must come.

In the balcony two listeners were not so deeply impressed; Miro-slawa Bukowska whispered to the peasant Seweryn Buk: "Always they sing of gentry in the manors. The real Poland is the peasant in the village. On that stage it's all fluff."

The next day the negotiators from Lithuania and Ukraine de-parted to write reports for their governing committees, and the other guests trailed off, leaving Paderewski and Szprot at the palace with the Bukowskis and Count Lubonski, and when it became apparent that the prime minister was determined to resign his high office be-fore he was forced out, all tried to persuade him that it was his duty to fight on, but he would have none of that: "They don't want me, and to tell you the truth, I don't think they need me."

In the discussion which followed, it gradually became clear that he was planning not only to quit his post as head of the government, but also Poland, forever, and this caused real dismay, for as Lubonski said: "Maestro, you are Poland."

"I was," he said quietly, and Bukowski reminded him of how in the dark years of 1909 and 1910 he had contributed all the money he made from his concerts in Berlin and Buenos Aires and Paris for the erection of a public monument in Krakow honoring the five-hundredth anniversary of the Battle of Grunwald when the Teutonic

Knights were driven back, and the old man said: "Matejko with his paintings, Sienkiewicz with his novels, I with my music, we tried to keep Poland alive," and Wiktor cried impulsively: "Yes, and Krystyna Szprot with her Chopin."

"She did indeed!" Paderewski agreed, blowing his fellow artist a kiss. "Great on Chopin, dreadful on Brahms." And Marjorie Bukowska, noting well the ardent enthusiasm of her husband, resolved that whereas there would in the future be much playing of Chopin in her theater, it would be played only by aspiring young male pianists and never again by visitors from Paris like Mademoiselle.

It was at the Bukowski palace that Paderewski finally determined to go into voluntary exile, and on the final night he said: "Poland drives out all its talented people. Frederic Chopin never saw this country again after the age of twenty. He wrote all his great works abroad. Adam Mickiewicz wrote his *Pan Tadeusz* in exile. Maria Sklodowska, whom I saw so often in Paris, won her two Nobel prizes there and not in Poland. I'm leaving because the nation is determined to fight one war after another. Against Lithuania over the matter of Wilno. Against the Ukrainians over the division of farmland. Against Czechoslovakia over a wedge called Cieszyn. And before long, against Russia over a matter of politics. Lubonski, slow your horses down or they will gallop away with you."

Marjorie, unwilling to see her gala week end in such disarray, pleaded with Paderewski to play for them one last time his Variations and Fugue, and when Krystyna Szprot added her entreaties with one calculated to warm the composer's heart—"I want to add it to my repertoire for America and Brazil, and I want to hear how you think it should be played"—he walked slowly to the theater, mounted the stage, and ran his fingers over the piano he had chosen as his own. Then, with the bare, heavy mastery which he sometimes displayed, he struck the keys, lining out the theme upon which he would build his twenty variations, but as he played he instructed Krystyna: "I like it slow, and heavy at the opening so that it sounds almost banal. Because you and I know what we shall do with it later."

On and on he went, speaking now and again when some critical point was reached and bringing all his listeners into the secret places where music was written. Lubonski, who had known most of the great musicians of his day, entertaining them in his home, simply allowed the sound to flow over him. Krystyna was enchanted by the complexities the great master had introduced into his music, providing something for any virtuoso who wanted to tackle his difficult composition, but at the same time she could hear herself playing certain variations rather better than he was doing, for she was in certain restricted ways a superior pianist. Marjorie hoped again that she might some day find a recording of the piece.

Wiktor sat enraptured, a veritable slave to every nuance. Chopin, he said to himself, was a dreamer, writing music that envisaged a day fifty years removed, either backward or forward. It evoked romance, the ringing of fairy bells. What I'm hearing now is the music of an extraordinary man who struggled to make today's dreaming come true. There's not a shred of romanticism. This is the statement of a practical man, a cynic who battled them all. Chopin may be the soul of Poland. This is the sinew and the strong trees in the forest and the workman plowing his field.

For the duration of the piece he continued thinking along these lines, accurately defining the two approaches to music, the two approaches to Poland, but when Paderewski finished his thundering fugue, Bukowski muttered to himself: "I prefer Chopin."

Paderewski had been right in his predictions about the future. In a series of twists and turns so bizarre that one could scarcely follow them, the new Polish nation launched an invasion of Lithuanian territory, with the announced intention of protecting Poles in that confused nation while at the same time aiding true Lithuanian patriots in establishing a secure state. This was a gambit difficult to explain, so negotiations between Lubonski and Jurgela, seeking a union of the two states, were shattered.

At almost the same time Polish patriots, for the best reasons in the world, felt they had to fight the Ukrainians in the Polish part of Galicia and some rather brutal events occurred, about evenly divided between the two armies but all calculated to make any future union of the two nations impossible. For a while Lubonski would see no more of Vondrachuk.

But war was a common commodity in these parts, and the battles far removed, so it was easy for attention to be diverted when a startling event focused attention on the Bukowski palace. Miroslawa Bukowska announced that she was marrying Seweryn Buk, the master's bastard son.

"You can't do that!" Wiktor protested, but his distant cousin, this tall, ungainly woman of twenty-nine whom no one could imagine as engaged in passion of any kind, was obdurate: "We're getting married."

"No priest will countenance such a thing," Wiktor growled, and it was apparent that he would take steps immediately to ensure that Father Barski did not perform any ceremony.

"I have supposed you would behave like this," Miroslawa said with lips pursed.

"You can't continue here," Marjorie said in defense of her husband's position, but as soon as the words were spoken she regretted them and would have softened her statement had not the house-keeper said: "I have no intention of staying. This is my formal announcement that I'm leaving."

"And where will you live?" Wiktor asked contemptuously. The answer indicated how deeply the Positivist malignancy had infected his cousin: "I shall live as the people of this land have always lived. Seweryn has a cottage—"

"I will not allow him, or you, to occupy—"

"Those days are past, Pan Bukowski. You no longer have the right to say who can and who cannot."

"I still own the cottages, remember that."

"But not the land that Janko Buk farms. Not the land on which his cottage stands."

"Is that one giving you his cottage?"

"No. But he's already given us land on which we shall do our own building."

"Seweryn Buk hasn't a zloty to build anything."

"I have," the determined woman said, and when Wiktor asked sneeringly: "You'd use your savings to build a house for a peasant?" she snapped: "Whose savings did you use to build this palace?"

It was then that Marjorie entered the conversation seriously: "I've always been distressed about Seweryn. Miroslawa, your mother begged me to ignore his mother, but I knew that a great wrong had been done to Jadwiga. My conscience warned me that I owed her . . ."

When Wiktor saw how this conversation was heading he stomped from the room, leaving the two women to discuss a problem which had never really been resolved.

"Are you determined to go ahead with this?" Marjorie asked as she rang for tea.

"I am. It's my salvation and the salvation of Poland."

"Don't mix the two, Miroslawa. Is it that you're growing older—"

"Because the two have never been mixed, there have been two Polands, one for the gentry, one for the peasants."

"Never try to correct a national situation by a foolish personal act."

"I'm sure people like me must have warned people like you in Vienna that if things continued, the empire would have to crumble. But you never listened."

"Predictions of disaster are easy to announce, but they rarely come to pass. I think you're acting this way because you're frightened you may never find a husband. Wiktor and I will take you to the little palace in Warsaw, where you can meet hundreds of men who would make good husbands."

"I am of this soil, Pani Bukowska."

"I wish you would call me Marjorie. If you do move out of the palace and live here in our village—"

"It is no longer your village. There's a new day, Pani Bukowska, and you don't seem to realize that."

"You are so determined?"

"I am. A new day is dawning in Poland and I shall consecrate it by giving Seweryn Buk the name he's entitled to."

"You're going to call him Bukowski?"

"No, he's going to call himself Bukowski."

Now Marjorie had to voice strong protest, and she summoned a servant to find Wiktor, and as he returned to the room she said abruptly: "Miroslawa tells me that after their wedding Buk is going to take her name—Bukowski."

"That's impossible!" Wiktor cried. During the quarter of a century since the birth of Seweryn Buk in 1896, the infant, and then the boy, and now the young man had been an agitation in this district. He had carried himself well, fitting easily into the Buk family, but everyone knew that he was really Wiktor's son and that brash Janko Buk had utilized him as a device for acquiring fields and a portion of the forest, so he was both resented and scorned.

At the palace, he was also a problem, a colorless, shapeless threat who bore the master's physiognomy but not his name, and Wiktor, coming upon him suddenly in some field, had often wished that the young fellow would go away . . . just vanish. But in those early-1900 days peasants were not likely to be going away to anywhere; they were tied to the land and that was that.

Now the skeletons were to be wrenched out of their hiding places, so that what had been talked of openly in the village would also be discussed openly in the palace. No matter what objection the Bukowskis raised, Miroslawa, who shared that name, remained resolute, and banns were published.

It could not be a wedding in the old style, Monday-through-Saturday, because the participants were not real villagers, and the riotous celebrations of a typical wedding would have appeared strange and improper for someone so austere as Miroslawa, but it was a three-day affair, with musicians paid for by Pani Bukowska and beer provided by her husband.

Father Barski, extremely eager, like most priests who sprang from humble families, to retain the support of castle and mansion, refused to perform the ceremony, and had he been an actual resident of the village instead of a casual visitor he could have prevented the marriage from taking place. He did not go so far, principally because his major patron, Count Lubonski, told him sardonically: "It's a gesture. It's a woman making a gesture, not one getting married for love. Be advised, stay clear."

A priest from a distant village came in some bewilderment to officiate, and when he saw the magnificence of the Bukowski establishment he prudently guessed that something must be terribly wrong in this affair, and he went to the Bukowskis and said: "If I am in any way offending . . ."

"Proceed," Pani Bukowska said, and when on the second day the ceremony was performed, she was present, lending her sanction to the celebration, and she brought her reluctant husband with her, advising him that it was much better to make amends openly. When the fiddlers began she danced with Count Lubonski, with her husband and, finally, with the startled groom.

Investigations had been made at Miroslawa's insistence, and it was determined that in many Polish marriages the bride who came from a family conspicuously more distinguished than the groom's could elect to retain her family name, with a hyphen, in which case the husband frequently assumed that more distinguished name also. The schoolteacher cited the cases of Maria Sklodowska-Curie, two-time winner of the Nobel Prize, and Ewa Bandrowska-Turska, well known as a singer throughout Europe. The peasant husband could borrow his wife's name and become Seweryn Bukowski-Buk, but since that sounded ridiculous, he would soon drop the hyphenated part and become what he should always have been—Seweryn Bukowski. It was not neat, and perhaps not legal, but that's the way it would be.

So once more the routine along the Vistula stabilized. Count Lubonski occupied himself in writing persuasive reports to the Polish leaders in Warsaw, to Witold Jurgela in Wilno, and to Taras Vondrachuk in Kiev, beseeching them all to display dispassionate leadership. Father Barski was slowly learning the intricate operations of the new Polish church as it endeavored to build one solid edifice upon the varied experiences which its Catholics had suffered when living for more than a century under three different jurisdictions. Those who had been part of Austria had been considered second-class citizens by the pompous Roman Catholic hierarchy in Vienna; those in Germany had been denigrated by the Protestants who ruled that country; while the souls under Russian rule had been treated with contempt by the dominant Eastern Orthodox church. Now the yokes had been cast off and the indigenous church was free to develop along its own historic lines of total fealty to Rome.

Since Father Barski saw that the next decades would be ones of redefinition and reestablishment, he found himself searching backward for the beginnings of his church when it came out of the western mists a thousand years ago to unify the bands of warring and wandering tribes who would call themselves to Poland. He was now thirty-four years old and vaguely aware that of all the priests in his region, regardless of age or position, he was the scholar, the knowing one, and although he had no clear vision of what rank he might obtain within his church, he did realize that to attain anything, he must retain the good opinion of the count, of the wealthy Bukowskis, and of the bishops in Sandomierz and Krakow. Therefore, he thought deeply and acted with great caution.

Wiktor Bukowski was not concerned with the petty wars with Lithuania, Ukraine and Czechoslovakia; his main interest was his horses. On Paderewski's last night in Poland, Wiktor had reluctantly gone with Marjorie to Warsaw, where they entertained the great man at the Palais Princesse and even tried to seduce him with the piano Marjorie had purchased for the occasion, but he did not wish to play, so the evening passed in mournful talk.

At one point he asked Wiktor, "What do you intend doing?" as if he were a boy in school, and Wiktor replied: "I'm told there's a good chance to sell Arabians in America."

"What Arabians?" Paderewski asked. "What are you talking about?"

"My horses. I've a lot of good money tied up in those horses . . ."

Paderewski broke into a generous laugh, his first of the evening. "Oh, I like that! One thinks of horses being tied to a wagon. But you change the idiom. 'A lot of good money tied up in the horses.' I like that play on words."

Wiktor had no idea of what the pianist was saying, but a nudge from his wife warned him not to pursue the matter further.

With Paderewski gone, Wiktor saw little reason to remain in Warsaw, and after a couple of concerts by an orchestra from Berlin and solo musicians who had fled the revolution in Moscow, he was hungry to get back to the Vistula: "I'm homesick, and that's a fact." So Marjorie allowed herself to be pulled away from what promised to be a gala season in Warsaw, with opera three nights a week and concerts constantly, but when she saw her husband once more on his fields with his horses, she was assured that she had done right in bringing him home.

She appreciated this even more when one morning Jadwiga Buk and her daughter-in-law, Miroslawa Bukowska, appeared at the palace asking to see the master, and when Wiktor came down from the room in which he had been taking his morning nap, the two women asked Marjorie to remain. "What we have in mind," Jadwiga said, "is that your fields are not doing well. Not really."

"And the villages," Miroslawa continued. "They're still your villages, in a manner of speaking . . ."

"They're not in good repair, Pan Bukowski."

"They could profit from closer attention, I suppose," Wiktor conceded with all the heavy formality he would have used at a meeting of the cabinet in Vienna. "But I'm kept rather busy, you know."

"I'm sure," Jadwiga said, aware that this frivolous man she had once known so intimately had never directed his attention on anything for long. "That's why Miroslawa and I—"

"Pan Bukowski," Miroslawa broke in, as it had been arranged that she would, "we think you should employ Seweryn, my husband—that is, as your manager."

Before Wiktor could respond to this amazing proposal, Marjorie cried: "A splendid idea! Bring some professional attention . . ."

"There could be merit," Wiktor said guardedly. "But why do you come to me with such a proposal? Where's Seweryn?"

Jadwiga said: "He never likes to push himself forward."

"Especially," said Miroslawa, "since the job is customarily reserved for gentry." And she could not keep herself from adding: "Which is why it is so often performed poorly. Like here."

Wiktor rose and stalked about the room, pondering this bold proposal and trying vainly to probe its weaknesses. He did not trust these two women, each more clever than himself, and he felt intuitively that he must protect himself from them, but before he could reject their proposal, Marjorie, who could be said to own the estates by right of marital purchase, said enthusiastically: "Wiktor, I think this is a most commendable idea. What would we do about salary . . . wages, that is? I have no concept of what's customary."

Again Jadwiga spoke: "The pay could be small until he proved himself. But he would have to have a house—"

"He just built one," Wiktor said.

"But not a proper one for a manager," Jadwiga said. Going to the window, she pointed to a space beside the stables. "He could build a real house there. With a cellar. Then he could watch your horses . . . the grooms, I mean, to be sure they did right."

The Bukowskis came to the window and looked toward the stables, where in a space between the western end and the river Jadwiga Buk had hammered in eight stakes, each with a small ribbon flying— the outlines of the home that would be occupied by her first son.

"But what would you do with the house already built?" Wiktor asked, with the hesitancy of a man who felt himself being sucked in by a great tidal wave over which he had no control.

"We'd give that to my son Jan, who's getting married soon," Jadwiga said. Then she added two thoughts which sprang from the heart: "You and I would be at ease, Wiktor, if we saw Seweryn in a proper house. A new start for a new Poland."

These words cut so deep that Wiktor had to look to his wife for guidance, and when she nodded, relieved that such a simple concession would alleviate her own sense of guilt, he cried impulsively: "We'll build the house! It would be a shame to waste those stakes with their little flags."

When the two women departed, Jadwiga knew she should keep her mouth shut, because no matter how sympathetic Miroslawa might seem and no matter how enthusiastically she had encouraged this expedition, she did remain a member of the gentry and thus a potential enemy of any peasant. But when they were a safe distance from the palace the older woman could no longer restrain herself, and catching Miroslawa in her powerful arms, she raised her in the air and did a little dance. "Oh, daughter! I went into that torn-down mansion twenty-five years ago a peasant girl with no shoes. Now I have my own house and fields. My second son will have his own house with a cement floor. And my first son will have a real house with a cellar." She embraced her daughter-in-law, then kissed her fervently on both cheeks. "It means something!" she shouted to no one. "It really does mean something."

Then, with the abruptness of a forest fire, an event of indecipherable complexity erupted, and life for everyone was severely modified.

Within eight months of having been engaged in brutal warfare against each other, General Pilsudski, semi-dictator of Poland now that Paderewski was gone, and Semen Petlura, hetman of the Ukrainians, joined forces as brother generals to launch a full-scale war against Russia.

How had this happened? Roman Catholic Poles and Ukrainians who followed various eastern rites disliked and distrusted each other, but they shared an intense dislike of Russian Communism, which they recognized as pagan atheism at its worst. Even non-religious citizens of both regions distrusted the promises of Communism, especially farmers, who knew that under this system they would lose their lands and control of their cattle.

So now when Russian armies seemed about to impose Lenin's new pattern on the east, a natural opposition developed in both Poland and Ukraine strong enough to submerge old animosities and even those of recent months. Pilsudski and Petlura marched forth to protect not only their own lands but all of Europe from the threat of Communism.

"It is," preached Father Barski, "a God-given opportunity to determine the history of this part of the world," and he encouraged all the men in his district to volunteer for the crusade.

Jan Buk, aged twenty-three, volunteered, and marched with the victorious army to Kiev, where the crucial battles would be waged. Seweryn Bukowski was also urged by the priest to volunteer, but his wife argued with the officials that as the manager of an estate producing food for the army, he could not be spared; secretly she told her husband: "It's the wrong war against the wrong enemy. Communism is the friend of the people. Pilsudski and Petlura are dictators, deceivers, protectors of the magnates, but don't say I said so in public."

Seweryn, listening carefully to all that was happening in his village, learned that several other peasants were also more attracted to the new Russian scheme of things than to the old Polish ways: "Father Barski and Pan Bukowski, of course they want us to fight to defend their interests. But those days are past."

Seweryn found great difficulty in determining what he thought about Father Barski; he liked the priest and had been taught by his parents to revere his occupation, but increasingly he respected Miroslawa's interpretation of events, for he had learned that she was usually right when men like Bukowski and Father Barski were wrong, and he suspected that in this sudden war, started without reason, Poland was wrong and Russia was right.

Despite such ambivalence, which surfaced in many parts of Poland, the Polish and Ukrainian armies swept to tremendous victories, driving the Russians from Ukraine and establishing in that perplexed and perplexing land a free government, the first in a thousand years of its turbulent history. On 8 May 1920, Pilsudski and Petlura actually captured Kiev, throwing the Communists completely out of eastern Europe, and ecstatic celebrations began.

They were premature. Because down from the north came a redoubtable double thrust of real Russian power. Headed directly for Warsaw were Mikhail Tukhachevsky's foot soldiers, with enormous weight of artillery and vehicles supporting them, but the more devastating force appeared in General Semyon Budenny's First Cavalry, a wild-riding, terrifying pack of horsemen who disorganized the Polish-Ukrainian armies, recapturing immense amounts of territory within a few days with savage cruelty; as if they were Tatars in the year 1240, they desolated the lands of eastern Poland and approached the fortified city of Zamosc, from which they could gallop on to Castle Gorka and the Bukowski palace.

By 2 August 1920, General Tukhachevsky's armies were within shelling distance of Warsaw, and he had reason to believe that the Polish defense might be in total collapse. It looked to him as if the Communist armies were free to sweep on to the Oder River and from there into disorganized Germany and the heartlands of Europe. It was a time of trembling.

A knowing French military observer, one M. Delacorte, sent a frightening report to his journal in Paris:

The perilous situation must be clearly understood. Warsaw is doomed. The Communist army of General Tukhachevsky will soon be joined by the dreaded cavalry of General Budenny, and this victorious force will enjoy a clear gallop to the Oder River. Germany not only is too weak to resist, but within that country at least half the disgruntled population might be expected to rise in favor of the Russians.

Within two weeks Tukhachevsky and Budenny could be on the borders of France, and England must prepare itself for this dread possibility. If the victorious Russians are able to enlist the support of the masses in one great revolutionary outburst, all Europe as we know it could be swept away.

Leon Trotsky, gadfly of the revolution, put it more succinctly in his battle order to the Communist troops: "Heroes, let us take Warsaw! Just sixteen versts more and we will have all Europe ablaze." He was right. Nine more miles and a stupendous victory would be in hand.

All knowledgeable observers shared this opinion. The fate of Europe really did hang in balance, and a fearful advantage worked on the side of the Russians, who were about to engulf Warsaw: they were a revolutionary force feeding on the wild excitement of people who felt themselves liberated at last, while the Germans, the French and the English were exhausted from fighting under old and sometimes outworn slogans. It was going to be an unfair battle between unequals, and the result, as Lenin predicted, "could be the Communization of all Europe before the new year."

At this juncture, word of the terror reached even Bukowo. Cried a messenger from Zamosc: "Our city is doomed. Budenny has it almost surrounded. Help! Help!"

Wiktor Bukowski, hearing the plea and learning also that Warsaw might fall, kissed his wife goodbye, selected his six best horses, and went to Janko Buk's cottage: "We're all needed. My son is still in Paris. Call yours."

For nine centuries the Bukowskis had given such orders to the Buks, and for nine centuries the serfs had dutifully marched off to war, holding their masters' horses, feeding them, and carrying the knights off the battlefield when they were wounded. Now the peasants were being summoned again, and Janko Buk obeyed, but with a difference: "Jan's already with the army. And I can't find Seweryn."

He could not be found for good reason: Miroslawa, still interpreting opposition to the Communists as an error, had hidden her husband and refused to reveal where he was. "He's in Sandomierz on your business," she lied, "and I have no idea when he'll be back."

So Wiktor had to leave without him, but he felt that it would be disgraceful for a gentleman of his position to go to war without a batman of some kind, so he ordered Jadwiga and Janko to produce their third son, Benedykt, and they did.

Away the three rode, each on a superb horse, with Benedykt leading three remounts. They went northeast until they forded the San River, and as they edged ever closer to the scene of battle, they accumulated others on horseback, peasants and gentry alike, riding together as they had always done during troubled times in these historic lands. They wore no uniforms, but each man did bring those accouterments which had proved useful in the past: guns, pistols, swords, daggers, heavy shoes, close-knit caps to serve as helmets, and the best saddlery in Europe. They were not prepared, but they were ready.

Twelve miles west of Zamosc they were intercepted by officers of the regular Polish cavalry, who welcomed them effusively; they were now a band of some two hundred volunteers and their value to the battle that impended could prove decisive. "You're to muster at Szczebrzeszyn," one of the officers said, and Wiktor broke into laughter. "What's funny?" the officer asked, and Bukowski, still chuckling, replied: "My wife. She's from Chicago and can never say that name."

"You must be Bukowski," the officer said. "Take command of these men."

So Wiktor Bukowski received a battlefield commission—well, a pre-battlefield commission—as major, and he fell easily into the role. He and Janko Buk were much older than most of the patriots, but they were skillful horsemen and no one was surprised when Major Bukowski announced that Buk would be his second in command.

At Szczebrzeszyn they found about six hundred other men like themselves, all nervous, all terrified when sounds of battle reached them from the east, but all prepared to ride straight at the oncoming Russians.

"None of that," a Colonel Stempkowski warned. "Budenny's men are impeccable horsemen and they've defeated us six times in this running battle."

"What are we to do?" Bukowski asked, relishing his new position.

"Are you Bukowski, owner of the big stud along the Vistula?"

"The same. This is my second, Janko Buk."

"You're practiced horsemen, not?"

"We are."

"I have a specific mission for you."

"We accept."

Colonel Stempkowski did not propose ever again to take the great Russian leader head-on, for he knew he must lose: "But if we can come at him from the south, and well to his rear, where he won't be expecting us, we can disrupt this gentleman's plans. We can disrupt them most confusingly."

Major Bukowski's irregulars were to ride well south to a village called Zwodne, ford a small stream at Labunki, and cut sharply north toward Jaroslawiec, where they could expect to find the rear of Budenny's forces. When they encountered them . . . well, they were supposed to create such havoc that word of it would rush to the front of Budenny's forces, which would then be faced with difficult decisions. Only then would the major force of the Polish cavalry be released.

"It all depends on you, Bukowski," the colonel said as he watched the undisciplined Vistula irregulars prepare for a battle they could not even vaguely comprehend. Wiktor rode in the lead, a dashing figure who encouraged his troops with waves of his right hand; Janko positioned himself on the flank, trying to keep his farmers in some kind of order; and Benedykt followed somewhere in the rear, tending the spare horses; and everyone moved with such easy abandon that the colonel shook his head and told his aide: "Poor fellows! You'd think they were heading for some country picnic."

General Semyon Budenny of Russia's First Cavalry was the world's ablest commander of mounted troops, a handsome man with monumental mustaches and a vast knowledge of previous cavalry battles. A student of Prince Rupert and J. E. B. Stuart, he had learned on the steppes how most effectively to throw his swift warriors against the weakest point of each enemy's position, and his uninterrupted surge from the other side of the Dnieper right to the gates of Zamosc gave proof of his ability.

He was a ruthless commander with one simple strategy: "Destroy the troops, burn the villages"—and if in prosecuting these ends he also ravaged the civil population, allowing or even encouraging rape, pillage and arson, his foes had to acknowledge that in the end he usually achieved a complete victory.

But now he realized that he must step up the speed of his offensive, for General Tukhachevsky had issued an incendiary threat at the gates of Warsaw: "On this day we shall revenge desecrated Kiev and drown the Polish army in its own blood. The pathway to world fire lies across the dead body of Poland. We shall have Warsaw by nightfall." If that happened, Budenny would have to subdue Zamosc, sweep on to a crossing of the Vistula at Bukowo, and close the Russian pincers about the heartland of Poland before galloping on to Berlin and Paris.

Budenny was a devoted Communist who never fully understood the movement of which he was such a powerful defender, but he did value it as a dynamic force which would enable Russia to gain the seaports on the Atlantic for which she had always yearned. "We shall be the ones to take Antwerp and Bordeaux and Le Havre," he assured his staff. "This next little target, then nothing to fear in Germany, and our troops on the English Channel before winter."

The three European journalists who had been allowed to travel with him, barely able to keep up with his dashing tactics, reported that nothing seemed strong enough to halt him: "He sets impossible timetables for the advance of his troops, then exceeds all his target dates. He is a modern Attila, a new Genghis Khan, and Europe will never be the same after he passes through."

His plan for Zamosc was simple. He knew he had crushed the foremost cavalry of Poland and Ukraine and that only second-echelon horsemen remained. But he also knew from careful scouting reports that in centuries past this hard little nut of Zamosc had withstood sieges by the Swedes, by Turks and by Ukrainians and that its walls did not easily surrender to the invader, so he did not approach it lightly.

Of course, at this period Zamosc no longer had outer walls of any dimension; the famous old battlements had been engulfed by the outward growth of the city, but its robust character and the quality of its citizens combined to make it a formidable bastion. On the other hand, once it was passed, an army would enjoy an almost unimpeded avenue into Germany. Zamosc was worth taking and worth taking quickly.

He would make a feint in force at the easternmost point of the city, trusting that this would draw the better Polish cavalry to that area. He would then send a light but noisy detachment to the north, creating the impression that this was to be the major assault, but at the same time he would himself lead his principal force to the south in a thundering rush which would disorganize any remaining Polish troops and allow him easy entrance to the city from the west. Obviously, this plan would mean that Budenny and his best troops would run into Major Bukowski's irregulars as they moved in unexpectedly from the south. It would be a fearfully uneven skirmish, brief and fatal, but now the two contingents were on their way in the dark of night and nothing could recall them.

At the precise moment when General Budenny's cavalry was riding forth to confront Major Bukowski's, Leon Trotsky assembled at Brzesc Litewski, ninety miles north of Zamosc, the representatives Lubonski of Poland, Jurgela of Lithuania and Vondrachuk of Ukraine to dictate to them the humiliating terms under which the victorious Red Army would allow the three defeated nations to exist. As Trotsky revealed in a cynical speech: "Words at Brest, swords at Warsaw."

Late at night, after formal sessions had ended with Communism's brutal demands on the table, the three envoys met in a shabby hotel to discuss their gloomy future: the Russian chairman had left with them the text of General Tukhachevsky's insulting battle order: "We shall drown the Polish army in its own blood."

Lubonski refrained from saying "I told you so," but memories of past discussions did make the air heavy, and now when he spoke from his vast knowledge of nations and their aspirations, he was listened to: "We failed in victory. Maybe we can salvage something from defeat."

"What?" Vondrachuk asked.

"I think that now more than ever we must unite our aspirations . . . form one nation along the American principle—each area protected in its vital interests and customs, but all under one supreme parliament."

"We would be overwhelmed by you two," Jurgela protested.

"And if you don't join us, you will be overwhelmed by either Germany or Russia."

"Then there is no hope for a small nation like us?"

"There is every hope. If you join us."

"But will Russia allow any of us to exist? After Warsaw falls and her armies get into France?"

"The larger she gets, the more certain it is she will have to organize into smaller units," Lubonski said with absolute assurance. "She will have learned her lesson from Austria."

"You think there will be a Lithuania? Or a Ukraine?"

Now Vondrachuk became the focus, and he said gravely: "If Warsaw falls, Ukraine falls. Russia will never allow us our freedom. We will never be a nation." He sat silent for some moments, then added: "And we wait tonight for news that Warsaw has fallen."

Count Lubonski could not accept this doleful prediction: "We must suppose that Warsaw has fallen and that Tukhachevsky's troops are on their way to Paris. All Europe is to be Communist. Well, in that moment it is more imperative than ever that we three hold together so that we can achieve the kind of Communism we prefer. If we do, there's still a chance for a decent national life. But only if we hold together."

He made his plea so passionately, and with such a wealth of experience and strength of character supporting him, that he almost persuaded his two national enemies to listen, but at this moment in the dead of night a messenger hurried in from Warsaw with the astonishing news that Polish forces were holding the city and even beginning to drive Tukhachevsky's armies back: "There's a real chance for victory!"

"Were you there?" Vondrachuk asked. "Did you see with your own eyes?"

"Of course not. The telegraph came as far as Biala Podlaska. There the Russians stopped it. They didn't want you to know."

"How did you get here?"

"On horse, stumbled right into the big meeting place and was almost arrested. But what I tell you is true."

The meeting continued, but now in a vastly different mood. Vondrachuk said: "If only Budenny could be defeated at Zamosc! By God, we'd have them on the run!"

And then everything would be changed, for as Jurgela said: "We wouldn't have to form any kind of union. Lithuania would have its own nation, its own parliament."

"Why do you say that?" Lubonski asked, feeling common sense draining out of the shabby room.

"Because if Russia loses at Warsaw, and Zamosc too . . . I mean, both arms of her thrust cut off at the same time . . ."

"Budenny does not have a habit of losing," Lubonski reminded the men.

"But if God grants us a miracle at Warsaw, why not a second one at Zamosc?"

Vondrachuk spoke: "Jurgela's right. If Russia absorbs two major defeats, she'll be too busy to worry about Lithuania and Ukraine. God, this night could be a turning point in world history."

"Men! Men!" Lubonski pleaded. "If by some miracle we do win a double victory, it will be more imperative than ever that we form a union to defend ourselves in the long years ahead."

"We would be very uneasy with Poland," Witold Jurgela said, and in this verdict he summarized the long years when thoughtless and ignorant Polish magnates dominated vast tracts of Lithuanian land, but he conveniently forgot those longer centuries when Lithuanian princes dominated Poland.

"Our Ukrainians," agreed Vondrachuk, "could not easily erase memories of our wars with Poland. Especially the wars of the last two years."

"Do you hear me," Lubonski asked with infinite patience, "reciting the horrors that visited Poland when your Cossack Chmielnicki invaded Poland? The hundreds of thousands he slew?"

"They were mostly Jews," Vondrachuk said, "and our people had to break out of the bondage your magnates imposed." He stopped, looked afresh at the count, and said: "Your Lubonski ancestors were among the worst, and now you come asking us to forgive these centuries of abuse?"

"I do," Lubonski said, and he hoped that his reasonable plea would encourage these obdurate men to forget recent history and look instead toward a promising future, but he achieved nothing, for at dawn a telegram arrived confirming what the messenger had reported: POLISH FORCES HAVE DRIVEN THE COMMUNISTS BACK FROM ALL WARSAW BRIDGEHEADS. A ROUT IS UNDER WAY.

Taras Vondrachuk fell to his knees, clasped his hands, and began to pray: "Let Budenny be crushed." Lubonski, listening to the prayer, suspected that it might be better for eastern Europe if Budenny were not crushed, for he could see in a Polish victory the end of any sensible discussion among the three nations. Arrogance would displace humility, and each would stumble along toward some common disaster which would engulf them all; they would be like simple sheep trying to exist within a circle of wolves.

But even as he phrased these prophetic thoughts, he visualized his rugged old castle at Gorka and the fine new palace at Bukowo and the Lubomirski wonders at Lancut and the peaceful villages between, and he did not want to see them overthrown by the Communists and destroyed, as they had been so often in the past: "God, let the miracle happen. Let Budenny's ravagers be crushed."

Semyon Budenny had no intention of being crushed. He never had been and he never would be. When word reached him, frantically and with the messenger gasping, that his partner Mikhail Tukhachevsky had suffered a major reverse at Warsaw, he gritted his teeth and told his men: "Not here."

Dispatching riders to his two subordinate commands, the one heading directly at the eastern approaches to Zamosc, the other circling to attack from the north, he gave stern orders: "It is essential that Zamosc fall by noon. To give encouragement to our brothers at the north." He therefore tightened his own formation and rode with even greater determination toward the victory he felt assured would be his when he struck from the south.

Major Wiktor Bukowski, fifty-two years old, six pounds underweight, still looked rather debonair. Dressed in the uniform of a Polish country gentleman, the kind he had worn when riding at Der Schmelz in Vienna and on the parade grounds inside the fort at Przemysl, he paused occasionally to smooth down his small mustache or brush the dust from his tunic. He knew that within a few hours at the latest he would lead his nondescript men into direct confrontation with the finest mounted army in the world, but he had no way of comprehending the power that the Russian cavalry would have. All he knew was that he must somehow impede it, and what cannon or gunfire he might meet in doing so, he did not care to guess. He was a Polish gentleman out riding on his best horse, and that was enough.

Janko Buk, who had experienced a wide variety of nonsense in his life, from the alleys of Vienna to the formal picnics at Castle Gorka, had a rather better understanding of what lay ahead than his one-time master. "Those Russians know how to use the saber," he whispered to those riding close to him. He did not want to frighten the troops behind or discourage in any way his leader, but he was apprehensive about the terrible power of Communist cavalry: "They didn't ride so fast from Kiev without killing somebody."

Benedykt Buk, only nineteen, had no concept of what such a battle might be; he rode his good Arab and led the three replacements. He had no idea whatever of how to keep in touch with Pan Bukowski or his father once the battle started, and since he had no weapons of his own, he supposed he was to stay clear of the fight, waiting till critical moments when someone came back for his spares. He hoped the older men would be able to find him, but as distances increased and confusion grew, he did not see how this was going to be possible. Indeed, he began to look upon the three horses he was leading as detriments which would prevent him from joining the battle. Another groom told him: "I think we're to protect the horses so they can be used in a hurry if we have to retreat." The rear of Major Bukowski's contingent was obviously not hopeful about the outcome, but even they could not imagine the fury with which Budenny's crack troops would soon fall upon them.

There was, however, one sign of hope: a rather large band of riders had mysteriously come out of the night to occupy Major Bukowski's right flank, and an even larger mass had evolved on the left flank, so that the Vistula men were in the dead center of a substantial force. It could not be termed an army, or even a regiment, for it lacked any military cohesion or leadership, but it was formidable.

Now a colonel from the regular cavalry rode across the front, west to east, advising the leaders of each contingent: "We will not charge first. Let Budenny's men come at us. Let them break their ranks. Then we cut at them from the flanks."

He asked if this was understood, but even as the improvised leaders gave their assent, he could see that the restlessness of the civilians behind would make discipline most difficult: "Major Bukowski, do you understand?"

"I do."

"Can I rely on you?"

"To the death."

And then, out of gloom to the northeast, came the dreaded horsemen of Semyon Budenny's advance guard, men easy in the saddle, with superb beasts to carry them forward. They had expected an unimpeded canter to the western approaches to the town and this sudden appearance of a real force of mounted adversaries surprised them. But they did not break. In orderly rank they approached to a distance from which they could calculate the strength of the Polish irregulars, then turned and rode back to Budenny himself, who was somewhat distressed to hear that he might have to fight his way to the west.

When dawn was well at hand, the Russians launched a fierce assault on the Poles, one that carried them deep into the civilian mob, and at first the slaughter was terrifying, but then the Polish farmers realized that if one escaped that first awful crush, one had a good chance of doing some damage to the disorganized Russians, and a counterslaughter began.

At the height of the melee, Major Bukowski was caught up in a great frenzy, and seeing an opportunity to inflict real hurt upon one of Budenny's exposed columns, he ignored his instructions, rallied his men, and galloped with terrible force right at the heart of the Russian position. It was crazy. It was impossible. It was a band of rural riders going up against the best trained horsemen.

With wild enthusiasm, Wiktor Bukowski, this frivolous man who had never accomplished a constructive thing in his life, this dilettante who had thought more of his waxed mustache or his tailored trousers than of Poland, led his tattered troops with a bravura which would have drawn respect from Julius Caesar or Hannibal. Always in the lead, always cheering his men, he created havoc among the astonished Russians. Miraculously, he held his horsemen together, shooting and stabbing as they galloped on, turning as a well-drilled team behind his dashing figure and raging through the enemy lines.

Bukowski's irregulars may have accomplished little in this first charge, killing only a few of the foe, yet they accomplished everything, because they diverted attention long enough for the real surprise of this morning battle to be effective.

From the west, obedient to plans spelled out long before, appeared a large body of real Polish cavalry; it had been held in reserve for just such a moment, and when the confusion of the Russians was greatest, agitated by the wild incursion of Bukowski's men, these professionals saw an opportunity they could not reasonably have anticipated, and they drove with great force at the disorganized Communists.

Budenny had been in tight spots before and had acquired his reputation as the foremost cavalry commander because he knew ways to extricate himself from trouble, so he ordered his men to ignore

Bukowski's gadflies and charge directly at the oncoming Polish regulars. A mighty clash ensued, and for the first time in this Russian sweep to the west, their horsemen were unable to rout the enemy. The Poles maintained their formations, and what was more ominous, they surged purposefully ahead.

Now Bukowski's men, a totally disrupted rabble, were able to hack and hew, creating enormous confusion, and they were soon augmented by other volunteer units which up to now had obeyed orders and refrained from frontal assault. The fight became a monstrous riot, with rural units of a hundred men or even a thousand completely out of control as they overran the Russian regulars. Had Budenny been free to turn his Cossacks on this Polish rabble, he could have annihilated them, but whenever he tried to do so, the Polish regulars coming at him from the west demanded his full attention, so the peasants and the farmers and the lesser nobility from the Vistula were free to ravage the Russians as they willed.

Always at their head rode Wiktor Bukowski, his superb horsemanship allowing him to move here and there wherever the informal fighting was thickest. He seemed immortal; Janko Buk, riding on his left flank, was shot through the head and tumbled from his horse, dead before he struck the ground, but Bukowski galloped on, picking up new companions, two of whom were also killed by Russian fire. He was indifferent to death, either his own or that of others, and as the battle raged, it was he who held the volunteers in whatever frail order they managed. He was a fearful force to have been let loose in such a situation, and he harried Budenny's men most savagely.

In any great battle or any war there comes a moment when the forces are evenly matched, when victory is a reasonable possibility for either side; then knowing men watch for the isolated incident which reveals that the tide has turned and is irreversible. Budenny now faced such a moment.

What information did he have to guide him? He knew that Tukhachevsky was in retreat at Warsaw. More important, perhaps, he was painfully aware that his last three requests for additional matériel had been unanswered because of a breakdown in the supply train. On the hopeful side, couriers assured him that the morning's northern diversion had been successful, but other messengers informed him that the middle contingent, driving directly at Zamosc, had accomplished nothing. Also, the damned Polish regulars, with an insight he could not credit, had anticipated his battle plan and had massed their major strength on the south, precisely where he did not want it, and they were holding their own or even pushing his men back.

Now, to cap it all, inside his own formation galloped this crazy Polish civilian followed by a gang of inflamed farmers who seemingly could not be stopped.

Upon his black horse, Budenny hesitated, and at this moment Wiktor Bukowski by sheerest accident headed straight for him. "Gun him down!" an aide shouted, and withering fire swept the irregulars, killing many but missing their wild-eyed leader. "Capture him! Shoot him!" But with great skill Bukowski evaded his assailants, dipping and weaving like a headstrong boy on his first bicycle.

At that moment Semyon Budenny realized that his rush toward the channel ports had ended. Disconsolate, he turned his black horse toward Russia, indicating to his subordinates that the battle was over. This crazy collection of tired Polish cavalry, peasants and gentry who seemed not to know what fear was, had saved Zamosc, but they had also saved Berlin and Stuttgart and Paris.

A titled Englishman who had monitored the two-pronged Communist offensive from a hotel inside Warsaw, a learned man who had led a battalion against Ludendorff during the Great War, reported to the French and British governments what he would later state in a book, which would be largely ignored in the west:

> The defense of Warsaw and the repulse of Budenny's cavalry at Zamosc constituted one of the decisive battles of the world. It not only saved Poland as a free entity perched between disorganized Germany and Communist Russia, but it prevented the latter from sweeping on to Paris and converting the entire continent into a Communist prison camp.

> I assure you that when General Tukhachevsky stood at the gates of Warsaw, with his shells landing in the city, I assumed that all was lost. And when he was supported in the south by the brilliance of Budenny's cavalry, I could see no hope for the reborn Germany or war-weary France. The fate of millions was determined by these almost unknown battles, and we shall all be permanently indebted to the heroic Poles who once again held back the pagan invaders.

At Brzesc Litewski, Count Lubonski refrained from making any such observations; his task was still to convince the Lithuanians and Ukrainians that their only hope for permanent survival was to unite with the Poles, but in the euphoria of victory he was again unable to gain an attentive hearing.

Witold Jurgela was ecstatic: "Now we're assured of a free Lithuania," and he would not listen when Lubonski, with his long knowledge of the minorities of the Austrian Empire, warned that Lithuania by itself was not a viable entity.

"We have the will," Jurgela exulted. "A thousand years of history reborn, a nation of ancient honor."

Lubonski was terse: "You have the will, and certainly you have the honor. But you do not have the industrial base. Or the army."

"Switzerland exists. Norway exists."

"They are not pinched in between Russia and Germany."

"Germany is defeated," Jurgela cried, at which Lubonski grew impatient: "Do you deny that German troops still occupy most of your land? Even after Versailles? And that before long they will occupy it again, in terrible force?"

"The nations of the world would not allow that."

"The nations of the world allow whatever happens, dear friend. And I know without question what's going to happen to your Lithuania. You'll have your freedom. Can't be denied. And your own postage stamps. And your paper money bearing the famous faces of your heroes. And you'll have editorials in your newspapers, condemning this or praising that. All that you'll have. And you know in your heart what else you'll have."

"What?" Jurgela demanded contentiously.

"Within two decades you'll have either Russia or Germany knocking on your door with a message. And it will read: 'The foolishness is over. Now you're a part of us.'"

"That would never be allowed," the Lithuanian insisted, and he dropped out of the conversation, for he had to make plans as to where he and his family might fit into the governance of the new republic.

Vondrachuk was brutally brief: "We've had too many wars between us, Lubonski. Magnates like you oppressing our people, now trying to worm their way back to recover their estates so they can continue the oppression. Your church leaders trying to subvert our churches. No, it's all finished, Lubonski."

"Tell me, with your collection of villages, with your twenty million people without a central leadership, with no great universities or intellectual traditions, do you really believe you can exist on the borders of a Communist Russia, with men like Trotsky and Lenin at your throat?"

Vondrachuk used almost precisely the words of Jurgela: "We have the will to exist," and Lubonski said with real sorrow: "I hope you can convince Russia of that."

Unwilling to see the discussions end so mournfully, he made one last desperate plea: "Vondrachuk, you know that in 1658 one of the wisest men you Cossacks ever produced suggested exactly the kind of union I propose now. It would have saved you then. It will save you now."

"That was a long time ago, Lubonski."

"But if we offered every item that you and Lithuania proposed then, wouldn't it be possible?"

"We were different nations then. We had not tasted freedom. And now there can be no going back."

So the maps were folded, the commission disbanded, and the hopes surrendered. The union which should have crowned the miracle at Warsaw and Zamosc proved unattainable, and the fault was no one's.

Lithuania would have its nationhood, briefly, tragically. Then seven hundred thousand of its people would be deported to various remote corners of Russia and in its death struggles it would vainly seek to ally itself with a losing Germany, and thus lose trebly.

Ukraine would become one of the world's great tragedies, a land in which the oppressors would allow ten million citizens to starve to death, where the native language would be outlawed, and where all kinds of depredations would be visited upon a distrusted and despised subject people. In despair, in 1939 the Ukrainians would try to side with Hitler in hopes that he might rescue them from Russian domination, and when this proved a fatal miscalculation, the revenge of the Communist victors would be harsher than ever.

Poland would be only a little better off. Unable to form an alliance with anyone, it would revert to what it had been a thousand years before, the imperiled land bridge between the Russians and the Germans. Its life would actually be even briefer than Lithuania's, for in 1939 it would be partitioned yet again, this time half to Germany, half to Russia.

Shattered dreams! Each of the negotiators had evidence which demonstrated beyond cavil that union was the only practical solution, but only old Lubonski, seventy and wearied with struggle, accepted the evidence, and he was powerless to persuade others. Even among his own Poles he was dismissed as a visionary; they still wanted to grab half of Lithuania, half of Ukraine, bits and pieces here and there along their borders, as if territory and not universal stability were the safeguard of nations.

Shattered dreams! On his mournful way home from Brzesc Litewski, Andrzej Lubonski experienced a general heaviness in all parts of his body, as if his musculature had decided to quit its business of holding the members together. He left the train at Lublin to consult with a doctor, but before the meeting could be arranged he collapsed, and it was obvious even to him that death was near. He thought of the gracious daughter of the Zamoyskis who had honored him by being his wife and he wished that he could talk with her about the dubious future, for she had been sagacious.

And then he thought of Castle Gorka, which he had defended about as well as any of his ancestors, and of his son Walerian in London: "I hope he will be capable . . ." And with that benediction, which could have been directed equally to the country he had served so honorably, he died.

IX

THE
TERROR

H OW CRUEL ARE THE REPETITIONS OF HISTORY. TOWARD THE close of the eighteenth century autocratic Russia, Prussia and Austria could not tolerate liberal Poland on their borders and united to obliterate her. In the middle of the twentieth century Nazi Germany and Communist Russia looked askance at the surprising progress of a free Poland and maneuvered to complete a new dismemberment.

In the years 1921–1939, after Poland had repulsed the Russian invasion of 1920, she accomplished a miracle. Her three provinces had been ruled for more than a century by three radically different foreign occupiers, yet the Polish people were able to unite these provinces in one reasonable system. Three disparate judicial, educational and administrative patterns had been reconciled. Land reform was initiated, social security established, health care organized, industry encouraged. A bold new seaport was built on the Baltic at Gdynia; aristocratic titles were abolished lest the old nobles regain an upper hand; liberated artists were encouraged to paint Polish canvases and produce Polish plays; and even the railroad system which used to have three kinds of trains—Russian, German, Austrian—was disciplined into one that conformed to European standards.

There was reason to hope that if this rate of progress could continue for another two decades, Poland might become one of the principal illuminations of Europe, but on 1 September 1939, Adolf Hitler's Nazis crashed over the border with such overwhelming superiority in manpower, tanks and dive bombers that the nation was quickly devastated and occupied. Poland's defense might have been more effective had not France and England, all that summer, pleaded with her not to mobilize, fearing that Hitler might be antagonized.

A brief ten days after their thunderous start, the Nazis, having met brave but futile resistance, stormed across the Vistula and occupied all territory around Bukowo, into which a contingent of their forward troops rushed, led by a civilian who announced himself to the villagers as Hans Yunger. When everyone was assembled in the village square he produced a carefully prepared document, from which he read the names of seven people to be arrested. Because the selection of these seven was so indicative of what was being repeated throughout Poland, their names will be recited here, with explanations of why they were on the list:

Ryszard Aksentowicz	57	Schoolmaster
Pawel Barski	54	Catholic priest
Miroslawa Bukowska	49	Notorious liberal
Szymon Bukowski	15	Son of the above
Barbara Ostrowska	19	University student
Roman Ostrowski	59	Leading farmer
Jakub Pisecki	33	Reported to have Jewish blood

Nazi soldiers were able, with help from some villagers, to locate six of the seven; Szymon Bukowski had disappeared into the forest, but no one reported this.

The six were told that they could take with them one small parcel which had to contain everything they would need for an indefinite stay in jail. They were then lined up in the village square to await the truck that would carry them off to imprisonment: Pani Bukowska was tall, thin, quietly aggressive, as if she had known all along that something like this would happen one day. Barbara Ostrowska was a soft, gentle girl studying to be a teacher, not pretty but gloriously youthful and bright of eye. There had never been any Jews in this village, and had Jakub Pisecki possessed the slightest degree of Jewish blood, it would have been known to his neighbors. Father Barski, now a secure, stable priest, looked the role; his parishioners believed the rumor that he was soon to be a bishop. The schoolmaster looked like one; the wealthy farmer was robust, stocky, square-faced.

They held their small packages before them as the truck wheeled up, but as it stopped, three young Nazis in gray-green uniform leaped out, knelt on the ground not six feet from the Poles, leveled their machine guns, and sprayed them with a terrible fusillade of bullets.

When the bodies lay slumped on the cobblestones, Hans Yunger said only three words, using Polish, which had been taught him in a special school for those officials who would govern Poland. Turning to a group of horrified men who had watched the execution, he snarled "Bury them," and to the general population, whom he surveyed coldly as he climbed into his staff car, he said "Obey."

The very next day Hans Yunger was back in Bukowo, this time to arrest six citizens at random, and as they stood waiting for the truck, he announced in his broken Polish: "Last night someone threw rocks at our trucks, an act of sabotage. This will not be permitted, now or ever."

The six were nondescript, just ordinary villagers, three men, three women. As the truck rounded the corner they saw that the windshield had been shattered, and they were rather pleased. And they were not surprised when the three young men in gray-green uniform leaped out and knelt before them, aiming the deadly machine guns. One farmer shouted "Poland will live" and a woman cried "You will suffer for—"

The bullets ripped through the bodies, making dents in the wall, after which Hans Yunger repeated his two-part order: "Bury them" and "Obey."

On the third day he performed the act which engraved his name and his countenance on the village mind forever: he appeared in his staff car, still in civilian dress, and posted on the door of the little church a list of one hundred and sixty-nine names, typed neatly but in no special order, men and women mixed together, each with proper age. No one under the age of sixteen was listed, and the proportion seemed to be older people, seventy percent; younger, thirty percent; men, sixty percent; women, forty percent.

This time Yunger had with him a proficient interpreter, who lined out the rules under which this region would now operate:

"This is a list of hostages to be shot if any Pole in this region commits any act of aggression or sabotage. Destruction of

German property, no matter how small, whether actual or attempted: six to be shot. Any physical act against a German soldier, no matter how small, whether actual or attempted: eight to be shot. The death of any German soldier or civilian, no matter the cause: twelve or more to be shot. Last night there was further destruction of military property, so the first six hostages will now be shot."

Again six ordinary villagers were stood against the wall; again the three young soldiers took their half-kneeling stance; and again the order was given to bury the bodies.

Bukowo never saw Hans Yunger after that third day. He had been sent there to strike terror into the hearts of the villagers, and he had succeeded. He would now move on to his next assignment, where he would perform just as efficiently.

His place was taken by a Nazi of much different character, SS Major Konrad Krumpf, a low-level functionary of the Gestapo whose job it would be to govern a set of seventeen villages for the duration of the war. He was a tense man of thirty-three when he drove his own small car into town, not at all the imperious commander that Hans Yunger had been. When the villagers first saw him they wondered how he had ever been accepted into the Gestapo or risen to the position he now held, but after he had been at work for a while they recognized his shrewd capacity to guess at what might be going on and his determination to stamp it out if it threatened the security of the Third Reich.

He was not tall, not heavy. He had thin sandy hair, weak eyes that required glasses and a weak voice that required him to scream when he wished to emphasize points. Villagers said "He soars like a lark," but he made himself understood. He had acquired a sober education at schools through his sixteenth year and through wide reading thereafter. As a boy he had supposed that he would enter his father's textile shop, but an offer of membership in the Gestapo at a time when they were eager to enroll anyone opened dreamlike horizons, and for some time now he had imagined that through diligent service to Hitler, Goering and especially Himmler, he might, in his fifties, attain a position of some importance. To prepare himself for competition with others who had attended university, he continued to read serious books and had acquired a vocabulary much larger than a man who had left school at sixteen might be expected to possess.

However, he was a realist, and knew that he was not as intellectually brilliant as some of his competitors in the Gestapo, or as gifted in political maneuvering, or even as masculine-looking as the stiff Prussians in the SS or the handsome Bavarians. But he knew he possessed two traits which many of them lacked: he had an innate sense of where his enemies, Polish or German, might be hiding and a cunning skill in frustrating them; and he had an almost rodentlike capacity for accumulating facts about everyone with whom he came in contact, assembling huge stacks of cards, in five different colors, on which were summarized the bits of information he had collected about them. These files were supervised by two gloomy, nervous clerks whose names were not even known to the villagers but whose laborious work dominated their lives.

No act was too trivial to escape the attention of Konrad Krumpf and his clerks, and when observed, it was written down. For example, he knew that Szymon Bukowski, the fifteen-year-old son of the liberal agitator Miroslawa Bukowska, had been among the seven to be liquidated on that first day and that he had somehow escaped. His card on the young man was voluminous, listing his friends, the books he read, his habits during winter and summer, where he might be encountered, and particularly the names of his relatives, no matter how far removed in blood line or geographical distance.

It was Krumpf's job to find this condemned man and execute him, and as he studied the cards pertaining to his target, he saw that Szymon was the presumed grandson of the local gentleman now dead, Wiktor Bukowski, who was known as The Hero of Zamosc because of his conduct at the siege of that city by the Russian Communists. So Krumpf went to the palace to pursue his ongoing investigation.

There he was greeted by a woman whom he had been instructed to treat with deference, for she was said to be a multimillionaire from Chicago and from a family potentially friendly to the German cause. Marjorie Bukowska, his cards told him—green in her case, indicating a person of high importance—was sixty-seven years old, a widow, an amateur patron of Polish culture, and the mother of the current owner of the palace, Ludwik Bukowski, thirty-nine years old and something of an enigma. The original list of leaders to be executed had said of Bukowski: "Not to be shot. Could prove to be of use."

Like many wealthy women free to tend their every need, Madame Bukowska had grown more beautiful as she aged, and now her slender figure and glowing white hair gave her an aura of great dignity as she came forward to greet the commander of her district: "Herr Krumpf . . ."

"Major," he corrected.

"I've never been able to read military designations," she said. "Do join me," and she led him into that grand hall dominated by the two huge paintings. He was awed by its majesty and in that first moment he hatched his plot. He, Konrad Krumpf, son of a merchant in Magdeburg, would live in this palace, and from it he would dispense justice to the Poles he supervised. To achieve this he must deal gingerly with the American woman and her Polish son.

"Madame Bukowska," he said easily as he settled into one of her comfortable chairs, "I must interrogate you on what could be a painful subject."

"Many things are painful these days," she replied.

"This missing man, Szymon Bukowski . . ."

"Szymon?" she asked brightly, almost laughingly. "He's not a man. He's a boy. Hardly old enough to drive an automobile."

"He's a fugitive, Madame Bukowska," and he said this with such finality that she made no further defensive comment. "I must ask you two questions."

"Please do," she said graciously, but before he could ask them the tea she had ordered arrived, and when Krumpf had balanced his cup on his knee, she said: "Now fire away."

"I have no weapon," he said, and she explained that she had been using an American idiom meaning "Ask me what you will," but that in the German they were using, it came out rather more ominous than she had intended. He laughed.

"Now to my questions. Do you know where Szymon Bukowski is hiding?"

"I do not," she said in the good German she had acquired in Vienna. She sipped at her tea, then said emphatically: "I would never have known where he was, Herr Krumpf. For I had little to do with him."

"Major Krumpf, if you please. But was not his father your husband's manager?" He had set his cup down and now held some cards, which he was studying as if to make sure of his facts.

"He was. And a very dependable one."

"And was not the unfortunate Miroslawa Bukowska who fell into trouble, was she not your husband's cousin?"

"Very remotely."

He glanced at his cards and nodded. "Where is your husband?"

She pointed to an equestrian portrait hanging on an end wall, away from the two great panoramas; it showed Wiktor in native costume astride his horse, with a caption which Krumpf rose to read: "'The Hero of Zamosc.'" He looked at his cards again and said: "Yes, he fought the Communists at Zamosc, I remember." And from the manner in which he enunciated his words, precisely but at a level somewhat higher than before, she deduced that he was not happy with Germany's present close alliance with Russia.

"He's dead?" he asked, although he well knew the answer.

"Many years."

"What I meant to ask, where is your son?"

"You must know that the governor general summoned him to Krakow. He's in Krakow."

"Yes, yes." He rearranged his cards and asked: "Now to my next question, the difficult one." He accepted more tea, then said: "This Szymon we seek, his father Seweryn Buk, later Bukowski, he was your husband's son, was he not? That is, he was your stepson?"

"Everyone in these parts knows that."

"So that Szymon is really your grandson, in a manner of speaking."

"I have never thought of him as such."

"Does his presence on your estate . . . well, does it in any way embarrass you?"

"Nothing embarrasses me. I'm sixty-seven years old and life continues to amaze me, but it never embarrasses."

"In Chicago," he began, pronouncing it Tchee-ka-goe with equal emphasis on each syllable, "you were very wealthy, yes? Then why are you still in this dreadful country?"

"Because I love it," she said quietly.

"And you would do anything to assist it?"

Turning so that she could look squarely at him, she said: "Yes, I suppose I would. You see, it's my country now."

"Would you be offended if I asked to . . . not search . . . but . . ."

"Look around?" She used a homely German idiom and he smiled, a thin, grudging smile which brought half-tears to his watery blue eyes.

"Yes, I'd like to look around. We're very concerned about this Szymon, you know."

It was during this inspection that Konrad Krumpf first saw the art treasures of the Bukowski palace, and although he ridiculed the two big Polish panoramas, terming them peasant painting, and denigrated the Claude Monet as degenerate Jewish art, he was astonished by the quality and beauty of the Rembrandt and the little Correggio: "But these are museum paintings! Madame Bukowska, your husband had flawless taste."

"I bought them," she said. "I studied art in Italy."

"Ah, Italy! What a perfect union, Germany and Italy. These two produce most of the art in the world."

He was on the point of advising her to get rid of the Monet, or at least hide it, because a new world of art was about to take command of Europe, one in which there would be no place for such immoral painting, when he saw for the first time the elegant Hans Holbein portrait of an English lady. The great German painter had chosen blue and gray as his dominant colors, with touches of red and gold, and the frame, which seemed a part of the painting, was one of those broad slabs of ebony beautifully carved in little squares which stood out from the rest of the wood, radiating light. It was really a complete work of art, very Renaissance, very German.

"That is a notable painting," Krumpf said with such enthusiasm that Marjorie was compelled to ask: "Where did you learn so much about art?" and he with obvious pleasure replied: "We are not all pigs, as your Jewish *New York Times* would have it." She wanted to know more, but he said, abruptly, that he had to leave, so they returned to the hall, and from the manner in which he surveyed it, with an almost proprietary interest, she was certain that she and her son would be seeing a great deal of SS Major Krumpf in the months ahead.

When the Nazis overran Poland that September they found themselves empowered to put into cruel operation a plan which Heinrich Himmler and Alfred Rosenberg had worked out in harsh detail.

Those sections of Poland which lay next to either Germany proper or East Prussia were to be completely denuded of Poles and resettled by Germans. What was to happen to the Poles living there? At first there would be mass expulsions; later there would be systematic extermination. As many as twenty million Poles would either be worked to death in labor camps or slain instantly. That part of Poland would never again exist.

There was temporarily an atrocious plan for creating an artificial Jewish state centering on Lublin, a city not far from Bukowo, where Jews would be herded until such time as they could be exterminated, down to the last woman and child. Himmler's figures showed a Jewish population in Poland of 3,547,896; every one was to be slain.

That left a large southern area well removed from the German borders and based on the triangle of cities—Warsaw, Krakow, Lwow—in which Bukowo was centrally located. This was given the curious name General Gouvernement, and why French was used to designate a so thoroughly German solution, no one explained, except that this name had been used in World War I for the area then occupied by the Germans, and now once more General Gouvernement served. It was governed by an able Nazi lawyer, Dr. Hans Frank, who maintained headquarters in the famous Wawel Castle in Krakow.

Dr. Frank was not a caricature, nor was he a sadist. He was a realist with a firm understanding of Polish history. His instructions to his subordinates were stated in clear, simple, legal terms:

> "The General Gouvernement will comprise all that is left of historic Poland, and it is essential that Poles residing here understand the nature of their new state. It is not a nation governed by law. It is a nation governed by the demands and desires of the Third Reich. The Pole has no rights whatever. His only obligation is to obey what we tell him. He must be constantly reminded that his duty is to obey.

> "With my full approval you are to apply ruthlessly every reasonable measure to keep the local situation under control, and this office will not enquire foolishly into the actions you deem necessary to keep all areas of the General Gouvernement pacified.

> "A major goal of our plan is to finish off as speedily as possible all troublemaking politicians, priests and leaders who fall into our hands. I openly admit that some thousands of so-called important Poles will have to pay with their lives, but you must not allow sympathy for individual cases to deter you in your duty, which is to ensure that the goals of National Socialism

triumph and that the Polish nation is never again able to offer resistance."

When deputies like Konrad Krumpf inquired in a general meeting what the ultimate plans were for this miserable, unhappy country, Dr. Frank was specific:

"Every vestige of Polish culture is to be eliminated. Those Poles who seem to have Nordic appearance will be taken to Germany to work in our factories. Children of Nordic appearance will be taken from their parents and raised as German workers. The rest? They will work. They will eat little. And in the end they will die out. There will never again be a Poland."

Dr. Frank encouraged the initial execution of all visible leaders, and he also ordered the rounding up of college professors, especially those of the prestigious Jagiellonian University in Krakow, assigning them to the most brutal of the concentration camps, where most of them perished. He also helped to establish the rules of retaliation that Hans Yunger had delivered to the citizens of Bukowo, and he commended those local leaders who enforced that rule.

But he did not, like many of his subordinates, practice cruelty for its own sake, and he did not for a very good reason. As he explained to his cadre:

"Long term, we work for the extermination of the Polish people. Short term, we must use them to help feed our soldiers. Therefore, farmers are to be kept at their fields, but the most rigorous rules are to be published in every community demanding that farm families keep for themselves only enough to sustain life. Everything else must be delivered to our representatives for shipment to Germany, and any farmer or housewife who connives to avoid this rule shall be shot. Each district commander is personally responsible for collecting the maximum food possible from his district. The farm population is to be preserved for the present, but when victory is ours we will settle with it."

When this order reached Konrad Krumpf in Bukowo he instituted his search for the querns. Bringing in sixteen extra Gestapo enlisted men, he lined them up in the village square, then summoned everyone in the area to stand at attention as he read the decree which would apply to his portion of the General Gouvernement:

> "Every item of every crop raised in this district belongs to the Third Reich and must be delivered to my assistants at locations which will be stipulated. Every grain of wheat must be brought to us, after which we will return you enough to live on till the next harvest. This means that no kitchen will be allowed to maintain its own quern for grinding wheat and making flour that might be baked into loaves for private use. It is now ten o'clock. You have till the clock strikes twelve to bring me all the querns you have in your possession, because at one minute after twelve these soldiers will begin searching your cottages, and if they find a hidden quern which has not been turned in, the owner will be shot."

For most of the villagers and farmers the situation was clear: turn in the little hand mills in which wheat had been ground for generations and from which the good bread of Poland had been made, or run the risk of being shot. From cupboards, from places in the corner behind the stove, women with tears streaming down their faces brought forth the treasured querns: two round flat stones set in a box small enough for a boy to carry, each top stone with a hole in its upper surface into which a wooden handle could be placed, which, when turned in a tight circle, caused the upper stone to revolve and grind the wheat until it became flour sifting safely into the bottom of the box.

Some of the stones had been used for almost a century, outlasting three or four of their owners' wooden houses, but all were treasured and each was surrendered with pain.

The order presented a problem for Jadwiga Buk, now seventy-two and still a determined woman; she delayed bringing forth the little mill on which she had ground her family's grain because she wanted to see what was going to happen to the querns that were surrendered. She was standing off to one side when at half past ten the first housewives came forward with their precious instruments, and she was horrified by what Konrad Krumpf did with them.

"Put them there," he commanded, and when they were placed on the ground, he directed the soldiers to smash the stones and toss the boxes into a pile that was obviously going to be burned.

This wanton destruction of the little machines which had served so well, this violation of the household gods who keep society together, so shocked Jadwiga that she cried: "Send them to Germany. Don't destroy them."

Krumpf did not halt his operations to check who had called out, but from the corner of his eye he saw that it must have been the Buk woman, and he could visualize her card: GRANDMOTHER OF THE SZYMON BUKOWSKI WE SEEK.

Jadwiga left the village square in great perturbation. The quern which she had inherited from her grandmother was one of the best, two marvelously flat stones set in a box made of some special hardwood; from the time she was a young child, grinding wheat in a quern like that was almost a pleasure, and when she grew up and married and had her two children, in addition to her first son, Seweryn, she taught them to love the process, for it seemed to her an essential act of wifeliness—to accept the husband's grain and convert it to nourishing food.

She simply could not condemn her quern to the destruction she had witnessed, and she endeavored to hide it, vainly. Her efforts were quite juvenile, and when the noon search began the SS men quickly found it. They dragged her into the square, where she was ordered to stand at attention as the stones were crushed at her feet and the hardwood box smashed and thrown onto the pile. She had not the courage to look down at the shattered stones but she did watch as the pile was set ablaze, and she was still staring in disbelief when the rope was thrown about her neck and she was hanged.

Because both his grandmother, Jadwiga Buk, and his aunt, Miroslawa Bukowska, had been executed by the Nazis, Jan Buk, inheritor of the farm, had to be looked upon with suspicion by Konrad Krumpf's men, and the three cards which summarized his case contained numerous entries. The blue proved that he was known to have dangerous associates, in this case his grandmother and aunt. The brown showed that either he or his family had attempted to hoard food. The purple, an ominous card, predicted that he would ultimately prove to be dangerous; and with dismal regularity men with purple cards were promoted to red: WANTED FOR ARREST. There was good reason to suppose that sooner or later Jan Buk would be so moved.

He was twenty years old, broad and solid like his ancestors, and a good farmer; if any would produce a surplus which might be hidden, it would be he. He also owned a forest from which branches could be taken by the Germans for firewood. But his greatest asset was his wife, Biruta, a peasant girl of the old type who milked and plowed with vigor.

On the day that Grandmother Jadwiga was hanged, Jan returned to the cottage with the cement floor, the one that Jadwiga had gained for the family, and sat soberly in the chair once occupied by the earlier Janko, the one who had worked in Vienna and been killed at the Battle of Zamosc. He sat there until Biruta returned after having watched the hanging, then stared at her inquiringly, saying nothing, and by a meaningful glance at one corner where cottage wall joined cement floor, she indicated that something of value lay buried.

His eyes riveted on the perilous spot, Jan listened as his wife spoke in whispers: "When Krumpf ordered that the querns be brought in, I gave them the old one my mother used. Our good one is hidden. But when we need to use it, we shall."

Jan, aware of the terrible risk his wife was taking, grasped her hand and pressed it. Then he kissed her, and the hidden quern was not mentioned again, but as he worked his fields he sequestered larger and larger quantities of wheat, which he smuggled home beneath his pants, and sometimes at night, he would awaken to hear in the darkness the turning of the stones and he would know that the Buks would once more have extra flour to bake into secret loaves for those in the cities who were starving.

In the other sections of Poland, those contiguous to Germany, terrifying rules against the movement of Poles were in effect: a Pole could be shot if caught on a train, or executed in a public square if caught moving about without a pass. No Pole could own a bicycle without a license from the Nazis indicating the specific streets on which he was allowed to ride to and from work. And even when on foot he had to step into the gutter if a German approached; if tardy, he could be shot.

In the General Gouvernement these harsh rules did not apply, for here the job of the Pole was to produce food, and it was realized that to do this, a limited amount of travel was obligatory. Nevertheless, the peasants were tied to their land, just as they had been a thousand years earlier, and it was assumed at headquarters in Krakow that this would continue sometime into the future, until the Polish race died out and its place was taken by Germans.

During 1939, 1940 and the first half of 1941 living conditions for farmers in the General Gouvernement were bearable; their food was taken from them, but they were always clever enough to steal just enough to sustain their strength. There was constant repression, and the list of hostages remained in the public square; nineteen had now been shot in retaliation for various offenses committed by hotheads, but the general opinion in the countryside was that it was useless to try to oppose the Nazis: "They have the guns and they're ready to use them."

They also had the ropes, and these made an even deeper impression on the farmers, because when a disobedient person like Jadwiga Buk was hanged, the Germans left her or his body swaying in the wind, this way and that, legs not tied together, until some morning when Konrad Krumpf would come by and shout in his high-pitched voice: "Get that filthy thing out of here." Then the villagers were allowed to bury the corpse.

In his seventeen villages Krumpf had now executed more than sixty Poles, but never viciously, as some commanders did, and never without just cause, as he interpreted the rules. But even so, he was not able to stamp out the first beginnings of resistance in the countryside, and the more he studied the instances of sabotage or major thefts of food, the more he was convinced that some mastermind like the missing Szymon Bukowski was in command, and that the acts were by no means isolated or accidental. Placing all his cards before him on the table in his headquarters, he studied them, and had to conclude that it was Bukowski, even though so young, who was somehow communicating with the farmers of the district and causing trouble.

On three widely different occasions he had picked up rumors of an underground cell which operated from hiding places in the Forest of Szczek, and he wondered if Szymon Bukowski might have anything to do with this. Gnawed by doubt and irritated that he had not been able to run the missing man down, he returned to the Bukowski palace to talk with its real owner, and not that rather difficult American woman who might once have been its mistress.

He had always found Ludwik Bukowski a pleasant man to do business with: smallish, well-groomed, perfect in his German, an apparent conservative who had nothing to do with the rabble, and recognized in Krakow as a potential friend. Now as Krumpf sat with Bukowski, he spoke frankly: "We have persistent rumors of an organized underground operating in these regions. Have you heard anything?"

"No. And I rather think I would have."

"Who could be commanding such a body of men?"

"I haven't the vaguest idea. Perhaps some patriot who dreams of reviving—"

"Could it possibly be Szymon Bukowski?"

"My goodness, he's only . . . what . . . seventeen?"

"Aren't you his uncle, in a manner of speaking?"

"There've always been twisted rumors . . ." He twirled his thumbs, looked at the portrait of his father, and said: "There always are, in a village like this."

"I've been thinking about this village," Krumpf said cautiously, "and I believe I ought to transfer my headquarters here."

Bukowski, who had a shrewd ability to anticipate trouble, said: "Isn't it rather far from your other villages? Also, the Vistula cutting you off on one side?"

"But the more interesting . . . I mean, the more critical things seem to happen here."

During the months of occupation Bukowski had tried to estimate just how far Krumpf's authority extended, and he had seen proof that the Gestapo man could order the execution of anyone who provoked him, but he also noticed that like most middle-class Germans, Krumpf was respectful of authority and had handled the Bukowskis and Count Lubonski with deference. Ludwik decided he could ignore the man's rather heavy-handed suggestions. "You'd probably find it rather dull here, so far off to one side."

Krumpf smiled, moisture showing at the edges of his eyes, and with carefully chosen words he said: "Dr. Hans Frank . . . the governor general, you know. He sent us a memorandum last week. He wants his representatives properly housed. With right of requisition anywhere in the General Gouvernement." He looked directly at the wealthy Pole and waited for a response.

Bukowski could not imagine sharing his palace with such a man, a murderer, a tyrant, so he said nothing. Then, when Krumpf's silence grew frightening, like that of a watching adder, he licked his lips and asked: "Have you identified any place in our territory you would deem acceptable?"

Krumpf rose, took his host by the arm, and walked him purposefully toward the room in which the Holbein portrait hung. "I have been thinking that I would like my office here. In this room. With this great German painting." And before Bukowski could respond, the

Gestapo man led him back to the hall, where they stood before the portrait of Wiktor Bukowski: "'The Hero of Zamosc.' I like that. Your father was willing to fight the Communist atheists. I liked this place from the first time I saw his portrait. But at that time chance made us allies of the Russian monster and I was not allowed to speak."

"I would have to consult my mother," Ludwik said feebly. "She owns the palace, you might say."

"Not at all. In the Third Reich—and the General Gouvernement is practically a part of Germany now—widows own nothing and title should properly pass to their sons. This is your palace, and I shall expect an answer from you."

"I will consult with my mother," Bukowski said with a surprising show of stubbornness. And he went to his mother's apartment, where the beautiful little Correggio graced her sleeping area. In his absence, Krumpf returned to the Holbein room, studying the floor plan to determine how his desk and files would be placed.

Ludwik and his mother found him there, sitting in a chair once used by Wiktor Bukowski, and he did not rise when they entered. Before they could speak, he said sharply: "To avoid any statement that might be regretted later, let me say this. I have been empowered by the General Gouvernement to requisition any quarters I require."

"I am aware of that," Madame Bukowska said quietly, "and my son and I hope that you will choose to stay with us, if the rooms suit your purposes."

"They do," he said, rising to give the Nazi salute. "Heil Hitler!"

By the peculiar rules operating in the General Gouvernement, any Pole to whom these words were spoken had to be meticulous in his response. He was forbidden to use the sacred phrase himself, but he was required to stand quickly, in a posture of supreme respect, hands at side, eyes straight ahead. The two Bukowskis stood at attention.

Laboriously Konrad Krumpf continued to file his notes on cards of five colors—red, purple, green, blue, brown—and the two clerks he had brought with him, or even ordinary soldiers, were allowed to study these cards and could make entries upon them. But he also maintained a sixth file on golden-yellow cards, and these no one ever saw but himself. He was reluctant to title the top card in this pile by one of its honest names: *traitors, betrayers, committers of treason, apostates;* or to use either of the two new words: *quislings* or *collaborators.* Instead, with Germanic ponderousness, he titled them MEN OF PRUDENCE WHO CAN BE EXPECTED TO ACT IN THE INTERESTS OF THEIR NATION. It was not a good definition of treason, but it was a justification.

On the golden-yellow cards he recorded the shame of Poland: those few who betrayed their friends for money; those few who sought to pose as Germans, not Poles; those few who believed that the war was lost and that Poland would continue to exist as it did in these terrible times; those few who sought advantage of one trivial kind or another; those few who by nature always sided with the victors; those who preferred Germany to Russia; and those dreadful few, who could have been found in any nation, who actually supported the doctrines of Adolf Hitler and worked to spread them.

From his villages, Krumpf had assembled the names of thirty-seven "Men of Prudence," not yet fully confirmed, and on the night that he established his permanent headquarters in the Bukowski palace he riffled the golden-yellow cards, nodding appreciatively at remembrance of those few who had actually volunteered to aid the Reich. When he passed the thirty-seventh card he came upon a dozen blank ones, each waiting for the name of its traitor, and at the last card he hesitated a long time: What about this fellow Bukowski? He speaks German well. He's never married, so he could possibly be a sexual pervert. Definitely he's subject to pressure. And from the ideas I've heard him express, I'm sure he's more favorable to our side than to Russia's.

Very strongly did he want to add Ludwik Bukowski's name to his list, for to snag a member of the gentry, and one who would be extremely wealthy when his mother died, would offset the anger he felt over the fact that he had not yet captured the other Bukowski, who was now spoken of openly as a leader of one of the forest gangs. It would be a neat exchange, but he hesitated before lifting the pen which would convert Ludwik into an acknowledged traitor, for this privileged list contained only persons who had committed open acts of loyalty to the Third Reich.

He would wait to decide about the master of the palace, a weakling whom he did not trust, but as he was about to wrap the golden cards in their protective covering, he paused to weigh another name as a possible entry, and over this one he pondered a long time.

Count Walerian Lubonski, of Castle Gorka up the river, was a difficult man to assess. His card in the green file, "Men of Importance," showed that he was fifty-four years old, sole inheritor of the Lubonski estates, son of a distinguished servant of the Austro-Hungarian Empire, which was almost as meritorious as having worked for Germany, and a man of pronounced leadership. A penciled note, in the handwriting of Hans Yunger, who had conducted the initial executions in Bukowo, said: "Do not shoot. Cultivate for future use." A similar note, appended to Ludwik Bukowski's card, had first aroused Krumpf's suspicion that this Bukowski might one day prove to be a "Man of Prudence."

Count Lubonski was much more complex. Gracious in the style of nineteenth-century diplomats, he lived spartanly at the old castle, his room overlooking the Vistula. He had one son, who had been at Oxford University at the outbreak of the war and who still resided in England as a postgraduate student; the reassuring thing about this boy was that he was not engaged in any way in the Free Poland movement which infected England.

On the brief and chilly occasions when Gauleiter Krumpf visited the castle, he found the count punctilious, obedient and aloof. Soldiers watched the castle continuously, one detachment being billeted in the Gorka farmhouses from which the peasants had been expelled, but they reported no subversive activities. And on the two occasions when Dr. Hans Frank, the governor general, visited Bukowo he stayed with Lubonski, who entertained him not lavishly but with proper deference. It was thought by the Gestapo in the area that Dr. Frank was saving Lubonski for some important gesture, when his obedience to the Nazi rule would carry weight with the locals.

Krumpf, uneasy at having a man of such obvious importance in his district but not under his personal command, kept careful watch on Castle Gorka, endeavoring to pick up any clues as to Lubonski's fate or, indeed, his own. Once when he asked a senior Gestapo official from Krakow: "What will happen to men like this Count Lubonski in my district?" the man had replied: "What happens? Like all the others. We use him till our position is secure from Berlin to the Kurile Islands, then we allow him to die. Slowly, inescapably he will die."

Count Lubonski had only one black mark prominently noted. In the flush of Nazi victories, when German armies stood poised at the gates of Moscow, at Leningrad, at Kharkov and at Stalingrad, prior to the sweeping pincers that would destroy the Russian nation, Heinrich Himmler and Dr. Rosenberg promulgated an ingenious plan whereby those young Polish girls who looked German—and because of constant infusions of Swedish blood and German in past centuries, there were many—would be deported to cities in western Germany, where they would serve in factories and become impregnated by German soldiers on leave. Their children, when born, would be taken from them and placed in good German homes to be reared as true Germans, thus replacing any manpower losses incurred on foreign battlefields.

Several thousand such girls had been rounded up and sent to Germany, where in due course quite a few of them did become pregnant, and since the mothers were never allowed to see their children, not even in the hospital, the plan was working well. But when Walerian Lubonski heard that Gestapo special forces were rounding up young blond girls along the Vistula, he hurried to Krakow without having been summoned, stormed into Wawel Castle and informed Dr. Frank, who had enthusiastically approved the new procedure, that if any girls were taken from his district, he, Lubonski, would personally intervene and ensure that everyone in Poland knew why he was being shot, if he was shot.

Dr. Frank backed down. In those areas contiguous to Germany, young fair-haired Polish girls were still snatched off the street and shipped like cattle to western Germany, some to factories, some to brothels, and their children were expropriated, but this did not happen in Lubonski's district.

Why don't they shoot him? Krumpf asked himself that question many times that first night in his new quarters, and the answer he came up with was a half-truth: Dr. Frank must be toying with him. The total truth was that Dr. Frank was exactly like his subordinate; as a man from the German middle class, he had a fawning respect for anyone with a title, a big house or a fortune, but he was also convinced that he was clever enough to bend that important person to his purpose. Could Krumpf have entered Count Lubonski's name with certitude in his golden file of German patriots, he would have been overjoyed, but like the cautious man he was, he refrained from doing so, for he had a nagging suspicion that the Lubonski case was far from settled. In the meantime, he would keep watch.

• • •

Krumpf's decision to move his headquarters to the Bukowski palace created many new problems for the family of Jan Buk. Now additional troops moved through the village, and surveillance of Polish movement intensified. Under directions from the General Gouvernement in Krakow, renewed drives were made to increase food production, and when a neighbor of the Buks was caught baking more bread than permitted by her quota, the assumption being that she was sneaking the extra loaves to the partisans in the Forest of Szczek, the woman was apprehended by Krumpf's soldiers, dragged to the village square, and hanged. Again, her body was allowed to remain dangling from the gibbet for seven awful days before Krumpf gave the order to take it down.

Jan Buk was one of the three men assigned to bury the woman, and that night he was awakened by two sounds which terrified him: from his own kitchen he could hear Biruta moving about and he knew she must be grinding illegal wheat, an offense for which she, too, could be hanged; and from the outside he was certain he heard the stealthy approach of steps, which meant that Krumpf's soldiers were spying again.

Trembling, he slipped into the kitchen to warn his wife to hide the quern, immediately, but before he could alert her the door opened quietly and a man slipped noiselessly into the kitchen: "Buk? Are you awake? Don't make a light."

It was Szymon Bukowski, creeping in as he sometimes did from his hiding place in the forest. He was in need of food for his men, desperately in need, and had come pleading to his cousin Jan Buk.

He was barely eighteen, not powerfully built, but a young man of enormous resolution. He moved like a panther, always alert, always checking his escape routes. He was tired and cold and hungry, and as he sat in the darkness, munching bread and cheese, he gradually became aware that Biruta was grinding wheat. "Thank God, someone is. They're drawing the net very tight."

"You know they hanged Zosia last week?"

"We know. We keep records."

"What's it like . . . in the forest?"

"We harry them. We let them know we're still in existence."

He told the Buks that in the autumn days of 1939 the men in the forest had been a brave lot, hoping that the Germans would break their teeth in the west and be forced to withdraw from Poland. "We dreamed. But by 1940 any hope of such victory . . . vanished . . .

gone. Now we had another dream. That Russia would save us from the east. I remember Piszewski warning: 'Russians will prove as bad as Germans.' But we continued to pray for their victory. Now it looks as if the Nazis are going to occupy all the Soviet Union. And where does that leave us?" Despair momentarily crossed his face. "German occupation forever."

"But you will still fight?"

"Won't you?"

Without speaking, Jan Buk indicated where his wife was grinding her wheat, and Szymon ceased his eating, rose, went to where she worked, and kissed her: "You will be the salvation of Poland."

Then Szymon asked Jan the question to which the answer could mean life or death for the Buks: "Will you help us?"

"To what end?"

"To keep hope alive. To make the Germans know we shall never surrender."

"Even if Russia falls?"

"Even if England and America fall. Dr. Hans Frank will never rule this land in comfort."

"But every time you strike, he executes a dozen hostages. My name is on the list now. Four more killings and I'll be shot."

Now the great moral question of the underground had been confronted, and Szymon Bukowski, a mere boy, gave the answer which he and his men had worked out in pain and anguish: "All our names are on the list, Jan. Every name in Poland is on the list. It's just a matter of time till those bastards kill us all. So we must go down fighting. We must resist them. We must never let them have an easy night's sleep."

"So you intend to keep on murdering stray soldiers?"

"We do so much more! Jan, you would be proud of what we do. We can commit sabotage that looks exactly like a normal accident, and they can't do anything to prevent it. Watch, we're going to strangle this country, slowly, bit by bit."

"Aren't you frightened?"

"No more. Two years in the forest, you're not frightened any more."

"But you keep looking at the door."

"Cautious, yes. You will have to be very cautious when you join us."

"I . . ."

"You've already joined us, actually." Szymon pointed to where Biruta patiently ground her wheat. "You stand with one foot on the gallows, now. Plant both feet and work with us."

The silence in the dark kitchen was broken only by the sound of Biruta at her quern, but now a soldier passed along the village street, his hobnailed boots striking the pebbles, and the grinding stopped. When he passed on, she resumed her work.

Jan Buk was being asked to join the partisans, not in any big or bold way, but as a minor messenger between units or a distributor of clandestine newspapers; he would not even see a gun until the day of open rebellion, but he was needed. His wife was needed too, as a supplier of food to the men in the forest.

It was an invitation that might lead to the gravest consequences. Death might come at any moment, even for such a casual meeting as this, and to what reasonable end? Victorious Nazi battalions now threatened Stalingrad. Leningrad, despite its heroic resistance, seemed about to surrender and only the fiercest patriots believed that Germany could be defeated in the field, and yet the Polish underground preached that if pressure was constantly applied, and if Russia was able to stabilize its front, and if the Allies ever accomplished anything, there might be a chance, a remote chance, to regain freedom. As one pamphlet pointed out: "Once we were in captivity for one hundred and twenty-three years, yet we prevailed. We shall prevail this time, too."

So, with only the bleakest of prospects, Jan and Biruta Buk cast their lot with the partisans. Rarely had the oppressed of any nation groped so hopelessly for the light that might lead them out of a pit so deep.

Szymon said he would arrange at once for Jan to smuggle messages into Krakow and for Biruta to deliver bread. Within three days Jan was on his way to Krakow, where the underground maintained headquarters in an ordinary house less than three hundred yards from Wawel Castle, where Dr. Hans Frank orchestrated his grand design for the extermination of the Polish people.

There was great excitement in the General Gouvernement these days, when Nazi troops prepared to subdue all Russia, and vast plans were spelled out in Dr. Frank's offices for the incorporation of huge additional territories into the General Gouvernement. Frank had proved himself to be an able administrator, quick to prevent the mass uprisings that had occurred in other parts of occupied Poland. He had been assured by both Himmler and Hitler himself that his reign would be extended and prolonged, no doubt for the remainder of his working life.

When total victory came he would consider moving his headquarters to Lwow, which he preferred as a center of operation because it contained only a limited number of Poles, all of whom could be made to disappear. By that time, too, all Jews in the Lublin pale would have been exterminated, and if enough pure Germans could be moved in to replace them, what had once been eastern Poland would be a decent place in which to live. Farther east would be unpalatable: too many Russians there.

So at the very time that Jan Buk became a runner for the Polish underground, Hans Frank began to tighten up his administration of the General Gouvernement, and when Buk entered Krakow, which he did not know well, he had to be extremely careful where he went. He was not afraid of being arrested for traveling with limited papers; as a farmer bringing food he was entitled to show his pass and move fairly freely, but he did have to avoid any spot at which the Gestapo might conduct one of its sudden sweeps, trapping anyone on the streets within a cordon and arresting them all.

When this happened, and it did every other week or oftener, those inside the cordon were condemned. Either they were lined up against some city wall and machine-gunned in reprisal for a purported crime about which they knew nothing, or they were transported to Germany proper to serve out their lives as slaves, oftentimes in the underground factories where they would never again see daylight.

And sometimes the fierce raids occurred, on any street in any city, simply to terrify the citizenry and to remind them of Dr. Frank's basic rule: "Poland is no longer governed by laws. You are to keep silent and perform your duties as we determine them." On these wild, irrational raids the Gestapo would simply round up a score of citizens and execute them in some public place, so that the cowering Poles would remember that any German could kill any Pole for any reason whatever. One poor woman had a watchdog who protected her after her husband had been slain in such a raid, and this dog growled at the bigger dog owned by a German who had come to work in Krakow. The woman was arrested for anti-German activity and her dog was shot. When she protested weepingly, she, too, was shot.

So Jan Buk moved through Krakow with outward calm, as if he

had no fear, being a simple farmer in from the country, but with immense inner attention, and in six trips as messenger he avoided capture.

At intervals young Szymon Bukowski slipped out of the forest to consult with the Buks, always deep at night, and on one such visit he told Jan: "You must take a code name. Because our real names must never be spoken." At that moment the storks which inhabited the chimney pot of the Buk cottage, as they had done the chimneys of Bukowo for ten centuries, made one of their regular commotions, and Jan said: "I'll be Bocian," and henceforth he was known as Stork.

It was this name which was reported to Konrad Krumpf by one of his collaborators: "We have reason to believe that Szymon Bukowski is getting food supplies from someone near Castle Gorka with the code name Bocian." The location was wrong, the identification accurate, but the fact that Krumpf now concentrated his search efforts in the territory of Count Lubonski allowed the Buks a little extra freedom to conduct their underground activities. Biruta continued to bake her illegal bread and sneak it to the men in the forest, while her husband entered upon that dangerous and often tragic escalation which tempted a man first to run messages, then to derail a train, and finally to do outright battle with the Nazi troops.

At every step he took, Jan Buk was cruelly aware that his actions moved names higher and higher on that posted list of hostages and that he was, in effect, the executioner of those whom Krumpf apprehended and shot after the latest outrage against the Third Reich. In time he could well become the executioner of himself.

It was interesting that Krumpf never displayed the slightest reluctance to murder the next assignment of hostages, for he believed without question that Germany was intended by destiny, or God if one wished, to rule Europe and that Adolf Hitler had been brought to Germany from Austria to lead the nation into this supremacy. Therefore, the most trivial action against any German was an action against the ordained rule of the world, and no punishment could be too severe. Also, in the particular case of Poland, it was clear that this bastard nation must this time be totally removed from the map, with no possibility of reincarnation, so whatever steps he took to hasten that disappearance were laudable.

He was not a vicious man; in Magdeburg his family had long enjoyed a good reputation and his parents had raised him with an appreciation for German history and a conviction that Germans were inherently superior. He was a faithful Lutheran, but he had no animosity against Catholics, some of whom from the Munich area made excellent Gestapo officers. He did, however, despise Jews and sometimes wondered whether they were really part of the human race; he suspected not.

He was a bright man, but his watery blue eyes and straw-colored hair made him look something of a bumbling peasant, a fact he acknowledged, and this was one of the reasons why he had so firmly determined to live in the palace: to show his subordinates that he, too, was a gentleman. In his favor it should be said that he himself never tortured a prisoner, not even a Jew; if the man or woman was guilty of a crime against the Third Reich, that person was either hanged properly, or machine-gunned, or shot with a revolver behind the ear.

Counting the arbitrary sweeps in which the Gestapo rounded up citizens for mass killings, and the orderly shooting of hostages, and the executions for cause, like those of the women grinding illegal wheat, Konrad Krumpf had now been responsible for one hundred and eighty-three deaths in his villages, and he could not think of one that was not fully justified. If asked, he would have said: "I can imagine this rate continuing far into the future." For with the defeat of the Russians and the pacification of the eastern frontier, the General Gouvernement could begin the orderly extermination of the Polish people, just as the Jews were being handled now.

It was therefore with the greatest excitement that he learned that the man he wanted most, Szymon Bukowski, was indeed hiding in the Forest of Szczek and that he sometimes made nocturnal visits to his village of Bukowo. Sentries were posted, and one starry night in January he was caught as he left the forest.

He was taken directly to the Bukowski palace, where in the darkness Krumpf arraigned him, looked at his horribly beaten face, and told him: "You will be executed tomorrow at noon. But not before you are interrogated."

The interrogation, a brutal affair, was not conducted in the palace—that would have been unthinkable—but in a former schoolhouse, where the Gestapo beat the young man until he was almost dead but failed to elicit any significant information. It was obvious that he could not be executed at noon, even though the villagers had been alerted that a public hanging would be held at the gibbet, for more questioning was necessary.

This was a fortunate delay, because Governor Frank himself telephoned from Krakow directing that the terrorist be delivered to the Gestapo in Lublin, since they were more skilled in the interrogation of prisoners with secret knowledge, so with some regret Krumpf dispatched a truck to Lublin, where the Gestapo driver said: "I'm looking for Under the Clock," and the policeman looked at the rear of the truck and asked: "Terrorist?" and when the driver nodded, the policeman said, as he often did when trucks came in from rural areas: "Go straight down this street till you hit the square, look for the clock in the tower, and the door you want will be on the side street to the left."

On a Tuesday afternoon in February 1942, Szymon Bukowski, known terrorist, was delivered to Under the Clock in Lublin.

Jan Buk was in Krakow, working with regional headquarters of the underground, when he learned of his cousin's arrest and removal to Lublin. "They'll kill him. Especially if they send him to Lublin."

"Yes, and that raises a problem for us. Even a man like Bukowski, even he might speak under extreme torture. It would be perilous for you to return to your village."

"I think so, too."

"What we have in mind, and we've discussed this for some time . . . You're a powerful man, Buk. You have the temperament we seek."

"I could work in Warsaw." He paused. "I mean, Biruta could take care of herself."

"We're sure of that. But Warsaw has all the men it needs. What we want you to do is to go back to Bukowo."

"You just said . . ."

"The village, yes. It's too dangerous for you. But the Forest of Szczek? We have a promising group there, and we want you to lead it."

Jan Buk was twenty-two years old, a man who could read and write, a man of that stubborn character which often comes from wrestling with the soil. He had no fanatical hatred of the Nazis, only an unshakable resolve that they must somehow be expelled from his fields and from all of Poland. He realized this winter morning that this resolve would never leave him during his life and that whether

Szymon died in Lublin, or Biruta in Bukowo, or he in the forest, the fight would continue, remorselessly, imaginatively, brutally, forever.

"We want your group to have a name," the district commander said, "because we have major plans for your activity."

"My group?"

"Yes. You're the leader as of now."

Jan Buk stood silent, thinking of his village, and of the public square in which his grandmother had been hanged, and his aunt fusilladed on that first day, and he saw it as a village of peace, one in which many people had found satisfactory lives, and then he saw storks flying home from their winters in Africa and he thought that they, too, looked to his village as their home; they, too, sought repose.

"Use my code name—Bocian," he said, and thus the famous Stork Commando which operated out of the Forest of Szczek was born.

To protect his anonymity, the Krakow people forged several papers, which were inserted into Governor Frank's records by partisans who worked in Wawel Castle, and official word was sent back to Konrad Krumpf in the Bukowski palace that Jan Buk of his district had been swept up by a Gestapo raid and shipped off to Germany to labor in a munitions factory.

"We won't hear from that one again," Krumpf said, for life expectancy in such slave centers was not great.

Now the burden of running the Buk farm fell exclusively on Biruta, a woman of only twenty and with an imperfect knowledge of agriculture. Nevertheless, the Gestapo gave her a quota, which they said she must fill or the farm would be taken from her and she would be sent to work in Germany. But villagers would guide her in the spring plowing, instruct her in how she must apply for seed grain from the Nazis, and help her with her first planting. With them she prayed for rain and from them she would learn how to conceal part of her harvest to be sold for her personal profit. There was no need for her to reveal that she did not intend selling the grain; she would smuggle it to the partisans, and she suspected that other families were doing the same.

She worked hours which in normal times might have killed her, but she was kept strong by her faith: she was sure that if anyone could survive in the forest, or wherever he was, her husband would; and she was constantly encouraged by news of the bold moves made by the group that was now called throughout the district the Stork Commando. Its members appeared suddenly at some railroad crossing, dynamiting the tracks, or in some village where a German soldier was behaving with unusual brutality. It struck at those targets which would bring greatest discomfort to the Germans, greatest reassurance to the Poles, and Biruta Buk, dead tired from her animal-like labor in the fields, quietly shared her joy with the other villagers when the Storks humiliated the Nazis.

Fortunately, the operations of the commando were not associated in the German files with the village of Bukowo. The leader had not yet been identified, nor his hiding place discovered; it was assumed that the criminal gang must be somewhere in the Forest of Szczek, but that covered a large area, and Krumpf's experts believed the group must be getting its major support from the Castle Gorka district, and once more intensive searches were conducted there. Krumpf was infuriated when they revealed nothing.

And then late one night, almost at dawn, a soft footstep warned Biruta that someone was approaching her cottage. She experienced no undue fear, for she had not used her quern for some time and it was safely hidden, but she did sit up in bed, and she was there, arms clasped about her knees, when the door opened and her husband entered, his face discernible in the growing light.

He stayed in his home all that day, prepared to dash into the forest at the sign of any soldiers, but Biruta went to her fields as usual, and that night she talked with Jan about his activities: "Are you with the Stork Commando?"

"No," he lied, as he did to everyone.

"They're very brave. What do you do?"

"Like always. Carry messages mostly."

"How do you live in the forest? How do you eat?"

"Poorly. We shoot a few deer."

"Where do you get guns? Ammunition?"

"We raid German depots. We steal."

"But you don't have actual battles? I mean, real fighting?"

"No." He asked her what her life was like, and now she had to lie, too.

"We do well in the village. Hostages shot now and then, but not like it used to be."

"Food?"

"Plenty. Plenty."

"Do many women send bread to the partisans?"

"I know of none, Jan. I suspect several. We keep it very secret."

"Do you send any?"

"Krumpf watches our wheat like a hungry crow at harvest. I haven't touched . . ." She looked toward the sacred quern and showed her shame, and then she came close to tears. "Krumpf watches us constantly." She twisted her hands, then said: "You know he caught Szymon?"

"I heard." He sighed deeply and embraced his wife. "If you and I have troubles, think of Bukowski in Lublin."

After a while she said: "Some of us think that our Bukowski, the one at the palace, we think he's working with the Germans."

"I doubt that."

"He's got Krumpf living there . . . even before you left. You know that." When her husband said nothing, she asked: "How was the report spread that you were in Germany?" and he said: "I didn't hear that rumor," and she said: "Yes, and at first I thought it was true. How did you get from Krakow into the forest?" and he refused to explain, for the rule of the underground was: "No one is to know anything until the moment of action."

At two in the morning he prepared to leave, but had one final plea to make: "Biruta, sometimes we starve. We must have food. Could you speak to the women?"

"No," she said with stern finality. "I can trust no one. Krumpf has spies everywhere. You wouldn't believe that he could get Poles to spy for him."

"I can believe," he said.

So she made no promises about anyone else but she did say that she would steal what she herself could, and she would reserve it for him.

"No! I can't come back. Not for a while."

"I'll give it to the Storks."

"You do that. We'll get our share."

And suddenly a flood of great love came over these two, there in the utter bleakness of their situation. In the abyss of Polish hopes, when the enemy was proving stronger than ever, they trembled in each other's arms.

"They've taken our other priest, you know," she whispered. "Sent him to Auschwitz."

"Oh God, that poor man."

And in the darkness they prayed, and then, after a final desperate embrace, he returned to the forest, carrying food which he took reluctantly, for he had never seen her so thin.

In the city of Lublin at the corner of University and Basztowa streets there stood a rather impressive public building graced by a tower containing a good clock which struck the hours. In the cramped, dark, damp rooms in its cellar, the Lublin Gestapo had constructed a series of windowless cells and interrogation rooms, and none in the entire area of occupied Poland was as horrible, for criminals delivered here were not expected to leave this place alive.

When Szymon Bukowski was shoved through the small, low door leading to the cellar, he was greeted by a Gestapo functionary who clubbed him over the head with a brutal blow that might have killed a man less vital than he, then ordered two others to drag him to a holding cell. When he revived in the darkness, his head throbbing and his ability to speak impaired, he found that he was in the presence of another prisoner, whose voice indicated that the owner was a much older man.

"Professor Tomczyk," the voice said. "Roman Tomczyk of this city."

Szymon could scarcely make his tongue work, but managed to ask in muffled accent: "University here?"

"No," the voice said, and that was all.

Bukowski thought that perhaps the man was a spy, and would try to extract confidences, but there were no questions. And when light finally entered the cell, Szymon was amazed that this man could speak at all, for his face was horribly battered: "What happened?"

"The broomstick."

"Did they beat you with a broomstick?" The bruises looked too big and too flat for that.

"They put you on the broomstick. Then things happen." When Szymon tried to interrogate him, he diverted the questions: "Two things to remember, young man. Save your physical energy. Protect your psychological strength."

"How?"

"Never fight back. Let them do what they will. Never get angry. There will be a day of retribution. And a third rule, a very good one. Scream like hell when they beat you. It makes them feel superior."

"What is the broomstick?" Apparently it was too horrible to be discussed, for the man merely said: "You can survive, believe me, you can survive if you will husband your physical and psychological strength. Indulge in no excesses, not even hatred."

"How do you know?"

"I interrogated escapees . . . before they caught me. But don't you tell anybody anything . . . not even me. And it's known that I was head of the Lublin committee for two years. Tell no one who you are or why. Stay quiet and conserve your energies."

Before noon Bukowski learned what the broomstick was. He was taken from his cell, thrashed by two guards, who kicked and mauled him as they dragged him along, and delivered to a larger cell with lights. It contained four men, Gestapo he supposed, and two chairs with high, wide backs, facing outward one from the other. There was also a broomstick, a rather long length of some heavy wood like oak or ash, and with obvious delight one of the men brought this to where Szymon was standing, or rather, had been standing, for a savage blow to the back of his neck knocked him to the floor.

Adeptly, one of the men grabbed his feet and doubled his knees backward, whereupon his ankles were strapped together while the broomstick was passed under his knees. His body was then thrust brutally forward so that his elbows could be passed under the stick, and his wrists were lashed tightly and secured and forced back close to his chest. He thus formed a compact bundle, tightly compressed and twisted around the broomstick, whose ends the four men placed on the upper rims of the chair backs. Two men sat spread-legged on the chairs, holding the backs erect, and now Szymon was rolled back and forth as the four men rained blows upon him.

No one spoke, but from time to time one of the men sitting on the chairs would leap up, whereupon the weight of Szymon's bundled body would cause that chair to topple over; this meant that he would crash to the floor from a height high enough to terrify and bruise him horribly, but not high enough to kill him outright. Then he would be kicked numerous times, abused for being clumsy, and hoisted back onto the chairs. Again and again one of the men would jump up, sending him crashing to the floor. Once they placed him at the extreme end of the chair backs and started rolling him slowly toward the end, informing him of the distance still to be covered: "Thirty centimeters. Twenty. Ten. Whoooo!" and with a mighty shove they pitched him off. Since he fell a greater distance than when the chairs slowly collapsed, he was badly hurt and thought he might have a broken hip, but when they kicked him about the body he felt a new pain greater than that to the hip, and before he fainted he judged that he was still whole.

Of three hundred and sixty-seven prisoners interrogated during Szymon Bukowski's stay Under the Clock, one hundred and ninety died. Every one was listed in the careful records kept by the Gestapo as having died from Lungentuberkulose.

On three successive days Bukowski and Professor Tomczyk were each given the most savage treatment on the broomstick, and Szymon wondered how the old man survived, but whenever the latter was dragged back to his cell he simply lay on the floor, breathed as deeply as his damaged lungs would permit, and assured Szymon that nothing had happened: "It is not my responsibility to bring retribution to these men. We have created a God to whom we allocate that task and we must believe that He notes every action in this cellar and will in due course make honest restitution."

Szymon was too battered to comment, but the professor realized one weakness in his argument, and through lips shattered by kicks to the mouth he said almost incoherently: "And it does not matter, son, whether we are alive to see the restitution or not. It will come as surely as day follows night, and we are now in the night. It will surely come. That we must never doubt."

His remarkable faith helped keep Bukowski alive during these days of torture and interrogation, and during one afternoon of hideous abuse, he happened to be taken to the cell while Professor Tomczyk was still on the broom, and the old man was crying and weeping and screaming like a baby, which seemed to give his tormentors great pleasure, but later when he rejoined the old man in their cell, Tomczyk said: "Nothing happened. You must relax, son, and save your spiritual energies. I shall not survive, but you must, to bear witness. So save your energies, because God sees everything that happens in that room, and it is to Him that we look for deliverance."

Tomczyk proved a poor prophet; he did survive, and at the end of the interrogations he and Bukowski were taken out into an alley behind Under the Clock, thrown into a van, and hauled away as near-corpses to one of the fine buildings in Lublin, Zamek Lublin. It stood on a hill, a castle dating far back into history. It now served as both the major prison in the area and the court in which the destinies of prisoners were determined.

The court was convened on an upper floor of the castle, and as will be seen, this was significant, but more so was the fact that the trials were held in a very old chapel decorated with Biblical frescoes dating back to 1418, for this gave the proceedings an aura of religious sanction. Holy figures, representing justice, looked down on the judgments and watched their consequences.

The trials epitomized Nazi justice in general and the attitude of Germans toward Poles in particular. Two men, dressed in judges' robes, sat at a long marble table occupying the space where during five centuries the altar had stood. They wore red hats, which gave them a judicial appearance although neither had ever before been a judge. The older man, on the left as the prisoners saw him, wore heavy glasses; for a brief period he had been a lawyer's clerk in Hamburg; the young man on the right was a Gestapo functionary, and it was he who determined the course of the trial and its outcome.

Some forty prisoners had been assembled in the chapel at seven in the morning, and there they sat, as if at prayers, for two hours, and some whose kidneys had been damaged or even ruptured by the beatings Under the Clock began to experience extreme discomfort, but their guards would not allow them to move. With dismay Bukowski became aware that Professor Tomczyk had wet his pants, and then he saw that two others had done the same. This amused the guards, who cuffed the three men over the head most brutally for having misbehaved.

When the trials began they were shocking affairs. A prisoner would be dragged, literally dragged, by the armpits, his feet barely touching the ancient stones of the chapel floor, to a spot where he was thrown before the judges; some lost their footing and looked up from the floor itself in grave embarrassment, whereupon the young Gestapo judge shouted in a high piercing voice that the accused must stand before this court of the Third Reich.

Each trial lasted only six or seven minutes. A Gestapo officer announced what the charges were, a prosecutor heckled the prisoner, demanding answers to questions which assumed guilt, and the two judges harassed the man if he tried to reply. No witness was allowed to speak for the defendant, and if he endeavored to speak for himself, the Gestapo judge shouted him down.

The verdict came swiftly. In the week of Bukowski's trial an average of fifty-two men a day stood before the judges, or more than three hundred and fifty accused, and not one was found innocent; the judges felt that the Gestapo, Hitler's most valuable arm, would not have brought these culprits before the court unless they were guilty; the only legal problem was what their punishment should be.

Bukowski noticed that occasionally the Gestapo judge would consult a paper and whisper something to the other judge, and then the prisoner would be told: "You are to be taken to further imprisonment, where you will reveal what you have refused to tell us so far." These men were led off to the left.

The others, and by far the greater number, were ordered to execution, and it came swiftly. Upon pronouncement of the verdict, always by the Gestapo judge, two guards hustled the prisoner out the door to the right, which closed behind him with a bang. Within seconds there came another bang, this time very loud, from the muzzle of a revolver held close to a human head, then a moment of silence, then a crashing sound as the dead body was pitched headfirst down a stairwell to an open area below. Then the two guards returned to the courtroom to await the next verdict.

Szymon noticed one peculiarity which betrayed what the verdict was going to be. Whenever the young Gestapo judge, after whispered consultation, decided to impose the death penalty, but before he announced it, the civilian judge would take off his heavy glasses and stare at the accused. It was as if, having tried a ghost with only ghostly evidence against it, the judge wished to catch a glimpse of the real human behind the charges. Dangling his glasses, the inquisitive judge would watch the condemned man as he was taken from the courtroom, listen for the pistol shot, then replace his glasses almost as if to say: "Well, that finishes that. Let's get on with the next one."

Professor Tomczyk was summoned first, and he presented a pitiful sight, a frail old man who had wet his pants, his face badly bruised, his eyeglasses twisted from a blow he had received in this courtroom, his knees trembling, not from fear but from lack of food during the preceding five days of torture. But he stood erect and almost defiant as the so-called legal procedures swirled about him. He was charged with having led the opposition in Lublin to the new rule of the Third Reich and with having aided Jews to escape eastward into Russian areas.

It was clear from the rantings of the prosecutor that Tomczyk was to be executed, but at the moment of judgment the Gestapo judge consulted his list and announced in that piercing voice that this prisoner was of supreme danger to the new order and would be remanded to further imprisonment and interrogation. Tomczyk was led off to the left, and Bukowski supposed that he, Bukowski, would never see him again.

Now two guards cuffed him on the back of his head, causing stars to dance in the courtroom, and he was dragged forward. The strong shove he received at the end caused him to fall on the stones, where he looked up at his judges. Since these would probably be the last human beings he would ever see, he wanted to savor each moment, each revealing impression. He did not listen to the accusations, for they were preposterous and in no way related to what he had actually done while operating from within the Forest of Szczek: destruction of a troop train, the murder of two members of the Gestapo, the spiriting of Jews away from the Krakow ghetto, the theft of wheat and other consumables. Instead he focused on the faces, and saw not beasts devoid of human characteristics, but two men caught up in the passions of their time: a man who should have been a legal assistant in some small German town and never a full-fledged lawyer or judge, and a man who should have spent his life as a minor and ill-regarded political hack in some rural district, the kind who was sent for beer and sausages in the late afternoons. By the fate of revolution and war they were now dispensing supposed justice in a city they had never before heard of and to a people they despised.

Profoundly sad that men and their systems could be so cruel, Szymon tried to straighten his bruised shoulders and accept the death so wrongfully imposed upon him, but he noticed that the civilian judge had not removed his glasses! He was not going to be shot! Then came the high, whining voice: "The prisoner has not told us where his hiding places were. Further imprisonment and interrogation."

He had not the slightest idea as to what awaited him behind the left door, but when he was shoved through he found himself in a small stone-walled room which looked as if it had once been used as a robing closet for the priests who officiated in this chapel, and there he waited with some dozen others as the trials in the courtroom proceeded, and with every echo of the pistol shot that sent some other Pole pitching headlong down the stairwell, he shuddered. In Zamek Lublin four hundred thousand Polish men and women would be tried by judges like the two Bukowski had seen and less than nine thousand would be found innocent.

When the trials ended and the gunfire ceased, a new group of guards appeared in the little stone room, heavy boots and heavier voices, and they assumed control of the prisoners sentenced to further incarceration: "Line up. Keep silent. Move smartly."

They were taken down two long flights of stone stairs and out into the Lublin sunlight, where some two hundred other prisoners from various parts of Poland were waiting. In ragged military formation they walked eastward out of town, some older men falling by the way, for the pace was sharp and steady.

"Get up!" the guards said only twice to the fallen men, and if they could not, they were shot, their bodies left behind as the long file moved on.

At the edge of Lublin a spur of the railroad which connected Krakow with Brest-Litovsk had been converted into a huge unloading platform, and here several thousand prisoners from the south of Poland and even from Hungary and Czechoslovakia were being driven from the boxcars that had carried them great distances, and these, too, joined the procession, which now started a long tramp eastward.

Bukowski walked beside Professor Tomczyk, aiding him when it looked as if the old man might collapse, and in whispered consultation they tried to decipher what was happening. "Many of them must be Jews," Tomczyk guessed. "From other countries, maybe. They don't look Polish."

"Where are we going?"

"Majdanek, I think."

And for the first time Szymon heard the name that would be engraved in letters of fire upon his heart. "Majdanek," he repeated. "What is it?"

"A big camp our people in Lublin helped build east of the city." Tomczyk paused, then added: "It was really built by Russian prisoners captured on the eastern front. They worked five months, and on the day they finished the barracks they were shot. Every man. Five thousand, four hundred and sixty-three in one day." They walked in silence and then the old man said: "My group kept the records." More silence, then a nudge so deftly given that the Gestapo guards could not detect it. "Someone in that crowd from my unit is counting each of us as we go past. You are being recorded, Szymon. Tonight, somehow, our numbers will be radioed to the Polish government in London."

It was a long, tiring march from Lublin to Majdanek, and some of the new prisoners from the boxcars could not negotiate it; they were shot. Others who talked in ranks were clubbed with rifle butts, and many limped from the bruises of previous tortures, but this tragic column came at last to Majdanek, that once-beautiful field of corn and wheat that was now enclosed by three concentric fences of barbed wire, two of them electrified with enough power to kill any passing animal which touched them.

At the main gate to the camp things happened with startling speed: "All women and children here. All Jews here. Men under thirty here." The sorting out was swift and amazingly accurate.

A guard spotted Bukowski standing with the non-Jewish men under thirty and snapped: "Can you drive a car?"

"Yes."

Szymon received a blow to the head, and the instruction: "Here you say 'Yes, sir,'" after which he was told: "Over there. That truck."

He moved quickly to a long flatbed truck with wooden strakes that formed low sides; if Bukowski or his neighboring farmers had had such a truck, they would have used it to haul manure. It had no driver.

"Take it over there and wait," the guard said, and Szymon moved his truck to third position behind two others that were also waiting.

The guards now had all the Jews separated and were herding them quickly to a low stone building, well built and of good design, marked BATH HOUSE. Here the Jews were ordered to undress, to take a medicinal shower that would kill any lice acquired in the boxcars during the long trip north, and Szymon caught glimpses of their naked pale-skinned bodies, like those of city people who rarely saw the sun. As he waited in his truck he watched an unceasing flow of new arrivals head for the bathhouse.

Nineteen minutes after the first batch of Jews had entered the bathhouse, the three flatbed trucks with the shallow sides were edged forward, toward the far end of the bathhouse, where four Gestapo guards ordered the drivers to dismount and help with the task at hand.

Inside the actual shower room, yet another contingent of Gestapo men, this time in gas masks, were busy tossing naked bodies out through small doors, from which the men waiting outside grabbed them, head and feet, tossing them deftly into the waiting trucks. Bukowski worked with a strong German who counted, each time:

"Eins . . . zwei . . . drei"—and through the air the newly dead body would fly. Twenty-one minutes after arriving at Majdanek, the Jews from Hungary and Czechoslovakia were dead.

When his truck was loaded with fifty-four dead bodies, men, women and children indiscriminately, Bukowski was ordered back to the wheel, and by the pale wintry light he followed the two lead trucks up a kind of alleyway between the barracks, arriving at last at the gateway to another solidly built structure, where a man with an unforgettable face awaited. He was Eric Muhsfeldt, about thirty years old, with a pinched, triangular face, square at the top, pointed at the bottom and with almost no chin. He had big ears, a low hairline, wide eyes which saw everything and a generous mouth which smiled easily. He was in command of this building, and since these were the first deliveries of the day, he was eager to get started. Congenially, and almost jovially, he greeted the first two drivers, then saw Bukowski still in regular dress: "You're new, eh? You'll catch on."

When he directed the first two trucks to unload their cargo, men came out from the building to take charge, and one by one the dead bodies were carried inside. "You want to see?" Muhsfeldt asked Bukowski, almost as if the latter were his brother. And when Szymon stood inside, facing the five effective brick-faced ovens with the gas jets blazing below, he was awed by the mechanical ingenuity displayed in the design of this crematorium.

Corpses were moved in orderly fashion from the receiving gate to the five gaping mouths awaiting them. When an oven was crammed, the entrance door was locked shut with heavy metal clamps, elegantly designed, and the fierce heat was allowed to do its job. When only ashes and bones remained, equally efficient doors on the other side, each bearing a neat brass sign indicating that they had been built by Cori of Berlin, were opened and the ashes were removed by four Polish prisoners using long-handled shovels.

Less than an hour after a Jew stepped inside Majdanek, he could be fertilizer heading for a collection dump outside the electrified barbed wire. "But you'll find many Jews still inside the camp," Muhsfeldt assured Szymon. "We had to handle these so quick because we had no more room."

That evening he was formally processed, which meant that all his clothes were taken from him and thrown in a heap for later distribution in Germany. In return he was given only three items, each made from a flimsy material conspicuous for its broad convict stripes in black and white: a cap, a large shirt and baggy pants. One young prisoner who had been a university student and done field work in Italy studied himself in stripes and whispered: "Now I look like the Siena cathedral," but Szymon, who knew nothing of architecture, did not understand.

In gathering dusk the new prisoners were marched down the camp road to their quarters, and it was a mournful experience to pass almost a mile of barbed wire, horribly tangled, forming three different fences, one behind the other, inside of which stretched what seemed like an endless row of low, massive barracks. The first impression was one of bleak immensity, for the plan was that when Majdanek was completed, it would hold two hundred fifty thousand prisoners, year after year, for as long as any Poles survived. The Jews, by that time, would have long since been exterminated.

For the present it consisted of six fields, tremendous in size and surrounded separately by their own barbed fences. Each field contained twenty-two identical barracks carefully aligned, for this was an orderly camp.

Szymon had been assigned to Field Four, and when he reached the heavily guarded gate which led through the wire he noted that the guardhouse was decorated with the famous SS sign, in which the letters had been drawn to look like two bolts of lightning, and by a huge swastika. The Nazis want us to remember who's in charge, he said to himself. When the gates were locked behind him he was taken to Barracks Eleven, which would be his home until he died, for it was not intended that he or any of the others in that camp should emerge alive.

He walked into a room of enormous size, and stood still for a moment, shivering in the wind that seemed to come from every direction through the cracks in the walls. Double-decker wooden frames stretched in two lines, seemingly to infinity, bare planks on which five hundred and fifty slept jammed side by side, each man allocated exactly twenty-six inches.

While he waited for a sleeping space to be assigned him, a prisoner in charge of handing out blankets to the newcomers whispered: "Most of us in here are Poles, like you and me. But one thing I want to warn you about." He was toothless and could have been thirty years old or eighty. "I seen you driving the death truck to the crematorium. You keep that up, in no time you'll be dead."

"Why?"

"They find men can't stand it. They go crazy. Do crazy things."

"What do you mean?"

The whispering man did not answer that question. "So when they see that a team of drivers and oven men are about used up, they wait till you're together, then herd you into one of the rooms and release the Zyklon-B."

"What's that?"

"The new supergas the German chemists invented. Zyklon-B. Kills quick and painless, I'm told. So into the room you'll go with the others who've been handling the ovens. Psssst! Here comes the Zyklon-B, and ten minutes later, guess who's in the oven?"

Szymon could scarcely absorb such dreadful information, but his informant continued: "Another thing. Whatever you do, stay out of Barracks Nineteen."

"Are they especially tough there?"

"They're fatal. That's where the other barracks send their men who look as if they're going to die."

"What happens in Nineteen?"

"Nothing. That's the problem. They stick you in there, feed you nothing—and *psssst*! Three days later, guess who's in the oven?"

But before sleeping spaces were assigned, all prisoners were led out to a feeding area, where the planned horror of Majdanek was revealed: men who had spent twelve hours at grueling labor, many with pick and shovel, were given as their main meal of the day a small bowl of watery soup containing no meat, no fats, just a cube of black bread whose principal ingredient was sometimes sawdust. Those who had been in camp for some months finished by licking their bowls avidly, seeking even one additional morsel of nourishment.

Szymon had suffered great pain from the beatings he had recently taken and the bruises from the broomstick, but he experienced an even greater pain that night. He was unbearably hungry, and from the faces about him he could see that all the others were too. And as a newcomer in one of the most crowded barracks, he was assigned no plank, just a narrow area on the damp ground, with only one blanket so thin that the man next to him said: "You could read through that one."

With the blanket wrapped tightly around him and rearranged a dozen different ways throughout the night, trying desperately to gain just a little more warmth, Bukowski spent his first night on the cold ground, aware that if this continued for long, he must die of pneumonia.

It was incredible that men who were expected to labor for the Third Reich, regardless of what work they were to do, should be so abused; Bukowski would not have treated one of his cows this way and then expected her to give milk. Toward morning, as he lay shivering uncontrollably, he realized what the program at Majdanek really was. They want us to die. They want all the Poles who might do any constructive work to die. Leaving only slaves. Despite the aching cold and his tormenting bruises, he laughed bitterly: They'll find few slaves in this country. They'll have to kill us all.

Half an hour before dawn he participated in a routine calculated to speed the dying: he and all the others were rousted out, those from the damp ground confused after the sleepless night, and mustered in long lines before their barracks. There they stood, some without shoes, for an hour and a half while roll calls were taken and orders given. They grew numb. They needed to go to the latrine. They were ravished by hunger. Their feet and legs were aching. But if they moved or fell, they were beaten and returned to the ranks, where they must somehow continue to stand, waiting for the roll call to be finished.

As Szymon waited, he noticed that the immense open space between the two rows of barracks was kept completely clean, not a shed or a blade of grass intruding upon the bleak expanse. However, between Barracks Six and Seventeen, in the middle of this barren waste, stood a single stout pole with a heavy crossbeam at the top. When the barracks commander was at the other end of the line Szymon whispered: "What's that?" and the man next to him said: "A gibbet."

Each field had one, and here from time to time camp officials liked to conduct public hangings: "A good execution, well-handled, brings the prisoners to attention. Excellent for discipline, and a hanging is clearly more effective than a shooting." The executions were held now in one field, now in another, so that during any one month each field could anticipate two or three. On this day the hanging would occur in Field Four.

It was customary for all prisoners in a given field to form a square around the gallows, to which the condemned man, his guards and the field commander would march stiffly. At each hanging the commander would announce the reason why this particular man had to be hanged, and someone in the camp, some Pole of extraordinary heroism, would write down in a secret place the name of the condemned and the charges against him. This morning the man was Onufry Unilowski and his crime was that he had spoken against the food being served and had tried to start a riot.

He was a young man—the secret records of the underground showed that the average age of those hanged at the public gibbets was nineteen—and he met his death bravely, shouting as he stood with no hood over his head: "Resist! Resist!" A Gestapo guard bashed him in the mouth with a gun butt and the white stool on which he was standing was kicked away. He did not die quickly, for camp officials wanted their prisoners to see the prolonged agonies which awaited them if they caused even a trivial disturbance.

Bukowski remained on the death truck for five weeks, during which he still had to sleep on the ground with only that shadow-thin blanket. He could feel weakness creeping into his bones, assaulting his joints, but he was sustained by Professor Tomczyk, who lay beside him: "Szymon, you must try to tell yourself that this is not happening. Do not fight it all the time, or you will weaken all your defenses."

"The killing all day. The starvation. The sleepless nights."

"The sovereign law, Szymon, is to survive. Avoid the gibbet. Avoid Barracks Nineteen. Say nothing. Do nothing. Like a bear in winter, you must go into moral hibernation."

The old man was able to do this, ignoring the cruelest deprivations, but one morning at roll call, when, hungry and cold, he could scarcely stand, he almost lost his composure. Down the line, checking on everyone, came the commander of Field Four, a big, stoop-shouldered Gestapo man who selected those who were to be hanged on his gibbet, and on this morning he was looking for diversion. Spotting Tomczyk and remembering that he had been a professor, he suddenly grabbed the old man's glasses, threw them to the ground, and stamped on them with his heel, grinding them into the pebbles. "You won't need glasses any longer."

If Tomczyk had made one movement, even a twitch of the face, he would have been hanged within ten minutes, but with the discipline he had acquired during the interrogations, he nodded his head slightly in deference to the commander and somehow indicated that he was ashamed of having been a professor, or one who had read books. The fatal moment passed, and it was a man from Barracks Seventeen who was hanged.

But when they were together in Barracks Eleven that night, Szymon saw that Professor Tomczyk was weeping, not crocodile tears to gratify his tormentors but the real tears of a distressed old man, and when Szymon asked why, Tomczyk said: "Because I will never again be able to read a book."

"You'll get other glasses when you get out," Szymon reassured him, but Tomczyk said with awful foreknowledge: "I will never get out. Thousands of us, hundreds of thousands, will never get out. They will never allow us even to see a book, let alone read one." He took Szymon's hands. "Learning is a beautiful thing. Wisdom keeps the world functioning. Get learning. Get wisdom. For on you young people the future of Poland depends. Us old ones, they'll kill us all to halt the flow of learning."

Field Four was under the command of SS Captain Otto Grundtz, one of the best men in the business. With extreme severity he operated his set of twenty-two barracks in a way which quickly stifled any protest. He was a big man, thirty-five years old, and the combination of bulging eyes and bristling black eyebrows made him look menacing even when conducting routine inspections. He had been one of the early Nazi bullyboys, adept at smashing Jewish stores or liberal meetings, but he had been categorized from the first as a mere brute with little likelihood of any serious promotion. He was ideally suited, his superiors felt, for concentration-camp duty, and since Nazi plans called for camps to be permanently maintained in both Germany and the conquered countries, men like Grundtz could look forward to many years of employment.

Even in Germany, where education was important, he had not attended school beyond the age of twelve and felt no need to repair the loss. He read nothing, discussed nothing, cheered when told to, and was careful to preserve an unblemished record with his superiors. But he was not a dull man. When a new procedure was to be introduced, he studied it more carefully than the other field commanders and instituted it with a minimum of dislocation.

For example, when the camp commandant found that the barracks were becoming overcrowded because prisoners were dying more slowly than anticipated, it was Grundtz who devised the strategy for Barracks Nineteen. He told his twenty-two subordinates, each of whom supervised a barracks, that they must watch constantly for prisoners who were assigned to especially onerous tasks on diminished rations and not to allow them to waste slowly away, which might take months, but to observe the moment any man fell into unconsciousness: "He is not to be revived. Carry him as he is to Barracks Nineteen." There the man was to be dumped, and left to die.

On some mornings as many as fifteen or sixteen bodies would be hauled away from that barracks alone. It was efficient; it was quiet; and it furthered the objective for which Majdanek had been established.

Morning inspections, with the men standing at attention, became a time for Otto Grundtz to walk slowly down the line, shoulders hunched, big body moving forward, eyes peering out from beneath those heavy brows, trying to pick out which men might be moved on to Nineteen. When he made his decision, there was no review, which was why the prisoners in Field Four tried to use what little strength they still had not to appear sick or weak during these inspections. Among the men, Barracks Nineteen was known as "Otto Grundtz's infirmary. Cure guaranteed."

Unlike the other concentration camps which the Nazis built in Poland—unspeakable Treblinka, which was simply an extermination center, in and dead the same morning; or Belzec, which specialized in torture; or Auschwitz, where hideous procedures were encouraged; or its terrible appendage Birkenau, whose gas chambers were able to accommodate 60,000 bodies in any twenty-four hours—Majdanek was a relatively humane center. True, it did kill off 360,000 unwanted Jews and Poles, almost as many of the latter as of the former, but outright torture for its own end was not permitted. A field commander like Grundtz would have been reprimanded had he instituted anything like the infamous little cell at Auschwitz, where at dusk camp officials would cram into a tiny room with one high window some sixty prisoners chosen at random, then lock the door—and expect to find forty suffocated or trampled to death by morning. There was nothing like that at Majdanek. Prisoners were inducted into the camp in an orderly fashion. Jobs were assigned, such as working at the crematorium or in the shoe-repair shop, one being considered about the same as the other, and after a testing period, the strongest and ablest men were selected for work at one of the German commercial factories that had grown up around the camp perimeter in order to profit from free slave labor.

For all prisoners food rations were kept at a minimum so that disease would the more quickly finish them off; vast epidemics of various fevers and choleras swept the camp at intervals, killing six or seven thousand at a time, especially the many children who found their way into Field Five, where they were sequestered with the women. And of course, the constant regimen of ten and twelve hours of heavy labor, with less than nine hundred calories of food a day, did speed the deaths of any with even the slightest impairment. One abscessed tooth when there was no dentist and no protein to produce white corpuscles could kill a man overnight.

Szymon noticed at the gas chamber that the Zyklon-B the Nazis were using was made by the German firm of Tesch & Stabenow and that what he supposed were careful instructions came with each shipment. The gas was delivered in neatly labeled cylinders bearing a bold skull and crossbones plus a verbal warning that the gas could be deadly if not used with extreme care.

He was at the gas chamber one morning, loading his flatbed with dead Jews, when a Dr. Eigenstiller, who served as traveling expert for Tesch & Stabenow, arrived to check on procedures at Majdanek and to compare their operations with those at the other camps that were the principal users of his company's product. He told the men supervising the chamber: "You must keep the nozzles clean. That way you get a more even distribution of the first application, and that's important if you want an orderly procedure."

Eigenstiller did suggest one improvement that had worked well in the other camps: "Pack your undesirables in more closely, using about one square foot per person. Giving them three separate blasts assures you a more even distribution and doesn't waste the Zyklon-B. You'll see the advantage when you open the doors. The bodies remain upright. They can't fall down, so you'll avoid that jungle of arms and legs."

There was one regrettable aspect of the system for which no solution had yet been found: "When an undesirable dies of strangulation, which is what this is, technically, his bowels often empty automatically, also his bladder, and we have found no way to prevent this. It is absolutely essential therefore that you hose out the chamber after every use. After every use! Otherwise contamination builds up and any communicable germs the undesirables may have brought with them get a chance to multiply."

On the whole, Szymon heard him reporting to the camp commander, Majdanek was doing an efficient job, and after sharing drinks and sandwiches with the SS men running the place, Eigen-stiller left in a staff car to check what improvements might be needed at Treblinka.

Shortly thereafter Heinrich Himmler himself visited Majdanek, poking his fat little belly and pig-set eyes into many corners, and what he found delighted him: "This place is beautiful! Everything works!" In his enthusiasm he announced that the Fuehrer had far-reaching plans for this camp: "It's to be enlarged tenfold. We want a quarter of a million Poles behind barbed wire, constantly replen-ished. We'll build a chain of factories around the perimeter to manu-facture many of the goods we'll need in Germany."

To guards like Otto Grundtz, who were encouraged by this pros-pect of endless employment of a congenial nature, he explained: "Your work in such an enlarged camp will advance our program in two ways. You'll accelerate the death rate of the Polish swine. And by keeping their men away from the women during the years of normal reproduction, you'll lower the birth rate drastically. Give us twenty-five years—just twenty-five—and we'll be on our way to settling the Polish problem permanently."

So Majdanek went its prosaic way. It would be open about three years, perhaps a thousand days, which meant that not fewer than three hundred and sixty persons had to die each twenty-four hours to maintain the standard. But it didn't really work that way, because on certain days there were unusual events which speeded the process and compensated for those days when perhaps only a hundred died.

One such event occurred shortly after Szymon's arrival. Maj-danek housed many Gypsies, collected assiduously from various parts of Europe, and they were housed in segregated barracks in Field Six, where they received extra rations and special privileges. Since they were excused from heavy labor, they seemed actually to prosper in camp, and this caused envy and even animosity among the other prisoners.

The reason they were so carefully nurtured was bizarre, but un-derstandable if one accepted Nazi philosophy. Dr. Alfred Rosenberg, philosopher of the party, was the son of an illiterate German shoe-maker who had not been able to earn a living in Germany proper but who had done so in Estonia, where his son was born. Rosenberg's amateurish studies led him to the mystery of the European Gypsy, and he became convinced that these strange people out of Asia were a race completely apart. And what made them especially worthy of study, Rosenberg preached, was the unquestioned capacity of their women to produce healthy babies with great regularity and with some kind of immunity which defended the children against normal diseases. "We must," argued Rosenberg, "determine the secret of the Gypsy woman, because then we can apply it to our German women and help them produce a master race of blond, moral, strong Nordics." He was convinced also that Germans, Norwegians and Swedes, but no others, sprang from a race of pure Nordics who inhabited a cold Arctic continent which vanished sometime around A.D. 400, having contributed to the world the superior race that was now destined to conquer Europe and rule it justly.

He ordered any camp which contained a concentration of Gypsies to conduct interesting experiments on the women and especially their child-bearing processes, but regrettably, nothing substantial came of this, so one day in disgust he sent to centers like Majdanek a coded message which read: RESEARCH ON GYPSIES CONCLUDED. HARVEST HOME ACTION.

The telegram was delivered at Majdanek at seven in the morning, and by nine all the Gypsy quarters were vacated. Nine hundred and sixteen of these curious, talkative, gesturing people were led to a hill at the far western edge of the camp, lined up carefully—names and numbers registered—and machine-gunned.

The Nazis who ran the individual fields at Majdanek did condone one practiced brutality, and since it contained an element of amusement, it was also approved by the commandant. It would occur at the close of day, when the prisoners were exhausted from their heavy labors and no food. A two-hundred-pound guard called The Dancer sometimes appeared unannounced and arbitrarily, first in this field, then in another, and in a high-pitched feminine voice, shouted at the slaves as they stood at muster before their barracks: *"Stillgestanden, Mützen ab, Augen links!"* and the captives had to stand very still, take off their caps with their left hand just so, and turn eyes and head to the left.

As they stood so, The Dancer moved down the line trying to detect any irregularity. Satisfied, he cried in that high voice: *"Mützen auf!"* and the men replaced their caps and looked straight ahead.

Then came the terrifying moment, for The Dancer now moved back, folded his arms, and inspected the men standing before him.

Finally, on no selective principle that could be ascertained, he chose some prisoner, moved menacingly before him, studied him for about a minute, then with his left thumb wet with spit, marked a spot on the man's body: behind the right ear perhaps, or on the left side of the belly, low down, or directly over the heart. Twice he would indicate the target spot with his spit.

Now he showed why he carried his nickname, for he would move well away from the prisoner and begin the dancing shuffle used by prizefighters, weaving this way and that, uttering small grunts as if a true fight were in progress, licking first his left thumb, then his right, and all the time marking his target.

Finally, with a piercing scream, he would lunge forward with all his considerable force, swing his right fist with terrible power, and strike the prisoner hard on target.

Invariably the man would be knocked to the ground, for in his weakened condition there was no chance of withstanding such a blow, but this falling seemed to infuriate The Dancer, for he would stand over the prostrate prisoner and revile him in screeching tones: "Get up, coward bastard Pole afraid to fight! Get up and fight like a man!"

With this he would begin to kick the fallen man, hard, heavy blows of the boot to the head and kidneys and heart, screaming for the man to get up and fight like a decent German . . . like a man. And all the while he danced back and forth like a boxer.

In Field Four he had killed five men, three by kicking them to death, two by terrible blows which ruptured the heart—and the men of this field, not knowing how many others he had killed in the other areas, often felt that the most hideous sound on earth was that high-pitched cry *"Stillgestanden, Mützen ab, Augen links!"* for they knew it threatened another indecent death.

An especially gruesome aspect of The Dancer's performance was that when it became known to the guards in other fields that he was about to box, these men ran to where he was conducting his evening "inspection," forming a kind of cheering section and even making small wagers as to whether he would be able to kill his target with one blow. "A clean knockout" that was called, and the watching guards applauded when he achieved it.

One evening after the usual brutal day of work, Bukowski returned to Field Four, where the guards had gathered to watch The Dancer, and found himself selected as the target, marked just below the heart with that spit-wetted left thumb. Two of the guards cheered their man on and two others arranged a bet as to whether or not Bukowski could survive the forthcoming blow. Szymon, watching the weaving shuffle as The Dancer maneuvered to attain maximum power in his right arm, prayed: Let me withstand this. Body, grow strong. And he looked The Dancer right in the eye as the guards cheered and the terrible blow fell.

He had never experienced such a paralyzing, thunderous smashing. Resistance was impossible, and he felt himself going down as if a woodsman had chopped off his legs. Don't faint! he ordered his failing body, but he could feel blackness sweeping over him. Don't faint or he'll kick you to death.

He did faint, but just for a moment. Then he felt the deadly boot crashing into his head, and surprisingly, this revived him. With a fortitude he did not know he had he raised his hands, fended off the next kick, and slowly regained his feet while The Dancer screamed at him: "Filthy fucking Pole! Why don't you stand up and fight like a man?"

One morning Bukowski arrived with a load of corpses at the crematorium, to find that no one was working inside. Eric Muhsfeldt was there, of course, as chief of the installation, but he had no helpers; Gestapo guards had appeared suddenly that morning and driven the oven workers into a small room, where Zyklon-B was released. Now, before work could begin, it was necessary to remove those bodies from the room and place them in the ovens.

Bukowski was detailed to this duty, and when he was finished, Muhsfeldt, with his triangular face, staring eyes and smiling lips, said: "I want you to work with me now. I've been watching you, and you're very good."

Bukowski, knowing this to be a death sentence—all in Majdanek were under that sentence, but to work in the crematorium meant that it would come hideously sooner—thought for a moment that he must protest, but he knew that if he did, Muhsfeldt could order him shot, so he temporized: "I'd like working with you, sir, but first I must take my truck back."

"Of course! You'll start tomorrow. I'll tell your commander."

Szymon, trembling, drove the truck back to the gas chambers to pick up his next load of Jewish corpses, but as he waited in line he chanced to see the pile of shoes left by the doomed Jews before entering the baths. He knew that these shoes would be taken to the shoe-repair shop, where the sound ones would be mended for use in Germany, and on the spur of the moment he left his truck, a crime in itself, and went up to the officer in charge.

"May I speak, sir?"

"What is it?"

"Some of those shoes. They could be saved."

"I know that. That's what I have my men doing."

"I used to be a shoemaker. I could fix that shoe," and he pointed to one almost worth salvaging.

"You could?"

"Yes. I fixed shoes that were in much worse shape than that." Then he had a brilliant thought: "In Poland, you know, we don't have good shoes."

"Not like good German shoes," the Nazi said. "Come with me."

"My truck."

"I'll find another driver. Drivers are plentiful. Good shoemakers, not."

He led Szymon to a small, low concrete building outside the triple barbed wire where six emaciated camp slaves were going through the painfully slow motions of repairing shoes. With thumping heart and almost animal cunning, Szymon surveyed the work area, spotted a pair of pincers like those he had once watched his village shoemaker use, picked them up, and reaching down for one of the shoes lying on the floor, began pulling away the worn sole. When the officer's attention was diverted, Szymon whispered to the man nearest him: "Protect me," and that man took from the pile the mate to Szymon's shoe and began the procedures which a skilled shoemaker would follow. Szymon aped him, whereupon another man said, in the officer's hearing: "This one knows how to fix shoes."

He got the job, but at close of day, when he should have gone with the guards back to Field Four, he sought permission from his officer to detour to the crematorium: "I should explain to Muhsfeldt. He would be expecting me and I would not want him to think . . ."

The shoe-repair officer laughed at the idea of anyone's apologizing to a chinless wonder like Muhsfeldt, who was kept at the crematorium because he was good for nothing else, but the officer also liked Bukowski's attitude, so he assigned two guards to return him to his quarters via the burning place, and they watched as Szymon apologized. He did not want Muhsfeldt to harbor any grudge that might cause the angular-faced man to order his death, and the crematorium man, for his part, seemed pleased that the Pole had come to apologize.

"I could have used you," he said, the narrow space between his hairline and his eyebrows wrinkling with obvious irritation. "But I always come last. They don't like me because I work here, but this camp couldn't function without me. We average about three hundred fifty bodies a day, and did you ever stop to think how many men it would take to dig that many graves day after day? It would bankrupt the camp." He pointed to his five ovens, their metal work gleaming, and said: "These are the most sensible thing in this camp."

He was sorry to lose Bukowski: "But around here the officers always come first. If they need you to fix shoes . . ." He showed Szymon his own, which were not good.

"I'll fix them," Szymon said, and that night he returned to Barracks Eleven certain that he had gained a few more months of life, and he was right, for ten weeks later all the crematorium crew of which he would have been a member disappeared, and Professor Tomczyk explained why: "The Nazis want no one alive who could report specific details. When surrender nears—and believe me, it will come—you watch! Then they'll shoot whoever is left here."

Bukowski's feeling of good fortune in escaping imminent death was dampened by the decline he saw in Professor Tomczyk. As the old man grew ever weaker, he was in danger of being nominated some morning for Barracks Nineteen and accelerated death. But at morning muster, when he stood in the snow for ninety minutes, he drew upon some inner reserve whose power dumfounded Bukowski: How does he do it, that frail old man with the bruised and broken body?

Otto Grundtz, who monitored everyone in Field Four, always seeking those who could be more quickly killed off, as if to fulfill his quota, had seen Tomczyk as a likely prospect, and assigned him to the great concrete rollers, two massive cylinders with iron pipes set through their middles. They were used for smoothing the camp roads, and work on them was the cruelest that could be devised, for in cold weather prisoners, with no gloves, had to grasp the freezing iron pipes, and then summon all their energy to start the rollers forward and keep them going. It would have been murderous work for a young man consuming thirty-five hundred calories a day of fat and protein. On nine hundred calories of thin soup, it was a sure sentence of death.

But Professor Tomczyk refused to die. And he refused to be placed in Barracks Nineteen: "I will defeat them." And he began that series of instructions which no man who survived Barracks Eleven would ever forget. He became a professor again, urgently teaching as if he must within a limited time impart all he knew to younger men who would carry on the obligations he had assumed. In whispered discussions at night, or in casual observations to his fellows as he strained at the concrete rollers, he taught his lessons:

"The most important thing to do when this nightmare ends— and it will end—is to rebuild. Every item that they destroy, you must rebuild. Because rebuilding is an act of faith, an act of commitment to the future. If they've destroyed a schoolhouse in your village, and they've burned down many, rebuild it first of all, because a schoolhouse is a pledge to the future.

"And our beautiful buildings, if they destroy them, rebuild them, because they are testimony to the greatness we once knew. Rebuild a church or a historic palace even before you rebuild your own homes, because you've learned here that a man can live anywhere, under any conditions. Homes can wait, but the edifices which warm the civic heart can be lost if not attended to at the proper time.

"Rebuild, rebuild. And most of all, you young fellows, rebuild your own lives. Love your wives when you get home and have many children. This is not the end. Otto Grundtz is not the god who oversees the fields of Poland.

"Rebuild. Rebuild. Think now of what you will rebuild as soon as the evil ones depart. Imagine churches and palaces and schoolhouses. And most of all, imagine the children you will make, and educate, and send on their way."

He was incessant in this teaching, a dying man who refused to die until he was sure that the spring fields had been sown with good seed.

He was really remarkable, the younger men around him thought. Sixty, seventy years old, probably weighed less than a hundred pounds, but there he stood at muster, his feet freezing in snow, and there he worked at the icy handles of the great concrete rollers, and each day it seemed that he must collapse and be moved the final distance to

Barracks Nineteen. But at the next day's roll call he would report: "Present."

It was his opinion, in these darkest days of the war when Germany's triumph seemed universal, that two things would happen:

"Like Napoleon, Hitler will go too far into Russia, and before I die I will see his armies heading back this way. Mark my words, you young fellows, you will be liberated sooner than you know by men coming from the east. The barbed wire will be torn down. The gibbets . . . [He stopped, as if he knew how close he was to those gibbets.]

"At the same time the Americans will strengthen the west. You'll see American bombers over this camp. Yes, you will see airplanes right up there. This you must never doubt. So what if the Germans have reached the Volga River? Mark their retreat. You will hear about it."

On one point he was insistent:

"You must remember the name and look of every Nazi who worked in this camp. If any of you escape, and I pray to God you will, first thing you do is not eat a big meal or visit your wife. First thing, you get someone to write down all the names. Karl Otto Koch, who came here from Buchenwald. Max Koegel, who was our commandant, and Hermann Florstedt, if I have his name right. And Otto Grundtz, who commanded Field Four, and don't forget the medical doctor, Heinrich Rindfleisch. Promise me to record Otto Grundtz, the worst of them all. And find out the name of The Dancer.

"Because when liberation comes you must see that these men are brought back here to Majdanek and hanged. They must be hanged from the very gibbets they profaned. Because they did not profane me, or harmless Jakub Grabski, whom they hanged last week. They profaned the human race, and the memory of Jesus Christ, and the souls of the little children they have massacred in Field Five. For this terrible crime of profanation of all that is good in life, they must be hanged. You must commit yourselves not to revenge but to the service as God's exemplars here on earth. These men have profaned God, and they must be punished."

Until word of what Professor Tomczyk, this walking ghost, was doing reached the ears of Otto Grundtz, he merely continued to observe the old man, noticing that each day he seemed feebler. But his head was still held high and the sunken eyes still flamed. He had seen phenomena like this before in Field Four; the average Pole was a pathetic thing, a subhuman type who wilted in adversity and did not resist being dragged off to Barracks Nineteen. With no food at all, the man would just stay asleep, comatose one day, dead the next—and no harm done. But a few men, sensing death upon them, seemed to pour all their energy into their hearts, and their eyes and their voices. These men died on their feet; he concluded that in some devious way they must have got German blood into their life systems. Perhaps in centuries past, some German warrior had come this way, leaving his precious seed, which had continued uncorrupted; he could imagine no other explanation for the behavior of men like this Tomczyk.

Once he satisfied himself that the old professor was spreading lies and cultivating anti-German attitudes, he knew that he must be stamped out, so on one cold morning after the inspection was finished he directed his guards to bring Tomczyk to the headquarters of Field Four, the small stone house outside the fences, and there he interrogated him. "What is your purpose in disseminating lies about the Third Reich?" he began, and to his amazement the old man collapsed and cringed like a frightened child. He wept, he pleaded, he threw himself upon the mercy of the commander, and whatever Grundtz proposed, no matter how contrary to what he had been preaching to the men in the barracks, Tomczyk agreed.

"Poland is a fifth-class nation not worth preservation."

Tomczyk nodded.

"It is Germany's destiny to bring order to the east."

Tomczyk nodded.

"A superior race must under God's will subdue and rule an inferior."

Tomczyk agreed.

And slowly, as Grundtz continued, laying bare his soul and identifying the drives which motivated him and justified him in slaughtering hundreds and thousands, he began to realize that this man was making a fool of him, leading him on, encouraging him to divulge the horrible sickness in his soul.

In the end Grundtz was screaming at Tomczyk, who stood placidly agreeing with everything: "You are laughing at me. You've been tricking me. You don't believe a word of what I've been saying." With a mighty blow, he knocked him clear across the room, then pulled him to his feet and began hitting him about the face and head, but Tomczyk did not stop smiling, and agreeing, and nodding whenever he had a chance to control his head.

Exhausted and somewhat ashamed of having lost his temper with such an old fool, Grundtz smoothed down his rumpled uniform, resumed his seat at his desk, and looked up at the old man who, miraculously, was still able to stand. "I know what you really think. You think the Russians will drive us back one day. You think the American bombers will destroy Germany. That's what you think, isn't it?"

"No," Tomczyk lied, "that's what you think."

Now real screaming began, real hammering punishment, until Tomczyk's face was distorted and knocked sideways. When at last he fell unconscious, Grundtz shouted for his assistants: "I want every Pole and every Jew in Field Four in formation at the gallows, now!" When the men said that some were working outside the fences, he shouted: "Get them!"

So a guard ran to the shoe-repair shop and brought the two Field Four men who worked there back to the gibbet, and the squared lines were formed, and the little white stool on which the condemned man would take his last stand was put in place. The prisoners were confused as to what was happening, for there had never before been a hanging except at morning muster, but here came Otto Grundtz with three guards who were half-carrying the victim, and voices whispered in hushed affection: "It's the old man."

For the first half of the walk from gate to gallows, his feet dragged, but when Tomczyk reached the waiting square and moved past his own men, he braced himself, tried to control his almost crippled legs, and walked with awkward dignity through their ranks and to the gallows.

"This man has been spreading lies against the Third Reich," Grundtz bellowed. "He has proved himself an enemy of the new order. He has forfeited his right to life."

It was the cynicism of the sentence which infuriated Bukowski, the infamous insincerity at a time of death. In Germany's eyes, every man in that field had forfeited his right to life by being either a Pole or a Jew, and to specify any further fault was insane. He wanted to scream against the lunacy, but, helpless, he stood silent.

When Tomczyk mounted the gallows, the prisoners could see his face, how it had been abused, jaw knocked to one side and broken, teeth kicked out, and they were sickened, but as the noose was put about his neck the old man shouted: "Rebuild! Rebuild!" And he was trying to shout it again when the stool was kicked away.

The iron discipline with which Konrad Krumpf governed the movement of food through his seventeen villages made it more and more difficult for Biruta to sequester any of her wheat kernels or grind them into flour for the baking of illegal bread. Also, Krumpf's fanatic determination to reduce further the local use of fallen branches, so that more could be shipped to Germany, meant that she could seldom use her oven. Krumpf maintained a watch on chimneys, and if unauthorized smoke was seen emerging from them, his men were ordered to break into the offending kitchen and confiscate whatever was being baked and to arrest the woman if any loaves were being made beyond quota.

So the midnight quern ceased operating, and the men in the forest had to forage even more for their existence. One night, against his better judgment, Jan Buk sneaked into Bukowo to plead with his wife for more bread, and she had to inform him that Krumpf had made this impossible.

"What shall we do?" Buk asked in desperation, and they considered for some moments the possibility of throwing themselves on the mercy of Ludwik Bukowski at the palace.

"He's a Polish patriot," Jan reasoned. "He'll see he has to help us stay alive," but Biruta pointed out something her husband had apparently forgotten: "Konrad Krumpf lives in the palace," and he surprised her by actually laughing: "That's where we always do our best work. Under their noses." And in the darkness he told her in broad general terms, so that she would not be able to divulge secrets if questioned, of how the men always attacked a train near some German headquarters or stole from a commissary close to the Nazi barracks: "They feel secure in numbers and leave themselves vulnerable." She remarked that he was using bigger words now, and he said that he was working with bigger men, men of education and savage purpose, but then the question of more food returned, and she had to tell him truthfully: "We in the village suspect that Ludwik Bukowski is collaborating."

"If so, he should be killed," Jan said without hesitation.

"But we're not sure."

"You think it would be fatal to approach him?"

"I wouldn't, Jan. Because no one can trust him."

"But the old woman? The American?"

Biruta pondered this question a long time, then conceded: "All we know of her is good. She helps us with the babies." Then she added quickly: "But as I told you, Krumpf lives there."

It was almost a challenge, to grab food from under Krumpf's nose.

"Approach the old woman. Plead with her."

Jan was so famished that he accepted with no embarrassment or apology his wife's last bit of bread, her final scrap of cheese, rationalizing that in the village she could eat somehow, whereas in the forest he could not. But as he wolfed down the last morsel he chanced to look at her and saw that her mouth gaped with hunger.

"My God! What are we doing to Poland?" he cried, and with both arms he reached out for her, kissing her furiously and almost sobbing upon her shoulder: "Forgive me for eating your food."

She could not speak. In the darkness she could only return his kisses, and as she did so, a stalwart woman who refused to acknowledge fear, he realized the peril in which he had placed her through his pressure on her to provide him with bread, and in the passion of that moment of intense love he left her, uncovered the quern and clutched it to his breast. "It is too dangerous to leave here. If you were lost, Biruta, I would . . ."

"Don't speak it," she said, placing her fingers on his lips. "You'd fight on, that's what you'd do, and we both know it." But the quern that would have ensured her death was taken into the woods, where the partisans could not use it, for they had no grain to grind.

The wisdom of Jan's action in removing the grinding stones was demonstrated two weeks later when Konrad Krumpf organized a master sweep through the village, his men probing into corners overlooked before. Four cottages away from Biruta's the investigators found a buried quern, and without even granting the woman a trial, they hanged her from a village tree. Their eyes ablaze with victory, they descended upon the Buk cottage, and soon they found the secret hiding place in the corner where wall met floor, and when they ripped it open they expected to find grinding stones; instead they came up with a chain made of woven hair from a cow's tail on which was suspended a curious pentagon-shaped medal dating back to some pre-Christian time.

"What's this?" a soldier asked, and Biruta said truthfully: "We've always had it."

"Why was it hidden?"

"It's our good-luck charm."

This was too complex for the men, so they summoned Krumpf, and as soon as he saw it he surmised that it must be some early Germanic medallion, a souvenir of the time when Teutonic greatness began, and he snatched it from the soldier. As he stomped off with his prize, Biruta thought: How strange. A man from this village, centuries ago, took that medal from a pagan. Now the pagans have reclaimed it.

Like Professor Tomczyk in his final desperate days, Biruta felt a consuming urge to share with the children of Bukowo whatever knowledge she had acquired, and she realized that she could teach them only if she could set up some kind of illegal school. In the parts of Poland outside the General Gouvernement, even the speaking of Polish was punishable by beatings and long imprisonment; if persisted in, it could mean death, for those areas were now officially part of Germany and neither Poles nor their language existed, but in the General Gouvernement, which was to remain semi-Polish until the race died out, oral use of the language was grudgingly permitted, though any printing of it or education in it was forbidden, and this meant that schools for children no longer functioned.

As Konrad Krumpf had explained when the villagers first protested: "In the future, Poles will not be going to college or even high school. You will grow food and make things for use in Germany."

Biruta herself had had an imperfect education, no more than seven years of partial schooling, but she so appreciated the tremendous difference even that little had meant in her life, an understanding so superior to that of her mother, who had started work at five, that she was now determined the children in her village would learn to read and write. So she organized an informal, secret school, which met at odd hours in odd places, and when she saw the bright little faces looking up at her, grave faces aware of the forbidden thing they were doing, her heart grew big with pride and she taught with an efficiency she did not know she possessed. She loved the children and wanted to see them grow in knowledge, and the villagers encouraged her because they knew that even if Krumpf did discover the clandestine school, he would punish her and not the children.

It was through this school that Biruta had met Madame Bukowska from the palace. Biruta was with her children one morning, all of them just standing in the village square looking at things their teacher had been telling them about, when Madame Bukowska had walked past, stopped, and inquired as to the children's health.

The villagers had always known the Madame as an interested, generous woman. They knew that she was not Catholic, but it was always she and not her son who had helped the priest in whatever programs he had arranged for the children. It was she who purchased little books in Warsaw and candies for the feast days. She refrained from attending the large religious festivals of the church, holding that they were reserved for the believing Poles, but she did often appear at Sunday Mass, occupying the place which had been reserved for Bukowskis since the church began seven hundred years ago.

In the weeks following that first meeting, Biruta had occasionally seen the great lady and always treated her with deference, not because she felt any subordination to the Madame, but rather because it was possible that one day she might need the American's help. Now was such a time, and for three anxious days Biruta awaited her next encounter with the lady of the palace, and one morning she saw her coming into the square.

Madame Bukowska dressed with elegant touches, a hat just a little larger than one might expect, a bit more lace or filmy material, and never in the funereal black that Polish widows seemed to prefer. In fact, the villagers often wondered why she remained in Bukowo when her wealth would have entitled her to live anywhere pleasant in the world. One day she had explained to the priest: "This has been my home since 1896. That's almost half a century. Also, my paintings are here, and this is the land I love." Then she had looked back toward the palace: "I built that building, from plans I sketched on a schoolgirl's tablet. I cannot leave it now it's endangered."

As the great lady of the district passed through the square, Biruta accosted her: "Madame, may I speak with you?"

"Of course. What do you hear from your husband in Germany?"

"He was allowed to send only one card."

"Of course." She spoke Polish with a delightful, almost childish accent. "These are trying times. Your name again?"

"Biruta Buk."

Marjorie Trilling Bukowska was silent for a moment, recalling those distant days when as a young bride her life was entangled with that of the Buks. "Let me see, your husband's father . . . no, his grandfather. Didn't he fight with my husband at Zamosc?"

"He was killed there."

"So he was. So your grandmother . . . his grandmother, that is, must have been Jadwiga?"

"Yes. She was hanged over there."

"Yes, yes." She could visualize Jadwiga, young and arrogant and so very capable. She remembered Jadwiga most forcefully, for she had learned some of her Polish from that sturdy young woman.

"Madame," Biruta said in a burst of confidence, "our children are starving. They must have food."

"Indeed they must. No matter what happens, children must not be allowed to go hungry."

"I was wondering if you . . ."

"If I could give you some extra food?" To Biruta's surprise she broke into laughter. "Dear child! Don't you know that Konrad Krumpf lives with me? That his men watch like hawks everything I do? Because I'm an American and they suspect me, even though they live in my house. I could not give you even a crust, Biruta, not even from my purse now, for over there they are watching me. And if you are seen talking with me too long, those clever men will sooner or later guess about you and your school."

"School?" Biruta repeated in astonishment.

"Yes, your school," and the slim, erect woman in the faultless dress walked away.

For six days they did not see each other, but on the seventh, Madame Bukowska passed Biruta in the square, and in the briefest possible exchange, told her: "I know you want the food for the men in the forest. I cannot help, but Count Lubonski might." And she was gone in a flutter of gray and creamy lace.

Before Biruta could bring herself to do anything about the startling suggestion made by Madame Bukowska, the two women met again. Biruta was with her children—not in any formal structure, but more like an earnest mother showing her offspring the trees and the storks nesting on the chimneys—when Madame Bukowska passed idly by, stopped to admire one of the little girls, and said: "If you want to feed your husband in the forest, do see Lubonski. That one's a great patriot."

"My husband is in Germany," Biruta said. "And I have no school."

"I shall pray for you ... and your husband ... and the little ones," Madame Bukowska said, and tears filled her eyes, but regardless of whether they were real or not, Biruta could take no chances: "My husband is in Germany, and I have no school."

For two weeks she continued to teach her students, at night, in the early morning, now in some barn, now boldly in the church, and then she slipped through the forest to Castle Gorka and asked to see the count, and when Gestapo sentries guarding the castle demanded to know the nature of her errand, she said boldly: "He wants to hire a maid," and they forced her right into the castle and shouted for the count. When he appeared from an upper floor the Nazis asked: "Are you expecting someone looking for work?" and upon seeing the young woman, he said instantly: "I'm seeking a maid," and they left her with him.

"What causes you to risk your life?" he asked when they were upstairs and alone.

"Madame Bukowska sent me."

"For what reason?"

Now came the terrible moment when she must trust a man to whom she had never before spoken, a man whose credentials she did not know, a man who could cause her to be shot within the next few minutes if she judged him incorrectly. But the fate of all Poland seemed to hinge upon her that day, and whereas she had known instinctively that the Bukowski palace was corrupted and must not be touched, the same instinct assured her that Castle Gorka was an inherent part of Poland and could be trusted.

Taking a deep breath, she said: "The men in the forest are starving."

Without altering his expression in the slightest, Count Lubonski replied: "I conduct no traffic with partisans. Now get out of here," and he called for the Gestapo to remove the girl, but before they reached the second floor he told Biruta in calm, even tones: "In the barn away from the river and near the beech trees we keep wheat and sometimes a freshly slaughtered pig."

When the Gestapo arrived he told them: "This one won't do. She doesn't know how to bake. If you come upon a young woman who can bake in the German style, let me know." And Biruta was dismissed.

She returned to her village with thundering heart, but the problem now was how to deliver the message to her husband, and she pondered this perplexing question for some days, because there seemed no rational way by which she could get into the Forest of Szczek or find her husband if she did, for Krumpf maintained patrols which even skilled woodsmen like Jan Buk had difficulty penetrating. She thought of sending some child sneaking through the trees, but in the end she concluded that she and only she must undergo the danger of such an excursion.

For several days she made herself conspicuous in the village square, lest anyone had missed her when she went on the secret trip to Castle Gorka, and then one evening as the sun was going down she studied the disposition of Krumpf's troops, and as soon as darkness fell she headed into the forest.

Her plan was to continue in a straight line, using the stars as her compass, until she was intercepted by someone. If it turned out to be a Nazi patrol, she was dead. No, she told herself repeatedly to nerve herself for what might happen, I would not be dead. They would torture me first, maybe pull out my fingernails or cut off my toes. No, I would not be dead. But I will not betray our men. I will not betray my husband. She walked through the night, catching glimpses of the guiding stars now and then through breaks in the trees, and she encountered no one. During the first segment of daylight hours she slept at the foot of a huge beech tree, but by midafternoon she was back on the trail, heading always eastward, and toward dusk the great Forest of Szczek lived up to its name, for she heard a clinking sound, and when she crept toward its source she spied from behind her tree a small group of young men who were obviously not Gestapo patrol and who might be partisans.

For more than an hour, as darkness deepened, she studied the men, and when she heard them speaking Polish she judged that she could make her frightening gamble. Remaining behind her tree lest they fire at her in fright, she cried: "Polish men! I am over here." And still from the safety of the tree she waved a hand.

They ran to her, seized her, and led her to their quarters, where they tried to determine who she was, while at the same time she was endeavoring to find the same answer about them. Gradually her suspicions abated and she satisfied herself that they were indeed partisans, but whether they were members of her husband's group she had no way of ascertaining. She could tell them his name, but they might know him only by his code. In fact, she did not even know the name of the group to which he belonged, for he had not wanted to burden her with that fatal knowledge in case the Gestapo interrogated her. But she did know that somewhere in this considerable forest her husband was hiding, and starving.

"My husband is with you," she said, and now they had to be suspicious, for she could well be some silly village girl whom Konrad Krumpf had suborned to act as his spy. Everyone in Poland had to be an object of supreme suspicion, and she was not excused.

They questioned her for a long time, and now she had to be circumspect, lest one of them be trapped by the Nazis and tortured for information. So the battle of misinformation continued, the men lying to the woman, the woman to the men, and that night nothing was settled, but next morning when she intimated that she might be able to deliver food, they had to pay attention.

They decided, after much angry debate among themselves, that they must take this woman to another camp, and although two of the most outspoken members warned against it, still not convinced she wasn't a spy, the others prevailed, and they walked a far distance through the woods, and after signals had been given and answered, they took a carefully prescribed route to where a larger group lay in hiding, and in the bright noonday sun filtering through the treetops, Biruta saw her husband and ran toward him joyously and embraced him and started to weep with overwhelming joy, mumbling through her tears: "You will have food."

At Majdanek it was always understood by the Gestapo officers running the camp that they must provide the factories whose branches had been erected outside the gates with a steady supply of slave laborers for whom the employers paid nothing but whom they were obligated to provide one meal a day. The firms who participated in this scheme were some of the most respectable in Germany; before the war they had operated subsidiaries of distinction in cities like London, Sydney and New York, their advertisements appearing proudly in such magazines as *Life* and *The Illustrated London News*.

Prisoners who were detached from Majdanek to work in these plants entered a bizarre world, for they worked all day in what was an almost normal situation, even given a real lunch, then returned at night to barracks where Otto Grundtz still dominated their lives. They were also threatened by a curious fact of human behavior: the German civilians who operated the plants were never in actual charge of the slave laborers; that job was handled by a Gestapo detachment. But since any Poles assigned to the factory were already stigmatized as being criminals, their civilian bosses were prone to treat them as such, and more Majdanek men lost their lives because these civilians brought arbitrary charges against them than were shot because some Gestapo guard took a dislike to them. It was a risky game, working in the civilian plants, and Majdanek men learned that they must jump to any task and show enthusiasm and pay great deference to their civilian supervisors, or they would die.

The compensations, however, more than offset the risks. Men worked on tasks which made sense, and not the cruel make-work of the camp. They worked with other intelligent human beings and saw the results of that work. And they received real food, not ersatz stuff that was only marginally digestible.

The deadly temptation, of course, was sabotage. Since the plants produced armaments, anything that retarded the process helped Germany's enemies, and if a product could actually be destroyed or rendered useless by inserting some defective part, it was the same as if an Allied shell had struck the plant. So sabotage occurred constantly, and men were killed at their machines for attempting it. A civilian inspector would suddenly scream: "This is sabotage!" and a Gestapo guard would run up, listen for a few seconds, put a pistol to the back of the offender's ear, and fire—right in the factory.

And yet almost every Polish worker devised some new and hellishly clever way of obstructing the system. Shells would leave munitions plants after the most careful inspection, then blow up just as they were being fired, killing an entire crew. Or the gearbox of a truck would suddenly grind to a halt, its various parts fused together in one lump. Sabotage was an infinite game of chess, played with death as the adversary, and some Poles played it with exquisite skill. But there were also some German overseers who possessed a fiendish ability to anticipate it.

When Szymon Bukowski was detached from his shoe-repair job and delivered like a sack of sand to the Berlin Electric Laboratories, whose plants in Pittsburgh and Chicago had made superb components before the war, he entered a contradictory world, for he had two supervisors who earnestly wanted him to master their machines and who gave him every encouragement to do so. They were highly trained men, experts in their specialty, who recognized him as their equal in basic abilities and potentially their equal in ultimate mastery. For them to have a prisoner like Bukowski was a privilege.

They accepted no nonsense: "One suspicion of sabotage, Bukowski, and you'll be shot. You've seen what happens." But they never ranted, like many of the other supervisors: "You're making this machine for the greater glory of the Third Reich." They did their work because a good machine was an admirable accomplishment of itself, and they intended to make the best. There was not much sabotage in their division because they rid themselves quickly of men who had no respect for good work and treated with friendliness those who did.

However, Bukowski quickly learned that something was badly wrong in this section of the B.E.L., and one day he even overheard the two men referring to one serious aspect of the problem. One said: "If we could only keep a man like Bukowski permanently," and the other replied: "It's that damned Mannheim." Bukowski began to look about him and discovered that his managers were right; as soon as a Majdanek prisoner became proficient in the intricate processes of assembling electrical devices, he was taken off the job and returned to the camp, where he was given the most menial tasks or the most brutal and destructive heavy labor, as if Otto Grundtz was determined to punish him for his vacation at B.E.L.

Then it happened to him. Just when he had mastered all the procedures in his section at B.E.L., he was yanked off the job and assigned to the heavy concrete rollers that graded the camp roadways. Also, it seemed to him, he invariably found himself in the kitchen lines that received the worst food, and he realized that any strength which he had acquired at B.E.L. was dissipating.

He was therefore pleased when he was again assigned to the cadre at B.E.L., and when he reported there he was further pleased that the managers of his old section recognized him and requisitioned him for their assembly line. Soon the good lunches at the factory restored both his energy and his enthusiasm, and he was once more almost happy at his work. The evening and morning torments that Otto Grundtz applied to all men taken away from his daytime jurisdiction could be borne, but there was another problem which disturbed him mightily. With Professor Tomczyk dead, he had no older man with whom he could discuss his dilemma, but he did seek out a prisoner whose intransigence he admired, a forester from the Tatra Mountains.

"I think the things I'm making go into German tanks. Inspection is constant and they shoot any saboteur. What is my duty?"

"Burn the damned factory down."

"Even though they're watching every move?"

"Burn it down."

Szymon received little helpful guidance that first time, and not much during later discussions. The mountain man was simplistic and advocated that everyone react as he did. Late one night he whispered:

"The governor general, Hans Frank himself, came to Zakopane and us mountain men were told to dress in colorful costumes, so bagpipes paraded and we danced and the girls flared their skirts like it was four hundred years ago, and Frank cried: 'This is the real Poland!' and he went back to Krakow and gave orders that a free state was to be erected in the mountains, with every consideration. Brotherhood of Mountain Folk, it was to be called, and we were to wear our costumes all the time and every boy was to be taught the bagpipes, and when peace came, tourists from all over Germany would come to admire us. We were to do a lot of woodcarving too.

"By God, he meant it! He established the Brotherhood of Mountain Folk and made that horse's ass Krzeptowski king of our new nation or president or something, and documents were printed up, and stamps were to be issued.

"Do you know what we did? We held a meeting in a barn and said: 'There's only one thing to do about Krzeptowski. Hang the dumb bastard.' So while the Gestapo was out of town we put a rope about the king's neck and hauled him sky-high and left him there. The Gestapo went crazy and shot half a dozen men and sent the rest of us here. A man who arrived the other day told me that Frank has decided not to go ahead with the separate kingdom. Said the mountain people weren't ready for it."

One morning as Bukowski stood in line for roll call before being taken to B.E.L., he noticed that the deadly square was being formed about the gibbet. Then he saw Otto Grundtz leading the forester to the gallows, and when the big, undefeated man stood on the stool he heard him bellowing: "Burn the fucking place down!" and the cries rang in Szymon's ears for many days.

Then one day after he had completed the normal tour of five months at the Berlin Electric Laboratories, followed by a hideous six weeks digging burial trenches for Jews shot in the fields, he was again returned to B.E.L. The two supervisors welcomed him with a half-bottle of really good German wine and made him a kind of super-visor, not of his fellow Polish workmen, for that job had to be filled by Germans, but of the flow of materials into and out of the plant, and it was while performing these duties that he found on the floor an important-looking document which he knew at once he was not supposed to read, but without attracting attention he bent down, scooped up the paper, and stuffed it in his trousers.

At mortal risk to himself, he smuggled the paper back to Barracks Eleven, but when he tried to read it he found that he could not, for it was in German, and for three days he could find no one to translate it, but finally a man at the far end of the barracks came, took it in silence, returning later to read it in whispers. "It's called 'Control of Calories,' written by Dr. Siegfried Mannheim:

> "We have established that a grown man doing hard manual labor requires thirty-five hundred calories per day, nicely distributed between fats, carbohydrates and proteins. In such a diet vitamins take care of themselves and no additives are necessary.

> "At Majdanek the diet for enemies of the Third Reich who are to be liquidated after their period of usefulness is nine hun-dred calories, which is satisfactory if the prisoner is to do brute work without regard for nervous control. However, when such men are moved into the plant of B.E.L., they are not capable of doing the delicate work we require. They ruin more than they make and not always because they are sabo-teurs. I believe that at least half the men who are regularly shot for sabotage committed theirs because they were too weak to prevent it.

> "Prisoners reporting to B.E.L. must have a daily intake of at least eighteen hundred calories. With that they can perform

our tasks, which do not require brute strength but do require eye and hand coordination.

"But now we face a problem. At nine hundred calories daily and hard work, the prisoners remain docile, concerned only with their next meal and childish plots to steal even one extra crumb. They are easily controlled. But at eighteen hundred calories they begin to regain strength and mental acuity, and first thing you know, they are complaining about ventilation, light, quality of the food, freedom and things like that. With our good food we create problems for ourselves.

"This seems like a vicious circle, but it can be broken. We must note carefully the date at which any man leaves Majdanek and enters B.E.L. and keep him on advanced rations for only five months, which seems to be the exact time when he begins to cause trouble. At the end of these five months he must be sent back to Majdanek and hard work, with a daily ration of nine hundred calories. This will break his spirit, and after seven months of this we can use him again at B.E.L. without fear of his causing trouble.

"From other plants which have used convict labor since 1937, there is evidence that after a man has been up and down this calorie ladder three or four times his usefulness at B.E.L. is exhausted. Psychologically and physically he seems ruined, insofar as good work is concerned. Therefore, at the conclusion of his last assignment at B.E.L. the prisoner should be returned to Majdanek, given the hardest labor possible, a daily ration of seven hundred calories, and be encouraged to disappear."

When the horror of the document was revealed, Szymon knew that it must somehow be delivered to the underground, for if it could be smuggled out to London, it would prove the inhumanity which was being exercised with full knowledge and support of distinguished German industries, but the man who did the translating refused to accept any responsibility for handling the document: "Too dangerous. They'll shoot you if they find you with it."

So the task remained Szymon's, and for three perilous days he carried the paper about his middle, where it became well stained with sweat. On the fourth day he ran enormous risks to slip it to a Polish woman who worked on the B.E.L. food line, and she in turn gambled her life to spirit it out of the factory, where other members of the underground displayed their own heroism in moving it out of the country and eventually to Washington.

There an official of the State Department, Jefferson Rigaud Riverton, studied the sweat-stained document as it lay on his desk, turned it over distastefully several times, then pushed it away with his fingertips, telling his assistant: "Jewish propaganda. And not very cleverly done. File it." Eleven years after war's end it would be found in a crowded drawer, but even then it would not be believed.

Calories had a similar effect on the Stork Commando, for after the men had made frequent raids on the remote barn at Castle Gorka and got decent food in their bellies, they developed a daring they had not had before, and one day just as the titanic battles were developing at Stalingrad, producing the first tremors to attack the Nazi leaders of the General Gouvernement, Jan Buk devised a sortie which delighted his men by its ingenuity and terrified the Nazis in Krakow by its boldness and its nearness to their headquarters.

Nineteen members of the Stork Commando slipped past the defenses of Krakow but did not go into the city itself; they went a short distance west to the prehistoric site of Tyniec on the Vistula, where under the shadow of ancient ruins they assembled a large raft made of logs and whatever floatables they could find. On it they piled an immense amount of dynamite stolen from various Nazi installations over the past year and a half. They covered this with the kind of hay used to feed cattle in winter, then donned heavy clothes and submerged themselves in the river, leaving two farmer types atop the raft to guard the hay.

The seventeen swimmers propelled the raft rapidly toward the city of Krakow, and when they reached the big bridge that connected the south side of the river with the north, they hid under its protecting arches and at night conveyed their dynamite to a plant that generated electricity for much of the city. With great patience and almost unbearable risk they managed to cut wires, avoid alerting guards or activating signals, and plant their charges right against the walls. From a distance so short it would have terrified a professional dynamiter, they detonated a tremendous blast which destroyed much of the plant. Then, with forged passes, they slipped into the crowd that gathered to watch the fires and with brazen dexterity made their way out through Gestapo cordons, returning to their forest.

The fury which Governor General Hans Frank felt when a plant on his doorstep was dynamited did not endanger the Stork Commando, for his intelligence officers assured him that the partisans must have come from the Katowice area, since none could have penetrated from the east, and he initiated harsh reprisals against the westerners. He did, however, transmit to all his subordinates a surprisingly accurate estimate of his own:

> "Because security in Krakow is so intense, I think we must assume that the terrorists came from outside, possibly from a good distance. I rule out nothing, not even as far away as Warsaw. Therefore, regardless of where your command is, I want you to assume that it was your people who committed this crime. Remember that nine Nazi workmen died in this blast, so we are dealing with murder. Act accordingly."

When Konrad Krumpf received these instructions he interpreted them as encouraging him to do something that he had intended for a long time. There was no possibility that partisans from his district could have committed the crime, but there was good reason to suppose that some of the Poles of his village were passing foodstuffs to partisans hiding in the forest. He therefore ordered a renewed search for hidden caches of wheat or private querns which were converting that wheat into flour and bread.

To the captain of the searchers he confided: "Someone, it doesn't matter who, has suggested that this woman Buk might be bringing food to the partisans. She might still have a grinding mill." The captain interpreted this, no doubt correctly, as an invitation to bear down on Biruta in hopes of extracting information, so after another thorough search of her cottage, which again disclosed nothing, he ordered her taken to the interrogation quarters at the far end of the village, and there he himself questioned her.

He did not torture her; that would become known in the village, to the detriment of order. He simply knocked her down with his fist whenever her answers did not please, and each time she rose from the floor, bleeding from the mouth and unsteady, he questioned her some more, then knocked her down again when her stubbornness persisted.

He continued this for several hours, always missing the true facts but always coming very close: "While your husband is working in Germany, you have a lover in the forest, don't you? He sneaks into your cottage at night, while we aren't looking, doesn't he? Is he strong and good in bed? Do you love him as much as your husband?"

She said nothing, and he hit her again, but now he changed his attack: "Who says your husband is in Germany? Has anybody seen him in Germany? I know about the postcard and the official report, but who really knows? Do you know what I think? I think your husband is here in Poland."

Again she made no response, so more blows rained upon her, until at last she simply lay still where she had fallen, unable to bear any more. But even then she refused to acknowledge even by wince or whimper that he had come close to the truth.

He let her lie on the cold floor for nearly an hour, after which, of her own accord, she rose as if to ask "What now?" and after a while he sent her home, warning her to tell no one what had happened at the interrogation, but her face was so bruised and her gait so unsteady that she needed to say nothing.

She had defeated his interrogation, yet unknowingly he had gained a significant triumph, for he had made her afraid to risk teaching her children. He thus deprived her of the last possible act she could perform to demonstrate her enmity to the German occupation.

She went back to her cottage, and sat there, no light lit, and stared at the floor.

On the late afternoon of 2 November 1943 the new commandant of Majdanek, SS Obersturmbannführer Martin Weiss, a soft pudgy man who did not like to look anyone in the eye, received in code a set of instructions which launched his tenure dramatically: SUBJECT UNDESIRABLES. YOUR CAMP BADLY OVERCROWDED. HARVEST HOME ACTION.

On 3 November when the prisoners mustered in darkness, Szymon Bukowski became aware of unusual movements, and before dawn Otto Grundtz came storming down the line picking out men at apparent random, whereupon the troopers who followed grabbed each man indicated, throwing him forward. Bukowski was so nominated, for what no one knew, but when he saw the others who had been chosen he realized that they were all younger men with modest strength still in their emaciated bodies, and he had to assume that they were going to be shot because they were taking too long in their dying.

When the selections had been made, twenty-nine of them, the men were marched away, as always happened when there were to be mass executions rather than individual hangings. When they reached the three lines of electrified barbed wire that marked the exit from Field Four, the gates were opened and they were led right through, then ordered to go left toward the execution ground, a hill where machine guns could dispose of many prisoners at one time.

It was now dawn, and walking bent against the bitter wind that blew in off the endless flatlands, Bukowski thought how pitiful it was to die for no reason at all. Professor Tomczyk had been hanged because he was trying to strengthen the moral resistance of the men in Barracks Eleven. The mountaineer from the Tatras had died because he was a real revolutionary. But this group of young men had done nothing specific, they had uttered no battle cries for freedom, nor had they opposed the Third Reich in any detectable way. They were simply being shot, and he remembered his resolve not to die in this supine way, but he could devise no way to escape. He was powerless, unable to make even a protest, and he knew it: I am so weak. I am ashamed.

But then from the far end of the camp, from the fields near the main gate, came two other lines, one of men shivering in the thinnest of rags, many of them barefoot and without caps—thin, wasted men. The second consisted of women and children, hundreds of them or even thousands, frail creatures, some too weak to walk by themselves; other women helped them. Spryest were the children, especially the young girls of seven and eight, who walked with a certain eagerness as if glad to be out of their constricted field at last.

Almost every adult person in the two lines looked near death from starvation, and it was clear that these prisoners had received even less food than those in Fields Three through Six, and Bukowski wondered why this had been. Then he saw with horror that everyone in these endless lines wore the Yellow Star. He was not going to be shot. They were.

The code name for Jew was *undesirable,* meaning that the leaders of the Third Reich had decided that there was no way by which these people of a different religion and, the Nazis claimed, a different race could be fitted into the great, clean Germany that was to evolve. Up to now, Majdanek had disposed of more than a hundred thousand Jews, but with the possibility that the Russian army might one day soon break through the German lines and overrun the great death camps like Belzec and Treblinka before the task of killing all the Jews in Europe was completed, the high command had decided, in a rush of panic, to get rid of all remaining undesirables now, when it could be done in an orderly way.

A thousand Jews marched up the hill that cold morning, then five thousand, then fifteen thousand, more than the population of some places on the map labeled cities, and the hardened men from Field Four, who had seen death in almost every guise, felt great pity for the old men and women who could barely struggle to their place of execution, and overwhelming grief when they saw the children, especially the young ones not old enough even to dress themselves. Szymon Bukowski was especially shaken by the awful parade, and as he approached the execution ground he did not know if he could control his emotions.

When he reached the top of the hill he saw that two squads of machine-gunners were in place on the western edge of a deep trench, and he realized that the Jews would be marched along the eastern lip, where they would be gunned down. His job would be to throw the piles of corpses into the trench so that the next batch of undesirables could be harvested.

The first contingent was a mixed group: about forty older men, a few youths, twenty women, and nine children from the age of two or three to fifteen. They stood in the dawn, facing their executioners, and the last sight they saw was the lovely skyline of Lublin, the medieval towers of the churches, the fine high profile of the castle in whose chapel men and women like themselves would be tried that day, and shot, and tossed down the stairwells.

Rrra-rrra-rrra-rrra! The machine guns stuttered. Bodies slumped forward. Otto Grundtz and two other Gestapo officials walked down the line of fallen, administering with their revolvers the *coup de grâce* to any body that moved. And then the cold, dispassionate voice of a superior commander: "Throw them in the ditch."

All day the lines moved up the hill, all day, at ten- or fifteen-minute intervals, groups of Jews took their places along the edge of the pit, and from the tangled bodies below they knew what awaited them. Some prayed. A few sang. Women reached to clutch children who were not their own, and boys and girls in their early teens simply looked bewildered.

Rrra-rrra-rrra-rrra! Hour after hour the dreadful killing continued, until more than eighteen thousand were slain, and as the lines began to dwindle, a man whispered to Szymon: "When the Jews are finished, they shoot us, you know. They always do. Want no witnesses." So as dusk approached, Szymon Bukowski, this honorable man, the son of a woman of superlative decency and the grandson of a woman who had stood for all that was good in Poland, found himself hoping that the fields would disgorge a few more Jews so that he could live a few more minutes.

But on this day they did not shoot the burial crew. Someone forgot to give the order.

Even when the deep pits with their awful plantings were covered over in the careful way a farmer piles earth over his seedlings so that crops will grow, and when the hill showed only slight mounds running parallel one to the other, the day's work was not finished; typists in various buildings compiled endless lists of those executed, their numbers, names, birth dates, regional derivations, dates of death and presumed causes—and not a single Jew died unrecorded:

NR.	NAME	VORNAME	GEBURTS-TAG	HAFTART	TODESTAG	TODESURSACHE
12,187	Grunwald	Neftali	28-3-12	Roman, Jude	3-11-43	Lungentuberkulose
188	Selig	Israel	1-4-22	Ungarn Jude	3-11-43	Lungentuberkulose
189	Kirschner	Solomon	14-3-22	Italien Jude	3-11-43	Lungentuberkulose
12,190	Blechman	Isidore	9-9-27	Nederl, Jude	3-11-43	Lungentuberkulose
191	Seidenwar	Judko	11-7-08	Greisch, Jude	3-11-43	Akute Herzschwäche
192	Blum	Dawid	23-6-07	Slowak Jude	3-11-43	Akute Herzschwäche
193	Brzosowski	Piotr	13-8-24	Polen Jude	3-11-43	Akute Herzschwäche
194	Jiszko	Antoni	19-3-26	Polen Jude	3-11-43	Grippe
195	Kozlowski	Stefan	7-7-27	Polen Jude	3-11-43	Grippe
196	Przebik	Stefan	4-5-05	Polen Jude	3-11-43	Grippe

The methodical masters of Majdanek saw nothing preposterous in recording that on 3 November 1943, an exact total of 18,431 people died at almost the same instant of tuberculosis, cardiac arrest or the flu, and that all of them happened to be Jews. SS Obersturmbann-führer Martin Weiss had executed his first important assignment with distinction.

· · ·

At seventy-one, Marjorie Trilling Bukowski had to admit that the tensions of war were affecting her health adversely, and she listened attentively when her son Ludwik recommended that she heed the invitations she had been receiving from friends in Chicago and return to the States, where better care would be available.

"How can I leave one battle zone and cross through enemy lines to another?" she asked, and her son's reply terrified her: "I have friends. There's a constant exchange of prisoners."

He has friends, she thought. And who would they be, that they can authorize such traffic? It was clear that he must be referring to his Nazi associates, and that raised the most difficult questions, for the only one of his German friends that she knew was Konrad Krumpf, and to associate one's self with him would be dishonorable.

She was forced to dine with Krumpf about four nights a week, but there were compensations: he provided the palace with large supplies of good food, and the meals gave her an opportunity to observe her son, whose uncertain future had always bothered her. He was like his father, not like her, a vague and ineffectual man whose refusal to marry or even to court seriously had perplexed her. Hesitancy about sex had certainly never been a weakness of his father, whose occupation in Vienna had been chasing pretty girls, and why Ludwik should have become confused in this vital area she could not specify, but she guessed it might have something to do with his falling between two worlds, her international interests and his father's rural concern with horses. All she knew was that for some sad reason Ludwik Bukowski, heir to two splendid palaces and a large income from funds invested in Illinois, was a most unsatisfactory man of forty-three. It was by no means clear how he would behave in the crisis which she could see approaching from the east, where Russian armies, to her alternate joy and apprehension, were beginning to gain impressive victories.

She was delighted that the German terrorists were tasting defeat, but as the daughter of an eminent American capitalist, she suspected that Communist victors would prove almost as vicious as the Nazis, and she wondered if Ludwik would be strong enough, or clever enough, to protect this marvelous palace from either the retreating Germans or the incoming Soviets. She had good reason to think not. So now, as she sat in the resplendent hall where Paderewski and

Caruso and Sarah Bernhardt had shared spectacular nights with her, with Ludwik at her right, Konrad Krumpf on her other side, she felt the world slowly falling apart and the stones of her palace falling with it.

She had only one hope. During the long middle years of her marriage with Wiktor Bukowski she had often felt as gloomy about his prospects as she now felt about Ludwik's, yet he had survived for that one glorious day at Zamosc and was now, as the portrait at the far end of the room proved, a permanent actor in Polish history, The Hero of Zamosc. But there had been a difference. Dear, weak, frivolous Wiktor had never faced real moral temptation; true, he had behaved rather poorly with the serving girl Jadwiga and not too sensibly with the pianist Krystyna Szprot, but the monumental moral questions of treason and the meaning of civic life had never confronted him. When the war bugles blew he mounted his horse, and kinetic energy took care of the rest. Poor Ludwik was going to have to confront problems infinitely more complex, and his mother was not reassured by what she saw as the lights grew dimmer.

"I've done what I promised," Krumpf announced one night at dinner.

"You mean with Berlin?" Ludwik asked.

"Yes. My message went direct to Goering and he's just let me know that he'd be delighted."

"Now I am pleased," Ludwik said, but when his mother asked about what, he became evasive.

Krumpf, however, proud of his accomplishment, was eager to talk. "When I first visited with you, Madame Bukowska, I told you how impressed I was, how favorably impressed, that is, with the Hans Holbein you have in my room. That you should have chosen a German painting for a place of honor pleased me very much. I thought of it a great deal, the honor you had paid our country, and I sent a report to Hermann Goering. He's making a major collection, you know."

Marjorie felt faint. This wormy little man, making deals behind her back regarding her paintings. She shivered to think of what he was going to reveal.

"For a year I heard nothing, and believe me, it's frustrating to be here at the end of the line, you might say, and hear nothing. I had rather hoped that Goering would become excited by the Holbein, or maybe the Correggio, but one of his aides told me when I asked during my visit to Berlin, 'Goering already has a big Correggio,' and he accented the word *big* like I just did." He laughed at himself, then confessed: "To tell you the truth, Madame Bukowska, I didn't know what I hoped to win for myself with this information about the Holbein. A promotion, maybe. A summons to be on Goering's staff, maybe. I really didn't know."

"Do you know now?" Marjorie asked acidly.

"Well, Goering's man assured me that if the field marshal takes a liking to the Holbein—and I sent three excellent photographs—the matter of the train might be arranged."

"What train?" She noticed that her son was most uneasy.

"Ludwik proposed it," Krumpf said with real enthusiasm, "and I approved immediately. I saw every reason to support the idea, and I did, in writing, to the field marshal."

"What train? What would it do?"

With calculating eye and swiftly moving gestures with both hands, as if he were a country auctioneer, Konrad Krumpf indicated the treasures in this grand room—the gold chairs, the centerpieces in their cabinets, the paintings, the silvery chandeliers—and by extension, the wonders in the rooms above. "Ludwik said that it would be a mortal shame if anything happened to these treasures . . ."

"You mean the Russians?"

"Oh, no! The Russians will never reach here. You can be assured of that."

"What did you mean?"

"Well, frankly, under the Fuehrer's plans for Poland, for its extinction, that is . . . I don't mean gentry of quality like you or Count Lubonski. I mean only the unspeakable peasant and the impossible shopkeepers in the villages. In the new Poland there'll be no place for a palace like this, a center of education and refinement."

"Where would the train carry the treasures?"

"To Berlin."

She wanted to say, with bitter force, that Berlin was being bombed nightly by the Allied planes and that her treasures would be much safer in Bukowo than there, but she refrained, conscious of the absolute power this unpleasant little man had over her. She asked simply: "Is that wise?" and received an answer which stunned her.

"I believe arrangements could be made for the train to pass right on through to Paris."

She could not believe what she was hearing, but then her son said:

"Goering has indicated that if we give him the Holbein and three of the statues, he will permit us to carry the rest of the treasures to Paris."

"What an extraordinary arrangement," Marjorie said. "Whatever would we do with them in Paris?"

"What do we do with them here?" her son asked.

"They grace a building which is inextricably a part of this land, this edge of the Vistula River, and no other. Each piece, Ludwik, was brought to stand in proper relation to each other. Those two paintings . . ." and she indicated the two magnificent panoramas that summarized so much of Polish history.

"Oh," Krumpf said. "We've already discussed them. Goering or nobody else would want them. They're purely local, with no significance at all. We wouldn't take that other big one, either, the one that's nothing but water lilies. But even leaving them behind, which we would have to do, Ludwik and I calculate we'd need seven goods wagons from here to Paris."

"I do believe that you and Ludwik might have consulted with me," she said. "They are my belongings, each item purchased with my money."

Krumpf did not have the gall to state the truth bluntly; had he been alone with her, he might well have done so, pointing out that she was a worn-out old woman who would soon be dead and commanding her not to meddle in decisions reached by her superiors with great difficulty. Instead he said: "Under the new rules this palace became your son's at the moment his father died. These are his treasures now, regardless of who paid for them. And he is being very wise, I think, in completing these arrangements now."

She could not keep herself from asking: "Before the Russians come?"

Krumpf's voice rose to a high scream: "You stop that! If you say that where others can hear you, you can be shot. For treason."

"I am sorry," she said honestly. "These are difficult times."

"They are," Krumpf said, resuming his customary manner. "And I think your son has been rather brilliant in handling this affair. A train of seven cars, all the way to Paris. I can tell you that when Ludwik first proposed giving the Holbein to Goering, I prophesied it wouldn't work. We'll be crating the Holbein tomorrow for a special truck heading for the mine outside Berlin where the field marshal is collecting the paintings for his new museum."

So it was Ludwik who had arranged this infamous deal, and as she looked to where he sat before the Matejko painting of Jan Sobieski on his way to Vienna, she wondered what other things he had done behind her back—what hideous price had he paid the Germans to have won their permission to obtain an entire train? And she began to count up the strange happenings at Bukowo—the capture of young Szymon Bukowski, the beating of Biruta Buk, the executions of the women grinding illegal wheat—and she saw that in every instance the clever identifications by the Nazis would be understandable if they had within the Polish community someone who was feeding them information. Could it really have been her son?

When the carpenters crated the Holbein, sending mournful echoes through the palace, she did not run to catch one last glimpse before the lid was nailed down; she carried that painting in her heart. But as she sat at dinner that night at one corner of the vast table which could have seated threescore, she felt terribly alone, even though Krumpf and her son were in their usual places, and when the German asked her why she was so sad, she said: "Painters do strange things. They put the image on the canvas and at the same time on the hearts of all who ever own it."

She left the generous table where Krumpf and some of his men ate extremely well, and wandered not to the upstairs, where her Rembrandt and Correggio and Jan Steen still waited, but down to the lower floor, where that narrow, poorly lighted gallery housed the portraits of Polish nobles long dead, and as she walked along with a flashlight, she illuminated each face and spoke to it as if the owner shared her misery:

"Radziwill, you damned Lithuanian conniver. You were always smarter than the Poles you competed with. I would have enjoyed crossing swords with you. You were clever and genetically prolific, and that's a good combination for those who would rule.

"Old Mniszech, it was you who determined who should sit on the throne of Russia. What a devious, powerful rascal you were. And Jan Zamoyski, I would have loved to be your daughter. We would have understood each other, you a minor noble who became head of the University of Padua and owner of whole cities and wise governor of men. What savage husband would you have found for me?

"And you, Czartoryski, how I admire you! Tyrant, manipula-
tor of princes, but always the defender of women's education
and the father of Lubomirska. I wish I had been educated at
your feet, old man."

And there in the darkness, when she allowed her torch to dim, she
burst into tears and asked aloud: "How could I love Poland so much
and Ludwik, my own son, love her so little?"

Signals flashing through her tired body sent unmistakable messages that her remaining days might be few, and she felt that she must
dedicate what energy she had to try to bring reason and responsibility to her son, and to this end she arranged to be with him whenever
possible.

"Ludwik, I can see now that someone like Goering was bound to
get some of our paintings, and you've probably done a clever thing in
buying him off cheaply."

"That was my thinking. You know, Mother, the future here is
extremely obscure."

"I don't think so. I think the Russians will sweep over here like a
hurricane. They'll probably burn the villages, but they'll leave this.
They enjoy museums."

"You think the Germans are doomed?"

"Of course I think so. I know America. I know her factories. Ludwik, when they get cranked up, as they say, they'll keep turning out
tanks and planes for twenty years, if it takes that long. I know my
nephew Lawrence in Detroit. If it takes till the year two thousand, he
and others like him will still be working."

"You believe that, Mother?"

"The amount of time? I don't know. The end result? There can be
no question. We will see American airplanes over this palace." She
paused, startled by her own vehemence and by the alteration it made
in her relations with her son and his adviser Krumpf. "I am sorry to
have disclosed my hand so openly, but I feel very weak these days and
thought it better be said."

Ludwik, trembling with apprehension lest the Germans learn that
his mother was a defeatist who could be shot—and Konrad Krumpf
was a man to do the shooting—could think of nothing to say. It
would be undignified to plead with his mother to keep her mouth
shut, for he knew she would not. And there was no way he could prevent her from voicing her opinions at table if she felt she was about to

die. The simplest solution would be if she really did die, and sooner rather than later, and he reached this conclusion not through callousness, but because he could see that the decisions which had to be made now were of a magnitude and definition which she was simply too old to understand. Marjorie Trilling, heiress of Chicago, had quixotically fallen in love with a nation she had never seen realistically, and now those days of romance and imagination were ended. She was as out-of-date as her palace, and he prayed that she would vanish without causing irreparable damage.

She sought certain assurances: "Ludwik, my family was a proud one. My grandfather was a country druggist, an apothecary, and he gave honest count in his prairie town. He couldn't do otherwise. The Bukowskis in this little village never had much, you know. Always had to jump and do what the various Counts Lubonski directed, but they were known as men of solid honor. I don't want you to do anything, not the slightest thing, Ludwik, that would scar our honor."

"Whatever do you mean?"

"I mean Krumpf. His job is to drag you down and destroy you. His job is to destroy Lubonski, to destroy everything Polish. He tolerates you because you live in a palace, and when he has no more use for you, he will cut your throat."

In the long silence that followed, Ludwik, inheritor of the palace, was forced at last to study the real moral issues that confronted him. Finally he said, very slowly: "I know that Krumpf is using me to gain a promotion of some kind, but principally to gain escape from here. I think he's terrified of the Russians. I think he will do anything to get away, and that's why I was able to get him to make the deal on the train."

"But what will you do with all these treasures in Paris?"

"Sell them."

His mother could offer no sensible comment, so she ignored the statement. If her son believed that he could find happiness by selling off his mother's possessions in a strange city, so be it. But she could speak about the graver issues: "Ludwik, you're Polish. You're not even half-American, because I became Polish years ago, heart and conscience Polish. So in saving yourself, you must not do anything to the detriment of your nation."

Ludwik licked his lips, looked at his mother finally, and promised: "You will not find my name on Krumpf's golden cards."

"What do you mean?"

"I came upon him one day when he was working, as usual, on his cards. Poles who could be trusted. Poles who would be shot if arrested. One color for each. And I noticed a small pile of much different cards and I asked what they were, and he quickly covered them up. But he did say: 'Those are the ones who will have positions of importance in the new Poland we shall create here, the German Poland.' And he said meaningfully: 'I hope your name will be on one of those cards soon—the people we treasure.' I could guess what a Pole had to do to get on that list."

The image of Konrad Krumpf hunched over his cards, ordaining who should live and who should die, was so compelling that Marjorie could think of little else during the remaining days of her life. Early one morning, after Krumpf had departed to supervise the execution of nine hostages in one of his villages down the river, she walked casually along the second-floor hall and looked into the Holbein room to see if Krumpf's secretary was there, and finding him absent, she entered as if to check the spare space where the painting had been, but when she satisfied herself that no one was likely to interrupt, she took a deep breath, hurried to Krumpf's desk, and began rummaging for the stack of golden cards.

Finally she found it with the neatly lettered top card proclaiming that the persons hidden underneath were people of prudence willing to act in the long-range interests of their country. Trembling, and aware of the suicidal thing she was about to do, she took paper and began writing down the forty-three names.

As she was at work, she heard footsteps in the hall, and assuming it to be Krumpf's secretary, who would occupy the room from then on, barring her escape, she supposed that she was doomed, but on the chance that something might happen to save her, she scooped up the cards, grabbed her paper, and darted into a closet, where she waited in darkness, trying to control the palpitations of her heart.

It was not the secretary. It was two minor Gestapo functionaries come to make entries in the card system, and they went to the very section from which she had taken the golden cards.

"Hello, the commander left the drawer open! He'd bite us if we did that."

"He's busy these days."

"Do you have Biruta Buk's card? She's a bad one."

"I can't understand why he just doesn't shoot her."

"I think he's using her as bait. She's passing food to the partisans, you know."

"Everybody knows. He'll trick her yet. You watch."

The men made their entries, returned the files, and closed the drawer. When their footsteps retreated down the hall, Marjorie went to the desk, spread her cards, and resumed transcribing them. When she was finished, and had replaced the file, she thought: I'm glad my son's name was not among them. At least he's not an actual traitor.

She folded the precious piece of paper and held it in her left hand as she walked down the hallway. She paused at the entrance to her theater, where she could hear Caruso singing and Paderewski at the piano, then descended to the great hall and looked as if for the last time at her two mammoth canvases, nodding to the defenders of Czestochowa and saluting Jan Sobieski. She walked casually from the palace, gazing with love at those sights which had always enchanted her. There was Wiktor's grandiose stable with its array of handsome carriages. There was the chimney on which the storks built their messy home each year. Beyond were the immortal beech trees, those castles of the forest. And straight ahead was the little village in which so much life evolved. She loved that village and its irregular square, and she loved the people who had occupied it, bold Jadwiga most of all. From this powerful woman she had learned her first real words of Polish, and in this square she had seen Jadwiga hanging by the neck.

She walked twice around the perimeter, pausing now and then to inspect shops that contained nothing, and then she spotted her target. Biruta Buk, limping from the punishment she had absorbed during her interrogation, unable to smile because of the wounds across her face, appeared at the far end and saw Madame Bukowska immediately. Sensing that the old woman would not be here without good reason, she walked slowly toward her, and as the distance between the two diminished, each could see in the other exactly what she had hoped to see.

Biruta had been beaten close to death, but she still walked proudly, almost defiantly. Madame Bukowska was old and tired and nearly worn out, but she still displayed that inner radiance which comes only from a life actively spent in defense of purposeful ideals.

When they stood face to face, Marjorie leaned forward like a village busybody to inspect with her right forefinger Biruta's scarred cheeks, but with her left hand, so that none could see, she delivered the fatal list of names.

"Kill them all," she whispered, and when Biruta gasped at such a message, Marjorie took her by the shoulders and turned her sideways so that light could fall upon her damaged face, as if she wished to see it more accurately. "They are the traitors. Kill them all."

Abruptly she dismissed the peasant girl as if she, Bukowska, were still gentry from the great house and Biruta the serf, and then resumed her passage about the square, but as she reached one of the corners she half-stumbled sideways, as if struck by a cart no one could see. Then she staggered twice, reached out for a handhold that was not there, and died in the sunlight.

When the apparently distraught son was told that his mother was dead, he could not prevent himself from thinking: God's mercy.

Because Poland continued to play such a vital role in the eastern theater of war, the attention of its patriots had to focus on what was happening along the battle lines in Russia, and every inch of territory regained by Soviet troops was greeted joyously by those partisans who saw in Communism the path that Poland must take when peace came, and with growing apprehension by those more conservative men who had begun to hear rumors of how the Russians were behaving in towns they recaptured.

At first Jan Buk sided with the pro-Communists, cheering the Russian victories, but when rumors of a massacre of Polish officers at a place called Katyn Forest began seeping in, he had to wonder: Hundreds, maybe thousands, murdered by the Soviets. Shot in the back of the head. He found it difficult to believe such accusations, and when the radical partisans explained that Germans had really done the killing, he accepted their version.

But then he heard the pro-Russians describing the way they wanted the new Poland to be, and he was not pleased with the prospect of surrendering his farm to the management of others, and he was downright displeased with their proposal to outlaw the Catholic church.

The debate took a sharp turn when the radicals started abusing the Allies for accomplishing so little in the west when the Soviets were fighting so valiantly in the east: "Cowardly Allies! Hiding behind their Channel. Afraid to tackle Hitler. Leaving the Russians to fight the war alone." Such speakers held the efforts of the English and especially the Americans in contempt, but on several occasions Jan heard others argue differently: "Watch! When the great push comes, those Americans are going to hammer Hitler." He could not make up his mind who was right.

However, at midnight on 17 August 1943 the British had performed an act in their western theater which bore no apparent relationship to the war in Poland but which did subsequently alter the whole complex of warfare along the Vistula, plunging Jan Buk into the very heart of the wider conflict of which he had previously been ignorant.

An immense formation of heavy British bombers from various air bases in England and Scotland had flown across the North Sea, crossed Denmark in darkness, and dropped down low over the inconspicuous village of Peenemünde at the edge of the Baltic Sea. Here they had dropped a tremendous freight of high explosives upon laboratories, manufacturing centers and barracks in which Adolf Hitler's most formidable secret weapon was being readied for the destruction of London. Damage caused by the mighty bombs was immense, fires started by the smaller incendiaries completed the damage, and although the German air force retaliated, the lumbering British bombers made their escape, bomb racks empty.

The raid did not obliterate Peenemünde, for its installations had been strongly built and cleverly camouflaged, but it did cause great anxiety, for if the bombers had come once with such striking success, they could come again. So a two-part decision was made: move the manufacturing elements for the secret weapon to underground sites deep inside Germany and move the testing of the weapon to some relatively unoccupied corner of Poland, from which the weapon could be fired onto empty land, Russian or Polish.

The site chosen by the German high command for the assembly and testing of the weapon occupied a polygon, one base of which was formed by a line between Castle Gorka and the Bukowski palace. Since test firings of the secret weapon might carry it far toward Przemysl and empty lands beyond, the experts who had been working at Peenemünde said: "An ideal location."

And now everything changed. Bukowo became a major battleground in the war. Where there had been one German soldier, twenty appeared to guard this vital secret. Where there had been two Gestapo men checking on the citizenry, there were now six. Railroad spurs were built overnight. Buildings appeared mysteriously, their roofs covered with forest branches to prevent detection from the air. Truckloads of workmen came from remote Polish villages and trainloads of technicians from Germany.

When six of Konrad Krumpf's villages were overrun by the new demands for secure space, so that every Pole had to be evacuated to find such quarters as he might, there was protest, and Krumpf personally warned that this must cease: "We must all make sacrifices for the Fatherland."

But the forced evacuation was so brutally carried out that serious objection had to be voiced; peasants were being treated worse than animals, and they said so. One village in particular, with the grandiose name of Nowa Polska, the New Poland, was especially abused, and its three leading farmers went to see Krumpf, who had always been attentive when the continued production of foodstuffs was involved.

This time the protesters met a man much different from their familiar, bumbling Konrad Krumpf. The high command, recognizing the supreme importance of the weapon which now dominated the Gorka-Bukowo polygon, had sent to supervise the operation a man with a brilliant record of administration and a ruthless determination to succeed once more. He was Falk von Eschl, forty-seven years old, scion of a family whose forebear had fought with the Teutonic Knights at Grunwald in 1410, Rhodes scholar at Oxford University in the 1920s, and diplomat in various capitals of Europe.

Tall, slim, a fine tennis player who had once been Baron von Cramm's doubles partner at Wimbledon, he was a man of unusual talents, especially that of self-preservation. Not a Nazi and often contemptuous of their grosser acts, he saw them as the only agency that had the power to lead Germany to a position of world dominance. His years at Oxford had satisfied him that Great Britain could provide no leadership at all, and the Americans he had met there, most of them Rhodes scholars like himself, were beneath contempt: "Country boors who know nothing, lack all character, and have no insights whatever."

The Nazis did not like him or trust him, but they did need him, for he had an uncanny perception of what steps ought to be taken to achieve sought-for results, as he now proved when the three farmers appeared before him to protest the destruction of their village.

"We will go there and see," he said in broken Polish, acquired by dint of forced study in the brief time since his appointment, and he allowed the farmers to lead him to their village. When he reached there, he indicated to his accompanying soldiers that they were to line the protesters against a wall and shoot them, and this happened within four minutes.

His troops then rousted all the villagers from their cottages, and every man was shot dead as he appeared. Six women who came screaming at Von Eschl were also pinioned, stood against the wall and gunned down. By this time the other women and the children were pacified through sheer terror, and in this condition they were expelled from the village while their homes were razed.

Falk von Eschl had the designated area cleared and ready for tests two weeks earlier than expected, and he spent this grace period training his personnel in their new duties:

> "Any Pole who trespasses into a restricted area without a signed pass is to be shot at the moment he is apprehended, and without further consultation. Anyone smuggling food is to be shot. For any sabotage, you are to execute six hostages. And if any Pole so much as touches a German soldier or workman in anger, appropriate steps will be taken. And you can assure the natives that such steps will become increasingly severe. The Third Reich is nearing victory, and what you accomplish here will make that victory possible.

> "You are here to protect the most precious secret our nation has today. It must be defended with your life. If any one of you betrays even one word of what you see, you will be shot. And if any Pole or any member of the so-called underground is allowed to catch even a fleeting glimpse of what we're doing, he is to be shot instantly."

While these draconian measures were being fine-tuned, Von Eschl had an opportunity to inspect the civilian areas bordering on the secret range and to give some attention as to where he might live during the extended period of his command. Naturally, he visited the Bukowski palace, but saw at once that it was too pretentious, and already occupied by Konrad Krumpf, for whom he had only contempt, and by the weak and silly owner, Ludwik Bukowski, whom the advance reports had described as worthless and to be ignored.

With the methodical and judicious approach for which he was

famous, he decided quickly that the logical place for his headquarters was Castle Gorka; it was clean and strong and not exhibitionistic like the palace; it was well situated in relation to where the work would be done; and its owner, even though a Pole, was a person deserving of respect, for he had traveled widely, he spoke both German and English, and he had a well-matured understanding of the world. He was probably also a secret supporter of the Polish underground; that made the relationship more exciting and in the long run it might be profitable, for if he could unmask a man like Lubonski, he would strengthen his claim to significant promotions when Russia and the Allies were finally defeated.

He summoned Lubonski to a meeting, and was astonished at how much like himself the Pole was: several years older, hair nicely grayed while his own was still black, most of his teeth apparently, the reserved bearing of a man who rode horses well, and that mastery of languages which marked the European gentleman. But there was a deeper similarity that intrigued Falk von Eschl: Walerian Lubonski gave the appearance of a man of fierce commitment who could absorb much punishment and still keep fighting.

"I've decided to make my headquarters in your castle," the German said. Lubonski nodded with just the right degree of deference. "You may continue residence, but only in the upper rooms." Again Lubonski nodded. "My men will convert two of your barns into barracks."

"Of course," Lubonski said.

"This fellow Bukowski, at the palace. Is he as stupid as he seems?"

"His father, you know, was a great hero at Zamosc. In the 1920 battle against the Communists."

"I didn't know that."

"It has been an excellent family. For a thousand years."

"That I did know. One of his ancestors fought at the Battle of Tannenberg in 1410."

"What we call the Battle of Grunwald," Lubonski said quietly.

"Where one of your ancestors fought, too."

"And one of yours, as well. With the greatest distinction. Von Eschl is an honored name along this river, especially with my family." When the German diplomat realized that this clever Pole had briefed himself on the Von Eschl record, it was his turn to nod graciously.

So the sparring began, and when Von Eschl had time to look into records with his customary diligence, he discovered a most disturbing fact: on several different occasions a Lubonski barn had been raided and food supplies stored there had been stolen. What attracted Von Eschl's attention was the fact that it was always the same barn, which led him to believe that there was some kind of connivance going on between the count and the partisans.

He therefore baited that particular barn with an extra supply of unground wheat and established near it a concealed bunker manned every night by men with powerful guns; but he was not able to conceal it perfectly, and one morning as Count Lubonski was leaving the castle he spotted the disturbed earth, which had been unsuccessfully smoothed down, and guessed what it meant. He alerted one of his servants, who alerted a woodsman bringing fuel to the castle for the German contingent billeted there, and this woodsman warned the Stork Commando that it could no longer obtain food from that cache.

Von Eschl, suspecting some intricate maneuver like this, drove over to the Bukowski palace to do something which irritated him immensely: he had to consult with Konrad Krumpf to learn what kind of record that stupid Gestapo underling had been able to compile on Lubonski, and for the first time he was able to inspect the remarkable card file assembled by Krumpf. It was extraordinary that this seemingly dull man had completed such a splendid work, and he ran through the purple cards with extreme care, noting every name that Krumpf had identified as potentially dangerous. Count Lubonski's name was not there.

"We've heard rumors," Krumpf said. "Persons who could be part of the infamous Stork Commando have been seen in the vicinity of your castle . . ." Von Eschl noted the subtle introduction of the phrase *your castle,* as if Krumpf were now throwing the problem into his lap. Perhaps the man was more clever than he had at first supposed.

"What are those other cards, the yellow ones?" As Krumpf's acknowledged superior, he reached for the small carefully guarded file, and although the Gestapo man objected to surrendering it, Von Eschl insisted, and after he had studied the cards, he assembled them into a neat pile and started shoving them back to their owner, but as Krumpf reached out to recover them, Von Eschl kept his own hand firmly on them.

"Is it wise to have such names in a list? I mean, in a list anywhere but your own head?"

"This file is secure. Only I touch it."

"I'm touching it, now."

"You're my superior. In this particular operation."

"If I were you, I would burn those cards. They're terribly dangerous. What I mean, these people are very vulnerable. Surely you see
that."

"Is that an order?"

"I would never give you an order, Major Krumpf. We're partners
in protecting a secret of inestimable importance."

"But you recommend burning?"

"I do," and Von Eschl casually lit a match and reached for a wire
basket. While he held the match, Konrad Krumpf with considerable
anguish held out the first card and watched it burn. Dropping that
card into the basket, he surrendered one card after another to the
flame until all forty-three were consumed.

"I feel infinitely safer," Falk von Eschl said. "If anyone had seen
those cards, even someone like me . . ." He paused. If this man had
been careless enough to maintain such a file, he might be stupid
enough to inform others of its existence. "Have you ever told anyone
about this file?"

"No. Not even my assistants knew."

"Not anyone? Not some village girl, perhaps? No one?"

"No one," but as Krumpf spoke he remembered that Ludwik Bukowski had once come upon him as he was consulting the cards, and
the hesitation that came into his eyes assured the older man that
someone else had known, and that the contents were no longer secure.

He said no more to Krumpf, but he did assign one of his best men
to make a detailed study of all unusual deaths within the villages
under Krumpf's command, and then the pattern stood forth in brutal clarity: "In this village a woman was run over by a runaway
wagon, but the bruises on the back of her head were not matched by
any wagon marks on her face or chest. In this village a man was shot
accidentally while hunting. This man drowned." From Krumpf's list
of forty-three traitors to the Polish cause, so far as Von Eschl could
remember names, eight had died mysteriously, and as he talked with
his agent he could not know that the Stork Commando was even
then executing a ninth, at the very edge of the polygon.

• • •

From London a Polish officer and an English scientist who had taken a crash course in Polish dropped by parachute into northern Czechoslovakia. They made their way, with the help of the underground of that country, into Poland and the Forest of Szczek, where the Pole told Jan Buk and his commando: "It is vital, more important than anything we have ever asked before, that we know for sure what's going on inside that forbidden area."

Buk said: "We're engaged in a vital process of our own. Wiping out collaborators."

"No longer," the Polish officer snapped. "You're to direct every effort to providing this man with solid information on what the swine are doing in there."

"But we know nothing," Buk said honestly. "We've counted the trucks and watched the trains, but we haven't even a guess . . ."

The scientist had to concede the common sense behind Buk's complaint; if the commando didn't know even the outlines of the thing whose details it was seeking, what possible intelligence could it collect? So he told the partisans: "If what the Germans are doing is so secret with them, it's doubly secret for us. We think Hitler's perfected a completely new kind of weapon with the capacity to wipe out London." He had been empowered by the Allied high command to divulge the problem to the men on the site if that became inescapable, so after two days of cautious assessment of the men and the leadership of the Storks, he concluded that if anyone could be trusted, these veterans of the forest could:

"When we hit Peenemünde with the most powerful armada we'd launched to date, we didn't really know what our target was. The Americans have cause to think the Nazis were making heavy water there, peroxide we call it, for some new kind of bomb. Devastating it would be, I'm told.

"We British are convinced that what they were building was a radically new type of flying bomb. Germany to London in one swoop. Tremendous explosive head in the nose.

"Your job and mine is to determine what in hell it is they *are* doing. If the Americans are right and it's peroxide, we'll see tremendous explosions when they test it. Something quite spectacular, I'm told. If we're right and it's a flying bomb, we'll see them flying through the air. So we'll listen and watch.

But I must inform you of this most stringently. We do not know, we cannot predict, what little fragment of information will prove most valuable. Something so small we'll overlook it, that might be the key that unlocks the riddle. And if we do not unlock it, London may be destroyed and the whole western effort abandoned."

The forest men were sobered by the gravity of the situation in which they were now involved, by its opaque definition and their own inability to penetrate the security rim established so effectively by Von Eschl.

"I heard about him at Oxford," the Englishman said. "Fantastically good. He'll stop at nothing to frustrate us."

For five weeks the men of the Stork Commando and this dedicated Englishman stayed in the forest, watching, listening, but learning nothing. Behind Von Eschl's perimeter they could see, from various treetops, much hurried activity but not a single object that would indicate what that activity involved. One daring man carried a small Leica camera aloft to photograph with long-distance lenses the terrain inside the stout wire fence which had now been erected for miles, and these undeveloped films were spirited back to London by messengers who risked death each day as they crossed Poland, Czechoslovakia, Austria and Italy before they reached the Allied air base at Bari. When they were studied by English and American experts, they revealed nothing.

So far, Von Eschl's security had allowed no intelligence to seep out of the polygon, and it had accomplished certain unexpected triumphs of its own. Convinced that Konrad Krumpf's list of Polish traitors had somehow been compromised and that Polish patriots were engaged in a process of killing them off, one by one, he used as a kind of bait a farmer who had betrayed several underground operations. The man, who had to be a likely target for execution, was allowed to go unattended to his field, and when the expected attack was launched against him from a grove of beech trees, the three Poles conducting it were overcome before they could harm him. One commando was killed, the other two tortured to death without revealing anything.

The increased Nazi forces also enabled Von Eschl to make broad sweeps into the forest, and two retreats of the Stork Commando were overrun, with loss of life. The English scientist, rescued narrowly from one by virtue of heroic covering action by his Polish friends, understood better the hardships these men had faced incessantly for so long. "The beaters do try to drive you into the guns, don't they?" he joked, but it was obvious that he was disheartened.

Then, on a bitterly cold day in December, the German scientists inside the polygon reached a point at which they must test one of their devices, and a number of Stork Commandos at various lookouts through the forest heard a vast, prolonged explosion, after which a monstrous cylindrical object rose slowly in the frosty air and soared to a great height, then began a swift descent toward an unoccupied area downrange.

With quivering excitement the English scientist assembled his spies and compared their interpretations of exactly what had happened, and aided by his learned guesses as to what the explosion must have been, he put together an accurate profile of what the dreadful V-2 rocket was going to be like when it struck London, but before his report even reached London, something much more dramatic occurred.

One of the rockets, headed toward Przemysl, soared into the air, became confused, turned about, and roared westward almost directly at Castle Gorka, but at the last moment it went north, crashing into the Vistula River some distance north of Bukowo. With heroic effort, Jan Buk and the Englishman, accompanied by four powerful swimmers, burst out of the forest, dashed to the river's edge, swam out to the foundering rocket, and sank it with a tangled mass of ropes and stones, then hid in the woods to laugh at six different detachments of Von Eschl's men as they dashed up and down each side of the riverbank looking for their wayward rocket.

A Polish farmer on the opposite side of the river, who had watched the rocket splash down near him, convinced the Germans that it had flown over his head and landed far inland, and off they went.

From the Warsaw underground a team of Polish scientists with cameras and intricate tools sneaked down to Bukowo, entered the river at night, swam to where Jan Buk guided them, found the rocket, dragged it to the western shore and dissected it. Burying the vital parts on the farmer's land, even though he knew this was a sentence of death if he was detected, they informed London that they had the guts and sinews of a rocket bomb. The hope was that the Allies might be able to counteract the devilish bombs when they began to hit London . . . if the information could be spirited out of Poland,

flown across Europe, and delivered to General Eisenhower's headquarters. For the moment such delivery was impossible, but the determined Poles spent long hours trying to devise some daring trick
that would help defeat the Germans.

Now the war raged toward its climax, and as tremendous news surged
out of Russia—"Leningrad breaks its siege, Vitebsk is freed, great
victories in Ukraine"—the individual battles of the Polish occupation accelerated. Count Lubonski, aware that his guest Falk von
Eschl was setting traps for him, continued quietly and bravely his
support of the underground, determined to set some traps of his
own; like cobra-and-mongoose the two distinguished gentlemen engaged in thrust and parry. Konrad Krumpf, holding on to a secret
letter which he hoped to use effectively, had to protect himself from
Von Eschl but at the same time keep Bukowski and his trainload of
treasures safe until such time as both could be moved out of Poland.
Jan Buk and Biruta had to be suspicious of everyone yet continue
their personal warfares against the invader. And inside the charnel
house of Majdanek, Szymon Bukowski had to study with the instincts of a ferret every whim that possessed Otto Grundtz lest that
capricious dispenser of death and life drag him some morning to the
gibbet in Field Four.

At the conclusion of his last assignment with the two compassionate managers at B.E.L., he noticed that they said goodbye with
what came close to affection: "Take care of yourself, Szymon. You're
a good worker." Then he learned that Dr. Mannheim had decided
that Bukowski had been up and down the calorie ladder so often that
he had become disoriented, as such prisoners invariably did, and was
thus of no further use to the Third Reich. When Szymon was returned to Majdanek this time, it was with instructions that he be
placed on a diet of seven hundred calories, given the most strenuous
work possible, "and be encouraged to disappear."

He was assigned to the concrete rollers, and day after day, with
bare hands, he had to grasp those ice-cold iron handles and exert almost superhuman effort with his team to move the massive rollers
back and forth so that the roads, in the words of Otto Grundtz,
"could be nice and a credit to the camp."

It was soon obvious that a prolonged assignment to the rollers
would kill Bukowski, even though he had started with his body in

good condition after his spell of decent food at the factory, and he began to connive at ways to conserve strength, to keep his mind a blank, and to waste his energy on nothing at all, to feel no resentment at the morning hangings, or at Otto Grundtz's brutalities, or even at the monstrosity of Majdanek itself, with its continued Zyklon-B administrations to the Jews and the constant burnings at the crematorium.

The terrible risk in the weeks ahead, he realized, would be that some morning Grundtz might find him in a coma and move him into Barracks Nineteen, where without regaining consciousness he'd soon starve to death. This, with the help of God, he would avoid. He had watched with horror as those eighteen thousand Jews had died passively at the pits, and he swore to himself that he would not allow himself to be killed that way. But even as he voiced this resolve, he remembered how powerless he had felt that cold November day when he believed that it was *he* who was about to be executed; poor Jews, they never had a chance.

For one spell of three weeks he thought of absolutely nothing day or night but a glass of cold beer he had once enjoyed in Sandomierz. He could see every drop of sweat on the glass, each millimeter of level as the foam subsided. He could hear the echo of the filled glass when it was placed before him, the changing tone as he set it down after each sip. He could taste the difference between the pure froth, the froth with a little beer mixed in, the beer with no froth. He spent twenty-one days drinking that glass of beer, and was so preoccupied with it that he did not notice the deterioration of his body, but others whispered: "It won't be long now. The rollers take everyone to Barracks Nineteen."

He then transferred his imagination to a supper served at the wedding of a well-to-do farmer, where huge platters of sauerkraut, sausage, boiled pork and pickles had been provided, one to each of six tables, and he had helped himself piggishly, moving from one to the other so as not to reveal his gluttony. He recalled this particular feast for two reasons: as a peasant, he knew that the acid bite of the pickled kraut was good for him, all peasants knew that and it was one reason why they survived so long; and he could see in the rich fat of the meats the strength that came from them.

Now when he absolutely lusted for something, anything, to eat, his mind oscillated between the two benefactions of that long-ago feast: the vitamins that keep a body alive and the rich fats that keep it strong, and after a while his mind focused only on the latter, and he imagined himself luxuriating with platters of butter, or grease, or pork drippings, or oil that rich people bought from Spain, or the golden globules at the edge of a roast, or plain lard.

"Oh God!" he cried one day as he toiled at the freezing handles of the roller. "I want something with fat on it." He knew that he could not go on much longer with this excessive labor unless he had some fat intake.

But then a miracle happened. Each barracks had at its entrance a good, strong cot provided with warm blankets, its own bucket of water and clean eating dishes. This was always occupied by some newly recruited Gestapo man whose job it was to keep order and forestall incipient subversion. For some time it had been the quarters of a weak-chinned city lad, but when he showed signs of cracking under the strain of watching so many of the prisoners die from starvation, Otto Grundtz requisitioned a new man, and he received a most unlikely replacement.

Willi Zimmel was a round-faced, towheaded, good-looking farm boy of nineteen, with flashing blue eyes and a congenial grin. He liked people, and was so gently simple-minded that he refused to see Majdanek as the charnel house it was.

In his Rhineland village he had been an early volunteer for the Hitler Jugend, whose mysticism and battle drills delighted him; he interpreted it as a kind of superior Boy Scouts, which he had intended joining before it was outlawed. He loved marching; he thrived on camping; military drill excited him; and he invariably considered heroic any older man placed over him. On two occasions his troop had been ordered to smash Jewish stores and beat their owners, but he did this with no malice, and now, suddenly promoted to full membership in the Gestapo, he felt no animus toward the prisoners he was to guard. As he told his mother in his first letter home: "They've all done something wrong and must be in jail for a while," and he refused to believe that every man in his barracks was slated to die.

When he first saw the physical condition of Barracks Eleven he was appalled at its messiness, those hundreds of double-decker planks, each with one filthy blanket, those lines of men who had not washed in months, the scores with infestations of lice about which they did nothing, and he took it upon himself to improve matters. But only through exhortation, never with any ration of soap or lice powder or better food: "Men, you must develop self-pride. You simply cannot live decently with lice crawling everywhere." He always harangued them as if they wanted the lice, as if they had plenty of soap but refused to use it. He assured them every morning at muster that if they would but wash themselves more carefully, look out for the cleanliness of their sleeping spaces and spruce themselves up generally, they would feel better.

Then, remembering the joy he had found in the Hitler Jugend programs of physical exercise, he initiated at morning muster a series of gymnastics made popular by the Sokols in the 1920s. In his well-fed condition he found these energetic movements invigorating, but his emaciated charges could not possibly follow them. In fact, it seemed to the disappointed Zimmel that only the man recently returned from Berlin Electric paid any serious attention to the fitness program, unaware, of course, that Bukowski did so because he was trying to follow Professor Tomczyk's advice: "Agree with anything they want you to do."

Bukowski realized that Willi Zimmel lived in a world of dreamlike simplicity where torture and starvation and hangings did not exist. He was the perpetual leader of a hearty boys' camp, and he saw the men who lined up before him each morning as skeletons only because they did not look out for their health. One morning when a man from Willi's barracks was hanged for no discernible cause, Bukowski heard Zimmel say: "He must've done something terribly wrong."

The preposterous morning exercises continued until one snowy morning when Otto Grundtz happened to see Willi Zimmel going through a series of wild distortions, devised by a Czechoslovakian instructor to train Olympic athletes, while all his ghostlike men but one watched lethargically, not even trying to wave their frail arms. They were a pitiful lot, gaunt, almost skeletal, many with sunken mouths, for Grundtz had confiscated all false teeth, since the materials, especially the metals, were needed in Germany.

He was enraged by what he saw, and bellowed: "What in hell is going on here?" and Zimmel replied: "I want them to look out for their health," and Grundtz screamed in German, which some of the prisoners would understand: "Stop it, you pig's asshole!"

Zimmel was mortified by such a command; he could hear those who knew German starting to laugh, but he also noticed that one man from his barracks had a look of compassion on his face, realizing that he, Zimmel, had merely been trying to help. And that brief look, for that hundredth of a second, would save Bukowski's life.

One morning as Zimmel was walking idly back from the main gate, he happened to see Bukowski straining at the concrete rollers and went over to him. "Isn't this heavy work?" he asked naïvely, and when Bukowski nodded, he asked: "Are you the one who used to be a shoemaker?" and Bukowski nodded again, but at this time nothing further happened.

A few days later, when Szymon was dragging the road in front of Fields Five and Six, he witnessed the arrival of some nine thousand women and children, the largest contingent of its kind ever to reach Majdanek, and in that mass of people he happened to notice a young girl, perhaps nine or ten, dressed in good shoes, a Russian-style woolen cap and a new overcoat. He never saw the child's face, but from the proud manner in which she bore herself, it was clear that she hoped to behave well.

Transfixed, he watched the child striding along, trying to keep up with the older women, her hands in the pockets of her coat, her head bravely erect as the horrors of the camp unfolded, and then she vanished in the teeming crowd entering Field Five, where he knew her fine clothes would be stripped from her, leaving her to sleep in a thin, miserable shift on bare ground, with only a frail blanket to ward off the pneumonia and the fatal bronchitis.

For the next week Szymon could think of nothing but that little girl, and by persistent questioning he learned that she and her group had come from the splendid walled town of Zamosc: "All Poles are removed from that area. Exterminated. Their place is being filled by German immigrants. Zamosc is to be a German town forever. A frontier fortress. No Pole to be allowed to set foot inside."

This statement was accurate. A vast area around that noble city was to be depopulated, then filled with loyal Germans, and the Polish citizens who had once lived there were being moved into Majdanek to be starved to death. They had done no wrong, but their land was coveted.

Now, as he dragged the massive rollers, tall as a man, he tormented himself with visions, imagining this little girl again, whose face he had never seen, and she filled his mind. Always he saw her in her new overcoat, still striding along, still trying to keep up with older people, her little body pressed forward to accept whatever was to happen. Then one day, as he was almost hanging on the frozen handles to stay alive, he imagined that she turned to look at him, and for the first time he saw that she was beautiful, and that she was a grown woman, and that it was she he was destined to marry, and for two semi-delirious days he imagined only his courtship of her, and their marriage, and of how in the evening she sat with needle and thread, mending her coat.

Always attentive, Otto Grundtz saw that Bukowski's mind was wandering, and he ordered Willi Zimmel to move him into Barracks Nineteen as soon as he showed the first sign of unconsciousness, but Szymon suddenly rallied, aware that he must prepare for the christening of his wife's first son, and that morning as he dragged the rollers he was present when the death truck stopped at the gate to Field Five and he watched as women in prisoner's garb threw in the bodies of newly dead companions to be taken to the crematorium, and as the wagon filled, Bukowski in his delirium thought he saw the little girl again, as she had been on that first awful day, still in her overcoat, still marching bravely, and when he saw her body tossed into the open wagon, he uttered a terrible cry.

This cleared his addled brain, and in quivering fury he left the rollers and followed the death truck up the hill to the crematorium. When it halted at the entrance to the ovens he watched as men came out to strip the corpses of any usable clothing, then toss the naked bodies into the waiting ovens, five carefully constructed steel-bound ovens from Berlin, each with its gaping mouth. His mind glazed, and when he saw that the next body to be lifted would be that of his little girl, flames seemed to engulf his eyes, and he heard himself screaming "No! No!"

Again his mind cleared, and he realized with new horror that he was far from his assigned duty and that if caught, he would be shot at once, so he started running back to Field Five, but this route took him right past the guardhouse from which Otto Grundtz conducted his business, and he was terrified, for the closer death came, the more he wanted to live.

And now, from the guardhouse, came the man who would send him to his death, and Szymon was prepared to do battle, when he heard a mild voice asking: "Where were you? I was looking for you."

It was Willi Zimmel, and he told him that the officer who ran the shoe-repair shop wanted him back again: "He said you were a good shoemaker." Almost too weak to follow, for on this day he surely would have passed into final coma had he returned to the rollers, Szymon accompanied Zimmel to the shop, where he resumed his old job and regained his sanity.

But he never forgot Field Five and the little girl in the overcoat, and when his calmer moments returned he swore that her death would be avenged. Planning how became even more obsessive than his former preoccupation with beer and food. Stupid acts like trying to murder Otto Grundtz he dismissed, but his gyrating mind did evolve six or seven reasonable alternatives, not one of which could he at that moment put into operation. Gradually, however, amid the storms that possessed him he came upon exactly the right revenge.

Having noticed a daring Pole he thought might be planning escape, he watched the man intently for a week, then whispered one night: "If you make it, tell the underground to wipe out one of the German settlements at Zamosc." The would-be escapee, knowing well that his chances were eighty-to-one against and that slow strangulation awaited him if he failed, was the kind of man who could appreciate what Bukowski was saying. The terrible rape of Zamosc must be avenged, but he gave no sign to Szymon that he had heard the whisper.

As the dreaded Russian armies drew ever closer, Konrad Krumpf realized that he had a difficult and tricky game to play if he wished to survive, with certain advantages. He must get a train into the area, which, in view of the way Allied bombers had been destroying German railroads, would require maneuvering, and he must get it packed with the palace treasures before Falk von Eschl at the castle could interfere. Then, and this could be most difficult of all, he must somehow manage to leave his post and ride with the train to safety in Paris. The obstacle to such an escape would be Von Eschl, who could be depended upon to anticipate it and forestall it.

Krumpf had made the reasonable deduction that Von Eschl intended to have him shot, and he did not propose to have this happen. So the two German officials sparred on every point. Von Eschl, actually no more than a civilian, had wanted Krumpf to move his headquarters into the castle, where he would be under easier surveillance. But Krumpf, aware of his motive and as an authentic member of the Gestapo with powers of his own, refused, for he was plotting the downfall of the arrogant plenipotentiary.

Von Eschl, now convinced that Krumpf had bungled with his famous golden cards, betraying an entire cadre of spies to the enemy, confronted him with the dismal figures: "In less than six months, of your group of forty-three valuable aides to the Reich, sixteen have now been shot or otherwise murdered, and I am wasting good forces to protect the remaining twenty-seven. Doesn't that tell you something?" Krumpf replied with a surprising show of wit: "It tells me that nothing I was supposed to protect"—and he accented the *I* heavily—"fell in my own backyard, where I allowed partisans to take it apart under my nose and send it God knows where."

But in a straight duel, Von Eschl, with his extraordinary influence, had the upper hand, which meant that Krumpf had to be especially clever if he was to escape with the treasures and with his life. He had two pawns to be played at the proper moment: Ludwik Bukowski; and a letter of major importance, addressed to him personally, about which Von Eschl could not know, and he was grimly determined to play them with daring and skill.

On the day the train arrived, he requisitioned all the villagers for the task of loading it, and farmers with wagons needed for tillage brought them to the palace, where the treasures of half a century were taken from their accustomed places and prepared for shipment. The paintings, the carved tables, the priceless rugs from Persia, the silverware from Venice, chandeliers from Prague, the bibelots in gold and amethyst from Vienna, all went into the wagons and from there into the seven boxcars of the waiting train. By dusk one of Poland's finest buildings had been denuded: originally the contents had cost more than three million 1896 dollars; they had been added to and were now worth five times that much, and all was being stolen from the Polish people, for whom it had always been intended. And what was most painful to the villagers who were forced to participate in the theft, it was being supervised by the son of the woman who had gathered the treasures.

Bukowski displayed no remorse. Moving from room to room, he checked to see that all items of value were taken, and when the walls were bare and the rooms echoing, he left the palace, not even pausing to think how fortunate it was that his mother had not lived to watch this raping and pillage.

But as he was ready to depart for the train which would take him from Poland forever, Von Eschl drove into the beautiful driveway, screeched his Mercedes-Benz to a halt, and rushed into the entranceway. "As commander of this district I have given orders that the train shall not be moved."

"And a commander much higher than you has given orders that

it shall," Krumpf said, his hand sweating as he reached for his letter. With his catlike wisdom he did not hand his enemy the real letter, but only a typed copy, and as Falk von Eschl took it, Krumpf said with nervous glee: "Look who signed it!"

Von Eschl read the bottom lines, gasped, then recovered quickly. "Hermann Goering never saw this letter. Any fool could have typed it," but Krumpf replied with a bravura which astonished even himself: "But only Goering could have sent the original."

For such insolence Von Eschl could have called for members of his special forces to arrest this man, but Krumpf, fighting for his life, had one more surprise. Pointing with trembling finger to a special line in the letter, he said: "You better read that carefully," and Von Eschl read: "The Holbein you sent is here. Bring the other gifts you spoke of to me personally." Leaving the copy with Von Eschl, Krumpf walked with apparent indifference toward the car that would carry him to the train, but he was shaking inwardly, for he knew it was possible that Von Eschl in rage might shoot him in the back. But the imperious commander of the polygon was not entirely free to act; in the cascading days ahead he might very well require Hermann Goering's support and he could not risk losing it over an individual as wormlike as Konrad Krumpf. With grinding anger he allowed Krumpf to enter his car and drive down the entrance lane of his Polish palace for the last time.

Krumpf and Bukowski and their seven boxcars of treasures were on their way to Paris.

The SS guards at Majdanek were skilled in spotting and frustrating escape attempts. For them it was a stimulating game, bursting in upon the plotters, beating them nearly to death, but saving them so that next morning their crumpled bodies could be dragged to the gibbet. There an officer would announce over the loud horn: "Ferencz Hunyadi, this Hungarian enemy of the Third Reich, tried to escape last night. See what happens to him." After his arms and legs were tied he would be suspended from the gallows by a loosely tied length of rope, so that he could struggle and choke for minutes before dying.

However, over the years, three hundred Poles did escape, and two months after the forced depopulation of Zamosc the dedicated man to whom Szymon Bukowski had whispered made good his flight by killing an SS guard, donning his uniform, wiping away the blood, and exiting by the main gate. Eight supposed accomplices were shot, but he made his way south, where he joined up with Jan Buk's commando. He announced himself simply: "Chalubinski, schoolteacher, Lodz," for he had served so long at Majdanek that he no longer used his first name, Tytus. The Nazis had transformed him into a man without nerves, a machine existing solely for revenge.

Within minutes of meeting Buk he started the litany that would not cease: "We must move east and wipe out one of the new German settlements outside Zamosc," and when Buk hesitated, he added: "We must let the entire German occupation know they will never have an easy night in any house they've stolen from us."

"You mean," Buk asked in amazement, "that we'd just take a village at random, surround it, and kill everybody?"

"Exactly what I mean. We must strike terror into their craven hearts." Again Buk hesitated, but Chalubinski would not relinquish his plan: "If we destroy one of their prize villages—'Our bright new Poland' and all that manure—we can make the entire occupation tremble. Then they'll know they can never subdue us."

"Are you willing to burn an entire village? And kill everybody in it?"

"If I had twenty men and the guns, I'd do it tonight."

He was so remorseless in his pressure that Buk felt he must call his leaders together, and when they sat in a circle to judge the debate, they saw two entirely different men. Chalubinski was tall and cadaverously thin, Buk of medium height and also thin, but he was not emaciated; men of the commando had not eaten well, but the men of Majdanek had been systematically starved. Chalubinski's fanatical face looked as if all humanity had been drained from it by the calculated terrors of the concentration camp, but Buk's still retained the square, open, peasant appearance of a man who had known poor treatment but never a carefully planned assault on his body and mind. The greater difference was not visible, for it lay in their hearts. Chalubinski's had been sorely damaged: he had watched six men he knew well hanged at the gibbet outside his Barracks Six. To escape he had killed the SS man with a pair of scissors. On one day alone he had helped dig graves for more than eighteen thousand Jews. For two long years he had doubted that he would ever escape. And worst of all, he had been alone, shared his thoughts with no one. Jan Buk, on the other hand, had always been with friends; in the forest he was with men he could trust; on his early forays into Krakow he had met with daring men like himself; he had seen his wife at intervals; and he had worked with enterprising people like the English scientist and Count Lubonski.

Society had helped to ennoble Buk, it had done everything to dehumanize Chalubinski, and this difference manifested itself in what the two men said to the commando.

Buk started quietly: "An entirely new operation has been proposed. Tell them about it, Chalubinski." When the schoolteacher was finished uttering his cold, harsh words, Buk said: "I'm sure you all see the two problems. If we do what he suggests, Hans Frank's retaliation will be terrifying."

Chalubinski cried: "Wrong statement! Hans Frank has already retaliated, in advance. He's already done his worst." And in brief, cruel sentences he told them of Under the Clock, and the chapel in Zamek Lublin, and the deaths of the Gypsies, and the one-day execution of eighteen thousand Jews.

"But he will do more of the same," a farmer warned.

"He will do it anyway," Chalubinski said, and now the commandos faced the first of the two moral dilemmas which would confront them in this operation: should they commit an act which would bring down vicious retaliation on the heads of innocent neighbors, even though the act had merit of itself, and when the viciousness was going to arrive regardless of what they did?

The men discussed this for a long time, and some suffered real anguish at the difficulty facing them, but before a resolution could be reached, Buk presented the graver problem: "If our commando wipes out an unsuspecting German village and kills innocent people, aren't we as bad as Hans Frank when he wipes out one of our villages?" This question carried terrifying overtones and the men in the forest handled it cautiously.

"We don't kill innocents," one man said forcefully, and he was so obviously concerned with the moral aspect of such a raid that he seemed to persuade many of his companions, who repeated the sentence approvingly. Buk, listening to ideas which he himself supported, thought of how only a short time ago these same men, upon hearing of a most wanton shooting of hostages, had wanted to commit almost any act of retaliation. Now, with an ugly opportunity before them, they drew back, and it became clear that the vote was going to go strongly against any attack on the Zamosc villages.

But before a decision could be voiced, Chalubinski moved Buk aside and explained in cold, shattering words what this proposed raid was all about:

"You men sound as if you were discussing a picnic. Would it be better to take potatoes or beets? Men, we're talking about the soul of Poland. Listen to what's been happening.

"As you all know, the Nazis decided to make Zamosc, on the border with Russia, a German stronghold, peopled only by Germans. To achieve this they had to expel from the city and the surrounding area more than one hundred thousand Poles. How did they do it? And what happened to these Poles?

"The eight thousand leading citizens were marched to a place in the city called The Rotunda and shot. Well, as you know, that's happened everywhere. But in the dead of winter the others were marched to concentration camps. I saw them enter Majdanek. I saw them starve to death. I saw them carted away to the crematoriums, so their ashes could be freighted back to Germany as fertilizer.

"But as you know again, that happens all the time—Auschwitz; Belzec, not far from here; Birkenau, maybe worst of all. It was what happened to the children that counts. It was the children that brought me here. They were placed in boxcars, thousands of them, and shipped to various camps, but it was winter, and there were no blankets, no food, no water, and the trains were delayed, and when the boxcars were finally opened, the children were found frozen to death."

There was a long, aching silence, and some men who had not seen their own children for months began to weep. Then came Chalubinski's hard, terrible voice: "We shall wipe out one of the villages they stole from the people of Zamosc. We shall destroy every cottage, throw down every stone. Because we must send the Germans a message that they cannot do such things to us ever again." His voice rose to a scream: "They cannot stuff our children in trains and freeze them to death!"

There was something wrong with that last sentence and the men knew it. The accusation was too sensational, so broad that his cry for revenge lost its force, and he sensed that the meeting was flowing away from him. But with a touch of schoolteaching genius he stumbled upon exactly the right note on which to end his plea: "And what do you suppose they're going to name Zamosc when they've made it German? Himmlerstadt."

The obscenity of this, the erasing of a notable Polish name and the glorification of one of the worst Germans ever to have been born was too much for the commandos, and men began to shout "No! No!" and to call for an immediate march on the stolen city of Zamosc.

But now Jan Buk asserted his leadership: "We do not massacre innocent civilians."

Chalubinski was waiting for this, and cried: "They're not innocent, and they're not civilians. It was people like them who brought Hitler to power. They applauded what he's done. And they glory in their new homes. They're front-line soldiers and they must be destroyed. And if Buk won't lead you, I will."

The men cheered and insisted that Buk join them in the assault, but he temporized, and this was the beginning of the serious tension between him and Chalubinski, who was infuriated by the delay Buk initiated when he proposed: "Let's forward this to headquarters," and when this was done he received a surprising response: "We've been considering such an operation for several months. Now is the time. Take your group and eliminate one of the new settlements."

One hundred and eight men were assembled from units in the forest, and they moved cautiously eastward, acquiring other underground units from Stalowa Wola and a few former residents of Zamosc who were continuing personal vendettas against Nazis who had expropriated their homes. Never showing themselves in groups of more than three, they drifted slowly into position, then found that their leadership had sent down twenty resolute men from Lublin.

Scouts surveyed the area, evaluating six different communities where German settlers tilled their new fields and tended cattle that had only recently belonged to Poles. Sometimes, seeing the neat cottages at night with lights dimly glowing, Buk lost all stomach for this mission, and Chalubinski, already convinced of Buk's unreliability, noticed the hesitancy and kept close watch upon him.

At ten minutes of two on a dark night the commandos formed a half-moon scimitar close to the northern edge of the chosen village, and posted sharpshooters at strategic spots to the south. With terrible resolve the scimitar began to close and men bearing the torches prepared to light them. The sharpshooters and machine-gunners to the south breathed deeply, their fingers on the trigger.

When Buk sensed that Chalubinski was about to leap ahead and start the attack, he jabbed his gun backward, catching the teacher in the gut: "I'll give the command," and Chalubinski, masking his anger, said grimly: "Be sure you give it."

When the force was so near the village that dogs might begin to bark, Buk called to his Stork Commando "Now!" and flicked his flashlight to signal the Lublin men on the wings, and with flaming torches these commandos fell upon the village, setting roofs ablaze and sweeping all areas with gunfire.

The enraged Poles, remembering what had happened to the children who had once occupied these cottages, never had to face the awful problem of whether they themselves were guilty of a similar crime, because their fire was so intense, their flames so wild and rampant, that no Pole ever confronted an individual German. There were a few screams, a few shadowy figures running in the night, until the waiting gunmen shot them down . . . then only silence.

The raid coincided with broadcasts from London telling of monumental Soviet victories in the east, and in the days that followed, Poles could tell when passing a German whether or not he had heard the two pieces of ominous news. When they saw one worried and looking cautiously here and there, they said of him: "That one has heard about Leningrad and Zamosc."

From the eastern front the Nazis were receiving bulletins that were even more ominous, for an Allied victory seemed to roar across the land like a firestorm blown in from the Asian steppes, gathering momentum with every mile, but from the western front, there was still reassuring news, because cities like London, from which the force of any Allied attack must come, found themselves in great danger. The V-2s were displaying awesome power, and it was therefore obligatory that the Stork Commando which had in its possession plans and parts of an actual V-2 deliver them to the Allied strategists in England, but in this effort they were consistently and brilliantly frustrated by Falk von Eschl, who had clamped down on all likely routes of exit.

And then one night when the Poles were sure that he would be engaged in an affair which the Storks were staging at the far end of the polygon, two Poles in rubberized swimsuits dug up the vital parts of the V-2 from the farmer's field, swam across the Vistula in darkness, and handed a woman cook from Castle Gorka a sheaf of drawings and a wrapped bundle of tremendous value. Without speaking one word, she accepted the packages from the dark and froglike men and took them into the castle, where she reported immediately to the count.

Lubonski could guess what the materials must be and knew he must get them to London, but how this was to be accomplished he did not know. Without opening the packages, he secreted them behind a panel which his family had often used in past centuries, and waited. That he would deliver the crucial materials properly he had not the slightest doubt.

Two nights later, when Von Eschl was again called to attend matters in his domain, the two frogmen who had been guarding the buried V-2 swam the Vistula once more, this time with a third member. It was Jan Buk, head of the Stork Commando, who was met in silence by the woman cook and led immediately to Count Lubonski's study.

"You are Buk of the next village?"

"Yes."

"Leader of the Stork Commando?"

"I do not know them. I hear rumors."

"Why do you come? At such risk to us both?"

"Tomorrow at half after one I shall appear at your gate, in uniform, in a stolen German staff car, and send you to London."

"How?"

"Be ready. Half after one. The timing is critical."

With that he was gone. He had told Lubonski just enough to command his attention, not one word more which might be betrayed if the count were caught.

That night Buk did not swim back across the river; he stayed in the forest with the men who had stolen the staff car and who had the proper forged documents. Satisfied that everything reasonable had been done on the Polish end, Buk went to sleep as easily as if he had done a day's work at the plow and eaten a good meal. His days and nights in recent years had been filled with such constant danger that he had learned there was not much he could do about it. Tomorrow he would try to drive a stolen car past a dozen sentries, and he hoped that luck would continue with him.

Walerian Lubonski slept easily, too. The men of his family had been trained to service, sometimes under arms, sometimes at a papal court, sometimes at the imperial palaces in Vienna, and it was in no way unusual that he should now be summoned to duty of the most stringent character. The possibility of death in this charade whose rules he did not even know was no greater than his ancestors had known at the battles of Grunwald and Vienna.

But at ten-thirty next morning he received a shock. Falk von Eschl sent word that he would take lunch at the castle, at which time he wished to discuss important matters, and customarily the German commander liked to eat late, which would make a one-thirty departure with Buk impossible. At first he thought that he must ask his cook to take Buk a message, if he could be found, but to have her moving about in daylight was too dangerous. Besides, if Jan Buk was clever enough to have arranged an escape as complicated as this one sounded, he would be clever enough to see Von Eschl's Mercedes-Benz waiting in the driveway.

Lubonski was therefore not unduly nervous as he awaited his German guest, and at eleven-thirty he checked to be sure the piece of venison the cook proposed to serve was in good order. It was, and he said: "Please see it's served promptly," and she nodded, aware that this simple request might mask a most complex situation. Had he asked her to stab Von Eschl with a carving knife as she brought in the roast, she would not have been surprised and would have complied.

At quarter to twelve good news reached the castle: Von Eschl had to attend a meeting in Krakow chaired by Dr. Hans Frank himself, and he wondered if lunch could be served at twelve-fifteen. In apology for imposing on Lubonski and then altering the time arbitrarily, he brought with him a bottle of good Traminer; the meal was congenial, two diplomats sparring to attain and defend advantages.

They spoke alternately in German, English and French, with Von Eschl throwing in an occasional phrase in Polish as a courtesy to his host. When Lubonski praised the wine, he did so in French; when he asked about the conduct of the war, he used German; and Von Eschl graciously responded in whatever language was most appropriate.

"Is it widely known . . ." he began in German, twirling his wineglass and studying it, not Lubonski. "What I mean is, among the generality. Is it known what we're doing in the polygon?"

"I scarcely know myself."

"The firings. Those tremendous blasts."

"I assume it has to do with some kind of advanced ordnance."

"Surely you've heard about the objects flying through the air."

"I've heard rumors. But I've seen nothing myself."

"In your opinion, could the Polish underground—I mean, in real army strength—could it mount an attack upon the polygon?"

"I would suppose our people would attempt anything. We're at war, you know."

"Not really. The pattern for the future has been well established. It's understood, I think. This is more a pacification."

Blandly Lubonski agreed: "Give my regards to Dr. Frank. He's stayed with me twice, you know."

"I do indeed. He speaks of you with great warmth." Von Eschl twirled his glass again, and still without looking directly at Lubonski, said casually: "You know, of course, that when the Russians are defeated . . ." He stopped, as if aware of how stupid this must sound when the Russians were advancing all along the battle line. There was a short silence, and then he changed direction completely: "There's good reason to believe that what we're perfecting in the polygon . . . it will destroy England's capacity to wage war, and then we'll turn it on Moscow and destroy her, too. Our victory is much closer than you think, Lubonski."

He said this crisply, defiantly, then went on: "Dr. Frank, who holds you in the very highest regard as a true Polish patriot . . . he has been wondering if, when we do crush the Russians, there might not be a place in our plans for Poland for a local man—someone of distinction, that is—for a local man to serve as our representative." He paused significantly, then said: "From this very castle, perhaps. It could be arranged, you know."

Lubonski feigned surprise and pleasure at having been considered for an assignment of such honor and responsibility. Desperately he wanted to comment on the preposterousness of a situation in which the Germans one day discussed shooting him as a potential spy—and he knew well that Von Eschl and Krumpf had discussed exactly that—and next day suggested him as a proconsul. But his task this day was not to puncture ridiculous balloons; he had packages to deliver to London and he must allow nothing to deter him. "If peace does come to these parts, it would be important that we get everything back to normal as fast as possible. Like the agricultural land your polygon preempts now."

The two diplomats were now speaking English, and each had a wide vocabulary of precisely used terms, so Von Eschl replied: "I believe it was the American President Harding who coined the word *normalcy.* Yes, we will want to restore normalcy as soon as possible. Not quite what it was before the war, of course."

"Of course not."

"There have been permanent changes, you know."

"Indeed I do. Every time I visit Krakow, I see the changes, and many of them for the better."

"Yes . . . yes. This could become one of the grand parts of Europe. A veritable breadbasket. Recreation spots in your mountains to the south. There will be a place for a man of good sense, like you."

"Speak well of me to the governor general."

"I will," Von Eschl said, and he was about to broach another subject of equal importance, the importing of more Polish peasants from the north to work the fields, when Lubonski looked at his watch, and this prompted Von Eschl to do the same: "Look at that! How rapidly time flies with good food, good wine and good conversation."

He ran down the stone stairway to the ground floor, saluted Lubonski, who stood in the doorway, and jumped into his waiting Mercedes. It had scarcely cleared the castle grounds when a second car of the same make and style drove up, chauffeured by Jan Buk in German uniform. A footman in the same kind of dress stepped down, opened the car door, and Count Lubonski with his packages departed.

Had the Vistula River been easily navigable, and had the Stork Commando owned a speedboat of any kind, the trip would have been an easy one, for the secret airfield used with some frequency by the underground lay about thirty miles up the river, on the right bank in an area of very small and scattered villages. It was frighteningly close to Krakow's airfield on the opposite side of the river, but activity at that Nazi base helped mask the flights into and out of Zaborow. People in the area were used to seeing planes.

To reach the camouflaged airfield by automobile was a much different matter, for obviously there would be no major roads and this required Buk to stop at numerous roadblocks, but he had the forged papers to pass and the iron nerve to look like a relaxed Polish driver for an important Nazi official. Also, Lubonski had the engaging trick of asking anxiously in his refined German: "Is the other Mercedes far ahead of us?" and when the guards replied: "Not too far," he answered: "No worry. We'll catch them before Krakow."

They skirted the city of Tarnow, keeping to the north toward Zabno, where they must cross the Dunajec, a rather large river, and they knew the bridge would be heavily guarded, but they brazened it and could now drive carefully down country roads, coming at last to a dead end, where waiting partisans took charge, driving the Mercedes away immediately and leading Lubonski to a hut in which he would wait with Jan Buk until the courier plane arrived.

The operation, utilized perhaps twice in three months, was known as The Bridge, for it connected Polish air units stationed at the Italian city of Bari on the Adriatic with their homeland. Over The Bridge came daring Polish officers bringing instructions to the underground, and out went messengers to the various Allied commands, but no one either coming in or exiting carried information of such critical importance as what Lubonski held in his lap. The destiny of nations depended upon his successful journey.

Night fell and the quarter-moon set and there was no plane from Bari. A military transport approached the Nazi base across the river, but nothing flew near Zaborow. Midnight came and Lubonski began to worry, but Jan Buk assured him that when such a plane was scheduled, it arrived, and at quarter past midnight the sleek black plane did signal. Discreet lights flashed on; the plane circled only once and landed with surprising speed, braking in jerks as it sped over the grassy surface. With some effort, the pilot wrestled it to a halt, whereupon dozens of men ran from areas Lubonski had not noticed, carrying tins of precious gasoline stolen from Nazi depots.

From the plane emerged three men whom Lubonski did not know; they were colonels come to help with the uprising that was soon to erupt all over Poland. Grimly they sped away.

Within twenty minutes Count Lubonski was strapped into his seat, saluting the brave young man who had brought him so far: "Goodbye, Buk. Good job."

They flew south over Czechoslovakia, across the middle of Hungary and right down the center of Yugoslavia, then above Dubrovnik and in to Bari, where a fast courier plane waited to whisk the count and his precious cargo on to London. This plane crossed Italy, Corsica and most of France, before arriving after dawn at a military airport near London. And all this was done, this crossing of seven countries, at a time when Field Marshal Goering was still claiming that his air force dominated the skies.

Had Count Lubonski been able to peer down through the darkness as they passed north of Paris, he would have seen a train chugging along, bringing many boxcars to that city, among them the seven containing the Bukowski treasures, and he might have reflected on the strange twists and turns of a war which led one man from a palace on the Vistula to behave in so vastly different a way from another man who lived in a castle only a short distance away, the one bringing goods to his own selfish advantage, the other bringing documents crucial to the salvation of the free world.

As soon as his plane landed in England, men from British intelligence whom Lubonski had known when he was in London in 1919 hurried forward to embrace him for his gallantry. Assistants took possession of his packages, rushing them directly to military and scientific laboratories, and he would see his rocket fragments no more. His friends asked: "You've had a rather grueling bit, would you be up to a strenuous day?" and he replied in English: "That's what I came for."

He was taken to the shabby offices in London in which the BBC constructed its nightly broadcasts both to the free world and to the countries still under Nazi domination, and there a gentleman in pipe and tweeds offered him morning tea, a sip of good whiskey and a startling proposal: "We want you to go on the air tonight at seven with a complete and honest report of everything you've done during the past twenty-four hours. Masked a bit, you know, but there it will be—all spread out."

When Lubonski asked why, the tweedy one called his assistants, and they were enthusiastic: "Names, routes, stratagems, fudged up a bit, but we can drive them crazy."

"Is this to be in Polish or German? I mean, whom do you want to confuse?"

"Both languages, Polish first, then German immediately after. To let the Poles know how daring their people are. To scare the living hell out of the Germans."

As soon as they described this aspect of their plan, Lubonski became excited, for in both the Polish and German versions he was invited to identify by name specific Nazi monsters whom the Poles had marked for death: "We want to panic them during these days of maximum confusion. We want to goad them into making wrong decisions."

So during the afternoon Lubonski told what he knew of the terror, reminding them always that he had only partial knowledge: "I was not myself interrogated Under the Clock in Lublin, but I know two men of the greatest integrity who were. Their escape . . ." He fell silent. Anything he might have accomplished in his relatively easy

exit was trivial and not worthy of mention when compared to the
adventures of someone who had undergone the broomstick treatment Under the Clock and lived to speak of it.

At five, exhausted not by his work but by his memories, he fell
into a deep sleep, and at quarter to seven he was awakened to make
the historic broadcast which would later be printed in nine languages
and strewn from the clouds over occupied Europe by a hundred different bombers:

> "Good evening, citizens of Poland and members of the Ger-
> man occupying force, I am Walerian Lubonski, Count of
> Castle Gorka, which stands on the right bank of the Vistula
> River between Krakow and Sandomierz. My father was that
> Count Lubonski who served for many years as a high official
> of the Austro-Hungarian Empire and who, as you know,
> loved Germany.

> "Yesterday at quarter past noon I dined in my castle with Falk
> von Eschl, special commander of the secret area known as
> Polygon. I fed him venison and he served me a fine bottle of
> Traminer. I give these details so that if he is listening, as I am
> certain he will be, he will be satisfied that I am who I say I am
> and that I am telling the truth.

> "At half after one he left for Krakow in a Mercedes-Benz
> driven by the chauffeur Reiglen. What he does not know is
> that fifteen minutes later I left, also in a Mercedes-Benz, sto-
> len from the high command in Krakow, driven by a member
> of the Stork Commando wearing a stolen Nazi uniform. With
> forged papers we drove south to Dukla and through the Car-
> pathian passes into eastern Czechoslovakia to a secret airfield
> at which Allied planes land regularly. One flew me to a French
> air base eighteen miles from the English Channel, and from
> there I hopped to London.

> "Falk von Eschl will be interested to learn that I brought with
> me complete drawings and selected important parts of the
> machine which landed in the Vistula not many weeks ago.
> They are now in possession of Allied intelligence.

> "I give these details for two reasons. To encourage my Polish
> fellow citizens. Victory moves closer every day. When I flew

over the Channel, I saw thousands of Allied vessels waiting for the crusade that will soon free Europe. In London, I have seen reports of great Russian victories which will soon free Warsaw. But I also seek to strike a mortal fear in the hearts of my German listeners. And I will be specific.

"Dr. Hans Frank, ruler of General Gouvernement, I brought out with me a copy of all your commands to the Polish people. Your own words condemn you, and one day soon you will hang.

"Falk von Eschl, guest in my castle, I brought with me details of your massacre of villagers at Nowa Polska. For that crime and others you will hang.

"Konrad Krumpf, I have full details of your many crimes during the years you occupied the Bukowski palace. I know you have escaped to France, but for your crimes you will be hanged.

"Walther Nocke, Gestapo commander of the cells Under the Clock, we have a complete dossier of your enormous crimes, and you will hang.

"Hans Fiddler and Ulbricht Untermann, judges at the infamous court in Zamek Lublin, your own people have kept a record of your assassinations, and you will hang.

"Arthur Liebehenschel, commandant at Majdanek, your infamous crimes have been reported by prisoners who escaped your charge, and you will be hanged.

"Otto Grundtz, commander of Field Four, escapees who know you well have listed your hideous crimes, and you will be hanged."

On and on he went, giving specific names, specific crimes for which the accused would be hanged. Then he gave a promise:

"I will spend the rest of my life, if necessary, moving from country to country, from court to court, to testify against you, and I will bring my friends with me to give evidence until you are each and all hanged.

"There are among the occupying forces many fine Germans who have helped us Poles and I want to give them assurances. I shall not recite your names because to do so would hurt you with the monsters who give you orders, but you will be able to identify yourselves, and just as I promised the others I will not die until I have helped bring them to the gallows, I now promise you that I will travel to any court in the world to testify that you were men of integrity and honor and compassion. You will come to no harm.

"We Poles do not seek revenge for the terrible wrongs that have been done us. We seek justice, and a warning to others that they can never act as Dr. Hans Frank and his General Gouvernement have acted. The day of retribution is close at hand and it will be as remorseless as you were cruel.

"To my guest Falk von Eschl, I suppose you will destroy my castle. Well, in past it was destroyed by Tatars, by Cossacks, by Swedes and by Hungarians, and always my ancestors rebuilt. We will rebuild. Like the other conquerors, you have failed to kill Poland. It will live forever."

Lubonski's first BBC broadcast evoked so many responses that he was invited to deliver a series on conditions inside Nazi-occupied areas, and this brought him into contact with representatives of many nations seeking to regain their freedom. On some days he felt that he was holding his father's portfolio in Vienna in the 1890s when the situation had been similar.

Customs change, he thought, but not the great basic problems, and nowhere was this truism more clearly demonstrated than in the recurring case of Poland-Lithuania-Ukraine over which his father, Andrzej Lubonski, had broken his heart. The strategic situation was precisely what it had been in 1920: the three isolated and defenseless units must unite as they had done in centuries past, or they must perish individually, but just as rampant nationalism had prevented any such union in 1920, it now forestalled any rational approaches.

His father had conducted exploratory meetings in Brest-Litovsk with Lithuanians and Ukrainians, and now he held his meetings in London, with equally mournful results. Each national unit was afraid of the other two, each was convinced that this time it could walk the tightrope between Germany and Russia, and each conceded privately that such hopes were futile. "History doesn't repeat itself," Lubonski lamented one night to a party of experts on eastern European affairs. "It is the same history, never broken, never halted."

Despite his despair over the future, he did find reassurance in the present, for he had never known better people than his illiterate cook, who had been so fearless in her partisan activities, or Jan Buk, who had handled the V-2 affair so professionally, and in gratitude for the smooth way in which Buk had led his men to capture the V-2 and then spirited it and Lubonski off to London, the count prevailed upon representatives of the Polish government-in-exile to award Buk a medal honoring his services; so on the next Bridge from Bari to the secret airfield near Krakow, a Polish colonel who was flying in to help direct the uprising in Warsaw asked to be taken to the Forest of Szczek, where he met privately with Buk and Chalubinski and presented the medal.

"Keep it hidden till victory," the colonel advised. "The Nazis wouldn't look kindly on a medal like this."

So Buk kept it buried, but one day Chalubinski said: "I'd like to see that medal," and Jan dug it up.

"The last gasp of a Poland that's dead," Chalubinski said, shoving it back.

"It shows King Jagiello," Buk said. "He was our hero."

"The medal . . . Lubonski . . . that London gang . . . Buk, they're all from the last century. There's going to be a much different Poland, believe me. The ones who come to help us from the east, they're the ones who'll build the real Poland."

"Who do you mean?"

"The Russians. The Communists. They'll have no truck with such medals."

"Do you want me to throw it away?" Buk asked angrily.

"No. It suits you, that medal. And a defunct count trying to regain his estates."

Buk refused to lose his temper, but as a man of integrity he had to defend Lubonski: "At Majdanek, from what you say, you behaved well. Believe me, at Castle Gorka, Lubonski did too, and this commando is active today only because of the help he gave us."

"He better stay in London when peace comes. He won't be wanted here." Although Buk did not seek a confrontation, he felt impelled to say: "Your new Poland will be a sorry show if it can find no place for men like him," and Chalubinski growled: "You don't seem to realize. A totally new kind of man is going to organize Poland," and Buk asked, almost contentiously: "Who?"

Then it came out: "With Russian aid, socialists and men who understand Communism will build a new society here, one that will be gloriously better."

Very quietly, as if aware of the danger into which he was projecting himself, Buk said: "I am suspicious of any aid which comes from Russia."

This infuriated Chalubinski, who asked with reason on his side: "Do you reject the great victories the Russians are giving us? The salvation which they will soon hand us?"

"I shall accept the soldiers marching in, but I want them to march out again."

They were back in their camp now, but the idea that Soviet aid could be in any way injurious to Poland was so outrageous to Chalubinski that he kept up his harangue in a loud voice, whereupon an old man among the partisans—he was forty-nine, but years of deprivation made him seem sixty-nine—began to speak hesitantly, but as he proceeded, those about him listened, for he summarized their thinking:

"Always in the village at night when we talked about Poland . . . I mean in those days that you did not know, when Poland did not exist. Always we asked: 'Which would be better, to live under Russian rule or German?' And our old men who had known both told us the truth.

"They said: 'The Germans are the cruelest people on earth. They murder. They slaughter. And they do it all in the name of civilization.' They warned us that life under the Germans was to be avoided at any cost.

"But always they said that in the long run, as years passed and the first fury subsided, life with the Germans could reach compromises. Continuance was possible. It was never pleasant, but it was possible, for there was music and celebrations and you could travel to Berlin, and if you did things their way, you survived and could even have a good time now and then.

"But with the Russians, there was no hope. Only the dead hand of oppression, the unrelieved weight of Russian insensibility.

Work, work, work. One stupid rule after another. Never an alleviation in a special case. Do it their way or die.

"I myself have lived under the Russians, and it's like being in a tomb—a large tomb, yes, with perhaps a little room to move around, but a tomb nevertheless. Russians can make an entire nation a tomb. They're geniuses in building tombs.

"So if I have to choose between Germany and Russia, all I can say is: 'I don't want either, but I think I don't want Russia a little stronger.'"

With an impulsive swing of his right arm Chalubinski reached out and slapped the man across the face: "You could be shot for speaking against the only nation that can help us!" A general confusion might have ensued had not Jan Buk stepped forward to end the discussion. "I think the new Poland will find a place for all of us," he said, but Chalubinski, with his deep convictions about the future, warned: "Not for your man Bukowski, who fled with all those treasures. And your silly Lubonski is no better. Good riddance to both of them."

Buk had no desire to prolong an argument which he deemed fruitless, but he could not keep from visualizing the two men whom Chalubinski had lumped together—Ludwik Bukowski slithering off to Paris in a Nazi train laden with stolen treasures, Walerian Lubonski flying in a small plane to London to continue his honorable warfare: My God, can't he see the difference?

The war ended along the Vistula almost a year earlier than on the western front, for by 20 July 1944 it was obvious to everyone that Soviet troops would enter Lublin in a day or two, and the Polish citizens of that city who had suffered so cruelly when the Nazis were victorious would now have an opportunity to observe how these same Nazis were going to conduct themselves in defeat.

Suddenly German soldiers began to seek Polish friends, reminding startled housewives of how they, the Nazis, had always befriended the Poles and of how, on a certain day, this Nazi or that had brought children presents. Great fear showed in the German faces, and one captain went from house to house establishing friendships and stating his name clearly: "Gunter Kratzky. I am Gunter Kratzky of a little village near Dresden." But at the last moment, when he found that

Soviet soldiers were only six miles to the east, he panicked and fled.

Others remained unchanged. Walther Nocke went down into the cells at Under the Clock, counted the prisoners awaiting torture or in the middle of it, and found nineteen men and two women. "Shoot them all," he ordered, and he participated in the killing.

In the prison cells at Zamek Lublin four hundred and sixty-three prisoners awaited trial, but the civilian judge with the thick glasses could stomach no more senseless killing. He said: "Let them all go," but the young Gestapo judge who had screamed during the trials held in the chapel handed down an edict that all were guilty, so every prisoner was legally executed by gunfire as he or she stood motionless behind the cell gates.

At Majdanek any late-arriving Jews had already been liquidated during the preceding three weeks, so camp officials decided there was no necessity for a general assassination, but individual field commanders like Otto Grundtz were encouraged to clean out everyone they did not like, either by hangings at the gibbets or by point-blank gunfire. Grundtz sought one man he disliked intensely, this Szymon Bukowski who had escaped Barracks Nineteen by maneuvering an assignment to the shoe-repair shop, but he could not be found.

Willi Zimmel, the physical-fitness fanatic, had hidden him.

As Count Lubonski had predicted in his broadcasts from London, trials of the lesser Nazi officials were held in Lublin itself, and at lightning speed. But he was not allowed to participate; indeed the Russians forebade him to appear, since they had established their own courts and wanted no participation by democratically inclined Poles fighting from abroad. A few local Poles, selected because of their unswerving devotion to Communism—Tytus Chalubinski was one—were allowed to help the court in minor capacities, but Poles in general were excluded. It was a Russian victory and the Kremlin insisted that there be Russian justice.

Arthur Liebehenschel, the last commandant at Majdanek, was hanged close to the office from which he had issued his bloody orders. Reconstructed records would show that his efficiently run camp had been responsible for the deaths of more than 360,000 prisoners. These could be divided in various dichotomies. Religion: 140,000 Jews, 220,000 Christians. Or nationality: 274,000 Poles, 86,000 foreigners. In this last group citizens of fifty-two different nations were represented, from Albania and Austria to Spain, Turkey and Uzbekistan.

Walther Nocke, from Under the Clock, fainted at the sight of his gallows, while the civilian judge who had taken his glasses off to wait for pistol shots wept and pleaded for mercy on the ground that he was only obeying orders. The young Gestapo judge remained fiercely defiant, and from the gallows he predicted that without German leadership, Poland would collapse in weeks. In vile language he was describing what he thought of the country and its people when the rope caught his neck.

Otto Grundtz was hanged from the gibbet which he had so often commanded at Field Four. A solemn square of prisoners from the barracks gathered to watch, many too emaciated to stand, and those ghostly figures from Barracks Nineteen who wanted to see their monster meet his death were brought there on stretchers. Grundtz died bravely. With composure he stood on the white stool which he himself had so often kicked away and glared from beneath his dark eyebrows at his prisoners, until a man he had abused most cruelly cried: "Let me do it!" and this man, too weak to mount the gallows, reached out with an appallingly thin right hand and jerked the stool away.

When the hangings ended, Szymon Bukowski discovered to his amazement that he wanted to remain in Lublin, for Professor Tomczyk had awakened him to larger responsibilities than those available in a village like Bukowo. Within two weeks of the liberation of Lublin a university was operating, for as one of the new professors, a man from Majdanek, said: "We have so much catching up to do." A course in architecture was offered, even though for the moment there could be no drawing tables or drafting materials, and Bukowski, remembering Tomczyk's death shout—"Rebuild! Rebuild!"—enrolled.

With seven other students as emaciated as himself, he stayed at the home of Professor Tomczyk's widow, and she did her best to feed the young scholars, but there was still very little food in Lublin, and often they ate poorly, but one glorious day Mrs. Tomczyk found a chicken, and one of the students was able to fetch some bits of pork from the country, and she announced: "Tonight we have our victory celebration," and she prepared a real Polish feast, pork and sauerkraut with coriander seeds mixed in, a plate of chicken parts, a fine soup made from the various fats.

But when the students were seated, with Bukowski occupying the chair Professor Tomczyk would have used had he been here, and the soup was served, suddenly Bukowski started to shake, and then lowered his head, and the others were aware that he was sobbing, uncontrollably. No one spoke, for in these days of sudden peace people did strange things, nor could anyone guess what awful memory had assaulted their friend. But after a while the shaking ceased and with some effort he regained control. Pointing to the rich soup on whose surface floated globules of yellow fat, some as big as a golden Austrian crown, he said: "I would have strangled my brother for a bowl of soup like that."

German troops were able to retain control of the villages along the Vistula for a few days after the fall of Lublin, and at Castle Gorka, Falk von Eschl, aware that Count Lubonski had predicted in his London broadcast the destruction of his home, refrained from burning it, and even when men under his command appeared with large loads of dynamite salvaged from the polygon, he refused to give them the order. In haughty silence he climbed into his Mercedes with his driver, leaned out to salute the castle, and departed. He crossed the Vistula at Sandomierz and hurried west to the temporary security of a major German army, which was itself retreating. When he was gone his men, guessing at what his wishes must have been, piled dynamite around the tower and under all the stone rooms. They detonated a tremendous blast which threw segments of the battlement into the Vistula, leaving behind only the jagged stump of a castle gaping at the sky, as its predecessors had done in 1241, in 1510, in 1655 and in 1708.

The Bukowski palace, now vacant and denuded, was grabbed at eagerly by two Nazi companies fleeing the Russians. A Captain Plischke was in command, and at first he tried to maintain some kind of order, but since his troops could see only disaster ahead, everyone except Plischke got obnoxiously drunk and stayed that way for several days. One sergeant, loathing everything Polish and scornful of Plischke's attempts to preserve discipline, sat on a box in the big empty hall and stared at the two large canvases which had been left in place, and he became so enraged by the Matejko portrait of Jan Sobieski riding to Vienna that he whipped up a machine gun and started blasting the painting, killing all the Polish warriors. Hearing the shots, other soldiers rushed in, and when they saw what their sergeant was doing, they broke loose what weapons they had and joined the firing. They concentrated on Sobieski's big mustachioed face and blew it apart. They then turned to the Jozef Brandt painting of Czestochowa, riddling all the heads there, too. Then the sergeant shouted: "It's those bastards in the cellar I want," and he led his executioners' squad down to the long hallway, where the Nazis blazed their guns at the noble gallery of Polish heroes. Barbara Radziwill's brother had his face blown off. Maryna Mniszech's bold kinsman took fifteen bullets through his ample body. The glorious layman Zamoyski was exploded and Czartoryski had his face shredded.

"That finishes the Poles," the sergeant bellowed, but in his moment of victory he looked down the darkened corridor to see that Captain Plischke, hearing the fusillades, had come to investigate, and he was obviously disgusted by the behavior of his troops. Grasping his revolver in his right hand, with his left he pointed to the sergeant, as if condemning him: "You! Halt this destruction!" This was a dangerous moment, when anything might have happened, but a fat corporal who had not participated in the shooting said loudly: "Let's go up and see if there's any more beer."

This dissolved the tension, and the men started to move off, but the sergeant, bristling from the reprimand, swung his machine gun around as if to blast his captain, but he never had the opportunity, for Plischke coolly put two bullets through him, and he fell in a crumpled heap beneath the portraits he had savaged.

The suddenness of the pistol shots and their reverberating echoes down the corridor reminded the men that this was still war, and almost automatically they began firing at a captain they had never liked. Because they were drunk, their first bullets missed, and Plischke said calmly: "Men, come to your senses!"

But now more bullets, scores of them, came whining past the portraits, knocking Plischke to the dark floor, where three final shots from close in ripped his head.

The fat corporal, awed by the amount of blood streaming from the two dead bodies, cried: "Leave them! Let's get out of here!" but a tough enlisted man who had done much of the firing gave stronger counsel: "We'll burn this place before the others see what happened."

Not realizing that the retreating Wehrmacht would be too preoccupied with its own safety to worry about the deaths of one more captain and sergeant, he rushed upstairs, took what dynamite he could find, and began putting it in those spots where it would cause maximum destruction, and he would have blown up the entire palace had not outposts rushed back to warn: "Russians coming through the forest."

Hurriedly he ignited those explosives already in place, rushed outside, and watched with grunting pleasure as large portions of the palace crumbled: "There's one thing the Russians won't get." Then, seeing the magnificent stables still untouched, he used the last of his dynamite and gasoline to set them ablaze, so that when he led his remnant in retreat across the Vistula, the Nazis could look back at the blazing ruins along the shore, as if this were the last act of some turbulent and brooding opera.

He had lacked time to destroy the great hall. Headless, but still in command of his troops, Jan Sobieski continued his march toward Vienna.

One of the most touching moments of victory came at the village of Bukowo when the men of the Stork Commando were finally free to leave the Forest of Szczek, for when the villagers saw that this man whom they had believed dead was still alive, and that other man for whom they had prayed was not, there was wild and pitiful weeping; and when the men who had endured so much saw the ruined palace and the charred spots where their cottages had stood, they, too, wept. But the most powerful moment came when Jan Buk, heroic leader of his commando, walked the length of the village square, no longer wary of spies, no longer afraid of being captured by Nazi patrols. He simply walked past a row of cottages bearing in his arms the once-fatal quern which could now be restored to its proper place.

At last he saw Biruta, saw the deep scar across her face, and without calling out he went up to her, holding before him the symbol of their hearth. She took it, and then fierce tears coursed down her cheeks, for she better than most could appreciate the significance of its return; across his shoulder she could see the ravaged cottages from which women no less brave than she had been dragged to the hanging tree. Quietly she led her husband back to the home he had defended so stubbornly, and when she inserted the wooden handle into her top stone, she began to grind wheat from the fields she had tended, afraid no more of the noise she was making, and when the rich brown flour was milled, she kneaded it and baked that fine dark bread which makes men and nations strong.

In the years to come, many Polish communities would erect memorials to the heroism of the resistance, and most of them, seeking to avoid militaristic memories, preferred to feature some gallant woman striding forward with her children, undaunted. Biruta Buk could have posed for them all.

The happiness of the Buks was brief, because a few mornings after surrender a staff car roared into the village and a Russian official descended, with a list of persons to be arrested. Because the selection of these eight was so indicative of what was being repeated throughout liberated Poland, their names will be recited here, with explanations of why they were on the list:

Lionel Aksentowicz	32	Schoolteacher and supporter of General Bor
Bartosz Wysocki	22	Known member of the reactionary Home Army
Lucyna Grabska	20	University student. Member, Youth of All Poland
Janusz Glowacki	44	Priest
Konstanty Buczek	29	Member, Polish Peasant Party right-wing
Mikolaj Konarski	30	Member, Service for Poland's Victory
Zdzislaw Daraz	33	Outspoken opponent of the Lublin Committee

Obviously these names had been designated not by Russians, but by radical Poles who wanted to be sure the new state would be headed in their direction. It was the eighth name which evoked cries of great protest from the villagers:

Jan Buk	27	Accepted medal from London reactionaries

The only man who could have known about that medal was Chalubinski, the fanatical schoolteacher from Lodz; in their forest arguments he had classified Buk as a reactionary and had so reported him to the Russians.

When Soviet soldiers were sent to fetch Buk from his fields, Biruta ran to the official in charge, crying: "Everyone here knows he was a patriot in the forest," but the Russian said: "This is the new Poland now. We identify who are patriots."

"New Poland, old Poland," Biruta cried in despair. "Will it never just be Poland as we knew it?"

"Everything's going to be better now," the Russian said. "Everything in order."

"Five years ago the Germans made the same promise." She had more to say, but now the soldiers dragged her confused husband into the square and lined him up against a wall with the other enemies of the state, where the official harangued them: "You are enemies of the Polish people who now own this country and of the Soviet government which has given you your freedom. You will be taken to camp until your reeducation is completed."

The prisoners were not allowed to say goodbye to their families or to take with them any personal possessions, and when Biruta realized that she was going to lose her husband again, she tried to stand with him, but the Russian soldiers pushed her away so violently that she stumbled and fell. Jan moved to help her up, but was stopped by bayonets.

A military truck now wheeled up, and when it halted before the wall, three young Soviet soldiers in brown uniforms leaped out, formed a cordon, and loaded the Poles into the back of their truck. The prisoners were moved eastward toward Siberia, and were never heard from again.

X

BUKOWSKI
VERSUS BUK

THE FOUR WEEKS DURING WHICH THE BUKOWO TALKS ON THE
possibility of establishing a farmers' union were in recess were a
time of unprecedented excitement for Janko Buk, the farmers' spokesman. Japan television invited him to Tokyo for a pair of broadcasts;
with some reluctance the Warsaw government issued him a passport
and the Kremlin allowed him to fly across Siberia to the Orient.

He was awed by the immensity of Russia, for as he told the Intourist man who accompanied him from Moscow to Tokyo: "You
can fly across Poland in minutes. To cross Russia takes days."

"You Poles should keep that in mind," the Intourist man said.

Tokyo was an astonishment. The number of people was staggering, but it was the amount of goods in the stores, the rich variety, the
abundance of food and the fact that the Japanese people seemed to
have money to buy whatever they wanted that impressed him most
deeply. The official from the Polish Embassy who met the plane explained: "They're living on borrowed time. This is all going to collapse. Capitalism at its exploitative worst."

Polish officials coached Buk carefully on what he could and could
not say on television, but he listened and forgot. On the screen, with
a beautiful Japanese girl beside him interpreting his simple sentences,
he made an agreeable impression: "I'm a farmer like your rice farm-

ers I saw yesterday. We were damaged by floods last year and are doing our best to recuperate. We do have shortages, yes, and we've been hit as hard as you by the rise in petrol prices. My wife can seldom find the goods she needs, and we're all damned worried."

The Japanese television producers were so pleased with him, they asked if he would fly to Osaka for an additional two performances, and the embassy people were so relieved that he hadn't upset the turnip cart that they encouraged the detour. From there an American television network invited him to fly to New York, offering him two days' rest in Hawaii, where once more he was staggered by the amount of goods in the stores, by the freedom of action he saw everywhere, but especially by the stores that conducted their business in Japanese standing side by side with American ones.

Suspecting that this was some sort of trick, he asked if he could enter one of the Japanese shops, and his impromptu visit became something of a sensation when a local reporter heard about it, drummed up someone who could speak Polish, and conducted an interview right in the store: "I am amazed that the Japanese are free to come here and sell their goods so openly." Outside, the man pointed to twenty passing automobiles, and eleven were Japanese. "This is a miracle."

When the reporter asked if they didn't have Japanese goods in Poland, he replied: "We have scarcely any goods from foreign countries. Not even from our good neighbor Russia."

The network arranged for him to stop over with the Polish community in Detroit, where he received several shocks. First, he found himself in an area as large as some Polish cities, populated mostly by Poles, with excellent Polish restaurants and many sights that reminded him of Krakow. Second, he was invited to listen to a Polish-language program on radio and then to see one on television, but they distressed him so sharply that he had to complain: "I spend three years in Poland and never hear a polka. I spend two days in Polish America and hear nothing else. What happened to Chopin and Penderecki?" Third, he found the Poles in Detroit almost bursting with enthusiasm for a Polish-Russian war, and he had to tell them: "Nobody in Poland or Russia wants such a thing. You hear none of that talk over there." When he was asked if Poland was afraid, he replied: "We are. We can field an army of how many? Twenty thousand? And the heaviest gun our soldiers have is a deer rifle. Russia has eight hundred thousand men on our borders, with tanks, flame throwers, heavy artillery and dive bombers. We are very afraid." Fourth, and perhaps most important, he discovered that about half the Polish families he met had two cars, and in some cases, three. Even boys sixteen had their own cars. "How do you pay for them?" he asked, and they spread before him the figures on wages, income and the cost of second-hand cars, and he realized that if a Warsaw worker set aside only the same proportion of his salary as the American worker did, he could buy not even a bicycle.

He asked if there were any Polish farmers, and his hosts took him out to a farm near the Canadian border, where he methodically listed the description, cost, and cost of operating every piece of machinery, with the price of gasoline factored in. He could not believe his results. Then he went to four different machines and indicated peculiar parts which might break, and he wanted to know how long it would take to get a replacement and at what cost, so the farmer, a man named Dabrowski, drove him right in to the nearest town, where there was a John Deere representative and an International Harvester dealer, and in these shops Janko saw bin after bin of spare parts. Some of the prices seemed high, but as Dabrowski said: "That's how they make their money. Sell you the big machine cheap and then keep selling you parts for the next twenty years at a stiff price." But there the parts were. Every item Buk had specified could be obtained within an hour, except one, and as the John Deere man said to Dabrowski: "We've never had a single call for a thing like that. It never breaks."

"But let's suppose it does break," Buk said to Dabrowski, who interpreted.

"But it never does," the man insisted.

"Mine did," Buk said, staring right at the man, who brought down a large catalogue in which every component of the machine was listed, and there the part was, drawn in beautiful detail and numbered: 31-XZ-493-8271. Janko wanted to know specifically whether he could get that part, how much and how soon, and the manager said: "I'll have to call Chicago."

During the phone conversation Dabrowski told Buk that the manager was making apologies, saying that he had never before heard of such a part breaking, and then apparently the man in Chicago said the same thing, for the manager placed his hand over the phone and said: "He tells me he's never heard of that part breaking."

"So you have no spare?" Buk said triumphantly, but the manager returned to the phone and after a while said: "The company keeps six in stock, just in case. They'll fly one here by the afternoon plane."

"How much?"

"Thirty-two dollars, forty-seven cents."

"Who pays the air freight?"

"On a remarkable case like this, we do."

Then Janko Buk smiled, the gap between his teeth making him look like a naughty boy. "Tell him, Dabrowski, why I asked so many questions," and when Buk's visit was explained, the manager called several of his clerks and they stood admiring the plucky Pole: "Give the Russkies hell. We're with you all the way." And one woman asked: "Are you really going to be on television? What station? When?"

When they were back in Dabrowski's car the American warned: "Don't take what he said too seriously. These equipment dealers always promise you they'll get the spare part by this afternoon. Usually arrives three days later."

"Do you think they really did have six spares?" Buk asked.

"Probably. That's how they stay in business. But if they don't . . . to keep you happy, they'd take a part from one of their other tractors," and Buk said: "That's exactly what we do in Poland."

His visit to New York was a delight, with a charming young woman as interpreter always at his side. The network men asked if he'd like to visit a Polish restaurant, and he said: "Anything but." To their amazement he selected an Argentine one on the grounds, as he explained: "I'll never have another chance." The beef was so delicious that the network men thanked him for his daring. When they took him to a store where he could purchase gifts for his children, he stood dumfounded at the variety and at the fact that at least half of them came from foreign countries. He never rested easy with this concept of almost free movement of goods between nations.

His two appearances on national television were so self-controlled, and so clearly the performance of a man suddenly projected into a position far beyond his normal capacities but who was struggling to catch up, that three unexpected opportunities resulted.

The leaders of American labor wanted to talk with him and give him good advice, but as he listened to these tired and frightened old men he kept thinking that they had little right to advise Lech Walesa or him: We Poles are fighting on the frontier of entirely new situations and we're doing it with some courage. These Americans, with nothing to risk, weren't even clever enough to handle that air controllers' strike properly. That's not what I call solidarity. But out of politeness, he did listen.

He was startled one morning when the Polish ambassador himself appeared at his room in the big hotel on Sixth Avenue. "President Reagan invites you for lunch at the White House."

"What could I say to the President of the United States?"

"I'll be there to interpret."

"I mean, why me?"

"Because you've become an important man in the world, Janko. You represent something exciting and new. And I must say, Janko, you handle yourself well. All Poland's proud of their farm boy."

He flew with the ambassador to Washington and had an enjoyable, amusing and relaxing meal with the President, who was better versed on farm matters than anyone he had so far met in Honolulu, Detroit or New York. Also, everyone at table told funny stories, the prize being taken by Janko Buk himself, who relayed a story which Szymon Bukowski had told during their meeting at Bukowo:

> "Leonid Brezhnev needed a haircut, so he went down to the ground floor of the Kremlin and plopped into the chair. It was understood that at such times the barber was to say not a word, just cut hair. But this morning, after a few snips, he said: 'Comrade Brezhnev, what are you going to do about Poland?' No reply. Some minutes later: 'Comrade Brezhnev, what about Poland?' Again no reply. Then, pretty soon: 'Comrade Brezhnev, you've got to do something about Poland.'
>
> "At this Brezhnev jumps out of the chair and tears away the cloth: 'What's all this about Poland?' and the barber says: 'It makes my job so much easier,' and Brezhnev screams: 'What do you mean?' and the barber says: 'Every time I mention Poland your hair stands straight up on end.'"

He liked Reagan and was photographed several hundred times with him, but he doubted that Reagan would last very long in either Warsaw or Moscow, where the competition was brutal.

It was the third unexpected opportunity which left the deepest impression. Back in New York, on the night prior to his return to Europe, he was invited to meet with a group of serious scholars, diplomats and businessmen, all of whom had visited Poland and studied its problems. They dined in an exclusive club atop a soaring sky-scraper, with the beauty of a New York night spread out below them.

"What's going to happen in Poland?" the men wanted to know, but the first two hours were spent in their offering their guesses. A young man from Krakow teaching at New York University whis-pered interpretations as the various men spoke, and he relayed a por-trait of disaster.

"The world banks are simply not going to extend any further credits," an international banker predicted. "Poland owes . . . how much? Twenty-five billion? Not a chance of any more."

"And that means no replacement parts . . . for anything," an in-dustrialist said.

"They can still get some from East Germany. With blocked cur-rency."

"East Germany," said a man well versed in the area, "will drag its feet. On orders from Moscow."

Now the ugliest question of the evening was broached: "Do you think that Moscow is orchestrating the disaster in Poland?" The questioner was a sophisticated reporter from *Time*.

"Well, they're certainly not making it any easier."

A labor-union expert on international affairs said: "The critical point came a few weeks ago when Solidarity sent that message to workers in the other Iron Curtain countries." Some of the men did not know about this, so he elaborated: "Solidarity leap-frogged over the heads of the government in Poland and over the heads of govern-ment in Czechoslovakia, Hungary, Rumania and East Germany. They spoke directly to the workers of those countries, intimating that what Solidarity had accomplished in Poland, they could accomplish in their countries."

One man, who heard this news for the first time, whistled. "That's incitement to counterrevolution if I ever heard any."

"It is," the labor-union man said. "So we shouldn't be surprised if Russia does everything possible to frustrate Poland. To prove to the other countries that if they go the Solidarity route, they can expect bread lines and confusion and perhaps even troops in the street."

"No!" several experts cried in unison, and one by one they ex-plained that Russia had by no means a free hand in Poland: "They have to worry about Afghanistan, and believe me they're bleeding there. Just as we did in Vietnam. And they have to worry about China, which remains their major danger. And two new factors must be taken into account. The election of Karol Wojtyla to the papacy has changed a lot of things. You know, he said that if Russian troops invaded, he'd fly to Warsaw. He represents considerable force, shot in the belly or not. And another funny thing. Our election of Ronald Reagan poses the same kind of problem for them. They don't exactly know how to estimate Reagan. They're not sure what he might do if they go too far."

They then turned to Poland itself, and these men whose job it was to calculate the real position of nations agreed that Poland was in just about the sickest condition of any that they had seen in a long, long time. "If it was only food," said one man who knew the country well, "they could correct that in one growing season. Rationing. Giving the farmers priority in things they need. Cleaning out the channels of supply. But it's so infinitely more than food. It's the whole damned stew. It's turned sour, and maybe the only corrective is to throw it all out and start with fresh ingredients in a fresh pot."

One man asked how long it would require, if everything went well, to make the corrections.

"Most hopeful scenario, if all goes well, three years."

"Can Poland endure the mess for three years?"

"It has to," the Pole teaching at NYU said. "It has in the past. It will now."

The men turned to Buk, seeking his estimate of the situation, and he said softly: "I am amazed that in New York City, I should find so many men who know my country so intimately. You speak of things we don't even speak of among ourselves. And I suppose there are in Moscow tonight men just like yourselves who know as much as you do."

"Well . . ." a German diplomat said cautiously.

"So what does a farmer on the scene think? He thinks that things are terrible. And he sees no signals from Warsaw that they're going to get any better."

The men plied him with questions, and every one of his answers hung together cohesively with every other, leading to the unmistakable conclusion that the system itself had begun to show signs of fatal strain. Nothing was working properly, but even Buk did not place his finger on the terrible weakness that underlay everything else. A Hungarian scientist now working at the Massachusetts Institute of Technology was the first to voice the problem.

"The fatal weakness that I observed when I was there last year and again this spring is that practically no one in Poland does a full day's work, except maybe a few farmers who are selling their surplus on the black market. For one conspicuous thing, most factories are shut down two or three days a week because of strikes or shortages. But more important, those who do work put in only four or five honest hours a day, and even in those four hours their performance is apt to be inadequate.

"One of my colleagues filmed a television show in Poland. Where he would have used four men in America, five in England, he was forced by the government to use eighteen in Poland, and not a damned one of them did anything. It was disgraceful. He even had to carry his own umbrella and chair. It's that way with everything.

"Some of us have been working on an index of what percentage of an eight-hour day people really work in various countries, modified by how much they do accomplish in any given hour in which they do work. Combined figures like this can't be too accurate, but you may be interested in our provisional estimates using 100 as top norm.

"Singapore 92.6; Taiwan 89.7; Korea 83.3; Japan 82.1; West Germany 78.8; France 72.7; United States 70.3; Great Britain 40.4; Poland 33.3; Zaire 29.6; Chad 19.9. I have the others, but that's a sampling."

"What about Mexico?" someone called, and he replied after looking at his notes: "That would be 55.6. They refuse to work any harder. Oil makes them think they're rich."

The men focused on that low figure for Poland, only one-third as much productive effort per man as in Singapore, and whereas there was some slight shifting of the figure up or down in relation to other countries, the consensus was that the index was fairly accurate.

"How do you estimate Russia's productivity?" the German economist asked.

"Insufficient evidence," the Hungarian replied.

"You must have an idea."

"About 55 or 60. Better than Great Britain, worse than the United States."

"And your own country, Hungary?"

"There's a problem. It stands right with the United States, about 70 even. That's why we occupy such an enviable position within the bloc."

The men asked Buk what he thought of the figures and he said he was amazed at the relatively low position of his country, but then conceded that he knew nothing about factories, whereupon one of the men asked: "But you know about farms. What index figure would you put on your agricultural production?"

"I would say 30.0," Buk said, and when some of the men whistled, he said: "We really have no incentive to produce one potato more than we eat ourselves. My grandfather produced twice as much as I do, and I'm ashamed of myself. But the system has broken down."

The Polish professor admitted that he was confused: "As a loyal Pole, I don't like to hear my country criticized so harshly, but as a scholar, I'm forced to admit that your evidence is accurate. My beloved country is in one hell of a shape." He then advanced two interesting theories:

"Starting in 1772, when the divisions of Poland began, every Pole who found himself under the domination of Russia, Germany or Austria devised clever ways to circumvent the rule of the oppressor. Lazy on the job, break the machine, irritate the boss. After 1795, this continued, remember, for one hundred and twenty-three years.

"During World War II, when the Nazis occupied us, sabotage became a skilled art. In 1944, when Communism took over, with Russian masters once more, the same brilliant capacity for quiet sabotage was exercised. Today, when the people believe that government is opposed to their interests, they know a million ways to frustrate the government. Poles are the world's master saboteurs.

"And another thing. In the postwar period, right up to 1975, for a Pole to survive on wages the government allowed he had to have two or even three jobs. Work 0800 to 1300 here, then duck out and work 1400 to 1800 somewhere else. Then at night work 1900 to 0100 at a third job. But never really work at any of them. Catch as much sleep as you can on each.

"I was with the Labor Bureau when we got our first big computer. We cranked in the entire work force and found that with a population of slightly less than thirty-six million, we had fifty-three million full-time employees. That's when we stopped the moonlighting, but the evil habits our people acquired in those years persist."

An American military man asked: "Do you see any hope for Poland in the years immediately ahead?" and the scholar replied: "No. I think we shall have to plunge into the depths, reorganize in some unforeseen way, and slowly reestablish ourselves in some other posture." The general asked: "How soon could this be accomplished?" and Buk said: "I see no hope during the next five years."

Buk went to bed that night like many a world traveler before him: he had obtained a clearer view of his homeland by leaving it and seeing it through the eyes of others. He could scarcely sleep because of the doleful things he had heard these men say, for he feared that they were right in their calculations.

He was awakened early on the final morning by a group of men in a flurry: "You've got to change your airline tickets. You're to leave Kennedy at noon instead of tonight at seven."

When he asked why, they beamed. "Our man in Rome has finally arranged it! Imagine! Jan Pawel Drugi has said he'd be honored to greet you. At the Vatican. Tomorrow at three." Buk lowered his head. He could not believe that a Pope, and one so dangerously wounded, would want to meet him, but before he left the hotel, newsmen around the world were announcing to their nations that the Pope had invited Jan Buk to the Vatican for a discussion of Polish affairs.

At the airport, not the ordinary two or three television cameras waited but a dozen, each demanding of Buk some profound statement on Polish politics, and for the first time during his improvised trip around the world, he had to acknowledge that for this moment at least he had become a man of some importance.

It confused him. He could be sure of only two things: the democracies were trying to use him as a cudgel against the socialist states, especially Russia; and despite his introduction to the global thinkers at the meeting last night, he was still a farmer from the banks of the Vistula with a very imperfect understanding of how Poland functioned, let alone eastern Europe or the world. He did not allow notoriety to disorient him.

"Are you really going to see the Pope?" several newsmen shouted, and when the cameras were aligned he said: "Jan Pawel Drugi has graciously extended an invitation. Yes, I am to see him tomorrow."

The name Buk used was unfamiliar, and several correspondents asked: "Who? Who?" and a man from the Polish Embassy explained: "Jan Pawel Drugi. You say it John Paul Second. The Italian says it Giovanni Paolo Secondo. But to the whole world he is our beloved Polish Pope."

When Janko Buk was strapped into the Alitalia plane he began to appreciate the wonderful thing that was happening: he was flying to see the Holy Father, that simple, forthright Polish son of old peasant stock who came from a village not far from Bukowo and whose church life had been spent in Buk's Krakow. Janko could not remember ever having seen the future Pope during his visits to Krakow, a city of great importance to anyone from Bukowo and one much more likely to be visited than Warsaw, but he could have. He wondered if Cardinal Wojtyla had been present at either of the two great convocations at Czestochowa which he had attended as a pilgrim, and he supposed that he must have been. At any rate, Jan Pawel Drugi had been a neighbor, and it was always good to visit with a neighbor.

When the plane landed at Leonardo da Vinci south of Rome, more newsmen wanted to talk with Buk because the situation in Poland had deteriorated during the suspension of talks, and there was much speculation as to when and how Russia would invade. Three weeks earlier he would have avoided any such inquiry as being beyond his scope, but now, remembering the explanations which had so impressed him the night before, he said in carefully enunciated phrases: "I'm sure that both sides want to avoid any kind of confrontation. Poland's position is exciting these days, but not very strong. On the other hand, the Soviet Union is not entirely free to act as she might wish. Afghanistan and China on her southern frontier. Two new imponderables on her world scene. President Reagan in Washington, Jan Pawel in the Vatican. An amusing fellow in New York said he'd give me a strategy free. 'You farmers go ahead with your strike. Cut the food supply in half. Russia wouldn't *dare* to take you. Wouldn't even *want* to.'"

When the reporters laughed, he added: "I know of no one in Poland, and I suspect I'd find none in Russia, who is talking arrogantly at this moment. Desperately we are both trying to find workable ways. In Detroit, I met many Poles who talked violently, but not the

Poles in Poland. When I meet with the Holy Father, I shall ask him only one thing, to pray for peace."

Several reporters asked if he knew the new Pope, and Buk said: "Farmers from little villages do not know cardinals from big cities. But what I've heard about him I love, and when I think of the great danger he ran when the gunman fired at him, I love him even more." The newsmen thought he sounded like an uneducated farmer who was getting a crash course in diplomacy.

Next day at two-thirty in the afternoon a cavalcade of automobiles gathered at the hotel where the Polish group was staying, but most of the cars contained newsmen. They sped through narrow streets, then along the splendid boulevard that followed the Tiber and across the bridge into the minute area of Vatican City. They headed directly for St. Peter's, then turned sharp right and went up the very narrow street that took tourists to the Vatican art museum, and through huge gates that swung open for the two lead cars but not for those that followed.

They now entered a series of paved roads that led through gardens and up a hill, then through another stone portal that gave upon a cobbled courtyard completely surrounded by buildings of various colors and with varied façades. Here the two cars stopped as Swiss guards inspected the credentials of the occupants, after which Janko Buk and two of his companions were led to a most inconspicuous door and into a small vestibule, where hidden television cameras gazed down at them.

An elevator door slid quietly open, providing entrance to a really small lift which took them quietly up two stories, where it opened noiselessly, allowing them to step into a large, almost empty but tastefully decorated hall. Two priests who did not speak Polish led them through several anterooms, decorated in Renaissance style, and into a fine, narrow room with red-and-gilt chairs, paintings of churchly figures and three sculptures of holy scenes.

Here they waited, talking in whispers, until a brash young Polish priest hurried in with loud, jovial greetings: "No need to talk in whispers. Prayers don't come till later." He acted as if he were truly glad to see Janko Buk and gripped him warmly with both hands. "You are accomplishing wonderful things. Where is Bukowo?"

Buk, relieved to be able to talk about mundane matters, explained that his unimportant stretch of the Vistula contained three rather splendid buildings much visited by tourists: "Castle Gorka of the famous Lubonskis, Baranow Castle of the even more famous Leszc-zynskis, and in between, the lovely palace of our own Bukowskis."

"Never heard of any of them," the young priest said. "I come from Gniezno."

"Where Christianity began in Poland," Buk said.

"That's right!" the priest said with real enthusiasm. "I have no idea what the Holy Father will want to talk with you about, but you realize, of course, that it will be confidential."

"How am I to address him?" Buk asked.

"Your Holiness is always proper. Holy Father is used. And of course, his fundamental title is one we all share. Father. No other word characterizes him better."

"How is he?" Buk asked, but before the young priest could reply, an older priest, the Pope's constant companion during the years before his elevation to the Vatican, came in to announce that His Holiness would see the visitors now, but when Buk followed the two priests from the waiting room, he found in the reception room not the Pope but two Vatican photographers. This was going to be a historic meeting and they were responsible for catching proper mementos of it.

Everyone stood silent, and then a door at the far end of the room swung open and a sturdy man dressed all in white except for his red slippers hurried into the room as if he were twenty, stopped in delight, looked at this visiting farmer, and said: "Janko Buk, I am so very pleased to see you!"

Nudged by his companions, Buk stepped forward, knelt, and kissed the Pope's left hand. The cameras caught this, six different pictures in a quarter of a minute, but they were even more careful to catch the next important tableau: Pope Jan Pawel embracing Janko Buk, resident of his one-time diocese. It made an excellent photograph, something out of Florence or Venice in the fifteenth century but one fraught with contemporary meaning.

All else was subsidiary. It was the photograph of two men embracing—not Janko Buk embracing the Pope, but both embracing equally—that conveyed the message: a simple man endeavoring to start a farmers' union was welcomed in the Vatican regardless of how he might be received in Warsaw or Moscow.

After pleasantries about Poland and Krakow, with the Pope smiling constantly, Janko asked if the gunshot wounds had healed, and the Pope said they were healing, rather nicely he thought, and then the Pope asked how President Reagan had looked, and Janko said:

"You'd never know he had been shot." At this the Pope nodded sagely and smiled.

Janko repeated the joke about Brezhnev and the barber, and the Pope chuckled, responding with a joke about himself in Mexico. It seemed to the two companions that most of the visit was being wasted in laughter, but finally the Pope asked how the talks were going, and Janko made a highly improper reply: "The reason they broke off, Holy Father, is that I insisted the Bishop of Gorka participate."

The Pope realized that this was a subject about which he must not speak during a critical period, so he smiled and shrugged his shoulders, but he had to say something, so he was noncommittal: "He is a saintly man."

Janko said: "Many people in the area think he'll be cardinal one day."

The Pope broke into laughter at this huge impropriety and grasped Janko by the hand. "I hope you're more politic in your discussions with the government."

"I'm sorry, Your Holiness. But our side wanted the bishop to participate because he is a saintly man. Mere talking isn't going to settle this." No one said anything, so Janko asked: "Have we your prayers?"

"All Poland has our prayers," the Pope said, and the meeting ended, with another series of flashbulbs and handshakes and blessings, but as the Pope went far out of his way to accompany Janko to the elevator he said: "My prayers are with you, particularly. You've chosen a most difficult course." He neither condoned the course nor condemned it.

Back at the hotel, Janko was told that Austrian television had invited him to Vienna: "No fee of any kind, but they will put us up at a good small hotel near the Schönbrunn." So another change in itinerary was arranged, and the men flew into Vienna, which in many ways was the most disturbing visit of the entire trip. Two experiences had a devastating impact on Buk, so that he remembered them vividly even when President Reagan and Jan Pawel were becoming distant images.

The first was a trivial thing. Prior to his appearance on Austrian television he walked down Vienna's resplendent pedestrian street in the heart of the city, Kärntnerstrasse, and as he strolled slowly past the opulent shops offering goods of the highest quality from all over the world—he could think of scarcely anything he might want for his wife that was not available—he began to wonder how this city, which was only a day's drive from Warsaw, could have so much and his own so little.

Austria had only seven million five hundred thousand population to Poland's nearly thirty-six million. In available land Poland was four times as large, and in raw materials infinitely richer. Polish workmen were as skilled as Austrians and their political leaders as well educated. Both countries were Catholic, both had good railroads, excellent airplanes, and neither had an aggravated minority.

But there the identities ended, for Vienna was a city of lightness and music and newspapers freely admitted from all over the world, and hope and bursting joyousness, while Warsaw, from what Janko Buk had seen of it, was not. Most important, Vienna was feeding itself and was distributing its goods equitably; Warsaw was not. Some vast difference separated these two cities, only three hundred and fifty miles apart, and Janko Buk wanted to know what it was.

He was diverted from finding out by the intrusion of a brief trip he had not expected to make to a village he had never heard of. Traiskirchen lay a short distance south of Vienna, some twenty miles from the beautiful Neusiedler See, and it contained an immense army barracks dating back to the time of Emperor Franz Josef. To it had been brought, in the old days, those lads from occupied Poland who had been conscripted into the Austrian army for their obligatory term of duty, twenty-five years.

Now it was occupied by those energetic young Poles who had left their country as refugees, determined to spend the rest of their lives anywhere but in Poland. Nearly a thousand of these escapees waited in these forlorn barracks for the joyous news that America or Canada or Brazil or especially Australia or New Zealand had agreed to accept them as immigrants.

Very gingerly Janko Buk stepped among these refugees, living like outcasts on charity from the United Nations, for he had to classify them as traitors, but when he talked with them and heard them describe the desolation of spirit which had driven them to flee the country they loved, he came close to tears. These had been some of the best young people in Poland; he could see that from the bright faces of the young wives who had encouraged their husbands to take this dreadful gamble; he could see it in the attitudes of the many children who were now lost to Poland; and he could hear it in the hard, implacable words of the men: "I will not go back. Even if I starve here, I will not go back to that prison of the spirit."

"Does the world know about this camp?" Buk asked the men with him.

"We didn't know about it. And it's only one of three. The flight of our talent is continuous."

"But does anybody know about it? I never did."

"The world has other things to worry about."

"But this ought to be known in Poland," Buk protested. Leaving his companions, he mingled with the idle refugees, wanting to know how this one had escaped, how that one had managed to bring his wife and two children with him, and he discovered an astonishing fact: none of them had *escaped.* They had simply asked for passports, said they were going on vacation, and then thrown themselves on the mercy of the Austrian government as political refugees. Not one Pole he met had fled the country, in the traditional sense that men fled Russia or East Germany; they had all walked out, as if from a doomed village or from a city that had lost its way.

"It almost sounds," Buk said, "as if the Polish government wanted you out of the country."

"They certainly didn't try to stop us. Fewer mouths to feed. Fewer people of the type who might cause trouble."

Buk was so distressed by this that against his better judgment, for he was not an exhibitionist, he confided to a group of about twenty young men who were sharing their experiences with him: "I'm Janko Buk. The farmer."

Word flashed through the yard, enclosed by a high chain-link fence, that the farmer who'd been to see the Pope was here, and several refugees produced Austrian newspapers showing Buk on the front page. Now he had an audience of hundreds, most of whom wanted to know how Jan Pawel looked and how he was recovering from his bullet wounds. Several ardent patriots wished to explore the rumors which had been floating through Poland when they left: that the Pope had been shot by Italians who resented his occupancy of the Vatican, or by Russian Communists, or by a Bulgarian infiltrator under the pay of the Orthodox bishops, or by a demented nun, or particularly by agents of the Polish government who had gone to Turkey to hire the gunman for their plot.

Buk, who had heard none of these theories, gave it as his opinion that the gunman had pretty clearly been acting on his own, and several men jeered: "That's what they said about President Kennedy," but when they volunteered who the conspirators in that case had been, their guesses were as wild and as fascinating as before. One man insisted that Kennedy, too, had been shot by a demented nun.

But when the chatter and the nonsense ended, there remained the dreadful fact that these barracks which had once housed Polish recruits taken under duress were now filled with some of Poland's finest, who had placed themselves within the confines voluntarily, and Buk felt he had to address this tragedy: "Men like me, all over Poland, we're trying to correct things."

"We wish you luck."

"But don't you have any desire to help?"

One man answered for all: "I've been to Rumania. I've been to Czechoslovakia. And, God forbid, I've been to East Germany. And in that entire system there is no hope."

"Poland is not like those countries," Buk insisted.

"In some respects, it's worse."

But the men were hungry for news about their homeland, and after the negatives had been voiced, rather bitterly Buk thought, they wanted to hear about the strikes and the reaction of the two governments, Poland and Russia. They listened to every word Buk said, and several men complimented him: "You have courage. But what do you expect to accomplish?"

And Buk retreated to a saying popular in his village: "'A Pole is a man born with a sword in his right hand, a brick in his left. When the battle is over, he starts to rebuild.' After every war we rebuild. After every disaster we regroup. I do wish you would return home and help us regroup."

"There is no hope," the refugees said, and Janko Buk left the barracks sick in spirit.

That night the Austrian television people arranged an informal dinner at a popular Viennese restaurant called the Balkan Grill, where a sturdy country meal was provided, featuring great platters of mixed meats and hefty vegetables. Steins of beer were served, and when Buk leaned back to survey the littered table, he felt the same sickness, for this was another discrepancy he could not explain: Vienna gorged with food, nearby Warsaw facing terrible shortages.

When talks resumed, television crews from all over the world, including Moscow, descended on Bukowo, so many that some had to be housed in Castle Gorka up the river, some down at Baranow Castle, and all wanted to interview Jan Buk, but they found a much more sober farmer, and one Paris reporter wrote: "In the four-week break he gave himself a university education." He did not posture, nor did he fulminate; he showed that he was deadly serious in his endeavors to find a solution to the problem of food.

The second session began with a tour of the Bukowski palace for the reporters, and selected television cameramen were assigned as a pool to take pictures for all the networks. A spokeswoman from the cultural branch of the Warsaw government explained what was being shown, and she started with the great hall, where the visitors were delighted by the two huge facing canvases *Jan Sobieski on the Route to Vienna* and *The Defense of Czestochowa.* They formed a stunning pair.

"But I read somewhere they had been destroyed," a Japanese newsman said.

"They were," the spokeswoman said, "and your question gives me an opportunity to pay tribute to the man who resuscitated them." To everyone's surprise she pointed at Szymon Bukowski, who stood with his hands clasped at his waist.

"After the German occupation, in the years from 1950 through 1970, Pan Bukowski, now a minister of government, was responsible for the rebuilding of Poland's destroyed treasures. It was he who rebuilt Castle Gorka, where some of you are staying. You've seen photographs of how the Nazis left it. He then rebuilt beautiful Baranow to the north, which many of you know. He rebuilt parts of Lublin and of Stalowa Wola. But his heart, I do believe, was in the rebuilding of the palace we are now in."

She pointed to the Matejko painting of Jan Sobieski and said: "This painting has always been a national treasure. We revered it. But in the last hours of the war German soldiers stationed here took their machine guns and riddled every one of those men. We've put a photograph over there of how the painting looked when Pan Bukowski got to it. Not very pretty."

She allowed time for those who wished to study the ghastly sight of the great painting as it had appeared in 1944. Then she brought the reporters back to the painting itself: "Every figure you see there was first patiently rewoven by women from this village. By that I mean, we stretched the canvas out on an immense table and we rewove every missing fiber. I did the head of Brat Piotr, a wild and famous priest who accompanied Sobieski. It took me five weeks, but when I was finished we had a canvas on which some very skilled artists could re-create the face of Brat Piotr as Matejko had painted it a hundred years ago."

"Who did the head of Sobieski?"

"Some woman like me."

"I mean, who repainted it?"

"Some artist like the man who did Brat Piotr."

She invited those who considered themselves expert in art to study the two paintings, then she led everyone to the rooms where copies of the Correggio, the Rembrandt and especially the Holbein were displayed as they had been in the time of Marjorie Bukowska, and she made this point: "The palace is very old, perhaps back to 1450, but it had to be rebuilt so many times that we scarcely know what we have at any given intersection of the walls. We do know that it took its present form in 1896 when young Wiktor Bukowski, serving in Vienna, married the extremely wealthy daughter of the American ambassador. Oscar Mandeville Trilling, his name was for you American reporters. From Chicago. Grain and real estate and railroads, I believe."

She answered further questions about the Trillings, then said: "We are grateful to Madame Trilling Bukowska for what she did in reconstructing such a fine palace, but many of us treasure most what she did in the long gallery downstairs." She led the group down to the portrait gallery, where the thirty-one worthies of Polish history lived again. She told briefly of that last day when the Nazi troops ran wild, and she showed where the bloodstains of the murders had been allowed to remain on the old carpet. Then she led the reporters past the noble heads, the great paunches held in by golden sashes, the fierce mustaches, and gave brief introductions to these glorious wild men of Polish history: "Radziwill, one of the founders of the Lithuanian family—one married the sister of your Jackie Kennedy. Mniszech, who helped decide who should be Czar of Russia. This is Leszczynski, twice elected our king, twice rejected. He became father-in-law to one of the kings of France."

"Louis XV," a French reporter volunteered.

"And so it goes," she said. "Remember that every portrait here was bullet-ridden that day. But Pan Bukowski would not allow that desecration to remain. He ordered them all restored, and I wove the fabric for this fine fellow. I can never remember his name."

Some reporters felt afterward that this tour, instructive though it might be, had been a ploy on the part of the government to inflate Bukowski as their negotiator, but even these doubters had to concede that his work of restoration along the Vistula was triumphant. "These are three of the most congenial monuments in Europe," the French critic wrote. "Not grandiose. Not stupefying. But extremely real. That they should have been rescued from the debris of war will be a permanent tribute to Polish doggedness. Architect Bukowski made not a single mistake in his buildings. Now we shall see what he can do with his recalcitrant farmers."

This series of meetings, much enlarged in attendance, was held in the great hall, with Jan Sobieski looking down in stern supervision, and they were entirely different from those four weeks earlier. Jan Buk was no longer an embattled farmer; he was now a statesman, so acknowledged by other statesmen around the world. He carried weight where before he had carried only conviction.

But Szymon Bukowski was not the same man, either. Stiffened by his series of hammer-blow consultations with leaders of the Polish government, who themselves had sought secret instructions from Russian envoys who had slipped into the country, he was in no mood to make irrelevant concessions, and in the opening minutes he announced his first decision: "We recessed our discussions four weeks ago because Pan Buk asked that a high official of the Catholic church be brought into our meetings. This request is denied. Our two teams are competent to make all decisions."

To the surprise of the delegates, Janko Buk made no objection, and for a good reason: Bukowski had not accompanied the reporters down to the gallery; he spent that time seeking out Buk and assuring him that together they two would meet with the Bishop of Gorka that night, after the plenary session ended. When Buk asked where, Bukowski confided: "Secretly. At the castle."

With that prickly question settled, the morning session continued, with Bukowski standing forth as the man in command. He made two striking statements: "The people of Poland and the world must know that this country stands solidly and irrevocably with our great Soviet partner in our determination to bring social justice into the family of nations. We are united now and forever in that resolve, and anyone or anything that imperils that union is an enemy of the Polish people. I'm not saying that our farmers who are making certain demands are false to the cause. Not at all. They're discussing honest problems in an honest way. But those enemies of the state who try to inflate these discussions into a form of revolution, or who endeavor to use them as a wedge between Poland and Russia, are enemies of the state and will be so treated."

His second major statement caught the attention of all the delegates, and of the world press, when they heard a summary of what he had said: "We've just heard Pan Buk speak of his visit to Detroit, where he met many Poles who emigrated there in the bad days before we had social justice in Poland. And he spoke of his fellow countrymen who had automobiles, sometimes even two automobiles to a family. Well, let me tell you two things about such evidence. First, any family that has two automobiles anywhere in the world does so at the expense of the workingman. They are prospering on the blood of the workingman."

"But these were workingmen," Buk interrupted.

Bukowski took no notice. "Second, every impartial observer knows that America is heading for a major depression. The devices they're trying won't work. If Pan Buk returns to Detroit this time next year, he'll find his Poles selling both their cars in order to eat. America has solutions to nothing. Only the socialist republics of the world who believe in equality and freedom and peace have the solutions, and we must not be blinded in these days of relative discomfort to that basic fact."

A tough lion of a man with gray mane, this graduate of the cruelest academies the world had produced in recent years—exile in the Forest of Szczek, torture in Under the Clock, starvation and genocide in Majdanek, plus the agony of surveying a destroyed land before starting to rebuild it—was not disposed to surrender the social gains he believed his country had made since it passed under Russian control. He was especially forceful when he called upon his countrymen to remember how their ancestors had lived under the dictatorship of the magnates and the despotism of Prussia, Austria and czarist Russia: "Look back to how we lived in villages like this a hundred years ago. The dirt floors. Meat twice a year at Christmas and Easter. Bowing when the gentry forced us into the gutters as they passed. Polish forbidden to be spoken. No newspapers. Our colleges closed down. And everywhere the secret police sending our fathers and grandfathers off to permanent exile. That's the Poland my mother fought against. And I shall fight till I die to prevent its return."

At the noon break the television people wanted to cluster around Buk, hoping to stage a photograph of him standing beside a clever poster which some local cartoonist had created; it showed a clearly recognizable Janko Buk shaking hands with President Reagan, and the words in English: JANKO THE YANKO. It was a tricky little play on words, because Buk's first name was pronounced Yanko, of course, and since Polish has no word beginning with a *y,* the *Yanko* had to be pronounced in the American fashion, which made it the same as the other. Children in the waiting group outside the palace were crying "Yanko the Yanko" and sometimes "Djanko the Djanko." In either case, they were having fun and the television crews wanted to catch the frolicking.

But Bukowski had decided that from here on he would dominate the picture sessions, and he brought two sober companions before the cameras to help him summarize the morning's talk: "We confirmed our loyalty to the concept of social democracy and our alliance with the Soviet Union. About that there must be no confusion."

The afternoon session took up in sober detail the implied problems and difficulties of trying to organize and run an agricultural union, and again Bukowski steamrollered the opposition, which insisted that it could be done. When reporters heard of his hard line they began to write that whereas the earlier session had been Buk *versus* Bukowski, this one was surely Bukowski *versus* Buk, with the behind-the-scenes power of the Russian bear dominating the discussion. Bukowski, when asked about this, said merely that tomorrow the reporters would witness the real cohesion of the Polish people. When they asked what he meant by this, he said merely: "You'll see."

Since Buk still refused to lodge in the palace with the other delegates, preferring the familiarity of his own cottage, it was not difficult for him to slip away after dusk, but he had to wait in the car that would carry him and Bukowski to their meeting with the bishop. After a while the latter made his escape and they sped with dimmed lights to the town of Gorka, where the bishop was waiting.

They met not in the castle, as Bukowski had first indicated, for that was filled with reporters, and not in the bishop's palace, for that would have compromised the Communist Bukowski, but in a bare committee room provided in secrecy by the mayor.

The Bishop of Gorka was, as Jan Pawel Drugi had said in the Vatican, a saintly man. Sixty-three years old and with a face that looked as if it had been carved of wood and allowed to weather as the central figure in some treasured roadside shrine, he wore his white hair combed forward in the Julius Caesar style, which was appropriate, for his tall, lean figure resembled that of the aging Caesar when the daggers came at him.

He was a wise man, one who had fought enemies all his life, inventing ways to circumvent their ugly intentions and still preserve his own more humane and generous ones. As he had told a group of touring Scandinavian reporters the previous year: "When you had to survive under the Nazis as a young man, and under the Communists as an old one, and when you've spent your ecclesiastical life being tutored by the revered Cardinal Wyszynski, who was in jail a good deal of the time, and Cardinal Wojtyla, who knew how to resist and smile, you learn something . . . or you perish."

His reputation for saintliness stemmed from his unwavering support of his people, no matter what difficulties they fell into. He was indeed the ideal village priest, and his elevation to bishop had been a mistake which many in and out of the church now acknowledged; that he should be selected for promotion to cardinal, as Jan Buk had suggested to the Pope, was not even under consideration, for the lower his status in the hierarchy, the greater his contribution to the spiritual life of his country.

He was regarded by the multitude of Poles with reverence because of his simplicity, by the Polish Communists with apprehension because of his opposition to many of their policies, and by the Russians, who had to deal with these terribly difficult men Wyszynski and Wojtyla, as a source of comparable danger. To abuse this tall, almost ghostly figure would have created exactly the kind of opposition they sought to avoid.

The bishop, eager to meet the two men from his district who were playing such important roles in the present crisis, hurried forward to greet them as if he were being honored and not they: "Two men from the Vistula, causing all this commotion!" Buk genuflected and brought the bishop's left hand to his lips; Bukowski, to whom the gesture was distasteful, bowed and then extended his own hand to shake the bishop's.

"You were kind to arrange this meeting," Buk said. "As he will tell you," he said, smiling at Bukowski, "it almost broke up the sessions when I suggested it."

"I would not have wanted that," the bishop said as he led the men to their chairs. "In these dolorous times it's important that we all keep talking." He smiled, then paused as the mayor's assistant brought in tea, but no doilies, currant juice or small cakes. "How are the meetings going?" he asked when they were alone.

Bukowski replied: "Not at all well. Our differences are quite fundamental."

"They always are, if the meeting is worth anything. What are they this time?"

"They cut to the heart of Poland's future."

"Thank God that somebody's worrying about the future of this land."

"But in the wrong way," Bukowski said.

"Explain, please."

"My friend Buk here, and his Solidarity men at Gdansk, want to take steps that would alter the basic structure of our country."

"Well, if one looks at the bread lines—the lines for everything— isn't some alteration advisable? Isn't it even . . ." The bishop paused a perceptible moment as if loath to use the harsh word he could not evade. "Hasn't it become inevitable?"

Bukowski stiffened. "This is to be a socialist republic, that's basic. It's to remain in close alliance with the Soviet Union. That's forever. And if what Buk proposes endangers those two fundamentals, he becomes an enemy of the state."

The bishop extended his hand to touch Bukowski's. "But isn't what your side is doing, doesn't that endanger the state even more? Can we tolerate food riots this coming winter?"

"There will be no food riots," Bukowski said. "We won't allow them."

"One never allows or disallows the rioting of hungry women. There the riot is, right in your lap, and you either shoot the women down or you accommodate them. Mr. Minister, I'm not only honored that you've come to talk with me, I'm really quite excited, for it gives me a chance to share my views with a high official of the government. Mr. Minister, we are in deep, deep trouble."

"And that's why we wanted to talk with you," Buk interrupted.

The bishop sighed. "I am so glad you're talking. I'm so very pleased you asked me to join you, even if you were afraid to do so publicly. Because nations sometimes really do stand at crossroads, and I think this autumn of 1981 has been such a time for Poland. I've been reading, these days, about other periods when fate hung in the balance. In 1658, Poland-Lithuania joined Ukraine in a union—

sagacious laws, social justice, protection of minorities, Roman Catholics, Uniates and Orthodox, each church with its guaranteed rights. However, it lasted six months, torn apart by jealous, narrow-minded men, the Polish magnates the worst of the lot, with Count Lubonski of this very town leading the wreckers. Well, we tried again in 1920, and this time our Lubonski was the principal builder, but again it all came to ashes . . . shadows . . . despair. I often wonder, as I read, what proportion of their goods the Lithuanians and Ukrainians would give today to be living safe with such a union? I wonder how much we Poles would give had we been wise enough to bury our prejudices in 1658 or 1920?"

"Those chances are lost," Bukowski said. "We live in a new world now."

"Indeed we do," Bishop Barski granted, "and it is the protection of that world, such as it is, that concerns me. You men, together and individually, you must do nothing that will destroy your world. You must move with great caution."

"We understand the gravity," Bukowski said quickly. "And I'm terrified that this man's drive to disrupt the countryside—"

"No!" Buk cried. "It's your rules that are doing the disrupting."

"Are you two so far apart?" the bishop asked, and before they could give their answers he gave his: "Surely the three of us can find common ground . . . I mean we three in particular." And as he spoke he allowed his left arm to stretch forward rather awkwardly, but far enough so that the men could see that ugly purplish line of identifying numerals which had been tattooed upon it in the concentration camp, and when he was satisfied that each of his visitors had seen it, he spoke at some length.

"Szymon Bukowski, in the interrogations at Lublin and at Majdanek you went through two of the worst hells that this earth can provide. That you survived when so many others didn't is a tribute to your courage and the strong body your parents gave you. But I am equally impressed that on your release you dedicated yourself to the rebuilding of our nation. Here in Gorka, I see your reconstructed castle every day, and it's a monument to you. On my visits I see what you accomplished at Baranow, that dear little gem, and at the palace. Few men are ever given the chance to build their own memorials. You were offered that chance, and you built exceedingly well.

"Because of what you saw during the war and the occupation, you became a Communist, a very wise one I'm told. I suppose you understand the theory rather better than you do its application, but because you were so savagely treated at Majdanek, you exercise your own authority with gentleness and even love. Poland can be grateful that so many of its Communist leaders are like you and not like the Nazi officials who terrorized this land in their day.

"Mr. Minister, there is no warfare between you and me. I know you and I love you for the brave man you are. Your governmental decisions? Well, that's another matter.

"And you, Farmer Buk. What a distinguished son of Poland you are. Did you know that on the dreadful morning when the Nazis arrived in your village and lined up the people to be executed, your great-aunt Miroslawa—that's Pan Bukowski's mother—did you know that the man who stood next to her when the machine guns fired was my uncle, Father Barski of this parish? Yes, I dedicated myself to the priesthood that awful day. I told my mother: 'They've killed Uncle Pawel. I must take his place.'

"So we three are bound together in ways we might not recognize at first. We are three men of this soil, products of the fertility of this fortunate land. We've followed three very different paths, but we have all come to the same critical moment, in a bare little room on the banks of the Vistula: a member of the government, a bishop of the church, a local farmer who gallivants about the world appearing on television and meeting presidents and popes. Tell me, Pan Buk, how was the Holy Father?"

"President Reagan has recovered from his bullet wound. Jan Pawel Drugi has not. He was thin and I think he was in pain."

"What did you talk about?"

"We laughed most of the time. I told him two jokes and he told me two jokes, and we spoke of you."

"You did?" The bishop's two hands reached out to clasp Buk's. "And what was said?"

"I said we thought, in these parts, that you should be a cardinal."

"My heavens! And what did the Holy Father say to that?"

"He laughed."

"I should think he might. I'm barely qualified to be a bishop, and here you go promoting me to cardinal." He chuckled and said: "I read about it in a report from America. The Peter Principle."

"Saint Peter?" Buk asked.

"Heavens, no! This Peter was an advertising man, I believe. He said that organizations like the church or General Motors promote a man up and up till he reaches a spot which he is obviously incapable of filling, and there they let him rest. So that big organizations are constantly being run by men like me who have attained the demonstrated level of their incompetency."

He grew very serious: "But we three are competent to discuss the future of a nation we love. And I suppose that's why we're here tonight."

"The basic," Bukowski said firmly, "is that we must remain socialist and we must remain in tandem with the Soviet Union."

"But not dictated to by them," Bishop Barski said. "We've fought that battle in the church, and we've won."

"Russian Communism takes economic production rather more seriously than it takes religion."

"Don't you believe that! The pressures the Russians—and your own people, Mr. Minister—the pressures you put on the church were tremendous. Because Communism has always seen the church as competing for the souls of men like Farmer Buk here."

Bukowski dropped his arrogance. "Do you think the two can coexist?"

"They do coexist," Bishop Barski said.

"Happily?"

"How many married couples coexist in total happiness? Not too many, if I can believe my ears. But the years roll on and they live together and a sense of decency develops, and children of good quality are produced and brought to manhood, and I suppose that's what love is." He stopped to reflect on how this related to governments, then said: "I'd say, and I think Wyszynski would have said before he died, or Jan Pawel Drugi would say right now, that we've spent the last thirty years in reasonable relationships with you Communists in Warsaw and their Communists in Moscow. Not happily, no. But acceptably? Under the circumstances that Our Lord Jesus referred to— granting Caesar what is always due Caesar—yes, we have coexisted."

"That's what we want to do now," Jan Buk said. Up to this point he had been principally a listener as Bukowski and the bishop parried, but the meeting had been called by him to provide guidance in the areas of his concern. "Is it possible to have a farmers' union which will do for us what Lech Walesa has done for his factory people?"

Bukowski was overeager to settle that question quickly: "Nations do not allow farmers to have unions. No nation does."

"Up to now," the bishop said. "Go on, Buk."

"So far," Buk said accurately, "every gain that Solidarity has obtained for its city members has been at our expense."

"I wonder if that's true."

"It seems so to us."

"*Seem* and *is* are two vastly different words."

"Then let's consider what's actually happening. We farmers are being so savagely mistreated, paying more for all we need, getting less for all we grow, that we're going on strike. Yes, that's what I said. We are already on strike, producing less and allowing less of what we do produce to filter into regular channels of distribution. We're on strike, and if we continue, the people of Poland will go hungry."

"Are you proud of that?" Bishop Barski asked.

"I am mortally ashamed," Buk said.

"Then why do you do it?"

"Because it's the only way we can make men like this one listen to our complaints."

"Tell me," Bukowski broke in. "Do you know of any major nation that allows its farmers to combine in unions? Does Russia?"

"No, Russia does not," Bishop Barski said very quietly, "and I suppose that's why that great nation with all its power and all its marvelous agricultural land cannot feed itself. For two decades their farmers have been doing exactly what Buk says he's doing. They've been on strike, and not even machine guns can make them stop."

"How does this happen?" Bukowski asked.

"Because a field is like a human soul, Mr. Minister. It must be nurtured in specific and careful ways. It must be tended with love. The man cultivating it must respect it and want to see every seed mature. He must feel that if he does not do well with his field—his little field, the corner of the earth allowed him—all the rest of the earth will starve. And you cannot dictate that attitude, because if you try, you see what the cultivator of the field will say: 'To hell with this. Let the field rot.' It's an indecent thing to say, and I am broken-hearted to hear a man like Janko Buk say it, but that's what they say. And if I were a farmer, I think I would say it too. I would feed myself and say: 'To hell with you big-idea men in the city.'"

There was a long silence. Finally the bishop rose, went to the door and called for the assistant, who brought in a decanter of brandy and three small glasses. The men drank, still silent, until suddenly the bishop began to laugh. Rummaging in his pockets for a slip of paper, he said: "We must remember that Poland is a unique place. It sometimes produces extraordinary interpretations of events." He fumbled with the paper. "I've copied down a few lovely judgments I've come upon recently. 'At the Battle of Legnica against the Tatars in 1240, Boleslaw the Stupid placed his right wing under the command of his cousin Mieszko the Obese, who was not too bright and who ran away with all his troops at the flight of the first Tatar arrows.' Almost everything in the passage is wrong. It wasn't Boleslaw, it was Henry the Pious. It wasn't 1240, it was 1241. And Mieszko didn't flee because of the arrows. It was the mysterious black smoke from the giant's head. And how about this one? 'In their raid deep into Poland in 1655 the Cossacks did little permanent damage, killing only magnates, Jews and Roman Catholic priests, of whom they slew some twenty-nine thousand.' And this one which appeared the other day seems especially relevant for us tonight. 'The present disruptions will have limited consequences; only the people in the cities will starve, not those who live near villages where food will be available.' "

The two visitors understood what this wise old man was saying, but neither was prepared to comment on its application to himself. Finally Bukowski switched course completely to raise an extraordinary point, which caught Bishop Barski quite unprepared: "Tell me, Bishop, how do you react when you realize that Italy with its fifty-seven million population, at least half of it non-practicing Catholics, has about thirty cardinals running your church, while Poland with nearly thirty-six million population, most of it devoutly Catholic, is allowed only one?"

"Two, if you count the one serving not in Poland but in Rome."

"How do you view such a discrepancy?"

"I don't like it, but recently I've been able to find consolation. We may have only two Polish cardinals, but we do have one Polish Pope."

The men laughed, and Bukowski explained why he had raised such an issue: "I feel the same about Poland's relationship with Russia. We have only two Communist cardinals, but they do run the country." He then asked bluntly: "Would the church be willing to step in, and support the unions? Factory union or farmer union?"

This was about as difficult a question as Bukowski could have thrown at the bishop, for it was asking the latter to lend his imprimatur to what amounted to a new system of government, and Bishop Barski could see grave danger in this. Leaning back, then forward to pour himself some more brandy, he said very slowly: "Our church has survived in the modern world by refusing to ally itself with any one form of government. In a country like Italy, that would be a difficult course to follow. The Holy Father did break the rule and advise the Italians to vote against divorce and abortion, and they ignored him completely. He's better when he speaks on the general principles of good government and labor relations. Then they listen.

"It seems to me that whenever our church has taken a participatory stand this way or that in the actual governing of Poland, it has performed poorly. I doubt it will intrude now. Governing is up to you politicians, and I would advise my church not to allow itself to be used to fortify your position this week and your adversary's next week. Our job is to provide permanent solace and spiritual leadership to the people as a whole, whatever their government at the moment, so long as it stays within the bounds of moral decency."

"Have the Communists stayed within those bounds?" Janko asked.

"According to their definitions, yes."

"Can you, as a good Catholic priest, love the Communists?" Bukowski asked.

"I do. I love you, Szymon. If I had a son, I would want him to be a man much like you, fighting each battle as it roared at him from whatever new horizon. I bow down before you, Szymon, because I know . . . I know." Again his left arm revealed that horrible collection of purplish numbers, and Bukowski thought: Isn't it the damnedest thing? The Nazis were so orderly in everything, but they slapped their numbers on their slaves in such haphazard fashion. I'd think they'd be ashamed of such disorder, no two numbers lined up with any other two. Then, suddenly, in a blazing vision, he saw coming through this barren room the little girl from Zamosc, striding along so proudly in her good overcoat, which would soon be stripped from her, and as she disappeared through the wall he knew that he had nothing more to say this night.

At the meeting next morning Bukowski presented a surprise to his troublemaking farmers: from Warsaw he had brought with him one of the chief Communist theoreticians, a man of considerable intellectual and political strength, eager to do some serious headknocking.

He was a tall, cadaverously thin man in his sixties, with deep-set hawklike eyes, a furrowed face, a dominant chin which he kept thrusting forward when he talked, and a fierce addiction to Communism. He was Tytus Chalubinski, one-time schoolteacher at Lodz, long-time prisoner at Majdanek, and for a short time before the Russian armies arrived in 1944, a partisan fighting in the Forest of Szczek.

He sat beside Minister Bukowski as if to reinforce that administrator's flagging resolve, and it was he who spoke first: "Fellow workers, when you ask for more fertilizer and better pay for your produce, that's one thing. But when you threaten the state with a strike against its food supply, that's quite another. There is no place in Communist theory for a union of farmers. There is no place for a strike against the food supply of the nation."

Janko Buk, aware that the Polish and Russian governments were trying to overwhelm him, knew that he must fight back, and with whatever energy he possessed. "If Communist theory means that people must go hungry, Pan Chalubinski, then maybe you better re-study your theory."

Chalubinski flushed at this rebuke from a peasant and was about to lash out, but Bukowski reached forth a hand to restrain him, and after a brief pause the visitor from Warsaw allowed a wintry smile to possess his envenomed face. "Pan Buk, we have followed with interest your travels to Japan and the huly-huly girls in Hawaii . . ." Here everyone laughed, for he did a little dance with his ten fingers. "And we know you've talked with that warmonger President Reagan and with our fellow Pole in the Vatican, and all this must seem very exciting. You must have felt when you reached home as if you had three hundred million friends around the world. But now the mazurka is over. Now we come to hard realities, Pan Buk. Poland has only one real friend in all the world. Japan will do nothing to help us. China less, believe me. America will talk big, as she did with Hungary, but she will send you not one gun. And while the Pope is a fine man and a very brave one to have fought back against the assassins, he will not help you, either. And as for our good neighbors Czechoslovakia and East Germany . . . Let us not laugh. Our only friend in this world is the Soviet Union, and for us to take any action which might move us away from the protection of that friendship would be insanity."

Buk waited for the whispers to halt, then said: "Pan Chalubinski, surely friendship with the Soviet Union, which we all cherish, does not mean that our farmers have to make all the mistakes that their farmers have been making for fifty years. It can't mean that Poles must go hungry the way Russians go hungry."

This time Chalubinski's temper did flare, his face showing a deep red. "Pan Buk, I have not come here all the way from Warsaw to be insulted. No Russian anywhere in their great system of republics is starving."

"For the moment they escape by borrowing huge quantities of grain from America."

Chalubinski regained control. With disarming blandness he said: "Russia can have one bad season the way we in Poland had one last year. But the system itself is never impaired or modified by one bad year."

All morning Chalubinski hammered away at Buk, reiterating that in the grand design outlined by Karl Marx and Lenin, there was no place for a union of farmers, and finally he scored a most telling point: "All agencies of production, especially the land, belong to the people, who have wisely placed its management in the hands of the Communist party. It is not your land to abuse, Pan Buk."

When Buk stoutly advanced the argument that it was the government, and not he, who was abusing the land, Bukowski had to notice, with apprehension, that Farmer Buk seemed to have an almost physical dislike for Chalubinski and was taking delight in opposing even the good points the theoretician proposed, and he wondered what could have generated this automatic rejection. He could not know that from infancy Janko Buk had been familiar with the name and deeds of Tytus Chalubinski, for when his mother, Biruta, was able to talk with those former members of the Stork Commando who had not been banished to Siberia as enemies of the new Communist Poland, she saw clearly that it could only have been Chalubinski who placed Jan Buk's name on the list of those to be deported. No one else could have done it. No one else knew about the medal from London. And no one else had so consistently opposed Buk's leadership. It was obvious, therefore, that Chalubinski had murdered, so to speak, the heroic leader of the Storks, Janko's father. And now he, Janko, sought to test what this strange man was like.

The more he heard Chalubinski speak, the more clearly the philosopher's character stood out, and the more satisfied Janko became that this man was the type who could have sent a close companion to exile and death. Watching ever more closely, he saw the portrait of a fanatic, and as he listened to Chalubinski he could imagine him uttering the words that had doomed Jan Buk, and his bitterness toward the philosopher and all his preachings deepened.

But now the session took a sharp turn, which none of the participants could have anticipated, for Szymon Bukowski took command. Forcefully, and with a good deal of intelligence, he started to hew out the solution to the problems of the farmers. Ignoring Warsaw, and rebuffing Chalubinski when the latter grew too doctrinaire, he said: "Let us find a Polish solution to these matters."

Regaining the chairmanship that was rightfully his, he began a practical analysis of what steps must be taken, now, to protect the nation's food supply: "Always Poland will remain Russia's close ally, Respected Minister, so I need to offer no more reassurances on that point. And always we will find our solutions within the Communist doctrine, so we can put those matters to rest. On the one hand, we cannot allow our factory workers to disadvantage our farmers. On the other, we will not allow our farmers to hold the entire nation for ransom."

"Fine words," Buk cried sarcastically. "You've made Chalubinski happy, and you've obviously made yourself happy, but you haven't made me happy."

"No more of that, Pan Buk. We're about ready to spell out the course of action our government intends to follow with regard to its farmers."

"Beginning when?" Buk asked almost insolently.

Bukowski ignored him. "After lunch we have agreed to hear the complaints of certain women, a farmer who grows grain only for sale to the government and one who grows produce for sale in Krakow. When we've finished with them, Pan Chalubinski and I will deliver our report."

It was fortunate that Janko went home for lunch that day because he found his mother in a state of distress. She had heard that Tytus Chalubinski was in the village, the first time ever, and she was trembling to think that within an hour she would be testifying before the man responsible for her husband's disappearance. "What is he like, Janko?"

"Tall and thin and mean. Very intelligent, I think. Very harsh in doctrine, and obviously afraid of the Russians." Then he added: "About the age Father would have been." Janko had, of course, never seen his father, having been born after the hero's deportation by the

Communists, but in discussions with his mother they had always supposed that as a notorious free-commando leader, Jan would have been quickly liquidated by the Russians, who demanded total submission; they never thought of him as living in extended slavery; he was not the kind to have endured that.

"When I testify I shall throw the murder in his face," Biruta said, and her son replied: "Now that's foolishness, and you know it."

At lunch he told his wife and mother how penetrating Chalubinski's questions had been, at which his mother said: "You seem proud that the murderer was clever," and her son answered: "I'm always pleased to see a fellow Pole handle himself well."

As his mother combed her hair preparatory to the afternoon meeting at which she was to explain the plight of farm women during this difficult period, Janko happened to look at the small trunk in which he kept his clothes, and he saw that a shirt sleeve was hanging from under the lid, something which his wife would never permit, and as he went to the trunk to remedy this, it became clear that his mother had invaded what amounted to his private closet in search of a terrible item.

"Mother!" he shouted as she stood before the little wall mirror.

"What?" Her manner betrayed that she knew the answer.

"Oh my God! Give it to me."

"What?" she repeated, and remained facing the mirror as her son rushed over, frisked her as if he were a policeman, and found hidden in her pleated skirt the revolver he used when on patrol to protect the tractor.

"Oh my God!" Janko whispered, falling onto a chair and holding the weapon on his knees. He stayed that way for some minutes while the two women stood silent. Finally he looked at his wife and asked: "Did you know?" And Kazimiera nodded: "We were going to do it, the animal."

Janko remained sitting, trying to visualize what might have happened had his mother killed a high official of the party. The whole structure could have fallen apart. Everything that Szymon Bukowski had been trying to formulate during the last two hours of the morning session would have been lost, and countries like East Germany and Czechoslovakia would have been called upon to join the Soviet Union in stamping out the Polish rebellion.

"Oh God! You could have destroyed us all." Very carefully he returned the revolver to its hiding place, for under the disarmament laws insisted upon by the authorities, he was not entitled to own such a weapon, and then he went to stand before his two women: "You must do it with words, Mother. Crucify the bastard with words."

So when the afternoon session convened, with a pale and shaken Janko Buk sitting very quietly at the table while Szymon Bukowski continued to command with a mixture of force and brilliance that made him most effective, Biruta Buk was invited to make her statement as a working housewife, and she was forceful:

"I address my words principally to Pan Chalubinski, whom I have never met before. But he knew my husband well, Jan Buk of the Stork Commando, since it was he who reported to the authorities that my husband had received a medal from the Polish government-in-exile in London.

"The theories that Pan Chalubinski has been forcing on the farmers of this nation have failed in every respect. They have not produced more food. They have not created justice. They have provided no encouragement or hope. And they have not stocked our stores with things we need and which we could afford to buy if our food was properly priced and if our zlotys were worth anything.

"I am going to tell you, Pan Chalubinski, what my family must do without because of your planning. We have no dresses, no stockings, no cosmetics, no vodka, no oranges, no canned meat from New Zealand, no sewing needles, no penicillin, no paper tablets for our children's home study."

As Biruta continued to pour out the grievances of a Polish patriot who had watched her country slide toward chaos, the Communist leaders who faced her had varying reactions, which their stolid faces kept masked from witnesses.

A round-faced, stocky Russian cameraman, ostensibly a member of the television crew but actually a high official assigned to the Polish talks by the Kremlin, studied the fifty-nine-year-old housewife with disbelief: How dare this peasant woman come before an arm of government and publicly bring such charges? If she did this in Moscow or Kiev . . . Whssst! No one would ever see that one again. In Bulgaria they'd shoot her. In Rumania, silenced for good. We showed such people in Czechoslovakia where power rested and what happened when people criticized it. What's the matter with these Poles?

As a young man, he had been active in dragging seven hundred thousand Lithuanians from their homes and dispersing them one by one throughout the vast emptiness of the Soviet Union's eastern territories, and with their leaders gone, the back of Lithuanian resistance had been broken. Later he had done even more important work in Ukraine, where millions were deported to Siberia and other distant settlements, while millions more were allowed to starve. He believed in short, sharp measures, and when he returned to Moscow he would advise his superiors that a sudden rush of such measures was required in Poland now.

So he listened intently as Biruta dug her own grave. He would remember this woman who had insulted Chalubinski and by extension the Kremlin itself. He would note her well; she had a scar running from her left eye to her chin.

Tytus Chalubinski, unaware of how close to death he had been an hour before, listened to Biruta with a special interest. Was it true, as she claimed, that she was the widow of the man he had served with in the Stork Commando when it was operating out of the Forest of Szczek? He would try to verify this, for if it was true, she could prove to be dangerous; certainly her husband had been a right-wing reactionary with no vision whatever of a new Poland. He, Chalubinski, had indeed reported Jan Buk to the Soviets as too dangerous a fellow to be left running free, and the man's removal had been a prudent move: I'd make it again tomorrow. And if things deteriorate, I'll do the same with his widow.

But as he listened to Biruta's stern condemnations he had to concede that the Polish government had failed to keep factory workers and farmers in balance and that the latter did have substantial grievances. It was interesting, however, that he blamed this imbalance not on laggard legislation to help the farmer catch up, but on Lech Walesa and his gang of public enemies who had used their position to forge ahead. Tytus Chalubinski did not like anyone to forge ahead, ever, anywhere, for any reason. He saw society as an organized effort in which those who understood the great revolutionary forces of history made carefully studied decisions for the welfare of all the others. He could not accept that it had been the faulty judgments of his social technocrats that had brought Poland to its present crisis. He blamed it on last year's floods, on the cupidity of foreign bankers, on the intrusion into the governmental process by men like Walesa, and, if one wanted to be blunt about it, on the sentimental interruptions of that damned Polish Pope.

Biruta Buk symbolized everything that was wrong with Poland, and since he could not lay his hands on the other enemies of the state, he pondered how he might deal with her.

Szymon Bukowski, during the first stages of Biruta's tirade, was deeply irritated by her sweeping accusations and wondered how a man like this Janko Buk allowed any woman in his household, even his mother, to speak so bluntly. But as he listened to her forceful presentation of deadening data he began to realize that she was speaking for all the women of Poland, and when he closed his eyes so that he could not see her tense and angry face, he could imagine his mother, Miroslawa Bukowska of this village, orating in the precise words Pani Buk was using: My mother was a radical, a real Communist before her time, and I know she would have applauded the arrival of Communism. But she was also a realist, and if her men had been forced to work with no goods to reward them, she would have been the first to complain. Damn, but this woman sounds like my mother. Even more, like my grandmother. It's women like this who get lined up against a wall or hanged from the village tree.

When he opened his eyes again, he saw a much different Biruta Buk, a kind of permanent revolutionary whose ideals transcended Communism or Syndicalism or Anarchism or State Socialism. She, like his grandmother and his mother, was the embattled Polish woman, fighting terrible injustices which seemed always in the end to overwhelm them. He studied her face and noted again the scar that marred it, and he speculated as to which of her heroic ventures had left her with this mark of honor, and now as she continued to speak with unrelenting force, he listened more carefully. He did not like what she was saying, but he respected her for saying it:

> "Recently my son was in Vienna, not three hundred miles from here, and he saw a hundred stores containing a thousand things any husband or father would want for his family. How, how, Pan Chalubinski, can Austrians in their little country provide so much while we Poles in our big country are able to provide so little?

> "How does your planning justify itself if it makes the nation poorer and poorer?

"Let's leave the farmers out of this. If you boast about anything, it's that you know how to run factories. We've seen a
score of motion pictures proving how successful you are at
that. How is it that none of your factories is open more than
four days a week? How is it that they produce so little for us
to use?

"You have built a Poland whose cities starve and whose farmers find nothing they can buy. Are you proud of the system
you have given us, Pan Chalubinski?"

She sat down, and the Communist leaders were relieved that she had
not uttered any threats about a rural strike. Her speech was harsh,
but it could have been worse. Chalubinski, secretly acknowledging
the justice of some of her complaints, was stern in his rejection of her
favorable reference to Austria, and he reverted to a line of argumen-
tation popular in the 1950s to rebut it:

"It is unfair to compare corrupt, servile Austria with a great
socialist republic like Poland. The shops your son saw in Vienna, crowded with fancy goods no one really needs, are sub-
sidized by the larger corrupt democracies who obtain their
surpluses by grinding their workers into the dust, the way the
magnates of this nation used to keep us in slavery.

"Mark my words, Pani Buk, America and Brazil and France
and Italy are doomed, because their slave workers will see the
light one of these days and end the exploitation which alone
keeps those nations semi-viable for the time being."

Biruta started to shout "Those countries—" but Chalubinski silenced
her: "You had your chance to speak, now we wish to hear the others."
She rose to her feet, and retaliated: "I have not said one-tenth of
what you ought to hear, betrayer of Polish heroes." And with that,
she nodded deferentially to Bukowski and stamped out of the palace.
That one is doomed, the Russian cameraman said to himself.

When the second farmer finished his testimony, Chairman Bukowski
surprised the delegates by announcing a short recess prior to his closing statement for that day, and during the interval the Communist
leaders took Janko Buk upstairs to the room which had once held the
Holbein, and gathered about a desk like the one Konrad Krumpf

had used when doing his modest best to exterminate the Polish race, they laid down the law. It was one of those bare-knuckle sessions which often occurred behind the Iron Curtain when fundamentals had to be restated, and before it had been under way only a few minutes Janko felt faint.

BUKOWSKI *(who wanted to demonstrate that he could handle such a meeting):* Pan Buk, the games are over. If you persist, you will be destroyed.

CHALUBINSKI: You must understand without any confusion that Warsaw supports what Pan Bukowski has so accurately stated. You have put yourself in grave danger, Buk.

BUKOWSKI: We'll not tolerate any further nonsense. There will be no farmers' union.

CHALUBINSKI: Discussion of such a thing should never have been allowed in the first place.

BUKOWSKI: The leaders of our nation have been remarkably patient with agitators like you. *(His voice trembled and he was forced to lick his lips, for he knew that the next step would be a specific threat.)* Our patience has a limit, you know.

CHALUBINSKI: You farmers have put serious strains on the international fellowship of Communist nations, and if you continue, we can only expect them to unite in opposition to your heresies. *(Now, and for the first time in these talks, the true danger was exposed.)* Unless you draw back, Buk—you and Walesa, too . . . Well, you don't need me to remind you that one of these days you'll see troops marching in the streets.

BUKOWSKI: Have your eyes been dazzled by the fact that a cinema actor posing as the president of a large country invited you to lunch? Do you think for one minute that America will lift even one little finger to help you in a crisis?

CHALUBINSKI: Are you so stupid that you can't see the Americans are using you only to embarrass us? They don't give a damn about your welfare.

BUKOWSKI: You must cease your agitation. You must listen to what your true friends say. And you must obey.

CHALUBINSKI: The Soviet Union has been extremely patient with your disturbances. The Polish army has shown restraint. *(His voice grew noticeably sterner.)* But such concessions will soon stop. You are playing a most dangerous game, Buk, and before you know it, the whole thing could blow up in your face.

Janko Buk drew back from the desk and gave his adversaries his country-boy smile. Almost better than they, he appreciated the constraints under which they suffered. Russia was afraid to activate her tanks waiting in the woods because she could not anticipate what Red China might do in Asia if she was tied down in Europe. Chalubinski could do none of the things he so desperately wanted to do, because the citizens of Poland had turned against his ruling clique, and without Russian power to back him, he commanded little of his own; he and his gang had lost their legitimacy, and even Szymon Bukowski, a true patriot, would be loath to call for the military to restore order, since he could not anticipate what this might lead to or estimate how long a military dictatorship, once called into power, might wish to retain it.

Buk saw the limitations which inhibited his opponents but he did not yet know his own mind, and the Communists interpreted this confusion as acquiescence. Thus emboldened, they continued to hammer at him, each man making one harsh statement which summarized his position.

CHALUBINSKI: Keep in mind, Buk, that two nations are involved. The Soviet Union must consider the fate of many countries besides our little Poland. Bulgaria, East Germany and twenty others, who all depend upon Moscow for leadership. They cannot allow deviationism to grow on their doorstep. So what is Poland's responsibility? To stamp out any action which looks like a capitulation to capitalism or a move to the west. Poland's job right now is to affirm its allegiance to the Soviet Union and exterminate any who protest. I said exterminate, Buk.

BUKOWSKI: That's far too harsh a word, but the minister is right. The Polish government will not allow itself to be embarrassed by strikes and agitations. Those who continue to protest will do so at their own risk.

Chalubinski had the last word: "Do I need to remind you, Buk, that Russian tanks are right now in that forest over there?" and Janko replied from the long wisdom of peasants who lived beside the beech trees: "In the Forest of Szczek, there is always something hiding."

The men did not like the levity of this response and they asked if he understood the gravity of what they had been saying, and he replied: "I understand that you're frightened. Well, so am I."

They did not bluster or try to deny that they were frightened, but they did demand that he attend to their warnings and obey them.

When he carefully avoided making any promises, it was Chalubinski who made a gesture of conciliation: "We have a surprise for you, Buk, a most rewarding surprise." But he would not reveal what it was. Instead, he took Buk's arm and led him back to the conference room, his manner showing the other participants that they had been having an amiable conversation.

Then he startled the reassembled meeting with an announcement: "Under our democratic system, which ensures freedom for all, it is impossible to permit a union of food growers. That is forbidden, and the farmers' leader, Janko Buk, accepts this decision."

Everyone looked at Buk, who sat staring at the table.

"But what our government has agreed to do is initiate a council of farmers who will advise on rural policies and be your voice in Warsaw. This council will have plenary powers, and we will listen to it.

"The chairman of this powerful council is to be Pan Buk, who has demonstrated such a firm understanding of rural affairs." Across the table he smiled warmly at his proposed associate Buk, who was too startled to smile back, but when he saw that Bukowski was grinning approvingly, he knew he had better respond.

In that brief moment of hesitation Buk had time to assess his new position cynically and accurately: They're doing this to shut me up. I'll have a big office and no power. Nothing will change, and the factory people with Lech Walesa at their head will get all the privileges, and the farmers with nobody at their head will still get nothing. They've made fools of us farmers again, and I will not be partner to such fraud.

Still smiling, he said: "My mother, Pani Buk, who spoke here so forcefully . . . she's a heroine of the Polish resistance to Nazi terrorism. This afternoon she spoke truth about the mismanagement of our country, and as long as the weaknesses she identified remain uncorrected, I cannot leave my work here. I cannot go to Warsaw to serve as cover for your mistakes. I am a farmer, and I shall stay with my farm."

The three testifiers who had remained after Biruta's angry departure cheered, and two of the rather frightened men on Buk's side of the table clapped their hands. On the opposite side the Communist leaders sat stone-faced, waiting for the clamor to subside, and finally Chalubinski spoke. "Quick peace in Poland is the desire of all the socialistic democracies, who alone protect the freedom and peace of the world. As peace-seeking nations we cannot allow the superior standard of living we have achieved for our working people to be endangered by fraternal strife.

"Pan Buk, it is your duty to go to Warsaw as we have recommended. There you can perform a great service for all the peace-loving nations of our bloc. Your job is in Warsaw." Having said this, he leaned back with that bleak smile which indicated that the situation was resolved.

When Bukowski closed the session, Chalubinski rose, walked to where Buk waited and again took him by the arm, leading him to the front lawn where the television people waited.

"What's happened to the farmers' union?" a German reporter asked in Polish.

Chalubinski smiled. "No nation in the world permits its farmers to unite so as to control the supply of food. Among the social democracies such a union would be especially wrong. The people would not want it, so the government cannot permit it. The issue is dead."

At this news one of the French correspondents whispered: "Janko the Yanko has allowed himself to be converted into Buk the Rus." And on that gloomy note the discussions in the Bukowski palace drew toward a close.

When Szymon Bukowski, moving secretly and alone, slipped late at night into the bleak little committee room, it seemed even more desolate than it had during his earlier visit. But the cold place was made warm by the welcoming smile of Bishop Barski, who was already waiting for him. Szymon began to speak almost before he sat down: "I'm not here to seek counsel about our meetings. Chalubinski pretty well took care of that. And I'm not here to confess, because I'm no longer a believing Catholic. But I do very much want to ask you about something. You seem to be an understanding man."

"I try to be. But I barely understand myself, so what I provide is not understanding but sympathy." The bishop cleared his throat. "Yes, sympathy I do seem to have."

"Perhaps it's sympathy I need."

"I judge this does not relate to government policy? I tried to make myself clear last time that our church will not come down totally on any side in what is a governmental dispute."

"I understand that. Could I speak in some detail?"

"If you leave out the detail, you aren't really speaking."

"I was present at that notorious series of trials in Lublin when Majdanek and Zamek Lublin and Under the Clock were liberated by the Russians. The prisoners in Field Four elected me to speak for them, and I did. These men had been horribly treated and they demanded justice. So I was a principal testifier.

"By rotten luck the first man tried was a fellow named Willi Zimmel, a kind of dumb-witted, open-faced farm boy who had stumbled into the SS thinking it was a club of scouts. He saved my life. Hid me when a terrible brute named Otto Grundtz came searching for me on the last day to shoot me.

"So when Willi Zimmel was in the docket, fighting for his life, some men from Field Four came to me and said: 'We've got to hang that bastard,' and I suppose they had cause. But I didn't, for Willi had saved my life, and he saved it twice, because he also rescued me from the concrete rollers which would have killed me in a couple more days.

"I refused to say anything bad about him, but I wasn't saying much good, either, because I wanted these trials to produce results. I wanted men like Grundtz to hang but I wanted Willi Zimmel to live. And then I thought of exactly the right thing to say. I told the judges that the Nazi command didn't trust Willi because he was too lenient with the prisoners in his charge. And I related how Otto Grundtz had come along one morning and in front of us all had called him a pig's asshole.

"The judges laughed. The other witnesses laughed. In the docket Willi Zimmel laughed, a big dumb farm boy from some German village, and in the end he was acquitted. I had saved his life.

"But the men from my field who had wanted him hanged came to me and raised hell. 'You dumb fool,' they said accusingly, 'your joke let him get away.' And they warned me that if I did anything like that with Otto Grundtz, enabling him to escape, they would hang me in his place.

"The warning was unnecessary. No man in Field Four was more eager than I to see Otto Grundtz hang. I had this friend Professor Tomczyk of Lublin. Grundtz smashed his glasses on purpose so the old man could never read again. And he used to come slouching down the line, staring at us with dark eyes hiding under his huge eyebrows, looking for someone to hang on his private gibbet. I wanted to strangle him with my own hands.

"So when he moved into the docket to stand trial for his many crimes, and it was clear that I as a former prisoner under his command would be the major witness, I began to sweat and tremble, afraid that he would escape. The defense lawyer pleaded that Grundtz had only followed orders, and since the judges had already proved in the Zimmel case that they would find innocent Nazis not guilty, it seemed to me that I was personally responsible to see that this one did not escape.

"I testified to everything that I had seen Grundtz do, the hangings for no cause, the dragging of sick prisoners to Barracks Nineteen, where they were left to starve to death, everything. And then, because it seemed so long ago and so ordinary, all the killings, I invented three really horrible stories, and I saw the judge shudder. But most of all . . ."

Here Bukowski stopped. He reminded the bishop that he must remember that at the time of the Lublin trials he, Bukowski, had weighed barely a hundred pounds and, he said with a bitter smile, he was not in very good shape. He asked if he could have some brandy, and Bishop Barski left the room and rummaged for some. It steadied Bukowski.

"The judges looked at me, but so did Otto Grundtz, and he smiled. The worse my lies became, the wider his smile grew, as if he were saying: 'See! You're no different from me.' He knew what I was doing and why I was doing it, but he also knew that in a time of passion the Polish hero was no different from the Nazi torturer.

"My accusations were so appalling that the judges asked if I would swear to them, and I cried: 'I'll swear on the Bible itself,' and the Russian judge said: 'We don't need the Bible. Just tell us that all this actually happened,' and from the listeners several men shouted: 'It happened! He did worse to the men in our barracks.' And I pray to God they were telling the truth, because I wasn't.

"So Otto Grundtz was hanged. From the very gibbet on which he had himself hanged so many. And I waited there in the front line staring at him, and as he stood on the white stool with the rope about his neck he smiled down at me, still accusing me of being his brother, of being his Polish counterpart.

"He smiles at me at night. I cannot drive him from my conscience. He tried to murder me, and I murdered him. Is there anything I can do to get this hateful man out of my soul?"

Bishop Barski sipped his brandy, studied the glass, and said hesitantly: "A man runs a grave risk, Szymon, when he presumes to administer punishment. Because God may have plans which are quite different."

Bukowski was shocked. "Do you mean those monsters should have gone free?"

"No! No! It was proper that they should hang, because the foulness of their lives condemned them, not you or I."

"I would still be willing to condemn them. For the terrible things they did."

"But doesn't it seem strange, Szymon, that the large criminals at your Majdanek and my Auschwitz were hanged with great fanfare, while the little criminals who terrorized our villages along the Vistula . . . they all escaped?"

Bukowski's knuckles grew white. "I spent two years trying to find Hans Yunger, the man who shot my mother . . . your uncle. He vanished. We tracked him to Kiev, where he supervised the slaughter of eight thousand Ukrainians. But there he vanished." His tensed jaw muscles showed that he was reliving painful defeats, and when he could not speak, the bishop did.

"It was the same with the others. Konrad Krumpf, who ordered your grandmother hanged . . . he fled to Paris, sold some of the art treasures from your palace, bought his way to Paraguay, where he runs a big estate. Falk von Eschl, who supervised his terror from our castle . . . the judges could not believe that a man who spoke English so well, who knew many of their friends in the various governments . . . He was found guilty of nothing and is now living in Estoril, where rich American tourists idolize him."

The two men studied their brandy in a silence which was broken in a curious way: Bishop Barski clapped his hands and broke into a hearty laugh. Shoving his glass aside, he reached across the table and patted Szymon on the hand. "It's really quite funny, Bukowski, that you should consult me about a Nazi monster whom you can't get out of your soul, because I have a little Jewish rabbi that I can't get out of mine." He laughed again and poured Bukowski another drink.

"You may not know it, but in Auschwitz, which I prefer to call by its Nazi name because it certainly had nothing to do with Polish Oswiecim, which was a placid little town before they came . . . Where was I? Yes, in Auschwitz the Nazis were particularly brutal with priests and rabbis, because they felt a need to ridicule and denigrate all religions except their own.

"This meant that priests and rabbis were often thrown together, and there was one horrible little cell with only one small window rather high up into which they crammed sixty or more men at dusk, expecting to find thirty-eight or thirty-nine of them suffocated by morning. Twice I spent a night in that cell, and if you told me now that I would have to do so again, I assure you, Bukowski, I would go screaming, hair-pulling mad. I think no one could survive that terrifying ordeal three times. I couldn't.

"I survived the first time—one of nineteen who did—because as I was about to be jammed inside, a little Jewish rabbi whose name I never knew whispered just four words: 'Stand opposite the window.' That was all. When I found myself inside, one of that scrambling mass, I saw what he meant, for all the big and powerful fellows were fighting for a place near the window, which allowed me freedom to take my place against the wall on the opposite side.

"Secure in position and tall enough to have my head slightly above the others, I learned two things. Such air as did come into the room drifted my way, and those struggling to intercept it at the window killed one another. There were fights for air, and stranglings, and bodies crushed when they fainted and fell to the floor. And there I stood, thanks to the little Jew, above it all, saved by the bits of air that came to me now and then.

"Toward morning, when it looked as if I might be one of the survivors, I began to look for my benefactor, but he wasn't in the cell. Of that I was sure, for he certainly wasn't one of those still standing, nor was he among the corpses piled on the floor. When I got out I found that he along with several others had been at the end of the line and could not be pushed in. They would be held over for the next night.

"I saw the little Jew on the work detail next day, lifting great rocks when we'd had no food, not even breakfast soup, and I'd had no sleep. When he saw that I'd survived, his eyes glowed and he started to come over to speak to me, but guards saw him move and they kicked him to death. Before my eyes, they kicked him to death.

"As he lay there in the prison yard looking up at me, his face torn apart and covered with blood, I wanted with all the force in my body to rush over and comfort him, to take him in my arms, for he had saved my life and he deserved that consolation in the moments when he was leaving his. But I could not. I had no physical or moral power. The cell had been too terrible, and I stood motionless as they kicked my savior to death.

"What was the last thing he did on this earth? He smiled at me. Through the blood that dimmed his eyes he smiled at me, as if to say: 'Be not afraid.' I seemed to hear this little Jewish rabbi using the words of Jesus Christ."

Bishop Barski lowered his head to the table, and whether he was weeping or praying, Bukowski could not determine, but it seemed certain that he was in communion with the rabbi who had saved his life. Later, when he had composed himself, he blew his nose and said: "I am with this nameless little man three or four nights a week when I try to sleep. And if I am indeed sympathetic to the trials of others, as some say I am, it's because of the counsel I take with him. He saved my life and I was powerless to save his." He studied his hands for a moment, then broke into laughter again. "Have you noticed how I always refer to him as the little Jew? He was. I was this tall and he came only to here. But in the council of God he was so very big and I so very small."

Suddenly he reached forward to take Bukowski's hands again.

"We can never exorcise the spirits that really matter in our lives. And maybe that's a good thing. Maybe your Otto Grundtz, maybe he is the crucial member of your life the way the Jewish rabbi is the vital member of mine."

"But the bearing of false witness. My lies about a doomed man, that continues to worry me."

"Lies? Who escapes them, Szymon? People come to me: 'My mother is dying of cancer. Can you console her?' So I go to the death room and see this tired old woman who's spent a long life working for others, and her time has come and she asks me: 'Will God cure my cancer?' and I assure her that He will. But I know I am lying."

"You lie to help save a life," Bukowski said. "I lied to help destroy one."

"Men like Grundtz destroy themselves. You merely nodded approval. Don't let him haunt you."

"I shall try," Bukowski assured the bishop, "but my other haunting is much more deadening, in a way. It comes from a much different source."

"Such as?"

"Well, I'm much like you. I never married, you know."

"I didn't know."

"I saw you looking at me in surprise at the conclusion of our meeting the other night."

"Yes. It was clear that some powerful crisis had come over the talks. You looked quite shaken."

"I was. Whenever the soul of Poland, her continued existence, that is, comes under discussion a little girl in an overcoat enters the room, and walks past me without looking, and vanishes through the opposite wall."

"Tell me about her."

"When I first got to Majdanek, I drove the death truck, dragged the bodies of Jews out of the gas chamber and delivered them to the crematorium. You know, I suppose, that when a man had been doing that long enough, they killed him because his mind started to go bad. But I was lucky, I was assigned other work, and I survived. But then they put me on the concrete rollers, and one morning, when I felt that I was at the end of my rope, I witnessed the delivery of a batch of women and children from the dispossessions at Zamosc.

"In that mass, some ten thousand I think, I saw this little girl, nine or ten perhaps, wearing a new overcoat and a Russian-style woolen cap. She was very brave. She was very brave. [For some moments he could not speak.]

"I never saw her again, Father. Not really, that is. But I kept thinking about her and I convinced myself that I did, and always she had on that overcoat. And then I imagined that she was a grown woman. And I married her. And in my madness I used to see us sitting together by the fire in an ordinary cottage, me tired from work in the field, she mending her overcoat. I do believe my obsession saved me from dying.

"I risked my life one day by quitting my work and following the death truck that carried her to the crematorium, but whether it was really she or not I cannot say, for I was so near death that I was not myself. But I was sure that I saw them lift her out as I used to lift out the bodies of children, and I waited until they threw her into the furnace. Into the ovens, that is, not the furnace. They wouldn't throw anyone into the furnace, because there was no furnace, so to speak. [He stared at the table, a man with a burden too heavy to bear.] I never married, you know."

"I didn't know," the bishop repeated, and then the two men sat in silence, veterans of the worst experience the women and men of their generation had known: Bishop Barski, a survivor of Auschwitz, that flaming hell of ingenious torture whose fires raged more intensely year after year; Szymon Bukowski, who had endured the ice-cold efficiency of Majdanek, whose terrors so methodically administered froze the soul. The two men may have triumphed over the fire and ice, but they carried scars external and internal that would never heal, and each man knew it, regarding both himself and the one who sat opposite.

"How did you gain the courage to survive Auschwitz?" Szymon asked, and the bishop realized that what the younger man had wanted to ask was "How did *we* gain the courage?" and he answered:

"Character is the sum of all we do before the age of twenty. You did certain things in those formative years which made you brave and durable. What did I do? When I was a student at Krakow, I used to go out into that glorious square at night and at six minutes to the hour stand silent and stare at the dark tower from which the trumpeter sounded the signal which saved the city from the Tatars.

"For six minutes I stood silent, imagining myself to be that trumpeter who gave his life to save others, and I speculated on how I might have behaved in his place. As you know, on the hour, through all these centuries, a living trumpeter sounds from the tower once again that fatal call. The beautiful notes echo across the city, and at the moment when they sound the sweetest, they end. The arrow has struck home. The trumpeter is dead. But our city is saved.

"I vowed then that if my testing time ever came, I would sound my warning. Without that boyhood commitment, how could I have survived the camp?

"And Poland is bound by these same rules. The bold things it did when young have determined how it shall act when mature. Oh, critics in foreign lands laugh at us and say that our *liberum veto* was preposterous, allowing one man to negate the work of ninety, but I think we governed ourselves with more justice than either Germany or Russia, and if you look at their Nazism and Communism, we certainly turned out better."

The two patriots contemplated this truth in silence, after which the bishop cleared his throat and said: "God and brave men have saved our nation in the past. What do you and our friend Jan Buk propose to help us escape this time?" His voice dropped a full register. "We're in terrible danger, Szymon. You know that."

"Chalubinski has made the big decision. No farmers' union. I'm making the decision almost as big. Every concession possible to restore some kind of balance. Buk has agreed to halt rural agitation and get back to the production of food. And from you, Bishop, we want one of the biggest concessions of all. We want you to appear tomorrow on the steps at the palace when we announce the agreements. All of us beg you."

"Even Chalubinski?"

"Especially Chalubinski. He says no government can rule unless there is a perception of legitimacy. And he says that in Poland, legitimacy is conferred by the Catholic church and by Vladimir Ilyich Lenin, although he said the names in a somewhat different order."

"He's right about legitimacy. That should be the first concern of any government, and if he needs my support to keep his shaky system functioning, I have no option but to oblige with what little I possess."

From the floor he lifted a cheap fabric briefcase which had served him for many years, and as he placed it unopened on the table he said in a completely different voice, as if he were an older professor endeavoring to instruct a favored student: "I'm sure you realize, Szymon, that any bold act you perform could place our nation in grave peril?"

"That's why I'm here."

"But I wonder if you appreciate how grave?" Before Bukowski could say that he understood the danger of Soviet intervention, the bishop opened the case and took out three books, one published in London, one in Stockholm, one in New York. Szymon could not read the titles, of course, but from the lurid covers he determined that they dealt with Nazi concentration camps.

"Remarkable books," Bishop Barski said, touching each in turn. "Written by men of ability. Look at the figures they've assembled." Taking the London publication, he riffled the pages, showing Szymon tables of persuasive data.

"What are they about?"

"They prove that places like Auschwitz and Majdanek never existed."

"What!"

"They prove to the satisfaction of those who wish to believe, and millions do, that the camps where you and I lived in hell never existed."

Szymon stared at the books, afraid to touch them. "What else do they prove?"

"That Auschwitz was a fable invented by lying Jews. That Majdanek was a great lie perpetrated by Poles who wanted to discredit Germany."

"So Otto Grundtz never existed?"

"No. You invented him."

Bukowski gasped, whereupon the bishop produced a single sheet on which the conclusions of the London book had been translated into Polish, and when this was placed in Szymon's hands he was stunned by the bold assertions:

1. No concentration camps ever existed. They were lies created by Jews and Poles.

2. If any camps did exist, they were detention centers such as are used by all nations to imprison criminal types who have committed specific crimes against society in general.

3. It is preposterous to claim that six million Jews died in these supposed camps, because there were never that many Jews in all of Europe.

4. It is equally ridiculous to claim that two million Poles died, because the Germans have never borne animosity toward the Poles and have always treated them well.

5. The total number of criminals who died in the detention centers, either through legal execution for specific crimes or from the epidemics which occasionally touched the camps, could not possibly have exceeded three thousand.

6. If concentration camps did exist, Adolf Hitler knew nothing about them.

7. In the long light of history, Hitler will be seen as a generous, wise, considerate and constructive leader who took bold steps to save Europe and the world.

When Szymon reached the final item he could think of nothing rational to say, for his mind went back to the November day when he stood by the trenches as some eighteen thousand Jews were slaughtered, and he could see both them and their assassins. But then his finger drifted to Item 5, which conceded that in all the camps taken together, perhaps three thousand criminals had died, and he stared at this figure for a long time, mumbling finally: "I used to handle three thousand corpses in a week."

Overcome with rage at the indecency of the books, he pushed them away and demanded in a harsh voice: "Who wrote that manure?" and Bishop Barski replied: "Some of the most persuasive men and women of our day. They believe what they say. And they convert others with what they preach."

In silence these two graduates of Auschwitz and Majdanek contemplated the staggering fact that in the future it might be believed that their camps had never existed. There had been no electrified barbed wire, no little room into which sixty had been crowded at dusk and from which fewer than twenty had emerged at dawn. And after a while these survivors began to laugh—ugly, convulsive laughs which turned at last into robust guffaws at the idiocy of the world, and when they had purged themselves Bishop Barski thrust the books contemptuously back into his briefcase.

He then rose and went to the map of Poland, which served as the sole decoration in this bare room. "Our task, Szymon, is not only to preserve the integrity of our history but also to defend the integrity of our terrain." With a broad-sweeping hand he indicated those eastern territories which had once belonged to Poland but which Russia had grabbed in 1945: Lwow, Brzesc Litewski, Tarnopol. "Areas of vast extent," the bishop said. "People of Polish heritage kicked out, bodily. Expelled. Hundreds of thousands. So that the area could be made Russian." The land thus wrenched away had been enormous, about half of what was then Poland, and Bukowski mourned its loss.

"And where did the displaced Poles go?" the bishop continued. "You know well"—and he indicated a large area to the west which had once belonged to Germany but which Russia had awarded Poland in compensation for the lost eastern lands: Szczecin, which the Germans had called Stettin; Wroclaw, which had been Breslau; Opole, which had been Oppeln.

"Do you think, Szymon, that this map of Poland is fixed? Has our map ever been fixed? If the two Germanys are allowed to unite, can't you see that they'll march again to recover their lost lands? If the Soviet Union becomes more irritated with us, don't you see that they'll send their tanks rumbling in, and once more our lands will be ripped away from us?" The two patriots studied the fragile map that contained so many correctible errors, and they could visualize the sweep of armies across it, the sound once again of hobnailed boots. "We must all of us be so careful of what we do . . . not to alert the sleeping tanks."

Throwing his arm about Bukowski's shoulder, he led the Communist leader to the door. "It seems to me, Szymon, that our situation today is precisely what it was in 1791. Then some patriotic Poles conceded that the nation must have a liberal, free form of government. And they drew up the finest constitution Europe had yet seen. And do you remember what happened?"

"I do. My mother taught me that along with my alphabet. Prussia and Russia were so terrified by the prospect of a free modern nation on their borders, they swept in and destroyed us."

"Even the children know that the Forest of Szczek is filled with Russian tanks. Waiting to destroy us again."

"They're everywhere. In carefully concealed positions. All over Poland, I mean."

"Do you see the analogy, Szymon? Today the patriotic men of Poland, like Janko Buk, are struggling for a better society, and once more there are nations who fear her, want to destroy her. I'm sorry to see you allied with the tanks in the forest."

The bishop, recognizing Szymon as wise and patriotic, did not wish to end his conversation on such a somber note, so as he walked Bukowski to the door he said: "Szymon, clear your mind of torments. Put the ghosts to sleep."

"That is not so easy."

"Think of it this way. The little girl from Zamosc died to save you. The little Jew from the synagogue died to save me. But Jesus Christ died to save us all."

When Bukowski neared the village on his way back, he stopped his car so that he might look at the ruins of the old castle, and he stayed there for more than an hour, just sitting in the dark, allowing images to flash through his mind: Bishop Barski and the little rabbi; the girl in her overcoat; the grinning Otto Grundtz; the grinning Nazis Under the Clock; the bowl of hot, fatty soup at Pani Tomczyk's; the big head of King Jan Sobieski torn to shreds by Nazi bullets, then miraculously restored to life by women's fingers and a painter's brush; and that long row of noble men in the dark gallery whom he had brought back to existence by his patience and his love of things Polish.

Violently he started his car and whipped it with screeching wheels up to the palace, where he rushed past the guards to go down into the gallery to see once more the restored faces of his friends, especially the two who had worked so diligently and with such superior ability for the welfare of Poland, Czartoryski, who had struggled to bring the nation into modern times, and old Zamoyski, who had done so many wonderful things.

"Brothers!" he cried to the stately figures. "All of you, we owe you so much." He went especially to old Mniszech of the big beard and bigger belly. "You old son-of-a-bitch! We could have done business together." He stood on tiptoes but failed in his purpose, so he looked for a box, and when he found a rickety chair he brought it to the portrait of the old tiger, stood upon the seat, and kissed Mniszech on the forehead.

"Give me your blessing!" he shouted to them. "I need your blessing this night!"

And then he ran from the palace and down the beautiful lanes to the village and crept to the cottage of Janko Buk, where he tapped softly on the window. After a moment he awakened someone inside, and cautiously the door was opened. It was Janko's wife, Kazimiera, the country girl, and she was perplexed, for it was still two hours before dawn.

"What is it?" she whispered, for the others were still sleeping.

"I came here before like this," he said. "Let me in."

"I'll fetch Janko," she said.

He grasped her arm. "It is not Janko that I seek."

He brushed past her and went into the house, where he awakened Janko and his mother. When they stood before him he said: "Years ago I came into this room at this time of night to beg you with tears in my eyes, Biruta, for food to keep my men alive."

"We gave you what we had," she said, drawing her nightdress about her.

"And I asked your husband, Jan, to help me fight the Nazis."

"And he did. We both did," Biruta said.

"Tonight . . ." He was trembling violently and in the dim light sweat showed across his face. "Tonight I have come on a much different mission. I have been alone . . . I am still a prisoner in Majdanek . . . I can no longer fight them all."

They stood in the near-darkness, exactly as they had done on that night when Biruta had worked the stones of her quern, making the forbidden bread for which other women in this village had given their lives. And Biruta and Szymon were as frightened now at the dangers which assailed their country as they had been then, but finally he found courage to say: "I can no longer bear the burden of these days alone. Biruta, will you marry me?"

Next day, 5 December 1981, at one in the afternoon, when the discussions ended and Szymon Bukowski stood before the television cameras to explain what had been achieved, he finished his terse announcements with generous praise for "your neighbor and good farmer, Janko Buk."

Buk took the microphone, and with a bow to Chalubinski, said: "Our little village has been honored to have such a distinguished visitor. Our talks have been amiable, which was good, because they dealt with vital subjects. I am pleased with what has happened here. It bodes well for our nation.

"I close with two personal announcements. I have been asked, as you heard yesterday, to leave you and go to Warsaw to serve in the government. I shall not go." He turned to face Chalubinski, who gasped. "I am a farmer, fighting for farmers' rights, and here is the battlefield.

"My second announcement is one which gives my heart joy. My mother, Biruta, who fought the Nazis for so many years and who bears scars to prove it, has agreed to marry Szymon Bukowski, who fought them in his own way and who bears his own scars. In these meetings I have found him to be a resolute man of honor and I am proud to have him join my family."

On the wedding day Jan Pawel Drugi from Rome sent a telegram conveying his blessing, but Tytus Chalubinski, brooding in his Warsaw headquarters, did not. He was outraged that a member of his team should be marrying this Biruta Buk woman who had so scathingly attacked him during the palace meetings. Now, from his desk, he took out a pile of index cards, golden-yellow, on which he had for some time been listing the names of those Poles who would have to be arrested when the inescapable crackdown came. The people named on those cards that were marked with a black cross would be sent to the concentration camps which would eventually be needed—and to this growing list he now added Szymon Bukowski and his wife, Biruta.

But for the time being the Russian tanks remained well hidden, deep within the Forest of Szczek.

JAMES A. MICHENER, one of the world's most popular writers, was the author of the Pulitzer Prize–winning *Tales of the South Pacific*, the bestselling novels *Hawaii, Texas, Chesapeake, The Covenant,* and *Alaska,* and the memoir *The World Is My Home.* Michener served on the advisory council to NASA and the International Broadcast Board, which oversees the Voice of America. Among dozens of awards and honors, he received America's highest civilian award, the Presidential Medal of Freedom, in 1977, and an award from the President's Committee on the Arts and Humanities in 1983 for his commitment to art in America. Michener died in 1997 at the age of ninety.

ABOUT THE TYPE

This book was set in Times Roman, designed by Stanley Morison (1889–1967) specifically for *The Times* of London. The typeface was introduced in the newspaper in 1932. Times Roman had its greatest success in the United States as a book and commercial typeface, rather than one used in newspapers.